25

8
10
2

39. 6

TELF

Praise for *At The Water's Edge*

'If I needed a reminder why I am such a fan of Sara Gruen's books, her latest novel provides plenty. Unique in its setting and scope, this impeccably researched historical fiction is full of the gorgeous prose I've come to expect from this author. And even after finishing, its message still resonates with me: the monsters we seek may be right in front of us. In fact, the only fault I can find with this book is that I've already finished it'

Jodi Picoult, bestselling author of *Leaving Time*

'I devoured this book. Sara Gruen has proven herself, once again, to be one of America's most compelling storytellers . . . You might be tempted to rush to get to the answers at the end – but don't – or you'll miss the delectable journey that is Gruen's prose'

Kathryn Stockett, bestselling author of *The Help*

'*At the Water's Edge* skilfully transports us to a small, tenacious Scottish village in the grip of war, and into the heart of Madeline Hyde, a woman who is a stranger to herself until forces convene to rock her awake. Sara Gruen is a wizard at capturing the essence of her historical setting, and does so here in spades, but it's Maddie's unexpected transformation that grounds and drives the novel. As her husband and best friend search the surface of the Loch, desperate for a sign of the elusive creature, Maddie learns to plumb her own depths, and comes fully alive to the world around her. Magical'

Paula McLain, bestselling author of *The Paris Wife*

'An intoxicating blend of history and legend set against the thrilling backdrop of a hunt for the world's most famous monster. Sara Gruen has an exquisite eye for detail, and she evokes the haunted – and haunting – landscape with her signature passion, freshness and scope. Atmospheric and gritty, the compelling tale of Madeline's struggle to redefine herself in a world gone mad will linger long after you turn the final page . . . I love this marvellous, marvellous book'

Joshilyn Jackson, bestselling author of
Someone Else's Love Story

'A rich, beautiful novel. Elegantly written and compulsively readable. A gripping love story, a profound examination of the effects of war on ordinary women and a compelling portrait of female friendship. This story . . . will keep you riveted until the very last page'

Kristin Hannah, bestselling author of *The Nightingale*

'I just could not put this book down . . . Sara Gruen is a wonder at building the atmosphere and her attention to detail really brings the Scottish Highlands to life. I loved the way she weaved tales of folklore and monsters into this touching and haunting love story'

Emma, Waterstones bookseller

At the
WATER'S
EDGE

Also by Sara Gruen

Water for Elephants

Ape House

At the WATER'S EDGE

SARA GRUEN

www.tworoadsbooks.com

First published in Great Britain in 2015 by Two Roads
An imprint of John Murray Press
An Hachette UK company

1

A CIP catalogue record for this title is available from the British Library

Hardback ISBN 978 1 473 60470 4
Trade Paperback ISBN 978 1 473 60471 1
Ebook ISBN 978 1 473 60472 8

Typeset in Janson Text LT Std by Palimpsest Book Production Limited
Falkirk, Stirlingshire

Printed and bound by Clays Ltd, St Ives plc

Hodder & Stoughton policy is to use papers that are natural, renewable
and recyclable products and made from wood grown in sustainable
forests. The logging and manufacturing processes are expected to
conform to the environmental regulations of the country of origin.

Hodder & Stoughton Ltd
Carmelite House
50 Victoria Embankment
London EC4Y ODZ

www.hodder.co.uk

For Bob,

'S tusa gràdh mo bheatha

One Crow for sorrow,

Two Crows for mirth,

Three Crows for a wedding,

Four Crows for a birth,

Five Crows for silver,

Six Crows for gold,

Seven for a secret, never to be told.

PROLOGUE

Drumnadrochit, 28 February 1942

AGNES MÀIRI GRANT,
INFANT DAUGHTER OF ANGUS AND MÀIRI GRANT
14 JANUARY 1942

CAPT. ANGUS DUNCAN GRANT,
BELOVED HUSBAND OF MÀIRI
2 APRIL 1909–JANUARY 1942

The headstone was modest and hewn of black granite, granite being one of the few things never in short supply in Glenurquhart, even during the present difficulty.

Màiri visited the tiny swell of earth that covered her daughter's coffin every day, watching as it flattened. Archie the stonecutter had said it might be months before they could put up the stone with the frost so hard upon them, but the coffin was so small the levelling was accomplished in just a few weeks.

No sooner was the stone up than Màiri got the telegram about Angus and had Archie take it away again. Archie had wanted to wait until the date of death was verified, but Màiri needed it done then, to have a place to mourn them both at once, and Archie could not say no. He chiselled Angus's name beneath his daughter's and left some room to add the day of the month when they learned it. An addition for an absence, because Angus – unlike the wee bairn – was not beneath it and almost certainly never would be.

There were just the two of them in the churchyard when Archie returned the headstone. He was a strong man, heaving a piece of granite around like that.

A shadow flashed over her and she looked up. A single crow circled high above the graves, never seeming to move its wings.

One Crow for sorrow,

It was joined by another, and then two more.

Two Crows for mirth,

Three Crows for a wedding,

Four Crows for a birth

Archie removed his hat and twisted it in his hands.

'If there's anything Morag and I can do, anything at all . . .'

Màiri tried to smile, and succeeded only in producing a half-choked sob. She pulled a handkerchief from her pocket and pressed it to her mouth.

Archie paused as though he wanted to say more. Eventually he replaced his hat and said, 'Well then. I'll be off.' He nodded firmly and trudged back to his van.

It was Willie the postie who had delivered the telegram, on Valentine's Day no less, a month to the day after the birth. Màiri had been pulling a pint behind the bar when Anna came, ashen-faced, whispering that Willie was on the doorstep and would not come inside. Willie was a regular, so Màiri knew from that very moment, before she even approached the door and saw his face. His hooded eyes stared into hers and then drifted down to the envelope in his hands. He turned it a couple of times, as though wondering whether to give it to her, whether *not* giving it to her would make the thing it contained not true.

The wind caught it a couple of times, flicking it this way and that. When he finally handed it to her, he offered it up as gently as a new-hatched chick. She opened it, turned it right side up and let her eyes scan the purple date stamp – 14 February 1942 – added by Willie himself not half an hour before, and then

```
MRS MAIRI GRANT 6 HIGH ROAD DRUM INVERNESS-SHIRE
DEEPLY REGRET TO INFORM THAT YOUR HUSBAND CAPTN
ANGUS D GRANT SEAFORTH HRS 4TH BTN 179994 IS
MISSING PRESUMED KILLED ON WAR SERVICE JAN 1 1942
LETTER WITH DETAILS TO FOLLOW
```

She took in only three things: Angus, killed, the date. And they were enough.

'I'm sorry, Màiri,' Willie said in a near whisper. 'Especially so soon after . . .' His voice trailed off. He blinked and his eyes drifted down, pausing briefly on her belly before coming to rest again on his hands.

She could not reply. She closed the door quietly, walked past the hushed locals and into the kitchen. There she leaned against the wall, clutching her empty womb with one hand and the piece of paper that had brought Angus's death in the other. For it did seem as though it was the paper that brought his death rather than simply the news of it. He had been dead for more than six weeks, and she hadn't known.

In the time between the arrival of the telegram and the return of the headstone with Angus's name on it, Màiri had begun to blame Willie. Why had he chosen to hand her the telegram? She had seen his hesitation. He would have been complicit in what, at worst, would have been a lie of omission, especially if it meant she could believe that Angus was still out there somewhere. Even if he was doing things she couldn't comprehend, things that might change him in the terrible ways the men who had already been sent home had been changed, she could believe he was alive and therefore fixable, for surely there was nothing she couldn't love him through once he came home.

They had lied to her about the baby, and she had let them.

Since she had first felt the baby quicken, she was keenly aware of its every movement. For months, she had watched in wonderment as little braes poked up from her belly, pushing their way across – an elbow, or perhaps a knee – a subterranean force that constantly rearranged the landscape of her flesh. Was it a boy, or a wee girl? Whichever it was, it already had strong opinions. She remembered the moment it occurred to her that it had been hours since she felt it move, on Hogmanay, of all days. At midnight, precisely when Ian Mackintosh struck in his pipes to form the first chord of 'Auld Lang Syne' and seconds before corresponding shots rang out from the doorway of Donnie Maclean, Màiri began poking her belly, trying to wake it, for they said that unborn babes slept. She yelled at it, screamed at it and finally, realising, wrapped her arms round it and wept. Thirteen days later, her pains started.

Her memories of the birth were vague, for the midwife had given her bitter tea mixed with white powder, and the doctor held ether over her nose and mouth at regular intervals, putting her under completely at the end. They told her the baby had lived a few minutes, long enough to be baptised. Their lie became her lie, and that was what went on the headstone. In truth, she'd probably lost both child and husband on the same date.

The promised letter never arrived. Where had he died? *How* had he died? Without the dreaded details, she had only her imagination – her terrible imagination – and while she wished she couldn't fathom what his last moments might have been, she could, with distinct and agonising precision, in a million different ways. Please God that they were moments indeed, and not hours or days.

The murder of crows descended in a noisy fluster, settling in a row on the stone wall, huddling into themselves, their blue-black feathers puffed and their heads tucked in as though they'd pulled up their coat collars. They stared accusingly, miserably, but without their usual commentary. Màiri counted them twice.

Seven for a secret, never to be told.

She knew then that she would never know the details, would never know what had happened.

A bone-chilling wind stirred the fallen leaves until they formed cyclones that danced among the graves. Màiri crouched and fingered the names of her child and husband in the black stone.

Agnes.

Angus.

A third of the stone was still blank, at the bottom. There was room for one more name, one more set of dates, and these would be accurate.

She stood without taking her eyes off the stone. She wiped her eyes and nose on the handkerchief, and kept it in her hand as she wrapped her arms round herself and walked through the black iron gate, leaving it swinging. She headed toward the inn, except when she got to the crossroads, she turned left instead of going straight on.

A light snow began to fall, but despite her bare head and legs she trudged right past the Farquhars' croft. She'd have been welcome there, as well as at the McKenzies', where she could see the fire glowing orange through the window, but on she went, teeth chattering, hands and shins numb.

Eventually the castle rose on her left, its majestic and ruined battlements like so many broken teeth against the leaden sky.

She had played within its walls as a child, and knew which rooms remained whole, where you had to watch your footing, where the best hiding places were, where the courting couples went. She and Angus had been among them.

The snow was heavier now, falling in clumps that collected and melted on her hair. Her ears were past stinging. She pulled her sleeves over her frozen hands and pinched them shut with her fingertips. Through the gatehouse, past the kiln, pushing through the long grass and scrub gorse, bracken and thistles, straight to the Water Gate.

She paused at the top, staring at the blackness of the loch. Thousands of tiny whitecaps danced on its surface, seeming to move in the opposite direction to the water beneath them. It was said that the loch contained more water than all the other bodies of water not just in Scotland but also in England and Wales combined, and it held other things as well. She had been warned away from it her entire life, for its depth came quickly, its coldness was fierce and the Kelpie lay in wait.

She picked her way sideways down the slope, letting her icy fingers out of her sleeves to hold up the hem of her coat.

When she reached the bottom, the water lapped around the soles of her shoes. The edge of the loch looked seductively shallow, slipping over the gravel and back into itself. She took a step forward, gasping as the water flooded her shoes, so cold, so cold, and yet it had never frozen, not once in recorded history. Another step, another gasp. Bits of peat swirled in the water around her ankles, circling her legs, beckoning her forth. Another step, and this time she stumbled, finding herself knee-deep. Her wool coat floated, an absurd umbrella, first resisting and finally wicking water, pulling her deeper. She looked back at the landing, suddenly desperate. If only she had a hat, she could throw it back onto the thorny gorse. If she'd had anything that would float, maybe they'd think it was an accident and let her be buried with her daughter. Maybe they'd think the Kelpie took her. And then she remembered that the loch never gave up its dead, so she spread her arms wide and embraced it.

I

Scottish Highlands, 14 January 1945

'Oh God, make him pull over', I said as the car swung round yet another curve in almost total darkness.

It had been nearly four hours since we'd left the naval base at Aultbea, and we'd been careening from checkpoint to checkpoint since. I truly believe those were the only times the driver used the brakes. At the last checkpoint, I was copiously sick, narrowly missing the guard's boots. He didn't even bother checking our papers, just lifted the red and white pole and waved us on with a look of disgust.

'Driver! Pull over,' said Ellis, who was sitting in the back seat between Hank and me.

'I'm afraid there is no "over,"' the driver said in a thick Highland accent, his *R*'s rolling magnificently. He came to a stop in the middle of the road.

It was true. If I stepped outside the car I would be ankle-deep in thorny vegetation and mud, not that it would have done any more to destroy my clothes and shoes. From head to toe I was steeped in sulphur and cordite and the stench of fear. My stockings were mere cobwebs stretched round my legs, and my scarlet nails were broken and peeling. I hadn't had my hair done since the day before we'd sailed from the shipyard in Philadelphia. I had never been in such a state.

I leaned out the open door and gagged while Ellis rubbed my back. Wet snow collected on the top of my head.

I sat up again and pulled the door shut. 'I'm sorry. I'm finished. Do you think you can take those things off the head-lights? I think it would be better if I could see what's coming.' I was referring to the slotted metal plates our one-eyed driver had clipped on before we'd left the base. They limited visibility to about three feet ahead of us.

'Can't,' he called back cheerfully. 'It's the blackout.' As he cranked up through the gears, my head lurched back and forth. I leaned over and cradled my face in my hands.

Ellis patted my shoulder. 'We should be nearly there. Do you think fresh air would help?'

I sat up and let my head flop against the back of the torn leather seat. Ellis reached across and rolled the window down a crack. I turned towards the cold air and closed my eyes.

'Hank, can you *please* put out your cigarette?'

He didn't answer, but a whoosh of frigid air let me know he had tossed it out the window.

'Thank you,' I said weakly.

Twenty minutes later, when the car finally came to a stop and the driver cut the engine, I was so desperate for solid ground I spilled out before the driver could get his own door open, never mind mine. I landed on my knees.

'Maddie!' Ellis said in alarm.

'I'm all right,' I said.

There was a fast-moving cloud cover under a nearly full moon, and by its light I first laid eyes on our unlikely destination.

I climbed to my feet and reeled away from the car, thinking I might be sick again. My legs propelled me towards the building, spinning ever faster. I crashed into the wall, then slid down until I was crouching against it.

In the distance, a sheep bleated.

To say that I wished I wasn't there would be a ludicrous understatement, but I'd only ever had the illusion of choice:

We have to do this, Hank had said. *It's for Ellis.*

To refuse would have been tantamount to betrayal, an act of calculated cruelty. And so, because of my husband's war with his father and their insane obsession with a mythical monster, we'd crossed the Atlantic at the very same time a real madman, a real monster, was attempting to take over the world for his own reasons of ego and pride.

I would have given anything to go back two weeks, to the beginning of the New Year's Eve party, and script the whole thing differently.

2

'*ive! Four! Three! Two!*'

The word 'one' had already formed on our lips, but before it could slide off there was an explosion overhead. As screams rose around us, I pitched myself against Ellis, tossing champagne over both of us. He threw an arm protectively around my head and didn't spill a drop.

When the screams petered out, I heard a tinkling above us, like glass breaking, along with an ominous groaning. I peeked out from my position against Ellis's chest.

'What the hell?' said Hank, without a hint of surprise. I think he was the only person in the room who hadn't jumped.

All eyes turned upwards. Thirty feet above us, a massive chandelier swung on its silver-plated chain, throwing shimmering prisms across the walls and floor. It was as if a rainbow had burst into a million pieces, which were now dancing across the marble, silks and damask. We watched, transfixed. I glanced nervously at Ellis's face, and then back at the ceiling.

An enormous cork landed next to General Pew, our host at what was easily the most anticipated party of the year, bouncing outrageously like a bloated mushroom. A split second later a single crystal the size of a quail's egg fell from the sky and dropped smack into his cocktail, all but emptying it. He stared, bemused and tipsy, then calmly took out his handkerchief and dabbed his jacket.

As everyone burst into laughter, I noticed a footman in old-fashioned knee breeches perched near the top of a stepladder, pallid, motionless, struggling to contain the biggest bottle of champagne I'd ever seen. On the marble table in front of him was a structure of glasses arranged so that if someone poured continuously into the top one, they would eventually all be filled. As a rush of bubbles cascaded over the sides of the bottle and into the footman's sleeves, he stared in white-faced horror at Mrs Pew.

Hank assessed the situation and apparently took pity on the fellow. He raised his glass, as well as his other hand, and with the flair and flourish of a ringmaster boomed, *'One! Happy New Year!'*

The orchestra struck up 'Auld Lang Syne.' General Pew conducted with his empty glass, and Mrs Pew beamed at his side – not only was her party a smashing success, but it now had a comic anecdote people would speak of for years.

Should auld acquaintance be forgot, and never brought to mind
Should auld acquaintance be forgot, and old lang syne . . .

Those who knew the words sang along. I had refreshed my memory that afternoon in order to be ready for the big moment, but when cork met crystal, the lyrics were knocked straight out of my brain. By the time we got to running about slopes and picking daisies fine, I gave up and joined Ellis and Hank in la-la-la'ing our way through the rest.

They waved their glasses in solidarity with General Pew, their free arms looped round my waist. At the end, Ellis leaned in to kiss me.

Hank looked to one side, then the other, and appeared baffled.

'Hmm. I seem to have misplaced my date. What *have* I done with her?'

'What you *haven't* done is marry her,' I said and then snorted, nearly expelling champagne through my nose. I had sipped my way through at least four glasses on an empty stomach and was feeling bold.

His mouth opened in mock offence, but even he couldn't pretend ignorance about Violet's growing desperation at the seemingly endless nature of their courtship.

'Did she actually leave?' he said, scanning the room a little more seriously.

'I'm not sure,' I said. 'I haven't seen her in a while.'

'Then who will give me my New Year's kiss?' he asked, looking bereft.

'Oh, come here, you big lug.' I stood on tiptoe and planted a kiss on his cheek. 'You've always got us. And we don't even require a ring.'

Ellis threw us an amused side-eye and motioned to Hank that he should wipe my lipstick off his cheek.

Beyond him, the footman was still balanced on the second to highest rung of the stepladder. He was bent at the waist, trying to aim the bottle at the top glass, and had gone from pale to purple with the effort. His mouth was pressed into a grim line. I looked around to see if reinforcements were coming and didn't see any.

'Ellis? I think he needs help,' I said, tilting my head in the footman's direction.

Ellis glanced over. 'You're right,' he said, handing me his glass. 'Hank? Shall we?'

'Do you really think she's left?' Hank said wistfully, his lips hovering near the edge of his glass. 'She was a vision tonight. That dress was the colour of the gloaming, the sequins jealous stars in the galaxy of her night, but nothing, *nothing* could compare to the milky skin of her—'

'Boys! Concentrate!' I said.

Hank snapped back to life. 'What?'

'Maddie thinks that man needs help,' said Ellis.

'That thing's enormous,' I said. 'I don't think he can hold it on his own.'

'I should think not. That's a Balthazar,' said Ellis.

'That's not a Balthazar,' Hank said. 'That's a Nebuchadnezzar.'

The footman's arms were quaking. He began pouring but missed. Champagne fell between the glasses, splashing on to the table and floor. His gloves and sleeves were saturated.

'Uh-oh,' said Hank.

'Uh-oh indeed,' said Ellis. 'Mrs Pew will *not* be pleased.'

'I rather suspect Mrs Pew is never pleased,' Hank said.

Rivulets of sweat ran down the footman's forehead. It was plain to see that he was going to fall forwards, right onto the glasses. I looked to Mrs Pew for help, but she had disappeared. I tried to signal the General, but he was holding court with a replenished cocktail.

I dug my elbow into Ellis's side.

'Go!' I said urgently. 'Go help him.'

'Who's she talking about?' said Hank.

I glared at him, and then some more, until he remembered.

'Oh! Of course.' He tried to hand me his glass, but I was already holding two. He set his on the floor and yanked his lapels in a businesslike manner, but before he and Ellis could mobilise, help arrived in the form of other servants bearing four smaller but still very large bottles and three more step-ladders. Mrs Pew glided in behind them to make sure all was under control.

'Now *those* are Balthazars,' said Hank, with a knowing nod. He retrieved his drink from the floor and drained it.

'No. Those are Jeroboams,' said Ellis.

'I think I know my champagne,' said Hank.

'And I don't?'

'I think you're both wrong. Those are Ebenezers,' I said.

That stopped them.

I broke into tipsy giggles. 'Ebenezer? Get it? Christmas? The holidays? Oh never mind. Someone get me another. I spilled mine.'

'Yes. On *me*,' said Ellis.

Hank spun round and set his glass on the tray of a passing waiter. He clapped his hands. 'All right, who's up for a snowball fight?'

We toppled outside and made snow angels right there in front of the Pews' home and all the cars and liveried drivers that were lined up waiting for guests. I gathered one snowball and managed to land it on Ellis's chest before screeching and running back inside.

In the vast foyer, Ellis helped brush the snow off my back and hair. Hank hung his jacket over my bare shoulders and the two of them guided me to a trio of ornate, embroidered chairs near a roaring fire. Hank, who had had the presence of mind to grab my mink stole on the way back in, shook it off and draped it over the edge of the rosewood table in front of us. Ellis went in search of hot toddies and I peeled off my gloves, which were stained and soaked.

'God, look at me,' I said, gazing down at myself. 'I'm a mess.'

My silk dress and shoes were ruined. I tried in vain to smooth out the water spots, and checked quickly to make sure I still had both earrings. The gloves were of no consequence, but I hoped the stole could be saved. If not, I'd succeeded in destroying my entire outfit.

'You're not a mess. You're magnificent,' said Hank.

'Well, I *was*,' I lamented.

I'd spent the afternoon at Salon Antoine having my hair and make-up done, and had eaten almost nothing for two days before so my dress would drape properly. It was a beautiful pomegranate-red silk, the same material as my shoes. It matched my ruby engagement ring, and all of it set off my green eyes. Ellis had given me the dress and shoes a few days earlier, and before the party I had presented myself to him like a flamenco dancer, twirling so the skirt would take flight. He professed his delight, but I felt a familiar pang of sorrow as I tried, yet again, to imagine exactly what he was seeing. My husband was profoundly colour-blind, so to him my ensemble must have been a combination of greys. I wondered which ones, and how many variations there were, and whether they had different depths. I couldn't imagine a world without colour.

Hank dropped into a chair, leaving one leg dangling over its arm. He pulled his bow tie open and undid his cuffs and collar. He looked like a half-drowned Clark Gable.

I shivered into his jacket, holding it closed from the inside.

Hank patted his chest and sides. He stopped suddenly and lifted an eyebrow.

'Oh!' I said, realising what he was looking for. I retrieved the cigarette case from his inside pocket and handed it to him. He flipped it open and held it out in offering. I shook my head. He took a cigarette for himself and snapped the case shut.

'So, how about it then?' he said, his eyes glistening playfully. 'Shall we go get us a monster?'

'Sure,' I said, waving my hand. 'We'll hop on the next liner.' It was what I always said when the topic came up, which was often, and always after boatloads of booze. It was our little game.

'I think getting away would do Ellis good. He seems depressed.'

'Ellis isn't depressed,' I said. 'You just want to escape Violet's clutches.'

'I do not,' he protested.

'You didn't even notice when she left tonight!'

Hank cocked his head and nodded, conceding the point. 'I suppose I should send flowers.'

'First thing in the morning,' I said.

He nodded. 'Absolutely. At the crack of noon. Scout's honour.'

'*And* I think you should marry her. You need civilising, and I need a female friend. I have only you and Ellis.'

He clutched a hand to his heart, mortally wounded. 'What are we, chopped liver?'

'Only the finest foie gras. Seriously, though. How long are you going to make her wait?'

'I'm not sure. I don't know if I'm ready to be civilised yet. But when I am, Violet can have the honours. She can pick a mean set of china.'

As I set my drink down, I caught another glimpse of my dress and shoes. 'I think maybe *I* need civilising. Will you just marry her already?'

'What is this, an ambush?' He tapped the cigarette against the top of the case and put it between his lips. A servant appeared from nowhere to light it.

'Mmm, thanks,' Hank said, inhaling. He leaned back and let smoke drift from his mouth to his nose in a swirling white ribbon that he re-inhaled. He called this manoeuvre the 'Irish Waterfall.'

'If I do marry her, Ellis and I won't have a hope, because you girls will gang up on us.'

'We won't be able to,' I said. 'The distribution will be equal.'

'They're never equal between the sexes. You already gang up on Ellis and me all by yourself.'

'I do not!'

'You're ganging up on me right now, at this very minute, single-handedly baiting the marriage trap. I tell you, it's the ultimate female conspiracy. You're all in on it. Personally, I can't see what all the fuss is about.'

Ellis returned, followed by a waiter who set steaming crystal glasses with handles on the table in front of us. Ellis flopped into a chair.

Hank set his cigarette in an ashtray and picked up his toddy. He blew steam from the surface and took a cautious sip. 'So, Ellis, our darling girl here was just saying we should go on a trip,' he said. 'Find us a plesiosaur.'

'Sure she was,' said Ellis.

'She was. She has it all planned out,' said Hank. 'Tell him, Maddie.'

'You're drunk,' I said, laughing.

'That is true, I will admit,' said Hank, 'but I still think we should do it.' He ground the cigarette out so hard its snuffed end splayed like a spent bullet. 'We've been talking about it for years. Let's do it. I'm serious.'

'No you're not,' I said.

Hank once again clasped his heart. 'What's happened to you, Maddie? Don't tell me you've lost your sense of adventure. Has Violet been civilising you in secret?'

'No, of course not. You haven't given her the chance. But we can't go now. Liners haven't run since the *Athenia* went down.'

I realised I'd made it sound like it had spontaneously sprung a leak, when in reality it had been torpedoed by a German U-boat with 1,100 civilians on board.

'Where there's a will, there's a way,' said Hank, nodding sagely. He sipped the toddy again, then peered into it accusingly. 'Hmmmm. Think I prefer whisky after all. Back in a minute. Ellis, talk to your wife. Clearly she's picking up bad habits.'

He launched himself from his chair, and for a moment looked like he might topple over. He clutched the back of Ellis's chair while he regained his balance and finally wafted off, drifting like a butterfly.

Ellis and I sat in relative silence, within a bubble created by the chatter and laughter of other people.

He slid slowly down in his chair until it must have looked empty from behind. His eyes were glassy and he'd turned a bit grey.

My own ears buzzed from the champagne. I lifted both hands to investigate my hair and discovered the curls on one side had come undone and were clinging to my neck. Reaching further round, I realized that the diamond hair comb given to me by my mother-in-law was missing. I felt a stab of panic. It had been a gift on our wedding day, a rare moment of compassion shown me by a woman who had made no secret of not wanting me to marry her son, but was nonetheless moved to give it to me seconds before Hank walked me down the aisle.

'I think we should do it,' Ellis said.

'Sure,' I said gaily. 'We'll just hop on the next—'

'I mean it,' he said sharply.

I looked up, startled by his tone. He was grinding his jaw. I wasn't sure exactly when it had happened, but his mood had shifted. We were no longer playing a game.

He looked at me in irritation. 'What? Why shouldn't we?'

'Because of the war,' I said gently.

'Carpe diem, and all that crap. The war is part of the adventure. God knows I'm not getting near it any other way. Neither is Hank, for that matter.' He raked a hand through his hair, leaving a swathe of it standing on end. He leaned in closer and narrowed his eyes. 'You do know what they call us, don't you?' he said. '"FFers."'

He and Hank were the only 4Fers in the room. I wondered if someone had slighted him when he'd gone to find drinks.

Hank took his flat-footedness in his stride, as he did most things, but being given 4F status had devastated Ellis. His colour-blindness had gone undetected until he tried to enlist and was rejected. He'd tried a second time at a different location and was turned down again. Although it was clearly not his fault, he was right that people judged, and I knew how this chipped at him. It was relentless and unspoken, so he couldn't even defend himself. His own father, a veteran of the Great War, had treated him with undisguised revulsion since hearing the news. This injustice was made all the more painful because we lived with my in-laws, who had perversely removed any chance at escape. Two days after the attack on Pearl Harbor, they cut Ellis's allowance by two thirds. My mother-in-law broke it to us in the drawing room before dinner, announcing with smug satisfaction that she was sure we'd be pleased to know that until 'this terrible business was over' the money would be going toward war bonds. Strictly speaking, that may have been where the money was going, but it was perfectly clear that the real motive was punishing Ellis. His mother was exacting revenge because he'd dared to marry me, and his father – well, we weren't exactly sure. Either he didn't believe that Ellis was colour-blind, or he couldn't forgive him for it. The nightmarish result was that we were forced to live under the constant scrutiny of people we'd come to think of as our captors.

'You know how hard it is,' he went on, 'with everyone staring at me, wondering why I'm not serving.'

'They don't stare—'

'*Don't patronise me! You know perfectly well they do!*'

His outburst caused everyone to turn and look.

Ellis waved an angry hand at them. 'See?'

He glanced fiercely around. To a person they turned away, their scandalised expressions trained elsewhere. Conversations resumed, but in dampened tones.

Ellis locked eyes with me. 'I know I look perfectly healthy,' he continued, his voice under taut control. 'My own father thinks

I'm a coward, for Christ's sake. I need to prove myself. To him, to them, to *me*. Of all people, I thought you'd understand.'

'Darling, I do understand,' I said.

'But do you?' he asked, his mouth stretching into a bitter smile.

'Of course,' I said, and I did, although at that moment I would have said anything to calm him down. He'd been drinking hard liquor since early afternoon, and I knew things could degenerate quickly. The carefully averted faces of those around us already portended a very unpleasant beginning to the new year.

My mother-in-law, who had missed the party because of a migraine, would surely start receiving reports of our behaviour by noon. I could only imagine how she'd react when she found out I'd lost the hair comb. I resolved to telephone the next day and throw myself on Mrs Pew's mercy. If the comb had come out in the snow, it was probably gone for ever, but if it had fallen down the back of a sofa, it might turn up.

Ellis watched me closely, the fire dancing in his eyes. After a few seconds, his angry mask melted into an expression of sad relief. He leaned sideways to pat my knee and almost fell out of his chair.

'That's my girl,' he said, struggling upright. 'Always up for adventure. You're not like the other girls, you know. There's not an ounce of fun in them. That's why Hank won't marry Violet, of course. He's holding out for another you. Only there isn't one. I've got the one and only.'

'Who the whatty-what now?' said Hank, appearing from nowhere and crashing back into his chair. 'Over here!' he barked, snapping his fingers above his head. A waiter set more drinks on the table in front of us. Hank turned back to Ellis. 'Is she trying to marry me off again? I swear there's an echo in here.'

'No. She's agreed. We're going to Scotland.'

Hank's eyes popped open. 'Really?' He looked at me for confirmation.

I didn't think I'd agreed, per se, at least not after I realised we weren't just joking, but since I'd managed to defuse the bomb and perhaps even save the evening, I decided to play along.

'Sure,' I said, gesturing grandly. 'Why not?'

3

The next morning, I was startled awake by the telephone ringing in the downstairs hallway. It was exactly nine o'clock, which was the very earliest time considered civilised. I clutched the covers to my chin, paralysed, as Pemberton, the butler, summoned my mother-in-law. I heard her determined footsteps, then her muffled voice, rising and falling in surprised waves.

I was entirely wretched – my head pounded, my stomach was sour and it was quite possible that I was still drunk. While I remembered much of the night before, there were moments I couldn't recall, like getting home. The realisation that I'd passed the point of being tipsy had come over me quite suddenly – I remembered being acutely aware that it was time to call it a night, but I did not remember leaving, much less the ride home. I had no idea how many – or few – hours I'd been in bed.

My ruined dress lay in a limp heap in the middle of the carpet, looking for all the world like a length of intestine. My shoes were nearby, one of them missing a heel. The white stole was flung over the edge of my polished mahogany dressing table, the fur spiked and dirty. I'd dropped my strand of pearls in front of my jewellery box, and both earrings, cushion-cut rubies surrounded by diamonds, were nearby but not together. A very large champagne cork was planted squarely between them. I checked my finger for my ring and then, with a sickening feeling of vertigo, remembered the hair comb. I burrowed my face into my pillow and pulled its edges over my ears.

At noon, the housemaid knocked gently on the door, then opened it a crack.

'I'm sorry, Emily. I'm not feeling up to breakfast,' I said, my voice muffled by the pillow.

'I've brought Alka-Seltzer and gingersnaps,' she replied, which made my stomach twist again. It meant that not only had we wakened the entire house when we returned, but also that our condition had been obvious.

'Put it on the table,' I said, rolling to face the opposite wall. I didn't want her to see me. I'd fallen into bed without even removing my make-up, as evidenced by the streaks of mascara on my pillowcase. 'Thank you, Emily.'

'Of course, Mrs Hyde.'

She stayed longer than I expected, and when she left, I saw that she'd taken the dress, shoes and mink with her.

The telephone rang sporadically throughout the day. With each call, my mother-in-law's voice became a little more resolute until finally it was brittle and hard. I shrank further under the covers with every conversation.

At nearly six thirty, Ellis staggered into my room. He was still in his pyjamas. His robe was open, its sash dragging on the floor behind him.

'Dear God, what a night,' he said, scrubbing his eyes with his fists. 'I'm a bit green about the gills. I could use an eye-opener. How about you?'

I suppressed a retch.

'Are you all right?' he asked, coming closer. His face was drawn, and there were dark semicircles beneath his eyes. I didn't even want to know how I looked – Ellis had at least made it into his pyjamas; I was still in my slip.

'Not really,' I said. 'Look what Emily brought on my breakfast tray.'

He glanced over and guffawed.

'It's not funny,' I said. 'It means they're all gossiping about us in the kitchen. And I lost your mother's hair comb.'

'Oh,' he said vaguely.

'Ellis, *I lost the hair comb.*'

When the gravity of this sank in, he sat on the edge of the bed and the last of his colour drained.

'What am I going to do?' I said, curling into a ball.

He took a deep breath and thought. After a few seconds, he slapped his thighs with resolve and said, 'Well. You'll have to telephone the Pews and tell them to be on the lookout, that's all.'

'I was going to. But I can't.'

'Why not?'

'For one thing, I can't get near the telephone. Your mother's been on it all day. God only knows what she's heard. And anyway, I can't call Mrs Pew. I can't face her, not even over the telephone.'

'Why?'

'Because we were *tight*! We rolled around in the street!'

'Everyone was tight.'

'Yes, but not like us,' I said miserably. I sat up and cradled my head in my hands. 'I don't even remember leaving. Do you?'

'Not really.' He got up and walked to my dressing table. 'When did you get this?' he asked, picking up the cork.

'I haven't a clue,' I replied.

On the main floor the telephone rang yet again, and I cowered. Ellis came back to the bed and took my hand. This time when Pemberton fetched my mother-in-law, her footsteps were brisk and she spoke in punctuated bursts. After a few minutes she went silent again, and the silence was ominous, rolling through the house like waves of poisonous gas.

Ellis looked at my clock. 'She'll come up to dress for dinner in a few minutes. You can call then.'

'Come with me?' I whispered, clutching his hand.

'Of course,' he said. 'Do you want one of your heart pills?'

'No, I'll be all right,' I said.

'Do you mind if I . . .?' He let the question trail off.

'Of course not. Help yourself.'

At ten to seven, forty minutes before we were expected in the drawing room for cocktails, we crept downstairs, both of us in our robes, glancing nervously at each other and hiding behind corners until we ascertained that nobody was around. I felt like a child sneaking down to eavesdrop on a party for grown-ups.

I telephoned Mrs Pew and sheepishly asked if she would please keep an eye out for my hair comb. After a slight pause, she said curtly that yes, she would. *As she had told me last night.*

When I hung up, I turned wordlessly to Ellis, who pulled me into his arms.

'Hush, my darling,' he said, pressing my head to his chest. 'This too shall pass.'

At seven thirty, we met at the top of the stairs. I had bathed and repaired my hair as best I could in the available time. I had also put on a touch of lipstick and rouge, since my face was so devoid of colour as to be nearly transparent, and dabbed some eau de toilette behind my ears. Ellis had nicked himself shaving, and there were comb marks in his wet hair.

'Ready?' he said.

'Absolutely not. You?'

'Courage, my dear,' he said, offering his arm. I curled my icy fingers in the crook of his elbow.

As Ellis and I entered the drawing room, my father-in-law, Colonel Whitney Hyde, raised his face and aimed it at the grandfather clock. He was leaning against the mantel, right next to a delicate cage hanging from an elaborate floor stand. The canary within was the colour of orange sorbet, a plump, smooth ovoid with a short fan of a tail, chocolate spots for eyes and a sweet beak. He was almost too perfect to be real, and not once had he sung during my four-year tenure in this house, even as his quarters were reduced to help him concentrate.

My mother-in-law, Edith Stone Hyde, sat perched on the edge of a silk jacquard chair the colour of a robin's egg, Louis XIV style. Her grey eyes latched onto us the moment we entered the room.

Ellis crossed the carpet briskly and kissed her cheek. 'Happy New Year, Mother,' he said. 'I hope you're feeling better.'

'Yes, Happy New Year,' I added, stepping forward.

She turned her gaze on me and I stopped in my tracks. Her jaw was set, her eyes unblinking. Over by the mantel, the ends of the Colonel's moustache twitched. The canary fluttered from its perch to the side of the cage and clung there, its fleshless toes and translucent claws wrapped round the bars.

Tick, tock went the clock. I thought my knees might go out from under me.

'Better . . . Hmmm . . . Am I feeling better . . .' She spoke slowly, clearly, mulling the words. Her brow furrowed ever so slightly. She drummed her fingers on the arm of the chair, starting with her smallest finger and going up, twice, and then reversing the order. The rhythm was that of a horse cantering. The pause felt interminable.

She looked suddenly up at Ellis. 'Are you referring to my migraine?'

'Of course,' Ellis said emphatically. 'We know how you suffer.'

'Do you? How kind of you. Both of you.'

Tick, tock.

Ellis straightened his spine and his tie and went to the sideboard to pour drinks. Whiskys for the men, sherries for the ladies. He delivered his mother's, then his father's, and then brought ours over.

'Tell me, how was the party?' his mother said, gazing at the delicate crystal glass she held in her lap. Her voice was completely without inflection.

'It was quite an event,' Ellis said, too loudly, too enthusiastically. 'The Pews certainly do things right. An orchestra, endless champagne, never-ending trays of delicious titbits. You'd never know there was a war going on. She asked after you, by the way. Was very sorry to hear you weren't feeling well. And the funniest thing happened at the stroke of midnight – did you hear? People will be talking about it for years.'

The Colonel harrumphed and tossed back his whisky. The canary jumped from one side of its cage to the other.

'I've heard rather a lot,' my mother-in-law said coldly, still staring into her glass. Her eyes shifted deliberately to me.

The blood rose to my cheeks.

'So, there we all were,' Ellis continued bravely, 'counting down to midnight, when all of a sudden there was a positively *huge* explosion. Well, even though we're a continent away from the action, you can imagine what we thought! We nearly—'

'*Silence!*' roared the Colonel, spinning to face us. His cheeks and bulbous nose had gone purple. His jowls trembled with rage.

I recoiled and clutched Ellis's arm. Even my mother-in-law jumped, although she regained her composure almost immediately.

In our set, battles were won by sliding a dagger coolly in the back, or by the quiet turn of a screw. People crumpled under the weight of an indrawn sigh or a carefully chosen phrase. Yelling was simply not done.

The Colonel slammed his empty glass down on the mantel. 'Do you think we're fools? Do you think we haven't heard all about the *real* highlight of the party? What people will *really* be talking about for years? About your *disgraceful*, your *depraved* . . . your . . . *contemptible* behaviour?'

What happened next was a blur of insults and rage. Apparently we had done more than just get drunk and make fools of ourselves, and apparently Ellis's moment of temper had not been his worst misdeed. Apparently, he had also crowed loudly about our decision to go monster-hunting and 'show the old man up,' stridently proclaiming his intentions even as Hank was using a foot to shove him into the back of the car.

The Colonel and Ellis closed in on each other across the enormous silk carpet, pointing fingers and trying to outshout each other. The Colonel accused us of going out of our way to try to embarrass him, as well as being loathsome degenerates and generally useless members of society, and Ellis argued that there was nothing he *could* do, and for that matter the Colonel did nothing either. What exactly did his father expect him to do? Take up a trade?

My mother-in-law sat silently, serenely, with a queerly calm look on her face. Her knees and ankles were pressed together in ladylike fashion, tilted slightly to the side. She held her unsipped sherry by the stem, her eyes widening with delight at particularly good tilts. Then, without warning, she snapped.

The Colonel had just accused Ellis of conveniently coming down with colour-blindness the moment his country needed him, the cowardice of which had caused him – his *father* and a *veteran* – the greatest personal shame of his life, when Edith Stone Hyde swivelled to face her husband, bug-eyed with fury.

'How *dare* you speak of my son like that!'

To my knowledge, she had never raised her voice before in her life, and it was shocking. She continued in a strained but shrill tone that quavered with righteous indignation – Ellis could no more help being colour-blind than other unfortunates could help having club feet, *didn't he realise*, and the colour-blindness, *by the way*, hadn't come from *her* side of the family. And speaking of genetics, she blamed *her* (and here she actually flung out an arm and pointed at me) for Ellis's downfall. An unbalanced harlot *just like her mother.*

'Now see here! That's my wife you're talking about!' Ellis shouted.

'She was no harlot!' the Colonel boomed.

For two, maybe three seconds, there wasn't a sound in the room but the ticking of the clock and the flapping of the canary, which had been driven to outright panic. It was a haze of pale orange, banging against the sides of its cage and sending out bursts of tiny, downy feathers.

Ellis and I looked at each other, aghast.

'Oh, really?' my mother-in-law said calmly. 'Then what, exactly, was she, dear?'

The Colonel moved his mouth as though to answer, but nothing came out.

'It's all right. I always suspected. I saw the way you used to look at her,' my mother-in-law continued. Her eyes burned brightly with the indignity of it all. 'At least you weren't foolish enough to run off with her.'

I was almost compelled to defend the Colonel, to point out that *everybody* had looked at my mother that way – they couldn't help themselves – but knew better than to open my mouth.

My mother-in-law turned suddenly to Ellis.

'And *you* – I warned you. As embarrassing as it was, I probably could have tolerated it if you'd just wanted to carouse, to sow some wild oats, but no, despite all the other very suitable matches you could have made, you snuck off to marry' – she paused, pursing her lips and shaking her head quickly as she decided what to call me – '*this*. And I was right. The apple doesn't fall far from the tree. It's positively shameful the way the two of you and that beastly Boyd fellow carry on. I despair of the grandchildren. Although, frankly, I've nearly lost hope in that regard. Perhaps it's just as well.' She sighed and went calm again, smoothing her forehead and staring into the distance to revel in her victory. She'd successfully dressed down every other person in the room and thought it was now over: game, set, match.

She was wrong. Had she looked, she'd have noticed that Ellis was turning a brilliant shade of crimson that rose from the base of his neck, spread beneath his blond hair and went all the way to the tips of his ears.

'Let's talk about shame, shall we?' he said quietly, ferociously. 'There's absolutely nothing that I – or Maddie, or anyone else – could do to bring further shame upon this family. You' – his voice rose in a crescendo until he was shouting again, pointing his glass at his father and shaking it, sloshing whisky onto the carpet – 'shamed all of us beyond redemption the moment you faked those pictures!'

The ensuing silence was horrifying. My mother-in-law's mouth opened into a surprised *O*. The small crystal glass she'd been holding slipped to the floor and shattered.

Tick, tock went the clock.

This is the story as I'd heard it:

In May 1933, an article appeared in a Scottish newspaper that made headlines around the world. A businessman (university-educated, the reporter was careful to point out) and his wife were motoring along the newly built A82 on the north side of Loch Ness when they spotted a whale-size animal thrashing in otherwise perfectly calm water. Letters to the editor followed describing similar incidents, and the journalist himself, who happened to be a water bailiff, claimed to have personally seen the 'Kelpie' no fewer than sixteen times. Another couple reported that something 'resembling a prehistoric monster' had slithered across the road in front of their vehicle with a sheep in its mouth. A rash of other sightings followed, sparking a worldwide craze.

The Colonel, who had been fascinated since boyhood by cryptozoology, and sea serpents in particular, came down with a full-blown case of 'Nessie Mania.' He followed the stories with increasing restlessness, clipping newspaper articles and making sketches based on the descriptions therein. He had retired from the military, and idleness did not suit him. He'd largely filled the void with big game hunting in Africa, but by then he found it unsatisfying. His trophy room was run-of-the-mill. Who didn't have a zebra skin hanging on the wall, a mounted rhinoceros head, or an elephant-foot umbrella stand? Even the posed, snarling lion was passé.

When the first published photograph of the monster, taken by a man named Hugh Gray, was denounced by sceptics as being the blurred image of a swimming dog, the Colonel was so incensed he announced he was going to Scotland to prove the monster's existence personally.

He prevailed upon the hospitality of his second cousin, the Laird of Craig Gairbh, whose estate was near the shores of the loch, and in a matter of weeks had taken multiple photographs that showed the curved neck and head of a sea serpent emerging from the water.

The pictures were published to widespread acclaim on both sides of the Atlantic, and the Colonel's triumphant return to the United States was marked with great fanfare. Reporters flocked to the house, stories ran in all the major newspapers and he was generally regarded as a hero. He took to wearing estate tweeds around town, which made him instantly recognizable as the celebrity he was, and joked, in a faux British accent, that his only regret was not being able to mount the head in his trophy room, explaining that since Scotland Yard itself had requested he not harm the beast, it would have been in bad taste to do so. The height of the frenzy was when he appeared in a newsreel that played before *It Happened One Night*, the biggest movie of the year.

Like Icarus, he flew too close to the sun. It wasn't long before the *Daily Mail* published an article suggesting that the size of the wake was wrong and making the scandalous accusation that the Colonel had photographed a floating model. Next came allegations of photographic trickery – so-called experts claimed the photographs had been touched up and then rephotographed, citing slightly different angles and shadows, variations in the reflections. Because the Colonel had processed his own film, he was unable to defend himself.

The Colonel swore by the veracity of his photos and expressed outrage that his honour was being called into question precisely because he'd been honourable enough to defer to the request from Scotland Yard. If he'd just gone ahead and shot the beast – and he'd brought his elephant rifle with him for that very purpose – no one would be able to deny his claims.

The final nail in the coffin of public opinion was when Marmaduke Wetherell, a big game hunter who had been on safari with the Colonel several times, arrived at the loch with a cadre of reporters declaring that he was going to prove once and for all that the monster existed, and then promptly falsified monster tracks using an ashtray made from the foot of a hippo – a hippo that the Colonel himself had taken down in Rhodesia.

Reporters and their impudent questions were no longer welcome. The Colonel gave up his tweeds and his accent. The sketches and newspaper clippings, so carefully glued into Moroccan leather scrapbooks, disappeared. By the time I came into Ellis's life, the subject was taboo, and preserving the Colonel's dignity paramount.

Of course, what was taboo to the rest of the world was anything but to our little trio, especially when the Colonel was acting particularly accusatory about Ellis's inability to serve.

It was Hank who came up with the idea of us finding the monster ourselves. It was a brilliant mechanism for blowing off steam that allowed Ellis to poke merciless fun at the Colonel, imagine himself triumphing where his father had failed, while simultaneously proving that he was as red-blooded as any man at the Front. It was a harmless fantasy, a whimsy we trotted out and embellished regularly, usually at the end of a long night of drinking, but never within anyone else's earshot – at least, not before the New Year's Eve party.

Ellis swallowed loudly beside me. My mother-in-law remained frozen to her seat, her fingers and mouth still open, the crystal sherry glass in shards at her feet.

The Colonel's face was tinged with blue, like the skin of a ripe plum, and for a moment I thought he might be having a stroke. He lifted a quivering finger and pointed at the door.

'Get out,' he said in a strange, hollow voice. 'Pemberton will send your things.'

Ellis shook his head in confusion. 'What do you mean? To where?'

The Colonel turned his back to us, resting one elbow on the mantel, posing.

'To where?' Ellis asked with increasing desperation. 'Where are we supposed to go?'

The Colonel's stiff back and complete lack of response made it clear that wherever we went, it was of no concern to him.

4

Ellis directed the chauffeur to the Society Hill Hotel on Chestnut Street. On the surface it looked fine: the façade and public areas were up to par, but our suite was faded and shabby and had only one bedroom. However, it was what we could afford on Ellis's reduced allowance.

Ellis bought a bottle of whisky from the lobby bar while the clerk was checking us in and began downing it as soon as we got upstairs.

I understood his desperation. If the Colonel cut his allowance completely, we'd be destitute. Regrettably, it was a very real possibility.

Ellis's crime against his father was twofold, and the parts were equally grievous. He had been caught railing against the Colonel behind his back, and then had accused him of fraud to his face. I didn't think the Colonel was capable of forgiving either separately, but together they were exponentially worse.

As we waited for our things to arrive, Ellis paced and drank, analysing and reanalysing what had just happened and generally working himself into a lather. At one point, when he allowed as to how he wouldn't have lost his temper if he hadn't been driven to defend me, I thought he was unfairly trying to shift the blame to me and said so, pointing out that I hadn't uttered a word throughout the entire fiasco.

He stopped and looked at me, both pained and surprised.

'My God,' he said. 'That's not what I meant at all. Of course it's not your fault. You did absolutely nothing. Her attack on you was completely gratuitous.'

'It's all right,' I said. 'She didn't say anything everyone else wasn't already thinking.'

'It's not all right, and I will never forgive her. Neither should you.'

I hoped he would change his mind, because his mother was currently our only hope of returning to grace. Although she demonstrated her affection in strange ways, her whole world revolved around Ellis and, to a lesser degree, around torturing me. Without us, her life would be a void. I was entirely sure that she was already attempting to intercede, but I'd never seen the Colonel in such a state and I wasn't sanguine about her chances.

Appealing to my own father was pointless. When I wrote to tell him that Ellis and I had eloped, I'd expected him to be upset and wasn't surprised when he didn't respond right away. It was months before it dawned on me that he wasn't going to. I'd seen him only once since, although we lived less than two miles apart. He was crossing the street, and when he saw me, he pretended he hadn't and turned the other way. From overheard fragments of conversation, I gathered his activities revolved almost exclusively around the Corinthian Yacht Club, allowing him to avoid contact with the fairer sex altogether.

At some point after midnight, I managed to convince Ellis that our things weren't on their way and we should just go to bed. Neither of us had so much as an overnight bag.

While the room was stuffy, it was also draughty. Ellis called me a 'blanket hog,' accusing me of repeatedly rolling away with the covers, at which point he'd grab them back and leave me exposed. After a few rounds of tug-of-war, which started out in good fun but deteriorated quickly, we ended up facing opposite directions on the edges of the bed with neither one of us adequately covered.

I lay awake worrying. When Ellis finally fell asleep, he snored so loudly I had to hold a pillow over my head, pressing it against my ears. There was an odd smell, sort of earthy and minerally. For the rest of the night, all I could think about was how many heads had lain on those pillows before my own.

We were roused by an understated yet insistent rapping at the door.

'Dear God,' croaked Ellis. 'What time is it?'

I peered at the radium-painted clock beside me. 'Nearly seven.'

'The sun's not even up,' he complained.

After a few more minutes of intermittent knocking, I mumbled, 'You'd better get it. They're not going away.'

He sighed irritably, then shouted, *'Coming!'*

He switched on the lamp and rolled out of bed, yanking the chenille bedspread off as though he were doing the table-cloth trick. He wrapped it round his shoulders and stomped away, slamming the bedroom door behind him.

I had a fair indication of what was going on because of the shuffles, bangs and clunks. It went on for nearly ten minutes.

When Ellis returned, he wadded up the bedspread and tossed it onto my legs. As he flopped back into bed, I tried to straighten it.

'Our things, I presume?' I asked.

'Our every worldly belonging, from the looks of it. Six carts' worth. We're going to have to turn sideways to get to the door.'

I tried not to panic – the Colonel would have given the order before he retired for the night, when his anger was still fresh – but a queasy feeling settled in the pit of my stomach anyway.

'I don't suppose you have any idea where your pills might have ended up?' Ellis asked.

'Would you like me to have a look?'

'Never mind,' he said miserably. 'It's all right.'

The lamp was still on, so I went to the front room.

The floor was almost entirely covered by trunks and suit-cases. Emily, Pemberton and the others must have been up all night packing.

I found my cosmetics case on a low table, along with my hatboxes. To my relief, it was organised immaculately, the pill bottle tucked discreetly under its tray. Poor Emily – we'd cost her at least two nights' sleep, which my mother-in-law would certainly not consider an excuse if her daytime duties suffered.

I handed the bottle to Ellis and sat beside him. He propped himself up on an elbow, shook two pills into his hand and swallowed them dry. Then he fell back onto his pillow.

'Thank you, darling. I'm a little on edge,' he said.

'I know. Me too.'

'Let's try to get back to sleep. In the morning – in the *real* morning – I'm going to have the largest goddamned lobster in the city brought up to us, along with a mountain of potato salad. Caviar, too. They can skip the plates and just bring forks.'

I made my way back to my side of the bed. When I crawled under the covers, Ellis switched off the lamp. We found ourselves much closer together than we had been before. He rolled onto his side and threw an arm across my waist.

'Well, what do you know,' he said. 'Maybe there are enough blankets after all.'

In the early evening, the concierge called to tell us that Hank was waiting for us in the lobby bar.

Ellis and I were no longer speaking, a result of my suggestion that he talk to his mother and try to pave the way for a truce. We rode the elevator in silence.

The boys drank bourbon sidecars, and I ordered a gin fizz. A few drinks in, as Ellis and I took turns recounting the disastrous repercussions of the party, the freeze began to thaw. Soon, we were finishing each other's sentences and apologising with our eyes. We were in the same mess, facing the same consequences. Although I was willing to capitulate sooner, it was just a tactical difference. We were upset with our situation, not each other.

I reached my foot out under the table and ran it lightly down his calf. His eyes brightened, and the edges of his mouth lifted into a smile.

'I'm still trying to wrap my head around the idea of your mother shouting,' said Hank. 'Are you sure it was your mother? The same Edith Stone Hyde I've known all these years?'

'The very one. And it was more like a hooting,' said Ellis. 'An overtaxed owl.'

'A broken-down woodwind,' I added. 'Frail, yet screechy.'

'I'd have paid good money to see that,' said Hank, lighting a cigarette.

'I wish I'd known,' said Ellis. 'I'd have offered you my seat.'

'Do you really think the Colonel and your mother had an affair?' Hank asked, blowing a series of smoke rings.

'Of course not,' I said. 'My gorgon of a mother-in-law

extrapolated that because at some point she caught him looking at her, which I'm sure he did. Everybody did.'

'Yes, but he also defended her,' Hank pointed out. 'To his wife.'

'So maybe he carried a little torch for her,' I said, 'which still means nothing, because who didn't? She had that effect on people.'

'Not your father,' Hank continued. 'I never did understand why she married him. She could have had anybody she liked. Gorgeous, pedigreed, a bank account the size of Montana . . . I can't imagine why she allowed herself to get hitched to an old fart like your father.'

'She wasn't pedigreed,' I said, throwing him a dirty look. Hank knew perfectly well that my mother had married up.

Hank looked outraged. 'Of course she was pedigreed . . . *in the Levee District!*' He broke down, cackling at his own joke.

'Ha ha,' I said flatly.

'No offence, darling girl. Money is its own pedigree. But back on topic, what if it's true? Maybe that's why your mother-in-law was so hell-bent against the two of you getting married. *Maybe*,' he said, waving his cigarette in circles, 'you're brother and sister.'

Ellis and I burst into simultaneous groans of disgust.

'Hank, that's not even remotely funny! Please. My mother did *not* have an affair with the Colonel.'

'How can you be so sure?' Hank went on. 'Maybe that's the reason your mother-in-law encouraged him to go monster-hunting. To get him out of harm's way, so to speak.'

'I'm sure she just wanted him out of the way, period,' I said. 'She probably packed his bags. She probably booked his passage.'

'You're both forgetting that it was his idea,' said Ellis. 'He couldn't get out of there fast enough. I'm surprised he didn't leave a Colonel-shaped hole in the front door on the way out. Can hardly blame him, though.'

'She *is* a trial,' I said.

'She's worse than that,' said Ellis, looking suddenly grim.

Hank leaned back in his chair and cocked an eyebrow. He looked first at Ellis and then at me. 'Your drinks are empty. Let me remedy that.' He snapped his fingers over his head until he got the attention of the bartender, then pointed at the glasses.

Ellis stared into his depleted drink, poking the ice cubes with his swizzle stick.

'So,' Hank said, rubbing his hands together. 'Given the circumstances, I think you'll be even more pleased to hear my news.'

'Unless you're about to tell me my father dropped dead, I highly doubt it,' Ellis said without looking up.

The waiter delivered fresh drinks. Ellis pulled his toward him, picked up the new swizzle stick, and went back to stabbing ice.

'Maddie, darling?' Hank said expectantly.

I sighed before dutifully asking, 'What news?'

'I've found us passage.'

'Passage to where?' I asked in the same disinterested voice.

I knew full well what he was talking about, and was trying to convey that I didn't want to play and was quite sure that Ellis didn't either.

'You know,' Hank said with a coy smile.

I went for the direct approach. 'Hank, we're not in the mood right now. That's what got us into this pickle in the first place.'

'Then get in the mood. We leave in three days.'

I put my drink down and took stock of his demeanour. He was deadpan, yet clearly pleased with himself.

'You're not serious,' I said.

'I'm in absolute earnest,' he replied.

'But it's impossible. There are no liners running.'

'Connections, Maddie, connections,' he said with a flourish. 'We're going on a Liberty ship. The SS *Mallory*, a freighter taking supplies. It's part of a convoy. And speaking of supplies, stock up on cigarettes and stockings, both nylon and silk. International currency, if you will.'

His continued straight face began to worry me.

'Hank, this isn't funny.'

'It's not meant to be.'

'We can't cross the Atlantic during the war—'

'We'll be perfectly safe. We're going to the Highlands. That's where they sent the evacuated children from the cities, for God's sake.'

I turned to Ellis. He'd abandoned the ice, and was now pushing the ashtray back and forth.

'Darling, say something,' I pleaded.

'Don't we need papers, or something?' he asked.

'Arranged for them too,' Hank said brightly. 'And a sixteen-millimeter Cine-Kodak movie camera. After we get our footage of the monster, we'll send the reel directly to Eastman Kodak and have them develop it. Voilà – would-be naysayers won't have a nay to say. We'll make history. We'll be famous.'

After a moment of stammering, I managed to ask, 'And what does Violet think about this?'

Violet was nothing if not sensible. She didn't even approve when we pulled entirely harmless pranks, like hiding some-one's yacht in the wrong slip, or turning the racquet club's pool water purple. She'd sent an apology after we had General

Pew's sailboat moved round to the back of his house, even though she wasn't there when the crime was committed.

'No idea. She's off doing something or other,' said Hank. 'Rolling bandages or the like.'

'You haven't told her,' I said in disbelief.

'Not yet,' said Hank, sipping his drink. 'I figured one day of misery was preferable to three.'

'She'll never agree to it.'

'I don't expect her to.'

'Hank, she's expecting you to *propose*. You can't just abandon her.'

'I will propose, just as soon as we get back. Frankly, I'm getting a little worried that she's rubbing off on you. I was hoping it would work the other way round.'

'Hank's right,' said Ellis, still pushing the ashtray around. 'You used to like adventures.'

'I do like adventures, but sailing into the war is hardly an adventure!'

'Then think of it as a scientific excursion,' Hank said calmly. 'Honestly, Maddie. We'll be perfectly safe. You can't imagine I would even suggest it if I weren't completely sure of that, and Freddie certainly wouldn't have arranged it.'

'Freddie?' I said with growing despair. 'What's Freddie got to do with this?'

'He's the one who made the arrangements, of course.'

While I was trying to wrap my head round Freddie's involvement in all this, Hank looked deep into my eyes.

'Maddie, darling girl. This is my last hurrah, my final bit of craziness before donning the ball and chain. And since my particular ball and chain seems intent on civilising me, surely you wouldn't deny me this one final caper?'

'Why don't we come up with something that won't get us blown to pieces? And who's to say that I won't rub off on

Violet after all? When the war ends, we'll force her to come with us. I'll buy a pair of hip waders and bag the monster myself – heck, I'll buy a pair for Violet and drag her kicking and screaming into the loch with me. Won't that be a sight?'

Hank leaned forward and pressed two fingers against my lips.

'Shhh,' he said. 'We have to do this. It's for Ellis.'

Ellis looked up suddenly. The fire was back in his eyes. 'Let's do it. Let's fucking do it. It fixes everything.'

'What? What does it fix?' I asked.

'Everything,' he repeated.

I could see there was no arguing with him – at least not there, and certainly not in front of Hank.

'I'll have one of those cigarettes,' I said, bobbing my foot under the table and glaring at the rows of glittering bottles behind the bar.

In a flash, Hank had the case open and extended. I let him hold it there for a few seconds longer than was comfortable, then grabbed one.

Hank leaned forward, completely cool, and flicked his lighter, a sterling silver Dunhill with a clock on its side. I sucked a few times, enough to get the thing lit, then pushed my chair back and marched toward the bank of elevators, letting my heels clack noisily on the marble. I ditched the cigarette in the first available ashtray because I hated cigarettes, which both Hank and Ellis knew. Asking for one was a statement. Ellis was supposed to follow me back to our suite. Instead, he stayed in the lobby bar with Hank.

I paced the room, trying to persuade myself that this was a joke, that Hank was just pulling our legs, but every instinct told me otherwise. He'd worked out too many details, and if it was a prank, he wouldn't have let it go on after he saw

Ellis's reaction – unless they were in on it together, but that seemed even less plausible. They hadn't had a moment alone to plan.

I just wanted everything to go back to normal, but the only way that could happen would be if we found a solution that let both the Colonel and Ellis emerge with their dignities intact. Collective amnesia would have been an option if the accusations had been limited to the drawing room, where the only witness was the canary, but they hadn't. The Colonel had been disgraced in public.

The part that frightened me most, that made me think Hank really had made solid plans, was his mention of Freddie. If anyone could manage such arrangements, it was Freddie Stillman, whose father was an admiral, but it was beyond me why he'd lift a finger to help. The four of us had been close friends, a quartet instead of a trio, during one blissful summer in Bar Harbor, Maine, until I rejected his completely un-expected proposal, and probably not as sensitively as I should have. Ten days later I eloped with Ellis, and we hadn't exchanged a word since. That was four and a half years ago.

I was surprised that Hank was still in touch with him, especially since it was rumoured that Freddie had set his sights on Violet before Hank rolled through and swept her off her feet.

Ellis returned hours later, entirely smashed, and confirmed my fears. This was no prank, and he was absolutely determined that we were going to go.

I pointed out, as gently as I could, what I'd hoped was obvious: that it made no sense whatsoever to throw ourselves into the middle of an ocean crawling with U-boats on a quest to find a monster that probably didn't even exist, especially as a way of proving his worth to people who were too ignorant to realise he was as honourable as any of them. We knew the truth. *I* knew the truth. It would be difficult, but together we could withstand the scrutiny until the war ended.

Ellis turned on me with such ferocity I almost didn't recognise him.

Of course there was a monster, he said. Only an idiot would think there wasn't a monster. Never mind all the sightings and photographs, including his own father's – which, by the way, were still the best of the lot – Scotland Yard itself had confirmed the beast's existence when they asked the Colonel not to harm it.

Even as he continued shouting at me, waving his arms round the tiny, luggage-filled room, even as I absorbed that he had essentially called me an idiot, what really caught my attention was that he'd done a complete about-face regarding his father's pictures.

I tried to process this as Ellis pointed at the wallpaper, which was curling at the corners, at the water stains on the ceiling, as he wiped his finger along the windowsill and then held it up so I could inspect the grime. I wondered if he'd believed his father all along and, if so, why he'd made such a terrible accusation the night before – never mind the things he'd said as we left the party.

I hadn't uttered a word since my initial plea, but he continued his tirade as though I were arguing with him.

Did I really want to live in this dump, sitting around like hostages, waiting to see if the Colonel was going to cut off his allowance completely? And what if he did? What then? Did I think it was all right to act like Scott Lyons, running tabs up to the hilt and then skipping out, moving from hotel to hotel? Because he certainly didn't.

We were going to Scotland, it was our only option, and

we would not set foot on this continent again until he had found the monster the Colonel had faked.

He stopped, red and sweaty, huffing and puffing and waiting for me to challenge him, but my brain was stuck on the fact that he'd flip-flopped on the subject of his father yet again, and all in a matter of seconds.

I had witnessed firsthand how badly society treated Ellis – particularly his own father – and was well aware of the toll it was taking. For four years, I'd stood by helplessly as the happy, confident young man I'd met in Bar Harbor eroded into the bitter, suspicious man currently raging in front of me, a man who constantly believed people were giving him dirty looks and whispering behind his back, a man who was increasingly irritated by my Pollyannaish platitudes because he recognised them for what they were. But because I'd watched this devolution happen in dribbles and bits, I hadn't realised until that moment that he'd already been pushed beyond his limits. What was currently at stake was his entire self-worth.

Hank was right. Ellis needed this.

I crossed the half dozen feet that divided us and put my arms round him, pressing my face to his chest. After a moment of shocked hesitation he put his arms round me, too, and a few seconds after that, I felt him relax.

'I'm so sorry, my darling, I don't know what came over me,' he said.

'It's okay,' I said.

'I should never have spoken to you like that. It's inexcusable. You did absolutely nothing wrong.'

'I understand, darling. It's okay.'

'Oh God, Maddie,' he said, breathing into my ear. 'Hank's right. They broke the mould when they made you. I can't imagine what I did to deserve you.'

For a moment, as absurd as it was, I thought he might want to make love, but from his chest movements I could tell he was starting to cry. I held him even tighter.

If finding the monster was what it was going to take to make Ellis feel whole again, then so be it. I just hoped there was a monster to be found.

And so, three days later, we sailed into the Battle of the Atlantic.

5

I saw my first rat before we set sail.

Although our cabins were in the officers' quarters, there were only two and they were tiny, so Ellis and I had to share a very small bed – a bunk, really – which would have made sleeping impossible even if the engine that powered the rudder wasn't immediately beneath us. There was a small washbasin in the cabin, but the bath facilities were shared. I was the only woman on board, so I had to wash myself at the sink. I was also so sick I couldn't keep so much as a cracker down.

When I wasn't hanging my face over the sink trying not to throw up, I was lying on the bunk with my arms wrapped round my stomach, doing my best to stare into the distance, which in this case meant trying to focus on some point beyond the cabin wall, which was altogether too close.

The day before we were supposed to land at the naval base in Scotland, German U-boats caught up with one of the other ships in the convoy and torpedoed her. We circled back to pull men out of the water, which was so slick with fuel it was actually on fire. The Germans were still there, of course, and we could feel the depth charges, which pitched us about until I feared capsizing and splitting up in equal parts. Unsecured items flew across the room. The electricity flickered on and off, and the cabin was so full of smoke I couldn't breathe without choking. The handkerchiefs I held over my nose and mouth came away the colour of lead. Ellis took pills by the handful – he'd refilled my prescription before we left, getting a great many more than usual since he didn't know how long we were going to be away, and the quantities he consumed alarmed me.

When the torpedoes came, Hank shrank into a corner with a bottle of whisky, saying that if he was going to die, he might as well die drunk. I shrieked each time a deck gun fired. Ellis put his lifebelt on and wanted me to do the same, but I couldn't. Having something bulky strapped round my middle impeded my breathing and increased my panic, and besides, what possible difference could it make? If the ship went down, the Germans wouldn't pluck us from the water, and even if they did, the poor men the SS *Mallory* had managed to save were grievously burnt and likely to die anyway.

I flew into a tear-filled rage: I threw an alarm clock at Hank, who ducked it wordlessly and lit another cigarette. I pounded Ellis's chest and told him he had tossed us into the middle of a war because his father was a stubborn, stupid, irascible old man, and now, because of him, we were going to be killed. I said I hoped the Colonel dropped dead in his House of Testoni shoes, preferably upon hearing that we had all been blown up, because he was a fraudulent, egomaniacal blowhard without so much as a drop of compassion for anyone else on this earth, including – and especially – his own son. I declared Edith Stone Hyde a self-righteous, bitter old cow, and said I hoped she survived deep into a lonely old age so she could reap the rewards of her treatment of us and its fatal consequences. I told Ellis that the second we hit solid ground, I was turning round and taking the next boat out of there, although even as I said it I knew I would never willingly get on another ship. I told him that *he* was the idiot, and that his – and his father's – stupid obsession with a stupid monster was going to be the end of us all, and if he could come up with a stupider reason to die, I'd really like to know what that was.

Ellis's non-reaction was almost more frightening than the torpedoes, because I realised that he, too, thought we were going to die. And then I felt guilty and cried in his arms.

When we finally reached land, it was dusk. For the last couple of days, I'd been worried we might be changing ships rather than docking, because everyone kept referring to our destination as the HMS *Helicon*, but apparently that was a code name for the Aultbea Naval Base.

I was so desperate to get off the ship that I staggered on deck while the wounded were still being unloaded. Ellis followed me, but at the sight of the burnt men, turned and went back below.

Some of the men no longer looked human – scorched and misshapen, their flesh melted like candle wax. Their agonised moans were terrible to hear, but even more horrifying were the silent ones.

One looked me in the eyes as he was carried past, his head bobbing slightly in time with the steps of the men bearing the stretcher. His face and neck were blackened, his mouth open and lipless, exposing crowded teeth that made me think of a parrotfish. I hated myself immediately for the comparison. His eyes were hazel, and his arms ended in white bandages just below the elbows. His peeling scalp was a mottled combination of purple and black, his ears so charred I knew there was no hope of saving them.

He held my gaze until I turned in shame, leaning my forehead against the salty white paint of the exterior wall. I pressed my eyes shut. If I'd had the strength to go back down to the cabin I would have, but I didn't. Instead, I kept my eyes closed and held my hands over my ears. Although I managed to block out most sounds, I could do nothing about the vibration of footsteps on the deck. I was excruciatingly aware of each ruined life being carried past. God only knew how these men's lives would be changed, if they even survived. I tried not to think of their mothers, wives and sweethearts.

When we were finally allowed to disembark, I stumbled down the gangplank and onto the dock. My knees gave out, and if Hank hadn't been there to catch me, I'd have gone off the edge. Everything in my vision was jerking back and forth. I couldn't even tell which way was up.

'Jesus Christ, Maddie,' he said. 'You almost fell in the soup. Are you all right?'

'I don't know,' I said. My voice was hoarse. 'I feel like I'm still on the ship.'

Ellis took my other elbow, and together they led me off the dock. I stretched out an arm and leaned against a white-painted lamppost. The kerb at my feet was also white.

'Maddie? Are you okay?' said Ellis.

Before I could answer, a man in a wool greatcoat and hat approached us. He was tall and broad-shouldered, with red cheeks, black leather gloves and an eyepatch. His one eye alternated between Ellis and Hank. 'Henry Boyd?'

'That's me,' said Hank, lighting a cigarette.

'Well, I knew it was one of you,' the man said in a melodious accent, leaving us to interpret the wherefores. 'I'll be driving you, then. Where are your things?'

'Still on board. The porters are back there somewhere,' said Hank, waving vaguely towards the ship.

The man laughed. 'I'm your driver, not your lackey.'

Hank raised his eyebrows in surprise, but the man put his hands in his pockets, spun on his heels and began to whistle. His earlobe and part of the cartilage was missing on the same side as the eyepatch. A thick scar ran up his neck and disappeared beneath his ginger hair.

Ellis whispered, 'I think you're supposed to tip him.'

'Freddie said it was all taken care of,' Hank said.

'Apparently it's not,' Ellis murmured.

'Well, somebody do *something*!' I cried.

Hank cleared his throat to get the man's attention. 'I don't suppose I could make it worth your while . . .'

'Oh, aye,' said the man, in a firm but cheery voice. 'I wouldn't say no to a wee minding.'

When our trunks and suitcases had finally been identified, collected and loaded – a feat of engineering that resulted in an ungainly mountain of luggage strapped to the roof and trunk of the car – our driver raised his one visible eyebrow and glanced at Ellis's waist. 'I don't think you'll be needing that any more,' he said.

Ellis looked down. He was still wearing his lifebelt. He turned away, fumbling as he unfastened it, and let it drop at the base of a lamppost. I felt his shame acutely.

The driver opened the rear door of the car and motioned for me to get in. A soiled blanket covered the seat.

'Slide on over then,' he said. He winked at me. I think.

Ellis got in after me. Hank took one look at the blanket before walking to the front of the car. He stood by the passenger door, waiting for the driver to open it.

'Well, are you going to get in, or aren't you?' said the driver, jerking his chin toward the rear.

Finally, reluctantly, Hank came round to the back. Ellis frowned and shifted to the middle seat. Hank got in beside him.

'Right, then,' said the driver. He shut our door, climbed into the driver's seat and resumed whistling.

6

After four hours and twenty minutes of utter, stomach-roiling misery, with the driver leaning maliciously into hairpin curves despite (or perhaps because of) having to stop no fewer than six times so I could lean out of the back of the car and be sick, he came to a stop and announced we'd reached our destination.

'Here we are then,' he said cheerfully, shutting off the engine. 'Home, sweet home.'

I glanced outside. It wasn't clear to me we'd arrived anywhere.

My stomach began churning again and I couldn't wait for the driver to come round and let me out, although he was obviously in no rush to do anything. I fumbled with the handle, yanking it back and forth before finally realising it twisted. When I flung the door outwards, I went with it, landing on my knees in the gravel.

'Maddie!' Ellis cried.

'I'm all right,' I said, still grasping the door handle. I looked up, through the strands of hair that had fallen over my face. The clouds shifted to expose the moon, and in its light I saw our destination.

It was a squat, grey building in pebbledash, with heavy black shutters on the windows of both floors. A wooden sign hung over the entrance, creaking in the wind:

THE FRASER ARMS
Proprietor A. W. Ross
Licensed to Serve Beer and Spirits
Good Food, Rooms
Est. 1547

My queasiness rose in urgent waves, and while I couldn't believe there was anything left for me to expel, I hauled myself upright and staggered towards a half barrel of frostbitten pansies by the front door. I crashed into the wall instead, hitting first with my open palms and then my left cheek. I stayed there for a moment, my face flattened against the pebbled surface.

'Maddie? Are you all right?' Ellis asked from somewhere behind me.

'I'm fine,' I said.

'You don't look fine.'

I turned and slid down the wall, my coat and hair scraping against the embedded stones, until I was resting on my heels.

Snow collected on my exposed knees. Somewhere in the distance a sheep bleated.

'Maddie?'

'I'm fine,' I said again.

I watched as Ellis and Hank climbed out of the car, regarding them with something akin to loathing.

Ellis took a few steps towards the building and read the sign. He raised his eyebrows and looked back at Hank.

'*This* is where we're staying?'

'So it would appear,' said Hank.

'It looks like a pile of rubble,' said Ellis. 'Or one of those long communal mud houses. From, you know, Arizona or wherever.'

'What were you expecting, the Waldorf Astoria?' Hank asked. 'You knew we were going to be roughing it. Think of it as a field camp.'

Ellis harrumphed. 'That would be putting it kindly.'

'Where's your sense of adventure?'

'Somewhere in the ship's latrine, I suspect,' said Ellis. 'I suppose Freddie chose this dump.'

'Of course.'

'He might as well have sent us to a cave.'

Ellis stepped forward and rapped on the door. He waited maybe half a minute, then rapped again. Almost immediately after, he began thumping it with his fist.

The door swung open and Ellis leapt to the side as a huge man in striped blue pyjama bottoms and an undershirt burst forth. He was tall, broad, and densely muscled. His black hair stuck up in tufts, his beard was wild and he was barefoot. He came to a stop, ran his eyes over Ellis and Hank, then peered round them to get a look at the car.

'And what are you wanting, at this time of night?' he demanded.

'We need rooms,' Hank said round the edges of an unlit cigarette. He flicked the top of his lighter open, but before he could get it lit, the man's hand shot forward and snapped it shut.

'You canna smoke outside!' he said incredulously.

After a shocked pause – the man had reached within inches of his face – Hank said, 'Why not?'

'The blackout. Are you daft?'

Hank slipped both the lighter and cigarette into his pocket.

'Americans, are you?' the man continued.

'That we are,' said Hank.

'Where's your commanding officer?'

'We're not being billeted. We're private citizens,' said Hank.

'In that case, you can take yourselves elsewhere.' The man turned his head to the left and spat. Had he turned to the right, he would have seen me.

'I believe it's all been arranged,' Hank said. 'Does the name Frederick Stillman ring a bell?'

'Not so much as a tinkle. Get on with you, then. Leave me in peace.' He turned away, clearly planning to leave us on the side of the road.

I choked back a sob. If I didn't end up in a bed after everything we'd been through, I didn't think I wanted to survive at all.

'Wait,' said Hank quickly. 'You have no rooms?'

'I didn't say that,' the man said. 'Do you know what bloody time it is?'

Hank and Ellis exchanged glances.

'Of course,' said Ellis. 'We're sorry about that. Perhaps we could make it worth your while.'

The man grunted. 'Spoken like a toff. I've no truck with the likes o' you. Off you go.' He shooed them away with the back of his hand.

From just past the car, the driver snorted.

'Please,' Ellis said quickly. 'The journey was rough, and my wife – she's unwell.'

The man stopped. 'Your *what*?' he said slowly.

Ellis inclined his head in my direction.

The man turned and saw me crouched against the wall. He studied me for a moment, then looked back at Ellis.

'You've dragged a woman across the Atlantic during a war, then? Are you completely off your head?'

Ellis's expression went dark, but he said nothing.

The man's eyes flitted briefly skyward. He shook his head. 'Fine. You can stay the night, but it's only on account of your wife. And hurry up getting that kit inside or I'll have the warden round for the blackout. *Again.* And if I do, I'll not be the one paying the fine, mark my words.'

'Sure, sure. Of course,' said Hank. 'Say, can you do me a favour and send out the porter?'

The man responded with a single bark of laughter and went inside.

'Huh,' said Hank. 'I guess there's no porter.'

'And this surprises you because . . .?' said Ellis.

Hank looked back at the car, whose suspension was significantly lowered by the weight of our belongings.

Ellis came to me and held out his hands. As he pulled me to my feet, he said, 'Go inside, find a seat and make that brute bring you something to drink. We'll be in as soon as we've got this mess sorted out.'

I let myself in. The heavy wooden door groaned in both directions, and when it clicked shut, I glanced around self-consciously.

There was no sign of the bearded man, although he'd left a kerosene lamp on a long wooden bar to my left. Glossy beer spigots ran down its length: McEwan's, Younger's, Mackeson and Guinness, along with a few I couldn't make out. One had a cardboard sign hanging round it declaring it temporarily unavailable.

The lamplight flickered off the bottles on the shelves behind the bar, reflected and amplified by the mirror behind them. It looked for all the world like there was an identical, inverted room just beyond, and for a moment I wondered if I was in the wrong one.

There were a number of tables and chairs in front of the bar, and a wireless in a chest-high console against the far wall. The ceiling was low and supported by thick, dark beams, and the floor consisted of huge slabs of stone. The walls were plastered, and even by the dim light of the lamp's flame, I could make out the faint raised edges of the trowel tracks. Thick black material covered the windows, and it dawned on me that the white-painted lampposts and kerbs I'd seen in

Aultbea were to help cars navigate at night during the blackout.

To the right was a large stone fireplace with an assortment of stuffed and mismatched furniture arranged in front of it. Victorian, from the looks of it – a couch and two wing chairs positioned across from each other on a threadbare Oriental carpet, separated by a low, heavy table. The contents of the grate were covered by an even layer of ash, but still cast a faint orange glow.

I made my way to the couch and perched on the very edge of it, holding my numb fingers toward the embers. They smelled like smoked dirt, and the logs stacked off to the side were not wood. I had no idea what they were. They were rectangular and striated, and looked like gigantic Cadbury's Flake bars, the much-coveted treat sent by the British grandmother of one of my classmates.

A dog with scruffy grey fur rose from nowhere, materialising directly beside me. I stiffened. It was enormously tall, and thin as a greyhound, with the same rounded back and scooped abdomen. It stared at me, its dark eyes mournful, its tail curled between its legs.

'Don't worry. He'll do you no harm.'

The bearded man had come through a doorway behind the bar. He picked up the lamp, crossed the room and set a glass of something fizzy on the table in front of me.

The low ceiling accentuated his height, but he would have been imposing in any circumstances. His eyes were an unlikely and startling blue under eyebrows as unruly as his beard. He remained barefoot and robeless, and apparently unbothered by it.

'You've had a rough journey then?'

'Yes.' I reached up instinctively to check my hair, although since I could see myself from the chest down, I had a fair idea of how I looked.

He nodded at the glass. 'Ginger beer. To settle your stomach.'

'Thank you,' I said. 'That's very kind.'

I felt his eyes upon me. After a beat of silence, he said, 'I suppose you've heard there's a war.'

A familiar bristle ran up the back of my neck. I turned to see if Ellis was within earshot, but he and Hank were still outside, beyond the closed door, having a heated discussion with the driver.

'I have, yes.'

'Your husband and his friend look able-bodied enough.'

'My husband and his colleague are here to perform scientific research,' I said.

The man threw his head back and laughed. 'Of course. Monster hunters. Absolutely brilliant. And here I was thinking you were war tourists.'

He set the lamp on the table and waved at a board of keys behind the bar. 'You can take two and three, or four and five, or two and six for that matter. It makes no difference to me. And be quick about it. I'll not have you wasting my paraffin.'

I was emboldened. I'd never met a man so rude.

'Surely you mean kerosene,' I said.

'I think I know what I mean,' he said, turning to leave.

'Wait,' I said quickly. 'Don't you want to know our names?'

'Not particularly. What I want is to be in bed.' He slapped his thigh. 'Conall, *thig a seo!*'

The dog went to his side, and they slipped into the shadows behind the bar.

I was still staring at the place they'd disappeared when Hank and Ellis lurched through the front door, carrying a trunk between them. They dropped it on the worn flagstones and looked around.

'Where's the light switch?' Ellis said, squinting as he searched the walls.

'I don't think there is one,' I said.

I watched Ellis's eyes as he scanned the various lamps and sconces around the room. They were all topped by glass globes – oil lamps, every one.

'Are you kidding me? There's no electricity?'

'I don't think so,' I said.

His eyes glommed onto the radio. 'What about that?'

'Maybe it runs on batteries. I don't know,' I said. 'Isn't the driver going to help you with the luggage?'

'He took off,' said Hank. 'Left everything in the driveway.'

'You could have just tipped him again,' Ellis said.

'I believe it was your turn,' Hank said.

Ellis glared at him.

'What? It's only money,' Hank said. 'Anyway, it doesn't matter now. He's gone, and we need help. Where's that charming Scotsman?'

'I'm pretty sure he went back to bed,' I said.

'But we need help. Did you see where he went?' said Hank, craning his neck. His eyes lit on the doorway behind the bar.

'Hank, please. Just leave him alone.'

7

'Good Lord, Maddie – what did you pack? I told you to bring stockings, not gold bullion,' said Hank, dragging one of my suitcases behind him and letting it bang against each step.

'Just some essentials,' I said.

I was at the top of the stairwell, holding the lamp as Hank and Ellis brought up our luggage. I was freezing and queasy, and the lamp swung accordingly. I was terrified I'd trip and set the carpet on fire.

'Along with anchors and anvils, apparently,' said Hank, dropping the suitcase and wiping his hands.

Ellis came up behind him with two hatboxes.

'That's everything,' he said.

'Not really,' said Hank. 'We still have to get it into the rooms. I don't know why Maddie wouldn't just let me rouse Paul Bunyan.'

'She doesn't like to discomfit the staff,' said Ellis.

'Why ever not?' asked Hank, looking at me with surprise. 'Isn't that what staff are for?'

'Well, I would say so, yes,' said Ellis.

'It's still not too late to get him, you know,' said Hank.

'Yes it is,' I said crossly. 'He said we could take any of rooms two through six, so can we please just do that and go to bed?'

'All right, darling girl,' said Hank, glancing up the row of doors. 'I was merely pointing out that it would be faster if we had help. No need to work up a lather.'

I wobbled toward a hall table so I could ditch the lamp. I was as dizzy as the moment I'd got off the ship. If I hadn't known it was impossible, I'd have sworn the building itself was swaying.

'Why do you suppose room one is off-limits?' said Hank.

I turned round to find him trying the locked door. 'Hank, stop! For heaven's sake. Somebody's probably asleep in there, and every other room is available.'

He continued to jiggle the knob. 'But what if this is the room I want? What if it's the only one with a decent bath—'

The door swung inwards, tearing the knob from Hank's hand. He took a long step backwards as a striking young woman with red hair burst into the hallway wielding a fire iron.

'And what the hell are you wanting?' she shouted in a thick accent. Her hair was tied into curls with scraps of cloth, and she was wearing a heavy white nightgown. She planted herself in front of Hank, grasping the poker with both hands.

'Henry Winston Boyd,' Hank replied without missing a beat. He held out his hand. 'The fourth. And you?'

She turned her head and bellowed down the hall. 'Angus! *ANGUS!*'

Hank took a step backwards, hands up in surrender. 'No, wait. We're fellow guests. We've just arrived. See?' He gestured towards our luggage, which was scattered up and down the hallway.

She assessed it, ran her eyes over Ellis and me and finally settled back on Hank. She stepped right up to him, brandishing the iron in his face.

'I'm no guest,' she said, slanting her eyes accusingly. 'I'm Meg, and I'm not on the clock until tomorrow evening. So I'll not be doing anything for you until then – and that goes for all of you.' She returned to her room and slammed the door.

After a beat of silence, Hank said, 'I think she likes me.'

'Just pick a room,' said Ellis.

'No, really. I think she does.'

The rooms were cramped and depressing: each had a dresser with a mirror hanging above it, a narrow bed with two night-stands and beyond that a small sitting area with a lumpy chair, fireplace and a single blacked-out window. The wallpaper was faded Victorian, the rugs threadbare.

Hank chose room two, while Ellis and I took five and six respectively. Although Hank didn't spell out why he'd chosen that particular room, it wasn't hard to figure out.

Despite everything we'd just been through, he was plotting a romantic conquest. I was already incensed on Violet's behalf – I was pretty sure Hank never *had* told her we were leaving – but at that moment I was close to outrage. Then it occurred to me that maybe Hank didn't think a dalliance with Meg would count as an infidelity. Perhaps he simply felt entitled, that he had the *droit du seigneur* over servants.

Various rumours followed Hank around, including one about a pregnant kitchen maid his mother had tried, unsuccessfully, to frame for stealing, and who disappeared shortly thereafter, presumably with a large sum of money. The highlight of the story had always been how Hank's mother had stashed an entire set of Georgian silver in the girl's room and then called the police. The actual cause of the situation was glossed over, dismissed with the vague explanation that 'boys will be boys.' In the narrative, the maid herself never quite seemed real to me, nor did the child. I wondered now if either ever crossed Hank's mind.

'I'm going to lie down,' I said, leaving the men to deal with the luggage.

My room was the final one on the left. I lit the candle on the dresser and fell on the bed, shoes and all, waiting for them to bring in my things.

'The door at the end we thought was a closet?' said Hank, dragging in a trunk. 'It's a bathroom. Thank God.'

'Shared!' came Ellis's voice from the hallway.

'With running water!' Hank called back. He looked at me and winked. 'Wait for it,' he whispered, holding a finger to his lips. 'Wait . . . Any second now . . .'

Out in the hallway, Ellis mumbled something inaudible.

Hank laughed uproariously. 'He always gets the last word. Or so he thinks. Anyway, the bathroom. It's indoors, and it's right next to you, you lucky thing.'

As much as I felt like collapsing, I had to at least get the soot off my face and scour my teeth. I revived myself enough to dig through my luggage and find what I needed – no easy task, since I'd undone all of Emily's good work in my panic to consolidate for the trip. We'd been warned that our storage space on the freighter was limited – an irony if I'd ever heard one, since the ship's raison d'être was storage. In the end, I'd found myself throwing things in randomly, frantically, sure that whatever I didn't bring would turn out to be vitally important.

As I left my room, I banged into the corner of the dresser so hard I cried out, and a horrible thought struck me. What if the waves never did stop? What if I was going to be like this for ever?

When I returned from the bathroom, Ellis was at the far end of my room, poking the empty grate with a fire iron.

'Empty, of course, and the radiators are off. A class act all round. No electricity, one bathroom, no heat. I'm going to get some wood, or coal, or dung, or whatever it is they're burning downstairs.'

'Please don't,' I said. 'The fellow who let us in seems sensitive about fuel.'

'So what? I can see my breath.' He presented his profile and exhaled, loosing a gossamer wisp of vapour.

'I'll be fine,' I said. 'There are lots of blankets. And I can always wear my robe to bed.'

'Are you sure? I don't mind dealing with Blackbeard.'

'Yes. I'm sure. Anyway, we'd probably burn the place down.'

Ellis cracked a slow smile. 'You mean like Hamlet House?'

During our honeymoon in Key West, an unattended cigar of Ellis's had nearly caused a catastrophe at a historic painted lady we'd nicknamed Hamlet House because the Prince of Denmark was a fellow guest. The prince, along with everyone else, was forced to change hotels, but since no one was hurt the incident became funny in the retelling, a part of Ellis's and my shared repertoire, a story we trotted out at parties.

I knew that by bringing it up, he was trying to stir a fond memory and make things better between us, but what he didn't realise was that remembering the fire in Key West just made me think of the horribly burnt men I'd seen carried off the ship only a few hours earlier.

'Yes, like Hamlet House,' I said.

'We didn't burn it down. Merely scorched a few rooms,' he said whimsically.

I climbed into bed and shuddered.

Ellis furrowed his brow, then set the poker in its stand and came to my side.

We'd made a fragile peace after finally outrunning the U-boats, a truce that consisted mostly of giving each other as much space as possible in a situation where there simply wasn't any, and talking only when absolutely necessary. But that didn't mean my breakdown on the ship hadn't happened, or that I wasn't aware of how horrifyingly quickly proximity had bred contempt, or that I wasn't still terrified and furious about being dragged along on this half-baked escapade. It was the stupidest and most dangerous thing we'd ever done.

It was also pointless. I'd realised it the moment the driver commented on the lifebelt that remained round Ellis's waist, and again when the bearded man asked why he and Hank weren't serving, and I knew that it would keep happening. The very thing we'd tried to escape had followed us across the Atlantic.

I opened my eyes and found Ellis staring down at me, his misery obvious. I knew he wanted comfort, a sign that things would go back to normal between us, but I couldn't give it to him. I just couldn't.

'Please, Ellis. I don't mean to be harsh, but I'm completely and absolutely desperate for sleep . . .'

His lips stretched into a sad line. 'Of course. I know you're exhausted.'

He leaned over to kiss my forehead, and in that instant my resentment shattered, leaving behind an awful, piercing regret.

No one had put a gun to my head and forced me to board the ship. I bore as much blame for my predicament as anyone else. He and Hank may have told me that nothing would happen to us, but I was the one who'd chosen to believe them.

'Ellis,' I said, as he turned to go. 'I'm sorry.'

'About what?' he asked, stopping.

'The things I said.'

He laughed quietly. 'Which ones?'

'All of them. I was just so frightened.'

He came back and sat on the edge of the bed. 'No need to apologise. I just hadn't realised I was married to quite such a firecracker.'

He laid a hand on my cheek, and my eyes welled up. I hoped I was wrong about how people over here would perceive him, but if I was not, I hoped I could somehow protect him from their judgement, make him unaware, or better yet, not care.

'I wasn't myself,' I said.

'None of us was, my darling.'

'Except Hank,' I said, sniffling. 'Hank was himself the entire time.'

'Ah yes. Dear old Hank. Ever the pill,' he said, getting up. 'Speaking of which, do you think you need one?'

'No, I'm all right.'

That was my cue to offer him one, and I would have, except that I had no idea where they were and didn't have the energy to look.

'Sleep tight, my darling. Tomorrow, Hank and I will find a decent hotel, and then all you'll have to worry about is regaining your strength.'

He picked up the candle and went to the door. I rolled to face him.

'Ellis,' I said as he stepped into the hallway, 'this feeling of still being at sea – do you think it's normal?'

He paused before answering. 'Perfectly,' he said. 'It will be gone in the morning. You'll see.' He closed the door.

As I lay in bed, I could no more stop the waves than escape the images and sounds of the wounded being marched down the gangplank, one after the other, in a seemingly endless line.

8

I woke up to the sound of a blood-curdling scream, and it was a few seconds before I realised it was coming from my own throat. My eyes sprang open, but it made no difference. None. The black was impenetrable, the pitching violent.

The engine wasn't running. Why wasn't the engine running?

Even if the whooshing in my head had been shrill enough to drown out the sound of the turbines, nothing would have been able to disguise the vibration. The thrum had been relentless – rattling brains, teeth and eardrums, just like the propellers of a plane – and its absence was terrifying.

I'd been dreaming that the SS *Mallory* took a direct hit, but now I realised it wasn't a dream. The cabin rocked madly, almost as though the freighter was turning, rotating like a corkscrew as it slid below the surface.

'Ellis?' I cried out. '*Ellis?*'

I felt the blanket on either side of me, but he wasn't there, which meant he was lying injured somewhere on the floor, thrown on impact. I had to find him fast, because the cabin had tilted so drastically I wasn't sure how much longer I'd be able to find the door.

I slapped the surface and edges of the bunk, hoping to identify which direction I was facing, and hoping Hank was trying to find his way to us as well, because I didn't think I could drag Ellis out on my own.

When my hands hit a wooden headboard, I was momentarily confused. When I found a bedside table with a lace runner, I fell onto my back, gasping with relief.

I wasn't on the SS *Mallory*. I was in a bed in a hotel room in Drumnadrochit, and the motion was all in my head.

I reached over and felt my way across the bedside table, seeking the candle before remembering that Ellis had taken it with him the night before. I got to my feet, thinking that if I could just find the dresser, I could then find the door. I had taken only a couple of steps when my foot landed on something and twisted out from under me. I fell on my hands and knees.

The door opened, and a female figure was suddenly in the doorway with light pouring in around her.

'Mrs Pennypacker? Is everything all right?' she asked.

I blinked at her, wondering why she'd just addressed me by my mother's name.

'My Lord!' She rushed over to help me up. 'What's happened? Are you all right?'

'Yes, thank you,' I said. 'I seem to have tripped over a shoe, of all things.'

Now that the light was no longer behind her, I could see that she was about my age, with a sturdy frame, pleasant expression and thick auburn hair swept into a snood. She had a smattering of freckles, and her face was browned by the sun.

'Shall I get your husband?' she asked, looking at me with concern.

'No, thank you,' I said. 'I just need a minute to get oriented. When I woke up I wasn't quite sure where I was, and then . . .' I waved a hand at the carpet, which was strewn with the things I'd taken out while searching for my nightgown and toothbrush. 'Well, I was in a bit of a rush to get to bed last night, and this morning I couldn't see where I was going.'

'It's the blackout curtains,' she said, nodding decisively and walking past me to the window. 'They're that dark you can't see a thing, although I suppose that's the point.'

She braced her fingertips on the inside edges of the window casing and coaxed out a solid square frame covered with black material. Light flooded the room.

'That's better, isn't it?' she said, setting the frame on the floor.

Strips of tape criss-crossed the panes of glass. After a second's confusion, I realised they were in case of a bomb blast.

'Yes, thank you,' I said, trying to suppress my alarm. 'Is that a wooden frame? I've always thought blackout curtains were actual curtains.'

'Aye. We use traditional curtains too, but then you have to pin the cloth all the way round so no light can get past. This contraption is much easier on the fingers. Angus made them after the last time we got fined – twelve shillings it was, all because Old Donnie had the temerity to push the curtain aside for a wee moment to see if it was still raining. *And* the warden is a Wee Free, *and* he's not from the glen, so there was no getting round that, I can tell you. Twelve shillings! That's more than a day's wages for a shopkeeper!' she said indignantly, catching my eye to make sure I understood.

I nodded emphatically.

'Now these,' she continued, 'you could put the sun itself right behind them and not one ray would get through. Angus stretched the material tight, and then painted the whole thing with black epoxy rubber.' She leaned over to tap its surface. 'That's like a drum, that is.'

'Is Angus the one with the beard?'

'Aye.'

'And he's the handyman?'

She laughed. 'I should think not. He runs the place!'

A. W. Ross.

It made perfect sense but hadn't even occurred to me, an assumption based entirely on appearance. I caught sight of myself in the mirror and felt ridiculous for judging. I looked like I'd been dragged backward through a hedge.

The ceiling began spinning again, and I dropped onto the edge of the bed.

'You've gone pale as a potato crust,' said the girl, coming closer to inspect me. 'Shall I bring up some tea?'

'No, I'll be fine. I'm still a bit dizzy from the ship, strangely enough,' I said.

'Aye,' she said, nodding gravely. 'I've heard of that. People getting stuck like that.'

A jolt of fear ran through me, even as I arranged my face into a smile.

'Don't worry,' I said. 'My husband and I sail all the time. I probably just have a bit of a cold – you know, an ear thing. It will pass. Speaking of my husband, is he up yet?'

'He's been downstairs this half hour.'

'Will you please let him know I'll be down in a few minutes? I need a moment to pull myself together.'

She glanced at my luggage. 'Well, with this lot that shouldn't be hard. I should think you could start your own shop, if you wanted to. If you change your mind about having your tea upstairs, just give me a shout.'

'I'm sorry, what's your name again?' I asked, knowing perfectly well she hadn't yet told me.

'Anna. Anna McKenzie.'

After Anna left, I remained on the bed, looking into the mirror from a distance of five or six feet. The face that stared back at me was haggard, almost unrecognisable. It was also jerking back and forth. I looked at the doorknob, a seam in the wallpaper, a shoe on the floor. Everything I tried to focus on did the same.

I was well aware of my tendency to become consumed by thoughts and knew I had to put what she'd said out of my mind. I'd been back on solid ground less than a day, which was nowhere near long enough to begin to panic. The seas had been so rough, and I'd been so ill, it made perfect sense that my vertigo would take time to resolve. At home, though, I'd probably have slipped off to see a specialist just to put my mind at ease.

If I told Ellis what was going on he would have suggested I take a pill, and while they were probably designed for moments exactly like this, I had staunchly refused to let a single one cross my lips from the moment they'd been prescribed.

Because of my mother, people were always looking for cracks in my façade, waiting – even hoping – for me to revert to type. My mother-in-law's shocking proclamation on New Year's Day was the first time anyone had been quite so explicit, at least to my face, but I knew what everyone thought of me, and I refused to prove them right. The ridiculous thing was that only I knew I didn't take the pills, so I wasn't really proving anything to anyone except myself. Ellis found them calming, so my prescription was filled often enough to satisfy Edith Stone Hyde, who rifled shamelessly through my things when I wasn't there.

The clock was ticking and Hank and Ellis were waiting downstairs, so I concentrated on the job at hand.

Ellis put great stock in my looks, teasing me that my only job in life was to be the prettiest girl in the room. I had always thought I was perfectly adept at doing my own hair and make-up, but apparently Ellis thought otherwise, and immediately after our marriage placed me in the hands of professionals.

I dug through my suitcases and trunks, collecting my 'lotions and potions,' as Ellis called them, and lined them up on the dresser. At home, he liked to open the jars and sniff the contents, asking the price and purpose of each (the more expensive, the better).

One time, I'd come into my room and found him at my dressing table with his face half made up. He let me finish the job and then, for a lark, he donned my Oriental robe, wrapped his head in a peacock-blue scarf and tossed a feather boa round his shoulders.

Emily was entirely nonplussed when she brought up the petit fours and I introduced her to Aunt Esmée. She gawped as I explained that Esmée was a long-lost relation and a *teensy* bit eccentric. After she left, we howled, wishing there was a way we could get Hank involved. We drank whisky from teacups and Aunt Esmée read my fortune, which involved a long journey and great wealth. I asked if there was anyone tall, dark and handsome in my future, and she informed me that my destiny involved a man who was tall, *blond* and handsome – as well as already beneath my nose.

I leaned toward the mirror to have a closer look, tilting my face back and forth. The trip had taken a toll on my complexion, and my left cheek had thin red lines running across it from when I'd smashed into the outside wall. I looked as though a cat had taken a swipe at me.

I patched and spackled as best I could. In the end, it was clear I'd used a heavy hand, but my face turned out better than I expected. My hair, however, was a different story.

I usually wore it parted to the side, with a wave that swept across my forehead, then up and over my ears before landing in a cascade of curls at the nape of my neck. This was courtesy of Lana, the hair savant at Salon Antoine, who set my hair twice a week. She would cover my head in rollers and put me under the dryer to 'cook,' while someone else touched up my manicure. When the rollers were out, Lana would coax and pat my hair into submission, spray it until it was as hard and shiny as glass and send me on my way.

Between appointments, all I had to do was make sure I replaced any bobby pins that came out and wear a hairnet to bed. If it was necessary to smooth the surface, I was instructed to use a soft-bristled hairbrush with caution, but if anything went wrong that I couldn't fix – especially with the curls – I was to go back at once.

Consequently, I hadn't done my own hair in four years and had no idea what to do with the stringy mess that sat atop my head.

In honor of Aunt Esmée, I wrapped a turban round it, pinned a garnet brooch to the front and went to join my husband.

I kept a hand on the wall to steady myself as I went downstairs, and paused at the bottom to get my balance.

The fire was burning brightly, and the blackout curtains – or frames – had been pulled out and stacked in a corner. The downstairs windows were also taped, and posters on either side of the radio warned that 'Loose Lips Sink Ships' and 'Careless Talk Costs Lives.'

Another flicker of fear ran through me.

Ellis and Hank were at one of the tables, poring over an Ordnance Survey map with several logbooks lying open. A duffel bag, tripod and various other pieces of equipment were on the floor, and they had their coats and hats thrown over an empty chair.

Hank watched as I wobbled over, and I hoped he wouldn't have time to come up with a joke about sea legs.

'Look who's up!' he said brightly.

Ellis stood and pulled out a chair.

'Good morning, sleepyhead,' he said, kissing my cheek. 'Or should I say afternoon?'

I smiled weakly and sat.

'You obviously got your beauty sleep,' he said, pushing my chair in and sitting back down. 'You look positively radiant.'

'It's just a bit of paint,' I said. 'You two look busy. What are you up to?'

'A little strategizing,' he said. 'Thought we'd scope out the area on foot, maybe rent a boat. If there's time, we might walk over to the castle.'

'Don't forget the newspaper,' said Hank.

'Yes, we're going to place an advertisement to find people who've had encounters. Help us establish a pattern. When and where the thing arises, weather conditions, et cetera.'

'I thought we were changing hotels,' I said, glancing at the equipment on the floor. 'Or are we going to send for our things later?'

'Yes. Well, neither, actually,' said Ellis. 'There don't seem to be any other hotels. Hank took an early-morning walk, and the village is the size of a flea. The girl in the kitchen says the next closest hotel is two and a half miles away, but it's full of billeted soldiers, and anyway, it doesn't sound any better than this. Apparently there's no electricity in the entire glen.'

I looked around to make sure we were alone. 'But what if the landlord doesn't let us stay?'

'It turns out Blackbeard is much friendlier in the morning,' Ellis said. 'Well, "much" may be putting it a bit strongly, but we've officially checked in for a stay of indeterminate length, so don't worry your pretty little head for another second.' He reached over and play-pinched my cheek.

For the first time, I noticed their plates. There was a pale rectangular slab on each, grey and slightly gelatinous. 'What is that?'

'Porridge,' Hank said brightly, poking it with his fork.

'Apparently they pour leftover porridge into a drawer and cut slices off it when it sets. Waste not, want not.'

'You're both in very good moods,' I said.

'Of course!' said Ellis, spreading his hands. 'We're here, aren't we?'

'Excuse me, Mrs Pennypacker,' said Anna, appearing at my side.

My mother's name again. I shot Ellis a look, but he was watching as Anna slid a small bowl of steaming porridge in front of me, along with a cup of creamy milk.

'I'll be right back with your tea,' she said.

'Well, would you look at that,' said Hank. 'Virgin porridge. Aren't you special.'

I stared at it. 'I don't think I can eat. My stomach's still iffy.'

'You have to,' said Ellis. 'You're thin as a rail.'

'Please. That's how you like me,' I said.

'Yes, but if you get too thin your face will suffer.'

I looked up, horrified, wondering if he was saying it already had. I was still trying to decipher his expression when Anna returned with a cup of tea.

'I brought a wee bit of sugar, ma'am,' she said, setting it in front of me. There were two cubes on the edge of the saucer.

Hank glanced up from his map. 'Her tea's stronger, too. I sense favouritism.'

'And rightly so,' said Ellis. 'She needs it.'

The back of my throat tightened. So much for my being 'positively radiant.' I picked up the milk to pour on my porridge.

Anna sucked her breath through her teeth, and I halted with the bowl in mid-air.

'If you don't mind my saying, ma'am, that's not the best way of going about that. Pouring the milk all over it,' she tutted. 'It's just not right.'

'Don't you have something else?' Ellis said testily. 'Ham? Eggs? A steak? My wife is poorly. She needs protein.'

Anna drew her shoulders back. 'We do not, Mr Pennypacker. Those particular items are rationed, and we weren't expecting guests. And for your information, milk and sugar are rationed as well – I only brought them out because I thought Mrs Pennypacker could use a little perking up, what with her motion sickness and all.'

'Thank you,' I said. 'That's very kind of you.'

'Fine. Never mind,' said Ellis, pulling the logbook towards him. When she didn't leave, he threw her an irritated glance and flicked the backs of his fingers toward her. 'I said that's all.'

She folded her arms and glowered at him. 'No, you did not. You said "Never mind." And I don't suppose you've given your ration books to Angus.'

'No,' said Ellis, without looking at her.

'Oh, aye,' she replied on an intake of breath. 'Well, I can't do any better for you until you do, and I'll have you know it's a criminal offence to waste food, so get that down you or I'll be forced to call the warden.' She lifted her chin and sailed round the bar and through to the back.

Ellis looked agog at Hank. Then he broke into giggles.

'I told you she wasn't all there,' he said.

Hank nodded. 'She does seem a few sandwiches short.'

'You needn't have been so rude,' I said. 'She's very nice, and she was about to show me, if you hadn't interrupted.'

Ellis looked stunned. 'Show you what? How to eat porridge? It's *porridge*. You eat it.'

'Oh, never mind,' I said.

Ellis stared at me. 'Shall I call her back?'

'No. I'm fine,' I said. 'But perhaps you can explain why, exactly, she thinks I'm my mother?'

Ellis laughed, and Hank nearly spat tea out of his nose.

'You're not your mother – thank God,' said Ellis, after they'd collected themselves. 'But I did sign us in using your maiden name.'

'And why is that?'

'My father wasn't terrifically popular around here after the *Daily Mail* fiasco. But don't worry. When we find the monster, we'll come clean.' He held his hands up and framed an imaginary headline: 'Son of Colonel Whitney Hyde Catches Loch Ness Monster; Hailed as Hero.'

'Say, Hero, think we can get back to work?' said Hank, stuffing his napkin under the edge of his plate. He circled an area on the map with his finger. 'Since this area is the epicentre of the sightings, I think we should start at Temple Pier, then either walk or row to the . . .'

As Hank prattled on, I considered the two bowls in front of me. If you didn't put the milk in the porridge, surely you didn't put the porridge in the milk? I dipped my spoon in the porridge, looked at the bowl of milk, felt stupid and gave up.

I put one of the sugar cubes on my teaspoon and lowered it slowly into the cup, watching the brown seep upward, evenly, irrevocably.

9

Hank and Ellis seemed almost relieved when I told them I wasn't going to join them. I would have been offended if I didn't know I couldn't walk straight.

They gathered their things and left in a whirlwind of activity. I hadn't seen Ellis this energised since the summer I'd met him. At the last second, Hank leaned over the table, grabbed his porridge and gamely chomped it down. Then he ate Ellis's as well, saying he wasn't keen on 'being frogmarched to the clink, at least not over a slab of drawer porridge.' Ellis kissed my cheek and implored me to eat my own porridge in whatever fashion I saw fit, and to make sure the staff looked after me. And then they were gone.

I had planned on asking Anna to draw me a bath, but after threatening to call the warden she never returned. I began to think she'd left the building.

I found my way up the stairs, grasping the rail and stopping several times. At one point I thought I was going to fall backward, and sat on the step until it passed.

There was a black line painted round the inside of the bathtub, about five inches up, which I assumed was a guide to how deep the water should be, but no matter what the temperature of the water, there wouldn't be enough to warm a person up. I decided it was a suggestion rather than a rule, put in the rubber plug and turned the taps on full. I left them running while I went to my room.

When I returned and tried to step into the bath, I discovered that the water coming out of both taps was icy.

By the time I got my clothes back on and rushed down to the grate, my teeth were chattering.

The fire gave off a fearsome heat, and I couldn't seem to find the right distance from it – too close and my shins and cheeks stung, too far and I got chilled through. At one point, my toes were burning and my heels were freezing all at the same time. I was cold, dizzy, queasy and filthy. It was hard to imagine being more miserable.

There was a newspaper on the low table, but when I tried to read, the words swam on the page. I gave up almost immediately, left it open on my lap and gazed into the fire. Its movement masked that of my eyes, and was the most helpful thing yet in making me feel steady.

The chimney stones were charred, and the fire, part coal and part mysterious other, hissed and cracked and occasionally let off an unlikely whistle. As I watched, a glowing red ember shot out, landed on the carpet and immediately turned black. A pair of brown utility shoes, thick wool socks and reddened shins appeared just where it had landed.

Anna was standing beside me, holding a plate and a steaming cup. She put them on the table in front of me.

'I couldn't help but notice you didn't eat your porridge, probably on account of not knowing how.' She glanced behind her and added, 'I slipped a wee dram into the tea. I thought it might help, as I also couldn't help but notice that you're still a bit wobbly.'

The plate held a coddled egg and a few slices of golden fried potato. Moments before, my stomach had been doing flips, but I was suddenly ravenous.

'But I thought eggs were rationed?' I said, glancing up.

'Aye, and butter, too, but we've hens and a cow at the croft.

I nipped back and told Mhàthair – that's my mother – that you were feeling poorly, and she said to give you this. She's also the midwife, so she knows such things. She says you're to start with the tea.'

'Thank you. That's very kind. Please send her my regards.'

Anna lingered, and then said, 'Is it really the monster your husband is after? My cousin Donald's seen it, you know.'

I looked up. 'He has?'

'Aye, and his parents, too,' she said, nodding gravely. 'My Aunt Aldie and Uncle John were driving home from Inverness when they thought they saw some ducks fighting in the water near Abriachan, but when they got closer they realised it was an animal – a black beast the size of a whale – rolling, and plunging, and generally causing a right *stramash*.' She illustrated with her hands.

'What happened then?'

'Nothing,' she said simply. 'It swam off.'

'And your cousin?'

She shrugged. 'There's not much to tell. He was a fisherman. Something happened one day when he was out on the loch, and he hasn't set foot on a boat since. And neither will he discuss it.'

'What about your aunt? Do you think your aunt will discuss it?'

'I should think she'd blather your ear off, given the opportunity. Why don't you invite her for a *strupag*? And Mrs Pennypacker? You were on the right track. You put the porridge on the spoon and then you dip the spoon in the milk. It keeps the porridge hot.'

'I'm sorry I didn't eat it,' I said. 'Is it really a criminal offence to waste food?'

'Aye, several years since. But don't worry, the milk will go into the soup, and your porridge went into the drawer. Conall was that pleased to lick the bowl he wagged his tail. Do you think you'll be needing anything else? Only I need to get back to the croft. You might not think there's much to do in January, but you'd be wrong. There's clearing stones, cutting turnip for the sheep, the milking, oh, it goes on and on . . .' She stared into the distance and sighed.

'There's just one thing,' I said. 'I'd love to have a bath, but there's no hot water.'

'There will be in about twenty minutes. I heard you banging about up there, so I lit the boiler. I'll take up some Lux flakes as well. You're only supposed to run the bath up to the line, but I think maybe this once you might run it deeper.'

I couldn't take offence – she'd seen me moments after I'd quite literally fallen out of bed.

'I'm off then. Meg will be back from the sawmill around four. Now get that down you,' she said, nodding authoritatively. 'I've seen bigger kneecaps on a sparrow, and if Mhàthair hears you didn't finish up that tea, it's the castor oil she'll be sending next.'

Although the tea itself tasted like boiled twigs – I supposed it was ersatz – the 'wee dram' helped so much that after my bath I lay down to have a rest. I was surprised to find myself drifting off, because I was excited. I couldn't wait to tell Ellis about Anna's relatives.

Several hours later, I floated out of my nap to the buzz of conversation and laughter rising from the main floor. I was surprised by the number of voices, since I knew we were the only staying guests, and decided the inn must also be a pub. I lit the candle, which Anna had replaced, and looked at my watch. It was evening, and I was hungry again. I hadn't had a proper meal since I left the States.

You're thin as a rail, Ellis had said.

I've seen bigger kneecaps on a sparrow, Anna had said.

I let my hands explore my belly – the hipbones that protruded sharply, the concave area between, the ribcage that loomed above.

Oh, Madeline. We really have to do something, my mother had said.

I was twelve and at first had no idea what she was talking about. I'd stepped out from behind the striped canvas of the changing tent on the beach at Bar Harbor and was breathless at the deep blue of the sky and even deeper blue of the ocean, at the laughter and shrieking of the children who played at the edges of the lapping surf, at the seagulls swooping and diving. I turned, alarmed at her tone. She shook her head sadly, but her eyes were hard. She pressed her lips into a thin line as she surveyed the parts of me that made me most self-conscious. They were the parts that were filling out but were not yet curvy. I was merely pudgy. I'd never felt a deeper shame in my life.

She'd have approved now, I thought, stretching my legs out. With my ankles and knees touching, my thighs didn't meet. And then I thought, No, she wouldn't. No matter what I did or who I became, she would never have approved.

Hank's and Ellis's rooms were empty, so I headed downstairs. I assumed they'd returned, discovered I was asleep and gone down for drinks. I was eager to tell them what I'd learned, sure they'd be pleased with me. Perhaps with the right type of persuasion, even Cousin Donald would tell his story.

As I stepped out of the shadow at the bottom of the stairwell, everyone fell silent. Hank and Ellis were nowhere to be seen, and other than Meg I was the only woman in the room.

There were a dozen or so burly young men wearing khaki uniforms sitting at the tables, and about six older men in civilian clothes perched on stools at the bar. Every one of them was looking at me.

I girded myself, feeling the men's eyes upon me and hoping they wouldn't think I was drunk as I made my way to the couch. Conall stared from his place by the hearth. He didn't raise his head, but his eyes darted and his whiskered brows twitched as I approached. At the end, when I sank onto the couch, I realised I'd only been slightly off-balance. I further realised that I had taken the stairs without incident, and then, with some alarm, that what I had thought was ersatz tea was almost certainly medicinal. While I wasn't happy about being dosed without my consent, I couldn't deny it had helped.

Meg was behind the bar, her hair carefully arranged in a cascade of red curls. I remembered the bits of rag tied in her hair the night before, and wondered if I could figure out how to do that. My own hair, still damp from my bath, was back under a turban.

Her periwinkle dress hugged her figure, and her lips and fingernails were scarlet. It was hard to believe she worked at a sawmill. She looked like a redheaded Hedy Lamarr. If she was at all open to Hank's advances, she didn't stand a chance. Hank would never be serious about a barmaid. He was so slippery he could barely bring himself to be serious about Violet. I had to find a moment to warn Hank off, and wished I'd said something that very first night.

'Can I get you something, Mrs Pennypacker?' she called over. 'A half pint? Or perhaps a sherry?'

'Nothing right now, thank you,' I said, and at the sound of my voice the men exchanged glances. I didn't blame them – surely they were wondering how and why an American woman had materialised in their midst. A hot flush rose to my cheeks.

A young man sitting at a table with a glass of beer called out in an accent as flat and un-Scottish as my own, 'Canadian or American?' and I found myself staring back with equal surprise.

Before I could answer, the front door opened and an elderly man came in, leaning on a walking stick.

He said to the room in general, 'There's rain in it today.'

'Aye, Donnie, that there is,' said Meg from behind the bar. 'A hauf and a hauf, is it?'

'Just a pint of heavy.' He made his way to the last empty barstool.

She pulled a glass from beneath the counter and held it under a beer tap. 'There's game pie tonight,' she said, 'so you can keep your ration book in your pocket.'

'Oh, that's grand, Meg,' he said. He began to struggle out of his coat.

'Can I give you a hand?' she said, coming round to help.

'I'm in need of one, Meg, surely I am,' he said, chuckling at his own joke. His empty sleeve was pinned up against his shirt. As Meg took his coat away, he climbed onto the stool. He raised his glass and turned towards the room. '*Slàinte!*' he said.

'*Slàinte!*' Everyone, young and old, lifted his glass.

At that moment, Ellis and Hank burst through the door, cheeks ruddy with the cold, coats and hats wet.

'—so if the ad runs on Friday,' Ellis said, 'we could potentially start getting responses on Tuesday. Meanwhile, we can revisit . . . the . . .' His voice petered out when he realised he was the centre of attention.

Hank let his hands drop to his sides, clenching and unclenching his fingers like a cowboy ready to draw. Behind the bar, Meg picked up a cloth and began to wipe down the counter. Our black-bearded landlord appeared in the doorway that led to the back, wearing a heavy ribbed sweater in dark olive.

After a silence that seemed interminable, Old Donnie set his glass down and slid off his stool. He picked up his stick and hobbled slowly over.

Tap, tap, tap, tap.

He stopped directly in front of Ellis. He was shorter by a whole head. He looked Ellis up and then down, and then up again, the skin of his neck stretching like a turtle's as he strained to see Ellis's face.

'You favour your father,' he finally said.

'I beg your pardon?' said Ellis, draining of colour.

'The monster-hunter. From 'thirty-four. I'm not that addled yet.' The broken capillaries in his face darkened. A fleck of spittle flew from his lips.

Meg's eyebrows darted up and she glanced at Ellis. Then she resumed wiping the counter.

'Now Donnie,' she said. 'Come take a seat and I'll get your pie.'

He ignored her. 'I suppose it's the monster you're after, is it? Or are you going to float a balloon and take a snapshot like your old man?'

Ellis's face went from pale to purple in a split second.

The old man spun and hurried toward his coat, his gnarled stick banging on the flagstones. 'I'll no be staying where this *bastart* is.'

'Did he just say what I think he did?' Ellis said. 'Did he just call me a bastard?'

'If he wasn't a cripple, I'd knock his block off,' said Hank.

'Your mammie's his wife, then, is she?' said Old Donnie. 'Only rumour has it he was an awful one for the *houghmagandy.*'

'Now, Donnie,' Meg said, sharply this time. 'There's no call for that. Come and have your pie.'

'You'll excuse the language, but there's no other way to get to it,' the old man said indignantly. 'The pathetic *creutair*, trying to make *striopaichean* of honest girls up at the Big

House, and not a shred of decency. And I don't suppose anyone will help me with my coat.' This last was delivered as a statement, although he set his stick against the bar and straightened up, waiting.

Mr Ross had been studying Ellis since Donnie's initial proclamation, but now he came round the bar and helped the old man into his coat. Donnie picked up his stick and stomped dramatically to the door before turning and declaring, 'I'll not be darkening your door again, Angus. Not while this one's in residence.'

Several seconds after the door closed behind him, someone said, 'Well, I suppose Rhona won't mind not having to come and collect him at the end of an evening.' A swell of laughter rose, and the men returned to their conversations.

Meg came round the bar and put the radio on, fiddling with the lit dial until she first found Radio Luxembourg, with 'Lord Haw-Haw' announcing in a perfect English accent, *Germany calling! Germany calling!'*

She switched to static immediately, then moved the dial around until she finally found Bing Crosby, crooning about moonbeams and stars.

Ellis, whose face had finally settled on a terrible shade of grey, came and sat next to me.

'And that, my dear, is precisely why I used your maiden name,' he said through gritted teeth.

Our landlord was once again studying him.

IO

Ellis maintained a cool, silent façade through dinner, and excused himself immediately after. When I rose to go with him, he told me firmly to stay and enjoy my sherry.

I didn't want to stay, and there was certainly no enjoying to be done – all I could think about was what we'd do if we were given the boot for lying – but I knew he wanted me to remain behind and try to save face. I lasted only a quarter of an hour. When I left, Hank was grinding his teeth and white-knuckling his whisky.

I knocked on Ellis's door.

'Go away!'

'It's me,' I said, speaking into the crack. 'Please let me in.'

He barked something about not being fit for human company.

I went to my own room, hoping he'd change his mind and come to me. When the rest of the house had shut down and my candle had burned to a nub, I gave up and went to bed.

I lay on my back in the dark under a mountain of blankets, listening to the rain pound the roof. I was wearing my two heaviest nightgowns but was still so cold I was dabbing my nose non-stop.

I had never heard the words *strìopaichean* or *houghmagandy* before but deduced from the context that the former was what my mother-in-law believed my mother to be, and the latter was the activity that defined her as such.

I'd long thought of the Colonel as an irritating blowhard, but it had never occurred to me that he might also be a lecher. The mere thought of the Colonel making overtures to hapless young girls was horrifying. The pasty skin, the jiggling belly, the moustache yellowed by tobacco—

I hadn't noticed it before, but if Ellis were bald, forty years older, sixty pounds heavier, and had an alcoholic's nose, he would look very much like the Colonel.

No wonder Ellis hadn't felt fit for human company. Learning that he was going to age like the Colonel must have been a terrible blow, yet there was no denying it, since Old Donnie had identified him as the Colonel's son the first time he laid eyes on him. But there were ways of delaying the transformation with diet and exercise – even hairpieces, if necessary – and there was time to worry about that later. We had a more immediate problem to address.

I flipped back the covers and fumbled in the dark for the matches, lighting my last inch of candle.

A moment later I was in the hallway, standing outside his door. As I raised my hand to knock, the door to Meg's room clicked open and a heavy-shouldered figure slipped out.

I jumped backwards, muffling a gasp.

The man was tall and had prominent ears, but by candlelight I couldn't see much else. He glanced at me, turned up his coat collar and slipped into the inky black of the stairwell. I rapped quickly on Ellis's door.

'*Ellis! Ellis!*' I said urgently, looking down the hallway. 'Let me in!'

A moment later the door opened and his face appeared in the crack. 'What's the matter? Is it your heart? Do you need a pill?'

'No, I'm fine,' I said, irritated that he'd automatically jumped to that conclusion.

'You didn't sound fine.'

I glanced one last time down the hall and decided not to say anything about the man leaving Meg's room.

'I am. I'm fine,' I said, 'but we need to talk.'

'About what?'

'You *know* what. Can I please come in? I'd rather not do this in the hallway.'

After a flicker of hesitation, he held the door open. By the light of my candle, I saw that his room was in roughly the same condition as mine, with his belongings strewn all over the floor.

'Watch your step,' he said, sweeping his hand toward the mess.

I made my way to the bed and set the candle on the table. When I climbed under the covers, Ellis said, 'What are you doing?'

I felt like he'd kicked me in the stomach. 'I'm just getting warm. Don't worry. I won't stay.'

He exhaled through puffed cheeks and ran a hand through his hair. Finally, he closed the door and walked to the far side of the bed. He lay on top of the covers with his arms over his chest, stiff as a slab of marble.

'You could at least have brought me a pill,' he said.

'I can go get one.'

'Never mind,' he said.

A few minutes later, when it became apparent he wasn't going to address the issue at hand, or any other, I asked, 'What are we going to do?'

'What do you mean?'

'Where are we going to go? We can't stay here.'

'Of course we can. Why wouldn't we?'

'Because we checked in under a fake name.'

Ellis exploded, sitting bolt upright and slamming his fists

on the quilt so hard I recoiled. 'It's *not* a fake name. It's your *maiden* name, as I explained to you earlier, so what, exactly, is your point?'

'My point is that I'm terrified we're going to be tossed out onto the street!' I said in a harsh whisper. 'And I'm sorry you're upset, but you have no right to take it out on me. None of this is my fault.'

'So it's my fault, is it?'

'Well, *I* certainly didn't do anything.'

The wind howled down the chimney. The window rattled in its pane.

'I'm sorry about the old man tonight,' I said. 'The whole thing was dreadful.'

Ellis was suddenly yelling again: 'I've half a mind to have him arrested! It's slander and libel and God only knows what else, making ridiculous, groundless accusations against someone who's not even here to defend himself. My father would *never, ever—*'

'I know!' I said, interrupting him in a whisper, hoping that it would encourage him to lower his tone. I laid a hand on his arm. 'I know.'

In fact I did not know. Was he incensed about the accusations of womanising, or the accusations of fakery? Or because he, himself, had been caught in a lie?

The rain picked up and changed direction, battering the glass like someone was flinging buckets of nails against it. Water dripped sporadically down the chimney and onto the grate, an occasional heavy *plonk*.

Ellis lay back down.

I was infinitely sorry I'd come and was about to climb from the bed when he suddenly rolled to face me, catching me off guard.

'Well,' he said, 'to answer your question, I certainly hope we can stay. There isn't anywhere else to go.'

'Maybe we can move to the estate? I'm a little surprised we didn't go there in the first place.'

'I rather suspect they got their fill of Hydes back in 'thirty-four, don't you?'

'Oh, I don't know. Your father is hardly the first man to try it on with a servant. Anyway, you're family.'

He laughed wryly. 'I'm a second cousin once removed. And no, even if they would have had us, which is highly unlikely, the point is moot. Apparently the house and grounds are crawling with soldiers.'

'It was requisitioned? Where's the family?'

'No idea,' he said. 'It's not as though we've exchanged Christmas cards over the years.'

He laid an arm across me, and I realised we were making up.

'So what did you do today?' he asked.

'Mostly I rested, but I've got exciting news – three of Anna's relatives have seen the monster, and at least two are willing to talk to us.'

'Who?'

'Anna. The girl who served us breakfast.'

'Hmm,' he said. 'How interesting.'

'I thought you'd be pleased,' I said. 'Maybe even excited.'

'Oh, I am. I'll definitely follow up,' he said. 'How's the dizziness? Do you think you'll be able to come with us tomorrow?'

'It's much better, and I'd love to,' I said.

'Good. We could use your sharp eyes.' He wriggled his way under the covers. 'Aren't you going to put out the candle?'

I realised he was inviting me to stay.

I blew out the flame and rolled towards him.

A few minutes later a soft rumbling began in the back of his throat, and before long he fell onto his back. The snoring grew louder. I lay awake for what seemed like for ever, blinking into the dark.

I tried to remember the last time we made love, and could not.

I thought about the man leaving Meg's room, and hoped she was being careful. If Hank got her into trouble, her reputation might be ruined, but she'd end up well off, at least by the time I was finished with Hank. If a regular working man got her into a predicament – well, I just hoped he'd marry her, and that they really were in love.

In the morning, Ellis was gone. He had removed the blackout frame, so I woke to daylight. It was almost ten o'clock, early by my standards.

Downstairs, Anna was scrubbing the windows with a wad of newspaper. An earthenware jug labelled DISTILLED VINEGAR sat on a nearby table. She had a plain cotton kerchief tied round her hair, knotted on top, in stark contrast to the bright Hermès scarf that was tied similarly round mine.

She glanced at me and turned away immediately.

'Good morning, Mrs Hyde,' she said pointedly.

'Good morning,' I said, slithering into the nearest chair. It was only then that I registered the absence of Hank and Ellis.

Anna was watching from the corner of her eye.

'They've gone out,' she said, attacking the window with renewed vigour. 'They said to tell you they'll be back tomorrow.'

I sat up, panicked. 'What? Where did they go?'

'Inverness, apparently,' she said.

'Where's that? And why?'

'It's fourteen miles up the road. And for what reason, I would not know,' she said, setting the wad of newspaper on the sill and wiping her hands on her apron.

'They didn't leave a note or anything?'

'Not to my knowledge.'

'Do you know if they cleared up the . . . confusion?' I asked, wincing at the final word.

She turned and glared at me, planting her hands on her hips. 'Do you mean about using a fake name? You'll have to ask Angus about that.'

I was struck through with terror. If the landlord made me leave, what was I supposed to do? Where was I supposed to go?

'Any chance you've brought your ration book down?' Anna continued. 'Only I can't help but notice that not one of you has handed one in, even though I mentioned it yesterday, and you were *supposed* to do it the moment you checked in. Although I suppose if you'll be going elsewhere, it doesn't much matter.'

'I'm not sure where Ellis put them,' I said weakly. 'I'll have a look in a bit.'

Anna kept her hands on her hips, staring at me with grave suspicion. I dropped my gaze into my lap.

'I'll get your breakfast then, shall I?' she said, before stomping past.

I put my elbows on the table and dropped my head into my hands. I couldn't believe Ellis would do this to me. There had to be some mistake.

Breakfast was a slab of drawer porridge and decidedly weak tea, with no milk or sugar. Anna dropped them in front of me with a clatter and went back to the window.

'Bacon, butter, sugar, milk – it doesn't grow on trees, you know,' she said, as though continuing a conversation.

My hands were back in my lap. I started picking at the chips in my nail polish.

'Or eggs. Or margarine. Or tea,' Anna continued. She surveyed the wad of newspaper in her hand and dropped it on the table. She crumpled up a fresh sheet, tipped the mouth of the jug against it and slammed the jug back down.

'I suppose tea does grow on trees, but not round here.' She nodded toward my cup. 'I've reused leaves for that,' she said.

For about fifteen seconds I thought maybe she was finished.

'I suppose I could make you a beetroot sandwich in the meantime, although I don't suppose National Loaf is up to your usual standards. Neeps, tatties, onions. Porridge, certainly – but no milk, mind you. I might be able to find a tablet or two of saccharine. And I don't suppose you've got a gas mask, have you?' She glanced quickly at me, intuited the answer and sighed grievously. 'I thought not. You're supposed to carry one at all times. You can get a fine for that. And I don't suppose the mustard gas will know the difference between you and a normal person.' She curled her lips on the last two words.

I finally looked up from my lap. 'Anna, I'm sorry. I don't know what to say.'

'Oh, aye. I'm not sure I'd believe it anyway.'

She might as well have slapped me.

Mr Ross came through from the back, wearing the same sweater as the day before, trousers of the same dark olive, and heavy black boots. It looked like a military outfit, although there were no badges or any other identifying information on it. He stopped momentarily at the sight of me, then continued as though I didn't exist, going to the till and removing cash. He flipped through a large ledger book, making occasional notes with a pencil. With a start, I noticed that the first two joints of his right index finger were missing.

Anna turned her attention back to the window.

'Shall I correct the spelling in the register?' he said without looking up.

My relief was so great I clapped a hand to my mouth.

'I'll take that as a yes?'

'Yes,' I said, barely managing to speak. 'Thank you.'

It was more than enough that he wasn't turning me out. He had no reason whatever to preserve my dignity, and this simple act of kindness caused my throat to constrict.

'Right then.' He slapped his thigh. 'Conall, *trobhad*!' The tall dog trotted round the corner of the bar, and the two of them left.

'You're very lucky, is all I have to say,' said Anna.

My innards twisted into a knot, and my hands and heart fluttered so badly I couldn't even consider lifting a fork, never mind a teacup. I pushed my chair back so hard it screeched against the floor and bolted upstairs, abandoning my breakfast.

'I've half a mind to call the warden for that!' Anna shouted after me.

I turned the lock on the inside of my room and leaned against the door, hyperventilating. My heart was racing so hard I thought I might actually keel over. If I did, it would not be the first time.

The first time had been when I was having lunch at the Acorn Club with my mother-in-law and five of her friends, including Mrs Pew.

My marriage was not quite four months old, at a time when I still deluded myself that my mother-in-law's gift of the hair comb indicated that she might eventually come to accept me, perhaps even grow fond of me. The ladies were discussing the despicable attack on Pearl Harbor and saying that, despite previous reservations, they now agreed wholeheartedly with the President's decision to become involved. I mentioned the sinking of the *Athenia* and suggested that we might have got involved then, given the number of Americans on board. My remark was met with silence.

After a long, pregnant pause, my mother-in-law said, 'You are, of course, entitled to your opinion, dear. Although I, personally, wouldn't *dream* of second-guessing the President.' She clapped her bejewelled hand to her bosom, letting her eyes flutter as she warbled the word 'dream.'

As the telltale heat rose in my cheeks, she continued, praising the club for reducing its seven-course luncheon to five in the name of the war effort. She encouraged the other ladies to chip in, telling them that she, herself, had instructed the kitchen staff to donate cans, as well as whatever pots and pans they weren't using regularly. There was a flurry of regret from all of them that they couldn't do more, especially from such a distance, followed by a discussion of the surprising results of Ellis's attempts to enlist.

'A complete shock, I can tell you,' said my mother-in-law. 'Imagine, all these years, and we had no clue. I suppose it explains why he's crashed so many cars – he can't tell if the light is red or green. He's terribly upset, but there's nothing to be done. Whitney, of course, is beside himself.'

There were murmurs of sympathy for both Ellis and the Colonel before Mrs Pew leaned in conspiratorially to say, 'Of course, there are those who *arranged* to be turned down.'

'Do you mean . . .?' said another in hushed tones. Instead of filling in the blank, she let her eyes flit across the room to where Hank's mother was having lunch with her own friends.

Mrs Pew blinked heavily to confirm. The other ladies went wide-eyed, the thrill of their double-cross palpable.

'Absolutely shameful. Flat-footed, indeed.'

'Nothing a pair of good boots wouldn't fix.'

'That one's been trouble from the word go,' said my mother-in-law. 'It's somewhere in the blood, even if his mother *is* a Wanamaker.' She lowered her voice even further. 'I wish Ellis would keep his distance, but of course he's never paid attention to a word I say.'

I was staring at the shrimp and avocado on the fine china in front of me when it hit me that she had almost certainly said those very same things of me, to these very women, perhaps at this very table.

The hair comb hadn't been a peace offering. I had no idea what it signified, or why they had invited me to lunch, but by then I was entirely sure there was a motive.

I remember staring at the glass bowl of salad dressing, the flute of champagne with lines of bubbles rising from tiny, random geysers on the sides. I remember realising that I had gone still for so long they were looking at me and that I should pick up my fork, but could not, because I knew I would drop it. Someone addressed me, but it was impossible to hear over the buzzing in my ears. Then I couldn't catch my breath. I wasn't aware of sliding from my chair, but was certainly aware of being the centre of attention while lying on the carpet looking up at a circle of concerned faces. And who could forget the embarrassing ride in the ambulance, its siren blaring?

A number of consultations followed, culminating in a visit by a doctor brought in from New York, who took my pulse, listened to my heart and asked me extensive questions about my family.

'I see, I see,' he kept saying, studying me over the top of his wire-rimmed glasses.

Eventually, he folded the glasses and slid them into his breast pocket. Then he informed me – right in front of Ellis and his mother – that I suffered from a nervous ailment. He prescribed nerve pills and said I was to avoid excitement at all costs.

My mother-in-law gasped.

'Does this mean she can't . . .? Does this mean there will never be . . .?'

The doctor watched as she turned various shades of red.

'Ahh,' he said, figuring it out. 'No. She can tolerate a

reasonable amount of marital relations. It's more a matter of avoiding mental excitement. Such a condition is not unexpected, given the maternal history.'

He packed his bag and put on his hat.

'Wait!' said my mother-in-law, leaping to her feet. 'When you say this is not unexpected, do you mean such conditions run in families?'

After a slight pause, the doctor said, 'Not always. Remember that each generation is diluted, and any children of this marriage will have only one grandparent who was, well, how shall I put this? Not quite our kind.'

Edith Stone Hyde let out a cry and sank back into her chair.

My nervous ailment immediately became a heart ailment, and although I rarely felt grateful to my mother-in-law, I did admire how quickly she'd taken it upon herself to rediagnose me – particularly as it maintained at least the illusion of distance between me and my own mother.

My mother was a famous beauty, with sea-green eyes, a button nose and Cupid's bow lips that parted over teeth like pearls. In some women, perfect features do not add up to an exquisite whole, but in my mother the sum effect was so stunning that when she married my father, a Proper Philadelphian, society seemed willing to overlook that her father was an entrepreneur who dabbled in burlesque (revised for historical purposes as vaudeville) and married one of its stars, and that her grandfather was a rumoured robber baron with connections to Tammany Hall. Her family had a fortune; his family had a name. The arrangement was not all that unusual.

I was aware from my earliest memory that my mother was miserable, although the sheer magnitude and artistry of it took years to sink in. It ran through her like rot.

To the outside world, she presented meekness and long-

suffering, subtly conveying that my father was a tyrant and I
– well, I was defiant at best, and quite possibly criminally mali-
cious, a situation she found even more heartbreaking than my
father's cruelty. She was incredibly nuanced – all it took was a
sigh, a slight misting of the eye or an almost imperceptible
pause for everyone to understand the depth of her anguish and
how nobly she bore it.

She was excellent at reading a room, and when the atmosphere was not right for garnering sympathy, she was witty and
engaging, the centre of attention, but never in an obvious way.
She'd run a finger up and down the stem of her wine glass
slowly, repeatedly, or cross her legs and move her foot in deliberate circles, drawing attention to her exquisitely turned ankle.
It was impossible to look away. She entranced men and women
alike.

At home, she sulked with extravagance, and I learned early
that silence was anything but peaceful. She was always upset
about some slight, real or imagined, and more than capable of
creating a full-blown crisis out of thin air.

I tried to go unnoticed, but inevitably we came together over
the dinner table. I never knew if her displeasure was going to
be directed at my father or me. When I was the offender, dinner
passed with icy silences and withering looks. I rarely knew what
I'd done wrong, but even if I had, I wouldn't have dared mount
a defence. Instead, I shrank into myself. On those nights, I got
to eat, although she scrutinised every morsel that went into
my mouth, as well as how it got there.

On the nights my father was in her cross hairs, the choreography was very different. Her contemptuous looks and snide
remarks progressed to masterfully crafted barbs, which he
would ignore until they ripened into cutting sarcasm, which
he would also ignore. She would then, her eyes brimming with
tears, wonder aloud why we both delighted in torturing her

so, at which point my father would say something precise and lethal, usually to the effect that no one was forcing her to stay – she needn't feel obliged on his account – and she would flee the table weeping.

My father would continue to eat as though nothing had happened, so it fell to me to fix things. I'd abandon my food and trudge upstairs to her locked bedroom, my dread increasing with every step. It always took some negotiating, but eventually she'd let me in and I'd sit on the bed as she regaled me with the ways her life was a wasteland. My father was capriciously cruel and incapable of empathy, she'd tell me. She would have left him years ago, except that he'd sworn she'd never see me again, had even threatened to have her committed to an insane asylum, and did I know what happened in such places? She'd given up every chance of happiness for my sake, out of pure maternal love, although I was clearly ungrateful. But she supposed she had herself to blame for that. I took after my father. I could hardly be blamed for my miserable genes, and since I was there anyway, would I be a dear and fetch her a pill?

Twenty minutes after running away from Anna and the drawer porridge, my heart showed no signs of slowing down.

I was slumped against the back of my door, still gasping for air. My hands and feet tingled, the edges of my vision sparkled.

I hated that I'd been prescribed nerve pills – hated that anyone had seen any kind of parallel between my mother and me – and although it filled me with self-loathing, I found myself crawling to my luggage and digging through it, throwing dresses, slips, scarves and even shoes over my shoulder in my search for the brown glass bottle that I knew held relief.

I found the pills and swallowed one, swigging water straight from the pitcher to get it down. I lay on the bed and waited.

After a few minutes, a comforting fog began to settle over me and I understood, in a way that frightened me, why Ellis and my mother were so fond of them.

I sat up and looked around me. My room was a mess. I'd been living out of my luggage since our arrival, taking for granted that at some point my hanging things would magically be hung, the rest folded neatly in drawers and my empty trunks and suitcases stored. I realised quite suddenly that this was not going to happen.

After I put everything away, I made my bed, although it was painfully clear that it was an amateur effort. I tugged the corners and patted the surface, but my adjustments only succeeded in pulling it further askew. I decided to quit before completely unmaking it again.

I had run out of things to do. I had some crossword puzzles, a murder mystery and a handful of books about the monster that Ellis had instructed me to read, but reading was out of the question – not because of dizziness this time, but because my brain was dulled.

I walked to the window and looked out.

The sky was bright, although a solid cloud the colour of graphite loomed in the distance. The row houses across the street were a combination of white stucco and pink limestone, with wide brick chimneys. Beyond the houses were hills dotted with sheep, and fields defined by rows of trees. In the far distance were even higher hills, uniformly brown where they weren't forested, their peaks obscured by cloud.

The cold was insidious and eventually I pulled a quilt from my badly made bed and draped it round my shoulders. I settled into the chair.

Perhaps Anna had misunderstood. Perhaps Ellis and Hank had just gone on a day trip. Perhaps they were finding a new hotel.

I heard footsteps in the hallway, and from the sound of doors opening and shutting and water running at the end of the hall, I gathered Anna was making up the other rooms. A few minutes after she went back downstairs I heard – and felt – a door close. I went to the window and watched her ride down the street on a dark bicycle with a big wicker basket, her coat-tails billowing behind her.

11

I found myself gripping the windowsill, light-headed and weak. The feeling came over me without warning – my brow was suddenly pricked by sweat and I realised I was going to either faint or be sick. At first I thought it was a reaction to the pill, then I recognised it as hunger. The showdown with Old Donnie the night before had left me unable to do anything but pick at my dinner, and other than the egg and few slices of potato Anna had given me the previous day, I'd eaten virtually nothing since we'd left the States.

I'd felt this way before, in my early teen years, and knew that if I didn't eat something very soon I'd collapse. Because there wasn't even anyone around to find me, I had no choice but to go to the kitchen and scrounge. I would find the drawer porridge and take just a small slice, the slice intended for my breakfast, to mitigate my crime as much as possible.

Halfway down the stairs, I was hit by the aroma of roasting meat. It smelled so good my mouth watered, and it almost brought me to tears – Anna had made it very clear what my diet would consist of until I produced a ration book.

The front room was empty, so I slipped behind the bar. I was pretty sure I was alone in the building but paused at the doorway anyway, listening for signs of life. I heard nothing and went through.

The kitchen was larger than I expected, as well as bright.

The walls were whitewashed, and the doors and window trim were cornflower blue. Copper pots, pans and ladles hung from hooks over a sturdy table in the centre of the room. A large black stove emanated a gorgeous amount of heat, as well as the heavenly aroma. There was a pantry on one side of the room, and in the opposite wall – quite literally – was a bed. It was completely recessed, with panelled wooden doors that slid on a track. They were currently open, showing bedclothes much more neatly arranged than my own. I supposed it was where Mr Ross slept.

I marvelled at the contents of the pantry – jar upon jar of preserved red cabbage, pickled beetroot, gherkins, marmalade, loganberry preserves, Oxo cubes, Polo and Worcestershire sauces, baskets of onions, turnips and potatoes, enormous earthenware jugs of vinegar with spouts, canisters labelled TEA, RAISINS and SUGAR – it went on and on, and I could see even more behind the glass doors of cupboards.

It was the basket of apples I couldn't resist. A bushel basket, full to overflowing. Most of the apples were individually wrapped in newspaper, but a few lay exposed on top, shiny, round and beautiful. I felt like Snow White, or maybe even Eve; but all thoughts of virtue and drawer porridge fell away when I laid eyes on that fruit.

I was in the act of lifting one to my lips when a female voice spoke from behind me.

'Find what you're looking for?'

I jumped and spun around, simultaneously dropping my hand and curling my wrist, hiding the apple behind my thigh.

Meg was standing just inside the back door, wearing a thick olive-colored coat and matching cap. She had a cardboard box labelled ANTIGAS RESPIRATOR slung over her shoulder by a length of string, which she set on a chair by the door. She put her hands on her hips and looked at me.

'Can I help you with something?'

'No, thank you. I was just . . .'

I swallowed hard and clutched the apple.

Her eyes ran down the length of my arm. Then she looked me in the face. After a pause of three or four beats she turned round and took off her coat, laying it over the back of the chair. 'When you have a minute, Angus wants me to show you the Anderson shelter.'

She removed her cap and fiddled with her hairpins, keeping her back to me. I realised she was giving me time to either pocket or return the apple.

I leaned into the pantry and placed it gently on top of the others. 'Shall I get my coat?'

'You can if you want, but I'm not taking mine. We won't be but a minute,' she said. 'He just wants you to know where it is so you can find it in the dark. The blackout, you know. Can't even use a torch to cross the yard. Although to be fair, using a torch during an air raid would probably not be the very best idea.'

Despite the pill, my heart tripped.

The Anderson shelter was out back, beyond a large vegetable garden. Except for a few rows of sturdy cabbages and chard, the garden was covered in straw.

The shelter looked like an enormous discarded tin can, half-swallowed in dirt and sporting a thin layer of anaemic sod. Moss clung to the sides and a thick piece of burlap hung over the opening.

'So here it is,' said Meg, lifting the flap. 'You can go in if you like, but there's not much to see. Just remember there are a couple of steps down and two bunks at the back. We've got torches and bedding, in case we have to spend the night. Keep your coat and shoes handy. Bedding or not, you'll be wanting them. I've got a siren suit myself. You pull it on over everything, zip it up and off you go. Have you got any clothing coupons left?'

I shook my head wordlessly.

'Well, never mind. I can get my hands on a pattern if you want to make one, although you'd have to come up with the material.'

Although it was just past four, the sky had turned the jewelled blue of twilight, and I shivered in a sudden gust of wind.

'That's that then,' said Meg. 'Let's get inside.'

She headed back, walking quickly. I broke into a jog to catch up.

'Make sure you come down for dinner tonight,' she said. 'We've a lovely haunch.'

'I can't have any,' I said, utterly miserable. 'I haven't got a ration book.'

'You needn't worry. It's venison.'

'Venison isn't rationed?' Hope sprang up like a bird taking flight.

'They can't ration what they don't know about,' Meg said, 'and Angus isn't one to let people starve.'

'You don't mean he poached it?' I was aghast the second the words rolled off my tongue.

'I said no such thing,' Meg said emphatically. 'But even if he did – which I did not imply in any way – the taking of a deer is a righteous theft. He used to be the gamekeeper at Craig Gairbh, you know.'

'Why did he leave?'

'He joined up. And of course, by the time he came back, the old laird had offered up the house and grounds to the military for the duration of the war. His son was killed, and the laird thought that was the least he could do, since he was too old to fight himself. He was a real warrior himself, back in the day.

So for the moment, there's no need for a gamekeeper. At any rate, the only difference between then and now is the title.'

'Was he the gamekeeper in 'thirty-four?' I asked.

She glanced over her shoulder and cocked an eyebrow. 'That he was.'

Which meant he had been there for all of the Colonel's shenanigans, making it all the more remarkable that he was letting me stay.

When we reached the building, Meg held the door open and let me go in first.

'It wasn't my idea,' I said weakly. 'I mean, the name thing.'

'Oh, aye,' Meg replied, nodding. 'From what I gather, your husband doesn't consult you about a number of things. I don't suppose you'll help with the blackout curtains, will you? Only it's getting dark already and I haven't even started the neeps and tatties.'

'Sure,' I said. Although I was taken aback, it didn't even occur to me to say no.

'Make sure they're nice and tight. Even a sliver of light will get us a fine. Or bombed.' She glanced at my face and laughed. 'It's just gallows humour.'

'Yes, of course,' I said, turning to leave.

'Wait a minute.'

She went to the pantry and came back, lifting my right hand and planting an apple in it.

I stared at it, nearly speechless with gratitude. 'Thank you.'

She picked up my other hand and inspected my nails. 'You look like you've been lifting tatties. I'll fix that for you tomorrow. "Beauty is your Duty," you know. Keep the fellows' spirits up. And what's going on under that scarf of yours, anyway?'

'Nothing good,' I said, clutching the apple so tightly I pierced its skin. 'Maybe you could show me how to set my hair with rags sometime.'

'Certainly. If you can stand sleeping on them, you can use my rollers.' She looked at me critically and nodded. 'You have a natural head for victory rolls. Go on then – I have to finish up dinner, as well as make myself presentable.'

I ate the apple down to a tiny nubbin, leaving the stem and seeds hanging by a fibrous ribbon of core, but it didn't make so much as a dent in my hunger. I hated the idea of going down to dinner on my own, but since Ellis and Hank had left me no choice, I did.

The barstools and tables were taken up by the same men as the night before (with the notable exception of Old Donnie), but this time none of them paid any attention when I joined Conall by the fire. Almost immediately, Meg set an enormous plate of food in front of me.

The venison roast was well done, brown through and through, and served with rowanberry jelly and an ample heap of mashed potatoes and turnips.

I was dizzy with food-lust. I glanced around to make sure there was still no one looking, then ate. It was a struggle to keep to a civilised speed.

The dog, who was once again lying between the end of the couch and the fire, watched with intense interest until I scraped the plate clean, then heaved a disappointed sigh. I'd wanted to slip him a couple of tiny bits while I was eating, but Mr Ross was behind the bar and occasionally glanced over. He did not strike me as the type to spoil a dog, and I was trying to be unobtrusive. I didn't want to do anything to make him change his mind about letting me stay.

When Meg came for my plate, she brought a glass of beer, telling me it would 'build my blood.' I'd never had beer before – our crowd considered it lowbrow – and I sipped it with apprehension. It was not unpleasant, and contributed to the warm glow I felt from finally having a full stomach.

It was the only thing I felt warm about. Every time the door opened I couldn't help looking, hoping it was Ellis and Hank, but it never was and I began to accept that they really had left me without two nickels to rub together, no ration book and no explanation.

I wasn't trying to eavesdrop, but since I was alone, I couldn't help overhearing bits and pieces of conversation.

The young men who occupied the tables belonged to a military lumberjack unit, the Canadian Forestry Corps, which had been deployed to supply the British army's endless need for wood, and Meg – who, in the name of duty, had donned a swing skirt, painted her lips red and drawn lines up the backs of her legs – worked with them during the day. The local men were older, several of them bearing obvious scars and injuries, presumably from the Great War. They sat on stools at the bar chatting with each other and paying no attention whatsoever to either the Canadian lumberjacks or me.

At ten minutes to nine, Meg turned on the wireless to let the tubes warm up. When the chimes of Big Ben announced the nightly broadcast, everyone fell silent.

The Red Army were advancing in south Poland despite intense fighting and were now only fifty-five miles from German soil. In one battle alone, they had killed more than three thousand German soldiers and destroyed forty-one of their tanks. In Budapest, over three days of fighting, they had captured 360 blocks of buildings and taken forty-seven hundred prisoners. On all fronts, 147 German tanks had been destroyed and sixty of their planes shot down. And in four days Franklin D. Roosevelt would be sworn into office for the fourth time.

Despite undisputed progress on the Front, my satiated contentment collapsed into unfathomable depression.

In Philadelphia, the war had seemed a million miles away. It was certainly discussed and debated, but it was essentially an academic exercise, conducted over cocktails, or lunch at the club. It felt like theoretical men fighting a theoretical war, and after Ellis was excluded from service we avoided the topic altogether out of concern for his feelings.

Experiencing the U-boat attack and witnessing the terrible injuries of the men who'd been pulled from the sea's flaming surface had thoroughly shredded any sense of detachment I might have had, but I was still having trouble comprehending the notion of three thousand dead in a single afternoon – and that was just enemy soldiers. I'd heard of death counts at least that large many times over during the course of the war, but until that moment, while sitting in a room full of uniformed men and aged veterans, I don't think I truly understood the human toll.

In bed, with my hair in Meg's rollers and my face slathered in cold cream, I had a sudden longing for Ellis, which was utterly ludicrous given that he was directly responsible for my current dilemma. Then I realised that homesickness was the real culprit. The mention of President Roosevelt had set it off.

I wanted to be in my bedroom in Philadelphia, before New Year's Eve, before any of this. I wanted to be safe, even if it meant enduring countless more years of Edith Stone Hyde.

Instead, I was alone in a building full of strangers in a foreign country – during a war, no less. If I disappeared, I doubted anyone would notice, never mind care. At home, at least my mother-in-law would notice if I disappeared – she might rejoice, but she'd notice.

I thought of Violet and wondered if she hated me, before realising that yes, of course she hated me. All she'd know was that I'd been brought along and she'd been left behind. I wondered what she'd think if she knew I'd trade places with her in an instant.

It then dawned on me that if Hank really hadn't told Violet about our so-called adventure, the only person on earth who knew where we were was Freddie. When Ellis's parents eventually investigated, they'd see that Ellis had emptied his bank account and that we'd left most of our belongings in storage at the hotel, but then the trail would grow cold.

If Hank and Ellis never came back, it was absolutely true that no one would notice if I disappeared.

Anna was mopping when I got downstairs the next morning. Without a word, she leaned the mop against the wall and went through to the kitchen. Breakfast was a piece of grey, mealy toast and another cup of tea made from recycled leaves, unceremoniously delivered.

Since I didn't have anything else to do, I brought a book down to read by the fire, a murder mystery called *Died in the Wool*. The title had seemed a lark when I packed it for the trip, but judging from Anna's expression, she didn't agree.

After I settled into the chair she mopped all round me, sloshing the grey water noisily in the bucket and wringing the rope mop quite clearly as a substitute for my neck. Finally, she rolled up the carpet so she could clean directly in front of me, all but asking me to lift my feet.

It was almost a relief when she planted her hands on her hips and said, 'Surely you're not going to waste another day?'

I closed my book and waited.

'Here's Meg and me both working at least sixteen hours a day, her at the sawmill, me at the croft, and then taking turns catering to the likes of you, and there's you spending your days lolling about by the fire waiting for your meals to be brought and your bed to be made.'

I moved my mouth, but nothing came out.

'Why don't you knit some socks for the soldiers, or at least blanket squares?' she asked accusingly.

'I can't. I don't know how to knit.'

'Well, *that's* a surprise.'

I set the book on the table. 'Anna, I don't know what you want me to do.'

'There's a war going on, but apparently it's all fun and games for you lot. I can't imagine what you're even doing here.'

Neither could I.

When Anna went back to mopping, I got my coat.

After finding the post office and enduring withering looks from the postman, whose fiery and unruly brows looked like caterpillars glued to his face, I sent the following telegram:

```
DR ERNEST PENNYPACKER 56 FRONT STREET,
PHILADELPHIA PA
DEAREST PAPA HAVE MADE AWFUL MISTAKE STOP AM IN
SCOTTISH HIGHLANDS MUST GET OUT STOP CANNOT BEAR
OCEAN AGAIN PLEASE SEND AIRPLANE STOP I NEED YOU
STOP YOUR DEVOTED DAUGHTER
```

The postman was even less impressed after I realised I had no way to pay him.

As soon as I left the post office, I began to wonder if I'd done the right thing. I hoped so, because the thing was certainly done.

When Ellis returned, I knew he would try to talk me out of going, but since he and Hank seemed intent on leaving me behind anyway, I couldn't see why they shouldn't leave me all the way behind, in the States. I supposed the only reason they'd brought me along in the first place was that Ellis couldn't afford to stash me anywhere else.

I couldn't go back to the inn until I was sure Anna had left, so I wandered around the village trying to find the loch.

The village consisted mostly of row houses and a few free-standing cottages surrounded by stone walls. There were only three stores, and stark reminders of the war everywhere: posters advising to 'Make Do and Mend' along with 'Dig for Victory Now!' were plastered on the walls of the Public Hall, and the lone telephone booth – bright red and looking like it had been plucked straight from a postcard – was shored up on three sides by sandbags. A group of fast, tiny planes came out of nowhere, zooming overhead in formation and causing me to shriek and duck into a doorway. The only reason I knew we weren't under attack was that the villagers paid no more attention to the planes than they did to me. Not a single person made eye contact with me. I wondered if they all knew I was the Colonel's daughter-in-law.

I came to a school. As I gazed at the children in the play-ground, I realised that every one of them, as well as all the adults on the street, had a cardboard box like Meg's slung over one shoulder by a piece of string. I thought of Anna's comment about mustard gas and felt suddenly naked.

Most sobering was the graveyard, which contained family stones with the freshly carved names of young men. There weren't many different surnames, and many of the names were identical. I counted three Hector McKenzies and four Donald Frasers, and wondered how many of the latter were connected to the Fraser Arms. Probably all of them, if you went back far enough. Old Philadelphia suddenly didn't seem so old.

There was one stone, still quite new, that I stood in front of for a long time. It was unusual not just because an infant, husband and wife had all died within two months of each other, but also because the date of the husband's death was vague – only the month and year were engraved on the stone, with a space left for the date. They had died three years before, so I imagined that he, too, was a casualty of war, and that in the chaos the specifics had been lost. There was only one date for the baby. She must have been stillborn, or died immediately after birth. The wife had died six weeks later. Perhaps she'd died of a broken heart. I wondered what it would be like to love that much.

The sky had turned threatening, so I wasn't surprised when the sleet started. I left the churchyard and headed up the road. Not long after, I became so light-headed I had to lean against a wooden fence post until the feeling passed. If I hadn't known better, I might have thought I was pregnant.

The furry white ponies on the other side of the fence came to greet me, pushing their inquisitive noses into my face and giving whiskery kisses for naught. There was nothing in my pocket but a soot-covered, crumpled handkerchief.

Eventually, I walked the long way round to the top of the road where the Fraser Arms was. As I skulked around the bend waiting for Anna to leave on her bicycle, I realised that I'd been all the way round the village and had yet to lay eyes on the loch. On the map, Drumnadrochit appeared to be virtually on its bank.

I'd harboured the hope that at some point in the afternoon I'd see the monster. Not that I had a camera or any way to prove it, and in a way I was glad I hadn't seen it, because it was not a noble wish. I just wanted to see it before Hank and Ellis did, to make them regret leaving me behind – and not just that day, or the day before.

It had always been Ellis and Hank, or Hank and Ellis, long

before our group included Freddie and whatever girl was currently swooning over Hank. It had begun years before that, when they were at Brooks together and then at Harvard. Even after Ellis and I married, I often felt like an afterthought.

I needed him to comfort me, to reassure me that I was wrong. But he wasn't there. He simply wasn't there.

13

Meg corralled me instantly and dragged me into the kitchen to fix my manicure.

'I wondered where you'd gone off to. Just having a wee wander, were you?' she said, pulling two chairs up to the corner of the table.

'Not very successfully,' I said. 'I never even found the loch. I thought we were right beside it.'

'We are, but it's behind the Cover,' she said.

'The Cover?'

'The Urquhart Woods. But no one calls them that. It's a dead giveaway that you're an outsider.'

'I think my accent already takes care of that,' I said.

She spread out a towel, shook a bottle of red polish and unscrewed the top. As she got to work on my left hand, she explained that while it wasn't officially possible to buy nail varnish, it was sold as 'ladder stop' at the chemist. The idea of using bright red lacquer to stop runs in stockings was so absurd I laughed, and she laughed, too, pointing out that there weren't any stockings to get runs in anyway. And then I felt guilty, because I was wearing a pair at that very moment.

She glanced at my face, then back at my freshly painted fingers, which lay draped over hers. 'This colour matches your lipstick perfectly.'

'I've always worn red.'

'Good. "Red is the New Badge of Courage," you know. And it brings out your lovely green eyes.' She tilted her head from side to side to inspect her handiwork.

Then she sighed. 'I'm down to the dregs of my own lipstick. At this point I'm digging it out with a stick, and there's none to be had in Drumnadrochit of any colour. I'll have to go to Inverness, although Lord knows when I'll find the time, or the coin.'

'I have an extra tube,' I said.

'Oh, I couldn't,' she said, setting my hand carefully on the towel.

'I insist! And anyway, I'm using your rollers.'

'Well, since you put it that way . . . You're lucky you can stand sleeping on them,' she said, looking up quickly. 'Your hair turned out beautifully. Those are some nice victory rolls, right there.'

I decided that when my father sent for me, I was going to leave all my stockings and make-up behind for Meg.

Dinner was trout, simply done, served with a generous helping of boiled kale and a heap of potatoes. Meg brought me a half pint of port and ginger.

Once again I cleaned my plate, and once again the tall, thin Conall, whom Meg had identified as a Scottish deerhound, released a disappointed sigh. He'd joined me by the fire as soon as I'd come down, and I was grateful for the company.

It wasn't until Mr Ross turned the radio on to let it warm up that I realised how late it was, and that Ellis still wasn't back. What had been a fleeting notion the night before returned more urgently, along with all my fear and bafflement. What if he didn't come back at all?

Before he absconded to Inverness it had never once occurred to me that Ellis might abandon me, but the more I thought about it, the more possible it seemed. If he did leave me, his mother would lobby that much harder for his continued financial support and eventual return to the family seat. A divorce was scandalous, but scandals could be swept under carpets. I could be replaced by a more suitable wife, and the Colonel and Edith Stone Hyde could have grandchildren who were not just three quarters of the right kind, but of entirely the right kind. Upon even further reflection, I realised that the whole purpose of the trip – restoring Ellis's honour – had been mooted the second he was caught in a lie, and that he might very well not want to show his face in Drumnadrochit again. But to leave me behind?

Disappearing without a word was a cowardly way to leave a woman. Beyond cowardly, given that for all he knew I'd been turned out that morning.

When the broadcaster uttered the words 'flying bombs,' it broke my miserable reverie. Doodlebugs had flattened hundreds of houses in East London, killing 143 people. Survivors were picking through the rubble with sticks, salvaging what they could of their personal belongings, and more than forty-five hundred people were sleeping on platforms in the Underground.

The lumberjacks and the locals, some wearing their uniforms from the Great War, stared at the radio in silent, united resolve.

Just after the broadcast ended, Ellis and Hank rushed through the door in a gust of wind and swirl of snow, giggling. Anger flared up in me.

'Darling!' said Ellis, spotting me immediately and coming to kiss me. I turned my face so his lips landed on my ear. His hot liquored breath wafted past my face.

'What kind of a welcome is that?' he said, struggling out of his coat and throwing it over the arm of the couch. He plopped down next to me and looked at my plate. 'Good Lord, Maddie. What did you do – lick it clean?'

Hank snapped his fingers in the air and said, 'Three whiskys! Make them doubles.'

Mr Ross ignored him completely. Meg raised her eyebrows and got three glasses from beneath the counter.

'None for me, thank you,' I said, lifting my port and ginger. 'I'm still working on this.'

Hank threw his coat on top of Ellis's and flopped into the chair opposite.

'Where were you?' I asked Ellis.

'In Inverness. Didn't that girl tell you?'

'Her name is Anna. And yes, she did.'

'Then what are you upset about? And where are those whiskys?' he asked, raising his voice and looking around.

Meg appeared with the drinks and slammed them down on the table.

Hank picked his up and took a gulp. 'What's on the menu?' he asked. 'I could eat a horse.'

Meg crossed her arms over her chest. 'I could get you a beetroot sandwich, I suppose,' she said.

'What did she have?' Ellis said, tilting his head toward my plate.

Meg lifted her chin. '*She* had trout. The last piece, as it happens.'

'We have ration books,' said Ellis, nodding encouragingly at Hank.

'Yes! Indeed we do,' Hank said, leaning over to dig through one of the duffel bags. He pulled out the books and fanned them like playing cards.

'So, what's on the menu now?' he asked, grinning.

Meg snatched them from him and said, 'Beetroot sandwiches.'

Ellis went stony-faced. 'Is this some kind of joke?'

'It most certainly is not,' said Meg.

'The hotel in Inverness had beef rissoles. *And* electricity,' said Ellis.

'Then I suggest you go back to the hotel in Inverness,' she said, spinning on her heel and striding off.

'Fine! We'll have the sandwiches!' Ellis called after her. He threw himself against the back of the couch and drank steadily, tipping the glass to his lips without ever putting it down. When it was finally empty, he set it back on the table.

He looked again at my plate. 'It's not like you to overeat. I hope you're not going to make a habit of it.'

I was too stunned to reply.

Hank shook his head. 'Darling girl, pay no attention. He's sozzled. Here, have a ciggy . . .' He held the case across the table in offering.

I intended to just brush it away, but both our hands were in motion and I somehow ended up smacking it. Cigarettes flew all over. The case bounced off Hank's chest.

The rest of the room went silent. All heads turned toward us.

'Ow,' said Hank, examining his chest. He brushed off his sweater and collected the cigarettes. 'Maddie, look what you've done. You've broken two.'

The landlord crossed the room in long strides and stood in front of us, hands on hips. He looked at Ellis for a very long time, and then at me and, finally, at Hank.

'Is everything all right, then?'

'You'd better ask her,' said Ellis. 'She's the one launching missiles.'

'Everything is fine,' I said quietly, staring at his heavy black boots. I could not look him in the face.

'You're sure of that?'

'Yes,' I said. 'Thank you, Mr Ross.'

'I beg your pardon?'

'Thank you, yes,' I said, thoroughly chastened. 'Everything's fine.'

After a slight pause, he said, 'I'm very glad to hear it.'

When he left, Ellis leaned toward me and said, 'Have you lost your mind? What is *wrong* with you? You can't go around lobbing objects at people in public!'

'I didn't mean to lob anything,' I said, looking desperately at Hank. 'It was an accident. I'm sorry, Hank.'

He nodded and waved dismissively. 'S'all right.'

'Well, I don't believe it *was* an accident,' said Ellis. 'You've been acting like a total bitch from the second we walked through the door.'

I caught my breath. Never in my life had anyone spoken to me like that. Even during her tirade on New Year's Day my mother-in-law had referred to me in the third person. And because everyone in the room was still looking at us, they'd all heard.

'Ellis!' Hank hissed, somehow appearing sober. 'Get control of yourself.'

As I stood, crossed the room and disappeared into the stairwell, I was fully aware that all eyes were on me, with the exception of my husband's.

This was by no means the first time Ellis had drunk enough to act outrageously – at one party, he'd overturned a full tray of drinks when he felt the waiter was serving them in the wrong order. The frequency of these episodes had increased steadily since his colour-blindness was diagnosed, but before that night he had never directed his rage at me. I had always been the one who could calm him down and persuade him it was time to go home.

I was doubly sure I'd done the right thing in appealing to my father, and hoped he wouldn't let me down. I also hoped that Ellis would find the monster during my absence, and that it would have the curative effect he was so sure it would, because if it didn't, I couldn't shake the feeling that I'd just had a glimpse of the future.

14

At ten the next morning I knocked on Ellis's door, hoping to catch him alone. He wasn't there.

As I descended the stairs, I could see Anna dusting a heavy silver candlestick on the mantelpiece, her face as pinched as if she'd eaten a green persimmon.

I wondered if she'd heard about the scene from the night before. Then I wondered how I was ever going to face any of the customers at the bar again, never mind Mr Ross.

Hank and Ellis were sitting at a table, wearing layers of heavy wool and hobnailed boots. Bags and equipment were heaped on the floor beside them, along with their coats, hats and gloves. I couldn't believe it. They were going to leave again.

I sailed past and took a seat by the window.

Ellis joined me immediately. 'Darling, what's wrong?'

I tipped my head at the pile of bags by Hank's feet. 'Were you at least going to leave me a note this time?' I said, trying to keep my voice down.

'About what?' He glanced over and looked back, surprised. 'That? That's our field equipment. We were waiting for you to get up. But I gather from your question you're upset we went to Inverness.'

'Without *me*,' I said in an urgent whisper. 'What if the landlord had thrown me out?'

Anna's duster was poised above the mantel, its feathers quivering. It was perfectly clear she could hear every word.

'I knew full well Blackbeard wasn't going to throw you out.'

'How?' I demanded, no longer bothering to whisper.

'I asked him, obviously.'

Anna slammed the duster down and stomped into the kitchen.

'You still could have left me a note,' I said.

Ellis reached across the table and took both my hands. 'Darling, that girl was supposed to tell you. And it's not like I was trying to keep anything from you – Hank and I only realised at breakfast that we needed to get ration books and gas masks immediately or we'd all starve to death, never mind the other possibility. It didn't even occur to me you'd want to join us. We had to beg a ride in the back of a paraffin van. It reeked to high heaven and we had to crouch the whole way. You'd have been miserable.' He tilted his head, trying to catch my eyes. 'Darling? Is something else the matter? You still look upset.'

'Well, I am. Of course.'

'About what?' he asked.

'What do you think?'

His face went blank. 'Maddie, I have absolutely no idea.'

'He doesn't remember a thing,' Hank called over from the other table. 'One too many libations, I'm afraid.'

'You called me a very rude name last night,' I said. '*Very* rude. *In public.*'

Ellis frowned. 'I would never do that. Surely you misheard.'

'I don't think she did,' Hank piped up. 'I'm pretty sure everyone in the room heard. Shall I join you, or would you prefer I continue to fill in the blanks by shouting across the room?'

'What did I say?' Ellis asked.

'I don't care to repeat it,' I replied.

Ellis squeezed my hands. 'Maddie, I'm so sorry. If it's true, I'd clearly had too much to drink – I would never slight you in my right mind. I adore you.'

I trained my eyes on the fireplace beyond him, but he took my chin and aimed my face at his. He raised his eyebrows questioningly, beseechingly.

After several seconds, I sighed and rolled my eyes.

'That's my girl,' he said, breaking into a wide grin.

'If we're all peachy again, can we get this show on the road? The sun is up, so the clock is ticking,' Hank said. 'Maddie, darling girl, while you look absolutely stunning, you can't tromp around the scrub in that get-up. Didn't you bring something a little more . . .' He stirred the air beside his head with one finger. 'I don't know, Rosie the Riveter?'

'Well that's more like it,' Ellis said when I came back downstairs.

Hank had gone to a local pier to arrange for a boat, and Anna had returned just long enough to drop plates of drawer porridge on the table.

I glanced down at my dungarees, safari jacket and utility shoes, and hoped she wouldn't come back out of the kitchen before we left. I felt ridiculous.

'Here,' Ellis said, handing me a bright red case made of leather. It had an adjustable strap and a shiny brass buckle. 'What do you think? Isn't it pretty?'

'It's very bright,' I admitted. 'What is it?'

'Your gas mask. The cases have been weatherised, since it seems to be perpetually raining or snowing,' he explained, tapping the lid of his own case, which was dark brown.

I took the mask out to examine it. It was made of pungent black rubber, with a clear plastic window at the top and a strange metal canister capped by a bright green disc at the bottom. Three white cloth straps came from the sides and top of the face and were attached by a buckle.

I had just put it on and was trying to adjust the straps when Hank burst through the door. He stopped just inside and assumed a look of pure astonishment.

'Ellis! You weren't supposed to find Nessie without me!'

I pulled the mask off and stuffed it back in its case. 'Very funny, Hank.'

'It was, actually,' said Hank. 'Nobody appreciates me around here. Let's start over. Pretend I just came in. Go on – turn around and then turn back.'

When Ellis and I obliged, Hank stepped forward and threw his arms in the air.

'And we are in possession of a mighty sea vessel, ours for the duration!' he announced grandly. After a few beats, he dropped his arms and continued. 'All right, maybe she's not so mighty, and maybe it's more accurate to say she's a lake vessel, but I do know she doesn't leak. I took her out for a little test spin.'

He clapped his hands in front of him. 'Chop, chop, my dearest sourpusses. We're wasting precious daylight. Let the adventure begin!'

15

We walked a few hundred yards north to Temple Pier, a tiny local dock, and set out in a battered rowing boat. The plan was to find an accessible piece of land near Urquhart Castle and start surveillance.

When I first laid eyes on the boat and the ladder leading down to it, I baulked. Hank and Ellis clearly sensed my apprehension – before I knew it, they'd handed me into it and pushed off, and instead of climbing into the bow behind Hank, Ellis sat next to me in the stern. This left the boat unevenly weighted, and when Hank started rowing, I stayed as close to the middle of the bench as I could, clutching my gas mask case with one hand and the edge of the bench with the other.

The water was eerily black and seemed to move against itself, the top layer gliding across the ones beneath. The bottom third of the oars disappeared with each stroke, and I found myself thinking of what might be lurking down there. I decided to focus on the shoreline instead. It was densely wooded, marshy even, and almost level with the water. Since we were headed south, I realized that it was the Cover, and that the village was right behind it.

'That's the Urquhart Woods,' said Ellis, pointing. 'Drumnadrochit is straight through there, although you'd never guess.'

The banks became steep immediately beyond the Cover and

remained so – three to four feet high, with thick scrubby vegetation that reached right to the edge and trees that seemed to rise straight from the water. We passed two sheep stranded at the brink, bleating and struggling to keep their footing. Their wool was thick and full of twigs, and their skinny black legs bent at odd angles as they tried to gain purchase. Their cries were pitiful, and sounded for all the world like people making fun of sheep.

'How on earth did they end up there?' I asked.

Hank glanced at them and shrugged. 'They're not exactly known for their brains.'

'Surely we're not just going to leave them there,' I said as Hank continued to row. 'Ellis?'

'There's nothing we can do about it, darling,' he said, prying my hand loose from the bench and holding it on his thigh. 'Anyway, sheep can swim. The wool makes them float.'

Hank was rowing mightily, and soon the sheep were just tiny dots on the bank. I twisted in my seat, continuing to watch and worry. Even if they got up the bank, how would they ever make their way back through the thorny scrub? I couldn't figure out how they'd got past it in the first place.

'Look!' said Ellis, touching my arm to get my attention and then pointing. I turned round and caught my breath.

The castle was on a promontory immediately in front of us – spectacular, massive and ruined, with a single tower that was missing its roof and much of its face. The surrounding walls and battlements were crumbling and jagged, their stones mottled with lichen and moss.

Ellis watched me take it in and broke into a mischievous smile. 'So enlighten us. Tell us everything you know.'

The blood rushed to my face. I hadn't read any of the books he'd asked me to.

'You haven't cracked a single spine, have you?'

'I'm afraid not,' I said. 'But I will. I'll start tonight.'

He laughed and patted my knee. 'Don't worry your pretty little head. I only got the books to keep you out of trouble on the trip over, although I can't say that was a great success.'

Hank snorted.

'Fortunately, I have all the news that's fit to print right here,' Ellis continued, tapping his head. 'I read everything in my father's library before the Great Purge.' He drummed his fingers against his lips. 'Hmm, where to start . . . Well, the part you can see from here was built between the thirteenth and sixteenth centuries, and changed hands many times. It was last used by Loyalists in 1689, and when they were forced to retreat, they blew up the guardhouse' – he made sounds like explosions and threw his arms over his head, causing the boat to rock – 'so the castle couldn't be used by Jacobite supporters ever again. There are huge chunks of it lying near the entrance.'

'Try not to tip the boat, Professor Pantywaist,' Hank said. 'This particular spot is more than seven hundred and fifty feet deep.'

I checked quickly for lifebelts and, seeing none, resumed my death grip on the bench.

Ellis went on. 'For our purposes, the interesting thing about the castle is that it was built on the site of an ancient Pictish fort tied to the earliest monster sighting ever recorded. Saint Columba was on his way here in the year AD 565 and several witnesses claim he saved a man who was clutched in the monster's jaws by making the sign of the cross.'

I shrank away from the water. 'The monster eats people? Why didn't anyone tell me?'

Ellis laughed. 'You have nothing to fear, my darling. The worst it's been accused of since is mauling a sheep or two.'

Knowing that Anna's cousin had been too traumatised to

ever get back on his boat or speak of his experience, I wasn't entirely reassured.

'Here we are,' said Hank, using one oar to turn the boat towards a small landing next to the castle. He held the boat steady while Ellis removed his boots and socks and rolled up his trousers.

Ellis nodded at Hank, who bared his teeth in a primal roar and dug both oars into the water, pulling so powerfully the veins in his face bulged. He drove us hard and fast toward the shore and when we hit, I almost came off the bench. The bow lifted, which dropped the stern even further, and I shrieked.

Ellis grabbed a coil of rope and jumped out. The water came up past his knees, soaking his pants to mid-thigh.

'Shit!' he yelped. *'Cold!'*

Hank laughed as Ellis sloshed out of the water. 'Approximately thirty-nine degrees, if I'm not mistaken. Sit in the bow next time, and you'll be closer. Better yet, you can row, Mr I-Was-on-the-Rowing-Team-at-Harvard.'

'Damned right I'll row,' said Ellis. 'Starting today, on the way back.'

He grabbed the bow, hauling the boat toward him. I could feel and hear the gravel scraping against the bottom.

'Works for me,' said Hank. 'There's a dock at the other end.'

'Ha, ha. You think you're so clever, don't you?' said Ellis.

'That's because I am,' said Hank. 'I keep telling you.'

Ellis continued to pull until the boat was solidly grounded. He wiped his hands on his thighs and said, 'That's it. Everybody out.'

Hank grabbed the tripod and a couple of bags and hopped off the side.

Ellis reached in for his boots, then helped me climb out.

'At least my socks are dry,' he said, glancing at his soaked trousers. He was grinning, beaming really, and it was like I'd been whisked back in time.

I was looking at the Ellis I'd met at Bar Harbor – before the war, before his diagnosis, before my own diagnosis, before the rift with his father. The charming, optimistic devil I'd married was still in there, and was apparently just as close to the surface as the Ellis who'd been so awful the night before.

I decided then and there to send a second telegram to my father that rescinded the first. I had to, even though I knew it would infuriate him, because I realised Hank had been right all along.

Ellis *did* need this, and I wanted to be there when he found the monster, to watch his restoration with my own eyes. Just as importantly, I didn't want Hank to be the only one tied to the memories of that glorious day.

Hank set up the tripod and screwed the camera onto it while Ellis spread out a blanket and pulled a variety of things from the bag – beakers, binoculars, compasses, a thermometer, maps and logbooks. Although I hadn't gone to college, it all looked terribly scientific to me.

I arranged myself on the blanket and looked out over the loch's glistening surface. If Hank was right about how deep it was, I was having trouble imagining it. Were its depths as low as the hills were high? The loch became so deep, so dark, so quickly, it seemed as impenetrable as the fortress beside us once was.

Ellis ran through the plan. 'First, we record the temperature of the water. Then we take a sample to see how much peat is floating at the surface. It affects visibility, and also tells us how strong the undercurrent is. Then we record surface conditions, weather conditions, wind speed and direction, et cetera. We'll repeat all of this once an hour.'

'And in between?' I asked.

Hank took over. 'In between we scan the surface of the water and watch for disturbances. If you see something, call "Monster!" We'll confirm its location by compass, and I'll begin filming. You two keep it in your sights at all times, in case I somehow lose it in the viewfinder.'

There were supposed to be three pairs of binoculars and three compasses, but one of the compasses was missing. Ellis gave me one of the remaining two, insisting that he and Hank could share.

When I finally admitted I didn't know how to use it, I expected some kind of smart-aleck response, or at the very least an eye roll. Instead, they simply showed me.

'It's easy,' said Ellis, guiding my hands. 'Turn it, like this, until the arrow points north. Now, imagine a straight line from the degrees markedaround the edge to the object you're looking at, and read the number next to it. And really, that's all there is to it.'

I successfully confirmed the location of a speck of shore on the opposite bank, which we decided would define one edge of my viewing area. I was to start there and scan to the left, slowly, carefully, before coming back and going just far enough past the landmark to ensure a little overlap with Ellis. Hank had no boundaries, which I thought hilarious, but since they hadn't made fun of me for my lack of technical knowledge, I refrained from making a joke.

A few minutes after we began, I thought I saw something and swung my binoculars back. A rounded thing was poking out of the water, moving steadily, and leaving a series of *V*'s in its wake.

'Monster!' I shouted. 'Monster!'

'Where, Maddie? Where?' said Ellis.

I leapt to my feet, pointing strenuously. 'There! Over there! Do you see it?'

'Use your compass!' Ellis cried.

'Keep your eyes on it!' Hank ordered, dropping his binoculars and getting behind the camera. He bent over it, peering through the viewfinder, cupping one hand round it for shade.

'I can't do both!' I said desperately. 'What should I do?'

'It's okay! I see it!' Ellis shouted. 'Maddie, keep your eyes on it. Goddammit, I think we've got it!'

He jumped up and held the compass right next to the camera so Hank could steal glances at it while aiming the lens.

'It's at seventy degrees,' Ellis said, coaching Hank. 'Still at seventy. Now it's just past seventy. Still moving. Call it seventy and a quarter.'

'Got it,' said Hank. He began turning the crank handle on the camera, quickly, at least two rotations per second.

I had my eyes locked on the object in the water. It flipped on its back, exposing whiskers and a black nose.

'Oh my God,' I said, utterly deflated. 'I'm so sorry.'

'About what?' said Hank, still cranking away.

'It's an otter.'

'Ellis?' Hank said, continuing to film.

Ellis picked his binoculars back up. After a short pause, he lowered them and said, 'She's right. It's an otter.'

Hank let go of the handle and straightened up. He shaded his eyes with his hand and gazed over the water. 'Oh well,' he said, sitting down. 'Never mind. At least we know Maddie's got sharp eyes.'

Ellis recorded the event in the logbook, Hank lit a cigarette and they passed a flask, which I declined.

'I'm sorry,' I said, after calling the alarm over a duck.

'It's all right,' Ellis said with false cheer. 'Better to have a hundred false alarms than to miss the real thing.'

He duly recorded it. He took the water's vitals again and we resumed our watch.

'I'm really sorry,' I said, after a floating log.

'Never mind,' said Ellis. 'I suppose it did look a little like a creature's back from that distance.'

When I apologised for the jumping fish, Hank said, 'Ellis, maybe you could take a quick peek at whatever Maddie's looking at before anyone calls the official alarm?'

'I don't think that's a good idea,' Ellis said, clearly dispirited. 'Because if it's the real thing, that kind of a delay would give it time to dive down. That's why my father only got three pictures.'

I stared at his back.

He really did believe his father. This wasn't just about fixing himself – it was also about vindicating the Colonel. How could I have been so clueless about my own husband? I sat beside him on the blanket, so close our shoulders were touching.

Hank sat next to us and lit a cigarette. 'That's all well and good, as long as we don't run out of film,' he muttered. 'Pass the flask, will you?'

Four and a half hours later, Hank had smoked eleven cigarettes, he and Ellis had finished a third flask and I had seen a twig, two thrashing ducks and a second airborne fish.

16

When the sun began to sink behind us, Hank declared it a day. They tried to hide it, but I could tell they were both out of patience with me and my false alarms, and I felt terrible for disappointing them. We barely spoke as Ellis rowed back.

I was also anxious about facing everyone at the inn, but there was no avoiding it. I couldn't even slip in unobtrusively because of my Rosie the Riveter get-up, never mind my bright red gloves and gas mask case.

It turns out I needn't have worried. I smelled perfume and heard giggling as soon as we cracked the door open, and when we stepped inside, no one gave us a second glance. A crowd had gathered, and this time it included young women.

'Well now, what have we here?' said Hank, casting his eyes around the room.

A dance was about to start at the Public Hall, and the excitement was palpable. Meg and the other girls had pulled chairs over so they could sit together, and were sipping drinks, praising each other's shoes, hair and outfits, and surreptitiously posing for the lumberjacks, who colluded by pretending they weren't looking.

One girl told how she'd dismantled an old dress her mother had 'grown out of' and transformed it into the latest style using a pattern from the most recent 'Make Do and Mend' booklet.

Another girl was wearing real stockings, which were the object of much admiration. She extended her leg for the other girls to examine, although there was a great deal of examination from the lumberjacks as well.

'They're lovely,' Meg said enviously. 'Look at the sheen on them. Are they silk or nylon?'

'Nylon,' said the other girl, pointing her toe in various directions.

'Where on earth did you find them?'

'My George sent three pairs from London. He says the girls are stealing them right and left, in plain daylight. Shopkeepers have to keep them under the counter.'

Meg sighed. 'And here we are without a single pair to steal.' She turned to a large and ruddy-faced lumberjack sitting at the next table. I realised he was the man I'd seen slipping out of her room. 'Rory, next time you're on leave, do you think you can get me some real stockings?'

'And risk being ripped limb from limb by roaming packs of thieving girls?' He flashed a grin. 'For you, anything.'

Meg turned her leg so she could examine the line she'd drawn. 'I suppose I've done well enough with gravy browning and a pencil. But if it rains, I'll have the dogs chasing me again, licking my legs.'

'I'll keep the hounds away, canine or otherwise,' said Rory, winking. 'Go on, girls, have one more drink. My treat.'

'Och, but you're an awful one!' said Meg, wagging her finger. 'Don't think I'm not on to you. We're all on to the lot of you!'

There were giggles all round as the girls blushed, each casting a shy glance at a different lumberjack. They cleared out together a few minutes later, laughing and excited, leaving only three older locals perched on stools at the bar.

One twisted round to watch the young men file out after the girls. When the door closed behind them, he turned back.

'Well, I suppose if there's a good time to be a sheep it's when you're a lamb,' he said with a sigh.

'Aye,' said the others, nodding sagely.

'Say, I don't suppose you want to go,' said Ellis, giving me a playful jab.

I tried to smile but couldn't. He'd meant it as a joke, but I would have given anything to be part of that pack of girls making their way to the Public Hall.

I'd never had female friends. My single best opportunity – boarding school – was a complete wash. What happened with my mother ensured I was a pariah before I ever set foot in the place. My next opportunity, the summer I graduated, was no better. It was clear the other girls were simply enduring me in order to gain access to Hank, Ellis and Freddie, and when I apparently took two of them off the market at once – breaking one's heart and marrying the other – most of the girls dissipated. Hank's sweethearts continued to tolerate me until they realised he wasn't going to marry them, but not one of them had tried to stay in touch after. Violet was the first one I'd felt at all optimistic about, especially since I thought Hank was finally going to let himself be caught.

I felt guilty again about how we'd left her behind.

There was a knock on my door shortly after I'd gone to bed and blown out my candle.

'Who is it?' I asked.

'It's me,' said Ellis.

It didn't happen often, but from the tone of his voice I knew what he wanted.

'Just a minute.'

I groped my way to the dresser, found the hand towel and

wiped the cold cream off my face. Then I began fumbling with the rollers.

'What are you doing in there?' he said.

'Nothing,' I replied. 'Just making myself presentable.'

'I don't care if you're presentable.'

There was no way I was going to get the rollers out in the dark, so I gave up and opened the door.

Ellis stepped in and took my face in his hands, pressing his mouth against mine.

He had shaved and applied cologne, a custom concoction he'd been wearing as long as I'd known him, and although his lips remained closed, I could taste toothpaste. His pyjamas were silk.

'Oh!' I said, pulling back in surprise. There was usually no preamble at all.

'What on earth?' he said, patting the sides and back of my head.

Because Lana had always taken care of the serious business of maintaining my hair, all Ellis had previously encountered on my head were bobby pins and a delicately beaded hairnet.

'Rollers,' I explained. 'I've been setting my own hair. If you give me ten minutes, I'll light a candle and get them out.'

'In the middle of nowhere, with no electricity, my intrepid wife still finds a way to be gorgeous,' he said. 'Hank's right, you know – they did break the mould when they made you.'

He pushed the door shut and slipped his arms round my waist.

'After our little misunderstanding, I thought we should make up properly,' he said in a low growl. 'Also, I was reminded today of just what a good sport you are. You have no idea what it means to me.'

He backed me against the dresser and pressed his hips into mine. There was no mistaking his intentions.

'Do you mean for going monster-hunting?' I said.

'Yes . . .'

'False alarms and all?'

'Just proves what wonderful eyes you have . . .'

'What about for tolerating Hank?' I asked. 'Am I a good sport for that?'

'Positively saintly,' he said in a hoarse whisper. He put his hands on my hips and began grinding against me. I leaned my head back, boldly offering my throat. I had never before done such a thing, and when he didn't kiss it, I wondered if he couldn't see it in the dark.

'What about my overactive imagination?' I continued. 'And my unseemly appetite?'

'There is absolutely nothing unseemly about you,' he said. 'Should we light a candle, or just try to find the bed? Is your luggage in the way?'

'No, the way is clear . . .'

'Are you just neater than me or did they put your things away?'

'I think I'm just neater . . .'

'Neater, prettier, quick as a whip . . .'

He guided me backwards. When we bumped into the side of the bed, I climbed under the covers and lay against the pillows.

He crawled in beside me, lifted my nightgown, and arranged himself above me. Then he nudged my legs apart with a knee, balanced on one arm long enough to pull down his pyjama bottoms and entered me. After a few pushes, he collapsed, gasping in my ear. A minute later he rolled off.

'Oh, Maddie, my sweet, sweet Maddie,' he said, caressing my shoulder.

I wanted to tell him that we couldn't be finished yet, that it wasn't my shoulder that needed attention, but I couldn't find the words. I never had, and I probably never would, because I wasn't entirely sure what it was that I needed him to do.

I lay wide-eyed in the dark long after he'd crept from my bed and gone back to his own.

During my teen years, when my mind turned to such things, I imagined the physical side of marriage would be very different than it turned out to be. Perhaps it was the forbidden novels passed around the dorms at Miss Porter's that set my expectations so high. Perhaps it was the whisperings about girls who had *actually done it* (and anyone who didn't return after a holiday was suspect). Perhaps it was the sight of dreamy film heroes turning their leading ladies into willing puddles of mush with a single, authoritative kiss.

I had high hopes for our wedding night, but it was a complete disaster, with Ellis cursing and thrusting limply while his mother wept theatrically in a room down the hall. I was too innocent to realise it at the time, but I don't think we even managed to consummate the marriage.

Our wedding night may have had extenuating circumstances, but in the months after, when there were none, I remained baffled and disappointed. Either it was over as soon as it began, or else he couldn't finish, which left him extremely ill-tempered. I kept hoping it would develop into something more, something that involved *me*, but it never did.

I thought he must be disappointed too, because the frequency had fallen off the edge of the earth as soon as he had the excuse of my diagnosis, and I never tried to start anything. It was no wonder we didn't have a baby.

17

The second day of monster-hunting was much the same as the first, except that it was snowing.

I was desperate to get to the post office, but couldn't think of an excuse to slip away. For all I knew a plane was already on its way to collect me.

I continued to see disturbances in the water, but grew reluctant to say anything. Hank could not hide his displeasure at wasting film, and I couldn't stand the look of disappointment on Ellis's face.

The third day was gloomy and dark, and the air was heavy with the threat of rain. Everyone was cranky and cold, and I was even more distressed about not having sent the second telegram.

A few hours after we set up, Ellis realised I wasn't pointing anything out and accused me of not pulling my weight.

Shortly thereafter, I saw a large disturbance very close to the opposite bank and raised the alarm. It turned out to be a swimming stag, which climbed out of the water and shook itself off, right on the landmark I'd found with the compass.

'Wonderful! Fantastic!' Hank cried, throwing his hands in the air. 'I've got twenty seconds of crystal-clear footage of a fucking deer. And that's the end of this reel.'

He wrestled the camera off the tripod, pulled out the film and chucked it into the water.

'What the hell are you doing?' Ellis said. 'What if we accidentally filmed the monster?'

Hank dug around inside the duffel bag. He pulled out another reel and another flask. 'We've filmed plenty of monsters. Maddie's "monsters," to be precise,' he said, making quotation marks with his fingers before shredding the film's yellow box in his haste to get it open.

'For God's sake, control yourself,' said Ellis. 'We need the original boxes to send to Eastman Kodak.'

'I wouldn't worry. Apparently we're going to have all kinds of empty boxes,' said Hank, thrusting the new reel into the camera and then struggling to put the side panel back on. He slapped it twice with the heel of his hand.

'We're not going to have anything if you break the goddamned camera,' Ellis barked. 'Stop acting like an idiot, and give me the fucking thing. It's not lined up properly.'

Hank swung his head round to face Ellis. His eyes were wide, his expression murderous. I thought he was going to throw the camera to the ground, or maybe even at Ellis. Either way, I was absolutely sure they were going to fight.

They stayed that way for a long time, their eyes burning and chests heaving. Then, for no apparent reason, Hank seemed to snap out of it. He reattached the side of the camera, screwed it back on the tripod and sat down.

Ellis picked up the flask and took a long swallow. He held it out to Hank, pulled it away when Hank reached for it and took several more gulps himself. When he once again held it out, Hank glared at him for a few seconds before snatching it from his hands.

I was dumbfounded. In four and a half years, I'd never seen Hank and Ellis turn on each other. There had been plenty of bickering and sniping, especially if one of them came up with a quip that hit too close to home, but this was entirely different.

They'd nearly come to blows, and probably would have if I hadn't been there.

I was too shaken to keep scanning the surface for disturbances, particularly since my sighting of the stag had caused the explosion. Even so, I ended up keeping my binoculars glued to my face, because Ellis noticed that I'd stopped looking. After that, he spent more time making sure my binoculars were moving than looking through his own.

I couldn't believe that sitting on the bank with a camera at the ready was their whole plan, but despite the scientific trappings and meticulous measuring of conditions, that did seem to be what they had in mind. That, and drinking, and blaming me for doing exactly what I was supposed to be doing.

Finally, I set my binoculars down and said, 'Why don't we try something different?'

'What's that?' Ellis muttered with a complete and total lack of interest.

'Why don't we bait it?'

He and Hank lowered their binoculars and turned to face each other. After a moment of silence, they said incredulously, and at exactly the same time, *'Bait it?'*

They burst into peals of hysterical laughter. Hank reached out and grabbed Ellis's thigh, giving it a hearty shake before falling backwards and bicycling his legs in the air. Ellis also fell onto his back, hugging himself and stamping his foot.

'Sure,' Ellis finally said, wiping tears from his eyes. He looked demented. 'We'll string a few sheep up over the water, shall we? Or do you think it prefers children? I'm pretty sure I saw a school in the village.'

'Better yet, why don't I just whistle for it?' Hank said, giggling maniacally. 'Maybe it will do tricks for us if we offer it a treat?'

'Whistle for it!' cried Ellis. 'Of course! Why didn't we think of that before?'

They began howling again, purple-faced, thumping the blanket with their fists.

I clamped my mouth shut and turned away. I'd finally realized what was going on. Although it was barely noon, they were completely sloshed.

An hour later, when the drizzle turned into bullets of water and Ellis and Hank's hysteria had turned back into deadly, drunken purpose, I couldn't stand it any more.

'I'm going back,' I said.

'We can't pack up now,' Hank snapped. 'There are several hours of daylight left.'

'I'll walk,' I said, climbing to my feet. My legs were achy and stiff from being folded beneath me. 'Where's the road?'

'Right up there,' Hank said, pointing over his shoulder. 'Turn right. It's only a mile and a bit.'

I leaned over to pick up my gas mask. Ellis was watching me.

'Hank, we have to take her.'

'Why?'

'Because it's raining.'

'It'll be raining on the boat, too,' Hank pointed out.

'What if she can't find the inn?'

'Of course she can find the inn. She's a clever girl.'

'It's all right,' I said. 'I'll find the inn.'

'Well then,' Hank said. 'If you're sure.'

Ellis was still looking at me.

'It's okay. Really. It's not that far,' I said.

Relief washed over his face. 'Atta girl, Maddie. You're the best. They broke the mould when they made you.'

'So everyone keeps saying.' I started up the hill, barely able to bend my knees.

'She's terrific, you know,' said Hank. 'Best coin toss you ever won. And now I suppose I'm going to be stuck with Violet . . .'

'You shouldn't complain. She's miles better than the mewling, needle-nosed sheep my mother had lined up for me,' said Ellis.

I stopped and turned slowly round. They were perched side by side on the blanket, searching the loch through binoculars, unaware that I was still there.

I trudged back to the village with my hat pulled down, my collar turned up and my hands stuck deep in my pockets. I kept my eyes on the road in front of me, watching the raindrops hit and join others before running off the pavement in rivulets.

I tried various ways of analysing what I'd just heard, twisting the phrasing in the hope that I might have misinterpreted, and finally concluded that I understood perfectly. I'd been won in a coin toss.

As outrageous as it seemed, when I thought back over our history, there was nothing to contradict it.

We'd all met the summer I left Miss Porter's, when I still hoped to go to college myself. Many of my former classmates were headed for Sarah Lawrence or Bryn Mawr, and while I wanted to be among them, I didn't have a clue how to go about it. I knew better than to expect help from my father, who hadn't even tried to get me into the Assembly Ball and who had apparently forgotten I was coming home for the summer. A few days after I returned, he left for Cuba, where he spent the summer deep-sea fishing.

Left to my own devices, I packed up and went to Bar Harbor, slipping into the tide of Philadelphians going to their summer houses. My father hadn't opened ours since my mother's *grand scandale*, and going, especially on my own, made me excited and nervous in equal parts. I'd essentially been kept in purdah since I was twelve, and this was my first chance to connect with my hometown peers. I hoped they would accept me, regardless of what their parents might whisper. The girls at Miss Porter's certainly hadn't.

I needn't have worried, because Hank, Ellis and Freddie took me under their collective wing immediately. They didn't give a hoot about my family's chequered history – indeed, Ellis and Hank had somewhat chequered histories themselves. While they all referred to themselves as Harvard men, Freddie was the only one who'd left with a degree. Ellis was what was euphemistically referred to as a 'Christmas graduate' – he flunked out in the middle of his freshman year – and Hank was expelled shortly thereafter for trying to pass off as his own a paper written by John Maynard Keynes. And then, of course, there was Hank's kitchen maid.

Hank was the clear ringleader, a virtual doppelgänger of Clark Gable with a dangerous streak girls found irresistible. Neither the rumours about the kitchen maid nor the plagiarism deterred hopeful debutantes or their parents, because Hank was the sole heir of his bachelor uncle, a Wanamaker who was the current president of the Pot and Kettle Club.

If Hank was Clark Gable, then Ellis was a tow-headed, clean-shaven Errol Flynn. He had been on the rowing team during his time at Harvard, and his physique reflected this. His chest was like chiselled marble. He also had a quirky sense of humour I found hilarious – a trait that he, in turn, found adorable.

And Freddie – poor Freddie. Although the men in his lineage had married exclusively beautiful women for generations, he was proof that such planning couldn't guarantee an outcome. His features were asymmetrical enough to be off-putting and the hair on his crown was already thin. He sported frightful sunburns, and, because of his asthma, was constantly sucking on his Rybar inhaler. I was never quite sure how he ended up being so thick with Hank and Ellis, but he was very kind and he doted on me.

I quickly became their confidante, little sister and partner in crime, although I was aware that a large part of my appeal was novelty. I was the only girl around who hadn't been paraded under their noses at cotillions, tea parties and clubs for the last decade, and they agreed unanimously that I was refreshing and modern precisely because my natural spirit hadn't been ruined by grooming for presentation. They toasted my father for neglecting to have me finished, as well as for having the good manners to be otherwise occupied in Cuba.

We spent our days playing tennis, sailing and dreaming up increasingly outrageous practical jokes. At night we went to parties, built bonfires and drank ourselves silly.

It was at a beach party, while we were lying on our backs in the sand watching fireworks, that Freddie suddenly popped the question. I was caught completely off guard – I had never even considered him as a romantic possibility – and thought he was joking. When I laughed, his face crumbled and I realised what I'd done. I tried to apologise, but it was too late.

Not a week later, Ellis asked me to marry him. He said that Freddie's proposal had made him realise how much he loved me, and while he didn't want to seem hasty, he couldn't risk another close call. I hadn't realised we were in love, but it made sense. I'd never felt more comfortable with anyone in my entire life – we could talk about anything – and it certainly explained his indifference towards other girls.

The instant I said yes, Hank spirited us away to Elkton, Maryland, the quickie wedding capital of the East Coast, but because of a newly instated waiting period, Ellis's mother managed to track us down. She turned up at the chapel wearing a purple mourning dress, crying hysterically. When she finally realised she couldn't prevent the ceremony from happening, she inexplicably pulled the diamond comb from her own hair and pressed it into my hand, curling my fingers round it.

While this drama was playing out, Hank snickered and Ellis rolled his eyes. They were dressed identically in tuxedos – even the roses in their lapels were indistinguishable – and I remember thinking that either one of them could have been the groom. How right I was.

I'd been won in a coin toss. There had been no duel, no joust. No ships had been launched, no gauntlets thrown. There were no passionate declarations, challenges or displays about winning my hand – just the toss of a coin.

No wonder the physical side of my marriage was virtually non-existent, and no wonder Hank was always around. When they'd realised there were Freddies in the world who might actually be serious about me, they'd decided one of them had to marry me just to keep things as they were.

A coin toss, for Christ's sake.

I was soaked through and shaking violently by the time I reached the Fraser Arms.

Anna was sitting at a table with a row of lamps in front of her, cleaning the glass globes with a rag.

'Back so soon?' she said, glancing up.

'Yes,' I said.

I closed the door and went straight to the fire. My teeth were chattering, my very bones chilled.

Anna's brow furrowed. 'On your own?'

'Yes.'

I was aware of Anna watching and girded myself. It was the first time I'd been alone with her since Ellis and Hank returned from Inverness, and I thought I might be in for another tongue-lashing. Instead, she came over and threw another of the mysterious logs onto the fire.

'Get yourself closer,' she said. 'Your knees are knocking. I'll fetch a cup of tea.'

I hadn't realised how cold my fingers were until I held them towards the flame and the feeling began to come back. It was like being jabbed with a thousand needles.

Anna brought a cup of strong, milky tea. I took it, but realised immediately that I was shaking too hard to hold it and put it down. She watched me a few moments longer, then went behind the bar and returned with a small glass of whisky.

'Get that down you,' she said.

'Thank you,' I said, taking a sip. The warming sensation was immediate.

We were silent for about a minute before she spoke again. 'And they left you to walk back on your own, did they?'

After a pause, I nodded.

She tsked. 'It's not my business and I'm usually not one for the blather, but it's weighing on me and I'm going to say it anyway. When your husband and that Boyd fellow went to Inverness, they never asked Angus if you could stay. I wasn't going to say anything, but then he lied straight to your face, and I thought you should know.'

I sat in silence, absorbing this. They'd wagered that Mr Ross wouldn't throw me out if I was on my own, and no thanks to them, they were right. I wasn't just their plaything, their pretty, fake wife. I was their unwitting pawn, theirs to strategically play.

There would be no second telegram.

18

After my stag sighting, we fell into a pattern that was as unwavering as it was stultifying. Ellis and Hank left with their equipment every day, presumably rowing to different vantage points around the loch, while I stayed behind and did nothing but grow increasingly depressed about the war and wait for my father to send for me. The weather was so remorselessly foul I didn't even feel like walking.

Hank and Ellis returned each evening obscenely smashed, and arguing incessantly about whose fault it was that they hadn't found the monster. It was like watching a snake try to eat itself from the tail up. One particular night, they arrived so sauced up it was hard to believe they were still on their feet. I was surprised they'd managed to row back, never mind climb out of the boat with all their gear.

Ellis was sure he'd seen the monster and Hank hadn't even tried to film it because *he* was sure it was just another otter, and definitely not large enough to be the monster. Ellis said that maybe there was more than one monster, and although this one might have been a juvenile, it would have been just as useful for their purposes. Hank said he wasn't going to waste film on yet another otter, and Ellis insisted again that it was a monster. An otter, a monster, an otter, a monster – on they went, round and round.

The next morning, I went downstairs and found the two of them sprawled next to each other on the couch. Hank hadn't even got dressed. He'd just thrown a robe over his pyjamas and stuffed his feet into slippers. He was unshaven and his hair stood in spiky tufts.

Ellis was in even worse shape. It appeared he hadn't made it upstairs at all, because he was wearing the same clothes as the night before. His shirt was untucked and his collar open. His belt and shoes were missing.

Hank pried one eye partly open as I approached.

'Morning, sunshine,' he croaked.

'Good morning,' I said.

Ellis grunted.

'I'm warning you right now, I'm not rowing today,' said Hank. 'I'm not even sure I can walk.'

'Me either,' said Ellis, draping an arm over his face.

They sat in silence for several minutes, not moving even as Anna set cups of weak tea in front of them.

She stood looking at them, and then shook her head. Her gaze moved to me.

'I'll be back with your tea,' she said. 'It's still steeping.'

After she left, Ellis said, 'I was thinking, maybe we've worn out that particular vantage point.' He neither lifted his head nor opened his eyes.

'Huh,' said Hank. 'Very possible.'

'Maybe we should take the day off and regroup, so to speak.'

'I think you're on to something,' said Hank.

'Let's reconvene later then, shall we?'

'Absolutely,' said Hank. He climbed to his feet, wobbled for a few seconds, then lurched toward the stairwell.

Ellis followed. 'Say, do you want to try some hair of the dog?'

'Can't hurt,' said Hank.

Anna brought me a cup of strong, sweet tea and returned to the kitchen. I gulped it, collected my things and headed for the door.

'And what do you think you're doing?' she said, reappearing behind me. 'I was just about to start your breakfast.'

'I'm sorry. I need to . . . not be here,' I said.

'They've gone back upstairs, have they?'

I nodded.

She tutted. 'Foolish men. Where are you off to, then?'

'I thought I might go up to Craig Gairbh and have a look at the Big House.'

'You canna go there!'

I was stung by her tone. 'I was just going to take a peek from a distance.'

'You canna go near it at all unless you want to get killed! It's a battle school now, and they train with live ammunition! Many's the morning I see tracer bullets crossing the sky when I'm out milking the cow.'

'Oh,' I said. 'I wasn't aware. In that case, I suppose I'll just wander around.'

Anna's outrage fell away. 'You stay there a wee moment, and I mean it – no running off on me.'

A few minutes later, she was back. She handed me an umbrella and pressed a paper-wrapped packet into my hand. 'It's just a bit of Spam in a sandwich. I added some drippings to the bread. You need fattening up. And mind what I said about the estate. There's a reason you don't see any green berets around town. Even the men don't get to come and go – except Angus, of course, but he knows the grounds like the back of his hand.'

I was as lost outdoors as I was inside, but I had to put some physical distance between my husband and me.

We were no strangers to alcohol at home, but he and Hank were now drinking outrageous amounts – dangerous amounts – and I wondered, again, what might happen if they never did find the monster.

Hank would be fine, of course, but Ellis had lost everything. Even if he somehow managed to redeem himself socially, I wasn't sure I wanted to be part of that life any more, not knowing that my whole marriage – what I'd always thought of as my salvation – was nothing but a pretty, pretty fraud.

And pretty it was: I'd lived in fabulous houses, been driven around in fancy cars and drunk only the finest champagne. I had a closet of designer gowns and furs. My life consisted of waking at noon, meeting up with Hank and Ellis and then bouncing from eye-opener to pick-me-up to cocktail to nightcap, and staying out all night at dances or parties before starting all over again the next day. It was full of luxurious trappings and shiny baubles, and that had blinded me to the fact that nothing about it was real.

Growing up as I had, how had I not seen that it was all posturing?

Society's love affair with my fragile, martyred mother came to an abrupt end just after I turned thirteen, when she left a note on my father's desk, secured by a glass paperweight, that informed him she was running off with a man named Arthur.

Seven weeks later, when Arthur was persuaded to return to his wife by means of social shunning and a few solid turns of the financial screw, my mother also slunk home. She had no choice. Although the money had come from her side, my grandfather hadn't left her in control of it.

My father retreated on an almost permanent basis into

his study, even taking his meals there, which left me to deal with her entirely by myself.

She took to her bed, and her weeping became more than I could bear. She was sure that she was the one who'd been wronged, and her indignation was huge – Arthur's lack of chivalry and bravery were incomprehensible. She'd have been happy to live with him in a cave, so passionate was her love, and he'd simply tossed her aside.

When she discovered that the thick letters she sent every day were being returned by the postman and then burned, unopened, by my father, she went off her rocker.

She was furious that Arthur couldn't even be bothered to read the words that pained her so to write. She was furious at my father, for his complete and utter lack of understanding and also, incredibly, because he, too, couldn't be bothered to read the letters, which she was convinced would move any human being with a soul to forgive her. And she was especially furious at June, Arthur's wife, for allowing my mother's former friends to surround and comfort her.

When none of this worked, she began writing to June instead, warning her that Arthur was feckless and unfaithful – he'd lured my mother in and was responsible for her ruin. She and June had been equally deceived. Couldn't June see how similar their situations were? Those letters were also returned unopened.

In the blink of an eye, my mother had gone from social darling to pariah. It was irrevocable, but she was incapable of accepting that. She showed up at public venues, presumably in a bid to convince people she was still the brave, stoic, tragic Vivian, but no woman would talk to her and not one man was allowed to.

The injustice of it, particularly when she found out that Arthur was being accepted back into society, pushed her entirely over the edge. She wished my father dead and cursed her own, consigning him to hell for locking her away from what was rightfully hers. She cursed the servants and fired the housekeeper, whom she suspected of being my father's spy, and whom he immediately rehired. She even cursed me, because if I was going to ruin her figure and keep her trapped in a loveless marriage, I could at least have been a boy.

My mother became essentially housebound, and I became an unwilling confidante. She sought constant reassurance. Was she losing her looks? Was her neck still tight? Because there was a surgery, a thing called a 'skin flap,' that was supposed to turn back the clock. Did I think she needed one? I did not, but she went to New York and got one anyway. She came back with her face pulled taut and, more alarmingly, full of ideas for the improvement of me.

It was a shame I had not inherited her nose, but there was a surgery that could fix that. I was contrary and worried too much – there was a surgery to fix that, too. It was an easy thing, a simple adjustment of the front part of the brain. I'd be in and out in an hour, and I'd be so much happier. All the best families were having it done. And if somehow that didn't do the trick, there was a promising new treatment in France that involved electricity. It was just that she hated seeing me so unhappy, particularly when a cure was available.

I did not take enough care with my hair, but a permanent wave would fix that. I was not thin enough, but for that, alas, there was no quick fix. I should never put more than the equivalent of three peas on my fork at a time, or one small disc of carrot. I should always leave two thirds of my meal on my plate and was never to eat in public.

She weighed me regularly and hugged me if I was lighter. These fleeting moments of affection were enough to keep me drinking my morning 'tonic' of apple cider vinegar and eating as little as possible, although occasionally I got so ravenous I would sneak down to the kitchen in the middle of the night and eat an entire loaf of bread. I once ate a pound of cheddar while standing at the sink.

Despite the occasional binge, over the next two years I grew four inches and lost five pounds. My backbone and hips protruded, and there was not – according to my mother – a more elegant neck in all of Philadelphia.

I was desperate to escape. Everyone else my age was already at boarding school, but my mother claimed she couldn't bear to be apart from me, not for a single day, never mind that I hadn't seen her the entire time she was off with Arthur. I had no friends at all. My father wouldn't look at me, and my mother wouldn't stop.

One day, I pulled out the Yellow Pages and looked up the address of a children's home. In retrospect, stepping out of a hired car in expensive clothing and declaring myself an orphan to the mother superior was probably not the best-laid plan. Certainly I was returned forthwith, and after that was literally a prisoner in our house – the servants were under strict orders to prevent me from going out and to inform my mother if I tried. They had nothing to worry about. I had nowhere to go.

Shortly after my attempt to flee, my father and I met in the hallway and instead of passing me by and grunting, he stopped. His eyes ran from the top of my head down to my feet and then back, dwelling for an uncomfortable period of time on my hips and chest. He frowned.

'How old are you?' he asked.

'Fifteen next month,' I said.

'You look like a damned boy. Where is your mother?'

'In the drawing room, I think.'

He pushed past me and stormed away, bellowing, 'Vivian? Where are you? *Vivian!*'

When he slammed the drawing room door so hard it shook the walls, I realised that something extraordinary was about to happen. I crept closer, eager to hear. Our housekeeper, Mrs Huffman, was further down the hall, with her eyes wide and her hand pressed to her mouth. We exchanged a look, agreeing implicitly to eavesdrop. She came up behind me.

There were none of the usual weapons of war: no cool but caustic innuendos, no carefully crafted barbs, and there were certainly no devastating silences. My father's opening salvo was a roar, and my mother's response was to cry hysterically.

I expected her to dash out at any moment, her face buried in a handkerchief, but instead her weeping turned into furious shrieking, punctuated by the sound of things smashing. At the height of a primal scream came the biggest crash of them all – it sounded like a billiards table had come through the ceiling. Mrs Huffman and I looked at each other in horror, but since the battle raged on, it seemed no one had been murdered.

From him: It wasn't sufficient for her to destroy his reputation by running off with another man? Did her hatred of him really run so deep it now extended to ruining the health of his only child?

From her: She was only looking after my interests, because he certainly didn't. He cared as little for me as he did for her – he'd never loved her, had only ever wanted her money. Was it her fault he was no husband at all? Was it so wrong to want to be loved?

From him: What money? If she was foolish enough to think the proceeds were worth tolerating her antics, she had a vastly inflated view of herself. The principal itself would not be worth the torment of being married to her.

A period of ear-splitting cacophony followed, during which they each tried, unsuccessfully, to outshout the other. Finally, my father thundered for silence in a voice so unexpected and frightening he got his wish.

When he spoke again, his voice simmered with determination and quiet fury.

He may have been doomed, he said, but as yet I was not, and since it appeared I was going to be his only child, he would not stand idly by as she starved me to death. I was going to boarding school immediately, tomorrow, as soon as it could be arranged.

The door opened so suddenly both Mrs Huffman and I had to flatten ourselves against the wall to avoid my mother, who streaked past, her face red and twisted, clutching a handkerchief.

My father emerged a split second later with bulging eyes and a glistening forehead. He stopped when he saw me, and for an awful moment I thought he might hit me.

He turned to Mrs Huffman. 'Pack Madeline's things. All of them,' he said, before swivelling on his heels and marching to his study. When he slammed the door, another door, somewhere upstairs, slammed even harder.

Mrs Huffman and I poked our heads into the drawing room.

It looked like a war zone. Every vase was smashed, every photograph shattered. The curio table was on its side and missing a leg and, most spectacularly, the grandfather clock lay on its face, its casing exploded, surrounded by splinters of wood, shards of glass, springs, coils and cogs.

As I surveyed the damage, an immeasurable thrill swelled up within me, the closest thing to ecstasy I'd ever experienced.

If nobody smoothed this over, I might actually get out, perhaps even with my nose and frontal lobe intact. For the first time ever, I decided not to go up to my mother, and I prayed – actually prayed – that neither parent would yield.

I did get out. Four days later. But not before finding my mother submerged in the bathtub, her hair floating around her like Ophelia's and an empty bottle of nerve pills by her outstretched hand.

I had broken down and gone upstairs less than an hour after the argument. She had gambled that I would come sooner.

A formation of planes whizzed past, startling me out of my reverie. Meg had told me that 'our own fellows' flew by all the time, and that there was nothing to worry about unless the siren was blaring. Nonetheless, it shattered what was left of my nerves.

I walked to the field of white ponies, who once again approached the fence to see if I had anything for them. I unwrapped my sandwich and offered up tiny pieces of crust, but they yanked their heads back in disgust. Realising that I'd just tried to feed them part of a meat sandwich, I murmured helpless apologies and then ate the crusts myself. Moments later, I devoured the whole thing.

When I passed the graveyard, a single crow appeared overhead, circling and cawing as though it had a personal grievance. It also seemed to be following me. Certainly it was still above me when I reached the entrance to the Cover, and I ducked down the wooded path simply to get away from it. I hadn't gone far before realising I was being ridiculous, and stopped to get my bearings.

The trees and vegetation were dense and the ground squelched beneath my feet. I was surrounded by the sound of rushing water, and although the trees were leafless, everything around me was iridescent green, verdant even, with moss clinging to the ground and fallen trunks and dangling in lacy tangles from branches.

The forest floor was dotted with beautiful toadstools. They were tiny and shaped like chalices, their outsides an unremarkable fawn, but their interiors were the most spectacular scarlet I'd ever seen. I picked a few and put them in my pocket. As I did so, I found the compass. It was all I could do not to throw it into the trees.

Before long, I came upon a fast-moving river and followed the path beside it. When it veered sharply to the right, I realised that by ducking and dodging, I could see the loch through the trees.

To get closer, I would have had to cross a stream that was feeding the river. There were stones suitably spaced, but I imagined myself slipping, breaking an ankle and not being found for days, which was entirely possible if Ellis's and Hank's hangovers lasted more than a day, or if the 'hair of the dog' turned into another bender.

The idea of not being found swelled into a frenzied panic when, after forty minutes of trying to find my way out, I realised I was going in circles.

I switched directions. I took different paths. I went back to the loch and used the compass to try to figure out which direction the village was, but the paths were hopelessly twisted and there turned out to be multiple rivers. I was Gretel, on my own, and it was too late to start dropping crumbs, because I'd eaten them.

Maybe Mr Ross or Meg would notice if I didn't show up for dinner – or maybe they'd just assume I was sleeping one off, like Ellis and Hank. Even if they noticed I was gone, they'd have no idea where to start looking.

What kind of an idiot wanders blithely into a forest?

I was about to sit on a log and cry when I caught sight through the trees of a woman kneeling on the opposite side of the river. She was washing what looked like a rust-stained shirt, rubbing it against a large upright stone. Her hair was tied in a kerchief and her clothes were old-fashioned – a long green skirt made of rough cloth, an apron and worn brown boots that went up past her ankles.

'Excuse me! Hello!' I cried, stumbling forward.

She stopped scrubbing and looked at me. Her eyes glistened with tears, and when she blinked, a single drop fell into the river. Her lips were slightly parted, exposing a snaggle-tooth. The whole effect startled me, bringing me to a temporary stop, but soon I was staggering along the winding path, hands on tree trunks, trying to get closer to her.

'Hello! Ma'am? Excuse me! I'm sorry to intrude, but can you please tell me . . .'

My voice trailed off when I came round a bend that should have put me directly across from her. She wasn't there.

I scanned the bank quickly, confirming by the uniquely shaped rock that this was indeed where she'd been. I looked around desperately, listening for the sound of footsteps or crackling branches. There was no sign of her, yet I couldn't figure out where she could possibly have gone, or what I had done to make her flee. It was as though she'd simply vanished.

'Please come back!' I shouted, but the only answer was the sound of rushing water and the cawing of the crow, which was still somewhere above me.

'I'm lost! Please!' I yelled one last time, before sinking to my knees and bursting into tears. I stayed like that for about ten minutes, sobbing like a child.

Eventually, I pulled myself together. I got up, wiped my

face with the backs of my gloves and brushed off my coat, which was muddied from kneeling. Then I straightened my scarf and staggered forward, using the umbrella as a walking stick.

19

When I finally found my way out of the Cover, the sight of open sky and the towering, rugged hills made me weep again, only this time with joy and a completely unexpected rush of gratitude to the divine.

Although nominally Protestant, I'd given up prayer many years before. The last time I'd prayed for something, my request had been granted, but the means of my delivery to boarding school had apparently required my mother's death.

Despite my dubious history with God, I was so grateful at being delivered from the Cover that I decided to stop by the church and offer up a small thanks – but only if it still felt right when I got there, and only without asking for anything specific, and only if there was no one else in the building.

I had just climbed the steps when I saw Mr Ross at the grave I'd found so tragic the first day I'd gone walking, the one with the young family whose members had perished so close together. He had his back to me, but I recognised his broad shoulders and unruly hair.

After a moment he knelt and placed his hand on the granite marker. He bowed his head and stayed that way for several minutes. Then he put something on the ground, rose and headed for the gate, where Conall was waiting. He trudged up the road toward the inn with the dog at his hip, never knowing I was there.

I descended the steps and went to the grave. He'd left a handful of snowdrops.

'Willie the postie came by with some letters for you. I set them by the register,' Meg said when I came in.

She was behind the bar holding glasses up to the light and then wiping them with a dish towel.

I hung up my coat and collected the letters. There were several addressed to Hank and Ellis, which I dropped on the counter, and one addressed to me, sent by airmail. I recognised the handwriting immediately. My relief was so great I almost dropped it.

I sat by the fire and tore it open.

January 18, 1945

Dearest Madeline,

I was most surprised to receive your telegram. I can't imagine how you think I could – or would, for that matter – arrange for an airplane to save you from your 'awful mistake.' Have you any idea what that would entail? Clearly not. I take partial responsibility for that, having shielded you from the realities of life as best I could. You embarked on a most foolish and dangerous endeavor without affording me so much as the courtesy of a discussion, thus depriving me of the opportunity of saving you from yourself – much as you did when you decided to get married behind my back and without my permission.

I had to learn of your most recent hijinx second- or even thirdhand from cohorts of Frederick Stillman amid rumors of nefarious and, dare I say it, arguably treasonous dealings. Until your telegram, I had no indication that you had even survived the journey. I have taken the liberty of informing the Hydes and Boyds that their offspring also survived, since you did not indicate otherwise.

I wish you had come to me, my dear, but since you did not, I can do nothing for you. I will not bankrupt myself to bail you out of a situation entirely of your own making and that any sane person would recognize as, well, not. Whether you intended it or not, you have once again made my life most difficult.
Most sincerely,
Your Father

P.S. You should probably know that your in-laws are furious, and your friend Freddie has his own fish to fry.
P.P.S. I agree that you should stay away from the ocean. I'm afraid I think you should stay put until the end of the war. I wish you luck.

I stared at the letter long after I finished reading it. He'd written and sent it the same day he received the telegram. I knew that it would be difficult and expensive to arrange for a flight, but it was certainly not impossible. The Germans didn't control the airspace, and military commanders flew back and forth all the time. He'd simply decided I wasn't worth saving, apparently without even taking the time to sleep on it.

I put the letter back in the envelope and tossed it into the fire. Within seconds it was engulfed in flames – white, orange, red – and then finally was just a rectangle of black melding into the charred logs.

I realised Meg was watching.

'Is everything all right?' she asked.

'No. Not really.'

She continued to stare at me, but I could not think of a thing to add.

I stayed by the fire through the rest of the afternoon and then into the evening, as the locals filed in and the lumberjacks arrived in groups. I was barely aware of them. I didn't even respond when Conall slunk over and plopped down at my feet.

'You haven't moved in hours,' said Meg, bringing me a glass of sherry. 'Is there anything I can do?'

'I'm afraid not,' I said. 'But thanks for asking.'

Meg stiffened. 'Here they come.'

I turned to watch as Hank and Ellis emerged from the stair-well. Although they'd shaved and got changed, they looked every bit as sepulchral as they had in the morning.

Meg came over immediately, bringing their mail and a letter opener.

'Two whiskys,' Hank said, taking them from her. 'Make them doubles. And keep them coming.'

The letters were responses to the advertisement they'd placed in the *Inverness Courier* from people who'd seen the monster and were willing to be interviewed, and the excitement of that – along with the whisky – brought them both back to life. They consulted their watches and decided that it was not too late to call. Hank waved Mr Ross over.

'We need to use the telephone,' he said.

'It's up the street,' said Mr Ross, stroking his beard.

'What do you mean it's "up the street"?' said Ellis.

'I mean it's *up the street,*' Mr Ross repeated, folding his arms across his thick green sweater.

'There's a telephone booth just a little ways up the road,' I said, not exactly clarifying, but hoping to defuse. 'It's not far. I think it takes coins.'

'It does,' said Mr Ross, nodding. 'Do you need change?'

'You don't have a telephone? You don't have electricity *and* you don't have a telephone?' Ellis said.

'Ellis, knock it off,' said Hank. 'You're giving me a headache.'

Mr Ross went back behind the bar. Our eyes met a couple of times, and after that I was careful not to look.

I wondered if he'd always worn a beard, and what he'd look like without it. I wondered why he didn't have a wife, for there was nothing wrong with him that a little feminine attention couldn't fix. I wondered what it would be like to be married to him.

I wondered what it would be like to be married to anyone other than Ellis. Had the coin fallen the other way, would I have let myself be persuaded that I was in love with Hank and married him instead? Probably. Either way, I'd have been bamboozled into a marriage as real as the monster tracks Marmaduke Wetherell had pressed into the shores of the loch with his hippo foot.

I was still lost in thought when the policeman arrived, and noticed only because Hank and Ellis fell silent. The tired-looking man, in his mid- to late fifties, stopped just inside the door.

'Bob!' Meg called from across the room. 'Bob the bobby! We haven't seen you in ages. Any news from your Alec?'

'Some. We've had letters. He can't tell us where he is, but he did say he's flying a Spitfire.'

'Well, that's something, isn't it?' said Meg. 'It's a pally ally you'll be wanting, I assume?'

'I'm afraid not,' he said regretfully. 'Joanie's had me sign the pledge. Also, I'm here on official business.'

'Oh?' said Meg.

The policeman cleared his throat and lowered his voice. 'Angus, do you think I might have a wee moment?'

'Certainly,' said Mr Ross, coming round the bar. He joined the bobby by the door.

Hank, who had his back to them, put his finger to his lips. Ellis gave a knowing smirk, and both of them rearranged themselves into better listening positions.

'It's about the . . . *incident*,' said the bobby, dropping his voice to a whisper on the final word. 'You know normally I wouldn't bother you with such things, but I'm afraid you did throw the water bailiff in the river.'

'Aye, that I did. And I'd do it again. He deserved it, speaking like he owned the place.'

'I've no doubt, no doubt at all,' said the bobby, shaking his head sympathetically. 'Only, he made an official complaint up at Inverness, and so I am forced to say something. And there it is. I've said something.'

'It's all right, Bob,' said Mr Ross. 'I understand.'

'Only, could you show just a wee bit more restraint next time?' The policeman held his forefinger and thumb so close they were almost touching. 'Perhaps in the future you could just dangle him the tiniest bit?'

'Certainly. Next time I'll just dip his toes. His socks won't even get wet.'

The bobby laughed and clapped him on the shoulder. 'That's grand, Angus. You know I wouldn't interfere if there hadn't been an official complaint. You know we all appreciate everything you do.' He lowered his voice again. 'My mother greatly appreciated the bit of salmon the other day.'

'Ach,' said Mr Ross, waving him off. 'That could have been anyone.'

'We know perfectly well who it was.'

Our landlord waved again and said, 'If your business is concluded sufficiently for the purposes of reporting to Inverness, how about a wee dram on the house?'

'But Joanie's had me sign the pledge . . .'

'Just a wee one. And you know what they say. Always carry a large flagon of whisky in case of snakebite, and further, always carry a small snake.'

'I've not heard that,' said the bobby. 'Who said that?'

'Some American film guy. Has a potato for a nose. A jowly sort of fellow.'

'Well, it's bloody brilliant. But what's wrong with a potato for a nose?'

'Absolutely nothing. And if Joanie finds out, I'll get you an adder. Or throw you in the river. Whichever sounds better at the time, in terms of needing a dram for consolation,' said Mr Ross, draping an arm across the man's shoulders and leading him to the bar.

'Well in that case I don't suppose it would do any harm,' said the bobby, a look of relief flooding his face. The men at the bar, the locals, pulled a stool up beside them and welcomed him.

'Poaching,' said Ellis, tapping his chin and staring at Hank. 'That carries quite a stiff penalty, if I'm not mistaken.'

20

When the siren sounded, I knew instantly what it was. With my heart pounding, I felt my way in the dark to the chair, where I'd laid out my coat and shoes. I was pulling them on when someone flung my door open and hit me in the face with the beam of a torch.

'Are you ready?' Meg yelled over the din. She was already zipped into her siren suit, which was made of black-and-red tartan.

'Ready,' I called back, hopping towards her while forcing my heel into a recalcitrant shoe.

The siren continued its deafening wail, rising and falling. Hank and Ellis staggered into the hallway barefoot and in their pyjamas. Hank was wearing only the bottoms.

'What the hell?' he said, shielding his eyes from the torch.

'It's an air raid. Come on! We've got to go!' said Meg.

'To where?' Ellis said, rubbing his eyes and looking confused.

'To the shelter!'

Meg and I pushed past them and ran down the stairs. I heard them clumping after us, cursing as they navigated in the dark.

Mr Ross appeared at the bottom of the staircase holding another torch.

'Come on,' he said, waving us urgently toward the kitchen.

When we were all at the back door, Meg and Mr Ross turned off their torches.

Meg went out first, and I could see just well enough to follow her. I stumbled and fell to my knees on the frozen earth. Someone – Mr Ross, I realised immediately – scooped me up and propelled me forward, clutching my elbow with his left hand and keeping his right arm firmly round my waist.

Meg had thrown the burlap flap back and was already inside. Mr Ross held me by the armpits and lowered me in, handing me to Meg.

'Mind your head. There's a bunk at the back,' she said, pulling me in deeper and leading me to it. 'There's another above it, so mind your head there, too. When everyone's in, Angus will get a light on.'

She sat beside me and leaned in close. I huddled against her and we clutched hands. It smelled damp and earthy, and was terribly, terribly cold.

Outside, the men were shouting. Hank and Ellis were arguing that they'd never laid eyes on the shelter in the daylight so how were they supposed to know where it was or how to get in, and couldn't Mr Ross shine the light on it for just a moment? He replied that he didn't care what the hell they did or did not know, and to get the bloody hell inside.

My voice came out as a raspy screech: 'Ellis! Hank! Get in here! It's two steps down. Climb in backward if you have to, but hurry up!'

'Get in, *amadain*!' Mr Ross bellowed. 'Just get in!'

'I would, if I could just fucking— Hey!'

There was some kind of kerfuffle at the front of the shelter, followed by a thud, and a vile stream of curses from Hank. There was another thud, and this time I heard someone scraping toward us.

'We're back here,' I said, reaching my arms out. My hands found the top of Ellis's head, and then his shoulders. He was crawling.

'There's a bunk right here,' I said.

'Conall, *thig a seo*!' Mr Ross yelled, and shortly thereafter he turned on his torch.

The burlap flap was closed. We were all inside. Our breath curled like smoke from our mouths, and Mr Ross's expression was so fierce that while I knew his eyes were blue, at that moment I would have sworn they were black.

When Ellis saw that the bunk we were sitting on was made up, he grabbed the top quilt with both hands and yanked it out from under us, nearly dumping Meg and me on the floor.

'Hey!' I said. 'Was that really necessary?'

'I'm fucking freezing,' he said, wrapping himself in it.

'Throw me one of those,' said Hank, who was crouched barefoot against the corrugated wall. 'I can see my goddamned breath.'

'Get it yourself,' said Ellis. 'I'm as naked as you are.'

'Oh, for the love of God,' said Meg, and without even thinking I turned to help her rip another quilt loose, this time nearly toppling Ellis. She balled it up and threw it overhand at Hank. He wrapped it round his shoulders and made his way to the back of the shelter, climbing onto the bunk above us.

The wailing of the siren continued.

'You've not got your gas masks?' said Mr Ross.

I glanced quickly and saw that Meg had brought hers.

'No,' I said. 'I'm very sorry.'

He tossed his into my lap.

My hands shook as I tried to put it on. The smell of rubber was stifling, my area of vision vastly limited and I couldn't get the straps over the rollers in my hair. Meg pulled her mask on in a single fluid motion and turned to help me.

'Hold still,' she said in a muffled voice. 'I just have to thread the straps through . . . There's one . . . There's another . . .

Wait . . . I've almost got it . . . And there you are. Nice and tight.'

The combination of screaming siren and having my head confined sent me spiralling into panic. It was as though I was back on the SS *Mallory* during the U-boat attack. I felt like I couldn't breathe, although clearly I could, because the inside of my mask was so fogged up I couldn't see a thing. When I tried to wipe it from the outside, Meg pulled my hands from my face and held them against her thigh. 'It takes a bit of getting used to. Just breathe normally and it will clear up.'

I closed my eyes and took deep, deliberate breaths.

'That's it,' she said. 'In through the nose and out through the mouth. In, and then out. That's better already, isn't it?'

When I opened my eyes, the window of my mask was starting to clear.

'What about me? I don't have a mask,' said Hank, from the bunk above us.

'You'd take one off a woman, would you?' Mr Ross snapped.

Hank was silent for a moment, and then added, in a tone that could be interpreted as chastened, resigned or both, 'I don't suppose there's any whisky in this tin can?'

Mr Ross threw him a look of disgust and turned off the torch. The starry sky was briefly visible as he went through the flap. A moment later he returned and switched the light back on. He'd retrieved a rifle and was crouched with it by the opening. Just as I remembered his missing trigger finger, I realised he was holding it by his left side.

'How long is this going to take?' Ellis asked. He was curled into a ball in the corner of the bunk, wrapped in the quilt. 'I think I'd rather take my chances inside.'

Mr Ross held his hand up for silence, listening, concentrating.

From far in the distance, over the siren's wail, came the *boom-boom-boom-boom* of large engines.

'Bloody hell,' he said, leaping to his feet and pumping the rifle.

'What? What's wrong?' said Ellis.

'A fucking Heinkel.'

The light went off and he slipped outside with an untranslatable growl. The booming got closer and louder until suddenly it was right over us and Mr Ross was shouting – and shooting – at it.

'Thall is cac, Mhic an Diabhail!'

After the second shot, the sound of the aeroplane changed from a steady set of booms to three followed by a gap. It continued on, limping into the distance.

Mr Ross climbed back inside the shelter and turned the torch on again.

'Did you just do what I think you just did?' said Meg.

He shrugged.

'Did you just shoot out an engine?'

'It doesn't matter if I did. He's got three more.'

'But with a rifle?'

'The *shite* was right over our heads. I could have jumped up and touched—'

He was interrupted by a huge explosion in the distance, followed immediately by another – a terrible sound that reverberated across the water and through the glen. I screamed into my mask and grabbed Meg, who gripped me just as tightly.

After about twenty minutes, which felt like twenty years, the siren rose to its highest pitch and stayed there, before finally dropping off into silence.

'What's that? What does that mean?' said Hank, who remained on the top bunk.

'That's the all-clear,' said Meg, removing her mask. She was pale. 'Sweet Mother of God. I wonder where that was?'

Mr Ross set his rifle down and simply shook his head.

'Please God they didn't hit anyone,' said Meg, pressing her fingertips to her temples.

'Aye,' said Mr Ross, nodding slowly.

I tried to pull off my mask, which wouldn't budge, so I yanked even harder. Meg stilled my hands and got me free. I'd forgotten she'd threaded the straps through my rollers.

Without a word, Mr Ross turned off the torch and left the shelter, leaving the flap open.

'Come on then,' said Meg. She and I felt our way to the front and climbed out. I could see Mr Ross's silhouette as he trudged across the yard toward the inn, Conall at his side. He never looked back.

Meg and I linked arms, feeling our way together across the frozen earth and trying not to step on the precious winter vegetables. Hank and Ellis followed.

Moments after I reached my room, there was a knock on my door.

'Maddie? Darling?' said Ellis.

'I'm getting ready for bed.'

'Maddie, please. I need a pill.'

I let him in.

'They're in the top drawer,' I said.

Ellis yanked it open and rummaged around until he found the bottle. I could tell from the rattling that he was taking more than one. He kept his back towards me until he'd tossed them in his mouth.

'Do you want one?' he asked, after gulping them down with water from the pitcher. It dribbled down the front of his pyjamas. 'Fuck!' he exclaimed, wiping his mouth with the back of his hand.

'I'm fine,' I said.

'You must be shattered. Here, take these.' He shook a couple of pills into his hand and held them out to me.

'Put them on the dresser,' I said.

I took my coat off, folded it in half and laid it over the back of the chair. Then I lined my shoes up beneath the chair's edge, where I wouldn't trip over them.

Ellis watched with narrowed eyes. 'Were those laid out for you?'

Instead of answering, I smoothed my coat, brushing off the frost.

'They were, weren't they?' he insisted. 'That's why you were able to get them on so quickly.'

He glanced at the dresser drawer he'd left open, at the clothes that had been folded until he'd messed them up. He stepped across the room and opened my closet, revealing dresses and other items on hangers.

'They've put your things away,' he said indignantly. 'You should see the state of my room. It's like they're refusing to do it on general principle.'

'I put my own things away.'

It took him a second to respond. 'You did what?'

'I did it myself.'

He blinked at me in disbelief. 'Darling, you know better than that. What were you thinking?'

He launched into a speech about the dangers of making excuses for the help, and how slippery a slope it was from there to familiarity, and then heaven only knew where it would end, but certainly not well. If Hank's kitchen maid wasn't proof of that, he didn't know what was. Mrs Boyd had nearly got into a legal pickle sorting that mess out. Maintaining a proper distance was crucial, and he certainly hoped I wasn't . . .

I stared in fascination, watching his tongue undulate behind his teeth. Once, a string of saliva attached itself to his lips and survived the length of a few words before snapping. His nostrils flared beneath his pinched nose-bridge. Deep lines appeared between his eyes, and when he tilted his chin so he could look down his nose at me, I could have sworn I was looking at his mother's head spliced on to his body, a living, breathing cockentrice that had climbed off its platter and spat the apple out of its mouth so it could yammer at me about how surely even I could see that my blurred boundaries not only encouraged the lower classes to be lazy, but threatened the very social structures our lives were built upon.

I realised that he'd stopped talking.

'Maddie?' he said, peering closely at me. 'Are you all right?'

'I'm fine,' I said, trying to shake the image from my head. 'It's just been a long night, and I'd like to get to bed.'

His expression softened. 'I'm sorry, darling. Sometimes I forget how fragile you are. I shouldn't have scolded you, especially right after . . .'

He left the sentence unfinished, having apparently decided that reminding me of the air raid would send me over the edge.

'Can you forgive me?' He took a step toward me, and I instinctively held up my hand. He stopped, but looked hurt.

I gripped the back of the chair and trained my eyes on the grate. There was no point in telling him that his behaviour in the shelter had been a degree worse than ungentlemanly. I wasn't looking for an argument.

'And now I'm the one who's sorry,' I said, turning to face him. 'I didn't mean to be prickly. I just need to sleep.'

'Yes, of course,' he said, becoming the epitome of chivalry. 'But if you need anything, anything at all, you know where to find me. And make sure you take your pills. Even if you're not having an episode, they'll help you sleep.'

As soon as he left, I went to the door and turned the lock. I also slid the bolt.

When I put the pills he'd set out back in the bottle, I was alarmed by how many were missing.

Twenty minutes later, there was another knock.

I turned my back to the door and pulled the pillow up around my face. If I ignored him, surely he'd assume I was asleep and leave me alone.

'Mrs Hyde?' said Meg.

Seconds later, I was standing at the open door.

'Meg – is everything all right?'

'Perfectly,' she whispered. 'Except my feet are freezing, and I thought yours might be too, so I brought you a pig.'

She thrust a hot-water bottle made of stoneware into my arms. It was indeed shaped like a pig, complete with snout.

'Thank you,' I said, clutching it. Though it made no sense, I shivered all the more for its heat.

'Best close the door now. I've only brought the two, and I'm not going back for more – not for the likes of them, anyway. I've got to be up and out in less than four hours.'

I shook my head in the dark. 'I honestly don't know how you do it.'

She let out a quiet laugh.

'Me either. No choice, I suppose.'

2 1

When I dragged myself downstairs in the morning, I found Ellis and Hank in unusually good spirits, not in spite of being wrenched out of their beds in the middle of the night, but because of it.

As they revisited the air raid over the breakfast table, the details matured. By the final retelling, Ellis had made sure that everyone else was safely in the shelter before coming in himself, Hank had positioned himself on the bunk above Meg and me to shield us with his own body and Mr Ross was barely present.

Anna's demeanour got stonier and stonier as she served and cleared breakfast.

Hank decided he would write to Violet, musing that perhaps the idea of his being in mortal danger would loosen her draconian premarital rules.

'You and she are premarital now, are you?' said Ellis.

'Well, *pre*-premarital, at least,' said Hank. 'But still, I think I ought to be able to sample the goods. What if I wait until the wedding night and then find I'm stuck with something subpar until death do us part?'

'*Hank*,' I said urgently.

'What?'

'In case you've forgotten,' I continued in a lowered voice, 'you're in mixed company.'

'Darling girl, when did you become such a prude?'

'I don't mean me.' I cut my eyes over to Anna.

'Oh,' he said, furrowing his brow.

He changed the topic to monster-hunting, but not before giving me an odd look. It was perfectly obvious that he hadn't registered Anna's presence at all.

The front door opened and a handsome ginger-haired man in shabby clothing came in. He nodded at Hank and Ellis, set the two baskets he was carrying on the floor and turned his attention to the door, swinging it back and forth until he identified the point at which it squeaked most loudly. He was young enough to be fighting, and I wondered why he wasn't – not that I would judge, but I was certainly sensitive to the issue.

'Well, whadya know,' Hank said to Ellis. 'It's George the vannie. Maybe he'll give us a lift again.'

'Aye aye, George,' said Anna, appearing behind the bar. 'And how are you getting on?'

'You're seeing it. Although it's right dank, the day,' he said, closing the door and carrying his baskets to the bar.

I couldn't help staring. He walked from side to side, almost like a penguin, swinging his right leg forward from the hip. The leg was false.

'And what have you got for me today?' asked Anna.

'Paraffin, naturally. Plus a packet from the laundry and some things from the butcher.'

'Well, let's see them.'

'There's mutton shanks and some lovely sausages,' said George, hauling them out and setting them on the bar. The meat was unwrapped with the price drawn directly on it.

Anna leaned over to sniff it. When she stood back up, she put her hands on her hips.

'And I suppose our sheets are also smelling like paraffin?' she asked accusingly.

'Just pitching in to save petrol,' said George. 'They'll air out. Put them in the meat locker and they'll be right as rain.'

'I'm to put the sheets in the meat locker, am I?' Anna said with a long-suffering sigh. It was apparently a rhetorical question, because she turned and took the meat through to the back.

'Shall I oil the door for you, then?' he called after her. 'It screeches like someone's caught a cat by the tail.'

He craned his neck, peering through the doorway and waiting in vain for an answer. Eventually he gave up.

'Well, I'm off then,' he said to the three of us. 'Tell her I'll be back to fix the door.'

'Say, I don't suppose you're going anywhere near the Horseshoe, are you?' Hank asked.

'I wasn't, but I suppose I could be.'

'Same terms as before? Perhaps a little extra for your trouble?'

'I'd be a fool to say no,' said George. 'Are you ready now, or shall I come back when I've finished my rounds?'

Hank drained his tea and lifted his duffel bag. 'Ready when you are. Why don't you drop us off at the telephone and collect us when you're done? We have some calls to make.'

Ellis kissed my cheek before he left.

Anna came back from the kitchen and cut the strings on the parcels of sheets. She flipped a few folds open and sniffed the creases.

'*Oof!*' she said, waving a hand in front of her nose. 'I'd hang these out the back if it weren't for the snow. Maybe if I leave the quilts off and open the windows for a few hours . . . And I suppose it's paraffin pie I'll be making for dinner tonight.' She glanced sideways at me. 'I can't help but notice you've not gone with them for a week and a half.'

'Can you blame me?'

'Not a bit,' she replied. 'They're that *sleekit* you might turn round and find they've left you at the side of the road.'

After a few seconds, I said, 'Anna, can you teach me to knit?'

She had started refolding the sheets. She stopped.

'Come again?'

'You once asked if I could knit. I can't. But I want to. I want to knit socks for the soldiers.'

'It's not as easy as that,' she said, looking at me strangely. 'It's difficult to turn a good heel. There are competitions over it.'

'What about squares? Surely I could learn to knit squares. Are those also for the soldiers?'

'Mrs Hyde—' she said.

'Maddie. Please call me Maddie.'

'I'm very sorry, but I don't have time to teach you how to knit.'

'Then can I help you with the housework?'

She shook her head vigorously. 'Oh, I don't think so. No, I don't think that would be wise at all.'

'But why?' I pleaded. 'When we first got here, you accused me of "lolling about by the fire," and it's true. It's what I do all day, every day, and it's driving me mad, but I'm stuck here until my husband either finds the monster or gives up on it. Please – your load would be lightened, and I'd be so happy to have something to do.'

She frowned. 'Your husband would never approve, and I don't suppose Angus would either.'

'They'll never know. I won't say a word to anyone, and I'll turn back into my usual idle self the second anyone else steps in the door.'

Her hands went still, and I knew she was considering it.

'Have you ever made a bed?' she finally asked.

'Yes,' I said. 'Well, once.'

She did a double take, then returned to folding. 'I suppose if I change the sheets, you'd only have to put the quilts back on. And Mhàthair did ask me to pick up a few things at the shops this afternoon . . .'

'I can do more than just put the quilts on. I can also put their things away.'

She gave a sharp laugh. 'Well, that would be an immense improvement. I've fairly given up hope in that regard.'

'So have they,' I said solemnly.

Her eyes widened. 'I beg your pardon?'

She stared at me, daring me to deny it. Instead, I nodded.

'Oh, no, they *never* did think,' she said indignantly. 'They could *not* have expected . . .'

'Yes, they most certainly did.' I raised my eyebrows for effect. 'And still do.'

Her eyes blazed. 'Well, in *that* case, I'll just get these on the beds and leave you to it. Because if you don't do it, I cannot see how it's *ever* going to happen, and if nobody ever does it, I'll never be able to sweep the carpets again.'

She scooped the sheets off the bar and sailed away, her bosom hoisted like the prow of a Viking ship.

I don't know if I was more astounded at having talked her into the idea, or at coming up with it in the first place.

While Anna changed the sheets, I flipped through the newspaper to see if there were any details about the bombs we'd heard drop. There weren't, but of course the paper would have already gone to press by the time it happened. There was plenty of other news though, and as I read it, my optimism about having found something to do with my days crashed into bleak depression.

The juggernaut that was the Russian army was now only 165 miles from Berlin, and Marshal Stalin had announced that in one advance in Silesia alone they'd left behind sixty thousand dead Germans and taken another twenty-one thousand prisoner. It was a victory for our side, but I could not feel anything but a grim acknowledgment of progress.

So many dead. Only two weeks earlier, I had found the idea of three thousand men killed in a single afternoon nearly impossible to comprehend. The sheer vastness of sixty thousand deaths was even more numbing. It made it almost possible to forget that each and every one of the dead had been an individual, with hopes and dreams and loves now snuffed.

I did not see how this could go on. The world would run out of men.

When Anna came back downstairs, I was sitting with the newspaper open in my lap, staring at the wall.

'You've not had a change of heart, have you?' she said.

'Not at all,' I said, forcing a smile. I folded the newspaper and stood. 'So besides straightening everything and putting the quilts back on the beds, what else should I do? Fill the pitchers?'

She frowned in temporary bafflement. 'Oh, you mean the *jugs*? Don't worry about that. I'll finish up after I've been to the shops.'

'It's okay, Anna,' I said. 'Even I can't mess up filling pitchers – or rather, jugs – and you can check my handiwork when you get back.'

She tsked. 'Oh, I'm not worried. Well, all right. Maybe I'll have a wee peek, but just for the first few days.' She dug a key out of her apron pocket and held it out to me. 'Here's the master.'

I took hold of it, but it was several seconds before she let go.

I started with Meg's room, which was easy because she was tidy, and worked my way down the hall.

Hank's room was about as I expected. His clothes were mostly
out of his luggage and scattered across the floor, and the rest
looked like they were trying to make a slithering escape. I piled
everything temporarily on the bed and began dragging his
trunks and suitcases into the closet.

One trunk appeared to be full of stockings and cigarettes,
but when it refused to budge, I dug beneath the top layers and
found dozens of bottles of liquor. They were buffered by straw
and cardboard, but I was surprised they'd survived the trip.
Hank's cache of international currency was so heavy I had to
get down on my hands and knees and brace a foot against the
bed to shift it, but eventually I forced it into the closet.

I was out of breath. Although the window was wide open,
my blouse was sticking to my back, and this was before I had
even begun to address the remaining mess.

It felt oddly intimate to be touching things like his socks
and pyjamas, never mind his underpants, but I soon got into
a rhythm. At least he'd thrown his dirty clothes into one pile,
so I didn't need to inspect anything too closely in that regard.

Just when I thought I'd put everything away, I caught sight
of something under the bed. It was a stack of postcards, and
when I picked them up I was shocked to find I was looking at
a naked woman. She was reclining on a chaise longue with her
legs apart, wearing nothing but a long string of pearls and a
tiara.

I glanced through the rest of them, fascinated. I had never
seen a fully naked body except my own – Ellis had always got
straight to business with as little displacement of clothes as
possible, and always in the dark – and was surprised at how
different they were. One lay on her back on a white horse,
letting one leg dangle so the camera could focus on the dark
area between her legs. Another was on all fours on a picnic
blanket, smiling over her shoulder at the photographer. Her

legs were parted just enough that her dangling breasts were visible between them, so large they almost looked weighted. Mine were tiny by comparison.

When I came to the final card and realised there was a naked man in it as well, pressed up behind the woman and cupping her breasts, I became suddenly self-conscious and eager to be rid of them. I pulled open the drawer of the bedside table and, as I did, saw a small package labeled DOUGH-BOY PROPHYLACTIC. I had always thought a prophylactic was a toothbrush, but when I saw the words 'for the prevention of venereal disease,' I realised it was something quite other. I dropped the postcards inside and closed the drawer. I didn't want to learn anything else about Hank, and was glad that I'd finished his room.

I braced myself for the next, afraid of what I might learn about Ellis.

Although I thought I was prepared for anything, I was wrong. When I opened Ellis's door, I stopped in my tracks, utterly stupefied. It looked as though a bomb had gone off. Clothes of all kinds, including his underpants, were strewn everywhere – flung over the bedposts, the back of the chair, even over the fire irons. There were heaps in corners, under the bed and in the middle of the floor. His shoes, toiletries and other sundries were scattered everywhere, and the only thing that had found its way on to the dresser was a slipper.

I couldn't imagine how he'd managed to create such a mess. Then, with a wave of nausea, I realised he'd done it on purpose.

I could see it clearly: every time he discovered that his belongings still hadn't been put away, he'd upped the ante by reaching into the trunks and throwing armloads of anything that came to hand into the air, kicking it all as it fell. How else to explain the toothbrush sticking out of a shoe, or the comb and hair pomade beneath the window? It was brutish, childish and destructive, and it frightened me.

I started in the far corner and worked my way out. I could think of no other way to approach the mess that wasn't overwhelming.

When I opened his top dresser drawer, I found a photograph of Hank and him standing on the beach at Bar Harbor, their arms slung casually over each other's shoulders and grinning into the sun. Beneath it was a photograph of Hank alone, standing shirtless on the deck of a sailboat with his hands on his hips. His chest glistened, his arms and shoulders were muscled and he smiled mischievously at whoever was behind the camera. There was no picture of me, although I must have been around.

In the next drawer down, I found several monogrammed handkerchiefs folded into packets. I opened them and counted more than a hundred of my pills. Then I folded them back up and left them where they were. I didn't want him to think that Anna or Meg had taken them.

I had been locking my door only at night but decided to start keeping it locked during the day as well. I wanted to see how long it took him to go through that many pills.

I wondered if anyone other than Anna had seen the condition of Hank's and Ellis's rooms. I hoped not. I could only imagine what she thought of them and, by association, me.

Both of them would come back and see that everything had been put away and think nothing of what the person who'd done it had seen or thought. Indeed, they wouldn't think of the person at all, except perhaps to feel victorious.

Although I'd unpacked my own things after only a couple of days, I was ashamed of how much I'd always taken for granted. I wondered how Emily was faring, and wished I could let her know how grateful I was for everything she'd done for me over the years. I couldn't imagine it was easy being Edith Stone Hyde's maid at that particular moment in time.

When the rooms were all finished and I'd replaced the quilts, closed the windows and put up the blackout frames, I slipped a few pairs of silk stockings from my own supply into Meg's top drawer.

22

When I returned to the kitchen, Anna looked at me in surprise.

'Surely you're not finished!' she said.

'I am.'

'And you've put all their things away?'

'I have.'

'Well, if that doesn't call for a cup of tea, I don't know what does. Get settled by the fire and I'll be right out. I think we deserve a proper *strupag*, don't you?'

'So, are the sheets still smelling of paraffin?' Anna asked, sipping daintily from a teacup decorated with primroses and edged with gold leaf.

She'd brought out oatcakes and jam along with the tea, which was the strongest I'd seen yet, all of it served on fine china. She'd even put a doily on the tray.

'I didn't smell anything,' I said.

'Good. Because the wash is not a job I'm keen on doing myself. There's some that won't send it out because they're afraid it'll come back with lice.' She harrumphed. 'Personally, I'm more afraid of what George will put next to it in that van of his.'

'Why on earth would it come back with lice?'

'Because the same laundry facility also does the wash for

the men at the Big House and forestry camps. It's mostly old folk and Wee Frees who worry about it, but I suspect the real problem is that sending your wash out smacks of being a luxury. I'm just grateful Mhàthair isn't of that opinion – she's about as strict as they come, being old *and* a Wee Free.'

The top log on the fire slid toward us, sending up a cascade of sparks. Anna rose and jammed it back into place with the poker.

'And stay there!' she scolded, watching it for a few seconds before sitting back down.

'That may explain the old woman doing her laundry in the river the other day,' I said. 'Although it seemed a very odd place to do it.'

Anna set her tea down. 'I beg your pardon?'

'I got lost in the Cover, chased in by a crow of all things. I thought it was following me.'

I was suddenly aware that the atmosphere had changed. I looked up to find that Anna had gone pale. I ran through what I'd said, wondering which part could possibly have caused offence.

'I'm sorry,' I said, panicked. 'I don't really think that.'

Anna continued to stare at me.

I put my tea down, afraid I would spill it. 'Please forget I said anything. I have an overly active imagination.'

'Who was doing laundry where?' she asked sharply.

'An old woman was washing a shirt in the river. She didn't answer when I asked for help. Then, when I tried to get closer, I couldn't find her. It was like she'd never— Anna, whatever is the matter?'

She'd clapped a hand over her mouth.

'Anna? What's wrong? Please tell me what I've done.'

'The Caonaig,' she said hoarsely. 'You've seen the Caonaig.'

I shook my head. 'What's the Caonaig? I don't understand.'

'Someone's going to die,' she said.

'No, surely not. It was just an old woman—'

'Wearing green?'

I hesitated. 'Yes.'

'Did she have a protruding tooth?'

I hesitated even longer. 'Yes.'

'Was she crying?'

This time I didn't answer, but apparently my eyes gave me away.

Anna shrieked and bolted into the kitchen. I called after her, and then ran after her, but she was gone, leaving the door flapping on its hinges. I ran back to the front door, but by the time I stepped into the road she was receding into the distance on her bicycle.

'What's going on?' Mr Ross said.

I whipped round. He and Conall had come up behind me in the street.

'She thinks I've seen the Caonaig,' I said helplessly.

'And what made her think that?'

'Because I saw an old woman washing a shirt in the river.'

He took a sharp breath that whistled through his teeth.

'But how can that mean someone's going to die?' I said desperately. 'It was just an old woman. I don't understand.'

'Anna still has two brothers at the Front,' he said.

Still?

I turned to look down the road, where she'd disappeared.

I went upstairs and hid in my room, but about an hour before Meg usually returned from the sawmill I began to panic. Anna had not come back, and she always started the dinner, which Meg then finished and served to the customers. Eventually, I crept downstairs again, thinking I'd at least better warn Mr Ross that there would be no food to serve, but there was no sign of him either.

I didn't know what to do, but since I'd somehow managed to cause the problem, I ducked into the kitchen and scoured the pantry for the makings of a meal.

I realised almost immediately that it was hopeless, not only because I couldn't find any of the meat I'd seen delivered that morning, but because even if I could, I wouldn't have had a clue what to do with it. I wasn't even sure how to start potatoes, and in about an hour upward of twenty men would start arriving, each of them expecting to be fed.

When Meg came in the back door, she found me leaning over the butcher's block table, my head buried in my hands. She quickly assessed the situation, her eyes landing on the empty range.

'Anna left early,' I said.

'What's happened?'

'I said something to upset her.'

'And what was that?'

'I'm not exactly sure,' I said miserably. 'But I can tell you I didn't mean to do it.'

I expected her to grill me, but instead she simply set her coat and gas mask on the chair and said, 'Right then. Can you get the tatties going?'

I blinked a couple of times. 'Yes. I think.'

'You think, or you can?'

'I think.'

The truth was, I didn't even know how to slice bread. During my ravenous adolescent raids of the kitchen, I'd torn the bread off in chunks, digging out the soft middle to eat first and then gnawing at the crust over the sink so I could rinse away the evidence.

Meg told me to fill the largest pot with water, add salt and forty potatoes and put it on to boil. She stoked the fire herself while instructing me to hurry up about it so my husband didn't come back and catch me where I didn't belong, because she had a feeling that wouldn't go very well.

Then she went out back to retrieve something she called 'potted hough,' for which she thanked the dear Lord, for she had some on hand and it was served cold.

The bar was abuzz that night with news of the bombing, which distracted somewhat from the mashed potatoes, which tasted as though I'd boiled them in seawater. I also hadn't realised I was supposed to remove the skin or dig out the dark spots, or that the knife was supposed to glide smoothly through before I declared them done, all of which Meg explained to me later. I saw more than one man lift a full fork, examine it with disbelief and then attempt to fling the potatoes back onto the plate to see how tenaciously they stuck. Poor Meg – although there wasn't a man in the room brave enough to complain, she was assumed to be responsible.

Conall, who'd joined me by the fire as soon as Hank and Ellis arrived, didn't seem to mind how gluey they were. I was convinced that he'd come because he knew I needed moral support, so to thank him I began slipping him tiny bits of mashed potato on the end of my finger, which he gravely licked. At one point, I thought I saw Mr Ross watching when I had a potato-dipped finger extended in offering. Apparently Conall thought so too, for he stared straight ahead and ignored it until his master's attentions were elsewhere. Only then did he tip his head towards me and let his tongue sneak out the side of his mouth.

Since the bombing hadn't made it into the paper, people

were adding their own bits of knowledge to the general story. Hank and Ellis listened with great interest.

Two bombers had flown down the Great Glen from Norway, targeting the British Aluminium plant in Foyers, a village several miles down the other side of Loch Ness. One night guard had been killed when the blast threw him into the plant's turbine, and another died of a heart attack.

When someone shared the news that one of the Heinkels had gone down in Loch Lochy almost immediately after, I gasped and looked at Mr Ross. He finished pulling a pint and slid it across the bar to one of the locals as though he hadn't heard.

'Well, whadya know,' said Hank, his voice betraying a sliver of respect. 'He shot down a bomber with a fucking rifle. I wonder why he's not fighting?'

'That's a very good question,' said Ellis. He twisted in his seat and said, 'Say, bartender, my friend here has a question for you.'

'Don't!' I whispered, utterly appalled.

'Why?' he asked.

'Because it's none of our business,' I hissed. 'And he's the landlord, for goodness' sake, not the bartender. Can't you show a little respect?'

But it was too late.

'And what would that be?' asked Mr Ross.

'You're pretty good with a gun,' said Hank. 'Why aren't you at the Front?'

The room went silent. Mr Ross simply stared at Hank.

It was Rory who finally spoke. 'That's funny,' he said slowly. 'We've been wondering the same about you.'

'Medically unfit,' Hank said, as though it were all a joke.

'You look healthy enough to me.'

'I have a condition called *pes planus*,' Hank said.

'Do you now?' said Rory. 'Is that Latin for yellow-belly?'

Hank jumped to his feet. The lumberjack also rose, but slowly. He was clearly more than a match for Hank.

'Hank, *sit down*,' I pleaded.

'And let him get away with calling me a coward?'

'If the shoe fits,' said Rory.

'Ellis, are you going to just sit there and let him call us cowards?' Hank said, outraged.

'He wasn't talking to me,' Ellis muttered.

'As a matter of fact, I was,' said Rory. 'Have you got some fancy diagnosis for lily liver too? *Planus lilicus*, perhaps?'

'I have protanopia,' said Ellis. 'I can't see colour. And for your information, I tried to enlist twice.'

'The lot of you should mind your own business,' said Meg, coming out from behind the bar.

'It *is* my business, if he calls me a coward,' said Hank.

She threw him an exasperated look, gave up and turned to the lumberjack. 'You can't fight him, Rory. You heard what he said. He's got a medical condition. You can't go round beating up invalids.'

Hank opened his mouth to protest, and Ellis whacked him on the side of the leg.

'They don't look sick,' said Rory.

'Well, you don't always, do you? George the jannie looked just fine until he dropped dead of a weak heart. You can't fight a man with *pes planus*. You might kill him on the spot.'

Rory stared at Hank for a long time. He finally returned to his seat. 'I suppose you're right,' he said with a sigh. 'It would be like kicking a puppy, wouldn't it?'

'Of course I'm right, you daft fool,' said Meg, slapping him on the arm. He responded by slapping her bottom. She whipped round and pointed a finger in his face, but he just laughed and blew her a kiss. She glared at him and sailed back behind the counter.

As the rest of the men returned to their conversations, Hank and Ellis sat in silence, both of them ashen.

23

Anna showed up the next morning and served breakfast as though nothing had happened. I wondered whether she'd decided that the deaths in Foyers had satisfied the Caonaig's ghoulish requirement.

I watched her surreptitiously, hoping that the fragile thing that had sprung up between us hadn't changed and that she'd still let me help with the rooms, but I had to wait to find out because Ellis and Hank were still there.

Neither of them said a word about their rooms having been put straight. Instead, they sputtered indignantly about why everyone thought it was all right to judge them when clearly Blackbeard was as fit as anyone else except for his missing digit, which just as clearly didn't prevent him from shooting a gun. They said all this right in front of Anna, as though she didn't exist, and I cringed with embarrassment. She was at the far end of the room, sweeping the hearth with a broom made of sticks. She acted impervious, but I knew she wasn't.

I had almost given up hope of them ever leaving when George the vannie showed up.

'I've oiled yon door for you,' he said, glancing bashfully at Anna and swinging it back and forth. 'Yesterday afternoon when I came back.'

'That's very kind of you,' she said, without looking at him.

He stared openly for several seconds, and from his stricken expression I could tell he was in love with her.

'Well, I'll be waiting outside then,' he said to Ellis and Hank.

'We'll be right out. Oh, say, do you still have a compass?' Ellis asked, turning to me. 'We're missing one.'

'It's in my right coat pocket,' I said. 'Hanging by the door.'

He went over and rifled through it.

'When did you go into botany?' he said, looking into his palm. He came back and dropped a handful of the red and fawn toadstools on the table. 'Throw these out. They look noxious.'

There was a flurry of activity as they got on their coats and hats and gathered their equipment. When the door finally closed behind them, the only sound was the rhythmic swish of Anna's broom against the stone floor.

I wanted to start a conversation and figure out where things stood, but even though Hank and Ellis had left, their presence lingered like a cloud of soot.

Anna finally glanced up and said, 'Those are elves' cups you've got there. They're not poisonous, but they're also not tasty. They dry well, if you want to keep a bowl in your room.'

'I'll do that. Thank you,' I said.

'So what *is* wrong with them?' she asked.

I didn't have to ask what she meant.

'Hank is flat-footed and Ellis is colour-blind.'

She raised her eyebrows. 'I see.'

'It's true. He can't tell red from green – it's all just grey to him. He didn't even know before he tried to enlist. There's absolutely nothing he can do about it, but people don't believe it. They think he's making it up. That's why we're here – he thinks that finding the monster will force people to recognise he's not a coward.'

'Does he now?' she said, and went back to sweeping.

For a moment, I could think of nothing to say. I realised I was finished making excuses for either of them.

'I suppose you've heard what they said to Mr Ross last night.'

'To who?'

'Mr Ross. Angus.'

She laughed. 'Angus is a Grant. What on earth gave you the idea he was a Ross?'

'The sign,' I said. 'It says A. W. Ross. And then on our first day here, you told me that he ran the place . . .'

'He *does* run the place, but the proprietor is Alisdair. Angus is just holding the fort until Alisdair gets back from the Front.' She leaned the broom against the wall and put her hands on her hips. 'Have you thought that all along?'

Someone knocked on the door, a solemn, slow rhythm.

Anna frowned. 'Well, I don't like the sound of that. Not one bit.'

She wiped her hands on her apron and answered the door. Willie the postie was on the doorstep, holding his hat in his hands. His face was grey.

'And for what reason are you knocking, Willie?' Anna said in an angry voice that did nothing to mask her fear. 'The door's not locked. Come in then, if that's what you're wanting. I haven't got all day.'

'I'm very sorry, Anna,' he said without moving. 'But you need to go home.'

'What are you on about? I see nowt in your hands but your hat.'

'You need to go home,' he repeated quietly. 'I've just delivered a telegram.'

Anna's knees buckled. She reached for the doorframe.

I shoved my chair back and rushed to her, grabbing her by the waist.

'Your parents need you,' Willie said. 'Go to them.'

She caught his wrist, gripping it so tightly her knuckles turned white.

'Which one was it?' she said frantically. 'Tell me that much.'

'Anna—'

'Was it Hugh or was it Robbie?'

Willie's mouth opened, but it was a few seconds before he spoke. ''Twas Hugh,' he finally said, lowering his gaze.

She dropped his wrist and twisted free of me. She took a step backwards, shaking her head, her eyes wild. 'You're wrong. It's not true! It'll be like Angus! You'll see!'

Willie shook his head helplessly. 'Anna . . .'

She took flight, bursting past him and out the door. When I tried to follow, Willie caught my arm.

'Let her go,' he said.

He was right. I had no business intruding. When he realised I wasn't struggling any more, he loosened his grip.

I craned my neck past the doorframe and saw Anna pedalling furiously away, her bicycle jerking from side to side with the effort, her hair flying in the wind.

She'd left everything behind – coat, hat, scarf and gas mask. If I'd known where the croft was, I would have taken them and left them on the doorstep, but all I knew was that it was some-where between the inn and the castle.

I searched for the master key, eventually finding it on a hook under the bar. Then I made up the rooms, moving through the tasks like a robot. When I was finished, I went back and did them again.

I lined the toiletries up at exact intervals on the dressers. I wiped the mirrors clean. I picked the wax off the candleholders and smoothed the surfaces of the quilts. And when there was nothing left to straighten or polish or dust, I went to bed.

*   *   *

I stayed in my room that evening, despite Ellis's insistence that I join him for dinner. I could tell from his tone that he was in a foul mood, and when I stopped responding his entreaties turned into accusations of mental instability. He threatened to send for a doctor if I didn't come out.

I did not, and a doctor never appeared.

Hours after everyone else had gone to bed, I continued to thrash, twisting the quilts round my feet and punching my pillow, trying to find a position that would finally allow me to rest, but nothing helped, because it was not my body that refused to go still. My throat was so tight I could barely swallow, and my eyes welled with tears.

I knew with absolute certainty that if I'd gone upstairs right away, my mother would still be alive. But if I hadn't gone into the Cover and seen the Caonaig, would Hugh also still be alive?

I crept downstairs and sat by the fire, which had been dampened with a layer of ash.

When Mr Grant found me, I was on the floor in front of the grate, hugging my knees to my chest. I didn't hear him coming, or even notice the light of the candle.

'Is everything all right?' he asked.

I jerked round, pulling my nightgown over my ankles in an attempt to hide my bare feet. My cheeks were slick with tears.

'What's wrong? What's happened?' He held the candle closer and looked me over.

The lump in my throat had grown even larger, and it was difficult for me to speak. When I did, my voice was strangled. 'I did it, didn't I?'

'Did what, lass?' He set the candle on the low table and knelt beside me, searching my eyes with his. 'What have you done?'

'I've killed Anna's brother.'

'And how do you figure that?'

'I saw the Caonaig – I didn't want to see her, but I did, and then when I told Anna, she knew right away what it meant. I thought she was just being superstitious, but it turns out she was right. If I'd just stayed out of the Cover, if I hadn't let that stupid crow chase me in, her brother would still be alive.'

'Oh,' he said, letting the word slide out on a long exhale. His expression melted into one of pity and sadness. 'No. No, lass. He would not.'

'But I saw the Caonaig—'

'You didn't do anything. It was the godforsaken war.'

'But Anna's already lost at least one other brother. How much loss are people supposed to bear?'

He shook his head. 'I'm afraid I don't know. It seems there's nothing so good or pure it can't be taken without a moment's notice. And then in the end, it all gets taken anyway.'

I looked wildly into his face. 'If that's the case, what's the point of even living?'

'I wish I knew,' he said with a wry half smile. 'For some time now, that's been a source of great mystery to me.'

I looked at him for a few seconds longer and then burst into tears – colossal, heaving sobs that racked my shoulders.

Before I knew what was happening, he'd wrapped his arms round me and pulled me to him, breathing heavily into my hair. I scrabbled onto my knees and threw my arms round his neck, pressing my open, sobbing mouth on the pulse that beat so strongly in his throat.

24

I t was an innocent embrace, I told myself for the thousandth
time, hoping that I would eventually believe it. For hours
after I returned to my room the night before, I'd lain in the
dark wishing he was there with me. I wanted him to hold me,
I wanted to fall asleep in his arms. I was aware of wanting
more, too.

Despite being awake most of the night, I got up early and
waited at my door until Hank and Ellis were in the hallway.
Then I joined them so we could all go down together. I was
incapable of facing Angus – I could no longer think of him in
formal terms – on my own. Even the thought of seeing him
in the company of other people left me light-headed.

When the three of us went downstairs, he was standing by
the front door talking with a very old woman in a language
both guttural and burbling. When he glanced at me, I thought
my knees might give out.

I couldn't look at him for fear of giving myself away.

The air was so electrically charged I was sure Hank and Ellis
would pick up on it, so I also couldn't look at them. That left
no one but the crone, who stared at me as if she were plumbing
the deepest recesses of my mind and unearthing all kinds of
terrible things.

'This is Rhona,' said Angus. 'She'll be here until Anna gets
back. She doesn't speak English.' And with that, he left.

'And the stellar service continues,' Ellis muttered, leading the way to our usual table. 'What are we supposed to do? Learn Gaelic? Play charades?'

'Why not?' said Hank. 'It's always porridge anyway, and I can mime that.' He put his hands to his throat and pretended to choke.

'Don't tell me you're getting used to this,' said Ellis.

Hank shrugged. 'At least they've started putting my things away.'

Ellis harrumphed. 'Talk to me when they start ironing the newspaper.'

Rhona served our breakfast in dour silence and otherwise ignored us completely. I wondered if she was the wife of the old man who'd blown our cover the first day. Even if she wasn't, it was clear she disapproved of us as much as he did.

She was ancient, with a dowager's hump and bowed legs. Her hair was white, her clothes black, her complexion grey. She smelled like wet wool and vinegar and, as far as I could tell, wore a perpetually sour expression. Her upper lip and chin were lightly whiskered, her face so weathered that her eyes appeared as mere slits under the weight of her lids. Even so, I caught an occasional flash of piercing blue – usually as I was fighting off the memory of being held by Angus, or despairing of Anna's brothers, and wondering how two such disparate thoughts could coexist in my brain.

'Maddie?'

Ellis was looking at me. His forehead was crinkled, and I realised he'd said my name at least twice, but I'd heard it from a distance, as though through a tunnel.

'Darling? Are you all right? You seem . . . I don't know, shaken, or distracted, or something. Are you having an episode?'

'No. Nothing like that. I just didn't sleep well.'

'Why not?'

'I was thinking about Anna's family. I was here when she got the news about her brother.'

'What about her brother?'

'He was killed in action,' I said. 'He's at least the second brother she's lost.'

'Ah,' he said, smiling sadly. 'I suppose that explains why you wouldn't come down last night. But I'm afraid these things happen, my darling. *C'est la guerre.* How are you now? Should I have sent for a doctor after all?'

I could only shake my head.

He patted my hand and turned his attention back to Hank.

I stared at him for a long time. If he wanted to end his search for the beast, he need look no further than a mirror.

I collected my things and escaped as soon as Hank and Ellis left with George, whom they'd apparently hired full-time, petrol restrictions notwithstanding. I wondered how fast Ellis was going through his remaining money. Perhaps Hank was already supporting us.

After I got outside, I was free of Rhona's penetrating glare, but found myself yet again with no destination, no goal and no purpose on a day when I desperately needed to be occupied. However, even if we'd shared a language, I wouldn't have had the nerve to ask Rhona about doing the rooms. She clearly despised me. Once again, I'd been lumped in with Hank and Ellis.

My brain was fevered, my system overwhelmed. My glass had been filled too full, too fast. The Caonaig, the death of Anna's brother, my embrace with Angus, never mind finally recognising the sheer callousness of my husband—

Even after he'd shanghaied me into a war, even after I'd realised our entire marriage was a sham, even after I'd watched him go below deck to avoid seeing the wounded on the SS *Mallory*, I had never believed him to be as cold-blooded as he'd just revealed himself to be. I'd always assumed his avoidance of all things war-related was guilt over not being able to serve, but now I realised that he just didn't care.

Even if he didn't think of Anna as quite human, had he never considered the fate of George's leg? Apparently not, since he'd interpreted my distress as a symptom of fragility.

I thought of the moment Angus pulled me to him, gripping me tightly, not at all as though I might break, even as I was sobbing into his neck. We clung to each other as though life itself depended on it, and maybe it did.

I looked up with a gasp.

It'll be like Angus, Anna had said, her face twisted in grief, less than a minute after laughing at me for getting his name wrong.

Was it possible?

I marched down the street, keeping my head down – especially when the lace curtain in a front window shifted by the width of a finger, as nearly all of them did.

If red was the new badge of courage, I was certainly a shining beacon of bravery, with my stupid red gloves and my stupid red gas mask case. I shoved my hands in my pockets and encountered the last of the elves' cups, which I flung to the side of the road for the crime of being red.

Red, red, everywhere. I wanted to be grey.

I found myself back at the headstone, staring at its etched granite as though I could force it to reveal its secrets.

AGNES MÀIRI GRANT,
INFANT DAUGHTER OF ANGUS AND MÀIRI GRANT
14 JANUARY 1942

CAPT. ANGUS DUNCAN GRANT,
BELOVED HUSBAND OF MÀIRI
2 APRIL 1909–14 JANUARY 1942

MÀIRI JOAN GRANT,
BELOVED WIFE OF ANGUS
26 JULY 1919–28 FEBRUARY 1942

I knew how many men in the village had the same names – I'd seen it myself on the other gravestones, and I knew that Willie the postie was called that to distinguish him from Willie the joiner and Willie the box because every one of them was a Willie MacDonald – but I couldn't shake the image of Angus putting snowdrops on the grave.

It seems there's nothing so good or pure it can't be taken without a moment's notice, he'd said, and there was nothing so pure as an infant. Was it possible he'd returned from the war only to find that everything he loved had been snatched by cruel fate?

I thought back to the night we'd arrived in Scotland. When I realised it was the third anniversary of the child's death, I was afraid I might break into pieces after all.

I was afraid that if I went back to the inn I might take a pill, so I headed down the A82, knowing that somewhere between the village and the castle was the McKenzies' croft.

Small houses dotted the hillside and I stopped briefly in front of each, wondering if Anna and her parents were inside. Eventually I reached the castle, and knew I had passed them.

The ruined battlements looked very different than they had when we'd approached them by water. There was a large dry moat round the castle, full of high grasses and scrubby weeds, and I lifted my coat and tromped down, across and up the other side, ignoring the thorns that snagged my hems.

Directly beside the entrance was a massive chunk of stone – or stones, really, because they were still stuck together with mortar, still rigidly holding right angles. It looked like someone had torn a large corner piece from a very stale gingerbread house and flung it to the floor.

I paused beneath the arched entrance, where the drawbridge had once been, imagining all the people who had passed in and out over the centuries, every one of them carrying a combination of desire, hope, jealousy, despair, grief, love and every other human emotion; a combination that made each one as unique as a snowflake, yet linked all of them inextricably to every other human being from the dawn of time to the end of it.

I walked through it myself and went straight to the tower. Within its gloomy interior, I found a winding staircase and climbed the worn steps carefully. They were so narrow I had to brace my hands on either side.

I stopped on the second floor to look out, but pulled back immediately.

Angus was standing at an arched gate that led down to the water. He stayed for a long time, staring at the loch, which was as flat as if it had been ironed. Then he leaned over, picked up his gun and a brace of rabbits and turned round. I ducked further into the shadows, although there was no reason – he plodded straight to and through the main gate without ever looking up.

The light snowfall turned into a flurry and, before I knew it, turned into a blizzard. I had no choice but to return to the inn – to stay in the tower would mean freezing to death.

Rhona was neither upstairs nor in the front room, and although I had been desperate to get away from her just a few hours earlier, my need for a cup of something hot now made me just as desperate to find her. I hoped I would be able to

pantomime what I needed, and that she'd be receptive to inter-
preting. I took a deep breath and entered the kitchen. When
my eyes landed on the big wooden table and the freshly skinned
rabbits upon it, I stopped.

Angus was standing shirtless at the sink with his back to me,
washing his arms.

I knew I should leave, but I couldn't. I was rooted to the
spot, watching the rhythmic, alternating movements of his
shoulder blades as he cupped water first in one hand and
then the other, sloshing it up past his elbows to rinse off the
soap.

I don't know what gave me away, but he whipped his head
round and caught me watching.

Despite my heart being lodged in my throat, I couldn't look
away. After several seconds he straightened up and – without
breaking eye contact – turned slowly, deliberately, until he was
facing me.

His chest and abdomen were a network of thick, raised scars
– red, pink, purple, even white. They were not puncture wounds.
Someone had jammed a serrated blade into him and ripped
through his flesh, over and over and over.

I stared, trying to comprehend.

'Oh, Angus,' I said, covering my mouth. I rushed a few steps
towards him before coming to a halt.

He smiled sadly and raised his palms. After a few seconds,
he turned back to the sink.

I reached a hand out as though to touch him, although a
good fourteen feet still separated us. The illusion was there,
though, and I let my quivering, outstretched fingers graze his
shoulder. When I realised what I was doing, I bolted to my
room.

I took my pills out and put them back no fewer than three
times. I did not know what to do with myself, and ended up

pacing between the bed and the window, turning on my heel as precisely as a soldier.

Had he answered my suspicion about the gravestone? Had he been assumed dead and somehow survived? And what in God's name had happened to him? I couldn't imagine, and yet I couldn't stop imagining.

25

Ellis thumped on my door as soon as he and Hank returned, demanding I join them for a drink. I tried to plead an upset stomach, but once again he threatened me with a doctor, saying that this time he really meant it.

As we walked toward the staircase, Ellis bounced off a wall. He was utterly soused.

We took our usual spot by the fire. His and Hank's initial excitement at interviewing eyewitnesses had gone sour after only three days and was compounded by Ellis's anger at not being able to view the site of the bombing, despite having travelled all the way round the loch to get there.

He relived their outing from the comfort of the couch, sputtering about 'pulling rank' and 'having someone's head' and other such nonsense. Eventually, his rant segued into the interviews themselves. He held his notebook open, stabbing it with a finger.

'Two humps, three humps, four humps, no humps . . . Horse head, serpent's head, whale-shaped, coils. Goddamned white mane, for Christ's sake!' He threw his arms up in frustration. 'Scales on another. Eyes of a snake, eyes at the ends of antennae, no eyes at all. Crossing the road while chewing on a goddamned sheep. Grey, green, black, silver. Dorsal fin, flippers, all arms, no limbs, tusks. Tusks, for the love of God!'

He glared at me as if I'd made the offending observation. When I didn't respond, he turned back to Hank.

'Vertical undulation. Flaring nostrils. Otters. Deer. Lovelorn sturgeon. Giant squid. Rotten logs exploding from the bottom. The only thing we haven't heard is fire-breathing with wings.'

'I'm sure we will,' said Hank. He was leaning back with his legs crossed, blowing rings of smoke.

'How can you be so calm about this? How the hell are we supposed to figure out what's true when so many of them are obviously lying to us?'

'We should stop paying them, that's how,' said Hank. He successfully blew a smaller smoke ring through a larger one. He leaned forward and poked me on the knee. 'Maddie, did you see that?'

'I did,' I said.

So did Angus, who was watching from behind the bar.

'If you'd learn to smoke, I could teach you all kinds of tricks,' Hank continued. 'Watch this—'

He exhaled a vertical loop before sucking it back into his mouth.

'*Hank, for God's sake!*' said Ellis. 'Get back on topic. If we don't pay them, they won't meet us.'

'And if we do pay them, they'll lie. If people are willing to meet with us just to tell their story, they're more likely to tell the truth.' Hank turned to me. 'What do you think, darling girl?'

'I really don't know,' I said. 'I can see both sides, I suppose.'

'What was that?' Ellis said, swivelling towards me. 'Would you please repeat that?'

'I said I really don't know.'

'No, you don't,' he said, 'and yet you're always offering opinions.'

I decided to ignore the insult and poked through the remainder of the pie. I was looking for pieces of rabbit, because

I didn't care for the mushrooms. Unfortunately, they were the same shade of brown.

A fully formed thought crashed into my head, a *coup de foudre*. I put my fork down and looked at Ellis, feeling my eyes grow wide.

He had decided upon sight that the elves' cups were noxious, but there was absolutely nothing noxious-looking about them other than their red interiors.

'Stop gaping,' Ellis said. 'You'll catch flies.'

'Ellis!' Hank snapped. 'What the hell is wrong with you? That's *Maddie* you're talking to.'

'If you'll excuse me,' I said, setting my napkin by my plate and rising.

Ellis scowled and shook his head.

'Shall I walk you up?' said Hank, rising quickly.

'No thank you. I'll be fine on my own.'

'Yes, of course,' he said, although he came round the table and touched my elbow. 'Maddie, he doesn't mean it. He's just being a knucklehead. He's under a lot of stress.'

'Stress,' I said. 'Yes, of course.'

I tried to wrap my head round the enormity of what I suspected. If I was right, not only would it prove Ellis immoral on a completely different scale, it would also negate the entire purpose of this foolish, arrogant venture. Finding the monster wouldn't restore his honour, because he had no honour to restore.

Over the course of the night, I became convinced.

He hadn't crashed cars because he couldn't tell if the light was red or green. He'd crashed cars because he was drunk. Likewise, it was no coincidence that the dresses and jewellery he bought me were almost exclusively red. He knew it set off my green eyes. And the only reason I could think of for him buying me a bright red gas mask case was that it matched my gloves.

The thing I found most abhorrent was that he'd made such a show about trying to enlist a second time, then acted so devastated when they'd turned him down again. The entire spectacle was designed to garner sympathy, which – incredibly – he seemed to think he deserved. It was a production worthy of my mother.

I made sure I was the first one down the next morning, bringing my coat, gas mask and gloves with me. I set the gloves on the table and waited. I was usually the last one down, so I didn't know who would arrive first.

To my relief, it was Ellis.

'Good morning, darling,' he said, kissing me on the cheek. 'You're up early. Big plans?'

I was momentarily shocked by his cheer. I wondered if he even remembered the previous night.

'Just tromping around the countryside,' I said, trying to match his tone. 'I wish I had my watercolours.'

'Your paintings would be entirely washed away by the rain.' He pulled a logbook out of his duffel bag and opened it.

I fingered my scarlet gloves, flattening the thumbs carefully against the palms.

'Yes, I suppose you're right,' I said. 'Which reminds me, I'm so glad you got a weather-resistant case for my gas mask. I'm sure a cardboard box would have dissolved by now.'

'Nothing but the best for my girl,' he answered.

'But I *am* curious why you got this colour.'

'To match your gloves, of course. Say, what do you suppose a fellow has to do to get some breakfast around here?' He craned his neck, searching for Rhona.

'But my gloves are green,' I said.

'No they're not, they're red.'

'No,' I said, slowly. 'They're green.'

He looked down at the gloves, and then lifted his gaze until it was locked on mine.

'Well,' he said, just as slowly, 'you told me they were red.'

'Did I?' I said, still playing with the gloves. 'That must have been another pair. These are green, and it's a rather odd colour combination. I feel a bit like a Christmas wreath.'

I looked up. He was unblinking, his expression cold as granite.

'Anyway,' I continued, 'if you find yourself back in Inverness, I could use a new pair. These ones have water stains all over them. And this time I *would* like red – did you know there's a saying, that red is the new badge of courage?'

Hank appeared beside me. 'What's up, kids?'

'What colour are these gloves?' Ellis demanded.

'What?' said Hank.

'Maddie's gloves. What colour are they?'

'They're red,' said Hank.

Ellis stood so suddenly his chair legs belched against the stone floor. He tossed his logbook into the duffel bag, pulled the bag onto the chair, then yanked the coarse-toothed zipper so hard it took him three tries to get it closed. He threw me a final searing glare and stormed outside.

After a couple of seconds, Hank said, 'Christ. You two aren't falling apart on me, are you?'

Instead of answering, I stared into my lap.

He pulled out a chair and sat. 'Is this about last night? He was just being stupid. He's under boatloads of stress. If the Colonel doesn't forgive him, he's seen the last cent he's going to until we find the monster. And even then, the Colonel still has to forgive him.'

'You underestimate the powers of Edith Stone Hyde.'

'I hope so, because he sent her a letter yesterday morning. That's why he got so snockered last night.'

I was shocked. 'He wrote to her? What did he say?'

'Well, he didn't show it to me, but I assume he threw himself on her mercy and begged for divine intervention with the Colonel.'

'I had no idea he was going to write to her.'

'He didn't want you to worry.'

'Because I'm so delicate?'

'Because he wanted to protect you.'

'Well, he has a funny way of showing it.'

Hank sighed. 'If you're talking about last night, they're just words, Maddie. You know he didn't mean any of it.'

'I don't know anything any more. I don't think he even remembers. He's taking my pills and washing them down with liquor.'

'What are you talking about?'

'I just told you.'

His eyes met mine with something like comprehension.

'When did this start?'

'He's always helped himself, but it's really ramped up since we got here.'

'I had no idea.' He stared into space. After what felt like an eternity, he took a deep breath and slapped his thighs. 'All right. Don't worry, darling girl. I'll straighten him out.'

'It's too late,' I said.

'I'll straighten him out,' Hank said firmly.

When the front door clicked shut behind him, I whispered, again, 'It's too late.'

Ellis returned to the inn that night sober and courteous to a fault. His calm exterior and placid expression were too calm, too placid, and I wondered whether he was masking terrible hurt or terrible anger.

I began to second-guess myself.

If he really was colour-blind and I'd accused him of faking it, I was no better than all the other judgmental people. But if he was faking it and knew I'd found out, I was as lethal to him as a loaded gun.

If the Colonel discovered that Ellis had lied to shirk duty, he'd disown him immediately and permanently, and there would be nothing Edith Stone Hyde or anybody else could do about it.

Either way, I'd made a mistake and was going to have to fix it.

When Ellis laid eyes on me the next morning, his expression confirmed how critical it was for me to get things back on an even keel. The second he saw me, his jaw clenched and he stared at his logbook.

I hated what I had to do, and hated even more that I knew how. I would be drawing directly from my mother's playbook.

'Good morning, darling,' I said, joining him. 'Where's Hank?'

He made a great show of licking his finger and turning the page.

'Sweetheart, please tell me what I've done,' I said. 'You left in such a hurry yesterday, and then you barely spoke to me at dinner. I know I've done something, but I don't know what.'

He continued to look down at the book, pretending I wasn't there.

'Except that's not true,' I said miserably. 'I do know why you're angry. It was my pitiful attempt at a joke, wasn't it? Ellis, *please* look at me.'

He lifted his face. His expression was glacial, his eyes hard.

'My joke about the gloves,' I went on. 'I was trying to be funny, not make fun of you. But I should have known better than to joke about your condition. It was awful of me.'

He had no reaction at all. He simply stared, his lips pressed into a grim line.

I had no choice but to barrel on, because I had no other plan.

'I thought if I told you my gloves were green, you'd think Hank had pulled a prank on you by picking the wrong colour case for my gas mask, but then it all went wrong. As soon as I saw your face I should have stopped, but I was so far in I kept going and tried to turn it around instead. It's all so stupid – I really do need new gloves, and I was just trying to come up with a clever way of asking. It was the vaudeville in me trying to come out, but I'm no star. I'm meant to be a supporting act. So rest assured that yesterday's performance marked both the debut and finale of my solo career in practical jokes.'

He finally spoke. 'Not vaudeville. Burlesque.'

My cheeks burned. 'Yes. Of course. It's just we don't usually call it that.'

'My mother always said that blood will out. I wish I'd paid attention.'

My mouth opened and closed a couple of times before I could respond. 'I suppose I deserved that, after what I said to you.'

He laughed once, a short, harsh bray.

The two of them didn't return to the inn that night or the next, so I had no idea if Ellis had bought my story about the gloves. They left no note or any other indication of where they had gone.

26

When Anna finally returned, five days after learning of Hugh's death, she accepted my condolences and otherwise simply carried on, although there was a heaviness in her step that hadn't been there before. She let me resume doing the rooms, for which I was very grateful, because I'd been losing my mind trying to stay out of Rhona's way and had no idea what I'd say to Angus if I found myself alone with him.

The crone apparently shared Anna's view about picking up after others, because Ellis's dirty socks and underpants lay exactly where he'd stepped out of them three nights before, and his pyjamas lay in a crumpled heap in the corner. Hank had at least tossed his clothes onto the chair.

Of the hundred pills I'd initially found in Ellis's room, only thirty-six were left.

Hank and Ellis returned that night. When they came through the door, I took a deep breath, steeling myself.

'Darling!' said Ellis. He swooped over and kissed my cheek before sitting next to me on the couch. He stank of paraffin oil, but not liquor.

'Did you miss me?' he asked.

'Of course,' I said, trying to read his face.

Hank plopped down on one of the chairs opposite. 'You'll never guess where we've been.'

'She doesn't care about that,' said Ellis, rubbing his hands together. 'Quick – get her prezzie!'

Hank dug around in one of the duffel bags and handed Ellis a thin gift-wrapped box, which he solemnly presented on the palms of both hands.

I pulled off the satin bow and lifted the lid. A pair of red kid gloves lay inside, on tissue paper flecked with gold.

The blood drained from my face.

'What do you think? Do you like them?' he asked.

'They're beautiful,' I said.

'More importantly, what colour are they?'

'They're red,' I said in a near-whisper.

'Good,' said Ellis, smiling broadly. 'That's what Hank said, too, but I never know with you two jokers.' He held a hand over his head and snapped his fingers. 'Bartender! Two whiskys. Actually, just bring the bottle.'

Angus glared, but pulled out two glasses. Meg picked them up and tucked a bottle under her arm, her expression conveying every word that didn't come out of her mouth.

The gloves were a message, obviously, but what did they mean? Had I managed to convince Ellis that I still believed he was colour-blind? Or had he interpreted my desperate soliloquy as a promise to keep his secret? Or was he actually colour-blind?

Over the course of the evening, Ellis drank almost a whole bottle of whisky, but he remained – at least outwardly – jovial.

He kept a proprietorial hand on my shoulder or leg the entire time, and it was a constant struggle to keep from shrinking away. I stole occasional glances at Angus, whose face was unreadable.

I'd been back to the graveyard twice since seeing his scars, and had myself mostly convinced that he was the Angus on the stone, the one who'd lost everything in the space of six weeks.

I thought often of our embrace by the fire, and wondered if he did, too.

They never told me where they'd been, and I didn't ask. Despite Hank's promise to straighten Ellis out, they fell right back into their old pattern of returning to the inn plastered and then continuing to drink until they were both in a stupor. Judging from his fast-diminishing stash, Ellis was also gobbling pills. By my estimation, he was taking anywhere from eight to ten a day.

On the night I knew he'd run out, he knocked on my door and asked if he could have one. After popping one into his mouth, he shook more into his hand and slid them into his pocket. From what remained, I figured he'd taken about fifty, enough to last him five or six days.

We achieved a tenuous kind of normal. Ellis seemed to have completely forgotten about the glove incident, and while he was consistently drunk, he never tipped into a rage.

Every day he looked for a letter from his mother, and every day it didn't come. He began to say he didn't need her anyway – he was more certain than ever that when he found the monster, he would clear both his and his father's names, and that the Colonel would welcome him back with open arms and chequebook.

Finding the monster in Loch Ness was all he cared about. He remained as ignorant as ever about the monster facing the rest of the world.

I began to iron the newspaper, in the hope that he – or Hank – might start to read it. They did not.

*　　*　　*

Although there was no question that it was selfish and cowardly to blinker themselves against the chaos and horror, there were times I almost understood.

At the end of January, the Red Army had liberated a network of death camps in Auschwitz, Poland, and the details that trickled out over the days and weeks were so excruciating I fought a very real urge to remain ignorant myself.

Hundreds of thousands of people – perhaps many, many more, because the reports were often contradictory – had been interned and killed, most of them simply for being Jewish. They'd been rounded up and transported in cattle cars, and assigned to either death or hard labour as soon as they climbed out. Death was by gas chamber, and the chambers and crematoriums ran night and day. Many of those spared immediate death died anyway, from illness, starvation, torture and exhaustion. There were rumours of a mad doctor and unthinkable experiments.

When the SS realised the Red Army were closing in, they tried to destroy the evidence. They blew up the gas chambers and cremator-iums and set fire to other buildings before retreating on foot, forcing tens of thousands of starving inmates – every last person who was capable of walking – to march further into Nazi territory towards other death camps. The only people they left behind were those they were certain were dying. They shot people randomly as they retreated.

Even the hardened soldiers of the Russian army were unprepared for what they found: 648 corpses that lay where they'd fallen, and more than seven thousand survivors in such terrible condition they continued to die despite immediate rescue efforts.

They discovered that the SS had burned the infirmary with everyone inside it, 239 souls in all. One of the six storage buildings the SS had not had time to destroy was filled with tons – literally tons – of women's hair, along with human teeth, the fillings extracted, and tens of thousands of children's outfits.

I despaired of humanity. Although the Allies were making progress, I thought maybe it was too late, that evil had already prevailed.

27

With Anna weighed down by fresh grief and my own days as available as ever, I took it upon myself to expand my household duties, although I kept to the upstairs so I wouldn't get caught.

I began sweeping the bedroom carpets with the witchlike broom, which turned out to be made of dried heather, and then, since I was sweeping anyway, did the hallway to the top of the stairs. Less than a week after Anna's return, I was doing the entire upstairs on my own, polishing the doorknobs, trimming and filling the lamps, gathering laundry, changing the sheets – even scouring the sink, tub and toilet with Vim powder. Meg repaired my manicure as necessary, so while my nails were shorter, they were as flashy as ever, and Ellis remained none the wiser.

I grew bolder, and one day decided to sweep all the way down the stairs, since that was where the carpet ended. Too late, I heard the clicking of Conall's toenails and a moment later was face-to-face with Angus. I was on the bottom step, in an apron, clutching the broom. I froze like a deer in the middle of the road.

A sudden widening of his eyes betrayed his surprise.

'Good afternoon,' I said, after a few beats of silence, trying to act as though we found ourselves in this situation all the time.

He frowned. 'And how long has this been going on?'

'A while,' I said, feeling the heat rise to my cheeks. 'Please don't blame Anna – it was entirely my idea. I just wanted to help.'

The corners of his mouth twitched and a twinkle crept into his eyes. He laughed before continuing on his way, shaking his head and followed by a visibly confused Conall.

I sank down on the stair, light-headed with relief.

I had been restricting my efforts to the upstairs only for fear of getting caught, but since Angus apparently didn't mind, I began to help in the kitchen as well. I always brought my coat, gloves and gas mask with me, so that if Ellis and Hank returned early, I could slip out the back and return by the front, pretending I'd been on a walk. This was Meg's idea, and Anna objected vehemently. She was adamant that it was bad luck for a person to enter and leave a house by different doors.

Although I was close to useless to begin with, I was a willing student and they were patient with me. I soon learned how to scrape, not peel, carrots and potatoes, and how to cube turnips. After my first brackish mishap, I learned how to properly salt water for boiling, and not just how to slice bread, but how to do it to wartime standards – vendors weren't allowed to sell bread of any kind, even National Loaf, until it was stale enough to be sliced thinly. Anna confessed her suspicion that National Loaf was not made of flour at all but rather ground-up animal feed, and I thought she was probably right. It would explain a lot about the dense, mealy bread that was commonly referred to as 'Hitler's Secret Weapon.' It was rumoured to be an aphrodisiac – a rumour many suspected had been started by the government itself to get people to eat it.

I learned that all tea was loose leaf and steeped more than once, and also that the strength of a guest's tea was directly related to Anna's feelings about the person. At that point, Hank and Ellis were drinking hot water with a splash of milk.

I discovered that in addition to Anna's many personal beliefs – she couldn't see a crow through the window without running outside to see how many there were and then analysing what the number meant – there were all kinds of universally accepted sources of bad luck. One of them explained why I hadn't been able to find any meat the day Anna thought I'd seen the Caonaig and run off before starting dinner. It was considered unlucky to store it inside, and so it was kept in a ventilated meat safe out back. I also discovered that Angus was responsible for the contents of many a meat safe.

In the hill just beyond the Anderson shelter was a tall, draughty dugout, which he kept stocked with venison, grouse, pheasant and other game, hanging it until it was tender. Anna and Meg took what was necessary for the inn and wrapped the remainder in newspaper, which Angus then left on the doorsteps of families in need, delivering the packets at night so no one would feel beholden.

I'd already figured out that Angus was poaching – how else to explain the visit from Bob the bobby, or the ample supply of game? – but I wasn't shocked, as I once might have been. My education at the hands of Anna and Meg included enough history that I understood the policeman's reluctance to enforce the law, and also that it reflected the prevailing attitude.

It started the day I asked Anna what made a croft a croft instead of just a farm, and got an unexpected earful:

'It *is* a farm,' she said indignantly, 'only not quite big enough to support a family. *That's* the definition of a croft.'

Meg shot me a glance that said, *Well, now you've done it*, and she was right.

Although the events Anna spoke of had taken place nearly

two hundred years before, she railed with as much outrage as if they'd occurred the previous week.

She said that in 1746, following the Battle of Culloden – the final, brutal confrontation in the Jacobite Rising – the Loyalists forced an end to the clan system so the Jacobites could never rise again. They seized their traditional lands and dispersed clan members, banishing individual families on to tiny tracts and expecting them to become farmers overnight. The former communal hunting grounds were turned into sheep farms and sporting estates, and anyone caught hunting on them was subject to severe penalties. The aristocratic shooting party's right to an undepleted stock was held to be more important than feeding the starving.

But it didn't end there. Beyond the physical displacement and the abrupt, forced end of the clan system was a methodical attempt to wipe out the culture. Speaking Gaelic became a crime, and the first sons of clan chiefs were forced to attend British public schools, returning with the same upper-class accent my father-in-law had affected during the heady days of his celebrity.

I imagined the Colonel strutting around in his estate tweeds with his smug sense of superiority on full display, and realised that the loathing Rhona and Old Donnie felt for him – and all of us by association – ran far deeper than anything he'd done personally.

'And *that's* why the taking of a deer is a righteous theft,' Anna said, wrapping up with a decisive nod. She had unknowingly repeated Meg's words from the day she showed me the Anderson shelter, and I finally understood.

The taking of a deer was a righteous theft because it was taken from land that was stolen.

Because of their overlapping shifts, I spent the first part of each day with just Anna and the latter part with just Meg, and during these times, our chit-chat sometimes turned to confidences.

From Meg, I learned that Anna's brother Hugh had stepped on a mine and what could be found of his remains had been buried in Holland. The other brother she'd lost, twenty-one-year-old Hector, had been hit in the chest by a mortar bomb during the D-Day landings. His body was never recovered, although a fellow soldier had paused long enough to grab his identification tags.

From Anna, I learned that Meg had lost her entire family – both parents and two younger sisters – four years earlier in the Clydebank Blitz. Five hundred and twenty-eight people were killed, 617 injured and 35,000 left homeless during two nights of relentless air raids that left a mere seven out of twelve thousand houses intact. Meg had been spared only because she'd already joined the Forestry Corps and was in Drumnadrochit.

I kept hoping one of them would offer some information about Angus's background, enough to confirm or refute my theory about the gravestone, but they didn't, and I couldn't ask for fear of giving myself away. I was fully aware that my desire to know wasn't based on curiosity alone.

28

Meg told us the young women at the Forestry Corps were so excited about the upcoming Valentine's Day dance that they had been reprimanded twice for their lack of concentration around the huge, engine-driven saws. I couldn't blame them. Several of the girls, including Meg, expected to be presented with rings, making their engagements official.

As the day grew closer, the lumberjacks' remarks became increasingly ribald. The night before the dance, one of them said something so off-colour it turned Meg into a redheaded fury. She leaned over Rory, who flattened himself against his chair, and scolded him harshly, even as he protested – correctly – that he hadn't said a thing.

'But you did nothing to stop him, did you?' she said, still holding a finger in front of his face.

He glowered at her, but his arms hung slack off the sides of his chair.

When she spun and flounced off, her red curls bouncing, the older men at the bar gave sombre nods of approval, and the rest of the lumberjacks – who understood that Rory had been reprimanded for all of them – went on their best behaviour.

Hank leaned in toward Ellis and held a hand up to the side of his mouth so his voice wouldn't carry.

'Who's the tough guy now?' he snickered.

Ellis was too distracted to be amused. Not twenty minutes

before, he'd excused himself and gone upstairs, only to return looking pale. I knew exactly what had happened. He'd tried my door and found it locked.

When I did the rooms that morning, I'd noticed he was down to five pills. I knew he must be desperate to get more and wondered why he didn't just come out and ask me, like he always did. Maybe he didn't want to ask in front of Hank, I didn't know – but whatever the reason, I was grateful because I couldn't have helped him anyway. I'd flushed the rest of the pills down the toilet.

On the day of the dance, Meg, Anna and I went to special effort to dress up the front room because we knew girls would be coming in. We put linens on the tables, and Anna created something called 'coalie flowers.' She blamed the lack of real flowers on both the weather and the war, and instead put four or five pieces of coal in glass bowls, added water, salt and ammonia, before finally pouring a mixture of violet and blue ink over them. It was a complete mystery to me how this alchemy would result in anything resembling flowers, but they were 'blooming' within the hour.

We didn't have enough to put on each table, so we decided that Meg would herd the girls towards the tables that had them, and steer the men – who wouldn't appreciate them anyway – elsewhere. The job was Meg's by default, because Anna would have gone home by then and I, of course, would be waiting by the fire for Ellis and Hank.

The coalie flowers were not our only efforts. Between the three of us, we'd managed to come up with enough eggs and sugar to make two glazed bundt cakes, which were resting in the dead centre of the wooden table in an attempt to keep them out of Conall's reach. The beast himself was sprawled across his master's bed, watching keenly. He was tall enough to reach anything he liked if we turned our backs, but there was no chance of that. We would have protected those cakes with our lives.

Meg and I had given up our egg and sugar rations for the week, which were enough to make one cake, but then Anna's hens went on a laying spree. Because they lived on a croft, the McKenzies got chicken feed instead of egg rations, so their supply was sometimes iffy, but on this occasion the hens came through like champs. Each of the dance-goers was going to get a proper slice, instead of just a taste.

As Anna prepared to leave, hours later than usual, her mood deflated.

'I don't remember the last time I had cake,' she said, looking longingly at them.

'Don't you worry,' said Meg. 'We'll put aside the very first slice, and it will be lovely and thick, too.'

'Thank you,' Anna said, still sounding glum. 'I suppose I'll be off then. Have a grand time – and mind you, I want to hear *all* the details tomorrow.'

Anna's parents were staunch Wee Frees, and she wasn't even allowed to wear face powder, never mind attend a dance. Music itself was not allowed, except on Sundays, and then it had to be for the sake of worship only, and sung unadorned. The senior McKenzies were so strict they confined their cockerel under a bushel basket on the Sabbath so he wouldn't get up to anything untoward with the hens.

I understood Anna's melancholy, because I also wished I could go to the dance, although that would require an alternate universe in which Ellis didn't exist.

At least I'd be able to witness the prelude. I was particularly looking forward to seeing the reaction to the cakes, since I'd had a hand in making them. Although I'd only cracked the eggs and stirred the batter, I'd never been as proud of anything in my life.

Because we didn't trust Conall with the cakes, I stayed in the kitchen to guard them while Meg went upstairs to get ready.

She returned looking like a Valentine's Day dream, in a figure-hugging dress printed with tiny red hearts, her hair carefully arranged and lips painted into a vermilion Cupid's bow. Her high-heeled shoes were made of red suede, with pretty lace-up fronts. They had to be brand-new – I couldn't imagine suede surviving a single day in that climate.

I also noticed she was wearing stockings, and a smile crept across my face. She followed my gaze, blushed and smiled back.

'What do you think?'

'I think Rory will be knocked off his feet,' I said. 'I think you'll be the belle of the ball.'

'Well, at least I won't have to worry about so-and-so over there trying to lick the gravy browning off my legs.'

Conall's tail slid back and forth.

It was my turn to get dressed for dinner, but I hesitated. I knew I wouldn't have another chance to talk to her alone, and I wanted to say something about her imminent proposal. I found myself tongue-tied, probably because I was distinctly unqualified to offer advice in the marriage department. Eventually Meg saved me.

'Now go on,' she scolded, flicking her fingers toward the door. 'Make yourself up properly. Tonight, more than ever, beauty is your duty! Even if it's wasted on your pair of Boring McBoringtons over by the fire, the others will notice. And your dress had better be fancy. And it had better be red, especially tonight! Remember, red is the new badge of—'

'I know! I know!' I said, cutting her off with a laugh. 'I'll wear red! And good luck tonight! Not that you'll need it!'

I sprinted off before she could reply.

I made up my face as though I really were going to a party, and chose a red taffeta poodle dress that didn't look expensive, because it wasn't. I'd bought it myself, off the rack, before Ellis took control of my wardrobe.

Finally, I used an eye pencil to draw a shaky line up the back of each leg. I wanted to fit in, not stick out, and that night, especially, I didn't want to steal anyone's thunder.

By the time Ellis and Hank came through the front door, their cheeks flushed with the elements and whatever else, the other side of the room was filling up.

'Well, would you look at that,' said Hank, coming to a halt.

The mood was electrifying. The girls, all impeccably groomed, were admiring the cakes, which had been presented but not cut. The lumberjacks also made noises about the cakes, but were really admiring the girls. I couldn't help wondering which ones were expecting rings.

Meg was standing next to a table of girls from the Forestry Corps. She leaned over to point out how the coalie flower had transformed since Anna conjured it into being, but I knew exactly what she was really doing. It took but a moment.

'Wait – those are real seams!' squealed one of the other girls. 'How on earth did you get your hands on stockings?'

The lumberjacks murmured surprise, as though they weren't already looking at Meg's legs. Having been given an excuse, they stared openly, hungrily.

'Oh,' Meg said, shrugging coyly. 'They magically appeared.' She turned her ankle to better display the back of her calf.

Hank and Ellis watched all this from just inside the door.

Finally, Hank dug an elbow into Ellis and they launched themselves towards the fire.

Ellis tripped on the edge of the rug and fell forward, catching himself on the back of a chair. He navigated his way around it, clutching it all the while, and dropped onto its seat. His eyes were bloodshot, his forehead was shiny and I was shot through with dread.

Hank was so busy looking at Meg that he planted himself squarely on the arm of the second chair before tumbling sideways into it, leaving his head hanging over one upholstered arm and his legs dangling off the other. After a few seconds of stunned surprise, he hauled himself upright.

Ellis looked me up and down. His eyes narrowed. His lip curled in disgust. 'What's this?'

I knew he meant my cheap dress and lack of stockings, but I feigned ignorance.

'They're going to a dance,' I said. 'It's Valentine's Day.'

'It's what?' said Hank. 'Oh shit. I should have sent something to Violet.'

'No, I meant this . . . *get-up*,' said Ellis, waving the back of his hand toward me. 'It's like a combination of scullery maid and streetwalker.'

I clamped my mouth shut. There was no point in explaining why I was dressed the way I was. There was no point in doing anything at all, except keeping quiet and hoping the moment would pass.

'Well, *I* think she's a sight for sore eyes,' said Hank, still fixated on Meg. 'If I'd known she'd be so excited about a pair of stockings, I would have given her a dozen. I'd have given her as many as she wanted. In fact, there's no telling what I might give that girl. With that face and figure, she could come up in the world, like Maddie's mother.' He swung his head briefly toward me. 'No offence, darling girl.'

'Don't take up with trash, Hank,' said Ellis, still staring at me. 'Blood will out. It always does.'

'What?' Hank asked vaguely. He was back to gazing at Meg's calves.

'You can't make a silk purse is what,' said Ellis.

'No, those are definitely silk. Look at those gams. I bet they're a mile long. They deserve nothing less than the finest silk . . .'

'Hank?' I said desperately. I waved, trying to get his attention. *'Hank!'*

He glanced quickly and said, 'You look nice, too, Maddie. Definitely a silk purse.'

'So, Maddie, this silk purse of yours,' Ellis said with deadly purpose, 'is it red, or is it green?'

Adrenaline blasted from my core to my extremities.

'I beg your pardon?' I said.

'It is *red*, or is it *green*?'

'It's a fine brocade, a veritable smorgasbord of colour,' said Hank, still completely oblivious to the parallel conversation.

'Maddie? You didn't answer me,' said Ellis. The corner of his right eye began to twitch.

'I can't,' I said, looking into my lap.

'And why's that?'

'Because you were right.'

'About what?'

'About everything.'

'Say it!'

'Fine! There's no silk purse! There's only a sow's ear!'

He gave a bitter laugh. 'Submission is a colour that suits you, my dear. You should wear it more often.'

'I suppose you would know,' I said, before turning towards the bar.

Meg was serving slices of cake to an admiring audience. Rory had still not arrived, and while she was putting on a brave face I could tell she was wilting.

'I'd have some of her cake, oh yes indeed,' Hank said with a low whistle. He swivelled suddenly in his seat. 'Say, kids – I just had a crazy idea! Let's go to the dance – it'll be like the servants' ball at Christmas. You two lovebirds can do your own thing, and I . . . well, I might just find a pretty little lovebird of my own. To tide me over, so to speak.'

He beamed expectantly at us. When neither of us answered, his smile fell away. His eyes darted suspiciously between us.

'Oh, come on,' he groaned, before glancing at the ceiling in despair. 'Are you two at it *again*? Let me guess. Ellis said something totally stupid, and now you're not talking to him. Hell, you're not even looking at him. Is this what marriage does to people? No wonder I want nothing to do with it. Neither one of you is an ounce of fun any more.' He sighed and turned back towards the bar. 'Now that one over there, *she* looks like an ounce or two of fun . . .'

29

At eight on the nose, twin brothers from Halifax dropped to their knees and presented matching engagement rings to their sweethearts. When the blushing girls said yes, the remaining lumberjacks burst into song, serenading the brides-to-be with 'O Canada.' No sooner had they started than old Ian Mackintosh nipped across the road and returned with his pipes, striking in and accompanying the young men as they followed up with a heartfelt rendition of 'Farewell to Nova Scotia.'

Ellis sipped his whisky steadily and continued to stare at me like he wanted me dead.

Halfway through 'A Ballad of New Scotland,' I could stand it no longer and rushed upstairs, locking myself in my room. I leaned against the door, panting.

Not two minutes later, with the pipes still blaring on the main floor, I thought I heard something and pressed my ear to the door. Ellis was swearing and stumbling in the hallway and sure enough came straight to my room. When he found the door locked, he began to pound it.

'Maddie! Maddie! Open the *goddamned door*!'

'*Go away!*'

I dove onto the bed, pulling my knees to my chest.

'Open the goddamned door! I'm fucking serious!'

I knew he was using the side of his fist because of the way

the door jumped in its frame. I wished I could light a candle so I could see if it was in danger of giving, but my hands were shaking too hard to strike a match.

'Maddie! If you don't open the goddamned door right now, I swear to fucking God I'll break it down – do you hear me?' he roared, renewing his assault.

I curled into a ball and pressed my hands to my ears. I couldn't scream for help – there was no possibility anyone would hear me over the booming of the pipes – but where the hell was Hank? Surely he'd noticed we'd both disappeared, and surely he'd been at least vaguely aware of the state Ellis was in.

Over a period that felt like centuries, the thumping slowed to an uneven staccato and, finally, stopped altogether. I heard a soft clunk as Ellis slumped against my door. He began to weep.

'Maddie? Oh, Maddie, what have you done? You're my *wife*. You're supposed to be on *my* team. Now what am I supposed to do? What the hell am I supposed to do?'

His fingernails scraped against the wood as he slid to the floor. He continued crying, but that, too, eventually petered out. A few minutes later, all I could hear was my own ragged breath.

Just as I began to believe he was out for the night, I heard shuffling on the carpet, then a pause.

I held my breath.

A terrible, primal scream preceded a massive blow to the door, followed by another and then another, as he repeatedly rammed it with his body.

When the wood started to crack, I scrambled off the bed, fumbling in the dark until I found the grate and the fire irons. Then I crouched behind the chair, clutching the poker and crying.

There was another tremendous blow to the door, and the clatter and thud of a body falling, followed by copious swearing.

Then I heard Hank. 'What the hell do you think you're doing?'

'I need to talk to my wife!'

'Get up, you moron,' Hank said calmly.

'I need! To talk! To my!' Ellis huffed and puffed, but could not seem to come up with the final word.

'You can't even stand up. Let's get you to bed.'

'I need to talk to her,' Ellis insisted, although he sounded suddenly out of steam. He moaned, then began sobbing again.

I crept over to the door, still clutching the fire iron.

'Good Lord,' said Hank. 'You're a complete mess. Give me your hand.'

Ellis mumbled something incoherent.

'No, you didn't dislocate your shoulder. If you had, I wouldn't be able to do *this.*'

There was a sharp holler of pain, followed by whimpering.

'See? But if you had dislocated it, you'd have fucking well earned it for being a knucklehead. Give me your hand. All right, upsy-daisy. Now, give me your key and *don't move.*'

There was a crash against the wall right outside my door.

'Jesus. Can you at least *try* not to fall over while I get your door open? Do you think you could handle that?'

Ellis was drawing heavy, wheezing breaths, so close it sounded like he was in the room with me.

The door to his bedroom opened, and Hank came back.

'All right. One foot in front of the other.'

After a few seconds of clunking and shuffling, I heard the violent screech of bedsprings. It sounded like Hank had tossed Ellis into his room from the doorway.

'Stay put,' said Hank. 'If you don't, I swear to God, I'll tie you to the bed.'

The door shut, and a moment later there were three polite raps on my door.

'Maddie?' said Hank.

'Yes?' I said, still crouched with the fire iron.

'Are you sitting by the door?'

'Yes.'

'Are you okay?'

I didn't answer. My heart was thumping so hard I was sure he could hear it, and I was shaking uncontrollably.

After a pause, he said, 'Okay, I get it. You're mad at me, but what was I supposed to do? Knock the bottle from his hand?'

'Yes.'

He sighed, and I heard him scratch his head. 'Yeah, you're right. This won't happen again, I swear. By the way, I locked him in. Want the key?'

'No. You can have it.'

'Get some sleep,' he said. 'He won't be bothering you again tonight. And Maddie? I really am sorry.'

He waited a while before going away, hoping, I suppose, that I'd tell him it was okay.

But I couldn't. Things weren't even remotely okay, and with Ellis out of pills, they could only get worse. Why, oh why, had I flushed them?

When Ian Mackintosh's pipes finally stopped, the gathering downstairs exploded with applause; they cheered, whooped and stamped their feet until the whole building shook.

Within minutes, the younger crowd had gathered in the street and gone on to the Public Hall, but even after they left, the men who remained at the bar – the older men, the locals – spoke and laughed in raised voices, excited by their participation in the impromptu *cèilidh*.

I made my way to the window, still in the dark, pulled out the blackout frame and opened the sash.

I heard accordion and fiddle music coming from the Public Hall, along with laughing, singing and animated conversations, including a few that sounded like arguments. Despite the icy air, I knelt by the window and rested my head on the sill, listening.

I felt a terrible pang of longing. Less than half a mile away, young people – people my age, people in love – were planning futures together, futures that would include all the perks of truly loving each other: intimacy, passion, children, companionship, even though there were sure to be trials along the way. Some of the couples might even end up mismatched and miserable, but at that particular moment they were as happy and joyful as the rest, and no matter how mismatched or miserable they turned out to be, I could almost guarantee that none of them would end up with a marriage like mine.

Footsteps came up the road, and I heard a man and a woman talking. They stopped at the house opposite the inn, and went silent for what I could only assume was a goodnight kiss. He whispered something and she went inside, giggling. He waited a few seconds after the door closed, and then whistled as he headed back down the road.

Eventually, I replaced the blackout frame and went to bed.

'You *liar*! You *whore*!'

A man's angry shouting jolted me awake, and I initially thought Ellis was back. Then I heard Meg crying and realised the man was Rory. They were in the hallway.

I jumped out of bed and lit the candle on my dresser. Then I stood with my ear to the door.

'I swear by everything that's holy, I'm telling you the truth—'

There was a smack, followed by Meg's sharp cry.

I grabbed the fire iron, which was still leaning by the door. 'You worthless, lying slut! Tell me who he is! *Tell me!*'

'There *is* no one else,' she pleaded.

'Then why can't you tell me where you got the stockings?'

'I *did* tell you, Rory—'

'You want me to believe they "just magically appeared"? What kind of a fool' – another smack, another cry – 'do you take me for? What else has he given you, or did you earn them? Is that it? Have you turned professional? What's your price, then? What does a pair of stockings buy a man?'

'Rory, for the love of God—'

'Is it that flat-footed bastard? I've seen how he looks at you. What room is he in? Tell me! *Tell me!*'

When Meg screamed, I yanked my door open and rushed out. The only light was coming from the candle behind me, but it was enough for me to see him haul back and punch her in the side of the face. She dropped to her knees, clutching her cheek, sobbing. She was completely naked. He was in an open shirt and underpants.

'Stop!' I cried. 'She's telling the truth!'

He glanced over his shoulder. Our eyes locked. He turned deliberately back to Meg, grabbed a handful of her hair and kicked her full force in the ribs. The sound of the blow was a terrible muted thud. She made an *oof* noise as the air was forced out of her.

'*I gave them to her!*' I shrieked.

He kicked her again, still holding her by the hair, then tossed her aside. She collapsed and made no effort to move, like an unclothed porcelain doll dropped in a nursery. As he pulled his leg back to deliver another kick, I raised the poker and tore down the hallway.

Before I could get there, Angus charged out of the stairwell and in a single motion had Rory pinned against the wall by his throat, dangling him so his feet were above the ground. Rory's hands swatted at and finally grabbed the hand round his throat, but he didn't make a sound. Angus's other arm remained at his side, his fingers splayed.

'What the fuck is going on?' said Hank, peeking out of his room with a candle. When he saw, he ducked back in.

I dropped the poker and rushed to Meg. She was conscious, but barely. I dragged her toward her room and crouched beside her, wrapping my arms round her, shielding her nakedness. She whimpered and covered her head with her arms.

There was a rhythmic thumping across the hall. I looked up, expecting to see Angus throwing punches. Instead, he continued to dangle Rory with one hand. The thumping was Rory slapping the wall behind him with open palms. His eyes bulged and his tongue protruded, and while the light was faint, his face was clearly not the right colour, and getting darker quickly. The slapping got slower, and finally ceased. A wet patch appeared on the front of his underpants, and urine trickled down his leg, over his foot and onto the floor.

It felt like an eternity, but it was probably only a few seconds later that Angus dropped him. He crumpled to the floor and remained utterly still. I was sure he was dead, but after a few seconds he jerked violently and clutched his throat, gasping for air. It was a terrible sound, grating and rasping.

Angus stood beside Rory, hands on hips. He was in blue striped pyjama bottoms, but no shirt. Not a one of us was properly covered, least of all Meg, and it made the horror of the moment somehow more real.

Angus poked Rory with his foot. 'I don't suppose I need to tell you what will happen if I ever find you darkening my door again,' he said.

Rory writhed on the floor, drawing ragged, scratchy breaths and still grasping his throat.

'I'll take that as a no,' said Angus, leaning over and lifting Rory by the armpits. He turned and threw him into the stairwell.

I held my breath during the series of bangs and thuds as Rory fell down the stairs. I was sure I'd just witnessed a murder, but moments later I heard the front door open and then click quietly shut.

30

Angus scooped Meg out of my arms as though she weighed nothing.

'Pull back the bedclothes,' he ordered, sending me scrambling across the floor. 'And you,' he said to Hank, who'd appeared in the doorway with a candle, 'bring that in and light the others.'

Angus laid Meg on the bed and drew the covers over her pale, naked form. She rolled onto her right side, crying quietly. Her left cheek was bloodied, her eyelid ballooning. Blood trickled from her nose, and her lip was split.

'Where else did he hurt you, *m'eudail?*' Angus said softly, sitting on the edge of the bed. He stroked the top of her head as though she were a child. She just wept.

'He kicked her in the ribs,' I said. 'Hard.'

Angus swung his head round. 'And what were you doing out there? You could have been hurt as well.'

'I was going to kill him.'

He stared at me for several seconds.

'I'm going to get Dr McLean,' he said, standing up. 'There's a first aid kit in the kitchen. It's tucked in behind the—'

'I know where it is,' I said. 'I'll get it.'

Angus nodded and turned to Hank, who had by then lit the other candles.

'You – fetch some logs from the peat stack downstairs and

get a fire going in here. And light the hall lamps. It's going to be a long night.'

I ran down the stairs, feeling my way in the dark to where I knew there was a torch. I located the white metal tin with the red cross and knocked over the soap flakes in my haste to grab it. As I sprinted back upstairs, I passed Hank on his way down.

I sat on Meg's bed, flipped open the lid and soaked some cotton wool with iodine.

'Oh, Meg, I'm so sorry. This is going to sting,' I said, before dabbing the gash on her cheek. She didn't so much as flinch.

Her left eye had shut completely in my short absence – the flesh above the socket had expanded and rolled over, creating a grotesque new lid. A trickle of blood ran from the corner of her mouth to the pillow and, with a fresh wave of horror, I wondered if she'd lost any teeth.

Hank returned with an armful of logs.

'I have to get some compresses,' I said. 'She's swelling badly.'

I got two large metal bowls from the kitchen and took them out the back, leaving the door wide open. I fell to my knees on the frozen ground and scooped up snow, throwing it into one of the bowls and punching it down until ice crystals formed and tore at my knuckles. When I couldn't pack it any harder, I ran back inside, pausing just long enough to kick the door shut with my bare foot. I paused at the sink to fill the second bowl with water, set it on top of the first and dropped a pile of clean rags into it.

When I appeared in the doorway with the stacked bowls, Hank turned his head, but otherwise didn't move. He'd managed to get a small fire going and stood awkwardly in front of it.

'Hank, the hall lamps,' I said.

He sprang into action.

I set the bowls on the bedside table, wrung out a cloth and draped it across Meg's forehead. I folded another and laid it on her cheek, right under her eye.

Then I sat beside her, stroking her tangled hair and making shushing noises until I realised my fingers were sticky with blood. When I investigated, I found that a chunk of her hair was missing, leaving a patch of bright red scalp exposed.

I cleaned that as well, before covering it with yet another cold cloth. Meg didn't react to any of it.

As I waited for Angus to return with the doctor, there was nothing I could do but sit with her, swapping the compresses when they were no longer cold and watching the water turn pink. I'd never felt so helpless in all my life.

Dr McLean banished everyone while he examined Meg, so the rest of us went downstairs to wait. As far as I could tell, Ellis had slept through the entire thing. That, or he was dead, but I saw no reason to check. If he was dead, he'd still be dead in the morning.

Hank and I sat by the dampened fire. Angus lit a lamp and paced. He'd pulled on a sweater before heading out into the night, but I knew Hank had already seen his scars. They were impossible to miss.

When Dr McLean finally emerged from the stairwell, I leapt to my feet.

'How is she?'

The doctor set his bag on the floor and adjusted his glasses. 'I've given her morphine, so for the moment she's comfortable, but she's taken a very serious beating. Do you happen to know the brute responsible?'

'Aye,' said Angus. 'And he's taken a wee beating himself.'

'Will she be all right?' I asked.

'She has a concussion, a great number of contusions, bruising of the spleen and kidney and at least three cracked ribs. She lost the top molars on the left side, and the bicuspids are loose, although they might take hold again.'

'We need to call an ambulance,' I said. 'Surely she needs to go to the hospital.'

'Ordinarily I'd agree,' said Dr McLean. 'But under the circumstances, if there's any possibility she can be cared for here, I think that would be preferable.'

'What circumstances?' asked Angus.

'The hospital is in Inverness,' the doctor explained, 'which is suffering from a fuel shortage and an outbreak of respiratory illness. Chest congestion is the last thing the poor girl needs with cracked ribs, so I'd strongly prefer not to expose her. But if you do keep her here, you'll need to watch her very closely.'

'What do we do?' I asked.

After a pause, I realised everyone was staring at me. I turned to Angus.

'I know you're busy elsewhere during the day, but between Anna and me, I'm sure we can manage. Maybe Rhona can come back for a while.'

'Maddie,' Hank said slowly. 'Are you sure you know what you're doing?'

'I know exactly what I'm doing . . . Angus?'

It was the first time I'd addressed him by his Christian name in front of anyone else. He looked hard into my eyes.

'Maddie . . .' Hank said in the background.

'Please,' I said to Angus. 'The doctor said she'd be better off here, and I'll hold up my end. I promise.'

He turned to Dr McLean and nodded. 'She'll stay here.'

* * *

Hank sat quietly as the doctor gave instructions for Meg's care.

We were to watch for signs of shock – paleness, a drop in temperature, a weak or rapid heartbeat. If that happened, we were to call an ambulance immediately, because it meant she was bleeding internally. Also, because of the concussion, we were to wake her once an hour for the next twelve hours to check her mental acuity.

'I would normally have you compare her pupils at the same time, but I'm afraid that won't be possible with the swelling. However, each time you wake her, she must take five or six deep breaths to ward off pneumonia. If she can manage to cough, all the better. She will not want to, but it's critical. I left morphine on the dresser. With your experience in the field, I assume you're comfortable administering it?'

'Aye,' Angus said grimly.

'Good. Well. Unless you have any other questions, I'll be off.'

He picked up his bag and went to the door. Angus walked with him.

'And the animal who did this – you say he's been dealt with?'

'For the time being,' said Angus. 'But if you should happen to be called out to one of the lumberjack camps tonight, may I recommend you take your time, or perhaps even a wrong turn?'

'Aye,' the doctor said. 'With the blackout, it can be very difficult to find your way in the dark. One might even say impossible on a night such as this. I assume you'll be paying a visit to the commanding officer tomorrow?'

'That I will,' said Angus. 'And I may well pay a visit to the man himself.'

The doctor nodded. 'Under the circumstances, I can't think

of a single reason to try to dissuade you. Good evening, Captain Grant.'

Hank looked up sharply, and my heart began to pound.

I was right. It was him – he was the Angus on the stone.

31

Although my heart was racing from learning the truth, the rest of me was bone weary. We all were, and slogged back upstairs in single file – I followed Angus, Conall followed me and Hank brought up the rear.

I stopped cold when I saw Meg. I hadn't thought she could look any worse.

'Dear God,' I said, creeping closer to the bed.

The doctor had stitched up the cut on her lip, as well as the gash that ran vertically down her cheek. The latter was terrible to behold – a makeshift black zipper, encrusted with blood and indisputable proof that she'd be permanently scarred. I wondered if the missing teeth would hollow out her face, and hoped to God she wouldn't lose the others. Despite all this, she appeared to be in a deep sleep.

Hank cleared his throat. He lingered in the hallway, just beyond Meg's door.

'So, do you need me to grab more logs, or . . .?'

What he was really asking was if he could go to bed, and I hated him for it.

'We'll manage,' said Angus.

Hank hung around a few seconds longer before disappearing. I could only imagine what he'd tell Ellis in the morning, but there was nothing I could do about it.

When Angus went to get more ice, I retrieved a quilt from

my own room, turned the chair round so it faced Meg, then settled into it, tucking my feet beneath me.

'You should go to bed,' Angus said when he came back. 'I'll sit with her tonight and Anna can take over in the morning.'

'I'd like to stay, if you don't mind.'

'I don't mind, but unless I manage a wee bit of rearranging, you'll probably be on your own in the afternoon.'

'That's all right.'

He stoked the fire, then crouched against the wall. I snuck a quick peek. He was studying me.

'So you were going to kill him, were you?' he asked.

'I meant to, yes.'

He gave a soft laugh. 'You surprise me, Mrs Hyde.'

'Maddie. I'm just Maddie. Anna and Meg have been calling me that for weeks, except when my husband is around.'

He looked at me for a very long time, and I wondered how much he had figured out.

'I'm afraid it's time,' he said forty minutes later.

Meg was difficult to rouse, but we finally managed it by calling her name and tapping the backs of her hands. Angus asked if she knew the date. She replied that it was Valentine's Day and began to cry.

It was her fault, she mumbled through broken lips. Rory had been in his cups, and she should have known better than to be coy about the stockings, never mind scolding him the night before. He was a good man, really he was – she was moving to Nova Scotia with him after the war. She'd seen the 'Welcome to Canada' film just the week before, along with all the other girls who were going to marry lumberjacks when the war ended.

'Hush now, *m'eudail*,' said Angus.

'What if he doesn't come back?'

Angus and I exchanged glances.

'You've got to take some deep breaths now,' Angus said. 'Only five, but they must be deep.'

'I can't,' she wept. 'You don't understand. It hurts.'

'You've got to, Meg,' I said. 'It's doctor's orders. You don't want pneumonia, do you?'

Angus and I helped her roll onto her back and held her hands, counting aloud as she valiantly filled and emptied her lungs. Her cries were heart-wrenching, but as soon as we counted to five, she turned onto her side and drifted off.

'Thank God for morphine,' Angus said. 'She probably won't even remember we woke her.'

'How long before her next dose?'

'Not quite four hours. I'll give it to her just a wee bit early to stay ahead of the pain. It's better than trying to catch up to it.'

As he sat back down, I wondered if he was speaking from personal experience.

'What will happen to Rory?' I asked.

'There's no saying. But I can tell you this – he'll never lay a finger on her again.'

The fire danced in his brilliant blue eyes and I knew Meg would be safe from Rory for ever, even if she didn't want to be.

With everything else that had gone on that night, it was hard to believe that Ellis was still locked in his room, quite possibly tied to the bed. I wanted to crawl across the floor to Angus and tell him everything. I wanted to ask him about his own family. I wanted to feel his arms round me, and to wrap mine round him. I wanted to feel the blood coursing through his veins as he vowed to protect me, because I would believe him.

*　　*　　*

Just after we woke Meg for the third time, we heard Anna moving about downstairs.

Angus climbed to his feet. 'Well, I suppose I'd better let her know what's happened. Then I have to go out for a while – I have a wee bit of business to take care of.'

A few minutes later, Anna raced up the stairs and into the room. When her eyes landed on Meg, she burst into tears. I rushed round the bed to hug her.

'It's evil, Maddie, that's what it is,' she said, crying into my shoulder. 'Pure evil. What kind of a monster would do such a thing? To our poor, sweet Meg, of all people. Meg, who has no kin at all.'

'I don't know,' I said helplessly. 'I really don't know.'

When Anna calmed down enough that I believed she'd remember the doctor's instructions, I left to get some sleep.

As I walked down the hall towards my room, I noticed that the door was ajar. I had been in a rush when I got the quilt, but the daylight behind it gave me pause. I clearly remembered replacing the blackout frame after eavesdropping on the dance.

I crept up to the door and gave it a little push.

My room had been completely torn apart. The dresser drawers were wide open and empty, the top one yanked out completely. Everything I'd kept inside – my personal littles, slips, nightgowns, stockings and books – had been flung randomly about the room. My dresses, trousers and sweaters had been ripped from the closet, and the suitcases and trunks I'd kept stored behind them had been hauled out, opened and overturned. Even my cosmetics case had been dumped, and then hurled with such force that one of the bronze hinges from the tray stuck out to the side like a broken wing.

Someone touched my shoulder. I spun round, flattening myself against the wall.

It was Ellis, of course. His face was gaunt and his complexion yellow. The expression behind his red-rimmed eyes seemed vaguely conciliatory, solicitous even.

'Maddie?' he said, inching forward and cocking his head. He forced his parched lips into a smile. 'What have you done with the pills, Maddie?'

My mind spun, but I couldn't hide what I'd done. I couldn't magically conjure up more.

'I flushed them,' I said.

His wheedling façade was replaced in an instant by fury.

'You did *what*? When?'

'I don't know. A while ago.'

'What in the hell possessed you to do such a stupid thing? *Jesus!*'

'You did,' I said.

He looked dumbfounded.

'Oh my God. Oh my God,' he said quietly, to himself. He ran a shaky hand through his hair and began gasping for breath.

I moved sideways, feeling the wall behind me and trying to find my door. My fingers found and curled round the edge of the doorframe.

He raised his face abruptly, looking at me with stricken eyes. 'What the hell happened to you, Maddie? When did you become so hell-bent on destroying me?'

My mouth opened and closed, but I couldn't find an answer.

He turned and launched himself down the hallway, weaving from side to side and banging into the wall when his legs failed to straighten.

I slipped into my room and bolted the door. Then I collapsed on the bed and surrendered immediately to a deep, dreamless sleep.

*   *   *

When I woke up and realized that almost nine hours had gone by, I rushed back to Meg's room. It was well past the time Anna usually returned to the croft, and close to the time hungry customers began to arrive.

She was curled up in the chair with my quilt over her legs, as I had been earlier. I paused at Meg's bedside, gazing down at her battered face.

'How is she?' I whispered.

'Angus gave her some morphine just now, so she's out again. He says we don't have to wake her up any more. Alas, he also says that when she is awake, she still has to take deep breaths and try to cough.'

I sat on the floor beside the chair, with my legs stretched out and crossed at the ankles. 'I'm sorry I slept so long. I can take over now. Has anyone done anything about dinner?'

'There's no need. Angus tacked a sign to the door saying "Closed Due to Illness" – illness, for goodness' sake.'

I could only shake my head.

Anna sighed. 'It must be very bad indeed since the doctor didn't give her castor oil. Before anything else, you get a dose of the castor oil. I don't even see that he's left a tonic – he always leaves a tonic. How is she supposed to recover without a tonic?'

She looked at me as though I should know. When I raised my hands to indicate that I didn't, she sighed again.

'Rhona's got a soup going downstairs and I'm sure Mhàthair is mixing up all kinds of tea right at this very moment, but Angus says we're not to give her anything until Dr McLean says it's all right.'

A quiet moan rose from the bed. We sprang to our feet.

Meg moved restlessly beneath the bedclothes. Anna wrung out a cloth and mopped her brow, then dabbed her lips with something from a small jar.

'Lanolin,' Anna whispered. 'We've no shortage around here. Unfortunately, it does leave you smelling a bit like a sheep.'

Meg went still again. Anna and I returned to our spots and stared into the flames. They were hypnotic.

Anna finally broke the silence. 'Are you cold? Do you want the quilt?'

'I'm all right, thanks. It's toasty in here. I don't think I've been this warm since I got to Scotland.'

'I suppose your house in America is very warm.'

'Temperature-wise, sure,' I said.

Anna peered sideways at me. 'Is everything all right? Only I couldn't help but hear the racket earlier, with your husband shouting and stumbling about the way he was.'

'No, not really,' I said. 'Things are actually pretty dismal.'

After almost a minute of sneaking expectant glances, Anna broke down. 'I don't mean to stick my nose where it doesn't belong, but sometimes it can help to unburden yourself.' She turned deliberately away, presumably to ease my confession.

I hesitated, but not for long. 'I think I'm going to get a divorce,' I whispered.

'A divorce!' Anna's head whipped round, her eyes so wide I could see the whites all the way round. 'You'll be like Wallis Simpson!'

I recoiled. 'I certainly hope not. I only plan on getting the one – if I can even figure out how.'

As Anna reflected on this, she turned back to the bed. Her eyes remained huge.

'I shouldn't have said anything,' I said. 'I've shocked you.'

'No,' she said, shaking her head vehemently.

As a silence swelled between us, I plunged into despair. I couldn't stand the thought of Anna not liking me any more.

'You think I'm awful, don't you?' I asked.

'Don't be ridiculous,' she said. 'It's plain to see how he

treats you. It just hadn't occurred to me there was anything you could *do* about it.'

I thought of the cockerel confined under his basket on Sundays, and realised that divorce was probably not an option in Glenurquhart.

'Does he know?' Anna asked.

'No, and I have to keep it that way for now, because after I tell him, I'll have to live somewhere else. If I can find some-where else.'

'Oh aye,' she said, nodding. 'I can imagine it would be miserable indeed to remain under the same roof once you've broken the news.'

I looked at Meg's swollen, bloodied face and thought of the cracking sounds the door had made as my enraged husband threw himself against it, trying to get to me.

'I'm worried it might be worse than that.'

Anna's eyes flew from me to Meg and then back again, widening in understanding.

We looked hopelessly at each other, then resumed staring at the fire. It cast long shadows that danced all the way across the ceiling before turning sharply down the far wall, like they were following the folded crease in a piece of paper.

Although in the scheme of things I'd said very little, I'd probably said more than I should have. But I wondered if what I'd told her might have set the tone for a few more confidences.

'Anna,' I said, 'I know it's none of my business, but will you please tell me what happened to Angus? I know he's the one on the gravestone, the one who didn't die. But I know nothing else.'

She frowned and blinked, studying me as she considered my request.

My face began to burn. I'd made a mistake, asking about

things I had no right to know. I turned towards the opposite wall, filled with shame.

Behind me, Anna sighed heavily.

'Well,' she said, 'you won't hear it from him, because he doesn't talk about it, and while I'm not one for the blather, it's not what you might call a state secret, so I don't suppose he'd mind.'

I'd imagined a million scenarios since the headstone first caught my attention, but none was as tragic as the truth. The only body beneath it was the infant's.

'Mhàthair helped deliver her, in this very room,' said Anna. 'It's almost certainly the last time there was a fire in the grate. The wee mite lived only a few minutes, God rest her soul. That was nearly the end of Màiri right there. Then, a month to the day later, the telegram came saying Angus was also gone. I was here when Willie delivered it. It's still in the lockbox downstairs. It came on Valentine's Day, of all days.'

'When did you find out it wasn't true?'

'Too late for our poor Màiri.'

The very first time I saw the grave I'd wondered if Màiri had died of a broken heart, and it turned out she'd done just that. Two weeks after hearing that Angus was dead, she walked to the castle, through the Water Gate, down the slope and into the loch. The frantic fisherman who saw her do it could not row fast enough to reach her, and her body was never found.

When Anna told me this, my heart twisted. I realised I'd seen Angus at both graves.

'Had they been married long?' I asked.

'They'd been sweethearts for years, but they only wed when the war broke out and Angus joined up. It had that effect on a lot of people.'

'My God. They weren't even married two years.'

'Aye. The war has cut short a great many things.'

She fell silent, and I knew she was thinking of her brothers.

'Did they have much time together before Angus shipped out?' I asked.

'Here and there. It wasn't until April of 'forty that the fighting really heated up, and it wasn't long after that that Angus was injured the first time.'

As Anna recounted what happened, I was struck not just by what she was telling me, but also by how well she knew it. Then I remembered the size of the village and how huge a tragedy this was, even in an age full of tragedy.

During the Battle of Dunkirk, Angus had gone back into the line of fire not once, not twice, but three times to rescue other members of his unit, despite having taken shrapnel in the thigh. His courage attracted the attention of higher-ups, and when he recovered, he was invited to join the newly formed Special Service Brigade.

Only the toughest made it into Winston Churchill's 'Dirty Tricks Brigade,' the elite and deadly group he formed for the sole purpose of creating 'a reign of terror down the enemy coast.' They trained at Achnacarry Castle, by then known as Castle Commando, under the fifteenth Lord Lovat, who based his techniques on the small commando units that had impressed his father during the Boer War.

Angus and other potential commandos were dumped off at the train station in Spean, seven miles away, given a cup of tea and then left to their own devices, in full battle gear, in whatever weather, to find their way to the castle. If they made it, they spent six gruelling weeks training with live ammunition, being pushed to the brink of physical exhaustion and beyond, as well as learning all the ways you could kill a man even if you didn't have a weapon.

Angus was shipped off after a leave of only a few days, which was nonetheless long enough to leave Màiri with child. Nine months later, he was grievously wounded – gutted, essentially – during hand-to-hand combat in France, collapsing only after slitting his opponent's throat with the edge of his metal helmet.

As Anna spoke, I could see it all in my head, unfolding relentlessly. I'd dreamed up countless versions of what had happened, but this was worse than any of them. I saw Angus doubled over, struggling to remain upright, using one arm to try to hold in his internal organs while slashing out with the other to fell the enemy soldier. I saw Angus collapsing, sure he was dying, his eyes open and trained on the blue sky, his thoughts on his wife and the child that was due at any moment, and may well have already been born.

Angus was hauled to safety by members of the French Resistance, but nobody knew for a long time – his ID tags had been torn off and lay somewhere among the rotting bodies that littered the cobblestoned streets. The fighting was so fierce the corpses could not be recovered for more than a week, rendering them grossly bloated and unrecognisable.

He had remained on the brink of death for weeks. It was a miracle he survived at all, but five months later, against all odds, he made his way back to British territory.

'My God,' I said, when Anna paused. 'And then he found out his wife and child had both died.'

'Aye,' said Anna. 'There was nothing anyone could have done about the child, but he blames himself to this day for what happened to Màiri.'

'That wasn't his fault,' I said.

'I know that, but he feels responsible anyway, like he should have been able to find a way to get word back, even though he was lying right *gralloched* somewhere in a French cellar. He hasn't touched the waters of the loch since. He'll only fish in the rivers. In fact, he won't set foot through the Water Gate.'

'Other than that, has he recovered? I mean, physically?'

'He's strong as an ox – I've seen the man haul a deer down the hill on his shoulders, Harris-style. The only reason he's not back at the Front is because they need him at the battle school. Only a commando can train a commando, so that's what he does, up at the Big House, most of the time. The rest of the time he's keeping us all fed.'

'Do you think he'll go back to being the gamekeeper? I mean, after the war?'

Anna shook her head. 'No. The old laird died, you know. Only a few months ago, but it was a long time coming. He never recovered from the loss of his son, the poor man.'

I remembered Bob the bobby's warning with a sinking feeling. There were no hunting parties at the estate – for obvious reasons – so no rich person was being robbed of a trophy head, and Angus was supplementing the diet of every last family in the village. It was a true case of righteous theft, and I hoped the new laird would have a change of heart. After everything else Angus had been through, it seemed beyond cruel not to let him go back to being the gamekeeper after the war. It was clear he knew and loved the land.

'Well,' Anna said wearily, 'now that I've blathered your ear completely off, I should probably get going. I'll fetch you a cup of tea first.'

'Anna?' I said, as she got to her feet.

'Aye?'

'Thank you for filling me in,' I said. 'Even if it isn't any of my business.'

'Oh, I don't know. I'm starting to think of you as one of us now.'

A lump rose in my throat. I thought that might be the nicest thing anyone had ever said to me – and meant.

32

When Anna brought the tea, she also handed me the newspaper.

'Since she'll probably just sleep, I thought you might want something to pass the time.'

After Anna left, I checked on Meg, laying a hand across her forehead and watching the rise and fall of her ribcage. Except for her ravaged face and the blood that matted her copper curls, she looked as peaceful as a sleeping child.

I settled into the chair with the newspaper.

IT WON'T BE LONG, NEARING THE END, and GERMANY'S APPROACHING DOOM, blared the headlines, although the articles themselves revealed a far grimmer reality.

There was a report from a war correspondent who was travelling with the Seaforth Highlanders as they fought along the Western Front, describing 'scenes of utter devastation' – of soldiers trying to clear minefields in torrential rains, of abandoned towns that contained only shells of buildings, of corpses piled high along both sides of the road. In another article, the very same battle was characterised by a stiff-lipped field marshal as 'going very nicely although the mud is not helping it.'

There was an article about the respiratory illness that raged through Inverness, as well as the fuel shortage. A recent cold spell had caused such a sharp rise in consumption that the municipal authority, the source of the city's firewood, ran out completely. Despite suggestions that emergency fuel supplies in the North should be made available to people in dire distress, nothing had been done about it. One government fuel dump alone had more than seven hundred tons of coal and a thousand tons of timber, yet the sick and elderly in Inverness had nothing at all to put in their grates or stoves.

Sprinkled among reports that the Red Army had killed more than 1,150,000 German soldiers in just over a month, and that Tokyo had been bombed again, and that two days of raids conducted by the Allied Forces had reduced the city of Dresden to rubble, were advertisements for the Palace Cinema on Huntly Street announcing two new movies, *You Can't Ration Love* and *The Hitler Gang*, which would be shown three times a day, and for vitamin B yeast tablets, because 'Beauty Depends on Health.' A purveyor of effervescent liver salts promised its product would 'gently clear the bowels, sweep away impurities and purify the blood.' A circumspect warning about venereal disease admonished that its rise was one of the 'very few black spots' on the nation's war record, although it wasn't offering advice on what to do about it.

Perhaps the most absurd juxtaposition of all was of a statement issued by Field Marshal Montgomery, declaring the war to be in its final stages, which was set immediately next to an article about a horse pulling a milk cart that had bolted while the driver was setting milk on a stoop. The horse made a mad dash 'along Old Edinburgh Road and down the brae' as milk bottles 'flew in all directions.' It failed to take the corner at the High Street and crashed, cart and all, through the front window of Woolworth's. While 'badly cut about the shoulder,' the horse was rescued by a policeman and several soldiers and was expected to make a full recovery.

The sheer scope of detail and information, as well as its seemingly random placement, was proof to me that the world had both gone mad, yet remained the same as it ever was.

Mass killings were described right next to information about laxatives. Cities were bombed, men slaughtered each other in knee-deep mud, civilians were blown to pieces from stepping on mines, but horses still spooked, people still went to the cinema and women still worried about their schoolgirl complexions. I couldn't decide if this made me understand the world better or meant I'd never fathom it at all.

Dr McLean came in the late afternoon and said that while he was no longer worried about her concussion, Meg was by no means out of the woods. We were still to watch carefully for signs of shock. He encouraged us to try to get some sustenance into her, although he also warned that we should be gradual about it. He nodded approvingly when I told him that Rhona was downstairs at that very moment working on a soup.

When he left, I followed him downstairs and went into the kitchen. He'd wakened Meg for the examination but followed it with an injection, and I wanted to get something into her before she slipped back out of reach. As soon as Rhona saw me, she ladled out a bowl of rich, fragrant broth and held it out to me with gnarled fingers.

'Thank you,' I said.

She returned to the soup, her back so stooped her face was nearly parallel to the steaming liquid. Her white hair was pulled tightly into a bun and parted in the centre, showing almost an inch of pink scalp. I couldn't even hazard a guess about how old she was. She could have been anywhere from seventy to ninety, perhaps even older.

I managed to get only a few spoonfuls into Meg before the morphine pulled her away from me.

At three minutes before nine, Angus brought an armful of logs upstairs.

I hadn't heard him come back. As far as I'd known, I was alone in the building. I then wondered what Ellis and Hank were up to, because to my knowledge they also hadn't returned. Perhaps they'd gone elsewhere after seeing the sign on the door.

Angus dropped the logs by the grate, brushed off his hands and went to Meg's side.

'How is she?' he asked.

'A little better,' I said, before relating the events of the doctor's visit. 'She had a tiny bit of soup earlier. She's been stirring for about half an hour, so I've been trying to get her to sip some water.'

'What time did Dr McLean give her the injection?'

'Around five.'

'Then she's due. That's why she's restless.'

I sat in the chair, watching as he administered it. This was the first time I'd laid eyes on him since Anna told me what had happened to him.

He filed a groove into the neck of one of the glass ampoules, snapped the top off and filled the syringe. Then he wrapped a length of rubber tubing round Meg's arm, slid the needle in and slowly depressed the plunger. After, he stood at the side of the bed, looking down at her.

'You should go,' he said, glancing at me. 'Get some rest while you can.'

'You're the one who should sleep. You were up the entire night.'

'If I'm not mistaken, I wasn't alone.'

'Yes, but I slept for nine hours after Anna came. I can easily last until morning, although I can't give her morphine. If you go to bed now, you'll get almost four hours before she's due again, and then you can go right back to bed.'

He put his hands on his hips, considering.

'Please,' I said. 'I insist.'

His eyebrows shot up. 'You insist, do you?'

'I promised last night that I'd hold up my end, and it's clearly your turn to sleep,' I said, nearly tripping over my tongue in my haste to explain. 'That's all I meant.'

'I rather preferred it when you were insisting.'

I glanced at him. He was grinning.

I lifted my chin, trying my best to channel the headmistress at Miss Porter's. 'In that case, I'm afraid I really must insist that you get some rest.'

He laughed quietly. 'Well, when you put it like that, I suppose I have no choice.'

He eventually did go to sleep, but not before replacing the bowl of ice, stoking the fire, and extracting a promise that I would get him if I needed anything else – or even if I just changed my mind about going to bed – and that in any case, he'd be back in just under four hours.

I curled up in the chair, which was deep enough that I could fold myself sideways and end up almost horizontal. It was only when I tucked the quilt under my legs that I realised I was still barefoot, still wearing the nightgown I'd donned the night before and therefore had paraded around like that all day – in front of the doctor, in front of Rhona, in front of everyone. Getting dressed simply hadn't occurred to me. Although I was embarrassed, at that moment I was also relieved. Keeping an overnight vigil would almost certainly be more comfortable in a nightgown.

Apparently, it was too comfortable.

The fire let out a loud snap and jolted me awake. A red ember sat on the carpet in front of me. I leapt from the chair, grabbed the poker and pushed it onto the stone flags.

After a quick scan of the room showed that nothing else was

on fire, my eyes landed on Meg. I looked and looked with rising fear, because I could not see any movement beneath the quilts.

I was at her bedside in an instant, hovering in blind terror. Her face was grey, her mouth slack. Her right eye, the one that wasn't swollen shut, was slightly open, displaying a sliver of white. I laid a hand on her ribcage, trying to discern movement, but my hand shook too violently for me to tell. I pressed three fingers to the side of her throat, seeking a pulse.

'Meg?' I said, and then again, loudly, 'Meg?'

I grabbed the hand mirror from her dresser and held it in front of her mouth. It jerked wildly despite my best efforts to keep it steady, but it was aimed at her face at least part of the time and I never saw so much as a hint of fog.

Seconds later I was stumbling down the stairs in the dark, feeling my way along the walls and screaming, *'Angus, Angus!'*

We ran into each other in the doorway to the kitchen. He caught me by my upper arms to steady me. 'What is it? What's wrong?'

'She's not breathing—'

He sprinted past and was thumping up the stairs before I even had a chance to turn round.

By the time I found my way back, he was sitting on the bed holding two fingers against the inside of her wrist.

I crept over, breathing heavily, too afraid to ask.

After an unbearably long time, he laid her hand down and felt her forehead.

'Her pulse is steady,' he said. 'She's a little hot, if anything. Probably from the fire. Shock has the opposite effect.'

I covered my mouth to contain a cry of relief.

'Oh, thank God! Thank God! I fell asleep and then when I woke up she wasn't moving, and I thought . . .' I sucked air through my steepled fingers before finishing in a whisper. 'I thought I'd let her die.'

'You didn't, lass. Everything's all right.'

My vision filled with swarms of gnats, then disappeared completely.

The next thing I knew, my forehead was resting on my knees and I was looking at the folds of my nightgown.

I was on the floor, and Angus was propping me up. He had an arm beneath my legs, lifting my knees, and the other behind my shoulders.

'Stay as you are until the blood comes back,' he said, when I tried to lift my head.

'I'm sorry,' I said. 'I don't know what happened.'

'You fainted,' said Angus. 'You went down pretty hard. Are you hurt?'

'I don't think so. I'm sorry.'

'Don't apologise. There's nothing to be sorry about.'

Sweat broke out on my brow and upper lip, and the buzzing in my ears grew louder. A wave of nausea ran through me.

'Oh God, I think I'm going to be sick.'

He grabbed the stacked bowls from the bedside table and set them on the floor next to me.

I was horrified at the thought of vomiting in front of him, but for a while it seemed inevitable. Eventually, mercifully, the feeling passed.

'I'm all right now,' I said.

'When did you last eat?'

'I'm not sure,' I said. 'Yesterday, I think. Although I had a cup of tea earlier.'

'Well, that will do it. Where did you put the first aid kit?'

'It's under the bed.'

A minute later I was nibbling the small square of emergency

chocolate. As soon as it was gone, I folded the foil wrapper and said, 'I think I can walk now.'

'And I think you should wait another minute or two.'

He took a facecloth from the bowl, wrung it out and held it against my forehead. After a moment, I took it from him and wiped the front and back of my neck.

'I think I really am all right now,' I said.

'Then let's get you to bed.'

He stood and offered me his hands. As he pulled me to my feet, I crumpled. He caught me with both arms and held me upright.

'Steady, there. Do you need to sit back down?'

'No,' I whispered, leaning heavily against him. 'I'm fine.'

'Take your time. Just let me know when you're ready.'

When I finally thought I could control my legs, I said, 'I'm okay now. Really, this time.'

'All right,' he said, keeping a firm grasp on me. 'One foot in front of the other. I can't get a candle, but I know the way. I won't let you fall.'

'You should know something,' I said as he steered me into the darkness of the hall.

'And what's that?'

'There are a few things on my floor.'

'What sorts of things?'

'Mostly clothes. My husband was looking for something this morning.'

Angus supported me into the pitch black of my room and through the flotsam.

'Here you are, then.'

I sank onto the bed and against my pillow. As Angus found and pulled the covers up over me, his hands grazed the top of my foot, my throat, my chin.

'I'm really sorry, Angus,' I said, after he wrapped me into a cocoon.

'For what? You couldn't help fainting.'

'No, for promising I'd look after Meg and then falling asleep.'

'Don't *fash* yourself.'

'But now you're not going to get any rest at all.'

'I got a couple of hours, and I'll grab a few more winks here and there. But I'm afraid there is something that *I* must insist on.'

'What's that?'

'No more missing meals. I can't have all of you out of commission at once. The inn doesn't run itself, you know.'

His words caused a bitter-sweet lump in my throat, my second of the day.

Although I couldn't see a thing, I knew exactly where he was. I could feel his presence, and for a moment I thought he might reach for me. I held my breath and lay absolutely still, waiting, hoping, yet also fearful.

When nothing happened, I said in a cracked voice, 'Angus?'

'Aye?'

For a short time I thought I might say something, even though I didn't have a clue what, but the silence rose and overwhelmed me, a vast, oppressive thing that billowed around me until I was sealed within it.

'Thank you for helping me back to my room,' I finally said.

'I'd best get back to Meg now,' he said. 'Sleep well, Maddie.'

A few seconds later, the door clicked shut behind him, and I was left gasping in the dark.

33

The next day, I stopped long enough to gather some clothes off the floor and get dressed before rushing to Meg's room. I was still trying to smooth the wrinkles from my skirt when I got there.

'Sorry I'm so late,' I said, batting at the creased material. 'I guess I really did have some sleep to catch up on, but with any—'

I glanced up, expecting to see Anna. Instead, I found an old woman with peppery hair sitting in the chair. She was knitting up a storm: *clickity-clickity-click* went her needles, which were fed by an endless strand of yarn that coiled out from a carpet bag beside her. A sock was forming beneath them.

She peered at me over the top of her wire-framed spectacles. 'I suppose you'll be the one from America, the one Anna's been talking about. Maddie Hyde, is it?'

'Yes. That's me.'

'I'm Mrs McKenzie, Anna's mother, but the folk around here call me Mhàthair. You might as well too. When it comes right down to it, we're all Jock Tamson's bairns.'

I moved closer to Meg. 'How is she?'

'Taking a bit of soup when she's awake, and also sipping tea.'

'One of your teas?'

'Aye. I've left some more with Rhona. Try to get as much of it down her as you can. It's for the bruising and swelling, and will only work for the first couple of days. Then I'll bring another.'

Mhàthair's needles never stopped moving, even when she was looking at me. I stared in fascination at the partial sock.

'Where's Anna?'

'At the croft. She'll be back later. Angus said you'd had a rough night, so I stayed on a wee bit to let you rest.'

'Thank you.'

'And now you're to get yourself down to the table. You've nowt on your bones at all. I've seen bigger kneecaps on a sparrow.'

It seemed Angus had told everyone about my fainting spell, because minutes after I sat down, Rhona shuffled out of the kitchen with a plate of scrambled eggs, a large slice of ham and a heap of fried potatoes. She set the plate down, pointed at it and then pointed at me.

She had just gone back into the kitchen when Hank and Ellis breezed through the front door. They were smiling, freshly shaven and enveloped in a cloud of cologne. Ellis looked preternaturally pink and healthy – it didn't seem possible given what he'd looked like the day before.

When they headed towards me, my heart began to pound. I felt like my mother-in-law's canary, trapped in its ever-shrinking cage.

'Good morning, darling girl,' said Hank, plopping himself onto a chair. 'Did you miss us?'

'Morning, sweetie,' said Ellis, kissing my cheek.

Bile rose in the back of my throat. I couldn't believe he thought we could go back to pretending nothing was wrong. Even Hank should have realised that things were too far gone, but he barrelled on with whatever silly game he was playing.

'So did you?' Hank asked.

'Did I what?'

'Miss us? You know – because you love us and we spent the night at the Clansman? Don't tell me you didn't notice.' He blinked at me expectantly, then dropped his jaw in outrage. 'Oh my God. You *didn't* notice. Ellis, your wife didn't even notice we were missing.'

'I *did* notice.'

'But you didn't miss us?'

'I'm sorry. I was a little busy,' I said.

'Busy *sleeping* is what we heard,' Ellis said with a grin. 'We swung by to collect you in the afternoon, but the girl – not the injured one, the slow one from the kitchen – said you were having a nap. Apparently you needed it. You still look a bit peaked.'

I'm sure I did – I hadn't done my hair and face in two days. He, on the other hand, looked the picture of health. I didn't understand how that was possible. Had he come across someone with nerve pills at the Clansman? Certainly something had happened to restore the apples to my husband's cheeks.

'You didn't miss much,' Hank said, lighting a cigarette. 'Its only advantage over this dump was that it was open and we were starving. But wait – what's this?' He looked at my plate in wide-eyed amazement. 'Ellis, maybe we should have stayed here after all. I haven't seen a breakfast like this since we were on the right side of the pond.'

'Looks good,' said Ellis, reaching over and helping himself. 'Anyway, darling, go pack a few things and slap on some warpaint. We're going on a road trip.'

'We're what?' I said.

Hank also snagged some potatoes, popping them in his mouth.

'Oh, wow,' he said. 'These are really good.' He licked his fingers and reached for more.

'Anyway,' Ellis continued, 'we're going to Fort Augustus. One of the old farts at the Clansman last night told us the abbey there has manuscripts that describe the very earliest sightings of the monster. Apparently one of Cromwell's men saw it around 1650 – he recorded seeing "floating islands" in his log, but since there are no islands on the loch, the only possible thing he could have been seeing was the monster – maybe even several of them, which is interesting for all kinds of reasons. There are also Pictish carvings of the beast, which probably contain clues as well. There's obviously some pattern we haven't figured out yet, and it could be something as simple as migratory – it's a bit like code breaking, very complicated, but we're definitely circling it. In fact, we're so close I can practically taste it.'

I stared, unable to believe he'd just compared what they were doing to code breaking, or anything else related to the war.

'I can't go,' I said.

'Why not?'

'Because I have to look after Meg.'

Ellis leaned back and sighed. 'Darling, you *can't* look after Meg. But if it makes you feel any better, we can hire a nurse.'

'But I promised Angus—'

Outrage flashed across his face. '*Angus?* And when, exactly, did Blackbeard become Angus to you? Good Lord, Maddie. I can't even remember how many times I've warned you about getting friendly with the help.'

'Fine. I promised *Captain Grant* that I would help look after Meg.'

Ellis's expression switched from indignation to painfully aggrieved. He tore his eyes away. 'That was uncalled for.'

'How was that uncalled for?' I went on. 'He *is* a captain. Which means he's a commissioned officer – hardly "the help."'

'Regardless of rank, he's a poacher and a common criminal,

and I don't understand why everyone around here, including, apparently, my own wife, seems to think he's such a hero,' he said.

'Because he *is* a hero. You know nothing about him.'

'And you do?' he asked.

I stared straight ahead, at the far wall.

Ellis leaned forward and clasped his hands on the table, donning the insufferable face he always did when he decided my opinions were a result of mental frailty.

'I understand that you care about Meg and want to make sure she recovers,' he said patiently, 'but there's absolutely no reason you have to do it personally.'

'But I do. She's my friend.'

'She's not your friend. She's a barmaid.'

'Who happens to be my friend.'

Ellis hung his head and sighed. After several seconds, he looked back up.

'I know you're in a delicate state right now, but I wish you could see what is really happening.'

'I'm not in a delicate state. I'm *fine.*'

'But you're not fine, darling,' he said. 'You threw out your medication, you're having delusions, you're forgetting your station in life – please don't misunderstand, I'm not blaming you. I know it's not your fault. These are all symptoms of your condition. But these people *will* take advantage of you, if they haven't already, and as your husband, it's my duty to protect you. There's a hospital in Fort Augustus, quite well known, actually . . . I thought maybe you could check in for a while, just until you're back on an even keel.'

With a bone-deep sense of dread, I realised he was planning to have me locked up. He hadn't just come up with a solution that would provide him with endless pills, he'd also come up with a solution that would dismiss anything I might say about his colour-blindness – his behaviour in general – as a figment of my diseased imagination. As an added bonus, he would appear to be a loyal, martyred husband, deserving of pity and respect.

Poor, poor Ellis, saddled with mad, mad Maddie. The things he must have borne, and he never once let on. Such a shame – it was a love match, you know, against his parents' wishes, and then to have her turn out like her mother . . .

Everyone would shake their heads, demonstrating the appropriate level of sadness, while simultaneously feeling the thrill of vindication, because they'd all known it was inevitable. And then, one by one, the matrons of Philadelphia high society would make pilgrimages to the mansion on Market Street to snivel condolences at Edith Stone Hyde, who would hold up admirably, while secretly revelling in having been proved right.

I wondered if Ellis pictured me locked safely in the attic during all of this, like the crazy first wife of Mr Rochester, except drugged into submission.

The icing on the cake, the sheer beauty of his plan, was that I'd still be alive, so he wouldn't even have to marry again. It would be Hank's turn to put on a show. Poor Violet. I wondered if she'd slip as naïvely into the role as I had, and if she'd ever recognise it for what it was.

But Ellis's otherwise masterfully crafted solution had one enormous flaw: unless the Colonel forgave him, he would not be present at his mother's side to lap up sympathy. Without the Colonel's absolution, he still had nothing. Ellis had more at stake than ever in finding the monster.

There was an *Aroogah!* from the street.

'That's George. We should go,' said Hank, getting up.

'Please come with us,' Ellis said, looking me right in the eyes. 'I'm begging you.'

Aroogah!

'Ellis, we have to go,' said Hank.

'Darling, please change your mind,' Ellis entreated.

I shook my head.

After a pause, he climbed to his feet.

'I hate leaving you like this, even if it's only for a few days. But if you won't come, I have no choice. One way or another, we have to wrap this thing up so we can go home and get a fresh start.'

'Your plan won't work,' I said quietly. 'They won't lock me up, because I'm not insane. I never have been.'

He smiled sadly. 'I'll see you in a few days, darling. Take care of yourself.'

A few days. I had only a few days to come up with some way of extricating myself from this tangled mess, because despite my bravado , I wasn't at all sure he couldn't have me committed. And he certainly wouldn't let me divorce him – the proceedings would reveal all kinds of things he'd do anything to keep under wraps.

In the late afternoon, during one of Meg's waking moments, she asked for a mirror.

Anna and I exchanged glances.

'Why don't we give it a few days?' said Anna. 'Give Mhàthair's tea a chance to do its work.'

'I want to see,' said Meg. 'I already know it's going to be bad.'

Anna looked at me in dismay, and I shrugged my shoulders. I didn't see how we could refuse.

'Well,' Anna said, 'in that case, let's get you tidied up a bit.'

She worked at loosening and wiping away the yellowish crust that continued to ooze from the cuts around Meg's mouth and eye. I got my hairbrush, which had softer bristles than Meg's, and ran it carefully over her hair, taking pains to avoid the raw area, trying gently to encourage a wave or curl to form. Anna stood in the background, chewing her nails.

When I handed Meg the mirror, she looked into it and turned her face from side to side. She lifted her fingers to her ruined cheek, tracing the outline of the stitched-up gash, before hovering over the deep new hollow. Then she set the mirror on the bed and wept.

34

Two days later, Dr McLean decided to replace Meg's morphine with a bright red tonic.

As he put the syringes in a box with the remaining morphine, he paused and knitted his brow. He pushed the ampoules, both empty and full, around with his finger.

'Well, that's very odd,' he finally declared. 'I would have sworn I brought more than this. There should be four left. You've not accidentally double-dosed her, have you?'

'I should think not,' replied Angus, with more than a little affront.

'No, of course not,' said the doctor, shaking his head. 'I must have miscounted.'

A knot formed in the pit of my stomach. I knew exactly where they'd gone, and why Ellis had looked so improbably healthy.

When Anna saw the tonic, she nodded in satisfaction. To her, it indicated that everything was just a little more right with the world.

To Meg, it meant she could no longer sleep through the pain. Additionally, Dr McLean insisted that deep breathing was no longer enough. Now Meg also had to get up and shuffle the length of the hallway twice a day to ward off blood clots.

Meg bore this bravely, but it was clear that every step was

agony. Anna and I would flank her, holding her elbows and giving encouragement. When we got her back to her room, we'd help her into the chair, where she'd sit stiffly until she felt up to the task of lying back down, because lying down required using the muscles in her abdomen and back. Lifting, laughing, coughing, breathing – all of it caused pain.

Rhona had been a constant presence since the morning after Meg's injury, and she and Mhàthair made continuous adjustments to the soup we spooned into her. We consumed it as well, and its ever-changing nature was a source of mystery to me. One time, a pile of tiny lime-green leaves appeared on the corner of the big table in the kitchen. I fingered them absentmindedly, thinking they might be mint. They turned out to be the first spring shoots of stinging nettle, and I had to sit for hours with my hands submerged in a bowl of snow. This amused Anna and Meg no end, although Meg finally called an end to the merriment because she couldn't bear the pain of laughing any more. What they didn't notice was that my laughing had turned to crying.

There was no getting round it – a few days meant three, four at – most. My grace period was almost up.

Four days turned into five, and then six, and there was still no sign of Ellis and Hank. I almost wished they'd return just to get it over with, because a bolt of terror ran through me every time the front door opened.

Nights were even worse. My brain turned and turned, robbing me of sleep, yet I couldn't come up with a single solution. I had no money at all, either in a bank or on my person, so even if I'd known how to bribe my way onto another freighter, I didn't have the means. I also had nowhere to go at the other end.

Although there was no longer any need, I continued to sleep

in Meg's room. I was afraid that Ellis would come back and look for me in mine.

On the seventh day, when Rhona began assembling game pies, I realised Angus was reopening the inn.

I didn't see how he could. Even if Rhona prepared all the food, Meg was weeks away from being able to carry trays, and Rhona was simply too frail. Angus couldn't possibly serve and clear tables as well as tend bar.

When I came downstairs, he had the front door propped open and was taking down the sign, collecting the tacks between his lips.

'Is everything all right?' he mumbled, glancing at me.

'Yes. Everything's fine. I just wanted to ask something.'

'Ask away.'

'I notice you're reopening the inn, and I wondered if I could help. It's too much for one person, and Meg says she'll be all right on her own for a few hours, as long as I leave her with a book.'

Angus spat the tacks into his hand and shut the door.

'And what do you think your husband would make of that?'

'He'd hate it. In fact, he'd forbid it. But he's out of town.'

'I had actually noticed that,' he said with a quick laugh. 'But for how long?'

'I'm really not sure,' I said. 'I thought he'd be back a few days ago.'

'And if he were to come back and find you behind the bar?'

'There would be a scene, but I'm afraid that would be the least of my worries.'

Angus dropped the tacks onto the nearest table and looked at me.

'Maddie, is there something I should know? Because I can't help if I don't know.'

I wanted to tell him, but there was nothing he could do.

There was a long silence as Angus continued to stare at me, his hands on his hips, his expression stern.

'It's complicated,' I finally said, 'and when it comes right down to it, I don't think anyone *can* help me.'

'You're sure, are you?'

I nodded and said, 'I'm pretty sure, and in the meantime, I'm trying not to think about it. So what do you say? Can I distract myself by helping with the dinner service?'

'I'd be grateful for the help,' he said, his voice still serious. 'And if you change your mind and want to tell me what's going on, you know where to find me.'

A few minutes before six, when I was expected downstairs, I paused at Meg's door. I'd helped her move to the chair a little earlier, when she'd decided to read. Apparently sitting ramrod straight was more comfortable than being propped up in bed.

'I'm going down now. Do you want me to get you anything first? Top up your tea, or move you back to the bed?'

She looked at me over the spine of *Died in the Wool*, then set it face-down in her lap.

'Is that what you're wearing?'

'It was,' I said, glancing down at myself. I was in a navy blue dress that I hoped would be forgiving of stains, and shoes that were low enough that I probably wouldn't trip.

She tsked and frowned. 'You look like you've come from a funeral, for goodness' sake! You're supposed to lighten their mood, not darken it – change into something more appropriate, and then come back.'

'But they'll start arriving any minute,' I protested.

'Angus can pull pints while you make yourself presentable,' she said firmly. 'At least you've done your hair and make-up,' she added in a mutter, returning to her book.

I stood in front of my closet and considered my options. I picked out a periwinkle rayon dress with a pleated skirt and matching belt, and a pair of shoes whose heels were high enough to lengthen my calves, but that I hoped would not hinder my balance or speed.

Moments later, I stood in Meg's doorway with my hands on my hips.

'Will I do?' I asked.

I meant it rhetorically, but she ran a critical eye over the whole of me, from my hair to my toes and back again.

'Turn round,' she said, stirring a finger in the air.

I obliged, even as I heard the first customers arrive.

'The lines up your legs are a bit crooked,' she said. 'But otherwise, you'll do nicely.'

Although I had visions of china crashing to the floor and dinners sliding into laps, I was not a complete disaster. It was certainly awkward: everyone who came in was clearly taken aback at finding me behind the bar. I'm not sure they quite realised what was going on until they saw Angus tutor me on pulling pints and measuring drams, and I was the one to deliver them. In the moments between orders, I didn't know what to do with my hands, or even where to look. I felt like I'd been thrown naked onstage and forgotten all my lines.

When the curious and mischievous among them began placing orders with me directly, they addressed me as Mrs Hyde, even though Angus was openly calling me Maddie. It was a strange night for names all round, because when the lumberjacks finally began to trickle in – they usually arrived in a raucous crowd – they were subdued and addressed Angus consistently as either Captain Grant or Sir. I thought they must be testing the waters, to see if they were still welcome.

Willie the postie was the only one to make a direct

comment. He came to a dead stop just inside the door when he saw me. Then he marched up to the bar.

'What's this, then?' he said, looking me up and down. 'Are my eyes deceiving me?'

'What'll it be then, Willie?' said Angus, ignoring the question. 'The usual?'

'Aye,' Willie said, continuing to eye me suspiciously.

I got so that I could pull a pint without half of it being foam, and tried to remember what Meg did when there was a lull. I topped up the water jugs, took empty glasses back to the kitchen, and wiped the bar until my wrists ached, but what Meg did that I couldn't was chat and flirt and anticipate orders.

There was not a single local who didn't ask after her, although they did it individually and discreetly. It was clear they knew what had happened, although Rory's name was never spoken. Angus simply said that while she was improving, she was still feeling poorly, and that he'd pass along their good wishes. To a one, they responded with serious nods and expressions that underscored a wordless rage.

The lumberjacks did not ask, and their discomfort increased as the night wore on. It seemed to me they were trying to figure out if they should leave, and probably would have been relieved to do just that.

Conall was at his usual place by the fire, and by his hopeful look I realised he expected me to join him. His eyes followed me wherever I went, and over the course of the evening – after it finally dawned on him that I wasn't coming to sneak him bits of my dinner – he lost faith and dropped his head on the stones. It was all I could do not to take him a little something. We had a pact, and I felt terrible about breaking it.

When all the tables and stools were occupied and I was running back and forth between the front room and the kitchen, the hours began to fly. Before I knew it, everyone had eaten, I'd cleared the tables and I hadn't broken anything. I'd spilled just two drinks, and only one of them had landed on a customer – the piper, Ian Mackintosh, who was entirely gracious about it.

When nine o'clock rolled round, and Angus tuned the wireless to the nightly broadcast, I paused in the doorway to listen.

The Red Army were drawing ever closer to Berlin, and had cut railway lines and roads that led to the city. Dresden may have already been reduced to rubble, but the Allied Forces continued to bomb Germany 'night and day,' in the words of the announcer. British troops had taken Ramree, an island in Burma, and an important battle had begun on Iwo Jima, an island close to mainland Japan.

I slipped away before I could hear the number of casualties.

Rhona had the dishes stacked next to the sink, and I stood beside her to help. She seemed to have shrunk over the course of the evening, and was moving even more slowly than usual. If we'd shared a language, I'd have suggested that she rest her feet and let me do the dishes.

Conall had slipped in behind us, and when the last plate was washed, he heaved a heartbroken sigh and collapsed by Angus's bed, as though my cruelty had deprived him of the energy to even jump up.

If I'd done the dishes on my own, I would have let him lick a few.

After everyone left, I took a bowl of the latest incarnation of soup upstairs, along with a half pint of beer.

'Knock, knock,' I said, although Meg's door was open. 'I brought you a little something.'

She'd made her way back to the bed and lay facing the far wall.

'Unless it's morphine, I don't want it.'

I put the bowl and glass down and sat next to her. She'd lost what little colour she'd had earlier in the day.

'What happened? I thought you were feeling a bit better.'

'I was,' she said. 'I think I overdid it.'

'I brought you some soup. Do you want to move back to the chair?'

'No. I think the chair is what did me in.' She raised herself onto an elbow, slowly, haltingly. It was painful to watch. 'Just stick a pillow behind me. So, how did it go downstairs?'

'I think it went fine,' I said. 'I only doused one person.'

I held the soup under Meg's chin and fed her half a spoonful. She winced, manipulating her jaw carefully. Earlier in the day, Rhona had added finely diced pieces of potato and leek, along with a few other vegetables.

'Do you want me to pick the vegetables out?'

'No. I can mush them around. I just have to be careful.'

'Have a sip of beer,' I said, putting the soup down and handing her the glass. 'Someone wise once told me that it builds blood.'

'Maybe she wasn't so wise after all,' Meg said with a wry smile. She took a swallow and gave it back. 'So, when I asked how it went, what I really meant was . . .'

She fell silent. After a few seconds, she leaned back and closed her eyes.

I finally comprehended what her earlier surge of liveliness and corresponding collapse had been about.

'No, he didn't come, and I don't think he will. I don't think he'd dare.'

She nodded and blinked. Her eyelashes were moist.

'I'm so sorry, Meg.'

'Aye,' she said, sniffing. 'I suppose I knew that, and I suppose it's for the best, but God help me, in spite of everything, I still love him. It's not something you can just turn off.'

I held her hand.

'So you really don't think you can fix things up with your husband?' she asked.

A sickening feeling spread through me. 'I beg your pardon?'

'Anna said you were getting a divorce. Please don't be angry – it's just she's never met a divorcée.'

'She still hasn't! And she probably won't, because I'm not getting one!'

'You're angry!' Meg said with a sudden sob. 'I shouldn't have said anything.'

'No, no, no, don't cry,' I pleaded. 'I'm not angry, exactly, but I *am* a little alarmed. How many other people do you think she's told?'

'Possibly Angus, but I doubt it. She swore me to absolute secrecy.'

Angus. My heart lurched at the thought.

'Anyway, I'll tell her tomorrow you've changed your mind, and that will be the end of it. Was it just a rough patch then?'

'No,' I said. 'It's definitely permanent.'

'It might come round again. You never know. You must have loved each other at some point.'

I shook my head. 'I thought we did. But no, I'm afraid not. His affections have always been elsewhere.'

35

I was curled in the chair when the air-raid siren started its wail. There was no warning, and almost no warm-up – it went from silent to deafening in a matter of seconds.

'Oh God, oh God,' I said, jumping to my feet and looking wildly around. Meg's siren suit was stashed under the chair. I grabbed it, then stood helplessly at the foot of her bed. I had no idea how to wrestle her into it. Angus and Conall showed up seconds later, before I had a chance to try.

'Put that on yourself,' said Angus, when he turned the torch on me and saw what I was holding. 'And grab the gas masks.'

'The two of you go,' Meg cried. 'I can't make it.'

'The hell you can't,' said Angus. He thrust the torch at me, then scooped Meg up along with all her bedclothes and carried her away.

I pulled on Meg's siren suit, grabbed our gas masks and clumped downstairs.

A hazy bit of moonlight revealed the shelter's squat outline, and I ran ahead, holding the flap back while Angus climbed in with Meg. Then Conall slunk in, and I followed, letting the flap fall shut behind me.

I turned the torch on and leaned it up against the wall. Angus, stooping because the ceiling was so low, made his way to the bunks at the back and laid Meg on the bottom one. She turned on her side, writhing.

'Give me her gas mask,' he said, crouching beside her. 'And get yours on as well.'

He slipped Meg's over her battered face. She whimpered and curled up even tighter.

Angus reached beneath the bunk and pulled out a roll of brown canvas that was labelled FIELD FIRST AID. He unfurled it, revealing a variety of surgical instruments and containers strapped to the interior. A moment later, he was injecting something into Meg's arm.

'What was that?' I asked, kneeling beside him. 'Was that morphine?'

'Aye, a Syrette. A preloaded syringe. I jostled her something fierce getting her in here, and I see no reason she shouldn't sleep through this.' He glanced back at me. 'I said get your mask on.'

I was struggling with the straps when Angus twisted on his heels and did something to the back of my head. I reached up to investigate. He'd secured the place where the straps converged with a safety pin.

Several aircraft screamed overhead, one after another. I shrieked and covered my head. Angus threw his arms round me and I clutched him in a death grip, turning my face and digging the canister of my gas mask into his shoulder.

'Those are Spitfires – just Spitfires. There's nothing to fear,' he said. 'Let's get you up top. I've still got to get my gun.'

I gripped the edge of the upper bunk and he gave me a leg-up, as if helping me mount a horse. I struggled to find my way under the covers, but the gas mask made it nearly impossible to tell what I was doing.

'I'll be back,' he said, ducking away. I cried out, even tried to grab him, but a moment later he was gone. As even more aircraft zoomed overhead, I burst into tears, blubbering inside my gas mask.

The gun must have been in the dugout, because he was back almost immediately.

'It's all right,' he said, crouching by the flap. 'It's just more Spitfires.'

The siren was relentless, rising and falling, rising and falling, and after a few hours I grew numb to it, lulled into a stupor.

I lay on my side, watching Angus the entire time. He kept his head slightly down, listening carefully. Each time a plane roared overhead, he shouted over to me, telling me what it was. I didn't know the difference between a Lockheed Lightning and a Bristol Blenheim, but decided that if Angus wasn't outside shooting at it, it probably wasn't going to drop a bomb on us. I grew so inured to the siren's wail I was startled when it finally went steady, shrieking solidly at its highest note.

When it tapered off and fell silent, Angus set his gun down.

'That's that, I guess,' he said, climbing to his feet.

He made his way toward the back of the shelter and dropped out of sight to check on Meg. A few seconds later, he reappeared, folding his forearms on the edge of the bunk and resting his chin on them. His face was right in front of the clear plastic window of my mask, and I realised he'd never put his on. He hadn't even brought it out. His arms had been full.

'You all right then?' he asked.

I started to kick my way free of the covers.

'Stay put,' he said. 'Meg's asleep.'

'We're spending the night out here?' I asked, my voice muffled by rubber.

'Aye, what's left of it. It will be easier to navigate by the light of day, and I don't want to manhandle her again.' He tapped the window of my mask. 'You can take that off, you know.'

When I removed it, he took it from me and leaned over to put it back in its ridiculous red case.

'Are you warm enough up there?' he asked.

'Yes, but where will you sleep?'

'I'll nip inside and get a quilt.'

'Why don't you take the top bunk, and I'll move down with Meg?'

'No. She's curled up, and it would take some doing to rearrange her. We'll stay as we are.'

'There's enough room up here for both of us,' I said.

He popped back up. Our eyes met, and this time there was no separation at all, no plastic windows, green canisters, black rubber or anything else that might have disguised my words. I had no idea how they'd come out of my mouth.

He smiled, and the skin beside his eyes crinkled.

'I'm sorry,' I said, aware that my cheeks were blazing.

He held two fingers to my lips, then slid his hand round until he was cupping my cheek.

I gasped and turned in to his hand, pressing my face against it and closing my eyes. When I opened them again, he was staring right through me. His eyes were as penetrating and startling as the first time I'd seen him.

'Hush, *m'eudail*,' he said. 'Everything's all right.'

He pulled his hand free.

'Where are you going?' I cried.

'Back in a jiffy,' he said, slipping out of the shelter.

He'd left the torch on. Conall was sitting by the entrance, his head bowed like a gargoyle.

Angus returned with a quilt, which he wrapped round

himself. He crouched against the wall by the entrance and turned off the light.

'Good night, *m'eudail.*'

I reached up and traced the area of my face where he'd touched me.

36

On the ninth day, I began to wonder if something had happened to Ellis and Hank, and if so, if anyone would know how to find me. On the eleventh day, it dawned on me that they might not be planning to return.

It started out as magical thinking, but I soon convinced myself it wasn't that outlandish: Ellis had no home or money to return to, whereas Hank had all the money in the world, and would continue to have it wherever he was. They could change their identities, go somewhere exotic, find an opium den by the sea, leave the whole mess behind. I knew I was part of that mess, but if they really had run off together, never to return, why would they care what happened to me? Maybe they'd found some fondness for me after all, and had decided to set me free.

Of course, I wouldn't really be free until I managed to make it legal, but the idea shone as brightly as a sliver of light beneath a prison door. I was sure Angus would let me stay on until the end of the war – I worked as hard as anyone – but it was more than that. I felt at home at the inn, even welcome.

I couldn't bring myself to think beyond the war, when the proprietor would come back. My dearest hope, my deepest desire, was the one thing I couldn't let myself think about at all, in case I started to believe it was possible, because I knew it wasn't.

On the twelfth night of my husband's absence, I moved back into my room.

It was mid-afternoon, and Anna and I were up in Meg's room. We were making ourselves scarce because Rhona was concocting yet another soup, this one with a base of mutton shanks and barley. Between them, Rhona and Mhàthair appeared to have laid out an exact plan for Meg's recovery based on soup and tea. There were now four big pots simmering on the range, and they filled the entire building with an irresistible aroma.

Apparently it was not irresistible to Meg.

The three of us were sprawled on her bed playing Hearts when she wrinkled her nose and asked what the stink was. I told her about the new soup.

'Not Scotch broth!' she wailed. 'I haven't had real food in two weeks!'

Anna and I glanced at each other. This was the first time Meg had shown an interest in *any* food since her injury – real or otherwise.

'I'll be right back,' said Anna, leaping into action.

She returned shortly with a bowl of porridge and a coddled egg, both of them swimming in butter.

'I hope you enjoy it,' she said, handing the egg to Meg and putting the other bowl on the table. 'Because when Rhona tells Mhàthair, I'm done for.'

'Why?' I asked.

'Because their prescription of the day is cock-a-leekie, and no doubt I've undone all their good work.'

'This is marvellous,' said Meg, her mouth full of egg. 'I don't suppose there's another?'

'I'm afraid not, but I'll bring an egg a day from now on.'

'And if the hens don't cooperate?' I asked.

'I'll pick them up and squeeze until an egg pops out,' Anna

said, making strangulation gestures with her hands. 'And if that doesn't work, I'll remind them what happened to Jenny.'

'Who's Jenny?' I said.

'The hen in the soup. She stopped laying. Do you want to know the name of the sheep in t'other?'

'No! I most certainly do not!' I said.

'Elsie,' said Anna. 'She was a fine ewe. She'll also show up in potted hough, mutton hotpot and haggis. Oh, we'll be seeing Elsie for quite some time.'

'Stop!' I said, holding my hands over my ears. 'I'll never be able to eat again!'

'City folks,' Anna said, shaking her head. 'You never even met Elsie . . . I can see your cards, you know, when you tip them like that.'

'Behave yourselves, the both of you!' Meg said, trying unsuccessfully not to laugh. 'My ribs – remember?'

'Sorry,' Anna said in a sing-song voice. 'It's not my fault if some people can't—'

There was a knocking on the door downstairs, a solemn, familiar rhythm.

The three of us froze.

My mind began to race. Meg had already lost everyone, Angus had already lost everyone—

'Robbie,' Anna gasped, leaping from the bed. I scrambled after her, and had just caught up when she yanked the front door open.

Willie the postie was on the doorstep, holding his hat along with a telegram.

Anna slid silently to the floor. I dropped down beside her, wrapping my arms round her.

'Anna!' Willie said quickly. 'It's not for you.'

'What?' she said, looking up at him with shocked eyes.

'It's not Robbie,' said Willie. 'The telegram is not for you.'

'Oh,' she said.

'Mrs Hyde,' said Willie, 'I'm afraid it's for you.'

I climbed to my feet, confused.

'My deepest condolences,' said Willie, handing me the telegram.

Anna got up and closed the door, even though Willie was still standing there. I walked to the couch and sat down. Anna sat next to me.

The telegram was from a lawyer. My father had choked to death on a piece of steak fourteen days earlier. The lawyer was sorry the notification was so late, but my whereabouts had been somewhat difficult to discern. I was to confirm whether this was indeed my current location, and if this was where I wished details to be sent.

I set the piece of paper in my lap and looked blankly across the room.

My father had died on the night Ellis tried to beat down my door, the night Rory nearly killed Meg—

It was also the anniversary of Màiri receiving the telegram that turned out to be the end of her.

'Maddie?' Anna said in a hushed voice.

I handed it to her.

'Oh, Maddie,' she said after reading it. 'I don't know what to say. I'm so sorry. I'm so very, very sorry. Is there anything at all I can do?'

'I think I need to be alone for a while.'

'Of course. Whatever you want.'

As I stood, she laid her hand on my arm.

'That was Valentine's Day,' she said, her eyes opening wide.

'I know,' I said. 'It must be cursed.'

I walked slowly along the A82, stepping aside to wait as an impossibly long line of moss-coloured military vehicles rolled

past. They were lumbering and square-faced, the first dozen
or so with tarps tied over their loads and the rest transporting
soldiers. Men from every vehicle leaned out the open backs,
hanging by one arm, to whistle and make catcalls. More than
a few made vulgar comments, but there was no way I could
escape their attentions. I was trapped at the side of the road.

I turned to face the oncoming vehicles, because then I didn't
have to see the men's leering expressions. The drivers also
looked at me, but they were behind glass, so I couldn't hear
what they said. Finally, I saw the end of the line.

In all, twenty-eight vehicles had driven past. I wondered how
many of the young men would come back alive from wherever
it was they were being sent.

I kept walking.

The clouds were an intense grey, surging and changing, and
appearing in some places to roll out of crevices in the hills
themselves. It was astonishing how little it took for the same
landscape to take on a completely different cast. The hills, with
their fields and forests, were alternately bleak, looming, rugged
or majestic, depending on what the sky above them was doing.
At that moment, they looked aptly funereal.

It must have seemed strange to Anna that I did not cry.
Perhaps she thought I was having a delayed reaction. I considered the possibility, but dismissed it almost immediately.

I wondered if he'd been eating in his study when the meat
lodged in his windpipe, or if he'd gone back to taking his meals
in the dining room. Had he made any noise, or was he
completely silent? Perhaps he'd turned purple and staggered
around, trying to summon help. Perhaps he'd simply fallen
face-down into a spinach soufflé. I pictured these scenarios
with morbid curiosity, but not sorrow, and definitely not grief.

Although his letter to me had removed all doubt, I think I'd
always known that he didn't love me, and apparently his lack

of affection had engendered the same in me. There'd been a dearth of affection all round.

My mother certainly hadn't loved me, despite her extravagant claims. Her affections, such as they were, vaporised entirely during the seven weeks she was on the run with Arthur and returned, redoubled, only when she was forced to go back to my father.

Ellis had also never loved me. At least, not as a husband should love his wife, and recently, not at all.

I reached the castle. Although I hadn't consciously chosen it as a destination, I climbed up and through the dry moat and across the interior grounds without hesitation. I found myself standing at the opening to the Water Gate.

I picked my way down the hill, which was steep enough that towards the bottom I ended up in a graceless gallop to keep from losing my balance.

In the scrub to the side of the landing, there were dozens upon dozens of cigarette butts. I was heartsick at the thought of Hank and Ellis setting up on the very spot from which Màiri had stepped to her death – drinking, smoking and swearing, oblivious to everyone but themselves and their future fame.

I stepped forward, as Màiri once had, until my feet were at the water's edge. I took another step, just a little one, so that the soles of my shoes were submerged. I watched the water swirl around them, then looked up at the loch itself, black and rolling, endlessly deep.

What had Màiri's thoughts been as she walked in? When it was too late to turn back, when the water closed over her, had she regretted it or felt relief, believing that she was about to be reunited with her husband and child? I opened my mind, trying to channel her. I wanted to know what it was like to experience a love so deep you couldn't bear to exist without it.

I felt her then – I felt Màiri and the cavernous depths of her grief, and had an overwhelming urge to keep going, to walk into the loch. Her anguish was boundless, her sorrow without end. I was drowning in it. *We* were drowning in it.

I closed my eyes, lifted my arms and let myself fall.

A deep rumbling started in the water, like something was rising, followed by a great *whoosh* as it broke the surface. I opened my eyes, still falling – no way to stop then – and saw two blades of water curling from the edges of a channel that was being cut, but by what? Something was obviously racing across the surface of the water, but it looked like nothing was there. Before I could make any sense of it, the thing struck me in the abdomen, folding me round it and knocking me backwards.

I landed away from the water's edge, banging my head so hard my peripheral vision filled with tiny, sparkling stars. Although the wind had been knocked out of me, I staggered to my feet.

The surface of the loch was smooth, the stones on the landing dry. There was no sign even of a dissipating wake.

I scrambled up the hill, grabbing tufts of grass to speed my ascent. Only when I reached the top did I pause to catch my breath. I leaned against the inside of the ancient arch, periodically looking back at the loch and trying unsuccessfully to calm myself.

37

If Willie the postie was surprised by my dishevelled state when I entered his post office and asked about the possibility of making a transatlantic phone call, he didn't betray it. It was, after all, mere hours since he'd delivered the news of my father's death.

He explained that overseas calls were by radio only, and that the equipment was at the Big House.

'Thank you,' I said, putting my gloves back on.

'And where do you think you're going?' he demanded, angling his eyebrows fiercely.

'To the Big House,' I said.

He raised a hand. 'I'm afraid that's absolutely out of the question. The equipment is strictly for military use, no exceptions. It's not like a telephone box, you know. And anyway, you can't just go mucking about on the grounds of a battle school.'

'No. Of course not. I wasn't thinking.'

'You'll be sending a telegram then?'

I cast him an embarrassed look. 'I would, but I'm afraid my situation hasn't changed.'

'Ah,' he said, nodding. 'Under the circumstances, I think I can overlook the fee.'

'Thank you,' I said. 'That's very kind. I'll do my best to keep it short, but I'm afraid it might end up being rather long anyway.'

'I quite understand,' he said, preparing to take my dictation.

And I think he did understand, right up to the part where I asked the lawyer to please let me know what was involved in getting a divorce and whether I could do so from Scotland, and to please respond by either telegram or airmail, since I wished to settle both matters as quickly as possible.

Willie understood that part too, but it was a different type of understanding, one not tempered by empathy. His entire bearing hardened.

Despite the warnings, I couldn't help myself. I had to see Craig Gairbh.

I had no illusions about getting inside the Big House. I just wanted to lay eyes on the place. It was where Angus had lived before the war, and still spent his days. It was where he 'took' the game and fish so many villagers depended on to supplement their rations. It was where the Colonel had made such a nuisance of himself, all those years ago, causing the international scandal that eventually led to Ellis and Hank deciding we had no choice but to find the monster ourselves. It was the nucleus of everything.

There were no signs to direct me, although there were posts with holes in them where signs used to be, so I walked the periphery of the village until I found a dirt road that led into the forest. Because of my experience at the Cover, I took a moment to note where the sun was, as well as the relative positions of the hills, before winding my way in.

Ancient rhododendrons began dotting the side of the road, the tips of their droopy leaves pulled toward the earth by the weight of snow, but already bearing buds for the coming spring. In one clearing, a constellation of purple crocuses poked defiantly through the crusted ice.

About three quarters of a mile in, I caught my first glimpse of the house. I could see it only in bits and pieces, because the road was still twisting its way round and many of the trees between the house and me were coniferous. Still, I got an immediate sense of its scope.

I hurried round the bend to see more. The road grew wider and the thicket beside it disappeared, turning quite suddenly into a formal approach lined by hundred-year oaks. I stayed back, in the shadow of the woods.

I was no stranger to large houses, but this was enormous. From counting windows, I could see that the centre of the house had at least four main storeys, and the end towers even more. I could not begin to count the chimneys – I started at one end and lost track at sixteen, before I even reached the centre. Semicircular staircases with stone balustrades approached the main door from both sides, and another row of balustrades graced the roof's parapet.

This was no house. This was a castle.

The entire front garden – or what had been the front garden – was enclosed in barbed-wire fencing and crammed with row upon row of corrugated metal shacks. They looked like Anderson shelters, only much larger. An enormous stone fountain, dry of course, rose from the centre.

The fountain looked to be from the Baroque period, with three or four human forms kneeling under an enormous vessel. I crept up behind a large yew to get a better look, and tripped on an exposed root. I fell forward, catching myself on the tree's rough trunk. Only then did I see the sign nailed to it, directly above my hand. It was bright red and triangular, with a white skull and crossbones on top and a single word across the bottom:

MINEFIELD

I froze. My right foot was still partially on the root, leaving me precariously balanced. With my hand still firmly planted on the trunk, I looked down, studying my feet and the ground around me, wondering if there was any way at all of knowing where a mine might be buried.

A spurt of gunfire crackled in the distance, underscored by male voices: bellowing, primitive, and fierce.

I hadn't moved – was still standing with one foot teetering on the root and my hand braced against the trunk – when another round of gunfire went off, answered by a volley from a different, much closer location.

I think I screamed. I'm not sure. But certainly my careless attitude towards live ammunition had been replaced by sheer terror. Tracer bullets at night were one thing. Minefields and machine guns were quite another.

I was carrying my red gas mask case and wearing my red gloves, which would either make me visible enough that no one would shoot me accidentally, or else would make me an easy target.

Guided by sheer instinct, I twisted away from the tree and leapt toward the road in long strides. My feet landed in a thick carpet of leaves three times before I reached it, and each time I was sure I was going to be blown to smithereens.

When I found myself safely back on the road, I went completely still. I wondered if I'd been walking in a minefield the entire time, and how the hell I was going to escape.

As shots continued to ring out in the forest around me, my eyes lit on tyre tracks. I hopped into a rut and stayed carefully within it, placing each foot directly in front of the other. By the time I passed the last of the ancient rhododendrons, I was running flat out. My gas mask bounced behind me, hitting me in the back with every stride.

I stumbled out of the woods and onto the street, my legs pinwheeling as though someone had shoved me from behind. I went straight over the white painted kerb and crashed into the low stone wall beyond it.

I leaned against it, doubled over and wheezing, as a red cow with very long hair and even longer horns gazed placidly at me, chewing its cud.

Meg was standing by the end of the bar when I burst through the door and slammed it behind me.

'Maddie! Whatever's the matter?'

I peeled off my gloves, but my hands were shaking so hard I dropped them. When I leaned over to pick them up, my gas mask slipped off my shoulder and landed on the floor with a *thunk*.

'Leave them,' Meg said. 'Come and sit down.'

I left everything and wobbled over to the couch. I sat on the very edge and reached up to feel my hair, which was plastered to my forehead and neck.

Meg looked anxiously at the door. 'Why were you running? Is someone chasing you?'

I waved vigorously, still out of breath. 'No, no – it's nothing like that. Don't worry.'

She looked at the door one more time, then sat gingerly beside me.

'Then what is it?'

'Nothing,' I said.

'It's clearly *something*. You're all worked up. Wait here – I'll get a glass of water.'

'Please don't get up,' I said. 'What are you doing down here, anyway? You're not supposed to exert yourself.'

'I'm hardly exerting myself. I needed a change of scenery, so I brought down the crossword puzzles you gave me. Stay where you are. I'm fetching some water, and I'll have no arguments about it, either.'

I gulped it down noisily as soon as she handed it to me, not even lowering the glass when I had to pause for breath. When it was empty, I set it down and wiped my mouth with the back of my hand.

'Thank you,' I said, glancing over in embarrassment. I found Meg gazing at me with a combination of sympathy and sadness.

'Anna told me about your father,' she said quietly. 'I'm very sorry for your loss. It's perfectly natural to be rattled. You never know how you're going to react to news like that.'

'It's not my father,' I said. 'I don't care about my father.'

Meg watched me for almost a full minute. I realised how awful what I'd just said sounded, and wondered if she thought me heartless.

'Then what is it?' she enquired carefully.

I let out a desperate, nervous laugh. 'I'm not sure I should tell you.'

'Rest assured, I'll not be judging,' she said. 'I'm hardly in a position to cast stones.'

'You're going to think I'm crazy.'

'Well, I won't know until you tell me.'

I leaned in closer. 'I was attacked by the monster today.'

Meg's eyes widened. After a brief pause, she said, 'You were *what*?'

I threw myself against the back of the couch. 'I knew you'd think I was crazy! I didn't believe in any of this supernatural stuff before I came here. Then the Caonaig came for Anna's brother – there was never any doubt in Anna's mind that she'd come for Hugh, and she was right. And that damnable crow, signalling sorrow and chasing me into the Cover. And today, the monster – it rose straight out of the water and attacked me!'

Meg stared at me for several seconds, then got to her feet. 'I think we could both do with something a wee bit stronger.'

She poured two small whiskys and brought them over.

'*Slàinte*,' she said.

'Slàinte,' I said, clinking my glass against hers.

'All right, then,' she said. 'How about you go back to the beginning?'

I didn't know how far back she wanted me to go, so I started at the actual beginning, blurting out everything and barely pausing for breath. Everything, from how I felt nothing about my father's death because he had been completely indifferent to my existence, to my mother starving me for years, to her plans for fixing my nose and scrambling my frontal lobe, to the suicide attempt that I was supposed to foil, to discovering that Hank and Ellis had tossed a coin to see who had to marry me and now had abandoned me completely, to my belief that Ellis wasn't colour-blind after all, to realising I was crushingly in love with Angus, to my alarming experience at the bottom of the Water Gate, to sending a telegram to the lawyer asking how to go about getting a divorce and, finally, to wandering into a minefield because, for whatever reason, the Big House held some kind of gravitational pull I couldn't resist.

In the dead silence that followed, I realised what I'd done.

'Oh God,' I said, clapping my hands to my face.

'If you're talking about Angus, it's hardly a surprise,' Meg said. 'I've seen how you look at him.'

I turned away, panting through steepled fingers.

'And I've seen how he looks at you, too,' she added quietly.

My heart either skipped a beat or took an extra one.

I lowered my hands and turned back round. She was staring straight into my eyes.

'Go back a wee bit. Tell me exactly what happened at the water's edge.'

I told her again. 'And then, just as I was about to hit the water, it was like a boulder of air exploded from the surface, knocking me backwards. I know how crazy it sounds, but it's God's honest truth, even though I can't explain any of it.'

Meg nodded knowingly, solemnly. 'Aye. But I can. It wasn't the monster, Maddie. If it had been, it wouldn't have pushed you away. It would have dragged you in.'

I shook my head. 'But then what—'

'It was Màiri,' Meg said. 'She died three years ago today, at that very place. She entered your head and your heart to see if you'd be true to Angus, and when she saw that you would be, she pushed you to safety. Maddie, she gave you her blessing.'

38

In the space of one day, I'd gone from thinking that no one in the world had ever loved me to thinking that the man I was hopelessly in love with might feel the same way about me. It was more than just that, though – the ghostly intervention gave me hope that we were meant to be together. After the Caonaig, I was no longer inclined to ignore such a message.

Meg wanted to return to work that night, just to lend a hand, but Angus was having none of it. I had to agree – she'd only just had her stitches out, and I still caught her wincing when she thought no one was looking. Still, I was sorry she wasn't going to be there, because I felt in need of moral support.

A few minutes before six, when I took my place behind the bar, Angus came up beside me and laid a hand on mine. 'I heard about your father. I'm very sorry for your loss.'

'Thank you,' I said, looking up at him. 'And I, for yours.'

He nodded slowly, and that was it. He knew I knew everything.

As the evening wore on, I watched Angus's face, hoping for a sign that Meg's words were true. But he was understandably preoccupied, his expression unreadable.

It was clear that the local men also remembered the anniversary, for they placed their orders solemnly and with diffidence. The only chatter was at the tables of lumberjacks, some of whom had brought their fiancées.

At one point, when I was sprinting into the kitchen with a stack of empty plates, I ran straight into Angus. He caught my elbows to steady me.

'You all right?' he asked.

'Yes,' I said, in a pathetic attempt to sound casual. 'Not sure about the front of my dress though.'

He stared down at me, his eyes intense and unblinking. For the longest time, neither one of us moved.

When he finally stepped round me and returned to the front room, I dropped the stack of plates onto the table and leaned against it.

When the front door opened and closed for the last time, and Meg had gone to bed, I crept down the stairs as quietly as a cat.

I had prepared myself like a bride, brushing my hair until it was soft, rubbing scented lotion into my hands and elbows and donning a long white nightgown – modest, but with lace at the neck and on the ends of the sleeves.

The fire had been smoored, and cast but the faintest glow. The flagstone floor was cold beneath my feet, and I almost lost my nerve. I stood with both hands on the bar, gathering courage.

If I turned back, it would be like nothing had ever happened. If I kept going, I would be stepping into the great unknown.

Maddie, she gave you her blessing.

I slipped into the kitchen, and felt my way along the wall until I found one of the carved wooden doors that slid shut in front of his bed. In the darkness, I couldn't tell if they were open or closed. I let my fingers crawl along the wood until I reached the far edge.

The doors were open. I was standing right in front of him.

I found myself in a beam of blinding light, and jumped backward. When Angus saw it was me, he leaned the torch against the wall so it was aimed at the ceiling instead, then swung his legs round. He was wearing blue striped pyjama bottoms and an undershirt, just as he had on the night of our arrival.

'What's going on? Is everything all right?' he said, rubbing his eyes.

'Everything's fine,' I said, blinking quickly. The torch's glare had left two white spots in the centre of my vision.

'Then what is it?'

I dropped my gaze and bit my lip. After the better part of a minute, when the blind spots had mostly gone away, I forced myself to look up again. He was watching me with obvious concern.

'What is it, *m'eudail*?' he asked gently.

I steeled myself. 'Angus, there's something I want to . . . no, something I *need* to tell you. Something important.' I swallowed loudly and looked directly into his eyes. 'I know the situation is unusual and that under any other circumstances none of this would make sense, but nothing about our circumstances is normal, and I've come to realise that . . . that there are . . . that I have . . .' I clapped my hands over my mouth to stifle a cry. 'Oh God! I'm so sorry! I've never felt so stupid in all my life!'

In a flash, he was up and I was in his arms. 'Hush, *m'eudail*, you don't have to say a thing. I already know.'

'But how can you know if I can't even manage to tell you?' I sobbed.

·

'Because I just do,' he said. His heart went *thumpity-thumpity-thump*, inches from my ear.

Eventually he pulled back, keeping his hands on my shoulders. He stared into my eyes, and held my gaze until there was nothing on earth but his face. When he put his hands on my cheeks and leaned towards me, my legs almost abandoned me. I closed my eyes and let my lips part.

He kissed my forehead.

'*M'eudail*, you're grieving,' he said quietly. 'You're vulnerable. This is not the time for such things.'

I don't know how I made it upstairs. Certainly quickly, and certainly not gracefully, and when I finally reached my bed, I blubbered shamelessly, burying my face in the pillow.

There was a quiet knock on the door. Even though my sobs had subsided into quiet weeping, my ignominious retreat had certainly been loud enough to wake Meg.

'It's not locked,' I said.

The door opened, and the light of a candle cast long shadows at the far end of the room. Judging by its silhouette, the chair was almost as tall as the ceiling. I lay facing it, my knees folded nearly to my chest, my face and pillow wet with tears.

'Sorry I woke you up,' I mumbled.

'I'm not,' said Angus.

I jerked my head off the pillow and looked behind me. He was standing in the doorway, holding the candle.

'May I come in?'

I pulled myself upright, sliding backwards until I was against the headboard. I sniffed and wiped my face with shaking hands.

He set the candle on the dresser and crossed the floor to the bed.

'Forgive me,' he said.

I stared at him, trembling. Fresh tears rolled down my face.

He sat on the bed and ran a thumb across my cheek. I held my breath and closed my eyes.

'Forgive me,' he said again.

When I opened my eyes, I was looking directly into his.

'I was wrong, *mo run* – this is exactly the right time.'

He shifted closer and began kissing the tears from my cheeks in a slow, tender dance that moved from one side of my face to the other. Finally, when I thought I couldn't stand it any longer, he put his lips on mine.

They were warm and full and slightly parted, and I felt the quickness of his breath behind them. He kissed me over and over, with increasing urgency, his beard brushing against my skin. His hand slid down my neck and into my nightgown.

I gasped, and he stopped.

With his hand cupping my breast, he searched my face for a signal. It was a moment of excruciating sweetness, of torturous rapture, of exquisite need. It was unbearable.

I leaned forward, tugging at his shirt. He stood and pulled it over his head. I knelt on the bed, yanking at my nightgown.

'Wait,' he said, and this time I was the one who stopped.

He removed my nightgown, slowly, reverently.

I had never felt so exposed, yet I didn't want to cover myself. The candlelight flickered behind him, and his breathing grew even heavier as his eyes travelled my body, resting without shame on my breasts and hips.

'*Mo run geal og,*' he said. 'So beautiful.'

He untied his pyjamas and let them drop to the floor. I caught my breath. I obviously knew the anatomy, but other than statues, I'd never seen a naked man, never mind an aroused one. Angus seemed to sense that and paused, giving me a chance to look.

Finally, he knelt on the bed and put a hand behind my neck, supporting my head as he guided me backwards.

Moments later, when he was poised above me, he looked deep into my eyes and said, 'You're sure, *mo chridhe*? For this cannot be undone.'

'Yes,' I whispered. 'I am completely and absolutely sure.'

When he sank into me, I was so lost my body began to quake. I wrapped my arms and legs round him, holding on for dear life.

The next morning, it took me a moment to realise I wasn't dreaming. The candle had long since burned out, so we were in cave-like darkness, side by side, our naked bodies pressed together. He had one arm under my pillow and the other across me, his hand resting between my breasts. I lay very still, with my hands on his forearm. When he stirred, I clasped his hand to my heart and ran my fingers up his arm, marvelling at our different textures. Although he was still asleep, a pulsing nudge intensified until the length of him was pressed against my back.

I rolled over and pulled the sheets down, kissing his chest and tracing his scars with my lips and fingers. When I finally worked my way up to his mouth, he took my face in his hands and pressed his lips against mine, parting them so we shared the same breath. A moment later, he lifted me across him like I weighed nothing, setting me down so my knees were on either side of him. I put both hands on his abdomen to brace myself, more than a little shocked to find myself straddling him.

He reached up and ran his thumbs over my nipples. I sucked in my breath and almost didn't let it out again.

'Maddie, *mo chridhe*,' he said.

'Angus – oh my God,' I said in a broken voice. 'I don't know what to do.'

'You do, though. Let yourself come to me.'

I lowered my hips slowly, and stopped breathing altogether when I felt the tip of him pressing against me.

'Angus—'

'It's all right,' he said, stroking my face. '*Na stad*. I'm right here with you.'

He held himself steady while I took him into me, slowly, slowly, sliding down until he was buried so deep our hips met, then lifting myself up until I was afraid I might lose him, then sinking back down until we were joined again. I leaned forward and put my hands on either side of his head, breathing hard into the pillow beside his face.

He had his hands on my waist, and his hips rose a little higher each time I sank down, pushing himself deeper and staying there longer. I felt his blood pounding, as if our nerve endings had merged.

My legs were shaking violently, and just when I thought I was going to lose control entirely, he reached up and clasped my hands, intertwining our fingers, and guaranteed it.

The contractions overwhelmed me, so unexpected and intense I cried out, and he held my face, covering my mouth with his, pressing into me, faster, more urgently. When I felt his own surrender, I was shot through with an ecstasy so intense I thought my heart might actually stop.

After, as we lay in each other's arms, he stroked my hair and back. My face was buried in his neck, and every breath I took was suffused with his scent.

'Well,' he said, kissing me. 'I'm afraid that while I'd love to stay here for ever, duty calls.'

I caught his wrist. 'I love you, Angus Grant. With all my heart, I love you.'

He leaned over and gave me a long, lingering kiss.

'And I, you, *mo chridhe*.'

39

Meg knew exactly what had happened the second she laid eyes on me. She said nothing, just smiled in a knowing manner. It didn't help that I blushed and looked at the ground, or that I was wearing a turban because I hadn't set my hair.

I finished the upstairs chores at about the same time Anna finished the downstairs, and the three of us wound up round the kitchen table having a *strupag*.

Anna had spent the last few afternoons clearing rocks from the tattie beds at the croft, and was suffering from a stiff back.

'It's the buckets of stones,' she explained. 'They weigh more than buckets of milk, and you're always picking them up and putting them down, and then leaning over to collect even more . . . It's murder on the back, I tell you. I'll look like Rhona when all is said and done.'

'Of course you won't,' I said, although not as convincingly as I wished. Crofting sounded like a very hard life indeed.

'Stand up and lean over the table,' Meg said. 'I'll work those knots out for you.'

Meg stood behind her and massaged Anna's back, digging her thumbs into the areas just above Anna's hips.

'I'll come and help with the stones,' said Meg. 'Many hands make light work.'

'I should think not,' Anna said with righteous indignation.

'Dr McLean has not cleared you for any type of work yet, especially not clearing rocks.'

'Well, I can't just do nothing, can I?' said Meg. 'I'm sick to death of Maddie's crossword puzzles and their fiendish American spelling – why would anyone put an *e* in whisky, for goodness' sake? Anyway, Dr McLean is going to clear me for work any day now, which probably means I'm already perfectly capable.'

'Maybe I can help clear stones,' I said.

Anna and Meg looked at me, deadpan. A couple of seconds later, they burst out laughing.

'And get your hands dirty?' Meg practically crowed.

'I get my hands dirty all the time!'

'I didn't see you offering to help clean the range this morning,' said Anna.

'You didn't ask,' I said. 'And for your information, I was upstairs scrubbing the toilet. I didn't see you offer with that, either.'

'Oh go on,' said Anna. 'We're just having a bit of fun.'

'I know that!' I said, laughing. 'Don't be silly!'

Anna narrowed her eyes and looked me up and down. 'You're in a very good mood this morning . . .'

The front door opened, and after a few seconds closed again. Anna glanced at the clock.

'That'll be Willie with the post,' she said in a panic. 'And here I am all covered with soot and oven blacking!'

'Get a cloth and clean yourself up,' said Meg. 'I'll stall him.'

Willie was expected to pop the question at any moment, having already asked permission from Anna's father.

It was a mystery to me what the attraction was – it was easy to see why Willie was attracted to Anna, but what did Anna see in Willie? He had always struck me as an angry, orange gnome who was quick to judge and was also a good twenty years older than she was, but apparently she was madly in love with him. I supposed there was no accounting for Cupid's aim. I felt sorry for poor one-legged George, though.

Anna ran to the sink and began scrubbing her face. I followed to make sure she didn't miss a spot.

Meg returned, pale as beeswax.

'It's not Willie,' she said.

'Then who . . .?' I asked.

Meg looked despondently at me, and I knew.

'Dear God in heaven,' I said.

Meg stepped forward and squeezed my hands. 'He's not asked for you yet – when he does, I'll tell him you've gone walking.'

'No,' I said quietly. 'I'll go out. There's no point in delaying the inevitable.'

'What are you going to tell him?' Meg asked.

'I have no idea.'

'At the very least, wait until Angus comes back.'

I shook my head.

Meg watched me for a beat, then nodded. 'All right, but I'll be standing here with the heaviest saucepan we have, should you find yourself in need of assistance.'

I pulled my apron over my head and hung it on a peg. Then I walked through to the front room, my legs seeming to move of their own accord.

Ellis and Hank were settled by the fire in their usual places, as though they'd never been gone at all. Ellis sat on the couch with his back to me, and Hank sat in one of the wing chairs. He stood at once.

'Maddie, darling girl!' he said, raising his arms in welcome. When I didn't respond, he dropped them and frowned. 'What's the matter? You look like you've seen a ghost.'

'I feel rather as though I have. What are you doing here?'

Ellis shifted round to face me, draping his arm across the

back of the couch. 'That's an odd question. We're staying here, of course.'

'Well, no, in fact, you haven't been.'

'You knew we were going away,' said Ellis.

'You said you'd be gone a few days,' I said. 'It's been two weeks.'

'Thirteen days,' said Hank. 'But who's counting?'

'I was,' I said. 'I didn't think you were coming back.'

'Oh dear – you didn't think I'd abandoned you again, did you?' said Ellis. He raised an eyebrow and turned to Hank, adding, 'I told you she has quite an imagination.'

My knees buckled. A moment later, Hank and Ellis were steering me towards the couch.

'What's the matter? Are you having an episode?' said Ellis.

'Get her a glass of water,' said Hank.

'I can't,' Ellis replied. 'There's no one behind the bar.'

'Then get a glass and find a sink!'

'You mean in the kitchen? What if the hag's in there?'

'Then use the bathroom, for Christ's sake!'

Ellis glanced at Hank in a wounded manner, then went behind the bar for a glass. After pausing at the door to the kitchen, he changed his mind and went upstairs.

Hank perched on the low table in front of me. He leaned forward, resting his forearms on his thighs.

'Darling girl – what's going on? Talk to me.'

'There's nothing going on,' I said, although my voice betrayed me.

'It's not nothing, obviously. And if you don't tell me what's going on, he's going to think you're having an episode.'

I couldn't help laughing. 'He always thinks I'm having an episode. I don't care any more.'

'You don't mean that,' said Hank.

'Oh, but I do.'

'Fuck,' Hank said. He glanced quickly at the stairwell. 'Look, I think you should know that Ellis has been making enquiries. Actually, more than enquiries. Arrangements.'

'So, he's really going to try to have me locked up, is he?'

'No, he's going to have you treated.'

I was shocked into momentary silence.

'Treated?' I asked in a hollow voice, although of course I already knew.

'Given the severity of your symptoms, the physician he spoke to thought a permanent cure was the best solution. You wouldn't even have to stay in the hospital.'

You'll be so much happier, my mother had said. *An easy thing. In and out in an hour.*

'And what did Ellis say to the doctor to make him think that?'

'Well, for starters, that you flushed your medication—'

'I flushed the pills because Ellis was eating them hand over fist. I've had one pill in my life. *One. Pill.* He's always been the one who took them. Hank, you *know* that.'

'You've lost all sense of social structure, you're showing signs of paranoia—'

'*Paranoia?* Really, Hank?'

'—and you've begun having delusions.'

I stared at him and began nodding. 'So that's what this is really about.'

'What?'

'As if you don't know. I'm sending a telegram to the Colonel this very minute.'

'Saying what?' Hank asked.

'That Ellis isn't colour-blind! That he lied to get out of service!'

Hank went slack-jawed. 'Maddie, my God! Of course he's not faking it. That's a terrible thing to say!'

'Oh, please,' I said. 'How stupid do you think I am? You obviously planned it together, finding conveniently invisible ailments to keep you out of the war.'

'What are you talking about?'

'Flat-footed? Please.'

Hank sputtered in outrage. 'I *am* flat-footed. I've been wearing custom shoes my entire life!'

'You're each as bad as the other. I've had it.' I stood up.

'Maddie, stop—'

He said it with enough conviction that I did.

'Don't do it,' he said.

'Why? There will be no point in having me treated once everyone knows the truth.'

'Because it's *not* the truth, and this is exactly the type of rash behaviour Ellis is worried about. You get something in your head, and then you act on it without any regard for consequence, no matter who it damages. If you send a telegram to the Colonel, Ellis will just have you treated sooner rather than later – it's all been arranged, he only has to make a phone call – and then for good measure, he'll probably have Blackbeard hauled off as well.'

'Angus? Why?'

'Because of exactly that. The unsuitable familiarity. Ellis is sure he's been taking advantage of you, so he stopped by the courthouse to check the penalty for poaching. It's two years in prison per offence, by the way.'

I sat back down, slowly.

'So if it's a phone call away and there's nothing I can do, why are you even telling me?' I asked.

Hank sighed. 'I don't know. I guess because it *is* a phone call away. To warn you, I suppose, so you can try not to set him off. I was initially against the whole idea, but I have to be honest – Maddie, you're scaring me. Do you realise what you just accused me of? What you just accused Ellis of? It's like you consciously came up with the one thing that would hurt us the most. That's not like you. The Maddie I know wouldn't do that.'

Ellis came thumping back downstairs.

'Here,' he said, pressing a glass of water into my hands.

I pushed it back at him, spilling some onto his trousers.

He set the glass on the table and gazed at me with exaggerated concern.

'Darling, you look rattled. Do you need a pill? I picked some up while we were gone. Found a very nice doctor, top of his field.'

And then I knew it was true. I could see it running behind his eyes like a ticker tape – the false and self-serving concern that he would eventually convince himself was genuine, his enormous and growing satisfaction that I was, indeed, acting hysterically, along with his rewriting of history, so that he'd only ever done what was necessary for my happiness, because it was all he'd ever cared about—

It was like he was channelling my mother. I realised how much now hinged on my behaviour, and did my best to channel her too.

'No, I just have a bit of a stomach bug,' I said. 'I've been queasy all day. If you'll excuse me, I think I'll go lie down for a bit.'

'Do you want me to come with you?' he asked, using the same unctuous tone.

'No. I'm sure I'll be fine.'

'Maddie?' he asked. 'Were you in the kitchen just now, when we came back?'

'Yes,' I said, forcing a brief smile. 'I was looking for something to settle my stomach.'

'Ah,' he said, nodding. 'Of course.'

'I'll come down at seven, shall I?'

'Only if you feel up to it,' he said. 'Try to get some rest, darling.'

I rose in as dignified a manner as I could, and somehow
made it up the stairs.

Meg showed up within minutes.

I opened the door, then collapsed face-down on my bed.

'What's going on?' she said, closing the door. 'You should
have spoken louder. We couldn't hear a thing.'

'Bolt that, please,' I said.

She locked the door and sat beside me. 'What happened?
Did you tell him you were ending it?'

'No.'

'Why not?'

'Because I can't,' I said miserably. 'I have to reconcile with
Ellis, or at least pretend to.'

Meg jumped off the bed and spun angrily towards me. '*What?*
How could you? Do you have any idea what this will do to
Angus? Does he mean that little to you?'

'No, he means that much to me!' I whisper-shouted. 'And if
I ever do have a chance at a future with him, I'd like my brain
intact!'

Meg stared at me for a while, then sat back down.

'I don't think I follow,' she said.

'Do you remember when I told you my mother wanted me
to have a lobotomy?'

'Yes,' she said doubtfully.

'Do you know what a lobotomy is?'

'No, not exactly.'

'They put a tiny spatula up through your eye socket into
the front part of your brain and then twirl it around a bit –
and that's exactly what my husband is going to have done to
me the next time I do anything to upset him.'

Her mouth opened in horror. 'But surely he can't do that!'

'It appears he can, since he's got it all arranged. I was diagnosed with a nervous ailment a few years ago, and my mother was entirely nuts. Ellis sold the doctor on the idea without the doctor ever laying eyes on me. All Ellis has to do is make a phone call, and they'll come cart me off.'

'Dear Lord in heaven,' said Meg. She got up and walked stiffly to the chair.

'And you didn't tell him you asked about a divorce . . .'

'No, thank goodness. If I had, the ambulance would already be on its way.'

'And he doesn't know about you and Angus . . .'

'He suspects something, but certainly not the full extent of it.'

She slapped the arms of the chair, startling me. 'Then *why*?'

'Money, of course,' I said. 'And the *really* stupid thing is that I brought all of this on myself.'

'No,' she said, frowning. 'How could you have?'

'I was stupid enough to let him know that I don't believe he's colour-blind. If I tell his father, he'll cut him off without a penny. So he's come up with a plan that lets him dismiss anything I say as crazy talk – and, of course, if I were ever foolish enough to open my mouth, he'd make the phone call and take care of the problem. The only thing I can do is try not to upset him until I figure something out.'

'No, *this* is what we're going to do,' Meg said firmly. 'We're going to get you out of here. Anna's family will have you, I'm sure of that. Angus will spirit you over later.'

'It wouldn't work. He'd find me.'

'We'll make sure he doesn't.'

'He'd find me and have the rest of you arrested for kidnapping. And, of course, I'd be delivered to a hospital in the back of an ambulance and come back drooling. Drooling, but ever so obedient.'

'But you can't just sit about waiting for it to happen!' Meg said angrily. 'It makes no sense!'

'You don't understand. *He'd find me.* There's too much money involved – his own family's fortune is big, but sooner or later he's going to find out that *my* father is dead, and there's an *obscene* amount of money at stake there.'

Meg fell quiet for long enough that I finally turned back to her. Her pale eyes bored through me. She sighed and turned away from me, staring into the empty grate.

She obviously knew there was more to it, but what could I tell her? That there was nothing anyone could do to save me that wouldn't land Angus in prison for life? That his fate lay in the hands of my volatile, feckless husband, and in my attempts to pacify him?

After more than a minute, she began tapping a finger against her chin.

'Well,' she said, 'it's just possible there's another way.'

For the first time since flopping on the bed, I pulled myself upright.

'What? What is it?'

'Fiddlehead stew is a delicacy around here, very tasty indeed, especially with a few drops of malt vinegar. Of course, you have to be very careful not to cook it too late in the season or you risk bracken poisoning . . .'

Her eyes cut sideways at me, to see if I was following.

'But I suppose if the shoots were just a *little* bit iffy – maybe a week or two older than someone might usually use them, an inexperienced cook might decide they were still safe. And then somebody else might see the pot boiling, and – knowing that it was too late in the season to be cooking fiddleheads – come to the conclusion that someone was boiling up a batch of insecticide for the vegetable garden. And to be helpful, she might throw in a few rhubarb leaves.'

I blinked a few times.

'I don't think I can do that,' I finally said.

'Do what?'

'Kill him,' I whispered.

'Heavens no,' Meg said sternly. 'It would be an unfortunate case of kidney failure, a tragic misunderstanding.'

'Even if we make this . . . mistake,' I said in a strained voice, 'Angus is still going to think I betrayed him. At least until I figure something out.'

'I don't see how that's to be avoided, since you won't hear of being removed from the situation. If you won't let him do anything to protect you, we certainly can't tell him – if he thought for a moment you were being threatened, he'd take matters into his own hands, and then we'd have a body to dispose of, and not from anything nearly as neat and tidy as kidney failure. I can't guarantee that he won't take matters into his own hands anyway.'

'What if he stops loving me in the meantime?'

'I don't imagine you have to worry about that,' Meg said. 'But I also don't see that you have much choice, since you won't be talked out of doing nothing. Seeing you with your husband *will* crush him – that much I know.'

40

I could barely breathe when I descended the stairs that night, and as I crossed the small distance to the nook by the fire, I felt like I was climbing the platform to a guillotine. I wondered if Hank had filled Ellis in about our chat by the fire and my ill-advised accusations. I tried to convince myself that he wouldn't say anything – he knew what was at stake. He couldn't possibly hate me that much, even if it turned out he was flat-footed.

I tried to read Hank's face as I approached the couch, but he was giving nothing away. Ellis patted the cushion next to him.

'Sit, darling! I was beginning to wonder if you'd show up.'

'I'm sorry about earlier,' I said, flashing him a quick, forced smile before taking my seat. 'I'm sure that wasn't the welcome you were hoping for.'

'Don't be silly,' Ellis said. 'I should have sent word that we were going to be staying away longer. Is your stomach any better?'

'A bit.'

My attempt at an about-face probably would have been more convincing if I'd asked him about the trip and what they'd discovered about the monster, but I knew enough about what else they'd been up to that the conversation would have required a level of artifice I couldn't possibly sustain. For the moment,

I was just going to have to blame my lack of curiosity on an upset stomach.

Angus was watching the three of us intently, his face an inscrutable mask. I couldn't look directly at him – didn't want to give Ellis any reason to notice him at all – but in my peripheral vision I saw the way he clunked glasses down on the bar, the way he grimly went about his business.

I couldn't imagine what he thought. He must have known that things weren't as they seemed, but he also must have wondered why I didn't just tell him what was going on. I wanted to, desperately, but I was as good as shackled. Either he'd go to prison for life, or he'd kill Ellis and hang for it.

To a man, the locals were as stony and speechless as Angus, and when Willie the postie came in, he took his seat without so much as a glance in our direction – it was as though Hank and Ellis had never been gone, and the last thirteen days hadn't happened.

I was careful to avoid eye contact with the lumberjacks, who were clearly baffled at seeing me back in my old role as Mrs Hyde. I sent up a silent prayer that none of them would let on that I'd been working behind the bar, because I knew with absolute certainty that if anything would send Ellis off to the phone booth, that was it.

Fortunately, the lumberjacks were much more concerned with Meg than with anything that was happening by the fire. Earlier in the afternoon, Dr McLean had cleared her for work at the inn, although she could not yet return to the sawmill. She was painfully thin and moved carefully, but she'd made herself up and donned a bright dress, determined to carry on as usual. From the right, she was as gorgeous and perfect as ever. From the left – well, seeing her from the left made me want to cry.

'Shame about her face,' said Hank, lighting a cigarette. 'She was a real looker.'

'Can't say I noticed,' said Ellis. 'But she's definitely a wreck now.'

I wondered if the night he'd tried to break down my door ever crossed his mind, or if he had any idea what he'd planned to do if he'd succeeded.

When Meg set our plates in front of us, Ellis asked, 'Is this beef?'

'Venison,' she replied.

Ellis shot Hank a gleeful look.

I hated him. Oh, how I hated him. It seethed inside my belly like a squirming snake.

A quarter of an hour later, an old man in a ragged uniform stumbled in and announced with a drunken flourish that he'd just seen the monster.

Willie snorted. 'Here we go again,' he said.

'Are you doubting me, then?' the man asked incredulously.

'Oh, heavens no. What possible reason would we have to doubt you?' said Ian Mackintosh. Chortles ran down the length of the bar.

'Well, if that's how it's going to be, I'll just take my custom elsewhere.'

'You'll be walking the two and a half miles to the Clansman, will you?' said another.

'Well, I'll not be staying where I'm being insulted, that's for certain!'

Willie's orange eyebrows shot up. 'You'll be lucky to make it home, from the looks of it.'

The old man harrumphed and turned to leave, staggering towards the door.

Ellis and Hank exchanged glances. Ellis leapt up and rushed over.

'Excuse me, sir,' he said, touching the old man's elbow, 'I

couldn't help overhearing. Would you care to join us? We'd be delighted to hear about your experience.'

The man ran his rheumy eyes over Ellis, spent a moment concentrating and weaving, then poked him in the chest.

'I know you. You're the . . . I know who you are,' he said, struggling to form the words. 'I heard you were in town. Do you know, I met your old man. Nice chap. Very generous, if I recall.'

'Yes, that runs in the family,' Ellis said brightly. 'Do come sit.' He swept an arm towards the fireplace, as though inviting the old man into our drawing room.

'Well, I don't mind if I do,' said the man.

'Bartender?' Ellis said, snapping his fingers over his head. 'Bring the gentleman whatever he wants.'

I cringed. I could only imagine Angus's reaction, and it took every ounce of my self-control not to look.

Ellis took the old man's arm and parked him in the chair beside Hank. After introducing the three of us, he took a seat and leaned forward, rubbing his hands together. 'So, enough about us. Tell us about you.'

'The name's Roddie McDonald,' he said. 'And I should have known better than to say anything in a room full of sceptics.' He cast a disparaging look back at the bar, then leaned in to confide. 'This isn't the first time I've seen the monster, you know. I told your father about the other time. And very grateful, he was.' He nodded knowingly. 'Your father . . . he was a colonel, wasn't he? How is the old devil? He was in the Great War, like me . . . only now we're supposed to call it World War One.' He looked down at himself. 'This uniform . . . I wore it in the Battle of Liège, you know. It's the Home Guard for me, this time round. Too old, they say . . .' He looked directly at me, cupped a hand round his mouth and said in a loud, wet whisper, 'Just shows what they know. I'm as much of a tiger as I ever was.'

He winked, and like a scene from a *comédie grotesque*, Hank and Ellis threw their heads back and howled. Roddie looked alarmed, then just confused, and then he joined in, exposing rotting teeth and the gaps between them. I shrank into my seat.

'I'll just bet you are. Can't keep a good man down!' said Hank. He stopped laughing and cleared his throat. 'Now, start at the beginning and tell us everything.'

Although it was perfectly obvious that Roddie had come to the inn with financial gain in mind, I sensed immediately that something more was going on. He claimed to have seen the monster at the Water Gate, which should have upset Hank and Ellis since that was exactly where they'd been setting up shop, but they displayed not so much as a ripple of displeasure. Instead, they were attentive and encouraging, dazzling in their conviviality. I imagined them in tuxedos, holding court in some mansion on Rittenhouse Square.

Roddie clearly relished the audience, making wild expressions, inflecting dramatically and illustrating with his hands. 'Then, with no warning at all, the surface began to boil and churn, and suddenly the neck and head rose straight out of the water, not fifty yards away!' Roddie shook his head in wonder. 'Oh, it was a sight to behold . . .'

'The neck was long and curved, was it not?' said Ellis.

'Oh, aye,' said Roddie, nodding. 'Like a swan's. Only much, much larger. And its eyes—'

'Were they prominent?' Hank asked. 'Round and dark? Like a creature of the deep?'

'Oh aye,' Roddie said, nodding again. 'It had a fearsome look about it, like it wouldn't think twice about carrying you off.'

'How big was the fin on its back?' asked Ellis.

Roddie cackled and slapped his thigh. 'And how were you knowing it had a fin?'

'We've been doing some research,' Ellis said, glancing at Hank, and I suddenly understood. Interviewing doctors and visiting the courthouse was not all they'd been up to while they were away.

'Indeed, it did have a fin, and that alone was at least four feet long . . .'

In due course, Roddie confirmed that the monster's body was 'dark olive, with cygnet brown on the flanks, and a sort of speckling on the belly.' He'd gone from claiming he'd seen the head and neck of the beast from a distance of fifty yards to describing its whole body.

'Excuse me, darling,' I said. 'I think I'm going to head up now.'

Ellis looked at me with surprise. I couldn't remember the last time I'd called him 'darling,' and was sure he couldn't either. It was all I could do to force the word past my lips.

'But you haven't touched your dinner,' he said.

'I'm sorry,' I said. 'I'm still a little queasy. I'm sure I'll feel better after a good night's sleep.'

'Of course,' he said, rising. 'I'll walk you up.'

'No, please stay.' I laid a hand on his arm. 'This is important. Get as many details as you can. The sooner you flush the beast out, the sooner we can go home, and then everything can get back to normal.'

He watched with a curious expression as I bade goodnight to Roddie and Hank, and then continued to watch as I rounded the couch and headed for the stairwell.

He was not the only one watching. I nearly crumbled under the weight of Angus's scrutiny.

As soon as I closed the door, I threw myself on the bed. The scent of Angus lingered on my pillow. I buried my face in it and cried.

Hank and Ellis either had built a model or were planning to, and because of the description they'd coaxed out of Roddie, I knew exactly what it would look like. If they'd already built it, they would obtain their footage in a matter of days, and arrange to go home. But first, Ellis would have my brain scrambled, because he would be returning triumphant, with clear footage that confirmed the Colonel's pictures.

Father, son and bank account would be reunited, and Ellis would not let anything on earth get in the way of that – especially something of as little consequence as me.

41

I spent the night tossing and thrashing, twisting the quilts until they were a tangled pile. Every time the chimney whistled or the window rattled – every time I heard anything at all – I was sure Angus was coming to me, and then what would I do? Tell him everything, and hope to God he'd come up with a solution that hadn't occurred to me? Or just hope to God that what I told him wouldn't make him go straight down the hall and murder Ellis?

Eventually, I couldn't stand it any more and snuck down to the kitchen, feeling my way along the wooden doors of his bed until I reached the seam where they met. He'd shut himself in.

I leaned my forehead against the crack, thinking that he must know I was there – I felt his presence behind the doors as strongly as I felt the heart beating in my own chest, and even if he didn't sense me in the same way, surely he'd heard the shushing of my fingers running along the wooden panels, or the tiny clicks as the doors pushed against their tracks under the weight of my head.

If he did know I was there, he gave no indication. It was just as well, I told myself. Nothing could save me, and there was nothing I could do to Angus but harm him. I pressed my lips against the wooden door in a silent kiss, and crept back upstairs.

* * *

I heard Ellis and Hank talking downstairs the moment I stepped out of my room, and took a few breaths, steeling myself.

Being my mother's daughter, placating them should have come easily even if it was the last thing I wanted to do. Instead, I felt nauseated, lethargic, numb. It was as though my brain had already been compromised and nobody had bothered to tell me. I wondered what the procedure was like, and if I would retain any memories afterwards. I wondered if I would be able to form new ones.

Anna was sitting by the fire, polishing a full set of silverware that was laid out on a length of felt. She glanced up when I passed, making brief eye contact, and I wondered what Meg had told her.

'Good morning, my dear,' said Ellis, standing and pulling out a chair.

'Good morning, darling,' I said.

When I uttered the endearment, a flash of surprise crossed Ellis's face, just as it had the night before. Hank looked up and said nothing. His empty expression terrified me.

'You're obviously feeling better,' Ellis said, sitting back down. 'You look like Rita Hayworth going on safari. Got plans?'

'Yes,' I said, smoothing my dungarees over my thighs as though they were made of the finest silk. 'I thought I'd come with you today.'

'Really? Why?'

'Because I haven't seen you in ages,' I said. 'I've missed you.'

Hank and Ellis exchanged glances.

'This is probably not the best day for you to come along,' Ellis said.

'A girl could take that the wrong way, you know,' I said. 'I promise I won't make you waste any film.'

'The weather's terrible,' Hank said.

'He's right,' said Ellis. 'Have you seen what it's doing outside? The sky is grey as far as the eye can see. No chance of it clearing up.'

Either they were ready to mount the hoax, or Ellis had already pulled the trigger and the ambulance was on its way.

Angus walked out from the kitchen, saw me at the table with Hank and Ellis and spun on his heel with a disdainful bark.

Ellis stared after him. 'I honestly think he's the most unpleasant man I've ever met.'

Meg poked her head out from the kitchen. 'Will the three of you be joining us for dinner tonight? Only we're having a fine stew, and we've some proper bread for once.'

'Don't we always join you for dinner?' Hank asked with an amused smirk.

Ellis rolled his eyes and shook his head.

'Yes – when you're here, that is,' said Meg, 'but this is a local speciality and we've only the one good loaf for dipping – fluffy and white, and baked just this morning. There won't be anywhere near enough for everyone. Come down early, or I'll bring it up, because the rest will be getting beetroot sandwiches on National Loaf.'

'Why the special treatment?' asked Hank.

'Think of it as a welcome back,' she said, before disappearing.

'I think that lumberjack may have knocked a screw loose,' said Hank.

Ellis laughed. 'I think she always had a screw loose.'

A local speciality.

I wish I could say I dismissed the thought out of hand, but if my suspicions were correct, Meg was cooking up, quite literally, the only solution to my problem.

Could I let her? Could I live with myself?

I wondered if Rhona and Mhàthair were out foraging, or if they were already in the kitchen.

Hank and Ellis had just begun to gather their things when the front door opened and Willie the postie came in. He walked over to the fire.

'Good morning,' he said to Anna. 'It's a right *dreich* day.'

'Aye, that it is. I wish I could spend the whole of it by the fire,' she said, sighing. 'But the fields don't plough themselves.'

'You canna plough today – you'll be *drookit*!' Although he assumed an angry face, I knew enough about his feelings for Anna to recognise this as a display of affection.

'I've a raincoat. If I get too wet, I'll go in.'

'Make sure that you do,' he said, nodding sternly. 'I've some letters for your guests. Well, a letter and a telegram, anyway.'

'They're right over there,' Anna said, tilting her head at us as though Willie wouldn't otherwise find us.

'And which one of you is Mr Boyd?' he said, coming to the table.

Hank held out his hand, and Willie slapped a letter into it.

Even if the handwriting hadn't been impeccable, and even if it didn't still carry the faintest hint of Soir de Paris, the pale lavender of the Basildon Bond envelope would have given her away.

'Oh dear. It looks like my little songbird has finally tracked me down,' Hank said. He slid a knife beneath the flap. 'Probably begging me to come home. Well, it won't be long now, and then I suppose I'll have to slide a ring on that pretty little du Pont finger of hers.'

As Hank pulled out Violet's letter, Willie handed me the telegram. He held my gaze for long enough that I knew he was trying to tell me something. I took it with great reluctance.

'Well, go on, open it,' said Ellis.

I was motionless, clutching the telegram. I hadn't thought the situation could get any worse, but apparently I was wrong. Ellis was about to find out that my father was dead, and also that I'd asked about getting a divorce.

Hank unfolded his letter and began reading.

'Well, if you're not going to, I will,' said Ellis, snatching the telegram from my hands.

I covered my eyes. There were a few seconds of silence while they both read.

'What the hell? Your father died?' said Ellis. 'Why didn't you say anything?'

'Oh my God,' said Hank in a hollow voice.

'Oh my God!' shouted Ellis, slapping the table. 'Holy shit, Maddie. We're richer than Croesus. We're richer than Hank! But only because you're not a boy, and thank God we don't have a boy, or we'd have had to name him after your grand-father, surname and all, just to access the interest, and then the whole damned thing would have gone to the kid on his twenty-first birthday. But it seems your grandfather wasn't looking quite far enough ahead. Ha! You outwitted a robber baron, my brilliant, barren princess. Now we can buy our own house on Rittenhouse Square – the Colonel be damned!'

'She's left me,' Hank said quietly. 'She's fucking well left me . . .'

I peeked through my hands. Hank was pallid, gaunt. Ellis was leaping around the room like an idiotic leprechaun. He'd left the telegram on the table. I picked it up and read it.

He was right. I got everything free and clear, but only because I was the sole heir. If there had been a male anywhere in the picture I would never have seen a cent, unless the male in question was my own son, in which case I would have been destitute the moment he came of age. The lawyer suggested we meet in person once I got back to the States, but there was no mention at all of a divorce. I realised that was what Willie was trying to tell me – that the telegram was safe to read in front of my husband.

I set the telegram on the table and looked up. Hank had me locked in his gaze. He looked puzzled. His eyes were wet.

'She's dumped me, Maddie,' he said, shaking his head. 'She's going to marry Freddie. I don't understand. How could she do this to me?' His expression switched abruptly, and he slammed the table. 'Freddie! Damned Freddie! This must have been his plan all along! He wanted me out of the way so he could steal Violet out from under me! I'll kill him, Ellis – I swear, I'll kill him!'

He leapt up from the table as well, and suddenly Ellis was in front of him holding him by the shoulders.

'No, you won't kill him,' Ellis said calmly and slowly. 'We're going to get our footage, and then we're going to go home, and then we'll be world famous, and then you'll steal her back. That's what we're going to do.'

Hank stared into Ellis's eyes for a long time, huffing and puffing like an enraged bull.

'Let's get the hell on with it then,' he said.

'If you put it that way, I suppose I don't have much choice, although I was enjoying a moment with my lovely, rich wife,' said Ellis. He put his coat on, then kissed me on the cheek. 'Goodbye, my gorgeous golden goose. See you at dinner.'

When the door shut behind them, I was too stunned to move. Apparently so was Anna, who sat on the couch holding a serving spoon in one hand and a polishing cloth in the other.

Meg came through from the back, shaking her head in disgust. She went to the window and peered out at an angle, watching them walk away.

42

See you at dinner, he'd said.

I stayed at the table grappling with the concept, trying to parse it into something that wasn't cold-blooded murder. I tried to look at it from a purely rational point of view, as simply having to make a choice between organs – my brain or his kidneys. But it wasn't just his kidneys. It was his life.

I tried to look at it as self-defence, but it wasn't. If I allowed it to happen, it would be an execution, and a pre-emptive one at that, because he had yet to commit the crime.

I couldn't do it. Despite everything I stood to lose, I just couldn't sit by and watch him be poisoned.

I had only just come to that conclusion when the door burst open, hitting the wall behind it.

Two policemen strode in. A dark paddywagon was parked in the street beyond them, and through the rain, I made out the words INVERNESS-SHIRE CONSTABULARY painted on its side.

These were no Bob the bobbies – their uniforms were crisp navy with satin stripes running down the sides of their trousers, their pointed helmets emblazoned with silver insignia. Truncheons and handcuffs hung from their black belts, and when they came to a stop, water rolled off their slick uniforms, forming puddles around their heavy boots.

'Good morning, ladies,' said the taller one, nodding at us.

I almost couldn't breathe. Ellis had done it. He'd actually done it.

Was it because he hadn't liked the way Angus looked at us the night before? Had I not been convincing enough in my role as doting wife? Perhaps he'd returned from the trip already determined, and there was nothing I could have done anyway.

'And how can I help you gentlemen?' Meg asked.

I had to warn Angus, couldn't believe that I hadn't already—

'We're looking for Angus Duncan Grant,' said one of them. 'I believe he resides here?'

'He does for the moment. And what are you wanting with him?' asked Meg.

'Just a quick word is all.'

He sounded so pleasant, so polite, so matter-of-fact. It was hard to believe he was about to destroy Angus's life.

'I'll let him know you're here,' said Meg.

I stared after her as she went into the kitchen, and when I jerked back round, both policemen were watching me. I was sure they'd seen the panic in my eyes.

'Good morning, officers,' said Angus, coming around the front of the bar and sitting on one of the tall stools. 'I hear you'd like a word?'

Conall came with him, flopping down at his feet. The dog looked relaxed, but his eyes darted.

'Mr Grant—'

'That's Captain Grant,' Anna said, from over by the fire.

The policeman nodded at her, then looked back at Angus. 'Captain Grant, my name is Inspector Chisholm, and this is Sergeant MacDougall. We've had a report up at the courthouse about someone poaching on the grounds at Craig Gairbh.'

'I'm afraid I wouldn't know anything about that,' said Angus.

'The report named you as the perpetrator,' said Inspector Chisholm, 'and a quick summary of the evidence seems to suggest it's true. We took a wee stroll around the property, and couldn't help noticing that there's a well-stocked dugout in the hill behind. Two red deer, a pheasant and a capercaillie hanging, if I'm not mistaken. I don't suppose you'd care to tell us how they were obtained?'

'I took them from the hills,' Angus said. 'As I'm sure you've *jaloused.*'

'And that includes the grounds at Craig Gairbh?'

'Aye,' said Angus, nodding.

'Well,' said Inspector Chisholm, raising his eyebrows. 'I can't say I was expecting that. Your honesty is refreshing, but all the same, I'm afraid we're going to have to take you in.'

'I don't think that will be necessary,' said Angus, remaining entirely calm. He folded his arms over his chest, then stretched his legs out in front of him, crossing them at the ankles.

'I'm afraid I have no choice,' said Inspector Chisholm. 'The law is very clear on the matter.'

'And who's levelled the charges then?' said Angus. 'Because it certainly wasn't the laird.'

'And how would you be knowing that?' asked Inspector Chisholm.

'Because I think I'd remember doing it,' said Angus.

I was utterly confused. Judging from their faces, the policemen were as well.

'I beg your pardon?' Inspector Chisholm finally said.

'I don't think I can level charges against myself, and at any rate, even if I could, I'm fairly certain I wouldn't want to.'

'You're telling us you're the laird.'

'Aye,' said Angus, nodding. 'These three months. Son of the previous laird's late brother. Closest surviving male relative.'

I couldn't grasp it. I turned to Angus. 'But that night Bob the bobby came in – he gave you a warning for poaching,' I sputtered.

'That wasn't for poaching,' he said. 'That was for throwing the water bailiff in the river.'

I stared into his eyes as I realised what all this meant. Then I leapt to my feet.

'That bastard. That *rat* bastard! I can't *wait* to tell him!'

'Maddie?' said Angus. 'What's going on?'

'It was Ellis! He made the report! He was threatening to have you thrown in prison if I didn't turn back into his perfect society wife.' I stopped suddenly. 'And then he followed through. My God, the hospital is probably on its way for me right now.'

'Hospital? What hospital?' Angus demanded.

'Meg can tell you. I have to go,' I said, rushing past the officers to grab my coat.

'Maddie, *stop*!' said Angus. 'Don't go anywhere. I'm coming with you.'

'I'm sorry to interrupt,' said Inspector Chisholm, 'but could we trouble you for a wee bit of proof about this claim of yours before we all go about our business?'

'That can wait,' said Angus, striding towards the door.' Conall, *trobhad! Crios ort!*'

The dog scrambled to his feet, trotting to catch up.

'I'm afraid it cannot,' said Inspector Chisholm, reaching out and snagging Angus's upper arm. In an instant, Angus had swung round and was holding the other man's wrists parallel to his ears. Their faces were inches apart.

Sergeant MacDougall stepped forward with his hand on his truncheon.

After a few seconds, Angus released Inspector Chisholm, who straightened his sleeves and stared belligerently.

'I'll get your proof, and you'll be on your way,' said Angus. 'Meg, get the lockbox. I'll get the key. And Maddie, don't go *anywhere.*'

When he turned round, I took the opportunity to duck into the rain.

There were a number of things I wanted to say to Ellis – and Hank – before anyone else got there.

I ran for as long as I could, then continued at a jog, and by the time Urquhart Castle came into view, had slowed to a stumbling walk.

The sight of it gave me a second wind and I sprinted down and then up the slopes of the moat, through the gatehouse and across the scrubby weeds until I was at the top of the Water Gate.

Hank was on the shore, leaning over his camera with a raincoat tented over his head. Ellis was in the boat, which was half in the water. For a moment I thought he was preparing to get out, but then I realised they'd already unloaded their duffel bags, and the rope was coiled in the bow. He was heading out onto the water.

I hurtled down the hill, and before either one of them knew what was going on, leapt into the bow of the boat. I landed on my knees in collected rainwater and smashed my ribcage against the bench.

When I lifted my head to scrape the wet hair away from my face, I found Ellis staring at me in open-mouthed shock.

'Maddie! What the hell?' he said.

Hank came out from under his raincoat. 'Jesus Christ! What the hell are you doing here? We told you this wasn't a good day.'

Past the bench, on the bottom of the boat, was the miniature monster, with its curved neck and prominent eyes, its long fin and olive-green body.

I launched myself across the bench and grabbed it.

'Is this the reason?' I said, waving it over my head.

'Maddie, put that down,' Ellis said through gritted teeth.

'Gladly.' I threw it over his shoulder, as far from the boat as I could. It lay bobbing on its side, and I laughed. 'My God, it doesn't even work.'

Ellis just stared at me.

Hank sighed dramatically. 'Ellis, grab that thing, will you? We're running low on plastic wood. Maybe you could work on controlling your wife while you're at it.'

Ellis picked up the oars and began rowing towards the model, his eyes fixed on mine.

'Hey, *Hank*!' I shouted, my voice cracking with the effort. 'I want to talk to you! This business of controlling me. Does that include having my frontal lobe turned into a soufflé?'

Hank rolled his eyes. 'For crying out loud, Maddie. He just wants you to stop acting like a lunatic. If you can manage that, he's not going to do anything.'

'That's not what you thought yesterday. What's changed since yesterday?'

'He's just frustrated – we're all frustrated! – and we're all saying things we don't mean, including you. *Especially* you. But we're about to get out of this hellhole, so could you please just try to hold it together for a few days longer?'

'Was he frustrated when he called the courthouse? Because two policemen from Inverness came about half an hour ago to arrest Angus.'

Hank looked up sharply. 'Ellis? Is that true?'

'Why the hell are you asking him?' My voice, overtaxed, came out in broken shards. 'Do you think he's suddenly going to start telling the truth? He lied about being colour-blind to get out of the war, for Christ's sake!' My words echoed back to me, bouncing off the hills on the opposite shore.

Ellis stepped over the middle bench. I saw his closed fist

coming at my head, and the next thing I knew I was lying in water at the bottom of the boat, my vision filled with starbursts.

'Jesus Christ, Ellis!' Hank shouted. 'What the hell is wrong with you?'

I lay huddled in the bow, waiting for my sight to return.

'Get that fucking thing back here right now! Ellis, I mean it! *Get back here!*'

'Gonna have a quick word with my wife first,' Ellis called over, almost cheerfully.

'Ellis, if you don't bring that boat back this very second—'

'There isn't much you can do about it, is there?'

I hauled myself up on my elbows, my head wobbling. We were a dozen yards from shore. Ellis was sitting on the middle bench, staring at me, smirking.

'So it's true,' I said.

'I don't know what you're talking about.'

'You can see colour.'

He shrugged. 'So what? It doesn't matter.'

'It doesn't matter?'

'No one else will ever know. But don't fret about your appointment, darling – the facilities are quite luxurious.'

'Ellis!' Hank bellowed from shore.

'Once I get off this boat,' I said quietly, 'you're never going to see me again, except maybe in divorce court. You've got nothing left to hold over me.'

'Oh, but I do. You're incapacitated, which makes me your legal guardian. All I have to do is call the hospital.'

'The hospital can't take me away if they can't find me, and they won't.'

'Ellis! Turn around!' Hank roared.

'Oh, and by the way, Angus couldn't be arrested for poaching at Craig Gairbh because he is the *laird* of Craig Gairbh,' I continued. 'I suppose that makes you cousins of some sort, although I fail to see a resemblance.'

We locked eyes, as if seeing each other for the first time. The water lapped against the side of the boat, which was starting to bob.

'Ellis!' Hank bellowed. 'For God's sake, *turn around!*'

'Leave us the hell alone, Hank! I'll bring the boat back when I'm good and ready!'

'*Look!*' Hank screamed, and his voice was so guttural, so uncontrolled, we couldn't help ourselves.

He was filming furiously. He stuck his other arm out from under the raincoat just long enough to point. 'Over there! It was long and black and curved. It came up for just a moment – the wake has to be at least sixty feet long! Holy shit! This is it! I'm getting it! I'm fucking getting it! Ellis, this is going to be fucking *spectacular!*'

Ellis's expression shifted and he twisted in his seat. I grabbed the edge of the boat and leaned over to look. Something large, dark and rounded was moving quickly beneath the water. By the time I realised it was rising, it had rammed the bottom of the bow and flipped me into the air.

My mouth and nose filled with water before I fully comprehended that I was beneath the surface.

The cold was shocking. Thousands of bubbles, both big and small, rushed past me. It was air escaping from my clothing, and since I knew the bubbles must be going up, I must be facing down. I bucked instinctively in an effort to right myself.

The bubbles slowed, which meant that my clothes were becoming saturated. My one and only thought was to get free of my coat, but while I could bring my hands together in front of me, my fingers were too cold to obey. I could find the buttons, touch the buttons, even feel the thread that kept them attached to my coat, but could do nothing at all about unfastening them. Eventually, my hands drifted helplessly away.

I looked up at the surface and, as though through thick, wavy glass, saw Ellis standing in the boat holding an oar. It sliced through the surface and came to a stop against my chest.

With enormous force of will, I managed to bring my hands back in front of me and locked my fingers round its shaft, just above the blade. I kept hold of it and, after what seemed like an eternity, wondered why I wasn't moving toward the boat. Bewildered, I looked up and saw Ellis's determined face through the millions of tiny strands of peat in the water.

He wasn't saving me. He was making sure I stayed under.

I tried to push the oar away, but it was futile. He moved it to the centre of my chest and pushed me deeper still, until a final stream of bubbles escaped my nostrils. My consciousness flickered, the surface receded and then there was silence.

What happened next was like being sucked into an inverted waterfall. An arm swooped firmly round me and I was propelled upward, exploding through the surface with a deafening crash of waves. Then I was being hauled through the water, quickly, from behind.

'Hold on, *mo gràdh*, I've got you,' Angus said directly into my ear. His free arm backstroked steadily, his legs pumped furiously beneath us. I tried to take a breath, but my chest wouldn't budge. I couldn't even lift my hands to hold on to his arm.

My eyes drifted shut, and I fought to keep them open. One moment, I saw clouds churning and rolling above me looking for all the world like a living thing; and the next, nothing.

Clouds, nothing. Clouds, nothing. And finally, just nothing.

43

The next thing I was aware of was Angus's mouth covering mine, followed by me vomiting water. He flipped me onto my side and a spasm ripped through my ribcage, sending another stream of water flying from my nose and mouth. I drew a hoarse, gurgling breath – my first since going under.

Angus pulled me into a sitting position and wrapped his coat round me.

'What the hell?' said Hank, ducking out from beneath his raincoat tent. 'Jesus Christ – what happened? Maddie, are you okay?'

'No, she's not okay,' Angus barked. 'She's half-drowned and frozen. Give me your coat.'

Hank struggled out of it and thrust it at Angus. 'What happened? I didn't even see her go in.' He looked at me again. 'My God, her hands and face are blue.'

Angus wrapped me in the second coat and scooped me into his arms.

'I'm taking her to the corn-drying kiln,' he said. 'It's the intact room in the opposite wall. Run as fast as your legs will carry you to the first white house to the north. It's the McKenzies' croft. Tell them what happened and have them send for the bobby. He'll bring his car.'

As Angus carried me through the Water Gate, holding my head against his shoulder, I looked back at the loch.

Ellis was still in the boat, paddling like a madman with a single oar. The other was floating away from him.

Hank returned with Mhàthair, the two of them bustling in with armfuls of quilts and blankets. Before I knew it, Mhàthair had replaced the coats and swaddled me like a baby, depositing me on the edge of the ancient kiln and then sitting right next to me, pulling the edges of her own coat as far round me as they'd reach. I leaned against her, quaking with the cold, alternately drawing shallow breaths and coughing violently.

Angus wrapped a blanket round his drenched clothes like a kilt and paced. Each time I was racked by coughs, he rushed over to prop me up so Mhàthair could thump my back.

Hank crouched against the wall, pale. After a while, he climbed to his feet.

'I suppose I'll go see if I can get that fool back on dry land,' he said.

'If I were you,' said Angus, 'I'd grab my camera and leave that *amadain* right where he is.'

'I know that was a pretty rotten trick he tried to pull on you, but surely you don't want him to drown out there,' Hank said.

'I would like nothing more,' said Angus, 'although I expect he'll find his way back, if only to take care of the evidence.'

'If you mean the camera, I think it's pretty well protected by my raincoat.'

'I do indeed mean the camera. But it's not the rain it needs protecting from. In addition to anything else you might have captured on film was your friend's attempt to murder his wife.'

'What? No. That's ridiculous.' After a slight pause, Hank jerked round to face me. 'Maddie, is that true?'

I managed to nod.

He stared at me for a few seconds as understanding dawned. Then he turned and marched out the door.

From my perch on the kiln, I had a perfect view of the Water Gate. Hank crashed through the weeds, paused beneath its arch and looked down at the landing. Then he bellowed like a wild animal and tore down the hill. There were several minutes of angry shouting, amplified by the water but none of it comprehensible.

When Hank reappeared, he was changed. He plodded back to the kiln room with his face pointed at the ground and his shoulders slouched. His arms didn't even swing. He looked like an upright corpse.

He slid down the wall until he was crouching against it. He looked at the floor between his legs, resting his forearms on his knees and letting his hands dangle. They were bloodied and scraped.

'He made it back before I got there,' he finally said. 'He threw the camera in the loch.'

The rest of us remained silent.

He looked at me, his eyes bleak. 'You tried to tell me and I didn't listen. I thought I knew him. Can you ever forgive me?'

I remained huddled against Mhàthair, not even attempting a response.

'No, of course you can't,' Hank continued. 'I can't make it up to you, I know that. But I really didn't know – I don't even know when he found the time to slip off to the phone booth. We're almost always together. But I swear, if he called the hospital as well as the courthouse, I won't let them take you anywhere.'

'You!' Angus sputtered. 'You won't even get a crack at the *bastart* who's fool enough to show up trying to take Maddie away. Someone's brains will get scrambled, I promise you that. And I'll scramble the whole of that coward at the bottom of the slope, brains and all, while I'm at it. He'd better hope Bob the bobby locks him up right quick, before I get the opportunity.'

Hank watched Angus while he spoke, then dropped his head again.

When Bob showed up, Angus carried me to the car and Mhàthair and Hank followed. No one suggested we get Ellis.

As we drove back to the inn, Bob said, 'So you're telling me there was photographic evidence of the attempted murder, but it's gone?'

'Aye,' said Angus.

Bob turned to Hank, who was in the passenger seat, staring out the side window. 'And you're saying you didn't see a thing?'

'Just the monster,' Hank said despondently.

'But you were *right there*!' Bob slapped the steering wheel twice for emphasis.

'I was focused on filming.'

Bob glanced at him a couple of times in exasperation, then sighed. 'Well, there's one eyewitness, and fortunately the intended victim is still around to testify. I can certainly arrest him based on that.'

We reached the inn and pulled up in front of it, the gravel crunching beneath the cold, hard rubber of the tyres.

Bob twisted round in his seat, watching as Angus lifted me from the car.

'I'll fetch Dr McLean,' he said, 'and then I suppose I should go and collect the pathetic *creutair*. I canna remember the last time I had someone in my holding cell.' He sighed again. 'I suppose I'll be expected to feed him.'

As soon as Angus carried me up the stairs, Anna, Meg and Mhàthair wrested me away and banished him with orders to get himself properly dried off.

In short order, there was a fire roaring in my grate, they'd dressed me in a heavy nightgown and placed me under so many covers I couldn't move. They tucked stoneware pigs by my feet, and Mhàthair – after pressing her ear to my chest and shaking her head – disappeared for a while and returned with a steaming, smelly poultice that she shoved down the front of my nightgown. She put crushed garlic between all of my toes and wrapped my feet. When she replaced the quilts, she laid an extra one, still folded, across the bottom of the bed, weighing me down even further.

I withstood it all without protest. When I wasn't coughing, my lungs rattled. I was too weak to move, and lay with my eyes aimed vaguely toward the fire, drifting in and out of a fitful trance, reliving what I'd thought would be my final moments – the weightless, almost leisurely rolling in the water, the deafening *whoosh* of bubbles bursting up from all around me, the knocking of the oars inside the oarlocks. The first moments, when I tried to figure out how to survive, and the final moments, when I accepted that I would not.

Ellis had recognised an opportunity to get rid of me and seized it without a second's hesitation. My inheritance, his inheritance, his dirty little secret – all of it could be secured at once, with only a minute or two's effort.

Ellis would deny what he'd done, of course, touting my mental condition as proof that my testimony was unreliable, and saying that Angus had misinterpreted what was going on. He would probably even frame himself as a thwarted hero, claiming he'd been seconds away from hauling me into the boat, and that Angus's interference had subjected me to being in the water even longer.

I wondered how he'd explain the missing camera, or Hank's version of events, because while he might be able to cast doubt on my testimony, that was not true of Hank, and I doubted very much that he would be easily quieted.

Was it really the monster we'd encountered? We'd never know. Because of Ellis, no one would ever know.

44

My fitful trance was actually hypothermia, according to Dr McLean, although, with an appreciative nod toward Mhàthair, he declared me sufficiently warmed up to be past danger in that regard. However, he said I had pseudopneumonia from taking in water, and the important thing now was to prevent it from turning into real pneumonia, which could turn deadly in a matter of hours. He pulled a bottle of bright green tonic from his bag and set it on the dresser.

'This contains an expectorant. We want her to cough every-thing out.'

'What about castor oil?' Anna said anxiously.

The doctor shook his head. 'I'm afraid it won't help.'

Anna sucked the air through her teeth in despair.

Over the course of the night, my temperature rose and fell and I went from boiling to freezing in the space of seconds. I was racked by terrible coughing fits, and in between, felt my lungs crackle whenever I took a breath. I was at the complete mercy of my body.

I would clutch the covers to me, begging for someone to throw more logs on the fire. Then I'd kick the covers away from me, sometimes managing to hurl them to the floor. Mhàthair replaced them every time, calmly, gently.

She was in and out with poultices, alternating onion-and-vinegar mash with mustard plaster. When the unbearable heat rose in me, I flung them away. She replaced them in the same composed manner she did the bedclothes. She hovered in the background, doing mysterious things, seeming more like a pair of competent hands, a set of nimble fingers, than Mhàthair the actual person.

Angus never left my side. When I was sweltering and crying for ice, he mopped my brow and dribbled tiny bits of water onto my tongue. When my body bucked and heaved from the cold, he tucked the covers round me and stroked my face. There was not one moment the entire night when I could not open my eyes and immediately find his face.

At one point, in the wee hours of the morning, when I was so racked by fever that my jaw was clenched and aching, Angus laid a hand on my forehead and looked up in alarm.

Mhàthair also felt my forehead, then rushed from the room. Angus stripped the bedclothes back and held my limp body forward as he pulled my nightgown over my head. Then he wrung out cold facecloths and laid them all over my clammy skin.

A few minutes later, Mhàthair came back and I found myself propped up between them, being forced to sip some kind of tea. It was full of honey, but not enough to mask the bitter taste underneath. As they eased me back onto the bed, I was already slipping into a darkness as deep as the loch. The moment before everything disappeared, a pretty young woman with sad eyes appeared in front of me. She was floating, with her gown and hair billowing around her. It was Màiri – I knew it instinctively. She mouthed something to me and lifted her arms, but before I could make out what she was saying, she – and everything else – faded away.

The next thing I remember was waking up and not being sure where I was. I blinked a few times and found myself looking into Angus's blue eyes. He'd pulled the chair up to the bed.

Mhàthair reached over from the other side and laid a hand on my forehead.

'The fever's broken, thanks be to heaven,' she said. 'She's come through.'

Angus shut his eyes for a moment, then lifted my hand and kissed it.

'Never scare me like that again, *mo chridhe*. I thought I'd lost you, and I've lost enough to the loch already.'

Although my fever had broken, I was in no condition to get out of bed. The coughing alone was exhausting, as well as agonising.

Anna was knitting by the fire and I was resting my eyes when there was a rapping on the doorframe.

'Knock, knock,' said Hank. 'Are you receiving visitors?'

'I should think not,' Anna said sternly. 'Not when she's in this state.'

'I'm sorry. I didn't mean to be glib. Please, Maddie – may I have a word? Alone?'

'She's recuperating, you fool,' said Anna. 'Whatever it is can wait.'

'It's all right,' I whispered. My voice was nearly gone from all the coughing.

Anna stared at Hank for a couple of seconds, then held up the splayed fingers of one hand. 'Five minutes,' she announced. 'And not one minute more. I'll be in the hallway.'

She set her knitting on the floor and sailed out, throwing Hank a searing look as she passed.

He hovered uncomfortably, fidgeting, as though he didn't know what to do with his hands. I was afraid he might light a cigarette. Finally he walked round the bed to the chair. He plopped into it, crossed his legs and stared at the mantel.

'Did he really try to drown you?' he finally asked. 'I mean, are you positive?'

Only after the words were out did he look at me. I stared straight at him. He dropped his gaze and took a deep breath.

'Look,' he said. 'I know this doesn't change what happened, but I've decided to send a telegram to the Colonel. I'm going to tell him Ellis was lying about being colour-blind. There are tests, you know. He can't fake it for ever.'

After a pause, I said, 'What for? Revenge?'

'Because he deserves it! Because in addition to what he almost managed to have done to you medically, he tried to kill you! And he destroyed the footage! And he cost me Violet! He's cost me everything, probably even you!' He dropped his head and pressed his fingers into the corners of his eyes, as though he were about to cry.

I watched him, unmoved.

'He didn't cost you Violet,' I said. 'You were just as terrible to her as you were to me.'

He stopped trying to cry and looked up. 'I beg your pardon?'

'I know everything, Hank.'

'Well, apparently I don't. What are you talking about?'

'Were you heads or tails?' I asked. 'And more importantly, did you win or lose?'

His eyes went wide and unblinking. He stared at me for a long time. 'Jesus, Maddie. I don't know what to say.'

'I think I'd prefer it if you said nothing at all.'

Anna came back into the room.

'Bob the bobby is downstairs,' she said. 'He says he needs to speak to both of you right away, and since it can't wait and Maddie can't come down, he's asked me to check if it's all right for him to come up to the bedroom, even though I was very clear that it's not at all proper, and I wouldn't be a bit surprised if you said no.'

'It's all right,' I said. 'He can come up.'

I tried to remain calm, but was shot full of adrenaline. What if he'd come to tell us that Ellis had slipped away?

Angus and Anna led Bob into the bedroom.

He stood at the foot of my bed, holding his cap.

'Mrs Hyde,' he said, nodding a greeting. 'Are you feeling a wee bit better, I hope? Angus tells me you were quite poorly overnight.'

'Yes, thank you. I think I'm on the mend,' I said, although the effort sparked a fit of coughing. I rolled onto my side and Anna rushed over to thump my back.

Bob waited until I was finished and Anna had propped me up again. 'I'm very sorry to intrude like this, but I'm afraid a situation has arisen.'

'What type of situation?' asked Angus, and from the way his face clouded I saw that he'd jumped to the same conclusion I had.

'It's not what you're thinking,' Bob said. He gazed at his shoes for a moment, then looked Hank square in the face. 'Mr Boyd, was there any kind of . . . altercation down at the shore?'

'Sure, I knocked his block off.'

'But was he . . . conscious when you last saw him?'

'He was a little worse for wear, but definitely conscious. Mewling and obstreperous, even.'

'Yes, well,' said Bob, twisting his cap. 'I'm afraid that when I went back to make the arrest, I found the suspect deceased.'

Angus was by my side instantly, his hand on my shoulder. I reached up and clasped his fingers.

'What? How?' Hank demanded.

'He appears to have drowned in two inches of water,' said Bob. 'I've never seen anything like it. He was face-down at the water's edge. The rest of him wasn't even wet.'

Hank laughed bitterly. 'He was probably playing possum so you'd leave – he's not above doing that, you know.'

'There's no question that he's dead. The body's already at the morgue in Inverness. So the question now becomes how it happened.'

Hank's expression grew panicked as the implication sank in. He leapt from the chair.

'My God, you can't think I killed him!' he said. 'He was staggering around when I left, I swear! He must have fallen in after. I boxed his ears! That's all!'

He swivelled to face me, his eyes desperate and his fists clenched. 'Maddie! Tell him! For God's sake – you *know* I wouldn't kill Ellis! *Tell him!*'

'It's true,' I said. 'Hank would never kill Ellis. They're two parts of the same person.'

Hank stared at me, stricken.

Bob rubbed his chin for a while, thinking. 'Well, given the situation – and it is indeed a first for me – I suppose I could file it as an accidental drowning . . . Assuming there are no objections on the part of the family?'

He looked at me enquiringly. After a few seconds, I dipped my head in assent. Angus squeezed my shoulder and I clutched his fingers even more tightly.

Bob took a deep breath. 'Under the circumstances, I'm not sure what the right thing is to say. And while I know this is all very sudden, I'm afraid you're going to have to start thinking about final arrangements. Please let me know if there's anything I can do to help, anything at all.'

'Thank you,' I said quietly.

After Bob left, Hank headed toward the door, moving like a sleepwalker.

When his bedroom door clicked shut, I looked up at Angus. I knew something was coming, but nothing could have prepared me for the blood-curdling scream that rang through the building. I threw my arms round Angus's waist, waiting as the dreadful keening subsided into wild crying.

Angus held my head against him and stroked my hair. 'And what about you, *m'eudail?* Are you all right?'

I nodded. 'I think so. I don't suppose I would have wished this on anyone, but my God . . .'

'It's all right, *mo run geal og.* There's no need to explain. Not to me.'

I took his hand and pressed my cheek into it.

Down the hall, Hank continued to rage and grieve, but there was nothing any of us could do. There was not a soul on earth who could have comforted him, because he was worse than heartbroken. He'd been cleaved down the middle.

45

In the end, I sent Ellis home to his mother. I didn't want to attend the funeral, and suspected I wouldn't be welcome anyway.

Two days after Hank flew off with Ellis's body, Angus slipped into my room and my bed. He lay beside me, balanced on an elbow, stroking the hair away from my throat. He fingered the neck of my nightgown.

'Take that off . . .'

When I lay back down, he leaned over and whispered directly into my ear. 'I want to marry you, *mo chridhe*. To make this official just as soon as we can.'

He planted tiny kisses on my neck, working his way down. When he was almost at my collarbone, he took a small piece of my flesh between his teeth. I gasped, and every hair on my body stood on end.

'That's assuming you'll even have such a rough dog as myself,' he said, continuing his descent. He kissed his way to my left breast and ran his tongue over my nipple. It tightened into a little raspberry.

He raised his head. 'Although I suppose I didn't phrase it exactly as a question, that last comment of mine does require an answer . . .'

'But of course!' I said. 'I want to be Mrs Grant as soon as . . . oh!'

His mouth was once again on the move.

'Actually,' he said between kisses, 'you'll be the Much Honoured Madeline Grant, Lady of Craig Gairbh.'

The thing he did next left me unable to respond at all – at least, not with words.

We decided to wait a few weeks for the sake of propriety, but to all intents and purposes we were married from that moment on. Angus spent every night in my bed, although he slipped downstairs before dawn so as not to offend Anna's sensibilities.

The news from the Front made it clear that the war in Europe couldn't last much longer. City after city either surrendered or was liberated, and the Germans were driven ever deeper into their own territory. They were surrounded on all sides. They had also run out of men to recruit. They began drafting boys as young as ten from the Hitler Youth, and re-enlisting any soldier who had only lost his leg below the knee.

From there, it all fell like dominoes, beginning with a hit close to home. President Roosevelt died on 12 April and Harry S. Truman became the 33rd President of the United States.

Three days later, British forces liberated a complex of concentration camps at Bergen-Belsen and, according to an article in the *Inverness Courier*, found 'thousands of starving men, women and children, naked bodies lying four feet high stretching a distance of 80 yards by a width of 30 yards, cannibalism rife, disease and unspeakable cruelty rampant.' General Eisenhower implored members of the British House of Commons to come see 'the agony of crucified humanity' for themselves, because 'no words can convey the horror.'

On 16 April, the same day the Russians began yet another massive offensive, a desperate Adolf Hitler issued his 'Last

Stand,' in which he ordered troops to arrest immediately any officer or soldier who gave orders to retreat, regardless of rank, and if necessary to execute them, because even if they were in German uniform, they were probably drawing Russian pay. He told his forces, 'In this hour the entire German nation looks to you, my soldiers in the East, and only hopes that by your fanaticism, by your arms and by your leadership, the Bolshevik onslaught is drowned in a bloodbath.'

Twelve days later, Mussolini and his mistress were executed by firing squad after trying to escape to Switzerland. Their bodies were then hung upside down on meathooks in the Piazzale Loreto. A woman approached and cried, 'Five shots for my five assassinated sons!' before pumping another five bullets into Mussolini's already-battered corpse.

The next day, 29 April, American forces liberated Dachau, the first of the German concentration camps to be erected, and among the last to be liberated. Upon their approach, the Americans encountered thirty coal cars filled with decomposing bodies. Within the camp, they found approximately thirty thousand emaciated survivors, who continued to die at the rate of several hundred a day because their systems were too weak to take nourishment.

On 30 April, the Russians took Berlin and raised the Soviet flag over the Reichstag. Deep in their bunker, with the battle raging above them, Adolf Hitler and Eva Braun poisoned themselves and their dogs, after which Hitler shot himself in the head.

We huddled around the radio that night, every one of us breathing through our mouths. It was almost too much to believe. At long last – after more devastation and cruelty and callous disregard for human life than any of us could have possibly dreamed up – the hostilities appeared to be over. They were, in fact, although it wasn't made official for another week, when all remaining German forces surrendered unconditionally.

When Victory Day was finally declared, the collective jubilation became chaos. People ripped down their blackout curtains and set them on fire in the streets, sirens blared and church bells rang, victory parades turned into wild impromptu parties, people whooped and danced and sang, strangers made love in bushes off to the side of the road, bonfires raged and bagpipes called out triumphantly from every hill the whole night through.

At ten the next morning, Angus and I got married. The day after that, Anna and Willie did the same.

46

A few weeks after our wedding, I noticed that Angus had quietly had the gravestone with his name on it replaced with one that didn't. This time, it was I who knelt and traced the names of Màiri and her baby, leaving behind the handful of bluebells I'd just gathered from the Cover.

Knowing I'd paid homage to just one grave, I continued on to the Water Gate, picking more flowers on the way. After placing them at the water's edge, I stared across the loch's shiny black surface and wondered what, exactly, had happened to us out there. Was it Màiri? Was it the monster? Or was it something else entirely?

The monster – if there was one – never revealed itself to me again. But what I had learned over the past year was that monsters abound, usually in plain sight.

When Angus asked if I was ready to see my new home, I said that yes, of course I was, as long as he was entirely sure the army had removed all the landmines. He roared with laughter when I told him about my escapade, and told me that there hadn't been any mines in the first place – the signs were there to keep civilians out, as well as to keep the commandos in. The live ammunition, however, was real.

'What do you think?' he asked, when we rounded the bend and reached the oak-lined drive. The Nissen huts and barbed wire were gone, and it was the first time I'd seen the Big House in its entirety.

Angus's arm was round my shoulder, and he watched my face expectantly.

'Oh, Angus!' I said, skipping ahead of him. 'It's magnificent! Is it locked?'

'I don't think so,' he said, and then laughed as I ran ahead.

The double doors were huge and studded with brass. The entranceway was draped with carved boughs and vines, starting above the pediment and reaching almost to the ground. Just above that was an enormous coat of arms, and way up at the top, over a frieze of rearing horses flanking a shield, was a clock tower in a cupola that Angus told me was added in 1642. Each window was graced with a carving, and forty-foot Corinthian pillars ran up the wall between them.

When I walked through the front doors and found myself looking up at a vast, multi-storey gallery, I caught my breath. Generations of larger-than-life Grants glowered down at me from the oak-panelled walls, the frames that contained them separated by gilt curlicues. Most of them had ginger hair; all of them had Angus's striking blue eyes.

There was not one room on the main level that didn't have intricate plasterwork on its ceiling, and most were either painted or trimmed with gilt. Every detail was exquisite – from the ornate chandeliers to the medieval tapestries to the 'cabinet of curiosities' that once belonged to Louis XIV. The upholstered furniture seemed oddly shabby until Angus told me that it dated from the early 1700s, and that all the velvet was original.

I tried to imagine the Colonel's reaction when he first stepped inside all those years ago. When he looked up at the portraits of his ancestors, did his fantasies of finding the monster grow to encompass fantasies of becoming the laird? During his stay, as he harassed servant girls and adopted his upper-crust accent and commissioned estate tweeds, did he secretly ascertain how many male Grants stood between him and the title?

There was no doubt in my mind. Ellis probably had too.

Although the war was over, Europe remained in chaos: there were food shortages and transportation crises, a staggering number of refugees streaming from city to city, mass surrenders of German troops, hundreds of thousands of freed prisoners, as well as innumerable wounded soldiers who now faced the prospect of trying to rebuild their lives.

I'd never forgotten the wounded men on the SS *Mallory*, particularly the soldier who had caught my gaze and held it. He opened my eyes, awakening me to a reality I had somehow managed to avoid until that point. While Hank and Ellis carried on without a care in the world, it was men like the burnt soldier, Angus and Anna's brothers who sacrificed everything to save the rest of us. I wanted to give something back.

When I told Angus what I had in mind, he folded me wordlessly into his arms.

And so the plans were laid. For the next few years, the Big House at Craig Gairbh would be a convalescent hospital for injured soldiers.

EPILOGUE

Within two months, hospital beds and portable screens lined the halls and ballroom. The East Drawing Room became a surgery, and the Great Hall a burn unit. We moved into the servants' quarters on the top floor with Conall, and before long Meg joined us, having decided to become a nurse.

The patients both crushed and amazed me. I watched as a forty-seven-year-old sergeant, newly blind and learning to find his way around with a cane, first fingered the petals of a peony and then leaned over to bury his face in it. I held the hand of a boy who was not yet twenty as he cried in frustration after donning his prosthetic limb for the first time. I cheered from the sidelines during the frequent wheelchair races in the Great Hall. The library became a games room. One indomitable soldier, twenty-two years old, whose spine and left arm had been shattered, had one of us wheel him into the library each morning, then spent the rest of the day defeating anyone who dared take him on at chess.

I rooted for these men, and hundreds like them, as they passed through our lives and our home. It was a comfort to me to see them taking solace in the garden, or cooling in the shade of the fountain.

Meg was a great favourite with the soldiers, and she married a young corporal, who was also from Clydebank, the following Valentine's Day – an event that Angus and I had to skip for the happiest of reasons. I went into labour the night before, and just like that, Valentine's Day was redeemed.

Two of our children were born during that time, to the great delight of the soldiers. After all the horror, death and despair, the babies were the truest possible affirmation of life.

Life. There it was. In all its beautiful, tragic fragility, there was still life, and those of us who'd been lucky enough to survive opened our arms wide and embraced it.

AUTHOR'S NOTE

And now for the usual caveats about writing fiction based on real events:

I've appropriated some parts of the history of monster sightings. In particular, I transformed the 'Surgeon's Photo' into the 'Colonel's Photo,' and reimagined the Royal Observer Corps sighting completely. The British Aluminium plant at Foyers was indeed bombed during the war, but at noon rather than at night, and in February 1941 rather than January 1945. Similarly, while I tried to stay true to all other facts about the creation of the Special Service Brigade, Achnacarry Castle did not become Castle Commando until 1942.

While I did not fictionalise any of these, the facts and numbers associated with some of the battles and certainly the death camps are inaccurate in the book because I had to base them on the information that would have been available to my characters at the time, which was limited to the nightly BBC broadcast and what was reported in the *Inverness Courier*. The real numbers and full truth took years to come out and, as we now know, are even harder to comprehend than those that so horrified Maddie.

ACKNOWLEDGMENTS

I don't know if writing drives people crazy or if crazy people are driven to write, but I could not possibly have written this book without the help of the following non-crazy people, to whom I am for ever indebted:

My husband, Bob, my Rock of Gibraltar – without your unwavering support and belief, none of this would have been possible, and I certainly would not be able to continue.

To my sons, Benjamin, Thomas and Daniel, who are delightful and incredibly well-adjusted young men in spite of having me as their mother.

To Hugh Allison and Tony Harmsworth. It was as though some invisible hand guided me to you. Experts each on Scotland during World War II and the Loch Ness Monster, your willingness to answer my endless questions over the years was nothing short of heroic.

To Hugh's family members, who invited me in by the fire and made sure (for better or worse) that the level in my glass never went down: Hughie and Chrissie Campbell, Donnie and Joan Macdonald, Jock Macdonald and Alasdair Macdonald – thanks to each of you for your hospitality and for sharing your memories and mementos with me.

To the people who lived in Glenurquhart during the war and were generous enough to share their experiences: Duncan

MacDonald, Angus MacKenzie, Jessie (Nan) Marshall, William Ross and Bonita Spence.

To Lady Munro of Foulis, for graciously inviting me to Foulis Castle to discuss her experiences in the WAAF, and for allowing me to prowl around the castle's original kitchen with my camera.

To Siobhan McNab, for her timely and thorough archival work; to Fiona Marwick, from the West Highland Museum in Fort William; and to Sheila Gunn for providing Gaelic translations.

To my trusted critique partners: Karen Abbott, Joshilyn Jackson and Renee Rosen, each of whom has talked me off the ledge at least once, or, if I've already fallen over, pulled me back by my bungee cord. I can no longer count how many books we've collectively survived.

I would be remiss if I didn't also send a heartfelt shout-out to my dear friend David Verzello, who dropped everything to read this book every time I asked him to, which was often.

And a very special thanks to Emma Sweeney, my wonderful agent; Cindy Spiegel, editor extraordinaire; and to Gina Centrello and the team at Random House. All of you have the patience of Job and a keen understanding of the creative process, and you provided an unfaltering but gentle hand in guiding my book towards its finest form. I am also eternally grateful to Lisa Highton, my editor at Two Roads Books, who believed in this book from the very beginning.

To Cindy specifically – life threw me a number of curveballs over the last few years and I am grateful beyond words that you stuck with me. If I hadn't been sure of your support, I'm not sure I could have crawled through it. Thank you.

© Tasha Thomas

SARA GRUEN is the internationally bestselling author of *Water for Elephants* and *Ape House*. Her works have been translated into forty-three languages and have sold more than ten million copies worldwide.

Water for Elephants was adapted into a major motion picture starring Reese Witherspoon, Robert Pattinson and Christoph Waltz.

She lives in Western North Carolina with her husband and three children.

saragruen.com
facebook.com/SaraGruenBooks
twitter.com/SaraGruen

WATER FOR ELEPHANTS

**The gritty, compelling international bestselling novel of star-crossed
lovers and circus life, set in Depression-era USA.**

Selected for World Book Night UK 2015.

When Jacob Jankowski, recently orphaned and suddenly adrift, jumps onto
a passing train, he enters a world of freaks, grifters and misfits – the Benzini
Brothers Most Spectacular Show on Earth – a second-rate travelling circus
struggling to survive during the Great Depression, making one-night stands
in town after endless town.

Jacob, a veterinary student who almost earned his degree, is put in charge of
caring for the circus menagerie. It is there that he meets Marlena, the beautiful
young star of the equestrian act, who is married to August, the charismatic
but twisted animal trainer. He also meets Rosie, an elephant who seems
untrainable until he discovers a way to reach her.

Illuminated by a wonderful sense of time and place,
Water for Elephants tells a story of a love between two people that
overcomes incredible odds in a world in which even love is a luxury
that few can afford.

Stories . . . voices . . . places . . . lives

We hope you enjoyed *At The Water's Edge*. If you'd like to know more about this book or any other title on our list, please go to www.tworoadsbooks.com.

For news on forthcoming Two Roads titles, please sign up for our newsletter.

enquiries@tworoadsbooks.com

TwoRoadsBooks

The Stone Circle

Also by Elly Griffiths

THE DR RUTH GALLOWAY SERIES

The Crossing Places
The Janus Stone
The House at Sea's End
A Room Full of Bones
Dying Fall
The Outcast Dead
The Ghost Fields
The Woman in Blue
The Chalk Pit
The Dark Angel

THE STEPHENS AND MEPHISTO SERIES

The Zig Zag Girl
Smoke and Mirrors
The Blood Card
The Vanishing Box

OTHER WORKS

The Stranger Diaries

As Domenica de Rosa

One Summer in Tuscany
(previously published as *Summer School*)
The Eternal City
Return to the Italian Quarter
(previously published as *The Italian Quarter*)
The Secret of Villa Serena
(previously published as *Villa Serena*)

ELLY Griffiths

The Stone Circle

A Dr RUTH GALLOWAY MYSTERY

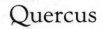
Quercus

First published in Great Britain in 2019 by

Quercus Editions Ltd
Carmelite House
50 Victoria Embankment
London EC4Y 0DZ

An Hachette UK company

A CIP catalogue record for this book is available
from the British Library

HB ISBN 978 1 78648 729 2
TPB ISBN 978 1 78648 730 8

10 9 8 7 6 5 4 3 2 1

Typeset by CC Book Production

Printed and bound in Great Britain by Clays Ltd, Elcograf S.p.A.

For Jane Wood

CHAPTER 1

12 February 2016

DCI Nelson,

Well, here we are again. Truly our end is our beginning. That corpse you buried in your garden, has it begun to sprout? Will it bloom this year? You must have wondered whether I, too, was buried deep in the earth. Oh ye of little faith. You must have known that I would rise again.

You have grown older, Harry. There is grey in your hair and you have known sadness. Joy too but that also can bring anguish. The dark nights of the soul. You could not save Scarlet but you could save the innocent who lies within the stone circle. Believe me, Harry, I want to help.

The year is turning. The shoots rise from the grass. Imbolc is here and we dance under the stars.

Go to the stone circle.

In peace.

DCI Harry Nelson pushes the letter away from him and lets out something that sounds like a groan. The other people in the briefing room – Superintendent Jo Archer, DS Dave Clough, DS Judy Johnson and DS Tanya Fuller – look at him with expressions ranging from concern to ill-concealed excitement.

'He's back,' says Clough.

'Bollocks,' says Nelson. 'He's dead.'

'Excuse me,' says Jo Archer, Super Jo to her admirers. 'Would someone mind putting me in the picture?' Jo Archer has only been at King's Lynn for a year, taking over from smooth, perma-tanned Gerald Whitcliffe. At first she seemed the embodiment of all Nelson's worst nightmares – holding meetings where everyone is supposed to talk about their feelings, instigating something unspeakable called a 'group huddle' – but recently he has come to view her with a grudging respect. But he doesn't relish the prospect of explaining the significance of the letter to his boss. She'll be far too interested, for one thing.

But no one else seems prepared to speak so Nelson says, in his flattest and most unemotional voice, 'It must have been twenty years ago now. A child went missing. Lucy Downey. And I started to get letters like this. Full of stuff about Gods and the seasons and mystical crap. Then, ten years on, we found a child's bones on the Saltmarsh. I wasn't sure how old they were so I asked Ruth – Dr Ruth Galloway – to examine them. Those bones were nothing to do with the case, they were Iron Age or something, but I got Ruth to look at the letters. She thought they might be from someone with archaeological knowledge. Anyway, as you know, we found Lucy but another child died. The killer was drowned on the marshes. The letter writer was a Norwegian professor called Erik Anderssen. He died that night too. And this,' he points at the letter on the table, 'reads like one of his.'

'It sounds like someone who knows you,' says Judy.

'Because it goes on about me being grey and sad?' says Nelson. 'Thanks a lot.'

No one says anything. The joys and sorrows of the last few years are imprinted on all of them, even Jo.

After a few seconds, Jo says, 'What's this about a stone circle?'

'God knows,' says Nelson. 'I've never heard of anything like that. There was that henge thing they found years ago but that was made of wood.'

'Wasn't the henge thing where you found the murdered child last time?' says Jo, revealing slightly more knowledge than she has hitherto admitted to.

'Yes,' says Nelson. 'It was on the beach near the Saltmarsh. Nothing's left of it now. All the timbers and suchlike are in the museum.'

'Cathbad says they should have been left where they were,' says Judy.

Judy's partner, Cathbad, is a druid who first came to the attention of the police when he protested about the removal of the henge timbers. Everyone in the room knows Cathbad so no one thinks this is worth commenting on, although Clough mutters 'of course he does'.

'This is probably nothing,' says Jo, gesturing at the letter which still lies, becalmed, in the centre of the table. 'But we should check up the stone circle thing. Nelson, can you ask Ruth if she knows anything about it?'

Once again everyone avoids Nelson's eye as he takes the letter and puts in his pocket.

'I'll give her a ring later,' he says.

'How did you know about the stone circle?' says Ruth.

Nelson is taken aback. He has retreated into his office and shut the door for this phone call and now he stands up and starts to pace the room.

'What do you mean?'

'A team from UCL were digging at the original henge site just before Christmas. They think they've found a second circle.'

'Is this one made of stone?'

'No,' says Ruth and he hears her switching into a cautious, academic tone. 'This is wood too. Bog oak like the other one. But they're calling it the stone circle because a stone cist was found in the centre.'

'What's a cist when it's at home?'

'A grave, a coffin.'

Nelson stops pacing. 'A coffin? What was inside?'

'Human skeletal matter,' says Ruth. 'Bones. We're waiting for carbon-14 results.'

Nelson knows that carbon-14 results, which tests the level of carbon left in human remains, are useful for dating but are only accurate within a range of about a hundred years.

He doesn't want to give Ruth the chance to explain this again.

'Why this sudden interest in the Bronze Age?' says Ruth.

'I've had a letter,' says Nelson.

There's a silence. Then Ruth says, her voice changing again, 'What sort of letter?'

'A bit like the ones I had before. About Lucy and Scarlet. It had some of the same stuff in it.'

'What do you mean "the same stuff"?'

'About corpses sprouting, shoots rising from the earth. Imbolc. The sort of stuff that was in Erik's letters.'

'But . . .' Nelson can hear the same reactions he witnessed in his colleagues earlier: disbelief, anger, fear. 'Erik's dead.'

'He certainly looked dead to me when we hauled him out of the water.'

'I went to his funeral. They burned his body on a Viking boat.'

'So it can't be him,' says Nelson. 'It's some nutter. What worries me is that it's a nutter who knows a bit about me. The letter mentions a stone circle. That's why I rang.'

'It can't be this circle. I mean, no one knows about it.'

'Except your archaeologist pals.'

'Actually, they've got funding for a new dig,' says Ruth. 'It's starting on Monday. I was planning to drop in for a few hours in the morning.'

It's Friday now. Nelson should be getting ready to go home for the weekend. He says, 'I might drop by myself if I'm not too busy. And I'd like to show you the letter because, well, you saw the others.'

There's another tiny sliver of silence and Ruth says, 'Isn't the baby due any day now?'

'Yes,' says Nelson. 'That might change my plans.'

'Give Michelle my best,' says Ruth.

'I will,' says Nelson. He wants to say more but Ruth has gone.

CHAPTER 2

Ruth reruns this conversation on a loop as she drives to collect her daughter from Sandra, her childminder. She has deliberately been keeping her interactions with Nelson to the minimum. She sees him every other Saturday when he takes Kate out for the morning but she manages to keep their conversation general and upbeat; they sound like two breakfast TV presenters handing over to the weather forecast. 'How are you?' 'Fine. Getting sick of this weather.' 'Yes, when's the sun going to come out?' But this latest development takes her back to a time that still feels dangerous and disturbing: her first meeting with Nelson, the discovery of the bones on the marsh, the hunt for the missing children, her last encounter with Erik. Over the last ten years she has, by and large, dealt with these memories by ignoring them but the discovery of the new henge in December, and now Nelson's mention of the letter, has brought everything back. She can still feel the wind on her face as she ran across the uncertain ground, half-land half-sea, knowing that a murderer was on her trail. She can hear Lucy's voice calling from deep underground. She can see the police helicopter, like a great misshapen bird, stirring the waters of the tidal pool that had taken a man's life.

Corpses sprouting, shoots rising from the earth. That's what Nelson had said, the words sounding strange in his careful policeman's voice, the vowels still recognisably Lancastrian even after more than twenty years down south. It had to be a coincidence and yet Ruth does not trust coincidences. One of the few opinions that she shares with Nelson.

Kate, her seven-year-old daughter, is drawing at Sandra's kitchen table and acknowledges Ruth with a friendly, yet dismissive, wave.

'I'm doing a Valentine's card,' she says.

Ruth's heart sinks. She has managed to forget that it is Valentine's Day on Sunday (VD she calls it in her head). In her opinion, the whole thing is an abomination: the explosion of bleeding hearts in the shops, the sentimental songs on the radio, the suggestion that, if you are not in possession of a single red rose by midnight, you will die alone and be eaten by your pet cat. Ruth has had her share of Valentines in the past but this doesn't lessen her distaste for the whole business. She's never had a card from Nelson; their relationship is too complicated and clandestine. *Roses are red, violets are blue. You've had my baby but I can't be with you.* She tries not to think about Nelson presenting his heavily pregnant wife with a vast bouquet (he will go for something obvious from a florist, red roses tied in ribbon and encased in cellophane). She wonders who is the intended recipient of Kate's artwork.

Ruth doesn't ask though and Kate doesn't tell her. She puts the card, which seems to show a large cat on a wall, in her school bag and goes to put her coat on. Ruth thanks Sandra and has the obligatory chat about 'thank goodness it's Friday, let's hope the rain holds off'. Then she is driving off with her daughter, away from the suburbs towards the coast.

It's dark by the time that they get home. When they get out of the car they can hear the sea breaking against the sandbar and the air smells brackish which means that the tide is coming in. Ruth's cottage is one of three at the very edge of the marshes. Her only neighbours are an itinerant Indigenous Australian poet and a London family who only visit for the occasional weekend. The road is often flooded in winter and, when it snows, you can be cut off for days. The Saltmarsh is a bird sanctuary and, in the autumn, you can see great flocks of geese coming in to hibernate, their wings pink in the sunlight as they wheel and turn. Now, in February, it's a grey place even in daylight, grey-green marshes merging with grey sky and greyer sea. But there are signs that spring is coming, snowdrops growing along the footpaths and the occasional glimpse of bright yellow marsh marigolds. Ruth has lived here for twenty years and still loves it, despite the house's increasing inconvenience for a single parent with a child whose social life now requires a separate diary.

It was on the beach at the edge of the marshes that the henge was first discovered. Ruth remembers Erik's cry of joy as he knelt on the sand before the first sunken post, the sign that they had found the sacred circle itself. She remembers the frenzied days of excavation, working desperately to remove the timbers before the sea reclaimed them. She remembers the druids protesting, the bonfires, the burning brands. It was during one of the protests that she first met Cathbad, now one of her dearest friends. And now they have found a second circle. Ruth worked on the dig in December and performed the first examination on the bones found in the stone cist. Now, during this second excavation, a lithics expert will look more closely at the stones and archaeologists will try to date the wooden posts. Ruth is looking forward to visiting the site again. It will never be the same as that first discovery though, that day, almost twenty years ago now, when the henge seemed to rise from the sea.

'Hurry up, Mum,' says Kate, becoming bored by her mother staring out to sea. 'Flint will be waiting for us.'

And, when Ruth opens the door, her large ginger cat is indeed waiting for them, managing to convey the impression that he has been doing this all day.

'He's hungry,' says Kate, picking the cat up. There was a time when he seemed almost bigger than her; even now on his hind legs he reaches up to her waist.

'There's food in his bowl,' says Ruth. But, nevertheless, she removes the perfectly edible cat food and replaces it with a fresh offering. Flint sniffs at it once and then walks away. He isn't really hungry – he has just consumed a tasty vole – but he does like to keep his human minders on their toes.

Kate switches on the television, a habit that never ceases

to annoy Ruth but she doesn't say anything. She starts to cook macaroni cheese for supper, one of her stock of boring but acceptable dishes. She tries to read the *Guardian* at the same time, propped up behind the pots which should contain tea and coffee but are actually full of mysterious objects like old raffle tickets and tiny toolkits from Christmas crackers.

She has left her phone in her bag by the front door but Kate calls to tell her it is ringing. She manages to catch the call in time. Frank.

'Hi,' he says. 'How was your day?'

'OK. Phil is more megalomaniacal than ever. I'm expecting him to make his horse a senator at any minute.' Phil is Ruth's boss at the University of North Norfolk. He adores publicity and is very jealous of the fact that Ruth occasionally appears on television.

'Same here.' Frank is teaching at Cambridge. 'Geoff now continually refers to himself in the third person. "Geoff is disappointed with student outcomes", "Geoff has some important news about funding".'

Ruth laughs and takes the phone into the kitchen.

'Frank was wondering if you wanted to go out for dinner tomorrow.'

'Ruth doesn't know if she can get a babysitter. Shall we stop this now?'

'I think we should. I could come over and cook?' Frank, a single father for many years, has his own small store of recipes but at least they are different from Ruth's.

'That would be nice.' Please don't let him mention VD.

'I'll come to you for seven-ish. Is that OK?'

'Great. Kate would like to see you before she goes to bed.' Which, on a Saturday, is becoming later and later. Ruth will have to bribe her with an audio book.

'See you then.' Frank rings off but seconds later she receives a text:

Are you pleased I didn't mention Valentine's?

Ruth doesn't know whether to be pleased or slightly irritated.

Ruth is glad that she has the evening to look forward to because the shadow of VD looms over Saturday. It's not one of Nelson's Saturdays so Ruth takes Kate swimming in King's Lynn and even at the pool there are red balloons and exhortations to 'Treat yourself to a Valentine's Day Spa'. At least she has arranged to meet Cathbad and his son, Michael, and, after their swim, the children play in the circle of hell known as the Soft Play Area and the adults drink something frothy which may or may not contain coffee.

'Are you taking Judy out for Valentine's Day?' asks Ruth, dispiritedly eating the chocolate from the top of her 'cappuccino'.

'No, but I'll cook us something special,' says Cathbad. In jeans and jumper with his long wet hair tied back in a ponytail, Cathbad looks like any ageing hipster dad. He still wears his cloak sometimes but Ruth has noticed that more and more, when he's with his children, especially Michael whose embarrassment threshold is low, Cathbad mimes a slightly offbeat version of conventionality. Apart from running a few evening classes in meditation and past life regression, he's the full-time carer for Michael, six, and Miranda, three, and seems to enjoy the role. Ruth often ponders on the fact that this apparently makes Judy a 'working mother' and Cathbad a 'stay-at-home father' as if mothers never have jobs outside the home and caring for children isn't work. Nelson is, presumably, a 'working father' though no one would ever label him in this way. Ruth's mother often used to describe her, rather apologetically, as a 'career woman' but Nelson, who is consumed by his job, will never be described as a 'career man'. Will Michelle go back to work as a hairdresser after this new baby is born?

Time to stop thinking about that.

'Valentine's is crap though, isn't it?' she says.

'I don't mind it,' says Cathbad, waving to Michael who is about to descend the tubular slide. 'I like ritual and saints' days. And it's another way of marking the coming of spring. Like Ash Wednesday and Imbolc.'

Nelson had mentioned Imbolc, Ruth remembers. But she doesn't want to tell Cathbad about the new letter.

'When is Imbolc?' she asks. 'Beginning of February?'

'It's flexible,' says Cathbad, 'but usually the first or second of February. It used to be a feast dedicated to Bridgid, the goddess of fertility, but then it got taken over by Christianity and Bridgid became St Bridget. In Ireland children still make rush crosses for St Bridget's Day.'

Cathbad grew up in Ireland and was raised as a Catholic but, like the feast day, he is flexible, incorporating both pagan and Christian traditions into his belief system. Ruth sometimes thinks that what he really likes is any excuse for a party.

'Are you seeing Frank this weekend?' asks Cathbad.

'He's coming over tonight to cook me a meal.'

'That's nice,' says Cathbad. His expression is bland but Ruth thinks she knows what he's thinking.

She takes pity on him. 'It's going well with Frank. We've got a lot in common.'

'He's a good person,' says Cathbad. 'He has a very serene energy.'

There's a brief silence during which Ruth knows that they are thinking of someone who could never be described as serene. She says, 'Michelle's baby is due any day now.'

'I know. Judy says Nelson is worse tempered than ever at work. It must be the worry.'

'Or maybe it's just bad temper.'

'No, he has a good heart really.'

'Let's hope the baby isn't born on Sunday,' says Ruth, 'or he'll have to call it Valentine.'

'I like the name Valentine,' says Cathbad. 'It's got a certain power.' His children, though, all have names beginning with M, for reasons that are not entirely clear to anyone, even him. He also has a twenty-four-year-old daughter called Madeleine from a previous relationship.

'Valentine Nelson,' says Ruth. 'I can't see it.'

'Of course 2016 is a leap year,' says Cathbad. 'There's a certain power in being born on 29th February. Funnily enough, in Ireland leap years are associated with St Bridget. She's said to have struck a deal with St Patrick to allow women to propose to men on one day of the year.'

'Bully for her,' says Ruth. 'I'm sure Michelle doesn't want to wait until the 29th to have her baby.'

She thinks about this conversation intermittently over the rest of the day. She doesn't envy Cathbad and Judy their relationship, or even Nelson and Michelle. By and large, she is happy with her life in her little cottage on the edge of the marshes with her daughter and her cat. If she has ever dreamed of a life with Nelson, the dream ended after the rapturous love-making and hasn't encompassed life in a confined space with a man who takes up too much room, literally and metaphorically. It's just that, on days like this, she does wonder if she'll ever have a romantic relationship again. But, at seven o'clock, there is Frank, bearing chocolates, wine and two steaks in a rather bloody bag. Kate has already had her supper but she insists on showing Frank her collection of Sylvanian animals and all her spelling/maths/reading certificates (this takes some time as Kate seems to win a new award every week). Eventually, though, Kate is tucked up in bed listening to Stephen Fry reading Harry Potter and Ruth and Frank have their meal.

It's a nice evening. They talk about work and the idiocies of their relative bosses. They talk about Kate and about Frank's children in America. Even Flint sits next to Frank and purrs at him loudly with his eyes closed. But, at eleven o'clock, Frank picks up his car keys and sets off home. They kiss on the doorstep, both cheeks like acquaintances at a smart party. Ruth locks the door, turns off the lights and goes upstairs, followed by Flint. What is happening with Frank? They had once had a proper relationship, complete with extremely good sex. Is Frank now just a friend who cooks her meals and takes her out sometimes? Is he seeing someone else, a stunning classicist from Christ's or an economist from Girton with a PhD and a thigh gap?

But, as Ruth is about to turn out the light, she sees that she is not in bed alone. On her pillow is a card showing a fat ginger cat on a wall.

'Happy Vallentines Day Mum,' it says.

Nelson is woken by a knock on the door. Three knocks actually. Staccato and self-important. Bruno, the German shepherd, barks in response. Is it the postman? But it's Sunday and – Nelson looks at the clock radio – 6.30 a.m. Michelle is asleep, lying on her back, her stomach a mound under the bedclothes. She is finding it increasingly difficult to sleep in these last days of her pregnancy and Nelson doesn't want to wake her. His daughter Laura, living at home while she studies to become a teacher, was out late last night and will be dead to the world. Nelson gets up as quietly as he can and pads downstairs in pyjama bottoms and a 'No. 1 Dad' T-shirt, a bit embarrassing but all he could find to wear last night.

'Coming,' he mutters irritably. Bruno is standing in the hallway staring at the door. He's actually not much of a barker; he prefers to assess situations and then act accordingly. Nelson thinks this could be because he came from a litter destined to be police dogs. 'Good boy,' says Nelson. He opens the door. There's no one there. Nelson looks up and down the street but the cul-de-sac is still asleep, no movement except for a ginger cat walking very slowly along a wall. The cat reminds Nelson of Ruth. He turns to go back into the house and it's only then that he notices the brown paper bag on the step.

In the kitchen, watched intently by Bruno, Nelson tips the bag upside down on the table. Inside is a stone with a hole through the middle and a note, black writing on red paper.

'Greetings,' it says, 'from Jack Valentine.'

CHAPTER 3

'It's an old Norfolk tradition,' says Tom Henty, the desk sergeant who has been at the station for as long as anyone can remember. 'Three knocks on the door and, when you go to answer it, there's nobody there but Jack Valentine has left a present, usually in a brown paper bag.'

'I've never heard of that tradition,' says Clough, halfway through his second breakfast of the day, 'and I was born and brought up in Norfolk.'

'It's an east Norfolk thing,' says Tom. 'I was born in Yarmouth.'

By now Nelson is used to the local belief that Norfolk is a vast place where the north, south, east and west regions are separated by massive, immovable barriers. As for Suffolk, it might as well be on a different planet.

'Whoever left me this is from east Norfolk then,' he says, pointing to the stone and the note on the briefing room table. Judy picks up the stone and looks through the hole.

'Cathbad would say that this is a witch stone. Stones with holes in are meant to be magical.'

Clough laughs and chokes on his Egg McMuffin but Nelson has learnt to listen to Cathbad's pronouncements.

'In what way?' he says.

'I'll ask him,' says Judy. 'I think they're meant to ward against evil.'

'I'll ask Ruth,' says Nelson, not meeting anyone's eyes. 'I'm going to drop in on the dig in Holme later. Just to follow up on that stone circle thing.'

Tom's thoughts are as slow and deliberate as his speech. 'Then there's Snatch Valentine,' he says now.

Clough chokes again.

'Present on the doorstep with a string attached,' says Tom. 'Child goes to grab the parcel but the string moves it just out of reach. Child chases the present until it's out of sight. Child is never seen again.'

There's a brief silence.

'Bloody hell,' says Clough, dusting himself for crumbs. 'That's a cheerful little story.'

'Where there's light there's dark,' says Judy. 'Some cultures believe that Father Christmas is accompanied by an evil imp who punishes bad children.'

'It's probably nothing,' says Nelson, 'but it worries me that it was delivered to the house. I haven't said anything to Michelle. I don't want to upset her. The baby's due any day now.'

No one says anything. They all know that, in the summer, someone else found Nelson's house, a man with a gun and a grudge against Nelson. Michelle and her daughter were both held at gunpoint and Tim, a police officer who had once been with King's Lynn CID, was killed. They all understand why Nelson has not told his wife about this new development.

'Do you think it's got anything to do with the other letter?' says Clough. 'The one about the corpse sprouting?'

'Don't know,' says Nelson. 'The first letter was typed, of course, so we can't get a handwriting match. But what are the odds of two nutters writing to me at the same time?'

'Pretty high, I would think,' says Clough.

Ruth drops Kate at school and drives back to the Saltmarsh, following the signs to the birdwatching trail. The car park, with its boarded-up ice-cream kiosk and notices about rare birds, reminds her irresistibly of the time when she first met Nelson. He had wanted her opinion about bones found on the marshes and they had driven here from the university – her first experience of Nelson's driving – parked by the kiosk and walked to the shallow grave where she had seen the dull gleam of an Iron Age torque and had known that this corpse, at least, would not be bothering the tall, rather intimidating, man at her side. She remembers Clough following them, carrying a bag containing litter found on the path. How alien they had seemed to her then, these grim-faced policemen, concerned only with what they referred to as 'the crime scene'. She knows more now, has attended many such scenes, but she knows that, in some ways, she'll always be an outsider.

There are several other cars in the car park, mud-spattered vehicles that look as if they might belong to archaeologists.

Ruth gets her oldest anorak out of the boot and puts on her wellingtons. As she does so, she feels a faint stirring of excitement. This is a dig; a place where, unlike a crime scene, she will always feel at home. It's a cold day, the air damp and grey, but it's not actually raining and this, in England in February, is also a cause for celebration. As she sets off along the gravel path between the reeds, Ruth wonders if Michelle's baby was born over the weekend. Would Nelson have let her know? The child will be Kate's half-brother, after all. Or will it? Whilst Nelson knows that the baby is a boy he doesn't – as far as Ruth can make out – know whether it's his or Tim's. If the latter, then the paternity will be obvious. Tim, as he was fond of pointing out, was one of the few black police officers in Norfolk.

The walk seems longer than it did nine years ago or maybe Ruth is even less fit. She glances at her wrist where a Fitbit, a Christmas present from her brother Simon and sister-in-law Cathy, sits smugly. She presses the button and it tells her that she has walked 2,007 steps since getting up (it tracks her sleep too). Surely it's more than that? She sometimes suspects Cathy, at least, of less-than-charitable motives in giving this particular present, a sort of mini-Cathy that nags her all day about doing more exercise. Ruth fears that her relationship with the Fitbit is already an unhealthy one. She worries about its good opinion of her (otherwise why not take it off?) but she also resents its chirpy bullying. *Almost there! You've nailed your step target for the day!* Never trust anyone, or anything, that uses that many exclamation marks.

She must have been going uphill (why doesn't the Fitbit give you more credit for this?) because suddenly she can see the sea, shallow waves breaking on the sand, seagulls flying low above the spray. The sun has come out and it sheds a hazy, Old-Testament beam of light on a small group of people standing just above the tide line. They are wearing hi-vis jackets and are grouped in a circle. Ruth walks towards them, stumbling over the sandy, grassy ground. She's about to call out but something stops her. The people seem very still and one of them, a man with a long blond ponytail, raises his arms to the sky. As Ruth approaches, he turns and Ruth sees a weather-beaten face, strong nose and bright blue eyes, eyes that seem to see into her very soul. Seagulls call, high above, and a sudden wind whips sand into Ruth's face.

'Erik?' she stammers.

CHAPTER 4

The man laughs and puts out a hand as if to steady her.

'My name's Leif Anderssen,' he says. 'I'm Erik's son. You must be Ruth Galloway.'

Erik's son. Ruth remembers that he had grown-up children, two girls and a boy. She'd kept in touch with Erik's wife Magda for a little while but their relationship hadn't been able to survive Erik's death and the events leading up to it. She hasn't heard from Magda in nearly five years and, besides, Magda wasn't one for talking about her adult children. She hadn't known that the son was an archaeologist but Leif Anderssen is very clearly in charge of this dig. He's a professor at Oslo University, he tells her, but has been seconded by UCL because of his expertise with stone artefacts. When Ruth had first approached Leif had been greeting the nature spirits, as he always does at the start of an excavation. Oh, he's Erik's son, all right.

'My father talked about you a lot,' says Leif as they walk towards the first trench. 'He always said you were his favourite pupil.'

Even after everything that has happened, Ruth can't suppress a small glow of pleasure.

The site is about a hundred metres west of the place where the henge was discovered almost twenty years ago. In December a team from UCL had discovered what seemed to be a second circle of wooden posts. Further excavation had uncovered the cist, a shallow rectangular pit lined with stones and containing a single urn and what looked like a fully articulated human skeleton.

'Cists are usually Bronze Age, aren't they?' says Ruth, panting slightly in order to keep up with Leif who, like his father, is tall and rangy.

'Yes,' says Leif. 'Later graves typically hold cremated remains. The fact that this one contained bones might mean that it's early Bronze Age.'

'Like the henge,' says Ruth.

'Yes, like my father's henge.'

This is, in fact, how Ruth thinks of the henge but she knows that, to others, the description would sound like sacrilege. Cathbad, for one, is of the opinion that the wooden circle belonged only to the sea and sky.

'It's possible,' says Leif, 'that the first henge was built to mark the death of an individual, like a cenotaph. It could be that we have found the grave of this person.' His English is near perfect; only the faint sing-song accent and the precision of his syntax mark him out as a non-native speaker.

'Have you had the dendrochronology results?' asks Ruth. Dendrochronology, the science of dating tree rings, was what gave them the date for the original henge.

'We're still waiting,' says Leif, 'but the wood looked similar: bog oak, intertwined with branches. Did you examine the bones?'

'Yes,' says Ruth. 'They looked old but we won't know for sure until we get the carbon-14 sample back.' She notices how, despite all the science at their fingertips, both she and Leif have fallen back on intuition; the wood and the bones had both 'looked' right.

'I heard that you thought that they might be female.'

'I'm pretty sure they are. The pelvic bones were intact and the skull definitely looked female; the brow ridges weren't developed, nor was the nuchal crest. From the size of the bones I'd say that it was a young woman, probably in her late teens.' She doesn't add that the skull has a particularly rounded and delicate chin which made her think that the owner had probably been rather beautiful.

They are at the trench now. Ruth can see the cist, solid slabs of stone interspersed with smaller pebbles, a dark void in the centre. A young archaeologist is kneeling down scraping away lichen but it looks almost as if he is in prayer.

'The roof stone was a metre wide,' says Leif. 'Quite a substantial tomb. Particularly for a young woman.'

Does Leif mean that a woman couldn't deserve an impressive memorial? Erik would never have implied such a thing. He knew that there are many prehistorical graves where women were buried with great care and ritual. And, even if some of these women had been killed as sacrifices to some cruel and faceless god, they were still important.

Ruth looks around her. The sand stretches away on either

side, grey and blue, giving way to windswept grass and marshland. The henge must have been visible for miles, silhouetted against the sky. She thinks of Erik's words: *The landscape itself is important. This is a liminal zone, between land and water, sea and sky . . .*

'Cists are sometimes called flat cemeteries,' says Leif, reading her mind in a way that she finds rather disturbing. 'They often occur in environments like this, flat land on the edge of water. It could be that the water represented rebirth or renewal in some way.'

Ruth feels that, with the reincarnation of Erik standing in front of her, she should steer clear of the subjects of rebirth and renewal. 'Have you looked at the grave goods?' she says briskly. 'There was an urn, wasn't there?'

'Yes,' says Leif. 'It contained seeds from wild fruit – blackberry, sloe and hazelnuts. Sustenance for the afterlife. There was something else though that I thought was significant.'

'Oh,' says Ruth, 'what?'

'A stone with a hole through the middle, found beside the urn. Such stones have powerful magical qualities.'

He smiles as he says this, reminding Ruth not of Erik, but of Cathbad.

'Stones like that have been found in Neolithic sites,' says Ruth. 'I was reading about a causewayed enclosure in Whitehawk, near Brighton. There were bodies buried there alongside fossils called shepherds' crowns, stones with holes through them too.'

'Hag stones,' says Leif. 'Odin stones. Holy stones. They have lots of names. They are meant to guard against witches and all kinds of evil. Some stories say that if you look through the hole you will see the fairy folk.'

Once again, Ruth feels that they are wandering along a slightly dangerous path. She does not want to discuss the fairy folk – or Odin – with Erik's son.

'Was it just one stone?' she asks.

'Yes,' says Leif. 'That makes it more significant, no?'

'Perhaps,' says Ruth. 'Could I look in the trench now? I'd like to see the layers.'

Ruth enjoys the chance – rare these days – of doing some actual excavation, the combination of heavy labour and precision, the feeling of working in the open air, the February sun surprisingly warm on her back even though her fingers and toes are soon frozen. She is just starting to work on an interesting section when a shadow falls over the neat line of soil and subsoil.

'Found anything interesting?'

Ruth straightens up. 'Hi, Nelson.'

He looms above her, blocking out the sun in his dark police jacket. Ruth tries to climb nimbly out of the trench but ends up having to take Nelson's proffered hand. His grip is very strong. Ruth lets go as soon as she is on solid ground.

'Is this the stone whatsit?' he says.

'The cist? Yes.'

'It's just a hole with some stones in it.'

It's lucky that Nelson says annoying things like this sometimes. It stops Ruth fantasising about him.

'It's probably early Bronze Age,' she says. 'A very significant find.'

'It's near the other one, isn't it?'

'Yes.' Ruth knows that they are both thinking not of the wooden henge, but of the child's body she found inside it. She remembers the moment with all her senses; the mist rising from the sea, the waterlogged ground under her feet, the seagulls calling high above, the little arm emerging from its shallow grave . . .

'Who's in charge?' Nelson is saying. He is pawing the ground like a horse, a characteristically impatient gesture.

'Well,' says Ruth, 'this might come as a bit of a shock . . .'

But it's too late. Leif is walking towards them, smiling a welcome, teeth very white against his tanned skin.

'Leif,' says Ruth, 'this is DCI Nelson from the King's Lynn police. Nelson, this is Leif Anderssen, the archaeologist in charge of the dig. He's Erik's son.'

Leif continues to hold out his hand and, after a second's hesitation, Nelson grasps it.

'DCI Nelson,' says Leif. 'I've heard a lot about you.'

'None of it good, I'm sure.'

'Not at all, my father had a great respect for you.' Ruth wonders how Leif can possibly know this, unless he was in closer contact with his father than she thought. Erik always used to say that he saw his children as 'free, independent spirits', which also seemed to be an excuse for rarely seeing them.

'It's all water under the bridge now,' says Nelson, employing a rather unfortunate cliché, given Erik's death from drowning. Erik's body had been found in a marshy pool only a few hundred metres from where they stand now.

'Indeed,' says Leif. 'The world turns and life continues. To what do we owe the honour, DCI Nelson?'

Ruth can see Nelson thinking as clearly as if there was a bubble over his head. She knows that he won't want to tell Leif about the letter but how else to explain his presence?

'I came to see Dr Galloway,' he says at last. 'I need her help on a police matter.'

'I should be going anyway,' says Ruth. 'I've got a seminar at twelve. Do let me know when you get the test results.'

'Of course,' says Leif. 'I hope to see you again.'

Ruth holds out her hand but Leif leans forward and kisses her on both cheeks. Even though he is standing behind her Ruth can tell that Nelson is glowering.

They sit in Nelson's car, which is parked next to Ruth's. Nelson drums his fingers on the steering wheel as Ruth reads the letter.

'It's very like the others,' she says at last. 'Even the quote from T. S. Eliot.'

'Where's that?'

'"That corpse you buried in your garden, has it begun to sprout?" I think it's from *The Wasteland*. Also the bit about our end being our beginning. That sounds like T. S. Eliot.'

'Your friend Shona. She helped with the literary stuff last time, didn't she?'

Ruth is silent for a moment. Shona Maclean, an English

Literature lecturer at the university, did help Erik with the letters last time but, over the years, she has allowed herself to forget this. At the time she had felt betrayed but friends are too valuable to lose. Shona has a child now too and that has formed another bond. After a holiday in Italy last summer, Ruth and Shona are closer than ever.

'Anyone can find quotes like this,' she says.

'Anyone who knew what the previous letters were like.'

'Who would have known?'

'We never made them public,' says Nelson. 'Didn't want any copycats sending us their lunatic scribblings. But word always gets out. Everyone in the station must have known.'

And Shona knew, Ruth thinks. And Cathbad.

'There are certainly similarities,' she says. 'The way he addresses you personally, the Biblical references. "Oh ye of little faith."'

'That's Doubting Thomas, isn't it?' says Nelson. 'The one who doesn't believe that Jesus has come back from the dead.'

'Full marks for religious knowledge.'

'He's one of my favourite characters. Always ask for evidence. Thomas would have made a good policeman.'

Ruth wonders whether Nelson is contemplating calling his son Thomas. Kate says the new baby will be called George but Ruth doesn't know where she got this information. Ruth looks at the typed letter, in its plastic sleeve, on her lap. *The year is turning. The shoots rise from the grass.* What did Leif say just now? *The world turns and life continues.* It's a fairly standard new-agey sort of phrase but there is an uncomfortable echo. Is it just a coincidence that Leif appeared at the same time as the letter?

'Actually the phrase occurs a few times in the Old and New Testaments,' she says. Her parents were evangelical Christians, fond of quoting the Bible. 'But it's nice to know that you've got a favourite saint.'

Nelson doesn't rise to the bait. 'There's another thing,' he says. 'You know it was Valentine's Day yesterday?'

'No,' says Ruth. 'Was it?' This is partly ironical (who could escape it?) but also she doesn't want Nelson to think that she spent the whole day waiting in vain for a card that never came.

Nelson misses the sarcasm anyway. 'Someone left a paper bag on my doorstep,' he says. 'There was a note with it. "Greetings from Jack Valentine." Apparently it's some sort of Norfolk tradition.'

'What was in the bag?'

'Just a stone.'

'With a hole through it?'

Nelson stares at her. 'How the hell did you know that?'

'There was a stone with a hole in found inside the cist,' says Ruth. 'We think it dates back to the Bronze Age.'

'So whoever sent me the letter might have known about the dig?'

'Maybe,' says Ruth, 'but those stones are fairly common. There are lots of legends attached to them.'

'I know,' says Nelson. 'Judy was telling me some of them. She gets it all from Cathbad. But it's a coincidence and I don't like coincidences.'

Ruth is about to answer when she sees a figure running across the car park towards them. It's the young archaeologist from the dig. Nelson winds down the window.

'We need Dr Galloway,' pants the archaeologist.

'Why?' says Ruth. But she already knows.

'We've found some bones.'

Ruth and Nelson follow the man, whose name is Vikram, back along the gravel path towards the sand dunes. The brief burst of sunshine has gone and the day is grey and cold again. When they reach the site they find Leif in the trench with two other archaeologists, a man and a woman. They stand aside for Ruth.

The bones are about half a metre down, white against the sandy soil. Ruth can see an arm, possibly a radius or an ulna. Silently Leif hands her a trowel and a brush and, for a few minutes, Ruth works to expose the bones. She doesn't want to excavate them yet because the context will be important. She can see already that there is a grave cut in the soil above. Someone has put this body in the ground deliberately. It takes about twenty minutes for Ruth to be sure of two things. One, there is a complete skeleton here. Two, it's relatively recent.

'How can you tell?' says Nelson, leaning over her shoulder.

Ruth points her torch to where part of the skull is visible. A piece of metal glints back at them.

'A filling,' says Nelson.

'Yes,' says Ruth. 'That will be useful for ageing. And there should be dental records too.'

There's a third thing too. The rounded ends of long bones, the epiphyses, are still growing in children as new cartilage gets added. In late adolescence these fuse with the main part of the bone. The bones are slender too, fragile-looking. Ruth is pretty sure that she is looking at the bones of a child.

CHAPTER 5

'We need to look at missing children from the last ten or twenty years,' says Nelson. 'Maybe even thirty. Ruth couldn't be sure of the exact age of the bones without doing more tests but there was a filling, the old silver sort.'

'They haven't been used since the eighties, have they?' says Judy. 'It's all white fillings now.'

'I haven't got any fillings,' says Clough, grinning to show annoyingly perfect teeth.

'That's amazing,' says Tanya seriously, 'given the amount of sugar you eat.'

'How old did Ruth think this child was?' asks Judy, who is taking notes on her iPad.

'She thought early teens, about twelve or thirteen. Apparently bones have end bits on them that disappear when children finish growing. Different bones fuse at different rates – I didn't follow it all – but the humerus hadn't fused and that usually happens at about fourteen. So we're almost certainly looking at a prepubescent.'

'Do we know if it's a boy or a girl?' asks Clough.

'Ruth says that she might be able to tell from the pelvic bones when she does the full excavation but apparently it's difficult with a prepubescent skeleton.'

'Can she get DNA from the bones?' asks Judy.

'Possibly. But again that depends on all sorts of things. You know what these archaeologists are like. They never give you a straight answer.'

The team are used to Nelson's impatience with all experts, including Ruth, but there is a palpable sense of anticipation in the briefing room. They have a body and there's a chance that they will be able to close one of the cases that all police forces dread, when a child apparently vanishes into thin air.

'If they've been missing for more than ten years we'll have done a review,' says Tanya, opening her laptop.

'That's true,' says Nelson, 'so we need to look at the neighbouring forces too. There can't be that many cases that are still open. I'll speak to my old sergeant Freddie Burnett. Who else was working here thirty years ago?'

'Tom Henty,' says Clough. 'He's been here for ever.'

'And Marj Maccallum,' says Judy. 'She came in to see me last year. When I was acting DI,' she can't help adding. 'Marj was a WPC here in the seventies and eighties, when such things existed.'

'I remember Marj,' says Nelson. 'She was still here when I was first made DCI. She was a good cop, very sharp.'

'I'll ring her,' says Judy.

'Good idea,' says Nelson, 'but there's something else I want you to do first. Clough and Fuller, you keep looking in the files.'

Both Clough and Tanya look briefly mutinous as Nelson ushers Judy into his office. Then Tanya turns back to her laptop and Clough finds a half-eaten Mars bar in his pocket and eats it thoughtfully.

Ruth is forced to cancel her seminar and so is met by Phil muttering about 'client expectations'. 'Now that people are paying nine grand a year they expect a better service.'

'They're not clients,' says Ruth, unlocking her office. 'They're students. I'll reschedule the seminar but I couldn't really leave the site. They'd just found a dead body.'

She can see that Phil is torn between wanting to know about the dead body and wanting to lecture her about time-keeping. In the end curiosity wins.

'Is the body modern?' he says, sliding into her office as soon as the door is open.

Ruth's office is so small that two people standing up make it feel crowded. Ruth sits behind her desk and, after some hesitation, Phil takes the visitors' chair. Her poster of Indiana Jones looks down at him disapprovingly.

'The bones don't look that old,' she says. 'I'll excavate tomorrow and send samples for carbon-14 and isotope analysis.'

'Is it a murder case then?' says Phil. Ruth knows that he is deeply envious of her links with the Serious Crimes Unit. Phil is also Shona's partner, which means that he is up to date with the gossip.

'Possibly,' says Ruth. 'DCI Nelson was actually at the

site when the bones were uncovered.' She hopes she isn't blushing.

'*Was* he? Why was that?'

'Just checking up on the dig, I expect. Do you know who's running it?'

'Someone from UCL?'

'Leif Anderssen. Erik's son.'

Phil's lips purse in a silent whistle. 'Erik the Viking's son? What's he doing in England?'

'He's an expert on stone artefacts, apparently. You know they found a stone cist in the centre of the circle?'

'I read the reports. They wanted my opinion but I didn't have time to visit the site. There's so much extra work now I'm Dean.'

Phil mentions his recent appointment as Temporary Dean of Natural Sciences roughly once every fifteen minutes.

'Lucky I've got so much free time, then,' says Ruth. 'The timbers and the cist look early Bronze Age. We're still waiting for carbon-14 on the bones in the cist.'

'Just like old times,' says Phil. 'You and Nelson hunting for a killer on the Saltmarsh.'

Ruth stares at him. Can he really be saying those words so lightly? Can anyone, even Phil, not be aware of how much the last case cost her, how many lives were lost or changed for ever?

'Let's hope it doesn't come to that,' she says. 'If you'll excuse me, I need to prepare for my next seminar.'

But after Phil has oozed out Ruth stays staring into space for the next ten minutes. Does the discovery of the bones mean that she is about to be involved in another murder investigation? What will it be like to be working closely with Nelson again, especially with Michelle's baby about to be born any day? The whole thing – the dig on the Saltmarsh, Erik's son materialising – feels uncomfortably like one of those dreams where the past replays itself but with certain details subtly altered. When she first dug on these marshes she was in her twenties, single, just about to embark on her academic career. Now she's still single but she has a seven-year-old daughter and an extremely complicated romantic past. Her career, too, seems to have stalled. She's a senior lecturer at UNN but it's a fairly lowly institution in the middle of nowhere. She should really be looking for a new job at a better university. She has written two books which were well received in academic circles even if they didn't trouble the best-seller lists. She gazes up at her poster. What would Indy do?

She is roused by a buzz from her wrist.

'Only 1,000 steps to go!' exhorts her Fitbit chummily. 'You're in it to win it!!!'

'You want me to interview Shona Maclean?' says Judy.

'Not interview exactly,' says Nelson. 'Just ask her a few questions. After all, she was involved the last time.'

'She wasn't charged though.'

'No, but I'm pretty sure that she helped Erik Anderssen with the letters. All that stuff from Shakespeare and T. S. Eliot. After all, Shona teaches English literature. Ruth says there's an Eliot quote in this one too.'

'Do you really think Shona could have something to do with the new letter? Why would she want to upset you? She's Ruth's friend. They went on holiday together last year.'

'Don't remind me,' says Nelson. 'I don't think Shona is necessarily involved but she might have some idea who's behind it. Erik Anderssen's son is running the dig on the Saltmarsh.'

'Is he?' Judy wonders why Nelson hadn't mentioned this earlier. She has only the vaguest memory of Erik although she was there when they pulled his body out of the water.

'He's called Leif,' says Nelson, with distaste.

'It's a Norwegian name,' says Judy. 'Is he an archaeologist?'

'Apparently so. Pretty pleased with himself too.'

'Do you think he could have written this new letter?'

'It's a bit of a coincidence that they both turn up at the same time. And there are things in the letter that were never in the public domain.'

'There are always leaks though. Maddie says that the local press know everything that goes on here.'

Madeleine, Cathbad's eldest daughter, is currently working on the local newspaper, the *Chronicle*. Maddie's mother was Cathbad's ex-girlfriend Delilah, who later married Alan and had three children, the youngest of them being Scarlet Henderson, the little girl whose body was found on the marshes ten years ago. Maddie has always felt that the King's Lynn police wasted too much time suspecting Scarlet's family of her abduction and murder and so she has strong opinions about police malpractice. But then Maddie has strong opinions about everything. It's one reason why Judy is glad that she's living in digs and not with her and Cathbad.

'Maybe,' says Nelson, 'but there are a few too many links for my liking. They found one of those witch stones on the site. It was buried next to the bones.'

'Do you think it's connected to your Jack Valentine parcel?'

'I don't know. It seems a pretty big coincidence, although Ruth says these stones are fairly common.'

'They are. Cathbad's got a collection. We keep them by the door because that's supposed to mean good luck.'

'You don't surprise me. But why would this Leif write to me or send me a stone in a paper bag? Just to make trouble? It doesn't make sense. That's why I want you to talk to Shona. Find out if she knows anything. But subtly, mind. We don't want her claiming police harassment.'

'You know her better than me. You should talk to her.'

'You'll do it better,' says Nelson. 'I'd just put her back up. And Cloughie and Tanya would be even worse.'

'She'd probably love to be interrogated by Cloughie.'

'I don't want to give her the chance to flirt or get on the defensive,' says Nelson. 'Just a nice woman-to-woman chat.' He says this like it's a new language.

'That's sexist,' says Judy, but she picks up her bag all the same.

'Is it?' says Nelson. 'But I said woman not girl.'

'You're learning,' says Judy. Very slowly, she adds to herself.

*

Nelson follows Judy downstairs and stops for a word with Tom Henty. To his surprise, Tom comes up with a name at once.

'Margaret Lacey,' he says. 'Aged twelve. Went missing in 1981. The year Charles and Diana got married.'

'How do you remember that?'

'You always remember the ones that weren't found, don't you?' Tom looks at him and Nelson finds himself nodding. He will never forget Lucy Downey or Scarlet Henderson. The lost girls.

'What do you remember about Margaret?'

'It was a street party for the Royal Wedding. That's why I remember the year. Margaret and her friend had been at the party in Lynn. They wandered off and no one thought much of it. Later, Margaret's mother – Kathy, Kelly, one of those names – went looking for her and turns out she hadn't been seen for hours, since she parted company with her friend by the quay. There was a massive police hunt but Margaret was never found.'

'Anyone charged?'

'No, there was a lot of suspicion of the parents, particularly the father, but no charges. There was the usual local weirdo but he had an alibi, as I remember. The case was reviewed in 1991, just before you arrived, but there were no new leads.'

'Tell me about the weirdo,' says Nelson. 'Did he have form?'

'Not really. A few cautions for prowling. This was before all this porn on computers malarkey. No, he was just a nutter who liked collecting stuff from the beach. The Stone Man, they called him.'

CHAPTER 6

Shona is surprised, but not displeased, to see Judy.

'No one ever comes to see me now that I'm part-time,' she says, clearing some books off a chair so Judy can sit down. 'Or were you looking for Ruth?'

'No,' says Judy. 'I wanted a quick word with you.'

Shona's office is similar in size to Ruth's but it's far less functional. There are throws over the chairs and a jar of spring flowers on the table. There are pictures too, a poster of woman drowning in flowers (Ophelia?) and several playbills in tasteful colours, which make the room seem more like a student bedsit than a lecturer's office. Even Shona's books are cosier than Ruth's, the orange spines of the Penguin classics and several shelves of leather-bound volumes. Judy fixes her eyes on the playbill over Shona's head. *Women Beware Women*.

Shona offers coffee – she even has a cafetière and proper cups – but Judy refuses politely. They exchange a few remarks about their children. Shona's son, Louis, is almost the same age as Judy's Michael. Then Judy says, 'I wanted to see you because DCI Nelson has received a letter.'

Shona is still smiling but Judy thinks that she has suddenly become very still.

'A letter?' she says.

'Yes. An anonymous letter. But the thing is it seems very similar to the ones Nelson received ten years ago, when Scarlet Henderson went missing.'

Shona says nothing. It was Judy who had questioned her about the letters and about the disappearance of Erik. Judy knows that they are both thinking about this now. Nelson was wrong; she is the very worst person to have this conversation.

'The first letters were written by Erik Anderssen, weren't they?' she says, after a pause.

Shona looks like she's going to deny this but then she shrugs and says, 'Yes.'

'With your help?'

'I supplied a few literary references.'

'And you were in a relationship with Anderssen?'

'Years ago,' says Shona. 'When we were working on the henge dig. I was a volunteer. That's when I first met Cathbad.' She looks at Judy. There's a definite challenge in her gaze. Is Shona implying that Cathbad had fancied her too? It's probably true; Shona is very beautiful, even if she is several years older than Judy. Cathbad's age, in fact.

'I was just wondering,' says Judy, trying to sound like this is a cosy 'woman-to-woman' chat, 'whether you had any idea who could have written this new letter. Some old friend or colleague of Erik's perhaps?'

'His son's working on the new dig,' says Shona. 'Ruth told me.'

'Do you know him, the son?' Judy doesn't want to let on that she knows his name.

'No,' says Shona. 'I never met any of Erik's family. Apart from his wife, of course.' Her voice is flat.

'Well if you do think of anything,' says Judy, 'can you let me know?'

'Of course,' says Shona. 'Anything to help the police.'

Judy does not like her tone.

Ruth is packing her bag. She supposes she should stay late as she missed most of the morning but she's damned if she's going to. Besides, she needs to pick Kate up from Sandra's. She hasn't got any lectures or seminars tomorrow which is why she will be free to excavate the body found on the Saltmarsh. Even so, she bets that Phil will make a thing of it. Or, worse, turn up.

She glances out of her window. It's only five o'clock but already nearly dark. Hard to believe that the clocks will go forward next month. The artificial lake, grubby and often litter-strewn in the daylight, looks attractive in this light, lit by the mushroom-shaped lights around its circumference. As Ruth watches, a man strides along the lakeside path, holding a child by the hand, another child walking behind him, occasionally patting a mushroom. It's rare to see children on campus and Ruth looks more closely before realising that she knows this family. It's Cathbad with Michael and Miranda. What's he doing here? Meeting his old colleagues in the chemistry department? As Ruth watches, another man approaches. He, like Cathbad, has long hair in a ponytail. The two men embrace warmly and the newcomer bends down to talk to Miranda. Michael, as ever, remains slightly aloof.

Ruth stands back from her window but she continues to watch. She wonders why Cathbad didn't tell her that he and Leif Anderssen are obviously close friends.

By the time Nelson gets back to his office, Tanya has put the Margaret Lacey file on his desk. Nelson reads through it quickly, noting dates and names. On 29 July 1981, Margaret Lacey, aged twelve, attended a street party near her home in King's Lynn. At some point during the afternoon she slipped away with her friend, Kim Jennings. Margaret's mother, Karen Lacey, reported her missing at eight o'clock that evening. Margaret had last been seen with Kim in front of the Custom House by the quay. According to one witness the two girls had been arguing but Kim insisted that they had parted amicably. Margaret had wanted to see the Punch and Judy man in the Tuesday Market Place and walked off in that direction. Kim went back to the street party. A massive police search started that night, combing the streets that were, presumably, still full of monarchist revellers. Frogmen searched the river and sniffer dogs tracked as far as South Wootton. The investigation, as far as Nelson could see, focused on the parents, Karen and Bob. There were two older children, Annie who had been fourteen at the time of Margaret's disappearance and Luke, who had been fifteen. Bob, who was a plasterer, was known to have a temper but he swore he'd never laid a hand on any of his children. He had been drinking in the pub most of the day, until alerted by Karen at about seven. There were several witnesses who claimed to have been with Bob but Nelson knows that drinking companions do not make good alibis. It would probably have been possible for Bob to have slipped out for an hour without anyone being much the wiser.

John Mostyn, the so-called Stone Man, emerged as a suspect quite early on, because of his previous convictions. He had also been seen talking to Margaret and Kim earlier in the day, 'showing them some pebbles he'd found on the beach'. But John had spent most of the day looking after his wheelchair-bound mother, Heidi, and she gave him a firm alibi. Some schoolfriends said that Margaret had talked about a boyfriend in London but this proved to be a false trail. Despite numerous appeals, Margaret was never seen again.

Nelson stares down at the file, now furry at the edges with age. Nelson was fourteen in 1981. They'd had street parties in Blackpool too but his mother had disapproved of them for some long-forgotten sectarian reason. Nelson remembers his mother and his sisters watching the wedding on television but he and his father had escaped to the park. They'd played football, he remembers, one against one, until some local lads had joined them. Come to think of it, that might have been the last time he'd had a kick-around with his dad. Archie Nelson had been an enthusiastic supporter of his son's schoolboy footballing career but he wasn't much of a player himself, childhood polio having left him with one leg shorter than the other. And, a year after the Royal Wedding, Archie was dead from a heart attack. It's an odd feeling. Nelson would have been only two years older than Margaret. He could have played football with her older brother, hung around on street corners with her big sister. Where are the family now? He emails Tanya and the answer comes back immediately. Bob Lacey died of cancer two years ago but Karen is still alive. She divorced Bob soon after Margaret's disappearance, married again and has two sons with her new husband. Margaret's sister Annie is married with children and lives in Lynn. Luke lives in London. John Mostyn is seventy and still lives in the house where he once cared for his mother.

Are they Margaret's bones that have been discovered buried on the Saltmarsh? Dental records should make identification possible even if they don't have DNA. At least this will give the family some closure, some remains to bury.

Nelson has left a message for his old sergeant Freddie Burnett. He suspects that Freddie is out on the golf course but, when he gets a call back, it transpires that Freddie is on holiday in Tenerife. 'Bit of winter sun,' says his old colleague, his voice mellow with vitamin D. 'You should try it.'

'Maybe I will one day,' says Nelson though he can't think of anything worse than a week of golf, cocktails and after-dinner entertainment. He tells Freddie why he is calling.

'Margaret Lacey,' says Freddie. 'Well, well, well.'

'Do you remember the case?'

'Very well. I was pretty sure who killed the poor girl too.'

'The father?'

'No, the prowler. John Mostyn.'

'He had an alibi.'

'His mother. She would have sworn black was white for him. No, Mostyn was the type. He was always hanging round the little girls. Pervert. Him and his pebble collection. If I had my way, I'd castrate the lot of them.'

Nelson tries to stop Freddie before he gets going on one of his crime and punishment diatribes.

'Well, if it is Margaret,' he says, 'we can reopen the case. There have been lots of advances in forensics since the eighties. We might still get the perpetrator.'

'I bloody hope so,' says Freddie. As Nelson is saying goodbye and wishing Freddie and his wife a pleasant holiday, his phone buzzes. It's Laura.

'Dad, you'd better come home. Mum says her contractions have started.'

CHAPTER 7

Laura meets Nelson at the door. She has her jacket on and car keys in her hand.

'Thank God you're here, Dad. Mum keeps saying that there's plenty of time but I don't think there is.'

Michelle is in the sitting room. She looks quite calm but she is staring intensely at the coffee table in front of her. Bruno is watching anxiously and there's an overnight bag by the door.

'Come on, love,' says Nelson. 'Time to get going.'

'It's fine,' says Michelle, not shifting her gaze. 'Contractions are still fifteen minutes apart.'

Nelson has such a strong attack of déjà vu that he almost feels dizzy. He and Michelle leaving their house in Blackpool in the middle of the night, Michelle in the early stages of labour with Laura, neither of them knowing what to do, Nelson breaking all the speed limits on the way. Laura had been born in a cubicle in A&E, there being no time to get to the maternity ward. Rebecca had taken her time, almost ten hours of Nelson pacing and questioning and absent-mindedly eating the ham sandwiches he had made for Michelle. Now Laura is a grown woman who is, even now, texting her sister in Brighton.

'Rebecca says hurry up. She wants to meet George.'

'We all do,' says Nelson. 'Come on, love.' He helps Michelle to her feet and they walk slowly out of the room, Michelle already doing her breathing, shallow pants that make Bruno cock his head with interest.

'Shall I come with you?' says Laura.

'No,' says Nelson. 'You stay and look after Bruno. I'll ring you as soon as there's any news. Don't worry.'

'I won't,' says Laura, worriedly.

He puts the blue light on the car and they are at the hospital in ten minutes. They go up to the labour ward where the midwife seems to spend an inordinate amount of time asking Michelle useless questions. The contractions are obviously closer now and lasting longer. Still the midwife writes slowly on her pad, stopping to answer an orderly's question about the birthing pool.

'We need to hurry up,' he says. 'The baby will be here any minute.'

'Don't worry, Mr Nelson,' says the midwife, 'we've got plenty of time yet.'

'It's DCI,' growls Nelson. Preoccupied as she is, Michelle finds time to give him a look.

'Michelle's in labour,' says Judy, reading Nelson's text.

'We should pray to Hecate,' says Cathbad. They are in the café at the University of North Norfolk. Leif is buying the coffee and, from what Judy can see, vast amounts of chocolate for the children.

'I thought Hecate was the goddess of witchcraft,' says Judy.

'Childbirth too.'

'That figures.' Sometimes Judy thinks that she would quite like another child (if she could stand another M name) but can't bring herself to go through pregnancy again. Besides, she wants to take her Inspector exam soon. She watches Miranda skipping along beside Leif as he manoeuvres his tray towards them. Miranda seems to have taken to Leif, which is unusual because the only adults she really likes are her parents. Actually, sometimes just her father.

'Why didn't you tell me that you knew Leif?' says Judy.

'You didn't ask,' says Cathbad.

Judy is used to answers like this – seemingly frank but actually frustratingly enigmatic – by now. 'I told you about the letter,' she says. She feels rather guilty about this. 'You could have told me that you were in touch with Erik's son.'

'I wasn't in touch with him then,' says Cathbad. 'He only emailed me today. I've met him once before, years ago, when he was still a student. And I wanted you to meet him. That's why I suggested meeting here, at the university.'

'What's he doing here?'

'Visiting a friend in the history department apparently.'

They have to stop talking because Leif and his tray have arrived. Michael sits reading on his Kindle. Judy feels conflicted (reading: good; technology: bad) but doesn't say anything. Besides, Miranda is making up for it by watching delightedly as Leif turns his paper napkin into a swan.

'Again!' she says.

'Do you want one, Michael?' asks Leif.

'No thank you,' says Michael politely.

'How long are you in England for?' Judy asks Leif as she sips her cappuccino. Ruth told her recently that, in Italy, it's considered shocking, almost rude, to drink cappuccino after midday. Judy is rather pleased to think that she's being a rebel for once.

'For as long as the dig lasts,' says Leif. 'Probably about two weeks.'

'What about the modern bones that you've discovered? Won't that delay things?'

'Ruth thinks that the excavation will only take a day. She seemed pretty confident.'

'She's very good at her job,' says Judy. 'She'll be very thorough.'

'She seems an altogether admirable person,' says Leif. Something in the way he says this makes Judy look at him sharply but Leif is smiling pleasantly while his hands are busy with another piece of origami. This time it's a frog for Michael. Despite his earlier refusal, Judy can tell that Michael is pleased with the gift.

'It's sacred land,' says Cathbad. 'That's what your dad would say. That's why you've found a second circle.'

'The second circle might have been a burial mound,' says Leif, 'with the cist at the centre. Or a sky burial.'

'What's a sky burial?' asks Judy.

'Bodies left in the open to be consumed by animals and carrion birds,' says Leif, taking a bite of chocolate brownie. 'They could be offerings to the sky gods or simply part of the natural cycle. Animals and plants feed on the remains, death and rebirth. We'll know more when we have the results back on the bones.'

'What about the modern bones?' says Judy.

'A policewoman's question,' says Leif, smiling.

'I prefer police officer,' says Judy. 'When do you think the modern bones were buried there?'

'Ruth thought they might have been interred fairly recently,' says Leif. 'She mentioned the grave cut. I suppose you are looking into your . . . what do you call them? Cold cases?'

'Yes, we are,' says Judy.

'I'd love to see the site,' says Cathbad. 'I have very happy memories of the first excavation. Despite what happened later.'

Leif seems quite moved. He puts his hand on Cathbad's. 'Come to the site,' he says. 'Come early one morning and we will salute the dawn together.'

'I'll have to do the school run first,' says Cathbad.

Nelson stares at the beauty spot on his wife's cheek. They are in the zone now. Michelle seems oblivious of him; she concentrates on breathing, occasionally waving her hands as if trying to conjure something out of mid-air. Just once, she stares at him, really stares, as if she's seeing him for the first time.

'If anything happens to me,' she says, 'look after the baby.'

'I will.'

'Promise!'

'I promise.'

But then, suddenly, she's pushing and it's all screaming, grunting and panting and horrible silences and then, just like in the films, a slithery rush and the first angry cries.

'A beautiful boy,' says the midwife.

She puts the baby on Michelle's chest, still with the umbilical cord attached. The room smells of blood.

'Does Dad want to cut the cord?'

But Nelson can't tear his eyes away from the baby. This miracle child. His son.

'Hallo, George,' he says.

CHAPTER 8

Ruth doesn't hear until halfway through the next morning when Clough turns up at the excavation. She has exposed the margins of the visible bones and has taken pictures next to a scaling rod for measurements. Now she is in the process of lifting out a femur. She's not sure if there's a complete skeleton; the bones aren't articulated, and don't seem to have been buried with any particular care. By contrast, the remains in the cist had clearly been arranged with reverence, almost in foetal position, with the grave goods, the urn and seeds, at their side. Ruth is more certain than ever that the modern bones were buried in a rush and fairly recently.

Ted, from the field archaeology team, stands by to number and label each bone. It's a sunny day, though bitterly cold, and Ruth plans to let the bones dry out in the sun for a while, which should harden them. She is concentrating on the job so doesn't see Clough until he appears at the edge of the trench. She sees his feet first, tough-looking boots that also manage to look as if they're at the cutting edge of fashion. That's how she knows it's not Nelson.

'Have you heard the news?'

'What news?' says Ruth, pushing the hair out of her eyes. She is simultaneously hot and cold and her back aches. She is desperate for coffee but Leif tells her that the site is a caffeine-free zone: 'No poisons, only good energy here.'

'Michelle's had the baby.'

'That's great.' Ruth wonders how she can voice the question that crowds all others out of her mind. Is there some subtle way she can ask, without offending or shocking Clough?

'Oh, and it's not black,' says Clough, climbing into the trench. 'So we know it's the boss's. I brought you some coffee.'

So even Clough knows! Does everyone at the station know? Were they having bets on whether Michelle's baby was Nelson's or Tim's? Clough's face gives nothing away. He hands over a Starbucks cup, which probably completely violates the karma of the dig, and looks around the trench with apparent interest. Ruth drinks the coffee gratefully. The baby is Nelson's. This means it will cement Nelson and Michelle's marriage for ever. She can't see Nelson walking out on a baby and, anyhow, does she still want him to walk in her direction? She doesn't know. At that precise moment she is conscious only of the caffeine making its way into her system and of the relief of standing upright, easing her back. The other emotions will come later.

'Born last night,' Clough is saying. 'Seven pounds, six ounces. Not as big as Spencer was.' Since becoming a father, Clough has directed some of his relentless competitiveness into boasting about his offspring. He hands Ruth his phone to show the photograph sent by Nelson last night. Ruth looks at the baby wrapped in a blue shawl, eyes closed, fists clenched. Nelson's son. Kate's brother.

'Mother and baby both doing well,' says Clough. 'They should be home later today.'

'That's great,' says Ruth again. 'I'll send some flowers.' She takes another swig of coffee.

'How are your bones?' says Clough, peering at the half-exposed femur, which Ted is clearing with a pointing trowel.

'Don't touch anything,' says Ted. 'I know what the police are like. And why didn't I get coffee?'

'I've never seen you drink anything that isn't beer,' says Clough. 'How old do you think the bones are?'

'We won't know until we have the carbon-14 results,' says Ruth, rather wearily, 'and even then we won't have an exact date. The burial looks fairly new but the bones are older. We'll do isotope tests on the teeth. That will tell us where this person grew up.'

'The boss said you thought it was a child.'

'Yes, from the look of the bones I'd say it's an early adolescent. The bones still have epiphyses on them and we've got teeth, which is a great help with ageing. The eruption of permanent teeth happens within fairly set timescales. I'll know more when we excavate the skull.'

'Girl or boy?'

'We can't be sure unless we get some DNA. Girls have shallower pelvises and less pronounced brow-ridges but this isn't always easy to discern in adolescents. These changes occur gradually during the pubescent years.'

'You know we've got a possible name? Margaret Lacey, a twelve-year-old who went missing in 1981. That's strictly confidential, by the way.'

Ruth is pretty sure that Clough shouldn't have told them at all but he's always been a terrible gossip. Having a name makes all the difference though. She looks at the skull, which is still embedded in the earth and thinks: Margaret.

'I remember Margaret Lacey,' says Ted. 'Disappeared during a street party, didn't she?'

'Were you living in Lynn then?' asks Clough. 'You'd be about the right age.'

'No, I was still in Bolton in 1981,' says Ted. 'That was before I had to leave.'

Ted always makes it sound as though he was chased out of his home town by a pitchfork-waving mob but, as far as Ruth can make out, he simply left to attend Liverpool University.

'Are Margaret's family still living in the area?' asks Ruth.

'The mother and sister are,' says Clough. 'Father's dead, brother's in London. From what you've said, I think we'd better warn Margaret's mum that this might be her.'

'Who's in charge now the boss is on paternity leave?' asks Ted, with a wink at Ruth.

Clough puffs out his chest. 'Who do you think?'

'Judy,' says Ruth.

Michelle and George are home by lunchtime. Nelson drives them back as if he's advertising a safer roads initiative. Rebecca has come up from Brighton and she and Laura have attached blue balloons to the front door. Both sets of neighbours come out to welcome them.

'I feel like royalty,' says Michelle, getting carefully out of the car. She's still wearing maternity clothes but she has dry shampooed her hair and it glows in the sunshine. Both girls come out to hug her but they turn immediately to the occupant of the baby seat that is being proudly displayed by Nelson.

'He's gorgeous,' says Rebecca. 'He looks just like me.' And it's true that George, like Rebecca (and Kate) has inherited Nelson's dark hair.

'He's a bonny baby,' says Brenda next door, who likes to emphasise her Scottish ancestry.

'Can I hold him?' says Laura, who is trying to stop Bruno jumping up at his master.

'When we get inside,' says Nelson. 'It's a bit cold out here.'

After a few more pleasantries, the family go indoors; Nelson holding the baby seat with Bruno at his heels, Rebecca and Laura either side of their mother. Brenda turns to Alan, the other next-door neighbour. The cul-de-sac is not normally a very chatty place but the events of the last few months have brought them all a bit closer together.

'It's nice to see some happiness after everything that happened in the summer,' says Brenda.

'Yes,' says Alan. 'Michelle looked radiant, didn't she?' He has always had a soft spot for Mrs Nelson.

'I still think about that day,' says Brenda. 'That poor young man being shot like that. Tim Heathfield, his name was. Derek and I went to his funeral. The church was packed out.'

'Well that's all in the past now,' says Alan, trying to edge back inside.

'Poor Tim,' says Brenda, looking at the Nelsons' house, the balloons dancing in the breeze. 'I'll never forget him.'

It's late afternoon by the time that Ruth has finished her excavation. The scene-of-crime officers have left. Ted has numbered each bone and Ruth has filled in her bone chart. It seems as if they have a complete skeleton and, from the look of the skull and the pelvic bones, Ruth thinks it is that of a young female. The bones lie in paper bags, ready to go into the pathology crates. They are well-preserved, a factor that makes Ruth think that they were originally buried elsewhere, in a more anaerobic environment, with little oxygen to cause decay. There's nothing obvious to point to the cause of death. A healed fracture is evident on one humerus but this injury probably occurred in early childhood. The other bones show no abnormal signs of stress. The most precious clue is the presence of some blue household rope, strands that may have once bound Margaret's arms and legs. Traces of material were also found near the jawbone, possible evidence of a gag or even a means of asphyxiation. These fragments have been carefully bagged and documented. If DNA is found on them then the police might have a suspect at last. Ruth is just about to ring Clough when Ted says, 'What's this?'

Ted is taking soil samples and is kneeling looking into the crater left by the skull. Ruth comes to join him and, as she does so, she is aware that Leif is now standing behind them. Ted points at something white, half-embedded in the soil. At first Ruth thinks it's another bone but then she sees the pitted surface and realises that she is looking at a round piece of chalk. Ted picks it up carefully with gloved hands. The stone is the size of a small apple and there are two holes going through it. The positioning of the holes makes them look disconcertingly like eyes.

'A witch stone,' says Leif. 'Was it buried with the body?'

'I think so,' says Ruth, looking closer. 'This is a sandy beach, there's not much chalk around.'

'It looks like a skull,' says Ted. 'Maybe that's why it was buried there.'

'Maybe,' says Ruth. 'Let's bag it up and send it for tests. There could be DNA on it. Or fingerprints.'

'You think like a policeman, Ruth,' says Leif. 'It's clear that this is an offering of some kind.'

'Nothing's clear at the moment,' says Ruth, rather annoyed at this comment. 'Now, if you'll excuse me, I need to box up the bones.'

It rains later that evening. Michelle feeds George and goes to bed early. Nelson stays downstairs watching a Swedish crime drama with his daughters. He keeps falling asleep but he knows that the presence of the baby's cot in his room will mean that he wakes every hour in the night to check that George is still breathing. The trouble is, every time Nelson's eyes close he thinks of Ruth. Will she have heard about George by now? He sent texts and pictures to Judy and Clough. A massive bunch of flowers has already been delivered, 'From everyone at King's Lynn CID'. What did Judy say about news leaking from the police station? Presumably the whole town will know by now. He needs to tell Ruth. For one thing he wants Katie to meet her half-brother, though that will be tricky with Laura and Rebecca here. His head nods.

'Why don't you go to bed, Dad?' says Laura. 'We'll take Bruno out.'

His girls have been wonderful all evening, so excited about the baby, so kind to their parents. There's not a trace or resentment or jealousy in either of them. Maybe they would welcome Katie in the same wholehearted way.

'No, you're all right,' he says. 'I want to see if that Sven bloke killed the man dressed up as a moose.'

Ruth sits at her computer as the rain lashes against the windows. Kate is in bed, still oblivious to the fact that she is no longer an only child. Ruth has been expecting Nelson to ring all day but now it's nearly midnight and she knows that she won't hear from him. She should go to sleep – she has a nine o'clock lecture tomorrow – but she googled Margaret Lacey a few hours ago and now can't stop reading about the case.

'Family's anguish as Street Party Girl still missing.'

Margaret became 'Street Party Girl' very quickly in the days after her disappearance. Ruth was thirteen in 1981, almost the same age as Margaret is, was, would have been.

As Douglas Adams said, the problem of the past is largely one of grammar. A confirmed republican, Ruth is rather embarrassed to remember that she too had attended a street party, just off Eltham High Street. She remembers the bunting and a ribald song about 'Lady Di' but little else. Now Lady, later Princess, Diana is dead too and the whole thing seems like it happened in a different life.

To some papers Margaret was also 'Maggie' although there was no evidence that her family ever called her by this diminutive.

'Did Maggie have a London boyfriend?'

The answer was almost certainly no but some of Margaret's schoolfriends mentioned 'a boy in London', a 'penfriend' according to some. Ruth had almost forgotten penfriends. She'd exchanged letters with Beatrix in Germany for almost a year before the correspondence petered and died. Where was Beatrix now? she wondered. All Ruth could remember was that she'd been keen on 'prog rock' and *Starsky and Hutch*. At any rate, Margaret's penfriend never materialised. There was only one London train from King's Lynn that afternoon and none of the passengers remembered seeing a twelve-year-old girl wearing jeans and a Fruit of the Loom T-shirt. No CCTV in those days, of course.

There was TV though and Ruth manages to track down a documentary from 1988 called *The Missing* about unsolved cases. Margaret pops up on screen, first in her school uniform – purple blazer, fat tie, blonde hair in plaits – then in a bridesmaid's dress, her hair loose and curly. She was a pretty girl with a heart-shaped face and big blue eyes. In 1981, the days when Jimmy Savile was considered a lovably eccentric entertainer, many of the papers commented on Margaret's looks or speculated that she might have had 'admirers', despite being only twelve. 'She looked older,' said one report, lascivious even in print.

Margaret's mother, Karen, features strongly in the documentary. The father, Bob, doesn't speak much apart from, once, saying he'd like to kill the person who took his little girl. Ruth can see why Karen was chosen as spokesperson. She was attractive, like her daughter, with short blonde hair and an impressively straight gaze.

'Margaret wouldn't have run away,' she said, more than once. 'She was happy at home. Her brother and sister doted on her. She was the apple of our eye. We all adored her.'

Margaret certainly looked like the adored youngest child, the golden girl. Ruth is a youngest child too although it's hardly the same with two and, besides, she always felt that both parents preferred her brother, Simon, who got married, produced children and kept his atheism decently hidden behind dutiful churchgoing. Annie and Luke Lacey both appear on the documentary. Annie would have been twenty-one at the time but looked older, a solid-looking girl with an impassive stare. 'Someone knows what happened to my little sister,' she said, 'and we won't rest until we find them.' Luke, a year older, was more nervous, ducking his head so that his eighties fringe covered his eyes. 'It's not knowing that's quite hard,' he said, with rather touching understatement. 'It would be better really if we knew she was dead. Then we could grieve.'

Well now they might have a body and the grieving and the questions could start all over again. When Ruth had finished her excavation and gave it as her considered opinion that the body was that of an adolescent, probably female, who had died about thirty years ago, Clough said that he and Judy would visit Margaret's mother 'to prepare her'. How can you ever be prepared for news like that, even after thirty-five years? Ruth looks at the time at the bottom right-hand corner of her laptop: 00.28. She should go to bed. She knows, without looking round, that Flint is staring at her, wanting his late-night snack. But, when she shuts her laptop, she continues to gaze at the window, at the rain and the darkness.

CHAPTER 9

The sun rises over the marshes, turning the inland pools red and gold. The sand stretches out in front of them, rippled like a frozen sea. A flock of birds flies from the reed beds, zigzagging into the light. Leif raises his arms: 'Goddess of the earth. Bless our endeavours today.' Cathbad makes a suitable answer but he finds himself thinking, not of Brother Sun and Sister Moon, but of whether Judy will get to work in time after dropping the children at school and nursery. It was kind of her to offer to do the school run, especially when she has a possible murder case on her hands and Nelson is still away on paternity leave. He hopes that she remembers Michael's special vegetarian lunch box.

'The energies are good,' announces Leif. He selects a stone that is glimmering on the edge of the water. He weighs it in his hand for a moment and then sends it spinning into the sea. It skips over the shallow waves, once, twice, three times.

'A votive offering.' Leif turns to grin at Cathbad who has a sudden desire to pick up his own stone and send it spinning into the air, describing a perfect parabola as it flies. Stone skimming is a speciality of his, much admired by his children. He's surprised at the pettiness of his thoughts. He supposes that Leif, with his height and golden looks, arouses feelings of inferiority and competitiveness in other men. It's just a disappointment that he's not immune to such things.

'The new circle is very near the sea,' he says, as they turn and walk inland.

'Yes,' says Leif. 'Of course the sea has come much closer over the years but I think the setting is important.'

'Ruth said that the bones might be female,' says Cathbad.

Leif stops. 'The modern bones?'

'No,' says Cathbad. Judy has, in fact, told him the possible identity of the modern bones but he knows that this isn't in the public domain yet. He wonders why Leif jumped to this conclusion. 'She said that the bones in the cist were early Bronze Age and probably female, post-pubescent but still fairly young.'

'Yes,' says Leif, seeming to recover his poise. 'It's interesting that a young girl was buried here with such ceremony. There were grave goods too. An urn containing berries and seeds and a stone with a hole through the middle.'

'A witch stone?'

'Yes, or hag stone. Funnily enough, one was found with the modern bones too.'

They have reached the site and Leif takes the tarpaulin off the trenches. Cathbad looks at the clean lines, the layers of soil, the scaling rods laid on the grass. It reminds him of digging with Erik in the early days. Erik, despite his eccentricities, was very strict about methodology. You weren't even allowed to sit on the edge of your trench, Cathbad remembers, in case you spoilt the edges.

Leif shows Cathbad the cist, a rectangular space lined with stones.

'The bones were roughly in foetal position,' he says. 'The urn at her head, the stone by her feet.' The female pronoun makes all the difference, thinks Cathbad. He finds himself praying for the Bronze Age girl as well as for Margaret, if that is the identity of the later body.

'Were there wooden posts around the cist?' he asks.

'We think so,' says Leif. 'We've excavated six of them. This is a sketch of the possible shape.' He shows this, not on a notebook, but on his iPad, which seems rather sad to Cathbad. But the reconstruction is impressive, a palisade of posts in a roughly oval shape.

'It's not really a circle, is it?' says Cathbad.

'No,' says Leif. 'It reminds me of stone ships. Have you seen these? You get them in Scandinavia, around a thousand years BCE. The Jelling stone ship in Denmark is famous. It's a grave surrounded by stones in a leaf pattern that resembles a ship. It's thought to link to the Viking belief that the dead sailed to Valhalla over the sea. But some say that the burial also meant good luck and fertility for the surrounding lands. Ships in fields, they're sometimes called.'

Cathbad looks out across the flat marshland. He remembers guiding Nelson across the quicksand in the dark, using the ancient posts as a guide. He likes the thought that the Bronze Age grave might have meant good luck for the surrounding land. But he finds the notion of stone ships rather disquieting. He once had a very vivid dream – or hallucination – about Erik sailing a ship made of stone.

'I remember your dad so well,' he says now. 'He was a great influence on me. I switched from chemistry to archaeology because of him. He was my lecturer at Manchester.'

'He talked about you often,' says Leif. 'I think you were very dear to him.'

'Maybe,' says Cathbad. 'I was useful to him, at any rate. I've sometimes felt that things didn't end well between us. Maybe that's why I think of him so often.'

'Perhaps there is some way that we can achieve closure,' says Leif. He's looking intently at Cathbad. His eyes – so like Erik's – disconcertingly bright.

'Perhaps that's why you came here,' says Cathbad.

'I was summoned here,' says Leif. 'By the dead girl.'

'The girl in the cist?'

'No,' says Leif, 'the poor spirit whose bones we found the other day. I feel sure she is a girl and that she is calling to us.'

He smiles at Cathbad, a radiant beam that recalls Erik at his most messianic. But, at that moment, Cathbad does not find the memory reassuring.

Judy drops the children at their educational establishments without incident. She forgets Michael's lunch box but stops off at the Co-op to buy him a cheese sandwich and some grapes. She puts these in a police evidence bag which, for Michael, makes his whole day worthwhile. At the station, she finds Clough eating a bacon sandwich which makes her mouth water. Doing without bacon is the single worst thing about living with Cathbad.

'Want some?' says Clough.

'No. Yes. Just a bit.' Clough tears off a piece of bread and bacon, dripping with tomato sauce. It tastes like heaven.

They have arranged to call on Karen Benson, Margaret's mother, at nine o'clock. On the phone Judy only said that they'd made a discovery which might be linked to Margaret's disappearance. She also suggests that Karen has someone with her to receive the news. When they get to the neat terraced house they are met at the door by a large woman in a nurse's uniform who says that she's Karen's daughter, Annie Simmonds.

'Margaret's sister,' she adds, fixing them with a rather belligerent stare. It's obvious that Annie, at least, regards the police with suspicion. Karen is a gentler, more nervous, presence. She's a small woman and that makes her look oddly childlike, despite ash-grey hair and a face that bears the lines of a lifelong smoker.

Annie offers them tea which Judy accepts because she feels that it'll put the visit on a friendlier footing. If the bones do turn out to be Margaret's, they will be seeing a lot of her family in the next few weeks. Annie puts mugs in front of them, together with a plate of biscuits. Clough takes two. Karen gets out a cigarette and looks at it longingly.

'You know Pete doesn't like you smoking in the house,' says Annie. Karen puts the cigarette back in its packet. *Smoking Kills*, is the bald message on the gold box.

Pete Benson is Karen's second husband, a mild-looking man with white hair who looks older than his wife. He barely speaks as the women hand out plates and mugs. And he doesn't comment on the cigarette.

'Thank you for seeing us,' says Judy. 'As I said on the phone, we've made a discovery which we think might be connected to Margaret's disappearance. It's early days but we just wanted you to know so that you can prepare yourselves and so that we can support you.'

'Have you found her?' interrupts Annie. The question sounds as if she really expects them to have found Margaret alive. As if a blonde-haired woman in her late forties is about to come into the room with her arms outstretched.

Judy says, 'We've found some human remains which we think might be those of Margaret. I'm sorry. This must be a terrible shock.'

Karen makes a noise that is halfway between a gasp and a sob. Pete reaches over and holds her hand. Annie takes a sip of tea, eyes hard.

'We've found some bones on the coast near Titchwell,' Judy continues. 'The forensic archaeologist thinks that they might be the remains of a child Margaret's age.'

'An archaeologist?' says Annie. 'What's an archaeologist got to do with it?'

'The bones were found on an archaeological site,' says Judy. 'And the police often consult archaeologists in cases like this.'

'And you think it really might be ... that it might be Margaret?' Karen's voice is trembling.

'We'll see if we can get some DNA from the bones,' says

Clough. 'And, if not, we can check dental records. One way or another, we should have a definite answer for you.'

It's almost the first time Clough has spoken – he prefers to leave the family liaison stuff to Judy – and Judy is annoyed to see both women turning to him with respect and attention. Superintendent Archer hasn't put anyone in charge in Nelson's absence. 'Let's try a collegiate approach,' she said, when asked directly (by Tanya). But there's nothing that admirable about the way colleges and universities operate, as far as Judy can see.

'How long will it take?' asks Annie.

'About two weeks,' says Clough, plucking a timescale from the air. Karen and Annie take it as gospel.

'So in two weeks we'll know,' says Karen. 'We'll know . . . we'll know what happened to her.'

'Easy, love.' Pete looks at his wife rather anxiously.

'These things take time,' says Judy. 'I know it's very hard, the waiting.'

'We've waited thirty-five years,' says Karen, with a harsh laugh that turns into a smoker's cough. 'Our Annie's just become a grandmother. I'm a great-grandmother. But it's as if Margaret disappeared yesterday.'

Judy looks at the wall behind Karen's head, where a giant flat-screen TV is surrounded by framed photographs: children, grandchildren and pets. Her eyes are immediately drawn to a studio portrait of a blonde girl in a pink bridesmaid's dress. Margaret. Forever young, forever missing.

'It's tough on the mother,' says Pete, with the air of one passing on a state secret.

'Tough on everyone, Pete,' says Annie. 'Our Luke still has nightmares about it.'

'Well, hopefully we'll have some news for you soon,' says Clough, standing up. 'Thank you for letting us come round today.'

'Thank you, Detective Inspector,' says Karen, addressing Clough.

'We'll be in touch,' says Judy.

'You didn't correct them about the rank,' says Judy as they drive back to the station.

'I didn't like to upset them,' says Clough, 'not at this emotional time.'

'Bloody sexist. Assuming the man is in charge.'

'I know,' says Clough, driving carefully through the maze of streets. 'It's shocking. I'd write to the *Guardian* about it if I were you.'

'You're going the wrong way,' says Judy. 'It's left here.' Karen and Pete still live in the house where Margaret was brought up. Once council, it's now privately owned, as are many on the estate. But, while the pebbledash houses display signs of individuality – a conservatory here, a loft extension there – the overriding impression is still that of uniformity, row upon row of identical houses, each with their small stretch of garden, roads named after First World War Generals: Haig, Allenby, Marshall, Byng. Clough takes a right down Allenby Avenue.

'Where are you going?'

'I think this is the one.' Clough slows down as they pass

a corner house, the same as the others in the street except shabbier, a decaying sofa in the garden, dirty blinds at the upper windows.

'What . . . ?' begins Judy.

'This is the house where John Mostyn lives,' says Clough. 'The prime suspect.'

Judy wants to tell Clough that John Mostyn's not an official suspect so they can't stalk him like this but she's secretly impressed that Clough has both read the file and remembered the address. 'It's very close, isn't it?' she says.

'Yes,' says Clough. 'The families knew each other.'

'Incredible that Karen hasn't moved away,' says Judy.

'Maybe she didn't want to leave with Margaret still missing.'

Judy thinks of Karen saying 'it's as if Margaret disappeared yesterday'. Has she, all this time, been half expecting her youngest daughter to walk through the door, golden-haired and unchanged? Does she feel, on the nights when the wind and rain rush in from the sea, that Margaret is out there somewhere in the dark?

Clough pulls in at the kerb and they both stare at the end house. Judy knows from the file that John Mostyn has lived on his own since his mother died almost twenty years ago. The Stone Man, they called him, and she has a sudden vision of the house's occupant sitting calcified in his chair, flesh becoming stone.

'Let's go,' she says. 'Time enough to interview Mostyn when we have a DNA match.'

*

When they get back to King's Lynn police station, the duty officer – a newish woman constable – tells Judy that her daughter is waiting for her.

'What?' says Judy. She imagines three-year-old Miranda sitting in the waiting area, clutching her teddy bear.

'I thought you were too young to have a grown-up daughter,' says the PC, blushing.

'I am,' says Judy. But by now she has spotted the blonde hair and the parka and knows who is waiting for her.

'Hallo, Maddie.'

'Hallo, Mum,' says Maddie, grinning. Judy and Cathbad aren't married so, technically, Madeleine isn't her step-daughter but it would be churlish to point this out. Besides, Maddie has a perfectly good mother of her own so Judy isn't required to fulfil that role. What they have instead is a rather uneasy semi-friendship. Maddie's not that close to Cathbad either although she adores Michael and Miranda.

'Have you got a minute?' says Maddie.

'Of course. Come on up.'

'Hallo, Maddie,' says Clough. 'You still working for that crap paper?'

Maddie laughs but Clough has succeeded in putting Judy on her guard. She knows now why Maddie is paying her this visit.

The open-plan office is empty apart from Tanya, sulkily writing up some notes. Judy offers to make coffee and Maddie proffers her own herbal teabags. She follows Judy into the kitchen and says, 'I hear you've found Margaret Lacey.'

'Is that why you're here?' says Judy, splashing boiling water into a mug.

'Come on, Judy,' says Maddie. 'Just say yes or no. It would be such a scoop for me.'

'I can't say yes or no,' says Judy, 'because I don't know.'

'But you have found some bones. Cathbad told me.' Maddie always refers to her father by his name (or, rather, his druidical name). Her stepfather, who brought her up, is Dad.

'Look, Maddie.' Judy tries for a calming tone. Maddie's startling green eyes are fixed on her face. She has an intensity that sometimes seems to edge towards something darker. 'You can't mention the name Margaret Lacey in connection with these bones. Not until we're sure. Her family have suffered enough. But, if this is her, you'll be the first to know. After the next of kin, of course. Is that a deal?'

'What about John Mostyn?' says Maddie. 'He still lives locally, doesn't he? Will you bring him in for questioning? Get a DNA sample?'

'I can't say,' says Judy.

'John Mostyn could have killed Scarlet too,' says Maddie. 'He used to work for the paper as a photographer. He knew all about the henge dig.'

'He didn't kill her,' says Judy.

'Scarlet was found buried in the centre of a Bronze Age circle,' says Maddie. 'That's where you found Margaret too.'

'Maddie,' Judy lowers her voice, 'we know who killed Scarlet and he's dead too. Don't do this to yourself.'

'You'll never understand about Scarlet.' Maddie sweeps out of the room leaving Judy standing there, a mug of boiling water in her hand.

CHAPTER 10

Clough was right; it takes two weeks for the DNA results to come back. And it's a match. The bones found buried by the Bronze Age grave are the remains of Margaret Lacey, aged twelve. Judy and Clough break the news to Karen and, before the police put out an official statement, they drive out to the Saltmarsh so that the family can put flowers at the site. The archaeologists have been warned to stay away.

It's a misty morning, the sky streaked pale blue and pink, the sea limpid and calm. They walk in file along the gravel path. Judy leading, followed by Karen and Pete, Karen holding a bunch of flowers hastily purchased from a garage, Clough and Annie bringing up the rear. Judy visited the dig yesterday but is struck by how different the Saltmarsh looks in different times and moods. Today the sand seems completely featureless and, if she hadn't seen the measuring rods, she might not have been able to identify the site. They climb the sand dune, picking their way through beach-grass and plants that look like huge cabbages. Then the ground levels out and the trench – the grave – is there, just at the edge of the tide. Someone (Judy suspects Leif) has marked the place with a rough cross made from driftwood and tied together with grass. Karen lets out a small cry and then puts her hand to her mouth.

'Why was she buried here?' says Annie, out of breath from the walk but angry again. 'It's miles from anywhere.'

'Ruth, the archaeologist,' says Judy, 'thinks that Margaret was originally buried somewhere else and her bones transferred here fairly recently. She can tell by the preservation of the bones.'

'Then why are we here?' says Annie, sitting heavily on the grassy bank.

But Karen has walked up to the trench and has placed her flowers by the cross. Then she falls to her knees. Pete hesitates then goes to stand beside her. Clough and Judy keep a respectful distance away. After a moment, Annie gets to her feet and joins her mother. The three of them are silhouetted against the skyline, like a religious tableau, the woman kneeling, the man and the younger woman standing one on each side. Judy can hear them speaking but it's a few seconds before she recognises the words. The Hail Mary. The family are Catholic, she knows, but Karen told her that she hadn't been to mass since Margaret disappeared. But they are praying now, the rhythmic mutter counterpointed by the cries of seagulls and the sound of the incoming tide. Judy, who was brought up a Catholic, thinks that they will say the prayer ten times, a decade of the rosary. She feels her lips forming the words but stops when she sees Clough looking at her.

'Pray for us now and at the hour of our death.'

Karen gets to her feet. Then she crosses herself and heads back towards the sand dunes, without looking back. Pete, Annie and Clough follow but Judy takes one last look at the site. The beach is still deserted apart from someone walking by the sea's edge. Something about the figure reminds Judy of Cathbad and she realises it's because they are either wearing a hooded coat or a cloak. But Cathbad will be dropping Michael off at school now. Judy stays watching as the figure comes closer, walking slowly but with great purpose, footprints disappearing into the wet strand. When the cloak-wearer is almost level with the site, it turns towards the sea, raising its hands to the sky. The hood falls back and Judy sees bright hair gleaming in the hazy sunlight.

CHAPTER 11

Superintendent Jo Archer speaks to the press at midday. Nelson is due back at work the next day but she's not about to wait for him. She speaks fluently and well, asking the assembled journalists to respect the Lacey family's privacy 'at this difficult time'. Judy, watching from the back of the room, spots Maddie sitting near the front. Judy kept her word and telephoned Maddie two hours ago with the news about Margaret. When Jo invites questions Judy half expects Maddie to ask about possible links to the Scarlet Henderson case, but her stepdaughter keeps silent.

Someone asks about DNA.

'The technology has come on in leaps and bounds since the eighties,' says Jo, managing to convey the impression that this decade is only a distant memory to her. 'We're hopeful that there will be some DNA on the remains, or on objects found with them, that will allow us to reopen the case and catch Margaret's killer.'

This is a real teaser for the press pack. Several people ask about these mysterious objects but Jo says that she is not divulging this information 'at this point in time'.

'Will you be reinterviewing past suspects?' says a man from one of the nationals.

'Again, I can't comment on that,' says Jo.

But Judy knows that the answer is yes. They already have a DNA sample from Karen, that is how they were able to identify Margaret. Now they need DNA swabs and finger-prints from everyone involved in the case, 'to eliminate them'. Judy and Clough are going to call on John Mostyn. 'He doesn't have to cooperate,' Jo reminded the team, 'but it will be interesting to see his demeanour. He'll have heard on the news about us finding Margaret's remains.'

Judy notes that Jo expects everyone in the world to have seen her press conference but, when they reach the shabby corner house late that afternoon, John Mostyn says that he never watches or listens to the news. 'It's always bad,' he says. 'I prefer to think of nice things.'

John Mostyn is a slight figure who looks older than sev-enty. Judy's mother is a seventy-five-year-old spring chicken who does yoga and wears skinny jeans. Mostyn is shrivelled and frail-looking, wearing a baggy jumper and corduroys. His house, too, seems to teeter on the edge of squalor; the sitting room knee-deep in cardboard boxes, the kitchen a nightmare of sticky brown units and overcrowded surfaces. Judy and Clough sit at the kitchen table after Mostyn has moved several books, a bubbling vat of what looks like beer and a hamster in a cage.

'So you haven't heard that the police have found Margaret

Lacey's remains,' says Judy, trying not to look at the mountain of newspaper in the corner which seems to be moving.

Mostyn sits opposite them. His faded blue eyes look open and guileless. 'No. I hadn't heard that. Poor girl. But it's good for the family. After all this time.'

'We're contacting everyone connected with the case and asking if we can take fingerprints and a DNA sample,' says Clough. 'Just so that we can rule people out.'

'It's very simple,' says Judy as Mostyn is looking rather alarmed. 'Just a swab from inside your cheek.'

'Will I have to go to the police station?'

'It's very quick,' says Judy. 'You'll be in and out in ten minutes.' Nelson has told them to bring Mostyn to the station if possible.

'People will see,' says Mostyn, 'and they'll think I did it. They'll throw things.'

Mostyn and his mother had suffered abuse at the time of Margaret's disappearance. It's in the files and Judy has seen the headlines. 'Loner was last person to see Maggie alive.' 'Police question so-called Stone Man.' Such coverage probably wouldn't be allowed now for fear of jeopardising the case.

'We can send someone here if that's easier,' says Judy.

'The neighbours will see,' says Mostyn. 'People round here know everything that goes on.'

The same comment had been made in 1981 but, all the same, a girl had managed to disappear in broad daylight. Judy wonders whether Mostyn has become more paranoid with age and isolation. The house certainly doesn't look like it belongs to an entirely well man. She is sure that something is moving under that newspaper.

'I'll come into the station,' says Mostyn at last. 'Don't call for me. I'll make my own way.'

'That's very helpful,' says Clough, 'thank you. Shall we say nine thirty tomorrow morning?'

'All right,' says Mostyn. 'I'm up early most mornings. Beachcombing.'

Judy has already noticed the stones. They are everywhere, amongst the flotsam and jetsam in the room, stones of every shape and colour, from glittering hunks of quartz to tiny piles of pebbles, like the droppings of a petrified rabbit.

'Have you always lived near the sea?' she asks.

Mostyn smiles for the first time. His teeth are discoloured and rotten but the expression is surprisingly benign.

'Yes,' he says. 'I was born at Caister-on-Sea. It used to be a Roman port once. I found a Roman coin in the sand when I was a boy. I sent it to the British Museum and they wrote a nice letter back. I've got it somewhere.'

He looks around as if he might, amid the detritus of years, find the letter written some sixty years ago.

'You must have found some interesting things over the years,' says Judy.

'I certainly have.' Mostyn is still smiling but now he turns away and starts searching along a shelf packed with books and yellowing magazines. 'I've found shepherd's crowns, sea lilies, brittle stars, all sorts of things. I've got something here somewhere . . . Yes. Here it is.' He scrabbles under some ancient copies of *Punch*. 'Have this, my dear. For luck.' It's a witch stone, a perfect oval with a single hole running straight through the middle.

Outside, in the car, Clough says, 'My money's still on Mostyn. He's as creepy as hell.'

'He was scared,' says Judy. She is still holding the stone. It fits perfectly in her hand.

'Yes, but why was he scared?' says Clough. 'And, did you notice, he didn't ask where Margaret was found? Surely that should have been his first question. We've found Margaret. Where?'

'I did notice that,' says Judy. 'Well, if his DNA's on the rope, we've got him.'

'And he could have written that letter,' says Clough. 'He's interested in history. Remember what he said about the coin?'

Once again, Clough surprises Judy. She had thought that he was too revolted by the house to be listening closely to Mostyn's ramblings down memory lane. But he's right. Mostyn did show an interest both in history and archaeology. Not to mention the sea.

'And he's from east Norfolk,' she says. 'Caister is right near Yarmouth and Tom said that's where the legend of Jack Valentine is from. He could have left that witch stone on the boss's doorstep. He found this one for me. I bet there are hundreds of them in the house.'

'That house,' says Clough and shudders. Clough and Cassandra are extremely tidy, despite having a baby and a puppy. Judy often fears that her own household will one day descend into chaos. Cathbad keeps things fairly clean but he doesn't like to dust because he admires spiders. But, at the end of their interview with Mostyn, when the newspaper mound finally erupted and a furry shape emerged, Judy hadn't been able to stop herself screaming. 'Tuppence!' exclaimed Mostyn. 'That's where you've been.' He cradled the little creature in his hands and Judy saw that it was another hamster. Mostyn held out his hands and Judy stroked the quivering fur. Now she puts the stone in her bag and fumbles for hand sanitiser.

'He needs help,' she says. 'He's a hoarder.' She passes the plastic bottle to Clough.

'We should do a proper search of the house,' says Clough, rubbing the gel on his hands.

'They got a search warrant at the time,' says Judy. 'They didn't find anything. And thirty-five years have passed.'

'There's more than thirty-five years of rubbish in there,' says Clough, starting the engine.

On the other side of King's Lynn, Ruth and Kate are also waiting in a car. Ruth has collected Kate from school and they are on their way to see the new baby. The day after George was born, Nelson drove round with some photographs and explained to Kate that George was her half-brother, 'because you both have the same daddy'.

'But not the same mum,' said Kate, who likes to get things straight.

'No,' said Nelson. 'Michelle is George's mum.' He hadn't looked at Ruth when he said this. She wished she had left

Nelson to have this conversation in private but had thought that she should be there in case Kate needed some questions answered. But, if Kate had queries, she kept them to herself and favoured her parents with a rendition of 'Food, Glorious Food' from her acting class, complete with gestures.

Now they are sitting outside the Nelsons' house and Ruth is gathering her courage. Kate, clasping a wrapped present, is watching her intently.

'Let's go in, Mum,' she says.

'In a minute,' says Ruth. She has never been in this house before, although Kate has. It's a modern detached, square and somehow reassuring, like a child's drawing of a house. Hard to imagine the horrors that occurred behind this front door – white with patterned glass – last summer. The front garden is a neat square of grass, the driveway wide enough for two cars, Nelson's Mercedes and Michelle's Micra parked side by side. Does Nelson mow the lawn? Ruth is ready to bet that he does.

'Come on, Mum.'

'I'm coming.'

Nelson is obviously on edge too because he opens the door before they have time to knock.

'Come in,' he says, over-heartily. 'Michelle and George are in the front room.'

The front room. Ruth thinks this must go back to Nelson's childhood home. She's sure that Michelle calls it the sitting room or the lounge.

Michelle is sitting on the sofa, buttoning her blouse. The

baby, obviously satiated from his feed, lies in the crook of her arm, his mouth half open. Ruth can see dark hair and long eyelashes, both inherited from Nelson.

'Hallo,' she says.

'Hallo, Ruth,' says Michelle, rather tightly. But she gives Kate a lovely smile. 'Come and say hallo to Baby George.'

Kate approaches, holding the present out in front of her. 'He's asleep,' she says.

'He sleeps all the time,' says Nelson. 'Except at night.'

Michelle smiles. Ruth thinks that she looks tired but lovelier than ever; no make-up, the brown roots showing in her hair, eyes ringed with violet shadows.

Kate touches George's cheek. 'Hallo, baby.'

'Do you want to hold him?' says Michelle.

'Are you sure?' says Nelson but Michelle ignores him. Kate sits next to her on the sofa and Michelle puts George in her lap. The three adults stare at them, Kate sitting very upright, the baby still sleeping, the winter sun illuminating both their faces.

'I should take a picture,' says Nelson, breaking the spell. He goes to get his camera, obviously not trusting the moment to his phone.

'How are you?' says Ruth to Michelle.

'Oh, OK,' says Michelle. 'Tired. You know.'

'Yes,' says Ruth. 'I don't think Kate slept through the night for the first year.'

Kate is interested. 'Why didn't I?'

'I don't know. Sometimes babies don't.'

'George is quite good,' says Michelle. 'He slept from

midnight until five last night. It's just that Harry keeps waking up to check on him.'

Ruth had forgotten that Michelle calls Nelson Harry. The thought of them sharing a bed, the baby next to them, causes a wave of jealousy so intense that Ruth feels almost sick. Nelson comes back into the room and takes several pictures. Michelle reclaims her baby and puts him in a Moses basket on the floor. Kate unwraps the present, a cuddly giraffe, and plays with it herself. Nelson offers to make tea and this is declined, although Michelle asks for a pint of squash.

'You get so thirsty breastfeeding,' she says.

'I remember,' says Ruth, although she doesn't really. Nature seems to grant you amnesia about childbirth, which is probably the only reason why women go on to have more children. But Ruth is clearly only going to get one chance at motherhood so she wishes that she remembered the early days better.

Nelson brings squash and biscuits for all of them. Ruth sips the orange liquid. She hasn't drunk diluted squash since childhood. It reminds her of church youth clubs. Kate drinks hers quickly and puts the glass down on a coaster. Ruth is proud of her.

'Where's Laura?' she says.

Kate met Laura last year, although she doesn't seem to have worked out that she too is a half-sibling.

'She's at college,' says Nelson. 'She's training to be a teacher.'

'Rebecca was here last week,' says Michelle. 'She's working in Brighton.'

'I like Brighton,' says Ruth. There's a rather awkward silence. George saves the day by waking up and starting to cry. Nelson picks him up and pats his back with an experienced hand. Ruth averts her eyes.

'Give him to me, Harry,' says Michelle.

'We should go,' says Ruth.

Kate blows a kiss to George, who is still crying, though in an angry, raspy way.

'Bye, Michelle,' says Ruth. 'Thank you for letting us see George. He's beautiful.'

'See you soon,' says Michelle. She sounds distracted and probably lets this phrase slip accidentally from her social lexicon. Ruth is pretty sure that Michelle would be happy never to see her again. Michelle is fond of Kate though; Ruth will always be grateful to her for that.

Nelson walks to the car with them.

'Did you hear?' he says. 'They've confirmed the identity of the remains found on the beach. It is Margaret Lacey.'

'I heard the press conference on the radio,' says Ruth.

'I'm back at work tomorrow,' says Nelson. 'No rest for the wicked.'

Ruth doesn't believe a word of it. She thinks that Nelson can't wait to return to the fray. He looks as if he's already thinking about the case, about marshalling the team and finding Margaret's killer. He won't rest, Ruth knows, even though so many years have passed. Nelson sees her looking at him and smiles. Because he so often looks serious, the smile transforms his face completely.

'George is gorgeous,' says Ruth.

'He's not bad,' says Nelson.

'I'm happy for you,' says Ruth. 'For you both. Really.'

'I know you are,' says Nelson.

There's a charged silence broken eventually by Kate's peremptory tap on the car window. Ruth says goodbye and gets into the driving seat. Nelson is watching as they drive away.

CHAPTER 12

Nelson is at the station by seven thirty the next morning. By the time that Tanya gets in at eight thirty, Judy at eight forty-five and Clough at nine, he has created an incident room display with Margaret Lacey's picture at the centre. Arrows point out to her parents, Karen and Bob, the latter with RIP scribbled across his forehead. Sister Annie and brother Luke are also there, alongside Kim Jennings and John Mostyn.

'We need to interview Kim Jennings,' says Nelson, after acknowledging the team's greetings and congratulations. 'I've been reading through the transcripts and I think there was something she wasn't telling the police at the time. I've checked and she still lives in Norfolk. She's got a shop near the beach in Wells. That's your neck of the woods, Judy.'

'Yes,' says Judy. 'I'll go and see her.'

'And talk to Marj Maccallum,' says Nelson. 'She was a good officer. I'd like to have her take on the case.'

'What did DS Burnett say?' asks Clough, who, as usual, is chomping his way through a McDonald's breakfast. 'I remember him. Hard as nails.'

'Freddie thinks it's all down to Mostyn. Well, he may be right.'

'Mostyn's coming in at nine thirty to give a DNA sample,' says Clough.

'Good,' says Nelson. 'Let me know when he's here. I'd like to take a look at him.'

'He's an unsavoury specimen,' says Clough. 'Lives in a house full of cardboard boxes and rats.'

'They were hamsters,' says Judy.

'He took a liking to Johnson,' says Clough. 'Gave her one of those stones with holes in.'

'Did he?' says Nelson. He notes that the team who, according to Jo, have been working together in perfect harmony during his absence, are back to vying for position. 'Well, Mostyn was the original prime suspect but there was nothing at the time to tie him to the crime. He was seen talking to Margaret during the street party but he had an alibi for the whole afternoon and evening. Admittedly it was from his mother and, as Freddie reminded me, she might well have been prepared to lie for him.'

'I think that it was Mostyn who wrote you that letter and left the stone outside your house,' says Clough. 'He's interested in history and literature and all that. There were all sorts of books around the house. And he talked about finding Roman coins on the beach.'

'And he's from east Norfolk,' says Judy. 'So he'd know the Jack Valentine legend. And there was a witch stone found with the remains.'

'Yes,' says Clough. 'Ruth thought that it had been placed there deliberately because you don't find chalk on that beach. She also thought that the bones hadn't been there long. She reckoned they'd been buried somewhere else first, in anaer-whatsit conditions. It's in her report.'

'I've been reading it,' says Nelson. 'She thought the bones had previously been buried in peaty soil that was rich in nitrogen.'

'What does that mean?' says Clough.

'Horse manure,' says Nelson, 'or some sort of silage.'

'So we're looking for horse shit,' says Clough.

'Again,' says Judy.

'The stone and the rope are both promising leads,' says Nelson. 'Also the material found near the mouth. The killer's DNA could be on them. You've taken samples from the mother and sister?'

'Yes,' says Judy. 'They were the first people we went to.'

'We need to get the brother too,' says Nelson. 'He's a bit of a shadowy figure in all this. He was fifteen when Margaret disappeared. That's old enough.'

'Do you think he could have killed his own sister?' says Clough, always one for saying the unsayable.

'I'm just saying we ought to talk to him,' says Nelson, 'and get a DNA sample. Fuller, can you get on to it?'

'Yes, boss,' says Tanya. 'Is the case officially open again?'

'Yes,' says Nelson. 'It may be thirty-five years too late but we're going to get justice for Margaret. Let me know when Mostyn comes in, Cloughie.'

*

Ruth is also looking at a report. She is reading the results of the isotope analysis on Margaret's teeth. There is nothing too surprising as it confirms that the teeth belonged to someone who was brought up in Norfolk, specifically the coastal north-east region. This would fit Margaret, who was born and bred in King's Lynn. The carbon-14 report confirms that the bones are fairly recent but has nothing much to add to the investigation. The best hope of a lead lies with the bones themselves. If Ruth could find out where they had originally been buried, then it might point the police in the right direction. Ruth has a lecture in half an hour but she opens her desk drawer and gets out a map entitled 'Geology of Norfolk'. Ruth loves old maps, the pinks and greens, the lines showing contours, the crosses for churches and the picks and shovels for mines. Reading maps is an essential skill for an archaeologist. But now she is looking at soil. The area around King's Lynn is marked as 'tidal flat deposits' and she knows that this will be clay and silt, built up during the millennia north Norfolk was covered by the sea (Lynn is the Celtic word for lake), so the soil is shallow and lime-rich over chalk or limestone. But Margaret's bones were buried in richer earth and there were definite traces of nitrogen which could come from manure. This might mean farmland. Ruth searches further inland, where you would expect to find loamy clay soil with a peat surface. This would fit with the preservation of the bones, typical of waterlogged anaerobic conditions. Taking a pencil Ruth traces a circle around King's Lynn, taking in agricultural land near the River Great Ouse.

She is so deeply engrossed that she doesn't hear the knock on the door. Debbie, the department secretary, has to put her head round the door. 'Ruth?'

Ruth jumps. 'Sorry. I was miles away.'

'A letter's been delivered for you.'

'A letter?' In these days of email, actual post is rare. Her publishers send royalty statements where the earnings are so tiny, both in monetary and typeface terms, that they are almost impossible to find. But they write to her home address. If the post has come to the university, it must be a sales catalogue of some kind. But Debbie's face seems to indicate that this delivery is rather more intriguing.

Debbie hands over a white envelope. 'Hand delivered,' she says impressively.

Ruth waits until Debbie has gone and then slits open the envelope with her special Victorian paperknife – a present from Frank. Inside is a brief typed note:

You found Margaret. She called from the depths and you answered. Her soul is now at peace. May the Gods of earth, sky and sea bless you, Ruth.

Ruth stares at the words for a long time. She doesn't move until her Fitbit buzzes and exhorts her, bossily, to 'get up and stretch for ten'.

Kim Jennings' shop, called Little Rocks, is on the quayside at Wells, only a few hundred metres from Judy's cottage. She texts Cathbad and suggests meeting for fish and chips after her interview. It's a lovely spring day, the sea sparkling and the boats clinking in the harbour. Although it's only March there are a few tourists wandering around and taking photos of the beach huts. Little Rocks, with its window display of crystals and fridge magnets in the shape of crabs, is empty though. There are trays outside displaying stones and pebbles, some rough-edged, some polished to shine like jewels. Judy recognises a couple of the shepherd's crowns mentioned by John Mostyn. These are really fossilised sea urchins, grey stones with a darker pattern of rays protruding from the centre, like a star or the spikes of a crown. She looked up sea lilies and brittle stars too, though she can't see any of them in the shop. These fossils are usually found in sandstone and can look rather sinister preserved in the stone, like scaly claws or alien faces. The most attractive stones outside Little Rocks are chunks of amber, clear yellow or red-gold, some flecked with what might be the remains of tiny prehistoric insects. But still no one is buying anything.

Kim Jennings, a short woman with Cleopatra hair, says that business is bad. 'People browse but they don't buy. I think that's rude.' Judy sympathises but she can't see anything in the shop that anyone would actually want to buy, unless you fancy bracelets made from pebbles and books entitled *Crystal Healing: How to Attract Wealth and Reduce Stress*.

On second thoughts, maybe that would be worth a read.

Kim switches the driftwood sign on the door to 'Gone fishing' and leads Judy into a back room. They sit amongst cardboard boxes which reminds Judy of John Mostyn's house but Kim offers to make coffee, which certainly wasn't on offer at the Mostyn residence, and the parts of the floor which can be seen are, thankfully, free of rodents.

'You've heard that we've found Margaret's remains,' says Judy, accepting a cup of instant coffee in a mug proclaiming, probably erroneously, that 'Mermaids Exist'.

'Yes,' says Kim. 'I heard it on the news. Poor Margaret. You know, for a long time I really thought that she was still alive. I kept expecting her to turn up at my house as if nothing had happened. "Hi, Kimbo," she'd say, "what's the gossip?" No one calls me Kimbo now.'

'It must have been very hard for you,' says Judy.

'It was awful,' says Kim, winding a large onyx ring round her finger. 'For years I was just "Margaret's Friend", "The Last Person To See her Alive". Newspapers hassled me, people stopped me in the street.'

'But you didn't move away?'

Kim shrugs. 'Norfolk's my home. My family have lived here for ever. Why should I move away? And things died down after a while. But now you've found her, I suppose it'll all start up again.'

'I'm sorry,' says Judy. 'But it does give us a chance to bring Margaret's killer to justice. There have been so many advances in forensic science since 1981. We're really hopeful that new evidence will come to light.'

'I hope so too. For Karen's sake mostly. It's been hell for her.'

'Did you know Margaret's family well?'

'Yes, we were in and out of each other's houses all the time. Karen was lovely. The sort of mum who didn't care if you came in with muddy shoes. She was so pretty, really slim with feathery blonde hair, like someone from Pan's People. I used to wish my mum looked like that.' She laughs. 'My mum looked like a mum, that was all.'

'Did you know Margaret's brother and sister too?'

'Annie was a bit of a cow. She was always jealous of Margaret. I had a bit of a crush on Luke. All the girls did. He was blond too, and an ace footballer. He had loads of girlfriends though. He never noticed me. I was a dumpy little thing in those days.'

'What about Margaret's dad, Bob?'

'Bob was all right. He had a short temper though so we kept out of his way. Bob was a mate of my dad's and Dad said that he was devastated when Margaret went missing. He searched for her for years. I think that's what killed him in the end, not the cancer.'

'I know it's a long time ago,' said Judy, 'but could you bear to tell me again what happened that day, the Royal Wedding day, the last day you saw Margaret?'

Kim laughs hollowly but answers readily enough. 'I could recite this in my sleep. I even did a reconstruction for the TV with Annie being Margaret, even though she didn't look anything like her.'

'Just tell me in your own words,' says Judy. 'Try to cast your mind back.'

Kim looks up and to the right. A good sign, according to a neural linguistic programming course that Judy once attended, because it means that Kim is remembering past experiences.

'We were at the street party,' she says. 'It was a really sunny day, I remember that. The party was lots of fun at first, food and games and everyone having a good time. Then the grown-ups starting singing these old songs and it got a bit embarrassing. Margaret and I slipped away. It was after lunch, about three-ish. We went for a walk to the quay because we liked seeing the swans. There was a Punch and Judy show in the Tuesday Market Place and Margaret wanted to go but I hate that sort of thing. I went back to the street party and I sat with my mum and sisters. They were all singing Beatles songs. "All You Need Is Love". I still can't hear that song without wanting to cry. The last time I saw Margaret she was walking up by the Custom House, across the little bridge, her head up and her hair blowing in the breeze. She looked so beautiful, she really did.'

There's no envy here from Kim, the woman who remembers her twelve-year-old self as 'a dumpy little thing', just sadness. Judy sympathises with her over the Punch and Judy show, she hates that form of entertainment herself and not just because of the name; it glorifies wife beating, in her opinion.

'Did you argue with Margaret?' she asks. 'Some onlookers thought you looked as if you were quarrelling.'

'The police asked me this at the time,' says Kim, with a trace of impatience. 'We often used to argue, about silly things really. Margaret said I was posh because I had a pony, even though he was just a shaggy little thing left behind by some gypsies. I used to say that Margaret was big-headed, she thought she was so pretty, just because she had blonde hair and had her ears pierced.'

Some of the papers had even mentioned Margaret's earrings, Judy remembers, as if they were a sign of sexual precocity that would surely end in abduction and death.

'Was Margaret angry when you wouldn't go to the Punch and Judy show?' she asks.

'She was a bit annoyed,' says Kim, 'but nothing serious. She waved goodbye and blew me a kiss. I'll always remember that.'

She is silent for a moment, twisting her ring.

'Did you see John Mostyn on your walk?' asks Judy.

'That was earlier,' says Kim. 'He came up to me and Margaret and some other girls and asked if we wanted to see some pebbles that he'd found on the beach. He was always doing that but the stones were lovely sometimes. I think that's where I got my interest in crystals from.'

'I know you've told this story lots of times before,' says Judy, 'but is there anything that you've remembered over the years, something that came into your head, maybe something that doesn't seem to fit with the rest?'

'There is something,' says Kim, unexpectedly. 'Seahorse.'

'Seahorse?'

'It came to me about five years ago that Margaret had said something about a seahorse or seahorses. That's when I started collecting them in the shop. It was a sort of tribute to her.'

Judy dimly remembers the seahorses; keyrings and charms, a few cuddly versions with iridescent tails. It strikes her as oddly fitting that these tiny, beautiful, almost other-worldly, creatures remind Kim of her dead friend.

'But you can't remember the context of the seahorse comment?' she says.

'No,' says Kim. 'Memory's a funny thing, isn't it?'

'It is,' says Judy. As an expert in the art of forensic interviewing, memory is her job but she often feels as if she doesn't understand it at all. She thanks Kim for her time and asks if her parents still live in the area.

'Mum and Dad are still in Norfolk,' says Kim. 'They still live in the house I grew up in. It's not far from here. And, of course, Uncle Pete lives in Lynn.'

'Uncle Pete?'

'Mum's brother. He married Karen. Didn't you know?'

CHAPTER 13

Clough informs Nelson when John Mostyn is in the building. He gives it about twenty minutes and then goes down to the interview room where a young PC called Jane Campion is guiding Mostyn through the DNA procedure.

Nelson watches through the two-way mirror for a few minutes. Mostyn looks nervous, but that could be just because he's in a police station. He also looks so much like a stereotypical sex offender – scruffy clothes, unwashed look, shifty gaze – that Nelson is almost predisposed to think that he is innocent. It's no wonder that the police focused on him at the time, weird loner living with his mother, wandering round showing young girls his pebble collection. It's only a surprise that Roy Brown, who'd been the superintendent in 1981, hadn't locked him up as soon as look at him. Nelson remembers Superintendent Brown, known to the station as 'Chubby', and he wasn't a man to let lack of evidence stand in the way of an arrest. Freddie Burnett has already been on the phone demanding to know if Mostyn is going to 'get away with it again'. Strictly speaking, of course, it wasn't a murder investigation the first time round but now it is and Nelson is determined to do things by the book.

Nelson pushes open the door. Campion jumps and looks flustered, although she is a highly competent constable and is handling the procedure perfectly.

'Good morning.' Nelson addresses Mostyn directly. 'I'm DCI Nelson. I'm in charge of the inquiry into the abduction and murder of Margaret Lacey.'

He means to intimidate Mostyn with his rank and with the reminder that this is now, officially, a murder case but the man just blinks at him mildly.

'I know who you are,' he says.

'Thank you for voluntarily providing a DNA sample,' says Nelson. 'We're hopeful that we've been able to retrieve DNA from the scene. It means we'll be able to bring the killer to justice.'

'That would be good,' agrees Mostyn.

'And we'd like a handwriting sample from you too,' he says.

For a second a flicker of alarm seems to cross Mostyn's face.

'Handwriting?'

'Yes. Just a few words will do. PC Campion will show you what to do.' The words 'Greetings from Jack Valentine' were in capitals and there's probably not enough writing to get a match but Nelson wants Mostyn, if he is the sender, to know that they're on to him.

'Happy to help,' says Mostyn, recovering his poise.

'Thank you,' says Nelson. 'We'll be in touch,' he adds,

managing to make this sound more like a threat than a promise. He goes to leave the room and is surprised when Mostyn calls him back, 'DCI Nelson?'

'Yes?'

'Is DS Burnett still on the force?'

'No,' says Nelson. 'He retired some years ago.' And is currently sunning himself in Tenerife.

'Well, give him my regards,' says Mostyn. 'If you see him, that is.'

Cathbad and Judy are eating fish and chips in a tiny café overlooking the quay. It's lunchtime so the place is full and they're sharing the table with two pensioners and a greyhound in a tartan coat. For this reason, Judy doesn't mention the morning's interview. They talk about the children, how Miranda is enjoying nursery and how well Michael is doing with his reading.

'I think we should get him piano lessons,' says Judy. 'I'm sure he's musical.'

'Lessons are so prescriptive,' says Cathbad. 'Let him find out about music for himself. Maybe we should buy him a ukulele.'

'He can find out about music all he likes,' says Judy, 'but he won't be able to play an instrument properly unless he has lessons.' She has already earmarked a second-hand piano on Gumtree.

'I used to play the guitar,' says Cathbad, offering a chip to the greyhound. 'Erik taught me. And I played the accordion at school. '

Judy doesn't remark that, in this case, even Cathbad had lessons of a sort. She says, 'Are you going back to the archaeological site? Leif's site?'

'I don't know,' says Cathbad. 'It's a beautiful place and it's interesting archaeologically too. But, I don't know, it felt odd being there with Leif. Too many memories of his father, perhaps.'

Judy thinks of her trip to the site with Karen, Pete and Annie, the Hail Marys rising into the mist, the sad flowers in their cellophane wrapping. She remembers the figure that she saw on the beach, the hooded man looking out towards the sea. Had that been Leif, saluting the dawn?

'What was Erik like?' she asks. They have never really talked about him before.

'He was a visionary,' says Cathbad. 'He could make you feel as if you were seeing the landscape through ancient eyes. He was an amazing teacher too. He made you think, really think, throwing out all your old assumptions and preconceptions. I was quite dazzled by him, at first. But now I think that he exploited me, used me to do his dirty work. Shona too. She was in love with him, you know.'

'She still seems quite bitter,' says Judy. 'But she didn't have to help him write those letters. They wasted a lot of police time.'

'Love does odd things to you,' says Cathbad. Judy turns to smile at him but he's looking at the greyhound, offering it a chip.

*

Nelson's phone buzzes as he goes up the stairs. He sees 'Ruth' on the screen and so waits until he's in his office to call back.

'Ruth? What is it? Is it Katie?'

A deep sigh. 'No, it's not Kate. It's me. I've had a letter.'

'A letter? What sort of letter?'

'One that reads like it was from the same person who wrote to you. Listen.'

As Ruth reads, Nelson can almost feel his blood pressure rising. He remembers the letters arriving when Lucy went missing and then later with Scarlet. The same mocking, erudite, menacing tone. *She called from the depths and you answered.* It's the same person, he's sure of it.

'Is it typed?' he asks.

'Yes.'

'Did you touch it?'

'Yes, of course I touched it. How else would I have opened the envelope?'

'Well, don't touch it any more. Put it in a freezer bag or something.'

'I've put it in an evidence bag.'

'Good. Hand delivered, you say? I don't suppose anyone saw who delivered it?'

'No. The department secretary just brought it in. It was delivered to the main reception.'

'To you personally?'

'Yes. To Dr Ruth Galloway.'

Nelson can't stop himself smiling. Ruth does like people to use her full title.

'It does sound like the same person. "Out of the depths" – that sounds religious.'

'"Out of the depths I cried unto thee, O Lord",' quotes Ruth. 'Psalm 130. Also that bit about earth, sky and sea. That's from a hymn. "Holy, Holy, Holy".'

'I'm going to talk to that Leif,' says Nelson.

'Do you really think it's him?'

'Judy and Clough have got the idea that it's someone involved in the original case. A loner who collects stones. But I still think Leif Eriksson's our most likely suspect. Like father like son.'

'I don't think writing anonymous letters is the sort of thing that runs in families, Nelson.'

'You never know,' says Nelson. 'Take extra care at home. Lock all the doors.'

'The letter writer sounds pleased with me, if anything,' says Ruth. 'Maybe I'll find some flowers on my doorstep.'

'Remember the last time someone left something on your doorstep,' says Nelson. 'Lock the doors and make sure the security light's on. I'll come round to see you tonight.'

Marj Maccallum seems delighted to see Judy.

'I like to keep in touch with the force,' she says. 'And I'm always glad to see a woman officer doing so well.'

Judy can't help feeling pleased. Sometimes she feels that her career has stalled; with three detective sergeants at King's Lynn, there's not really anywhere for them to go. Her only options are to take her Inspector's exam or move.

Marj makes them tea and they sit in her sunny conservatory watching Mabel, Marj's stunningly white Westie, running round the garden.

'Lovely weather for early March,' says Marj. 'Almost warm enough to swim in the sea.'

Judy had inadvertently stepped into the sea at the weekend, when on the beach with the children. It had been like standing in melted ice. But Marj has the fit, weather-beaten look of someone who swims all year round.

'It is a lovely day,' she agrees. 'Thank you for seeing me. As I said on the phone, we're keen to talk to anyone who remembers the Margaret Lacey case.'

'I remember it all right,' said Marj soberly, offering Judy a biscuit. 'That poor girl. That poor family. Well, I hope that they find some peace now.'

'What do you remember about the investigation?' asks Judy.

'Superintendent Brown and DS Burnett were sure it was the prowler. John something.'

'John Mostyn.'

'That's right. But, I don't know. I thought we should have looked more closely at the family.'

'At the father, Robert Lacey?'

'No, not Bob. He was the type who might kill a man in a pub fight, but not his daughter. He worshipped Margaret. No, I always thought the brother and sister were a bit odd.'

'In what way?' Judy remembers Kim saying that Annie had been a 'cow' and jealous of Margaret.

'Annie was very highly strung. Well, that's a kind word for it. She was the sort who was always shouting or in tears. I remember her yelling at her mum that nobody cared about her, only about Margaret. She argued with her dad too but I heard that she didn't get on any better with her stepfather. The boy, Luke, just didn't seem that interested. Normally youngsters – especially boys – are excited about a police investigation, despite themselves, even if it involves a family member. They want to know about fingerprints, clues, all that stuff. But Luke kept himself to himself. I thought at the time that he might be hiding something.'

'That's what DCI Nelson said.'

'Well, he's a shrewd man, Nelson. Not a dinosaur like Chubby Brown. He'll dig down and get to the truth.'

It's odd that people use dinosaur as an insult, thinks Judy, as she drives back along the coast road. Marj used it to mean someone stuck in old ways but dinosaurs were experts at evolution, that's why they lasted nearly two hundred million years. Humankind is never going to match that. She looks at the sea sparkling in the distance and thinks again of the mysterious figure on the shore. Marj had said that Nelson would dig down to get the truth. But archaeologists seemed to dig for days and find more questions than answers. She wonders how much Leif Anderssen knows about his father's past.

Nelson is also thinking about Erik Anderssen. It's hard not to, seeing as how he's standing with Erik's son very near the place where the Norwegian archaeologist breathed his last. And very painful breaths they must have been. Drowning must be the worst of deaths and, even now, Nelson doesn't like to think about that night: the storm, the chase across the treacherous ground, the desperate search for the missing girl. Today, though, the marsh looks very different, the grass flecked with little yellow flowers and the sun shining on the distant sea.

'It does your soul good, doesn't it?' says Leif, breathing in and expanding his chest like an advertisement for body-building.

'I wouldn't go that far,' says Nelson.

He'd rung Leif as soon as he'd spoken to Ruth. 'I'm on the site,' said Leif, 'but you could meet me here if you like.' Nelson knew that he should delegate the interview to Judy and Clough. He has reports to write and teams to lead. He should, as Jo is always telling him, 'be the hub of the wheel and not one of the spokes.' But, on the other hand, he's the one with the history here. He's the only one who can really ask these questions about Erik. And, besides, the archaeo-logical site is also now a crime scene. Really it's his *duty* to be there.

The site looks busy today, full of people digging and sifting and brushing soil away from what look like very ordi-nary bits of stone. The trench where Margaret was found is directly in front of them. Ruth says that the grave was fairly new – something about cuts and infill – but it still seems odd to Nelson that someone made this potentially perilous journey across the Saltmarsh to bury the bones with these other prehistoric remains. Almost against his will he remembers something Erik once told him. *It's the landscape itself that's important. Don't you see?* And Nelson does see that there is something special about this place even though, in his mind, it's special in the way that accident hot-spots are special.

'Would you like a tour?' says Leif, waving a hand towards the diggers and the trenches.

'No, you're all right,' says Nelson. 'I wanted to talk to you because some letters have been received.'

'Letters?' Leif tilts his head. He's taller than Nelson, which is annoying.

'Letters that recall other letters,' says Nelson. 'The ones your father wrote.'

'My father wrote you letters?' Leif sounds interested, even slightly amused, but Nelson doesn't entirely buy the act. He thinks that Leif is also wary; his arms are crossed which Judy would say is a sign of defensiveness.

'Your father once wrote me a series of letters,' says Nelson, 'which significantly impeded a major crime investigation. He would have been charged with wasting police time if he hadn't . . . died.'

Leif glances over his shoulder at the marshland, bright with spring flowers. So he does know where his father died.

'I didn't know,' he says. 'We weren't always that close, my father and me. He was a free spirit.'

A phrase that, in Nelson's opinion, hides a multitude of sins. He says, 'Were you at the University of North Norfolk this morning?'

Now Leif really does look uncomfortable. He looks away, uncrosses his arms and crosses them again. Nelson waits.

'I did call in at UNN,' he says. 'I've got a friend there. In the history department.'

Nelson is not a betting man but he's willing to wager that the friend is female.

'While you were there,' he says, 'did you drop anything off at the archaeology department?'

'At the archaeology department? No. Why? Is this about Ruth?'

Nelson lets this hang in the air.

'Are you a fan of T. S. Eliot?' he asks.

'Who?'

'British-American poet,' says Nelson. 'Died in 1965.' That's what Wikipedia says, anyhow.

'Oh,' says Leif. 'The man who wrote *Cats*.'

Nelson is not sure if he is joking or not. 'If you say so. You've heard of him, then?'

'Vaguely. I don't know much about English Literature.'

'Speaking of which, are you acquainted with a lecturer in English Literature called Shona Maclean?'

'I've heard the name,' says Leif. 'I think she was a friend of my father's.'

'She's not your friend at UNN?'

'No. My friend's in the history department. Her name's Chloe Jackson.' Leif smiles, seeming to recover his poise. The sun gleams on his yellow hair. Nelson eyes him coldly.

'Can I trouble you for a sample of your handwriting?' he says. The letters were typed but he has the Jack Valentine note. Besides, he thinks the request might wipe the smug smile off Leif's handsome face.

On a scrap of paper which he finds in his pocket, Leif writes: *To DCI Nelson. Tireless seeker after truth.*

It's meant to be funny, Nelson realises, but it's interesting nonetheless.

Michelle is also enjoying the sunshine as she walks to the village hall. For one thing, it will lighten her hair. Not having time to get her roots done is the single worst thing about having a new baby. But the sun also helps with the depression that she felt settling on her that morning as soon as Harry had gone to work and Laura to college. It's a cloud that has been hovering over her ever since George was born. George is wonderful. He's beautiful and really very good. Sometimes Michelle feels her heart almost exploding with love when she looks at him. But there's also a feeling of isolation, almost of loneliness, that seems to be lying in wait for her, ready to pounce even when she's with her family. Michelle tries to give herself pep talks: What have you got to complain about? You've got a loving husband and two gorgeous grown-up children. You've got a job waiting for you, appreciative employers (Tony and Juan sent a baby hamper from Harrods with a note saying, *We miss you but enjoy this precious time with Baby*) and lots of friends. Your baby is healthy and your mother is coming down next week to help look after him. You should be counting your blessings. In answer to this Pollyanna-ish monologue, Michelle can only answer: but I don't have Tim.

Did she love Tim? Sometimes, now, when she thinks about his face and his smile, the way his eyes softened when they looked at her, she thinks that she did. He had certainly loved her. He gave his life for her. It's such a dramatic, Sunday School sort of phrase, but in this case it is literally true. He gave his life so that she and Laura could live. And she loves him for this. But she also knows that she would never have left Harry for Tim. Her love for Harry has been the most powerful emotion in her life for over twenty-five years, a quarter of a century. It's a strong plant, this love, even if it has become slightly thorny over the last few years. It would take more than Tim's grace and beauty to uproot it.

But what if the baby had been Tim's? This had been a very real possibility, something Michelle had hardly dared to admit, even to herself. If George had been Tim's it would have been awful. Everyone would have turned against her, Harry would have divorced her – and, no doubt, married Ruth – and even her daughters would probably have disowned her. But at least she wouldn't have this feeling that Tim has disappeared altogether and soon there will be nothing of him left. In her last months of pregnancy it was as if some essence of Tim was still wafting about, wanting to find out if he was the father. But now he's gone and that is almost the hardest thing to bear.

Maybe the mother and baby group will help. She remembers these gatherings from the first time round. Her NCT class and the local toddler group had proved invaluable sources of female friends and playmates for Laura and Rebecca. It had been hard to replace these friends when they'd moved down to Norfolk but she'd managed it, assiduously following up playground chats and meetings in the park or at the swings. But now, of course, those friends all have grown-up children, some are even grandmothers. She'd been horrified to see her friend Liz referring to herself on Facebook as 'Nanny Beth'. Who the hell was Nanny Beth? Not Liz who liked to drink cocktails and once confided to Michelle that she'd had to resign her gym membership after she'd had sex with her personal trainer in an empty squash court.

As soon as Michelle pushes open the door of the Nissen hut that calls itself the Village Hall and manoeuvres the buggy inside, she realises her mistake. These aren't mothers, they are *children*. Some of the women look younger than Laura, younger than Rebecca. They sit casually on the floor in their skinny jeans and crop tops, texting and chatting whilst their babies lie on their backs on a slightly grubby 'activity rug'. A child wearing a hijab looks up. 'Oh, are you Michelle? I'm Saira, the community midwife. Come and join us.'

Saira is friendly enough, offering tea and coffee, cooing over George, but she's so *young*. How can she be a qualified midwife? Michelle would have trouble trusting her to babysit.

Michelle accepts a cup of burnt-tasting coffee and sits on a beanbag. George is mercifully still asleep. She feels overweight and overdressed in her Boden jeans and loose jumper. She is sure that the lounging girls think that she is George's grandmother. Nanny Miche.

'How old is your little boy?' asks an infant with pink hair.

'Just over two weeks,' says Michelle.

'Ooh.' The girl peers into the buggy. 'He's a good size, isn't he? Lots of hair. Is he your first?'

'No,' says Michelle, slightly cheered. 'I've got two older girls.'

'How old are they?' says Saira.

'Twenty-two and twenty-four,' she says. There is a silence, broken only by George waking up and starting to cry. As Michelle picks him up, one of the youngest-looking mums, a waif with (natural) silvery blonde hair says, 'Shall I hold him so that you can drink your coffee?'

It sounds like the kindest thing anyone has said to her for weeks.

'Thank you,' says Michelle, passing George to the girl.

'I'm Star,' she says, juggling George skilfully. 'My baby's Ava. She's over there, asleep under the baby gym.'

Star. She even seems to be glowing slightly.

CHAPTER 14

Ruth doesn't tell Kate that Nelson might be coming round that evening because, that way, Kate won't be disappointed if he doesn't turn up. But, at seven o'clock, she hears the familiar squeal of Nelson's brakes and, despite herself, feels the familiar surge of excitement that comes with seeing Nelson on her territory. It has been at her cottage that all their most memorable encounters have occurred and, although she knows all that is in the past, Ruth stops at the mirror by the door to let down her hair, which has been scrunched up on top of her head, and check her teeth for spinach (she has been trying to add more greens to their diet).

'What are you doing, Mum?' says Kate, who is lying on the floor putting her Sylvanians to bed – unlike Kate they have a very strict bedtime regime.

'It's Dad,' says Ruth, opening the door.

'Daddy!' Kate throws herself into Nelson's arms.

'Hallo, love.' Nelson comes into the room with Kate wrapped round him. Ruth feels a pang. She realised a year or so ago that she would probably never be able to pick Kate up again. Not in the easy, casual way that Nelson does, anyway. Her back is feeling the effects of three decades of digging and Kate now comes up to her chest.

'Hi, Nelson,' says Ruth. 'Do you want a cup of tea?'

'That would be grand,' says Nelson, depositing Kate on the sofa. 'I can't stay long.'

'Are you going back to see Baby George?' says Kate.

'That's right.'

Ruth says nothing. She leaves Nelson and Kate to enjoy some time together while she makes the tea, trying not to feel resentful that Kate gets ten minutes of her father's company while 'Baby George' gets him all evening, all day, for the rest of his life.

In the end, though, Nelson stays until Kate goes to bed.

'Is Dad coming to say goodnight?' asks Kate, as Ruth tucks her in.

'I'm here,' says Nelson from the doorway.

'You can both read me a story if you like,' says Kate.

'Another time,' says Ruth. 'You can listen to an audio book tonight.'

She kisses Kate and leaves the room. Downstairs, she gets the anonymous letter, still in its plastic wrapping, from her backpack. That is what Nelson is here for, after all. To look at a possible piece of evidence. Ruth sits on the sofa, listening to Nelson's deep voice and Kate's laughter. Flint comes to sit next to her but goes off in a fluffy huff when he sees Nelson coming back down the stairs.

'That cat hates me,' says Nelson.

'Maybe he can smell Bruno,' says Ruth.

'The whole world can smell Bruno,' says Nelson. 'Is that the letter?'

'Yes.'

Ruth notices that Nelson holds the note at arm's length to read it. Does he need glasses? She can't imagine it somehow.

Nelson says, 'It certainly sounds like the same person. As you say, it's not threatening. Rather the opposite. But, all the same, someone knew that Margaret was buried in the stone circle and that person may well be the murderer.'

'I'm pretty sure that the bones weren't on the coastal site for very long,' says Ruth. 'From their preservation and general condition I would say that they were initially buried on cultivated land.'

'I read your report,' says Nelson. 'So someone, presumably the killer, buried Margaret and then dug up the bones thirty years later. Why?'

'So they would be found?' suggests Ruth. 'After all, that first letter tells you where to look.'

'Do you think the bones were buried at the site after excavations began in December?' says Nelson. 'There must have been a lot of digging going on. Surely they would have been found earlier if they were there?'

'Not necessarily,' says Ruth. 'You can only dig something up if you know exactly where to look. But I do think the burial was fairly recent. It's hard to tell because the soil was already disturbed but the grave was shallow and the infill looked new.'

'So someone could have found out about the dig and decided to bury the bones where they would be found?'

'I suppose so but who would have known? The dig wasn't even on the local news.'

'Leif Anderssen knew.'

'But how could he know about Margaret's murder? That was more than thirty years ago. He would have been a child, living in a different country.'

'I know,' says Nelson. 'But the letters do seem so much like the earlier ones. The ones his father wrote. And I'm not sure I trust Leif. I went to see him today.'

'You did?' Even for Nelson, this sounds like quick work. 'What did he say?'

'He denied all knowledge of the letters, of course. But he looked a bit rattled when I asked for a handwriting sample.'

'What good is that? The letter was typed.'

'Remember the note that was delivered to my house on Valentine's Day? "Greetings from Jack Valentine"? That was handwritten.'

'And was it a match?'

'I don't think so. The so-called expert says there's not enough of it to be sure.'

'So it's quite probable that Leif wasn't involved.'

'I suppose so.' Nelson glowers into the fire. 'It's just that these letters do sound a hell of a lot like the other ones. The ones Erik wrote.'

'I'm not so sure,' says Ruth. 'Some of the allusions are the same but I think the tone is different. The others were nastier, more threatening.'

She stops because she has heard something. Nelson hears it too and stands up. A car is approaching. This is rare enough to be slightly alarming. Hers is the only occupied house. Bob, the Indigenous Australian poet, is off on his travels and, as far as she knows, the weekenders aren't due until Easter. Headlights shine in at the window, disconcertingly bright, then the engine is switched off and footsteps approach.

'I'll go to the door,' says Nelson.

Ruth wants to protest but she feels unaccountably scared. Maybe it's because she was talking about those other, darker letters, maybe it's the thought that someone is out there, watching her. So she lets Nelson answer the door.

He opens it about an inch and Ruth hears a familiar American voice say, 'Oh . . . hi . . . I was looking for Ruth.'

She gets up and joins Nelson at the door. 'Hallo, Frank. Come in.'

'I was just passing,' says Frank. 'I've got takeaway.' He holds up a bag from a Chinese restaurant on the Hunstanton road.

'Just passing?' says Nelson. 'No one passes this godforsaken place.'

'I had a meeting at UEA,' says Frank, although Ruth would have told him that he doesn't have to explain himself to Nelson. 'I'm on my way back to Cambridge.'

'Your satnav's wrong then,' says Nelson. And it's true that Ruth's cottage is definitely not on the route from Norwich to Cambridge.

'Sit down, Frank,' says Ruth. 'I'll get some plates. Are you staying, Nelson?'

'No, I've got to get back,' says Nelson. He is still standing in the doorway though and makes no move to leave. Flint comes sauntering in and, with what looks like deliberate provocation, tries to sit on Frank's lap.

'Hallo, buddy,' says Frank.

Ruth turns to say something to Nelson – something easy and light to ease the tension in the room – but he has gone.

Nelson drives back across the dark marshes in a fury. What is that American doing, hanging round Ruth and Katie? Driving all the way from Norwich on the pretext of having a Chinese meal. He must be sleeping with Ruth. No doubt he wants to sweep her and Katie off for a new life in the States. Before Nelson knows it, Katie will be riding around in a yellow school bus, wearing a jumper with a letter on it and calling him Pops. Well, he won't allow it.

By the time he reaches home, he has calmed down slightly. After all, he is driving home to his wife and baby. He can't really control who Ruth eats Chinese takeaways with. Even so, there was something about Frank's familiarity with the house (and that bloody cat sucking up to him too) that makes him wish he could arrest him for something. There are lights on upstairs. Michelle must be trying to get George to sleep. Nelson presses the remote-control button to open the garage – something that never fails to give him childish pleasure – and drives in. He can hear Bruno barking from inside the house and hopes that the dog isn't driving Michelle mad. The trouble is that Michelle doesn't have time to take Bruno for walks during the day and, although they employ a dog walker – something that seems, to Nelson, to be the epitome of soft southern laziness – Bruno still has a lot of unused energy. Also, he has heard the car.

'Down, boy.' Nelson tries to restrain – or at least quieten – Bruno's ecstatic welcome. He'll have to take him out for a walk but it's nine o'clock now and he's starving.

'Hallo, Harry.' Michelle is coming down the stairs. She looks different but he can't work out why.

'Hallo, love,' says Nelson. 'Sorry I'm late. There was a lot to catch up. First day back and all that.'

'Shh.' He doesn't know if she's addressing him or the still capering dog. 'George is asleep.'

'Does that mean he'll wake up later?' says Nelson, in what he hopes is a muffled tone. He's never been good at whispering. It's a northern thing, he tells his daughters.

'I don't know,' says Michelle. 'But the point is he's asleep now. Do you want a beer?'

Nelson suddenly feels that he would like a beer very much. Michelle certainly seems in a good mood. It's been a long time since she's suggested anything as frivolous as alcohol and she hasn't complained about him being late. Also he realises what's changed about her appearance: her hair is loose and she's wearing a T-shirt instead of a baggy jumper. Michelle complains that pregnancy has left her with extra weight but Nelson actually prefers her figure like this. He goes in for a kiss as she passes. She laughs and moves away but it doesn't really seem as if she minded.

'Where's Laura?' he asks, following Michelle into the kitchen.

'Out with some friends. I've made a shepherd's pie. Yours is in the oven.'

'Champion,' says Nelson, getting a beer from the fridge. 'George must have been good if you had time to cook.'

'He's always good,' says Michelle, getting out a plate and a glass. 'But I do feel a bit better. Maybe it was just that the sun was out today. Oh, and I met a nice woman at the mother and baby group. She's called Star.'

'I don't think DCI Nelson is my biggest fan,' says Frank, arranging foil cartons on the table.

Ruth is in the kitchen looking for a bottle of wine. 'Nelson's not much of a one for small talk,' she says.

'No,' says Frank. 'I imagine his talk is pretty big.'

Ruth has located a bottle and is now looking for a corkscrew. Since when did she buy wine with a proper cork? Phil must have brought it on one of the rare occasions when he and Shona came to dinner. She thinks that she detects an edge to Frank's words. She has never told Frank that Nelson is Kate's father but she knows he knows. She has also never revealed the identity of the mysterious 'someone else' in her life, the reason she has never been able to commit herself to Frank. But, again, she is pretty sure that Frank has cracked the code.

She comes into the sitting room with bottle and glasses and puts them on the table. They share out the food in a companionable manner, chatting about takeaways in England and the US and about the respective merits of egg-fried versus plain rice. Then Frank says, spearing a sweet-and-sour something or other, 'Why was Nelson here tonight?'

'It was about the bones we found on the Saltmarsh,' says Ruth. 'I told you about them.'

'Pretty late to make a business call.'

'It's his first day back,' says Ruth. 'I think it was a long day.' She wonders if she is revealing too much knowledge about Nelson's schedule.

'Is there . . .' Frank stops and takes a gulp of wine. 'No. Forget it. Forget I said anything.'

'Well, you didn't really,' says Ruth.

'Ruth. Are you . . . Are you still involved with Nelson? I know I haven't got any right to ask.'

Ruth sighs. She knows that Frank doesn't have any right to ask. She knows that she doesn't have to answer. But part of her wants to explain, to see if the words make any sense when said aloud.

'We are still involved,' she says. 'Nelson's Kate's father.' Frank makes a slight movement but says nothing. 'So that means we'll always be involved in a way. But it's difficult. He's married. He doesn't want to break up the family. And I'm used to my own company. I wasn't even sure if I wanted us to be together. Then, last year, I did think that I wanted it. Nelson felt the same. At least, I'm pretty sure he did. But then Michelle, his wife, announced that she was pregnant and now they've got a newborn baby. I couldn't ask Nelson to leave his baby. I wouldn't want him to.'

She stops and reaches for the wine. The bottle is nearly empty and, though she knows it's not the best etiquette, she pours the remainder into her glass. Frank is driving anyway.

'It's a tough situation,' says Frank and Ruth has the impression that he's choosing his words carefully. 'I guessed some of it and, for what it's worth, I think you're doing a great job. Kate's a great kid and you're a great mom.'

'Thanks,' says Ruth. And she is touched, although there are too many 'greats' in that sentence and she's never been called a 'mom' before. It sounds like a character in an American sitcom.

'And I know you don't want a man in your life,' says Frank. 'But, if you did, I'd be keen to apply for the position.'

Ruth has to laugh. 'That's an academic speaking,' she says.

'I've got an impressive research record,' says Frank. 'Five books and numerous articles in scholarly journals.'

'You can send in your CV,' says Ruth.

Nothing more is said on the subject. Ruth clears the table, putting the cartons in the bin. Frank stacks the dishwasher and Ruth makes coffee. They drink it in front of the fire, the embers now glowing like tiny dragons.

'I should be going,' says Frank. Ruth looks at the clock on the mantelpiece. It's nearly midnight. She has work tomorrow and Kate has school. Frank is right, he *should* be on his way.

'Drive carefully,' she says.

Frank turns to her. His face is suddenly very serious.

'Ruth,' he says. And kisses her.

*

Nelson is dreaming. He's on the beach at Blackpool. It's just as he remembers it from childhood except that the sand stretches into infinity. He knows that, if he can only find the sea, he will be able to swim and escape from whatever is following him. He walks and walks but the water is always just out of his sight. Then, suddenly, he's on the beach by the Saltmarsh and a Viking longship is approaching. Leif Anderssen is at the front, his hair blowing back in the wind. As Nelson watches from the shore, Leif turns into Michelle and then Ruth. The longship becomes a boat on the Norfolk Broads and Ruth is beside him saying, 'Don't die, Nelson.' A bell is ringing, becoming more and more insistent. *Never send to know for whom the bell tolls; it tolls for thee.* He wakes up with a start. His phone is buzzing. Blearily he picks it up. 'Control', says the screen.

'DCI Nelson? A body's been found at the Canada Estate. Looks like murder.'

CHAPTER 15

It's five a.m. and, miraculously, George is still asleep. Nelson gets out of bed without waking Michelle. He grabs his phone and texts Clough and Judy, then heads into the bathroom for a shower.

The Canada Estate is a business park built on a brownfield site that was once a gasworks. There were initially grandiose plans that included apartment blocks, a park, even a school, but these projects were stalled by local objections and by the unarguable fact that there wasn't any money left to develop them. The few businesses that moved to the Canada Estate now exist in splendid isolation looking down on an empty plaza and an unfinished fountain. Nelson drives right into the circular space where two uniformed police officers and a man in a hi-vis vest are standing beside the fountain. The sun is rising over some abandoned cranes and the whole scene is bathed in a pinkish light.

'DCI Nelson.' He shows his card but he knows one of the officers, PC Bradley Linwood, by name and the other by sight. The third man introduces himself as 'Pat Eastwood, the night watchman'. They keep their distance and stand aside to let Nelson see the body that is slumped in the shallow stone basin, the head by the base of a half-finished sculpture that was meant to represent King's Lynn and the Hanseatic League. Nelson recognises the dead man immediately. It's John Mostyn and he's been shot.

Clough and Judy arrive within a few minutes of each other, Clough wearing a woollen beanie hat and looking like an off-duty boxer, Judy in her Barbour with the hood up. It's very cold in the empty plaza even though Pat Eastwood has made them all mugs of coffee from a kettle in his Portakabin. Nelson has made everyone move away from the body and is waiting for the scene-of-crime team to arrive but he gestures to his sergeants to come and look.

'That's him all right,' says Clough. 'Poor bastard.'

'Shot through the heart,' says Judy, leaning closer.

'One shot,' says Nelson. 'Looks professional.'

'Who found him?' asks Clough.

'Night watchman from the security company doing his rounds. Found the body here in the empty fountain. No sign of the assailant.'

'Was he shot here, do you think?' asks Judy.

'No. I think he was shot somewhere else and brought here. There are some bloodstains on the step that looks as if the body was dragged along. There's CCTV everywhere so if we're lucky we might get something. Pat, the security guy, says half the cameras don't work though.'

'Why bring the body here?' says Clough, looking round at the empty offices, half of them boarded up, most of them sporting 'To Let' signs. 'This place is a bloody wasteland.'

But Nelson is looking round too. The sheer wall of buildings forming a ring around the central space with the dry fountain in the middle.

The Stone Circle.

Ruth wakes up to Radio 4 telling her that Hillary Clinton is ahead in the race for the US presidential election. That's good, she thinks sleepily, when the final votes are counted in November she will look forward to waking Kate with the news that the most powerful leader in the world is a woman. There are still too many men in top posts, including in universities. Then she sits up. There are currently too many men in her bed. One, to be exact. Dr Frank Barker, visiting lecturer in nineteenth-century history at the University of Cambridge, is asleep next to her, as silent as a cat, his naked chest rising and falling gently. Oh God.

Ruth realises that she too is naked and grabs her dressing gown. It's seven a.m.; soon Kate will come bounding in babbling about school and asking Ruth to do her hair in a French plait. She must head her off. Kate knows and likes Frank but the sight of him in Ruth's bed would raise questions that Ruth is not yet prepared to answer. What happened last night? She doesn't remember much beyond Frank saying 'Ruth' and leaning in to kiss her. She remembers that she had been dimly worried about smelling of chow mein but

soon that had been buried with all the other everyday con-
cerns, drowned out by her overwhelming need for someone
to hold, someone to make her forget Nelson going back to
his newborn baby, someone to make her forget that she is
nearly fifty and, in the Bronze Age, would probably have
already been dead for twenty-odd years.

And it had been great, Ruth remembers, as she pads out
onto the landing to forestall Kate. The sex had been fun
and tender and unembarrassing; the best she could hope
for from someone who isn't Nelson. Flint is waiting outside the door, looking at her accusingly. 'Don't you start,'
says Ruth.

She opens the door of Kate's room. Her daughter is still
asleep, her face stern in repose, her cuddly toys arranged in
a neat line by the wall.

'Time to get up, Kate,' says Ruth. 'Your uniform's on the
radiator.'

Kate is awake immediately, one of the perks of being
seven and not forty-seven.

'I've got PE today,' she says. 'We're going to play dodgeball.'

Ruth has no idea what that is but she quails at the thought
of retrieving Kate's PE kit from the laundry basket. 'I'll put
your kit in a bag,' she says.

'The pink bag with Hello Kitty on it.'

'I'll see what I can find.'

Ruth has a lightning shower and then goes back to her
room. Frank is awake, rubbing his eyes. 'Hi, baby,' he says
to Ruth. *Baby?* What's happened to them?

'I must get dressed,' says Ruth. 'Kate and I need to leave at eight.'

'Do you want me to lie low up here?' says Frank, understanding at once.

'Please,' says Ruth, searching vainly for a clean top. She has a lecture at ten and doesn't want to look more than usually untidy.

By the time that Kate is up and dressed, the hastily ironed kit in the Hello Kitty bag, untidy French plait completed and breakfast made, Ruth feels slightly calmer. If they can get out of the house without Kate seeing Frank then all will be well. Ruth packs her lecture notes in her backpack and notices the letter, still in its evidence bag. Nelson must have forgotten to take it last night. She puts it in her desk drawer. *Thought for the Day* is on the radio, which means it's nearly time to leave.

'Have a last-minute wee,' she tells Kate. 'Use the downstairs one.'

Ruth puts on her coat and gets Kate's anorak, hat and scarf ready. It's still very cold outside in the mornings, the frost glittering on the window panes.

'I want to say goodbye to Flint,' says Kate, putting on her gloves.

'I think he's outside,' says Ruth. 'We'll probably see him in the garden.'

They make it to the car without incident. Frank's car is parked in front of the weekenders' cottage so Ruth hopes that Kate won't notice it. Ruth scrapes her windscreen with her gym membership card. It's the most use it ever gets.

Then she climbs in and starts the engine, the hot air dispersing the last flakes of ice.

'Let's go disco,' says Ruth, revealing her age.

'There's a man at your bedroom window,' says Kate informatively.

CHAPTER 16

John Mostyn has no known next-of-kin so Nelson applies for a warrant to search his house. When it arrives Judy and Clough drive to the estate in King's Lynn. As soon as they park in front of the pebbledash house they know that something is wrong. The front door is open, swinging gently on its hinges.

'Keep behind me,' says Clough, as they approach.

Judy ignores him. She hates it when Clough gets into one of his Jack Reacher moods. She pushes past him, although she is careful to put on gloves before touching the door.

There are bloodstains in the hall and, in the crowded front room, a bullet hole in the back of the sofa, where Mostyn must have been sitting when he was shot.

'This is the crime scene,' says Clough, getting out his phone to call the station.

'No sign of a struggle,' says Judy, looking round the room.

'How could you tell?' says Clough.

But, in fact, it is easy to see that the fragile towers of cardboard boxes haven't been disturbed. There's a narrow channel from door to sofa and both victim and murderer must have travelled the same way. Clough peers at the faded green chenille of the sofa.

'Bullet's not in there. Murderer must have pocketed it.'

'The boss said it looked like a professional job,' says Judy. 'Looks like Mostyn was just sitting on the sofa when someone burst in and shot him dead.'

'The door was kicked in,' says Clough. 'But the wood was rotten. It wouldn't have taken much force.'

Judy looks at the sofa. There's a dull red stain and a scorch mark where the bullet entered the fabric. Not much blood though. The killer had known exactly where to shoot. 'Come on,' she says, 'we'd better leave this room before we contaminate it any further.'

They retreat to the kitchen where the hamsters are on their hind legs in their cage as if they know something is wrong.

'Poor things,' says Judy. 'We'll have to find a home for them. Would Cassie like them? Make nice pets for Spencer.'

'You must be joking,' says Clough. 'Cassie hates mice. And Dexter would eat them.' Dexter is Clough's dog, a bulldog puppy. Cassie is his wife and Spencer his one-year-old son.

Judy looks round the kitchen. There are some signs of order in here, some vestiges of a daily routine. John Mostyn seemed to have lived on tinned soups; they are lined up on the worktop: mulligatawny, oxtail, pea and ham – flavours Judy did not know still existed. His bowl, spoon and cup are washed up on the draining board. He grew herbs in pots on the window sill and has a 1992 'Beaches of Norfolk' calendar on the wall showing February, Hunstanton. He obviously sat at the kitchen table to read and to watch a small colour television balanced on a pile of children's encyclopaedias. Judy examines some of the paperbacks ranged around the chair.

'Clough!'

'What?' Clough is looking out of the window for the SOC team.

Judy points to the books. *The Wasteland* by T. S. Eliot. *The Four Quartets. The Complete Works of Shakespeare.* The *Good News Bible. The Sunday Hymnal. The Enthusiast's Guide to Pagan Festivals. The Oxford Dictionary of Quotations.*

Clough shifts some of the papers on the table.

'Look at this.'

It's a typed letter.

DCI Nelson,

You have found Margaret but this is only the beginning. It is the best of times and the worst of times. You must finish what you have started. Courage, my friend. Remember we know not the day nor the hour . . .

'It's not finished,' says Judy.

'Why print out an unfinished letter?' says Clough. 'Mind you, there's no printer. No computer either.'

But, under a pile of BBC cookery magazines, they find a laptop, only a few years old by the looks of it. There's a printer too.

'We should seize the laptop,' says Judy. She takes a plastic bag from one of the many bags that are full of them and carefully slides the slim computer inside. The forensics team arrive and start to erect an awning over the front door. 'One way in, one way out,' that's the rule. The house is suddenly full of people in white coveralls.

'We'd better get back to the station,' says Clough.

'I'm taking the hamsters with me,' says Judy.

'So John Mostyn was killed by someone who broke into his house, shot him at close range and then drove the body some three miles to leave it in an industrial estate.' In the briefing room, Nelson is rattling through the facts with his usual deadpan delivery. Judy, Tanya and Clough watch him. In the background, the hamsters run wildly on their wheel.

'We might get some CCTV from the Canada Estate,' says Nelson. 'It's quite a way from the car park to the fountain.'

'And someone may have seen or heard the killer breaking into Mostyn's house,' says Clough. 'It was probably pretty late at night though.'

'Maybe not,' says Judy. 'After all, he was sitting on the sofa and not in bed.'

'He probably slept in there,' says Clough. 'I think I saw a sleeping bag.'

'He was sitting upright,' says Judy.

'Watching TV?' suggests Tanya. '*DIY SOS* was on last night.'

'The TV was in the kitchen,' says Judy. 'And I don't think that he was much of a DIY fan.'

'We'll have to see what the SOC team finds at the house,'

says Nelson. 'And we need to ask why the killer took the body to the Canada Estate. Surely it would have been easier just to leave it in the house?'

'Maybe they just wanted to distract us,' says Clough. 'Misdirection, like in magic tricks.' Clough rather fancies himself as a magician and, after a few beers, is prone to trying to do a trick with empty glasses and a pound coin.

'I think the location itself might be important,' says Nelson. 'The plaza was a circle surrounded by buildings. It's a kind of stone circle.'

He looks slightly embarrassed to be voicing such a Cathbad-esque thought but Judy is impressed. The boss is right, there was something rather symbolic about the placing of the body, the shuttered buildings, the empty fountain.

'But if Mostyn wrote the letters,' says Tanya, 'he was the one who was obsessed with stone circles.'

'Maybe someone else knew about the letters,' says Nelson. 'Remind us what the letter said, Judy, the half-finished one you found in the house.'

Judy has given the letter to Forensics but she has a photo on her phone. She reads the words aloud. '"DCI Nelson, You have found Margaret but this is only the beginning. It is the best of times and the worst of times. You must finish what you have started. Courage, my friend. Remember we know not the day nor the hour . . ."'

'It certainly sounds like the other ones,' says Nelson. '"Best of times" is a quote, isn't it?'

'Yes, it's the beginning of *A Tale of Two Cities*,' says Judy. 'By Charles Dickens. I looked it up.'

'What about "we know not the day nor the hour"?'

'It's from Matthew's gospel. "Therefore keep watch, because you do not know the day or the hour." I think it's about being ready for the Second Coming.'

'Mostyn certainly wasn't ready,' says Clough. 'He can't have expected someone to burst into his house and shoot him dead.'

'Maybe that's exactly what he did expect,' says Nelson. 'Maybe he knew that someone was coming after him. Finding Margaret's bones must have stirred up lots of memories and he was the key suspect at the time. We should have offered him police protection.'

'We offered to take him into the station yesterday,' says Clough, bristling slightly. 'But he said he wanted to make his own way.'

'Because he was scared,' says Judy. 'He said that he and his mother had suffered abuse when Margaret first went missing.'

'So who would have wanted him dead?' says Nelson. 'Someone who thinks – or knows – that he killed Margaret?'

Judy thinks that, despite his low-key manner, the boss is actually relishing being involved in a murder case again. Tanya and Clough too seem galvanised at the thought of a dead body. For her part, thinking of the tins of soup and the 'Beaches of Norfolk' calendar, she just feels rather sad. She must be losing her edge.

'If Mostyn wrote the letters,' she says, 'he wanted us to find Margaret. Why would he do that if he was the one who had killed her in the first place?'

'Maybe his conscience was bothering him,' says Clough.

'And how did he know where she was buried if he wasn't the one that killed her?'

'Remember Ruth thinks that the body was moved,' says Judy. 'So Mostyn might not have been the one who originally buried her. He might have known who it was though.'

'He knew too damn much for my liking,' says Nelson. 'About Lucy, about the original letters, where Margaret was buried. Maybe he knew too much for someone else's liking. Well, we'll know more when we hear from the geeks.' He means the Computer Forensics team, currently examining Mostyn's laptop. Judy wonders if she should make a point by pretending that she doesn't understand the term but decides that it's not worth the hassle.

'What about Margaret's family?' says Tanya. 'I'm seeing Luke, the brother, later today. I'm going up to London,' she adds, rather importantly.

'The streets aren't paved with gold, you know,' says Judy. Tanya ignores her.

'Margaret's father, Bob, was a suspect too,' says Clough. 'Maybe Mostyn knew that Bob had done it and someone killed him to keep him quiet.'

'Yes, but why now?' says Nelson. 'Mostyn had thirty years to inform on Bob Lacey. If he was intimidated, surely he could have spoken up after Bob died? But we can't ignore the possibility that the same person killed Mostyn and Margaret. We should keep looking at the original case, at least until we get the DNA results back from the remains. Judy, where are we with Margaret's friends and family?'

'I spoke to Kim Jennings,' says Judy. 'I thought I'd speak

to her parents too. The two families were close and Karen's second husband is Kim's uncle. I've tracked down Margaret's English teacher, Carol Dunne. She's a headteacher now. I though she might have some useful insights.'

'Good idea,' says Nelson. 'Talk to the sister, Annie, too. Cloughie, you liaise with the Forensics team and find out about CCTV. Judy, we need to tell Karen today about Mostyn, prepare her for the media making the link with Margaret. We've got about a day before this hits the press.'

'I'm not sure about that,' says Clough. 'I saw Judy's step-daughter outside just now. She must know something's going on.'

'That girl's as much trouble as her father,' says Nelson. 'Judy, can you talk to her?'

'I haven't got any influence over Maddie,' says Judy. 'Or Cathbad, for that matter. I suppose we could offer her an exclusive if she keeps quiet for twenty-four hours.'

'Good idea,' says Nelson. 'Though I can't imagine any relative of Cathbad's keeping quiet for that long.'

He's forgotten that my children are Cathbad's too, thinks Judy. But she too often finds it hard to remember that they are related to Maddie.

CHAPTER 17

'What do you mean, he's dead?' asks Karen Benson. 'Did he have a heart attack or something?'

Judy and Clough look at each other. They don't want to release too many details about Mostyn's death but Karen deserves to know some of the truth. Besides, it will be in the papers tomorrow.

'We are treating his death as suspicious,' says Judy, falling back on police-speak. 'I must ask you to keep this to yourself for the time being. We'll make a statement tomorrow.'

'Suspicious?' Pete Benson who, as usual, is sitting quietly by his wife's side, speaks up for the first time. 'Does this mean that he was murdered?'

'It's an ongoing investigation,' says Clough and, to Judy's irritation, once again husband and wife both turn to him as if the oracle has spoken. 'We just wanted to prepare you because, when this hits the press, people will remember that Mostyn was originally questioned about Margaret's disappearance.'

Karen looks up at Margaret's picture on the wall,

something that she does, almost unconsciously, every few minutes.

'I never thought he did it, you know,' she says. 'People were quick to point the finger at John because he was a bit odd but I always thought he was harmless. I couldn't have gone on living near if I thought he'd killed her.'

'I saw him a few weeks ago,' says Pete. 'We talked about gardening.'

'Was he interested in gardening?' asks Judy, thinking of the overgrown wilderness at Allenby Avenue.

'I don't think so,' says Pete. 'Stones were his thing. He liked collecting stones.'

Judy thinks of the hag stone that was her gift from Mostyn. It's still in her bag, warding off evil. She too hadn't thought that Mostyn seemed like a killer. But, as the boss had said, he certainly knew too much.

'Why did people suspect John of being involved with Margaret's disappearance?' asks Judy.

'I think just because he was odd,' says Pete. 'And he was seen talking to the girls that day.'

'He was talking to everyone,' says Karen. 'He'd found a fossilised sea urchin or some such thing.'

'Sea urchin?' says Judy. 'A shepherd's crown?'

'I don't know,' says Karen, looking confused. 'A sea urchin's the name I remember. I can picture it now. A grey stone with a sort of star-shape in it.'

'You don't remember a seahorse at all?' says Judy. Clough looks at her quizzically.

'No,' says Karen. 'I just remember John going round

with this sea urchin thing. He showed it to the girls and he showed it to me too. Then, later on, I remember him sitting with his mother, Heidi, at one of the long tables. John was devoted to Heidi. He looked after her so well, took her everywhere. She was in a wheelchair, you see. A nice lady. She could be sharp-tongued but she had a good heart.'

And Heidi had been John's most stalwart advocate, thinks Judy, giving him an alibi that even the dinosaur Superintendent Roy Brown hadn't been able to shake. She wonders what it was like for Mostyn after his mother died. Did he feel any sense of freedom or was he scared, all alone without his champion? At any rate, he'd stayed in the same house, letting the clutter silt up around him.

'Was John Mostyn with his mother all afternoon?' asks Clough.

'I think so,' says Karen. 'But I've been asked this so many times. What happened that afternoon, when I last saw Margaret, what time I told Bob, where Annie and Luke were. And I've tried to remember everything, I've written down times, drawn maps, but there are parts that are still a blur. I think John was with his mother all afternoon but I can't be certain.'

Karen's voice has become almost hysterical. She reaches for her cigarette packet. Pete puts his arm round his wife.

'It's hard,' he says, addressing Judy and Clough. 'It's hard being asked to remember all the time.'

'I hate to ask,' says Judy, 'but do you have any idea who could have killed John Mostyn?'

'No,' says Karen. 'I'm sorry he's dead. I'm sorry about everything.' She's crying now.

'Could it have been a burglar?' says Pete. 'There have been a lot of burglaries on the estate recently.'

But, as far as they could see, nothing had been taken from the house on Allenby Avenue. And no burglar, disturbed mid-crime, would have killed with a single shot and then taken the body to an industrial estate on the other side of town. Much as Judy disapproves of the word, this was an execution.

Michelle is sitting on a comfortable sofa, George on her lap. She is watching Star carefully adding what looks like a large thistle to a collection of leaves steaming in a teapot.

'What's that?' she says.

'Blessed thistle,' says Star. 'It's very good for increasing your milk supply. You are breastfeeding, aren't you?'

'Yes,' says Michelle.

'Fenugreek too,' says Star. 'And fennel and goat's rue. I've got so much milk that I could be a wet nurse, Mum says. I'm expressing too. What about you?'

'I hate expressing.' Michelle is not that keen on breast-feeding, to be honest, but she did it with the girls so she is determined to give George the same start. She'll stop after ten weeks though. She doesn't say this to Star because she's so obviously revelling in the whole experience of mother-hood.

They'd exchanged mobile numbers yesterday but Michelle had been surprised to receive a text from Star suggesting that they meet for a 'cup of tea and a chat' at her house. 'It'll be much nicer than that baby group.' Michelle had been even more surprised when she turned up at the address to discover that it was a large modern house on the Ferry Road.

'It's my mum and dad's place,' said Star, opening the door with her baby, Ava, on her shoulder.

Michelle approves of the sitting room. It's rather like hers, neat and comfortable with a fitted carpet, three-piece suite and an array of cushions balanced on their tips. Children's toys are spread out on a patchwork quilt and sunlight streams in from large picture windows. Star says that she prefers wooden floors and 'things that are jumbled up a bit.' But she says that she knows she is lucky to be living with her parents. She's twenty-one – younger than Michelle's daughters – and a single mother. 'But Ava wasn't a mistake,' she says, passing Michelle a mug of aromatic tea. 'I wanted a baby but Ryan, her father, wasn't quite mature enough to be a dad.'

Michelle had married young; she was only twenty-one when she met Harry, twenty-four when they married. But she can't imagine going it alone and conceiving a baby with a manchild who isn't mature enough to be a father. Harry has always seemed grown-up, he was already in the police when they met and seemed able to cope with anything. She'd thought of herself as sensible too but she doesn't think she ever had Star's poise, her sweet seriousness that makes her almost seem the older one in the friendship. And they are already friends, Michelle realises with a slight shock, after two meetings.

Michelle puts George down on the quilt and sips her tea. It's almost tasteless and smells of grass cuttings. It's comfortingly hot though and there are home-made biscuits on the tray. Star tells her about her meditation classes and they watch the babies lying on their backs making underwater starfish movements as they gaze up at the little glass stars hanging from the ceiling.

'I put those there,' says Star. 'I think it's good to look up at the stars.'

'Are your parents at work?' asks Michelle.

'Dad is. He's a teacher. Mum's gone over to Grandma's. She lives nearby. Mum's taken some time off work to help me look after Ava.'

'That must be nice,' says Michelle. She is looking forward to her mother coming down next week. Even at her age, there's something about having your mother around that makes you feel safe.

'It is nice,' says Star. 'Grandma's been lovely too. She and Granddad even say they'll look after Ava when I go back to work.'

'What do you do?' asks Michelle. It's not that Star doesn't seem capable, it's just that Michelle can't imagine her doing an ordinary, prosaic job. She's too ethereal and otherworldly.

'I'm a qualified aromatherapist,' says Star. 'I want to set up my own business. I'd like to teach meditation too. I've been going to these fantastic evening classes. They're really inspiring.'

'I went back to work when my girls started secondary

school,' says Michelle. 'I'm a hairdresser. If I'd stayed near my mum I might have gone back sooner. I didn't really want to leave the girls with anyone who wasn't family.'

'I know what you mean,' says Star. 'I read somewhere that it takes a whole family to raise a child. Mind you, Mum can be a bit . . .' She pauses, looking up at the twinkling stars as if trying to think of the right word. 'A bit domineering,' she says at last. 'Of course she's had a difficult time in the past. Losing her sister like that, I mean. I think she had a complete breakdown when she was still in her teens. It's made her very protective of me. I know that. I make allowances.'

She sounds like a mother talking about a teenage child. Would Michelle's daughters be as understanding about her? she wonders. If they knew about Tim, for example.

'Of course,' Star is saying, 'Mum's a paediatric nurse. She knows all about babies and childcare but Ava's *my* baby.'

Ava is a fairy child with a tiny heart-shaped face and Star's silver-blonde hair. Next to her George looks big and almost rudely healthy, although Ava is actually a day older.

'That's so nice,' says Star. 'Like twins. Friends for life.'

'They can grow up and get married,' says Michelle.

'We don't know what their paths will be,' says Star, sounding like Cathbad. 'Marriage isn't for everyone.'

A sound in the hallway makes Star look up. She picks up Ava, although the child is still happily gazing at the ceiling. A large woman in a red coat comes into the room, bringing a chill of outdoor air.

'Have you heard?' she is saying. 'Mostyn's been killed . . .'

She stops when she sees Michelle.

'This is my friend Michelle, Mum,' says Star. 'And this is George.'

'Michelle?' says the woman, clearly expecting something more.

'Michelle Nelson,' says Michelle.

'DCI Nelson's wife?'

'That's right.'

'Mum . . .' says Star, on a warning note.

'My name's Annie,' says the woman. 'I'm Margaret Lacey's sister.'

It is some moments before Michelle realises the significance of the name.

Ruth is glad to dive into the comforting world of the university. She had dropped Kate off at school with some relief. Kate had asked if the man in the window was Frank. Ruth said yes, he had called in last night after Kate was in bed. This much was true at least and, for the present, lost in thoughts of dodgeball, Kate had seemed content to let the matter rest. Ruth arrived at UNN in good time for her lecture on The Archaeology of Disease which was greeted with the usual mix of enthusiasm and bafflement by her audience. Now she is in her office preparing for her seminar on Osteology. She has pinned a diagram of a skeleton on her cork board because, in her experience, students often get the radius and the ulna confused.

She almost ignores her phone when it buzzes but there's always the thought that it could be Kate's school (a fall, a sudden temperature, a freak playground accident) or

Nelson. But the display says 'Roz', Ruth's forensics contact. She presses 'answer'.

'Hi, Ruth. Thought you'd like to know, we've got some interesting stuff back on your bones.'

She means Margaret Lacey.

'Oh yes,' says Ruth.

'We've found some pollen and vegetable matter.'

'That's great news,' says Ruth.

'Yes, and some of it looks very specific. If you carry out a botanical morphological survey it could go some way to establishing the original burial site.'

'That's a big help,' says Ruth. 'Can you send me a list of the flora and fauna?'

'I'm emailing it now.'

She wonders whether to ring Nelson but she's still rather embarrassed about last night, as if Nelson will be able to tell, even over the phone, how the evening ended. In the end she calls Judy.

'That's great,' says Judy, sounding slightly distracted all the same. 'Will this pollen and stuff help us find the exact place where Margaret was first buried?'

'Roz did say it was specific,' says Ruth. 'So I hope we should be able to narrow it down a lot.'

There's a short silence. Ruth wonders if Judy's driving. Then Judy says, 'Have you heard the latest development?'

'No,' says Ruth. 'What?'

'John Mostyn, our prime suspect, has been found dead. Shot. This is confidential for now, by the way.'

'Understood.' There's no one Ruth could tell anyway. Kate? Flint? Her thoughts veer towards Frank and away again.

'I'd better go,' says Judy. 'I'm on my way to do some interviews. Can you come in tomorrow to talk about the pollen and the other results? About ten?'

'Yes, I think so.' Ruth looks at her timetable. She'll have to miss a department meeting but it will be worth it. 'See you then.' She can hear her students scuffling outside the door. She sighs and gets up to let them in.

'Good old Ruth,' says Clough. They have been listening on hands-free because Judy is driving.

'Yes,' says Judy. 'If we can find out where Margaret was originally buried, that'll be a great help.'

'I still think Mostyn was the most likely person to have killed her,' says Clough. 'That's why he was killed. It was a revenge killing.'

'This isn't *The Godfather*,' says Judy. Clough is obsessed with the Godfather films and can quote them at length. In order to stop him doing so she says, 'Shall we see Annie next? Then I can go on to interview Kim Jennings' parents, if you've got other things to do.'

'OK,' says Clough, who is looking at something on his phone, probably a message from Cassie full of heart emojis and kisses. He's silent for a minute, scrolling, then he says, 'Why did you say that thing about seahorses, when we were talking to Karen and Pete?'

'It was something Kim said,' says Judy, taking the turning where the Campbell's Soup Tower used to stand. 'I asked her if there was anything random that she remembered from the day Margaret vanished. She said "seahorses".'

'Is that one of your cognitive interview things?'

'Don't knock it,' says Judy. 'I've got results that way before.' But Clough is looking at photos of his beloved dog Dexter and doesn't respond.

CHAPTER 18

At Annie's house, Judy is surprised to find Michelle loading a baby seat into her car. She is watched by a blonde girl holding a baby and by Annie herself, who has her arms folded and is looking rather critical of Michelle's baby-wrangling skills.

'Oh, hi, Judy.' Michelle has succeeded in installing George in the back seat and looks up, pushing her hair back with one hand. 'What are you doing here?'

'I was going to ask you the same thing,' says Judy. Clough is making faces at George through the window.

'I'm friends with Star,' says Michelle, with a trace of something that sounds like defiance. 'We met at a mother and baby group.'

Judy had loathed mother and baby groups, the fake camaraderie, the subtle put-downs ('Oh, I remember Jordan doing that months ago'). It's another reason not to have another baby.

'Star?' she queries.

Michelle points to the blonde girl, which turns into a

wave. This must be Annie's daughter. Judy remembers Karen saying that Annie had just become a grandmother. But Star looks young enough to be Michelle's daughter, younger than her daughters, in fact. Judy is quite impressed by this inter-generational friendship.

'I won't keep you,' she says. 'Bye, Michelle. Bye, George. Stop that, Cloughie, you'll give him nightmares.'

'He likes it,' says Clough, straightening up. 'He's a little cracker, Michelle.'

Michelle gives him a genuinely warm smile and a modified version for Judy. She says goodbye and drives away. Annie greets them as they walk up the drive. 'I know why you've come. It's about John Mostyn. I've just come from Mum's.'

That was quick, thinks Judy. Mind you, they would have been there sooner if Clough hadn't insisted on stopping for chips.

'I'm going to put Ava down,' says Star. 'She's almost asleep.'

'Have you winded her?' says Annie.

'Yes,' says Star, with what sounds like elaborate patience. She smiles at Judy and Clough and retreats into the house. Annie ushers them into a modern kitchen, all gleaming surfaces and concealed gadgets. They sit at the breakfast bar, where the stools are just a little too high for Judy. She hates having swinging legs like a toddler. Clough grins at her but doesn't say anything.

Annie makes coffee with a certain amount of cup crashing but it's delicious and she gives them biscuits too.

'So Mostyn is dead,' she says. 'God rest his soul.'

This isn't said in a very religious tone, more in the way that Judy's Irish father tags the phrase onto reminiscences about unloved relatives, but it's interesting for all that. It seems that Annie, too, thinks that John Mostyn was innocent.

'Oh, he was just a simple creature,' she says. 'Going round showing us stuff that he'd found on the beach. I never thought that he'd taken Margaret. Even Dad didn't think that and he suspected everyone at some point.'

'Did he?'

'Yes.' Annie frowns into her coffee mug for a moment. 'The whole thing sent him a bit nutty for a while. Well, it did all of us.'

'John Mostyn's death is confidential for now,' says Judy, 'but it will come out in the press and, of course, people will make the connection with Margaret. We just wanted you to be prepared.'

'Oh, we're used to it,' says Annie. 'The things the papers used to make up about Dad, about all of us. Even Luke. Implying that he might have ... Margaret was his little sister, for heaven's sake.'

Judy has read the press cuttings and, whilst there are several veiled hints about Bob Lacey, she can't remember ever reading anything about Luke. But there must have been rumours, she's sure. She remembers Nelson's comment about him being 'old enough'.

'Can you think of anyone who *did* think that Mostyn killed Margaret?' asks Clough. 'Anyone who might have felt strongly enough to kill him?'

'A lot of people suspected him at the time,' says Annie. 'They used to shout things at him in the street, throw stuff at his house. I remember his mother, she was in a wheel-chair, attacking these kids with an umbrella when they said something about John.'

Judy remembers Mostyn's frightened whisper. *People will see and they'll think I did it. They'll throw things.* She feels guilty all over again. Did they fail John Mostyn? Is this their fault?

'Can you think of anyone who felt particularly strongly?' says Clough. 'Maybe someone who could have got worked up by the recent publicity?'

Annie stares at them. She doesn't resemble her mother, or Margaret (although Star does), but suddenly there's an expression that reminds Judy of one of the pictures on Karen's wall. Margaret in flared jeans, sitting on a wall and looking straight at the camera.

'Everyone felt strongly at the time,' she says, 'but then people forgot because that's what they do. Everyone forgets.'

'Do you mind telling us your recollections of the day that Margaret went missing?' says Judy. 'We're reopening the case and we're doing everything we can to find her killer. We hope that her remains will give us some forensic evidence but anything that you can remember will help as well. Even if it didn't seem significant at the time.'

Annie gives them the stare again and, for a moment, Judy thinks she's about to refuse. But then she sighs and says, 'It was such a lovely sunny day. Everyone was happy. I helped Mum lay out the food for the party. Luke had dis-appeared off with his friends playing football. That's how it was in the eighties. Girls were still expected to help around the house and the boys got out of everything. I made sure that all my children learned to cook and clean, Matt as well as Sienna and Star.' She pauses, and Judy is afraid that she's going to go off on a tangent about modern parenting but, after an eloquent eye-roll, Annie drinks some coffee and continues. 'Margaret was there with her friend, Kim. They helped a bit but they were too busy being silly and messing around. When Luke came back, Kim got very giggly. She had a crush on him, I think. I can't remember when Margaret left the party. I was with some friends, we were singing, and someone had got hold of some beer. There was a boy I liked too, Jimmy Preston. I remember sitting on his knee for a bit. The first thing I knew was when Mum came over and asked if I'd seen Margaret. I said I hadn't. Kim wasn't there either – she'd gone home but I didn't know that – and I thought they might be at our house. I went home but there was nobody there. I started to worry then. Mum came back and rang Kim's parents but they hadn't seen her. Mum went to get Luke and Dad. I stayed home in case Margaret came back. It was strange, it was still broad daylight and kids went wandering off all the time then but even so I think I knew that something bad had happened. I remember sitting there in our kitchen and shivering, though it was a hot day. I think that, even then, I knew I wouldn't see her again.'

She stops and stares out of the window. Judy thinks that she's trying not to cry.

'We've heard that John Mostyn talked to Margaret that

day,' she says. 'Did you see anyone else with her? Anyone slightly unusual?'

'John Mostyn showed her his stones,' says Annie. 'He was showing everyone. Later on I saw him sitting with his mother. I told the police that at the time. No, I didn't see Margaret talking to anyone strange. There was no one strange there. It was just our friends and family.'

'This might sound odd,' says Judy, 'but did you hear anyone mention seahorses?' She doesn't look at Clough.

'Seahorses?' says Annie. 'No. Why?'

'It's something Kim Jennings said.'

'Oh her.' Annie turns away with a shrug. 'She's away with the fairies, that girl. Have you seen her shop in Wells? Full of old tat covered in glitter. No wonder no one goes in there.'

Tanya enjoys the trip to London. She likes the anonymity of travelling at midday, an enigma in her jeans and navy Barbour, too casual to be an office worker, too smart to be unemployed. She buys coffee and a bun at the Countryline café and reads *Private Eye* with an amused and worldly expression on her face. Sadly there are only two other people in the carriage to witness her sophistication: a teenage boy wearing headphones who occasionally twitches in response to some private rhythm and an elderly woman reading *Fifty Shades of Grey* with her eyebrows raised.

King's Cross is even more exciting because there's a chance that she, world traveller that she is, could be heading for St Pancras and the Eurostar. But instead she takes the Thameslink to Blackfriars, where Luke Lacey works as an accountant. They are meeting in his office, an anonymous building with a stunning view over the Thames. Tanya longs to live in London, to work within sight of St Paul's and Tower Bridge, to drink coffee in Covent Garden and shop at artisanal bread stalls in Borough Market. But Petra, her partner – shortly to be wife – would never leave Norfolk.

Luke was once a good-looking boy but there's little trace of that in the middle-aged man with greying blond hair who meets Tanya in reception. He was a football player too but Tanya, a fitness fanatic, looks with some disapproval at his spreading bulk, only partially concealed by an expensive suit. Luke Lacey is fifty this year and, in Tanya's opinion, he's just the right demographic for a heart attack.

'Thank you for seeing me,' she says. 'As you know we've reopened the case into your sister's death.'

'Yes,' says Luke. 'I'll be down to see my mother at the weekend. This is pretty hard for her.'

You haven't been conspicuous by your presence so far, thinks Tanya. It's Annie who has been supporting Karen.

'I know it's been a long time,' she says, 'but I'd really like your memories of the day that Margaret went missing.'

Luke looks at her, twisting his wedding ring. He has a wife, Rina, and two children, Betty and Felix. Tanya has been doing her homework.

'Is it true?' Luke says suddenly.

'Is what true?'

'Is Mostyn dead? That's what Annie said. She rang me this morning.'

So Clough was right. The news is out. Tanya doesn't see that there's any point in denying it, especially if Maddie Henderson is going to run the story tomorrow.

'Yes, he was found dead last night.'

'Found dead? Killed?'

'It's an ongoing investigation. I'm not at liberty to say more.'

Luke sighs and leans back in his chair. Tanya tries to read his expression. Relief? Anger? Fear?

'So, twenty-ninth of July 1981?' she prompts.

Luke sighs again. 'There was a street party. I was there for a bit, had some food, listened to the songs, but then I went off with my friends to play football. At the Loke Road rec. It was all we thought about in those days. Football. I thought I'd play for Man U one day.'

Glory hunter, thinks Tanya. Why not Norwich City? 'When did you last see Margaret?' she asks.

'I think it was at the party. She was sitting with her friend Kim and her family. They were eating cake. Kim offered me some and some of my mates laughed.'

'Did she have a crush on you?'

'I don't think so. She was a funny little thing, Kim.'

'Did you see John Mostyn at the party?'

'Yes, he was hanging around showing people his stone collection. That's what he always did. We used to laugh at him.' Luke and his mates had done a lot of laughing that day, thinks Tanya. She wonders when the laughter stopped. She remembers something in Judy's report from the first interview with Karen Benson and Annie Simmonds. Annie had said that Luke still had nightmares about Margaret's abduction.

She asks Luke when he first heard that Margaret was missing.

'Mum came down to the rec to see if she was there. It was late, about seven thirty, but it was still light. Mum was really worried, I could see that. So I said I'd help search. I went to the park with some of my friends and up as far as the allotments. I went home when it was dark and the police were there. Mum had fetched Dad from the pub by then.'

'Was your dad . . . ?' Tanya tries to find a tactful way to put it.

'He wasn't drunk, if that's what you mean,' says Luke. 'Everyone tried to make out that he was but he wasn't. He was just in the pub with his mates. That's what everyone did back then.'

Except for the women, thinks Tanya, who were presumably left clearing up after the street party.

'What happened next?' she asks.

'Dad and his mates went out looking for Margaret,' he says. 'I went with them. It was dark but we had lanterns and torches. The police were out too, loads of them. They were searching the river. Frogmen and everything.'

'What about Annie? What was she doing?'

'She stayed behind with Mum. Mum was hysterical by then.'

'Do you remember who else was there? In the house or taking part in the search?'

'It felt like everyone was there. The house was full of

people. Lots of the neighbours were there, some of my friends and their parents. The police too. I remember a policewoman trying to comfort Mum. The men all went out looking for Margaret and Dad wouldn't come home. He stayed out all night, walking through the streets. He was crying, swearing, shouting out Margaret's name. I'd never seen him cry before.'

'Did you stay with your dad all night?'

'Yes.'

No wonder Luke still has nightmares, thinks Tanya.

'Is there anything else you remember about that day?' she asks, following Judy's lead. 'Anything that might not have seemed significant at the time but has stayed with you?'

'Not really,' says Luke. He looks at her but Tanya gets the impression that he's not seeing the faceless corporate meeting room but the dark streets, the torchlight, his father sobbing. 'It was horrible,' he says. 'You can't imagine it unless you've been through it. One day we were a family of five and then one of us just . . . disappeared. If she'd been ill or in an accident it would have been terrible but there would have been an explanation. A reason. But Margaret just vanished. Suddenly it was just Annie and me again.'

'Were you close, you and Annie? There was only a year between you.'

'I suppose so. When we were young. Mind you, she was always trying to boss me about. She used to make me do things.'

'What sort of things?'

'If she'd fallen out with someone at school, she'd want me

to beat them up.' He laughs suddenly. 'I didn't, of course. If I'd beaten up everyone Annie fell out with, I'd have been expelled.'

'Does she have a bit of a temper then, Annie?'

Another laugh, this time without humour. 'You could say that. Mind you, she had a lot to make her angry. Margaret going missing, Mum and Dad getting divorced, Mum re-marrying. It wasn't easy for us, growing up.'

'I'm sure it wasn't.'

'But we've both turned out all right. Annie's a nurse, full of good works in the community. I'm . . .' He gestures towards the window as if the Shard and the London Eye are tangible signs of his success. Which perhaps they are.

'Annie's got children now, hasn't she?'

'Yes, three. And now she's a grandmother. Her daughter Stella, or Star as she calls herself, has just had a baby.'

'And what about Margaret?' asks Tanya. 'Were you close to her?'

Luke smiles and, for the first time, Tanya sees a trace of the teenage heart-throb. 'Oh yes. We all loved Margaret.'

Judy drops Clough at the station and drives to the address given to her by Kim Jennings. Kim's parents, Steve and Alison, live on the outskirts of King's Lynn, in a house that was probably once surrounded by fields. Now there's just a small paddock, containing a skewbald cob. Judy stands for a moment by the gate watching the horse chew the grass, shaggy and mud-splatted in its winter coat. She had a pony when she was growing up though she, like Kim

Jennings, could hardly be described as posh. She thinks of Ranger now; his whiskery nose, his untidy mane, his divine horsey smell. Maybe she should get Michael riding lessons as well as piano lessons? She holds out some grass for the skewbald but the horse, correctly identifying her offering as worthless, carries on grazing.

Steve and Alison Jennings are a comfortable-looking couple, probably in their sixties, wearing matching Aran jumpers. Judy remembers Kim saying, 'My mum looked like a mum' and now Alison looks like a grandmother and a very competent one at that. The couple seem to be caring for two grandchildren, an elderly dog and an angry-looking cockatoo. Judy is tempted to ask them if they want some hamsters as well.

She asks about the horse instead. 'That's Patches,' says Alison. 'We got him from a riding school that was closing down. He's getting on a bit but the grandkids love to ride him.'

'Kim mentioned that she used to have a pony.'

Steve smiled. 'That was Cuddles. Kim named him. He was a little sod really. He'd been abandoned by some gypsies. We used to have quite a few rescue horses at one time.'

Judy, an enthusiastic patron of Redwings, a wonderful Norfolk horse sanctuary, warms to the couple. Alison brings in tea and home-made cake and Judy asks about Margaret.

'I remember her so well,' says Alison, expertly moving a crawling baby from the sleeping Labrador. The other child, aged about three, is watching *Peppa Pig* with the sound turned off. 'She was such a pretty young girl. I know everyone says that and, of course, looks aren't important, but that's how I remember her. So blonde and lovely, like an angel.'

'She was a nice girl too,' says Steve. 'Always very polite. Please and thank you and all that.'

Margaret hadn't always been polite to Kim, Judy thinks, teasing her about being posh and probably about having a crush on her brother. But maybe she was the sort who knew how to be nice to parents.

'Your brother-in-law married Margaret's mother, didn't he?' she says to Steve.

'Yes,' says Steve. 'We always thought Pete was a confirmed bachelor but when Karen and Bob got divorced he started courting Karen immediately. They make a good couple, I think.'

Judy doesn't think she's ever heard anyone using the word 'courting' in ordinary conversation or say 'confirmed bachelor' without meaning 'gay'. She thinks of the colourless man holding Karen's hand and saying 'It's tough on the mother.' Perhaps Pete was what Karen needed after the more volatile-sounding Bob.

She asks the couple what they remember about the day Margaret disappeared. Neither of them asks about John Mostyn and she hopes this means that the murder hasn't hit the press yet. Maddie has agreed to wait until tomorrow before breaking the news in the *Chronicle* but these days it's usually on Twitter or Facebook where a story first emerges.

'We were all at the street party,' says Alison. 'It was such a lovely day. Everyone was so happy about Charles and

Diana getting married. So sad when you think how that turned out. And Diana was only nineteen. That seems quite shocking now. Tammy, Kim's older sister, got married at twenty-one and I thought that was too young. Her kids are grown-up now.' She gestures at the baby, now on Steve's lap, and the TV-watching child. 'These are our great-grand-children.'

Kim is married, Judy knows, but she doesn't have children. There's a third Jennings daughter, Christina, but she has emigrated to Australia.

'Did you see Margaret at the street party?' she prompts.

'Yes, she sat with us for a bit. She always liked coming to our house. I think it was a bit more ordered than home, a bit quieter.' Kim had liked Karen Lacey, Judy remembers, because she was pretty and didn't mind mud on the carpets. She can imagine that the Jennings family, staid and conventional, had a similar appeal for Margaret.

'Margaret and Kim went off to look at the swans,' says Alison. 'We didn't think anything of it. We let our children wander then.'

'There were no mobile phones, you see,' says Steve, as if Judy can't possibly remember a time before such technology. 'You couldn't keep in touch.'

'Kim came back after about an hour,' says Alison. 'I think I asked about Margaret but I can't be sure. I felt terrible about that at the time. But you can't know what's going to happen, can you? We went home at about six. Chrissie was quite little and she was tired out. Kim had one of her headaches. Karen rang us at seven-ish asking if Margaret was with us. I said she wasn't. I rang back about an hour later and Karen was in a terrible state. So Steve got in the car and went to help look for Margaret.'

'We searched for hours,' says Steve, 'and, well, you know the rest.'

'Was Pete at the street party?' asks Judy. 'Did he help with the search?'

'No,' says Steve. 'He lived out Swaffham way then.'

'What about Bob Lacey? Did he help search?'

'Yes,' says Steve. 'I think he was in the pub most of the afternoon but Karen went and got him. Bob was a good man.' Steve fixes Judy with rather a stern look. 'People said all sorts of things about Bob but he was a good man, devoted to his family. He was frantic that night, literally tearing his hair out. Well, that's understandable. I would have been the same if it was one of mine. I think he stayed out all night, him and his lad, Luke. But we all helped. All the local men.'

It was the men with the search parties and the women at home with the children, thinks Judy, as she drives away with one last wistful look at the horse. She was only three years old in 1981. She doesn't think that she missed much.

CHAPTER 19

Judy's next stop is to see Carol Dunne, the woman who was once Margaret's English teacher but is now head of a primary school in Gaywood. St Paul's is a happy-seeming place, with a fence outside that looks like coloured pencils, a brightly coloured mural in reception and children's artwork on the walls. On the field a group of children are playing an energetic game of what looks like football but involves a beachball and several hoops. It reminds Judy of the school attended by Michael and Kate and shortly to be honoured with Miranda's presence. She senses that it's not league tables that dominate here but a genuine concern for pupils' well-being. This impression is reinforced when she meets Carol Dunne. She knows that Carol taught Margaret in 1981 so now must be at least in her mid-fifties but the woman looks like a teenager, with blonde hair tied back in a ponytail and the kind of energy that Judy can only achieve after three double espressos.

'I remember Margaret so well,' says Carol, moving a pile of poetry books so that Judy can sit down. 'She was very bright. She loved reading and used to come to my after-school drama classes. I was devastated when she went missing. It was my first teaching post and I suppose I got too attached to my pupils. I left at the end of the year and decided to transfer to primary. That was easier to do in those days.'

'And now you're a headteacher,' says Judy.

'That's not such an achievement,' says Carol with a smile. 'Stick around long enough these days and they make you a headteacher. It's a job no one wants with all the paperwork and the hassle from the government.'

Judy is not deceived. People say it's easy to progress in the police force but the top jobs are still dominated by men. For Carol to have become a headteacher at a relatively young age is still pretty impressive. She has been at St Paul's for eight years and the school is rated 'outstanding' by Ofsted. Judy has checked.

'You may have heard that we're opening a murder inquiry into Margaret's death,' says Judy. 'I'm try to build up a picture of Margaret and her family. I know it's difficult after so long but it really does help. Did you teach Annie and Luke too?'

'I taught Annie,' says Carol. 'She was in the fourth year, as we called it then, coming up to O Levels. She was bright too, very determined, not as sunny a character as Margaret. Funnily enough I taught Annie's children here. Matthew, Sienna and Stella. They were nice kids. Matt and Sienna both went on to university. Stella was always an original. I don't think she went on to university but I'm sure she's doing something interesting with her life. She calls herself Star now.'

'You said that Margaret had a sunny character?'

Carol smiles. 'She was one of those children who seem blessed. She was the baby of her family and everyone seemed to dote on her. She was clever, pretty, good at sport. Everyone wanted to be her friend.'

'What about Kim Jennings? She was Margaret's best friend, wasn't she?'

Carol pauses before replying and the late afternoon sun shines through the coloured glass in the window. Carol shields her eyes and her hand shines orange and purple and green. She gets up to pull down the blind.

'Kim was a nice girl,' she says, with her back to Judy. 'She was in Margaret's shadow, of course, but never seemed resentful about it. Poor Kim. It was awful for her when Margaret disappeared. Everyone looking at her, asking her questions. Her parents moved her to another school eventually.' She sits back down at her desk.

Judy thinks of Kim saying, 'She looked so beautiful, she really did.' The adult Kim also seemed remarkably lacking in bitterness. Is she happy, running her shop full of quartz and seahorses? Judy hopes so.

'What about Margaret's parents?' asks Judy. 'What were they like?'

Again, Carol seems to hesitate for a second. 'I didn't know them very well. It's not like a primary school, where you see people at the school gate. Her mother came to a parents' evening once. I thought she seemed a nice woman, she'd had little formal education herself but she was keen for her children to do well. And they have. I hear Luke's an accountant in the city.'

'Really?' says Judy, not adding that Tanya is probably interviewing Luke Lacey at this moment.

'Annie too,' says Carol. 'She's a paediatric nurse.' She laughs. 'I try to keep up with my ex-pupils.'

'What about Margaret's father, Bob?' asks Judy.

'I never met him,' says Carol, 'but I saw him on TV a few times after Margaret went missing. He seemed utterly devastated.'

'What do you think happened to Margaret? ' asks Judy.

'I don't know,' says Carol, with a certain headteacherly sharpness in her voice, 'I'm not a detective. The police and the press at the time seemed determined to pin it on Bob or on that poor simple man who collected stones.'

Is 'simple' a PC term? wonders Judy. It's the adjective Annie used too. She decides to take a risk. 'John Mostyn, the so-called Stone Man, has been found dead in suspicious circumstances,' she says. 'That's classified information for the present.'

Carol opens her eyes wide. 'Does this mean he did kill Margaret?'

'We don't know,' says Judy. 'We don't know anything at the moment but it certainly seems as if his death might be linked to Margaret's.'

'I never thought he did it,' says Carol. 'The Stone Man. It was just the strong ganging up on the weak. You see enough of that in the playground.'

Judy thinks of the press crowding round the police station

when they sense a story. That feels like bullying too sometimes. But, then again, the police have to be accountable.
As do schools.

'At the time,' she says, 'what did you think had happened
to Margaret?'

Carol thinks for a moment, adjusting a glass ornament on
her desk that is so horrible that it must have been a present
from a pupil.

'I think I thought it was an accident,' she says at last.
'That she fell into the river or something. I found it hard to
believe that someone could have deliberately taken her and
killed her. I still find it hard.'

Sadly, Judy finds it all too easy to believe.

It's getting dark by the time that Ruth leaves the university.
She's left it a bit late, catching up with marking, and now
she's anxious to get to the childminder's before the agreed
pick-up time of five thirty. Not that Sandra minds if she's
late, it's more that Ruth will feel that she has failed at one
of her many daily mother tests (test one: don't get caught
with a lover in your bed). As she fumbles for her new-
fangled Renault key a voice behind her says, 'Ruth?'

Ruth jumps and drops her keys.

A tall figure emerges from the shadow of the trees and
picks them up. It's Leif.

'Sorry to startle you,' he says. 'I wondered if I could have
a word. There's something I'd like to discuss with you.'

'I need to collect my daughter now,' says Ruth. 'Can we
do it another time?'

'Could I come with you?' says Leif. 'I came by bike.' Ruth sees that he's carrying a bulky bag presumably containing a fold-away bicycle.

'All right,' she says, slightly ungraciously. 'I can drop you off in Lynn.' She doesn't want to turn up at Sandra's with a long-haired Viking in tow.

Leif puts the bike in the boot and gets into the passenger seat. Ruth drives through the darkening campus, the mushroom lights coming on around the lake. There's a party in the students' union tonight. You can see posters for it all over the place. 'Spring has Sprung. Let's celebrate!' The student equivalent of Imbolc.

Ruth asks about the dig. Leif says that they are getting on well and are hoping to be able to commission a facial reconstruction of the woman whose skeleton was found in the cist. He knows a fantastic archaeologist sculptor in Sweden. 'He's called Oscar Nilsson,' he says, 'and he has a gift for conveying the actual character of the person. It's so important to have a face, then people can form a relationship.' Ruth shudders, thinking of faceless things, voices in the dark, hands reaching from the sea. There's something about Leif's presence that seems to disquiet her.

This feeling is reinforced when, a few minutes later, Leif says, 'I wanted to talk to you about my father.'

'Did you?' says Ruth, concentrating on one of the many roundabouts on the way to King's Lynn.

'When Dad died he left a letter for me,' says Leif. 'A lot of it was personal. We weren't that close. My parents were free spirits and that's not always easy for the children. But, in the letter Dad said that he was proud that I'd decided to become an archaeologist. He said that, if I could, I should come to north Norfolk to look at the henge circle. He also said that I should get to know you. He was very fond of you. My mother was too.'

'I was fond of them both,' says Ruth. Her mouth feels dry. She had once been very fond of Erik and Magda. She had stayed with them in Norway, sitting in the hot tub under the stars, taking the universe apart and putting it back in a different shape. They were her mentors, her idealised parents. She had thought that Erik and Magda had the perfect relationship, equals, friends and lovers, something to be aspired to and emulated. But it turned out that this too was not what it seemed. Both Magda and Erik had other lovers. Erik had a long-standing affair with Shona, something neither of them had shared with Ruth. And then there were the letters. When Ruth had first recognised Erik's handwriting on the pages, it was as if a monstrous shadow had fallen on their relationship. It meant that the Erik she knew – wise, compassionate, almost magical in his intuitive powers – was only ever an illusion.

'He said something though that I didn't understand,' Leif is saying. 'He said . . .' Leif takes a letter from an inside pocket and reads aloud, '"If you do make contact with Ruthie, tell her I'm sorry and that I loved her. Perhaps you will dance with the stone wedding party and pour a libation on the earth for me."'

For several minutes and several roundabouts Ruth can't speak. *Tell her I'm sorry and that I loved her.* This must have been written long before her last encounter with Erik but it's as if he knew everything: about Scarlet, about Lucy, even about his own terrible death on the marshes. It's as if Erik has given her his blessing from beyond the grave. He was the only person who ever called her Ruthie, although Cathbad sometimes does it to wind her up.

'What does he mean by the stone wedding party?' asks Leif. 'I think I have translated that correctly.'

'I don't know,' says Ruth. 'When he was my tutor at university, Erik was always saying things that I didn't under-stand. It meant that he wanted us to look them up, to find out for ourselves.'

'Will you look this one up?' says Leif. 'I'd like to make a libation to my father.'

'I will,' says Ruth. It sounds like an oath. Or a wedding vow.

Judy too finds someone waiting for her. Maddie is leaning against Judy's red Fiat, ostentatiously making notes.

'Have you been to see Carol Dunne?' she says. 'She used to teach Margaret, didn't she?'

'Why are you following me?' says Judy. She is tired and wants to go home.

'You can't think that Mostyn killed Margaret if you're still interviewing people.'

'I can't discuss the investigation with you,' says Judy. 'You've got your exclusive for tomorrow.'

'Who do you think killed John Mostyn?' Maddie gives her an enchanting smile, head on one side.

'I can't possibly answer questions like that,' says Judy, getting into the car. 'Do you want a lift home? Come for supper if you like. Cathbad's got one of his evening classes tonight but the kids would love to see you.'

'You're all right,' says Maddie vaguely. 'I've got some things to do. Tell them I'll see them soon.'

But, as Judy drives away, Maddie is still standing by the school gate, apparently deep in thought.

CHAPTER 20

It goes against the grain on the first day of a murder investigation, but Nelson leaves the station at five thirty. He's been at work for twelve solid hours but he still feels that he should be there all night, directing operations, moving arrows on a map like a plotter in a Second World War film. But, realistically, there's nothing more that he can do until he has the forensics results. The crime scene is sealed and he's had officers making house-to-house enquiries all day. Tomorrow Mostyn's identity will be in the papers and the link to Margaret will be public. The forensics on Margaret's remains, particularly on the rope, may well point to her killer. If that turns out to be John Mostyn, then the dead can bury the dead. It's a chilling phrase, thinks Nelson. Margaret's funeral is set for next week.

Bruno is still with the dog walker so the house is quiet when he gets in. Michelle is in the sitting room with George; he's sleeping in his Moses basket and she is watching one of those programmes where people buy a house in Tuscany and then seem surprised that everyone there speaks Italian.

'Hallo, love.' Nelson kisses her. 'Good day?'

'Yes, I saw Star. You know, the girl I met at the mother and baby group.'

'That's nice,' says Nelson, rifling through the post. 'Where's Laura?'

'Out at an evening class.'

'What's she studying? Isn't training to be a teacher enough for her?'

'She did tell me but I can't remember. My memory's terrible these days.'

Nelson bends over the basket to look at George. After all his fears, it's a ridiculous relief to be able to recognise himself in the little face. He can't stop himself picking up the sleeping baby and cuddling him, inhaling his sweetly pungent smell.

'Don't wake him up,' says Michelle. 'I met Star's mother today too.'

'Did you?' says Nelson, putting George down. He wonders if Laura has made anything for supper. He really should learn to cook. It's bad enough being dependent on your wife, somehow shameful to expect your daughter to look after you. He bets that smarmy Frank is a gourmet chef, the sort who talks about parmesan shavings and drizzling olive oil.

'She's Margaret's sister,' says Michelle.

'Who is?' says Nelson, who is lost in a pleasant fantasy involving deporting Frank.

'Star's mother. She's called Annie and she was Margaret's sister. The dead girl. Your dead girl.'

His dead girl. The trouble is, that's what it feels like.

'I've never met the sister,' he says. 'What's she like? It's odd to think of her being old enough to be a grandmother. This is tough on the family. You know the original chief suspect has been found dead? That's why I left so early this morning.'

'Yes,' says Michelle. 'I think Annie mentioned that. She seemed very upset when she came in. She knew who I was immediately.'

'You didn't say anything about the case?'

'I don't know anything about the case,' says Michelle. 'But Judy and Dave arrived just as I was leaving. I suppose they wanted to talk to Annie about this man's murder.'

'Yes, they were going to speak to all the immediate members of the family. Just to warn them, because it'll be in the papers tomorrow.'

'It's horrible for them,' says Michelle. 'Having the past raked up like that.' The press coverage of Tim's death had concentrated almost exclusively on the 'dead hero' angle but, even so, Nelson knows that it was almost unbearable for Michelle. For him too, come to that. He wants to say something, to reassure Michelle that the past horrors are behind them but, whilst he is still thinking of the words, she gets up and smiles at him. 'Are you hungry? There's some pasta sauce. Laura made a big batch and froze it. It's got Quorn in it but you can't taste that really.'

Laura is lying on the floor. There's a skylight in the ceiling and through it she can see stars and wisps of clouds.

'Lose yourself in the universe,' says a voice that seems to come, not from beside her, but from somewhere in the ether.

Laura closes her eyes and tries to hang on to her mantra but it's difficult in the dusty community centre with the traffic noise outside and the Italian Culture Class singing *'Funiculì Funiculà'* in the next room. Last year, in the autumn before it got too cold, Cathbad took them into the woods at Sandringham and they had gazed up at the trees and it really was possible to feel part of the natural world and yet apart from it, both unthinking and yet deeply conscious. Cathbad says that you can meditate anywhere but she must be an undeveloped soul because, tonight, she can't stop thinking about that day's uni assignment, about George and Mum, worrying about whether Dad's collected Bruno from doggy day care. She tries again with her own personal mantra, listing amino acids in alphabetical order. Alanine, arginine, asparagine . . .

'Be aware of your breath,' says Cathbad. 'Be aware of the sensation of breathing. May everyone be happy. May everyone be free from misery. May no one ever be separated from their happiness.'

Usually his voice has a hypnotic effect on Laura but today she's not really feeling it. She opens her eyes and sees Star in lotus position, palms upwards, apparently at one with the universe. A feeling of entirely unspiritual irritation washes over Laura, like a dirty tide. She sits up. The two other members of the group, Malcolm and Felicity, are also fidgeting. Perhaps the Italian folk songs are too much for them too.

It's possible that even Cathbad feels it because he finishes the class a few minutes early, bowing in a slightly ironical 'namaste'.

'Are you all right, Laura?' he says as she rolls up her mat.

'Fine,' she says. 'No. I don't know.' There's never any point lying to Cathbad. 'I'm just a bit distracted.' Cathbad knows her parents, of course, but he'd never dream of asking if things were all right at home. Now, he says, 'Sometimes distractions are a way of pointing us in a certain direction. Maybe give some attention to those thoughts.'

'They're just trivial things,' says Laura. 'Like what I should have for dinner.' She thinks about food a lot, mainly about how to avoid eating it.

'Food is never trivial,' says Cathbad. Bloody Star is hanging about with a question about mindfulness so Laura shouts a general goodbye and heads for the door.

There's a man outside, standing in the little lobby with the fire extinguisher and the posters for long-forgotten fun runs. He's tall and muscular with golden-blond hair in a ponytail. He looks a bit like Thor in the Marvel films and is as out of place in this environment as if he were a real Norse god.

'Excuse me.' He has a faint foreign accent. 'Is this where Michael Malone, Cathbad, teaches?'

'Yes,' says Laura. 'He's in there.' She finds herself wishing that she wasn't wearing her oldest leggings, slightly frayed where Bruno tugged them out of the linen basket.

'Thank you,' says the man. 'My name is Leif.'

'Mine's Laura.'

'A beautiful name.'

Laura has never liked her name. It's too old-fashioned and has, to her mind, a slightly whiny sound, like the twang of a country and western guitar. In fact she was given the name because Michelle liked the song 'Tell Laura I Love Her'. But now she smiles and tosses her hair for all she's worth.

'Thank you. It's Laura Nelson actually.'

Now he can track her down if he wants to.

Ruth is at her computer, Kate is asleep upstairs and Flint is out on a night-time excursion. Outside her window the marshes are dark and silent and Ruth is looking up stories about the devil. Googling 'stone wedding party' brings up a variety of folklore and fairy tales, usually involving Saturday night revels that go on into the Sabbath. They remind Ruth of all-night parties at UCL. But the version that catches Ruth's eye involves the standing stones at Stanton Drew in Somerset. Stanton Drew is an impressive megalithic stone circle (actually three circles in total) and there is an appropriate legend linked to the site. There was said to have been a wedding at Stanton Drew, date unspecified but in that dusty era that Ruth sometimes ironically describes to her students as 'yore'. At the wedding party a mysterious fiddler, dressed in black, appeared and offered to play all night. The wedding guests danced, the music becoming more frenzied, until dawn broke on the Sunday morning and the fiddler, who was, of course, the devil, vanished in a puff of smoke leaving a circle of strangely shaped stones. The three largest are known locally as the bride, groom and preacher and there is a further group that is meant to represent the musicians. Frankly, it sounds just Erik's sort of place. Cathbad's too. The word Drew is apparently derived from the Celtic word for druid. Ruth is especially interested to learn that a geophysical survey in 1998 showed a series of concentric post-hole rings outside the main circle. So this site may once have been surrounded by a palisade of timber. Like Seahenge. Like Erik's henge.

Ruth stares at her laptop screen where the stones, misshapen and dark with lichen, do seem to be acquiring sinister proportions. Is this where Erik wanted her to go? Ruth remembers Erik once saying that the human journey is one from flesh to wood to stone. From the living body to the wood of the coffin to the stone of the grave. Maybe this is why there are so many myths and legends about petrification. Ruth thinks of *The Lion, the Witch and the Wardrobe*, one of Kate's favourite books. The White Witch turned her enemies to stone until Aslan breathed on them and brought them to life. There's too much overt Christian symbolism in the story for Ruth's liking but there's no doubt that this is a powerful scene; a room that was once full of statues suddenly teeming with life, lions roaring, giants wielding clubs, Mr Tumnus embracing Lucy. In Greek mythology, Medusa was famous for turning her enemies to stone, and then there's the basilisk, immortalised for a new generation by J. K. Rowling in the Harry Potter books, whose gaze is also meant to petrify, in both senses. Nearer to home there's the Lincoln imp, a mischievous creature that is said to have darted around the cathedral throwing things until an angel turned it to stone where it remains to this day, grinning from the wall. There is something primal about the thought that soft flesh becomes hard stone, dead but also everlasting.

She needs to talk to Cathbad. He'd understand all this stuff and he'd also understand why Ruth is considering trekking all the way across the country to look at some old stones. It's a pilgrimage of sorts and pilgrimages are not meant to be easy. She looks at the time in the right-hand corner of the screen. Nine o'clock. Not too late to ring. She's not surprised that Cathbad's mobile goes unanswered (he's very concerned about harmful vibrations and usually leaves it switched off, much to Judy's irritation) but when she tries the landline Judy tells her that he's still out at his meditation class. She sounds rather stressed and so Ruth doesn't stay on the line to chat. She looks at her Fitbit. Only two thousand steps today. She's felt rather twitchy ever since Shona asked her to become her 'Fitbit friend' which means she can see how many steps Ruth achieves each day. The app even gives you your rankings at the end of the week and Shona always wins. Ruth walks around the room a few times before giving up.

She goes upstairs to check on Kate (stairs give you extra points) and finds her fast asleep with her head on her cuddly chimpanzee. Flint, who is obviously back from his wanderings, is lying at the foot of the bed. He blinks at Ruth but doesn't get up. Ruth goes to her own room and stares out over the marshes. There are tiny lights glimmering at the point where the land meets the sea.

Phosphorescence. Will-o-the-wisps. Marsh lights. Cathbad would say that they are the ghosts of drowned children but there is also the legend of Jack O'Lantern, the miserable blacksmith forced to wander between heaven and earth, his path illuminated only by a spark of hellfire concealed in a turnip. The devil really does have all the best tricks as well as the best tunes. Ruth pulls the curtains and goes downstairs to bolt the door.

Nelson and Michelle sit in bed, watching an episode of *Breaking Bad* on Nelson's laptop. It's only half past nine, Laura is still out, but they both feel like it's the middle of the night. Michelle has been silent for about ten minutes. Perhaps she's asleep.

'Michelle,' says Nelson. She doesn't answer but he continues anyway. On screen a body floats in a swimming pool. 'I've been thinking,' says Nelson. 'We should tell the girls. About Katie. I should tell them, I mean.'

He looks at Michelle. She's not asleep, in fact she is staring at him intently. The dark roots make her blonde hair almost brown. She looks different, more serious somehow.

'Why tell them now?' she says.

'They'll know one day. You've been great to let me see Katie but, as she grows up, it's going to be harder to keep them apart. Also, I don't know, after last summer – all you and Laura went through – I don't think we should have secrets.'

Another silence and then Michelle says, 'Do you think I should tell them about Tim?'

When Michelle told him about the affair with Tim, Nelson hadn't felt in a position to take the moral high ground. And it had been such a strange time, they were all really just happy to be alive and the thought of the baby had sustained them. Even when Nelson had thought that George might be Tim's, he couldn't view his birth as anything other than a good thing, cosmically speaking, something bright to set against the darkness. Of course, there is jealousy and anger there too. Nelson hates the thought of Michelle sleeping with another man. He hates the thought of Ruth sleeping with another man, come to think of it. But Michelle has lived with jealousy over Katie for seven years.

'I don't think you should say anything about Tim,' he says at last. 'It's not as if he's . . .'

'Alive,' says Michelle.

'No,' says Nelson. 'What good would it do?'

'It might make me feel better,' says Michelle.

'Do you feel bad then?' says Nelson.

'Oh, Harry,' says Michelle, and he thinks she's near to tears. 'Of course I feel bad. I had an affair with Tim and now he's dead. He died because of me. I feel guilty all the time.'

'I feel guilty too,' says Nelson. But he doesn't say what for.

'But I'm happy as well,' says Michelle. 'Because of George. He's a miracle baby. Remember what that midwife called him? A menopausal miracle. I love him so much.'

Nelson wants to ask if she still loves him but George is a safer subject.

'He's a little cracker,' he says. 'I'll tell the girls at the weekend.'

'I'll help you,' says Michelle. 'I'll tell them that I'm happy for Katie to be in our lives.'

She is rewarded for this generosity by falling into a deep sleep but Nelson stays awake for a long time.

CHAPTER 21

Maddie's article appears in the *Chronicle* the next morning.

The man found dead at the Canada Industrial Estate is
confirmed to be John Mostyn, 70, of Allenby Avenue,
King's Lynn. His death is being treated as suspicious.
Mostyn was one of the main suspects in the disappearance
of twelve-year-old Margaret Lacey in 1981. Margaret was
last seen at a street party held to celebrate the wedding of
Prince Charles to Lady Diana Spencer. Despite an extensive police investigation, opened again in 1991, no trace
of Margaret was ever found. But, last month, archaeologists excavating a site near Holme in north Norfolk found
human remains which were later confirmed to be those of
the missing child.

Margaret's parents Karen and Bob Lacey never gave
up hope that their daughter would be found. Bob died
of testicular cancer in 2014 but Karen still lives in the
house that she once shared with Margaret and her siblings,
Annie and Luke. She said that the discovery of Margaret's

remains would allow them to grieve at last. 'It's been hard,' she said, 'in some ways time has stood still since Margaret left us. I still think of her as that twelve-year-old girl who loved dancing and ponies and dressing up. Now we'll be able to bury Margaret and have a place to remember her. Maybe our family can finally find some peace.' Margaret's funeral is set to take place on Monday 7th March at St Bernadette's Church, King's Lynn.

The discovery of Margaret's bones has sparked a major police investigation led by DCI Harry Nelson, the detective who led the hunt for four-year-old Scarlet Henderson in 2008. Scarlet's body was found buried on marshy ground near Holme. No one was ever tried for her murder. Police wouldn't confirm a link between Margaret Lacey and John Mostyn but they admitted that they are still interviewing suspects in connection with Margaret's abduction and death.

'Did we?' says Nelson. 'Did we admit that?'

'I love the word "admit",' says Judy, who is looking slightly rattled. 'No, but Maddie saw me leaving the school after talking to Carol Dunne and she must have realised that the investigation is still ongoing.'

'The girl's a pro,' says Clough. 'She's even managed to get a quote from Karen Lacey.'

'She's got all the tricks,' says Nelson. 'Like saying "no one was ever tried" for Scarlet's murder. That's because the man was dead, for God's sake. She makes it sound like we never solved the case.'

'No mention of Lucy,' says Clough, 'who we did find.'

'That's because it's still all about Scarlet for Maddie,' says Judy.

'She's given a date for the funeral,' says Tanya. 'I didn't think that was set yet. Have Forensics finished with the remains?'

'They said they would release them to the undertaker today,' says Nelson. 'Maddie must have some inside knowledge.'

'St Bernadette's,' says Clough. 'That's the Catholic church, isn't it?'

'Yes,' says Judy. 'Remember, the family are Catholic. I don't think they go to church much though.'

'We should all go to the funeral,' says Nelson. 'It would be good if we could have some involvement, just to show that the relationship with the police is good. Judy, could you approach the parents? Maybe suggest that someone does a reading?'

'They like Clough best,' says Judy. 'They think he's in charge.'

'Christ, I don't want to do a reading,' says Clough.

Nelson looks back at the article which has upset him more than he cares to admit. 'She makes the link between Margaret and Scarlet,' he says, 'not overtly, but she says Holme for both of them when Scarlet was really found nearer Titchwell.'

'Is there a possibility that Scarlet's killer could have murdered Margaret?' says Judy. 'It was twenty years earlier but there was Lucy in between. And it *is* a similar location.'

'He wasn't living in Norfolk in 1981,' says Nelson. 'I checked. He was in the Shetlands or some such place.'

'The letters make the link too,' says Judy. 'If Mostyn did write the new letters he seems to be deliberately invoking the previous ones.'

'How did he know about them?' says Clough. 'We never made them public.'

'My guess is the *Chronicle*,' says Nelson. 'Mostyn used to do some photography for them. That place leaks like a sieve.'

'Bloody press,' says Clough. 'Who needs them?'

'We do,' says a voice from the doorway. It's Super Jo, newspaper in hand. 'Can I have a word, Harry?'

Ruth is on her way to the police station, suppressing the faint surge of excitement that always comes with being involved in a case. This is about finding a child's killer, she tells herself, not about seeing Nelson and being part of the team. Besides, her meeting is with Judy. Nelson might not even be there.

But, after she has signed in and been escorted to a meeting room, there's Nelson scowling behind the table and Clough eating a cheese and ham sandwich.

'Judy's just gone out to get some more sandwiches,' he says, rather thickly. 'In case the meeting goes on into lunch-time.'

Ruth glances at her watch. It's eleven thirty. She needs to be back at the university at one. 'What does Judy think about going on the sandwich run?' she asks.

'We take it in turns,' says Clough. 'This is a non-sexist workplace. We've got a certificate.'

'This is a non-working workplace at the moment,' says Nelson. 'Let's get on. What have you got for us, Ruth?'

Ruth gets out her file with Roz's forensics results and her own notes. Judy comes in and distributes sandwiches and bottles of water. Clough grumbles about the lack of chocolate. Ruth wonders where Tanya is. She usually never misses a strategy meeting.

'Forensic examination of Margaret's bones found traces of pollen, spores and wildlife—' she begins.

Clough interrupts her with a pained expression. 'Wildlife?'

'When the body was previously buried it would have been consumed by worms and maggots. Insects would have nested in the hair. Traces of their eggs remain. In addition, pollen was found in the nasal cavity. I have a report from an expert palynologist—'

'A what?' This is Nelson.

'A pollen expert. She traced the pollen found on the remains to this specific area.' Ruth gets out her map, the three police officers lean over to look.

'That's basically all of Norfolk,' says Clough.

'There's a place called Scarning Fen, near Dereham,' says Ruth. 'It's a very important wildflower reserve because there are some plants there that aren't found anywhere else in the country. There was moss on the bones that only grows in Scarning Fen.'

Nelson is frowning at the map. 'So Margaret was originally buried near Dereham?'

'It looks like it,' says Ruth. 'And there were damsel fly

eggs too. Scarning Fen is one of the few places in England where you find the red damsel fly.'

'If we go to this fen place,' says Nelson, 'do you think you can find where Margaret was buried?'

'I doubt it after all this time,' says Ruth. 'Vegetation will have grown so much and the fen is still such a large area. But having a location will help, won't it?'

'It will help a lot,' says Nelson. 'We've only really been concentrating on Lynn so far. Now we can find out who has links to this Scarning area. People always choose burial sites for a reason. It has to be somewhere they're familiar with, maybe a place where they walk their dog or where they camped as a child. Alongside the forensics from the rope, this might help us close in.'

'Have you got the forensics results?' asks Ruth.

'Tanya's at the lab. She should be back any minute.'

'That's her now,' says Judy. 'She always hums the *Rocky* theme when she climbs the stairs.'

Seconds later, Tanya bursts into the room looking important.

'What have you got?' says Nelson. 'Don't mind Ruth. She's one of us.' Ruth keeps her professional face on but she feels her cheeks glowing. One of us. One of the team.

'Mostyn's DNA is on the bones,' says Tanya. She pauses for effect. 'It's on the stone too, the piece of chalk that was found in the grave. But there's someone else's DNA too. The second DNA's not on the bones but it is on the rope and the gag.'

'So Mostyn's not the killer,' says Clough.

*

Nelson offers to walk Ruth downstairs. In the incident room she's surprised to see a cage with two hamsters in it.

'Is it bring your pet to work day?'

'They were Mostyn's,' says Nelson. 'We seem to have adopted them. Cloughie's named them Sonny and Fredo.'

'*The Godfather*?'

'What else?'

They walk down the stairs which are rather grand, with ornate banisters, a relic of the time when this was a gracious town house.

'Is this a breakthrough?' asks Ruth. 'The forensics?'

'I hope so,' says Nelson. 'I had Jo going on at me this morning. Apparently there's "concern amongst stake-holders" that we're not making enough progress. There's an article in the *Chronicle* today that makes us sound like the Keystone Cops.'

Nelson often uses these slightly archaic references. Perhaps he watched a lot of black-and-white films as a child. Another thing Ruth will never know about him. She can imagine that Jo would not be happy about the article, which Ruth read online that morning. Ruth has a sneaking admiration for Super Jo, although she would never admit this to Nelson.

'Is it still OK to take Katie out on Saturday?' asks Nelson, as they reach the bottom of the stairs.

'Yes, of course,' says Ruth. She has almost given up correcting him about the name. 'Have you got any plans?'

'I thought I'd take her to Redwings.'

'Good idea. She loves the horses.'

'Rebecca's coming down on Sunday to see George.'

They are at the main doors now but Nelson seems to have something else to say.

'I'm going to tell the girls,' he says, not looking at her. 'About Katie.'

'Oh.' Ruth doesn't know what to say. She always knew that he would tell them one day, of course, but there's no denying that she's dreading it. Nelson's 'girls' are grown women, women who will now hate Ruth.

'Good luck,' she says at last.

'Thanks,' says Nelson, rather grimly. 'What are you doing at the weekend?'

'I'm going to Cambridge on Sunday. To see Frank.'

'I hope it keeps fine for you,' says Nelson.

He looks like a thundercloud, though, which Ruth can't help finding slightly comforting.

CHAPTER 22

It's hard to find the right moment. Early on Saturday morning Nelson checks on the crime scene in Allenby Avenue. The house, surrounded by police tape, looks lonely and innocuous. A uniformed constable yawns on the doorstep, straightening up when he sees Nelson approaching. Nelson rings Judy and asks her to visit Karen and Pete. 'Ask about the funeral and try to find out whether anyone's got any links to Scarning Fen.'

'I'm out all day,' says Judy. 'I'm not meant to be working this weekend.'

'Sunday then.'

'We're visiting my parents.' But she agrees to visit on Sunday morning. Then Nelson drives to the Saltmarsh to collect Katie. Ruth is friendly enough but seems rather distracted. She has a pile of papers on her desk and is obviously planning to catch up on work. After a few brief pleasantries Nelson installs Katie in the back of his car and they drive to Redwings.

It's a bitterly cold day but he enjoys walking through the

fields with Katie, trying to engage the horses in conversation. He buys her hot chocolate in the café and she takes him to see the pony that she sponsors.

'I had to get a new one,' she says, pointing to a black and white blob in the distance.

'Did the old one go away for a holiday?' says Nelson, treading carefully.

'No, it died,' says Katie. 'I think I'd like a donkey next.'

Before they leave, Nelson fills out the adoption forms for a donkey named Wiggins.

When he gets home, his mother-in-law has arrived, which is the cue for lots of hugs and George-worshipping. Nelson gets on well with Louise, Michelle's mother, a smart ash-blonde who still works part-time and drives a pink Fiat 500. Seeing Louise, Michelle and Laura together is like watching a time-lapse photograph but, from a distance, the three beautiful women could almost be sisters. Michelle seems energised by her mother's presence and cooks them all a delicious lunch. In the afternoon Nelson takes George out in his buggy with Bruno cantering along beside them. Coming home, the lights are on in the house and he can see his wife, mother-in-law and daughter drinking Prosecco in front of the television. Is this the last peaceful family day they will have?

Rebecca arrives on Sunday. She's the brunette, the rebel, the one who is most like Nelson. If there's trouble, it'll be from Rebecca. His chance comes in the afternoon. After another epic lunch, Louise offers to take George out for some fresh air. She says politely that she doesn't think she can manage Bruno as well so the dog stays panting in the sitting room, looking hopefully at the door. Michelle, looking rather nervous, sits in her favourite chair. Rebecca and Laura are on the sofa, Rebecca's legs on Laura's lap. Both are on their phones.

'Girls,' says Nelson. 'I've got something to tell you.'

When Judy and Clough call round to Karen's house on Sunday morning, Annie greets them at the door.

'Mum and Pete have gone to mass,' she says. 'Do you want tea or coffee?'

Both ask for coffee and Judy makes an attempt to chat to Annie in the kitchen.

'I didn't think your mum went to church on Sundays,' she says.

'She doesn't,' says Annie, crashing cups and saucers. 'This kitchen is a mess. I'm always on at Mum to let me redesign it.'

Karen's kitchen looks tidy enough to Judy but it's definitely outdated, with blue Formica cupboards and tiles with embossed vegetables on them. It's friendly though. It reminds her of her grandmother's house.

'They've gone to mass today because they like the priest,' says Annie. 'The one doing Margaret's funeral.'

Karen, when she arrives, confirms this.

'Father Declan has been so nice about the funeral arrangements,' she says. 'We thought we ought to go to church today. It seemed only polite.' Karen is smartly dressed in a black trouser suit with a leopard-print shirt. Maybe she's from the generation that dresses up for church but Judy thinks that Karen is the sort of woman who always takes trouble with her appearance. She remembers Kim Jennings saying that Karen used to look like one of Pan's People. Judy hadn't got the reference at the time but she looked them up and it turns out that Pan's People was the name of a deeply sexist dance group that used to appear on *Top of the Pops*. From old YouTube clips it appears that the dancers specialised in routines that took song lyrics extremely literally, acting out lines like 'clouds in my coffee' whilst wearing very little clothing. Still, Judy assumes that it was meant as a compliment.

'We'll both be at the funeral tomorrow,' says Clough, as they move into the sitting room with their coffees. 'We want to pay our respects. Our boss will be there too, DCI Nelson.'

'Oh, I've heard about DCI Nelson.' Karen sounds impressed. 'It's good of him to come.'

'He wants to be there,' says Judy. 'Margaret is very important to us.'

Karen and Pete exchange a glance. 'Father Declan was asking about readings,' says Karen. 'Annie is going to do one and we were wondering if you'd do the other, DS Clough.'

'What about Luke?' says Annie. 'He might want to do a reading.'

'I've asked him,' says Karen, 'and he doesn't.'

Clough doesn't look at Judy but she knows what he's thinking. He's pleased to be the one who was asked but, at the same time, he wishes that it wasn't him.

'I'd be honoured,' he says.

They talk for a little while about readings and hymns. Clough says that his favourite is 'Amazing Grace', which surprises Judy. Hers is 'How Great Thou Art', a soaring anthem that seems as much about the glories of Nature as it is about God. Karen says that they wanted 'All Things Bright and Beautiful', which Margaret used to sing at school, but that Annie had said that it was 'feudal'.

'All that guff about the rich man in his castle and the poor man at his gate,' says Annie. 'It's obscene.'

Judy agrees in principle but she can't help noticing that Annie seems to wield a lot of power in the family. She asks who else will be attending.

'Luke will be there, of course,' says Karen. 'With Rina, his wife, and their children. They're not staying here though. It's not smart enough for them. They'll book a hotel.'

Interesting, thinks Judy.

Karen and Pete have two sons: Bradley, who is thirty, and Richard, twenty-eight. Bradley is divorced with two small children. Richard, Karen tells them rather proudly, is gay and married to a man called Brian. The brothers will be carrying the offertory gifts at the funeral.

'Of course, they never knew Margaret,' says Karen. 'But they feel as if they do. I mean, she's everywhere.' She looks up at the photograph on the wall.

She's everywhere and nowhere, thinks Judy, like one of the song lyrics so beloved of Pan's People. She wonders what it was like for Bradley and Richard, growing up with this presence in the house, this much-loved ghost.

'Annie's children will all be there tomorrow,' says Karen.

'Matt's working for a building society in Norwich, Sienna's training to be a nurse. Like her mum. And there's Star.' She smiles. Judy remembers that Carol Dunne had also smiled when she mentioned the mysterious Stella who became Star.

'Star's just had a baby,' says Pete. 'A lovely little thing. She wants to bring her to the funeral.'

'It's ridiculous,' says Annie. 'I told Star Ava's far too young. She'll only cry and upset everyone.'

'I think Margaret would have liked it,' says Karen. 'She loved babies.'

Judy wonders who will emerge triumphant from the battle of wills between Annie and Star.

'We've just got a quick question for you,' she says. 'Do any of you have any links with Scarning Fen? It's a nature reserve in Dereham.'

'Scarning Fen?' Pete looks at his wife. 'I don't think so.'

'What's this about?' says Annie. 'Has it got something to do with Margaret?'

Clough and Judy exchange glances. 'It's just a line of enquiry,' says Clough, in the soothing tone that he has now adopted for the Bensons. 'Might well be nothing but we've had some forensic reports back. Remember we thought that Margaret might have been buried somewhere else before the Saltmarsh? Well, the forensics show that she might have been buried near Scarning Fen.'

'Forensics?' says Annie. 'What forensics?' She seems outraged at the thought of such a thing in relation to her dead sister.

Judy doesn't want to go into the wildlife eating the body or the pollen in the nasal cavity. 'Moss,' she says at last. 'Moss that's unique to the area.'

'Any family links?' says Clough. 'Anyone live in Dereham?'

'No,' says Karen, sounding quite shocked even though the town is only about twenty-five miles from King's Lynn. Judy thinks of Tom Henty, 'It's an east Norfolk thing.' And of John Mostyn talking about the Roman port at Caister-on-Sea.

Before they go, Pete asks if they've made any headway with catching Mostyn's killer.

'We're following several leads,' says Clough.

But the truth is that Mostyn's killer seems to have vanished without trace. There's DNA at the scene but that's no use unless it matches some currently held on record.

'If anyone can catch him, you can,' says Karen.

Clough says modestly that the team has a pretty good clearance rate. Karen and Pete look at him admiringly. Annie is frowning in the background.

Ruth and Kate have a good day with Frank in Cambridge. They have lunch in a pub and go on a tour of the more picturesque colleges. Kate is entranced by the chapel at King's College and Ruth allows herself a brief daydream involving gowns and punting and a first in natural sciences. Of course, these places are incredibly elitist but Kate is such a clever girl and she'll be state educated . . .

'Ruth,' says Frank. Ruth comes back to earth. Frank is staring at a stone gargoyle that reminds Ruth of the Lincoln imp but it doesn't look as if he's seeing it. 'What are we doing?'

'Sussing out the right college for Kate?'

'You know what I mean.'

Ruth does know what he means and she very much wants to avoid having this conversation. She looks round for Kate but her daughter is looking up at the vaulted ceiling, apparently deep in thought.

'Do we have to be doing anything?' she says.

'I don't know,' says Frank. He runs a hand through his thick grey hair. He's wearing a heavy jacket and looks bulkier and more dependable than ever. A silver fox, he's often called by viewers of his TV programme. Ruth can't think of an equivalent compliment for a greying woman but there's no denying that Frank is still very attractive.

'I'm nearly sixty,' Frank is saying. 'I suppose I want to know if there's any future in our relationship. There's a job going at Cambridge. A permanent post. I'd like to apply. I could easily settle here. My kids are all grown and transatlantic flights aren't that expensive. It's just . . . Can you ever see us living together? I don't know about you, but I thought the other night was pretty special.'

Ruth cringes slightly at the word and at the memory of hustling Kate out of the house so that she didn't meet a semi-naked Frank on the landing. She glances over to check that her daughter is still out of earshot.

'It was great,' she says, thinking that her own word is also rather unsatisfactory. 'It's just . . . I like being with you but

I don't know if I could live with a man again. I've got used to it just being me and Kate.'

'And Flint.'

'Well, Flint would move in with you like a shot.'

'Thanks,' says Frank, rather wryly. 'What about you?'

'Can't we take it more slowly? After all, we've only just started seeing each other again. And I do like you.' She laughs, embarrassed at how lukewarm that sounds, but Frank takes her hand.

'I like you too, Ruth.'

In Frank's warm west-coast accent it sounds a lot more positive.

He tells it very badly. He'd meant to start with Katie, how sweet she is, how fond they all are of her, but instead he finds himself blurting out that he had an affair with Ruth.

'Ruth Galloway?' says Rebecca, sitting up and putting her phone down. 'The archaeologist woman?'

'It was a long time ago,' says Nelson, not entirely truthfully. 'And it wasn't even a proper affair, well, anyway . . .'

'Katie's your daughter?' Laura is staring at him with a blank, traumatised look that is worse than anything he could have imagined.

'I know it's a shock,' says Nelson. 'But I want you to know that I love you girls – and George too – more than anything.'

'Does Mum know about this?' This is Rebecca, sounding angry which is actually almost a relief.

'Yes,' says Michelle, her voice admirably steady. 'I knew about it from the beginning.'

'And you let Dad see Katie?'

'Well, it's not her fault, is it?'

'Jesus, Dad.' Laura stands up. 'I can't believe this. I thought you were one of the good guys. I thought you two had the perfect marriage. And, all this time it's been a complete sham. You've had an illegitimate daughter. You had an affair. And what about Tim?'

'What about him?' Now Michelle does sound nervous.

'He must have been in love with you. You rang him that evening, didn't you? That's why he came to save us. That's why he died.'

'This isn't about Tim,' says Nelson.

'Yes, Tim was in love with me,' says Michelle quietly, 'but I always loved your father.'

'I know it's hard,' says Nelson. 'But we do still love each other. We're still a family.'

'Bullshit.' Laura, who never loses her temper, yells so loudly that Bruno shoots out of the room. 'We're not a family. I never want to see either of you ever again.'

She storms out of the room and, with an apologetic look at her mother, Rebecca follows her. Seconds later, the door slams and they hear a car starting up. Bruno barks and then the front door opens. Nelson goes to the hall and sees Louise manoeuvring the buggy over the step.

'We've had a lovely walk,' she says. 'Georgie's been as good as gold. Where are the girls off to? Laura looked upset.'

It seems to Nelson that even Bruno is looking at him accusingly.

CHAPTER 23

'Slow down, for Christ's sake. Where are we going anyway?'

'I don't know,' says Laura. 'Away.'

'Well slow down or we'll be away to the next world.'

Laura was always the sensible one, thinks Rebecca, it's very odd to see her like this; face set, hair flying, eyes glittering with tears. But she does slow down slightly.

'That was a shocker,' says Rebecca. 'Did you have any idea?'

'It had crossed my mind,' says Laura. 'I mean, why was Dad always taking Katie to places? He brought her to the house once when Mum was out. I made her a fish finger sandwich. She was very sweet, I have to say.'

'She's our sister,' says Rebecca. 'How weird is that? I can't believe you suspected.'

'Well, I've been living at home for the past year. It's been obvious that something's up. Even you must have noticed.'

Rebecca is stung by the 'even you'. 'You're always imagining things,' she says. 'Remember when you were sure you were adopted because the date on your baptism certificate was wrong?'

'I wish I was adopted,' says Laura, taking a mini-roundabout at speed. 'I wish they weren't my parents.'

'You don't mean that,' says Rebecca, clamping a foot on the imaginary brake. 'Where are we going anyway?' They are on the Fakenham road now, full of Sunday drivers taking their time to look at the view.

'To see a friend in Wells.'

'You haven't got any friends in Wells.'

'He's my meditation teacher,' says Laura. 'I want to talk to him. He's the only person who understands anything.'

'Meditation teacher?' says Rebecca. 'Have you gone a bit nutty since the Tim thing?'

'The Tim thing? Since a man was killed in our house, you mean?'

'Yes,' says Rebecca. 'That. I mean, you finished with Chad and you never go out with any of the old gang.'

Laura is driving more carefully now but her face (so like their mother, whatever she says about being adopted) is set and serious, jaw clenched. 'I have changed,' she says. 'It feels like I've grown up at last. Cathbad says—'

'Cathbad? *He's* your meditation teacher?'

'Yes.' Laura colours slightly. 'He knows a lot about meditation techniques.'

'But he's Dad's friend. And Ruth's.'

'Mum and Dad don't know. They're so tired at the moment that they only think about George. Or this old murder case Dad's working on.'

Rebecca thinks it's a good sign that Laura is now mentioning their parents in an almost normal voice. They are taking the country route, hedges on either side, the occasional glimpse of grey winter fields. As they approach Wells, they see the sea, still exciting even if you've lived within sight of it all your life. Fishing boats are beached on the sand but the tide is coming in, streams becoming rivulets, lapis-lazuli blue in the twilight. It seems like a different world.

'Remember getting the train here when we were little?' says Rebecca, as Laura negotiates the tiny streets. Some of the shops are still open and their family name is everywhere because that other Nelson, Admiral Horatio Nelson, hero of Trafalgar, was born in Burnham Thorpe, near Wells. Nelson's café. Nelson's sweetshop. Nelson's Seaside Souvenirs. Outside a shop called Little Rocks, tiny stones glitter.

'It's a very special place,' says Laura. She even sounds like someone who takes meditation classes.

But, when they park in front of a row of fishermen's cottages, Laura seems reluctant to knock on the door that is painted an unusual turquoise colour.

'Go on,' says Rebecca. 'After all, we've come all this way.' She's curious to see Laura with Cathbad. She remembers him as a slightly oddball friend of her parents. He once gave her a dreamcatcher; she still has it above her bed in Brighton.

Laura gives her a nasty look but she gets out of the car. Rebecca watches as her sister knocks on the door and waits. After a few minutes she knocks again. There's obviously no answer. Laura starts to walk back to the car but then she stops. A man is approaching. He's got long hair. Is it Cathbad? No, this man is younger and, even from Rebecca's viewpoint, seriously good-looking. He stops and talks to Laura. Rebecca can't hear what they're saying but it seems very intense. The man has his hand on Laura's arm, bending his head down to her level. Laura flicks her hair back and laughs, all traces of the heartbroken daughter vanished. Then she comes back to the car. Rebecca winds down the window and Laura hands her the keys.

'Can you drive home? I'm going for a walk with Leif.'

'With who?'

Laura gestures at the long-haired man who raises his hand in a friendly wave.

'You're going off with a complete stranger?'

'He's not a stranger. I met him the other day. He's a friend of Cathbad's. He just came to call but they're out. It's synchronicity.'

'Is that what you call it? What shall I tell Mum and Dad?'

'Tell them I'm dead.' Laura gives her a dazzling smile and turns back to Leif.

It's dark by the time that Ruth gets home from Cambridge. Kate, who has kept up a steady flow of conversation, falls silent just as they take the road across the Saltmarsh. It's as eerie as ever, the raised tarmac with the ground dropping away on either side. One false move and they would find themselves in a ditch, prey to whatever night terrors are roaming the marshes at night. There are no lights, only that faint glimmer out to sea which might be late-night fishing boats, or phosphorescence or something altogether more sinister. Ruth hears Erik's voice, floating back through the years. Fireside tales, from that first dig, when they found the henge.

The Nix were shape-shifters. Sometimes they appear as beautiful women, sitting combing their long blue hair, their voices luring sailors to death on the jagged rocks. Sometimes the Nix is a man playing a violin, a wild tune that the traveller must follow at his peril. The Nix can even appear as a horse, a brook horse it's called in Scandinavian legend, a beautiful animal, snow white or coal black, that appears in the water by a ravine or a waterfall. If you climb on its back you can never dismount and the horse will gallop away to the ends of the earth. On dark nights you can hear the horse's hoofbeats, steady and relentless, carrying its rider to hell.

Ruth turns on the radio, wanting to silence the hoofbeats. The *Archers* theme tune fills the car.

'Can we turn it off?' says Kate from the back.

Back home, Kate panics because Flint is nowhere to be seen but Ruth senses that he's around somewhere. And, sure enough, when Kate goes up to bed, Flint is stretched out on her Hogwarts duvet.

Kate asks for a story and Ruth reads her the beginning of *Northern Lights*, the first book in Philip Pullman's His Dark Materials trilogy. The series appeals to Ruth, as an atheist, but up until now she has thought it too dark for Kate. She needn't have worried. Kate adores it. She lies propped up on one arm, listening intently, stroking Flint with her other hand. And, although it's set in Oxford not Cambridge, Lyra's world with its dining halls, gargoyles, panels and secret doors, recalls their day wandering through King's, Trinity and St John's.

'Can you read some more tomorrow?' asks Kate as Ruth bends to kiss her goodnight.

'If you like.' Ruth foresees that she will be reading His Dark Materials for the next year at least.

Downstairs, Ruth pours herself a glass of wine and tries to settle down to some marking. It's Margaret Lacey's funeral tomorrow and Ruth feels that, as the person to discover her remains, she should go and pay her respects. But it means taking a morning off work and Phil is sure to comment. It also means seeing Nelson, even if only from afar. She wonders whether Nelson has carried through with his plan of telling his daughters about Kate. She wishes that she could ring him to find out. The urge is so strong that, instead, Ruth rings Cathbad. He rarely has his phone switched on but this time he answers immediately. He and Judy and the children have been out today, visiting Judy's parents, and Ruth can hear children's voices and Thing, Cathbad's dog, barking in the background. She feels grateful for her evening peace with Kate, Flint and Philip Pullman.

'I'd like to go to the funeral,' he says. 'I visited the site with Leif a couple of days ago and there's incredible energy there. I'm sure that Margaret's remains were placed there for a purpose.'

'That's what Nelson thinks.'

'I'm not talking about the police case, I'm talking about the deeper significance. Leif says that you found another girl's bones there.'

It's a few seconds before Ruth realises that he's talking about the bones in the cist.

'Yes. I think they're early Bronze Age. An adolescent female.'

'There you are then. Perhaps Margaret was put there for the same reason as the first girl.'

'Perhaps.'

'I'd better go now. Judy's calling. I'll meet you at the church tomorrow.'

Ruth clicks off the phone, feeling more disquieted than ever. She had a breakthrough with the forensics. The unique pollen from Scarning Fen will help the police discover where Margaret was first buried and, with luck, may point them to the killer. But they will be no closer to knowing why they were put in the henge circle in the first place. Perhaps, as Cathbad says, the location itself is the clue. If the circle was a memorial to the Bronze Age girl then maybe Margaret has been placed there for the same reason and by someone who understands the significance. She thinks of the anonymous note that she received. Nelson forgot to take it with him and so it's still in her desk drawer. She gets it out and reads the words again.

You found Margaret. She called from the depths and you answered. Her soul is now at peace. May the Gods of earth, sky and sea bless you, Ruth.

There's no doubt in her mind that Margaret's remains were buried in the stone circle because someone wanted them to be discovered. Did that same person want her, Ruth, to discover them? The words are so like Erik's. So much so that, even though she knows he couldn't have written them, Ruth feels that, in some way, they are a message from him. And Leif had an actual message from him. Erik wants Ruth to travel across the country to a stone circle and pour a libation on the earth for him. For the first time Ruth thinks of the similarity between the Satanic fiddler who played until the wedding guests were turned to stone and the Nix with his violin, luring sailors into the sea. All these stories have the same moral: don't be lured by beautiful music or beautiful women or even a beautiful horse; keep your feet securely on the path; don't be lured by words from beyond the grave.

This isn't getting her anywhere. Ruth puts the note, still in its plastic bag, back in her drawer and clicks on the file marked 'Exam scripts'. But before she has read two paragraphs about 'The role of animal bone in excavations' her mind starts wandering, crossing the halls and cloisters of Cambridge, accompanied not just by Frank but now by Lyra and her dæmon too. The night when Nelson came round to look at the note was the night that she slept with Frank. And now Frank seems to be contemplating a future together. Is this so unthinkable? She likes Frank a lot, he gets on with Kate and Flint, and they all seem to coexist fairly easily. She told Frank that she doesn't want to live with a man again and this is true. But maybe they can go on as they are, with Frank at Cambridge and Ruth at UNN, but on a more formal basis. Marriage? Ruth's mind skitters away from the word as fast as it can. Ruth's mother, Jean, used to bemoan that fact that she'd never be 'mother of the bride' but now Jean is dead and her emotional blackmail can't influence Ruth any more. Though, come to think it, hasn't Erik proved that emotional blackmail can work from beyond the grave? She won't marry Frank but maybe he can be a more official partner, they can spend weekends together, meet each other's families, especially if Frank gets that job at Cambridge.

Ruth closes her file and goes onto the University of Cambridge website. She scrolls through 'Job Opportunities' before she finds it. Lecturer in Early Modern History. It's not her era, she prefers prehistory, the days before the written word made interpretation a matter of scholarship rather than detection. But, two lines below, she sees: Lecturer in Forensic Archaeology. She clicks on the link marked, 'Person Specification'.

CHAPTER 24

The church is full for Margaret's funeral. Nelson, arriving with only minutes to spare, is rather embarrassed to see that a pew has been set aside for King's Lynn CID. He wanted them to have a high-profile presence but there's something shameful about taking a seat in the middle of all the grieving relatives. He hasn't even met Karen Benson, née Lacey, yet. That must be her in the front row, a slight woman in deepest black. The larger woman with her must be her daughter, Annie. He's not sure about the other occupants of the family pews. There's a blonde girl who looks like Michelle's description of her friend Star. She has a baby in her arms which seems rather inappropriate to Nelson. But then he's hardly Father of the Year. Laura didn't even come home last night. She texted Rebecca so he knows she's safe but will his adored first-born ever talk to him again?

Judy and Clough look up as he takes his seat next to them. Clough is clutching a sheet of paper. He has been asked to read and seems extremely nervous about it. Nelson remembers reading the lesson at Scarlet Henderson's funeral, all those years ago. He'd done it very badly, stumbling over the words, unable to look at the little white coffin in front of him. He sympathises with Clough. According to Tanya, who has been left behind to hold the fort, Clough has been having coaching from his actress wife, Cassandra. It doesn't seem to have helped with the nerves. Clough's left leg is jiggling frantically. Judy gives him a slight kick and he stops.

Nelson looks round the church and is surprised, and rather pleased, to see Freddie Burnett and Marj Maccallum sitting near the back. Freddie is dressed in a black suit, his face dark brown from the Canary Islands sun. Marj is wearing a waxed jacket that looks like she uses it for dog-walking. She gives Nelson the ghost of a smile.

And there, even further back, is a face that, even in these circumstances, still gives Nelson a jolt of . . . what? Pleasure? Recognition? Love? Ruth, wearing a dark coat, sitting next to Cathbad, conservatively dressed for once in a black suit. Ted, from the field archaeology team, is with them. Ruth doesn't smile at Nelson but he knows that she's seen him. Two fair heads shine out in the gloom of the church. Maddie, somewhere in the middle, and Leif Anderssen, standing at the back, arms crossed. Nelson can't see his expression but he is sure that it is irritatingly enigmatic.

The music starts and the undertakers begin their slow march up the aisle. Another white coffin, another heartbreaking floral arrangement. 'Daughter', it says in chrysanthemums and lilies. Nelson feels his eyes start to prickle. He would give his life for his daughters, all three of them, but will they ever forgive him? In the front row,

Karen lets out a low moan. Her husband puts his arm round her. A man in the row behind sobs into his handkerchief. Is that Luke, the brother?

Nelson remembers the priest, Father Declan, from a previous case. He's white-haired with a soft Irish accent and a deceptively sharp mind. Now Father Declan talks about Margaret. He didn't know her in person, he says, but he knows her from her family's memories, which are golden. Nelson thinks of the girl whom he has only known in death, her smile, her halo of hair. Everyone describes Margaret as a golden girl but gold can be dangerous, as any miner will tell you.

Clough goes up to do the reading, passing so close to the coffin that the lilies leave pollen on his dark suit.

'The souls of the virtuous are in the hands of God, no torment shall ever touch them. In the eyes of the unwise, they did appear to die, their going looked like a disaster, their leaving us like annihilation; but they are in peace . . .'

It's a curiously apocalyptic text for a child's funeral but Nelson is sure that Margaret's going was 'like annihilation' for her family. Clough reads clearly and well, not too fast and not too agonisingly slowly. Cassandra is obviously a good teacher.

'Well done,' he says, when his sergeant sits back down. Clough acknowledges this with a quick smile. The leg jiggling has stopped.

The large woman (it's Annie, he checks the order of service, gold type on white) takes the pulpit for the second reading, that bit from St Paul about love being patient and kind. It always reminds Nelson of Princess Diana's funeral and Tony Blair reading with those curious mid-sentence pauses that made the whole thing sounds like some sort of experimental poetry. He supposes it's fitting. This case started with Diana's marriage and now it ends with echoes of her death. Annie reads well but with a slight irritation in her voice as if it's not *her* fault that people don't understand about love. She steps down from the lectern, not looking at the coffin, and Father Declan moves across to read the gospel. Nelson stands up with the rest of the congregation, the choir singing 'Alleluia'. He watches the altar servers swinging incense and remembers when he used to do that job, the only enjoyable bit about serving on the altar; the rest of the time it was just a question of standing stock-still in a starched surplice. No wonder he stopped after a few years. But, now, the memory comes back to him and he finds himself mouthing the responses and touching his forehead, mouth and chest to indicate that he will live the gospel with mind, voice and heart. Clough looks at him curiously and Johnson, another lapsed Catholic, smiles to herself.

He had forgotten how similar a requiem mass is to the everyday kind. The same prayers and hymns, the same rituals and choreography. Two men with shaven heads who look like they have just been released from prison bring the bread and wine up to the altar. The offertory, it's called. Nelson wonders who the men are. They must be trusted family members if they're allowed a role. When the congregation begins its slow, swaying procession to the altar for holy communion, Nelson, Judy and Clough stay in their seats. Almost all of Margaret's family go up though. Are they still practising Catholics or is this just a nod to the solemnity of the occasion? Nelson thinks of his mother Maureen who, in his mind (and perhaps her own) is the earthly embodiment of the Holy Catholic Church. What would Maureen say if she knew about the rift with her adored eldest granddaughter? Worse still, what would Maureen say if she knew about Ruth and Katie? Maureen has met Ruth once but, for reasons of her own, remains convinced that Ruth is in a relationship with Cathbad, to whom she took one of her rare but unshakable likings. But, if everyone else knows, if there really aren't any more lies in the family, then Maureen will have to be told. She is threatening to come down in the autumn, to see Baby George, whom she persists in believing is an answer to prayer. 'A little boy after all these years. It was the same with you, Harry. How I prayed for a boy after two girls.' Nelson can see his sisters, Maeve and Grainne, rolling their eyes at that one.

More hymns, more prayers. Karen leans forward so that her head is almost on her knees. Annie pats her back. The baby starts to cry and the mother shifts it onto her shoulder. One of the convict men tries to distract it with his car keys. Then, at last, Father Declan is sprinkling the coffin with holy water and the undertakers are bearing it out of the church, followed by Karen, doubled up with grief, and the rest of the family. The daughter, Annie, is scowling, probably trying not to break down. The brother looks in a daze. The blonde girl with the baby smiles at Nelson as she passes.

'Who's that?' says Clough.

'I think she's Karen's granddaughter. She's a friend of Michelle's. From one of those mother and baby groups.'

Clough doesn't comment on the girl's youth and beauty but Nelson knows what he's thinking. In the church porch Nelson exchanges a few words with Freddie and Marj and then walks over to where Ruth and Cathbad are standing, watching the cortège drive away through the rain. He is sure that they are all thinking of the last funeral they attended; Tim borne away by a gospel choir, the Union flag on his coffin.

'Good of you to come,' he says.

'Well, I was there when she was found,' says Ruth. 'It seemed the right thing to do. God, it was so sad though.'

'Sadness is good,' says Cathbad. 'It's our way of saying goodbye.'

Nelson gives him a look but refrains from comment.

'Poor little angel,' says Ted, who is standing with them. 'May she rest in peace.' He makes a sketchy sign of the cross. Is Ted another lapsed Catholic? They're everywhere.

'Are you going to the burial?' Ruth asks Nelson.

'No, that's family only. There's a wake in the church hall but I think I'll give it a miss. I need to get back to the station. Cloughie can go. The family seem to have taken to him.'

'He read well,' says Ruth.

'He's been going to acting classes,' says Nelson.

Ruth smiles, probably thinking of Katie's ambition to be an actress. Rebecca loves acting too. Maybe now the three sisters can meet. If Laura ever comes home again.

Nelson realises that Leif has joined their group. 'Her soul is at peace,' he is saying. 'As the scripture reading said.'

Nelson is irritated. How can Leif know anything about Margaret's soul?

'Good to see you, DCI Nelson,' says Leif. 'How is the investigation going?'

'Very well,' says Nelson. 'We've made some significant forensic discoveries.'

'Science can be fallible,' says Leif.

'Yes,' says Nelson. 'But in my experience it hardly ever is. Excuse me. I'd better get back to work now.'

Ruth watches Nelson run down the church steps, his black coat flapping behind him. She thinks of all the times that she has seen Nelson hurrying, rushing from place to place, pacing the floor of his office like a caged animal, striding off into the distance. She doesn't think that she has ever, once, seen him ambling or strolling or taking an aimless walk just for the pleasure of the view. Even with Kate it's 'I'll race you to the gate' or 'Come on, love, Bruno wants a run.' Even when he's giving her a piggyback he doesn't walk, he canters or gallops. It must be very exhausting, being Nelson.

He was gone so quickly that she didn't have time to ask him whether he had told his daughters about Kate. It's hardly the place for that conversation anyway. People are drifting away now, some following the cortège, some making their way towards the church hall.

'Are you going to the wake?' asks Cathbad.

'No,' says Ruth. 'I have to get back to work.'

Judy comes over, looking very sombre in a dark suit. 'I'm dreading this,' she says to Cathbad. He puts his arm round her. 'Stay strong.' Ruth would punch anyone who told her to stay strong in these circumstances but Judy doesn't seem to mind. In the background, Clough raises his eyebrows at Ruth.

'Hi, Cathbad,' says a voice behind them. 'Hi, Judy.' It's Maddie, in a black coat with a red scarf wrapped round her neck. Her hair is in one of those complicated plaits that Ruth can never master and she looks glamorous and much older than usual.

'Hallo, sweetheart,' says Cathbad, giving her a kiss. 'I didn't know you were here.'

'I'm covering it for the paper,' says Maddie, brandishing a notebook as if in alibi. 'But I wanted to be here anyway. I met the family when I did an earlier piece on them. They're nice people.'

'Did they like your piece?' says Judy, her voice even. Ruth gets the impression that Judy was not a fan of the article.

'Yes,' says Maddie with a tilt of the head. 'I think it's so important for the family's voice to be heard.'

'This must be so hard on them,' says Cathbad. 'The mother looked devastated.'

'Yes,' says Maddie, her voice hardening. 'It's the hardest thing in the world.' Ruth knows that she is thinking of Scarlet, her half-sister. That's not surprising; Ruth has been thinking about her all day too.

'Hallo, Ruth,' says Maddie, suddenly registering her

presence. 'I hear that you found Margaret's remains. Can I have an interview sometime?'

'I don't have anything to say,' says Ruth.

'I'm sure you do,' says Maddie, giving her a look that doesn't seem entirely friendly. 'Are you coming to the wake?' She turns to Cathbad.

'Well, maybe just for a few minutes. Just to keep Judy company.'

But as Cathbad follows his daughter down the steps, Ruth wonders whether it's Judy or Maddie who needs his company more.

Back at the station, Nelson reads the post-mortem report on John Mostyn. Mostyn was killed by a single bullet to the heart. As Clough had said earlier, someone knew exactly where to shoot. Nelson wonders what will happen to Mostyn's body. No requiem mass for him, no police attendance. The only relative they have been able to trace is a cousin in Scotland. Mostyn's body will probably be cremated with only the undertakers present. Perhaps Nelson should go. It seems wrong to have a funeral with no mourners. Especially if Mostyn does turn out to be innocent of Margaret's murder.

Finding Mostyn's murderer looks as if it will be almost as difficult as tracking down the person who killed Margaret all those years ago. No one was seen entering or leaving Mostyn's house but the CCTV from the Canada Estate did capture a figure carrying what looked like a body towards the central fountain. At first Nelson had been excited by this but, in the event, the film was almost useless. The man, dressed in a dark coat with a woollen hat pulled down over his eyes, didn't look up at the cameras once. It was as if he knew where they were. The whole operation – and it did seem like an operation – was almost like a two-finger salute to the police. They couldn't even be sure that the figure on the CCTV cameras was a man, although he certainly seemed large and strong. The small bit of skin that could be seen looked darkish but they couldn't even be certain about that. The clothing gave nothing away; enlarging the image showed that masking tape had been put over the logo on the coat. The assassin had thought of everything. He even took the time to remove the bullet from the back of the sofa to prevent the gun from being identified. Clough's name for Mostyn's killer is Spectre.

The fact remains, though, that John Mostyn was murdered. Was it revenge for his supposed murder of Margaret Lacey, old emotions rekindled by the discovery of her body? But forensic reports on Margaret's remains definitely show the presence of a second person's DNA. Unfortunately, the report says that this second DNA sample has 'degraded', which means that it will be harder to get a match. However, this seems to point to the second DNA being older and therefore potentially that of the murderer. Mostyn's DNA is on the bones, which means that he handled them, presumably to move them to the stone circle, but the second DNA isn't on the bones – only on the rope and the gag – because, of course, the killer never saw Margaret's bones, these emerged many years after death and burial. Unless he was the person who moved them, of course. The killer laid his hands on Margaret's actual living, breathing body. And then she was living and breathing no more. Nelson thinks of the white coffin, the flowers spelling out the word 'Daughter'. He makes a silent vow to the dead girl, the golden girl, the angel.

I will avenge you.

It seems certain that it was John Mostyn who wrote the letters telling Nelson to search in the stone circle. Several drafts were on his computer and, searching his house, police have found scrapbooks full of old newspaper cuttings about both Margaret's disappearance and the death of Scarlet Henderson. 'Scarlet: police find body.' 'Scarlet: a family mourns.' Just reading the headlines brings it all back: the morning when they walked across the marshes at daybreak and Ruth led him unerringly to Scarlet.

In the scrapbooks there are pages from the *Chronicle* showing photographs taken by John Mostyn. There's one of the Saltmarsh: 'Lonely spot where the little girl's body was found'. Was it from the newspaper that Mostyn found out about the first letters? Nelson flicks through the file until he finds the letter sent on 12 February 2016.

Well, here we are again. Truly our end is our beginning . . . You have grown older, Harry. There is grey in your hair and you have known sadness.

It's not just the content that's the same, it's the tone,

the implication that the writer knows Nelson well and is somehow disappointed in him. *You could not save Scarlet but you could save the innocent who lies within the stone circle. Believe me, Harry, I want to help.* He thinks back to the one time he met Mostyn, when PC Campion was guiding him through giving a DNA sample. There had been something odd about the way Mostyn had looked at him, come to think of it. *I know who you are*, is what Mostyn had said. Did Mostyn really know him, in some profound and rather sinister way?

He looks at the last, unfinished, message from John Mostyn.

You have found Margaret but this is only the beginning. It is the best of times and the worst of times. You must finish what you have started. Courage, my friend. Remember we know not the day nor the hour . . .

Is this a threat or a warning? Mostyn was right, finding Margaret's body was only the beginning. They have buried her today so that, at least, is the end of one part of the story. But the second part is more difficult. They must bring Margaret's killer to justice. Did John Mostyn know who that person was? Was that why he was killed?

He hears voices in the incident room and goes in to find Judy and Clough back from the wake.

'It was so sad,' says Judy. 'I think Karen hoped that the funeral would give them some sort of closure but it just seems to have opened up all the old grief. Karen and Annie were both crying when we left.'

'Was the brother there too?' asks Nelson. 'What's his name? Luke?'

'Yes,' says Judy. 'Luke was there with his family who all seem to think they're too good for the Norfolk branch. Annie's grown-up children were there as well.'

'Yes, I think Michelle knows the girl with the baby.'

'Star? I spoke to her. She seems very nice, very together. The headmistress, Carol Dunne, mentioned her the other day. Carol was at the funeral too. And Kim Jennings and her family.'

'The place was packed,' says Clough. 'Lots of press too. I saw Maddie.'

Judy rolls her eyes. 'Maddie seems very in with the family. I left her chatting with Star, holding the baby and all that. Of course, she's not quite as big a favourite as Cloughie.'

Clough is eating some crisps left over from someone's leaving do. 'I'm starving,' he says.

'Wasn't there food at the wake?' says Nelson. He realises that he hasn't had any lunch. Does he dare send Leah, his PA, out for sandwiches?

'There was lots of food,' says Clough, 'but it didn't seem right to eat it somehow.'

'Been to a funeral, Ruth?' says Phil, when he sees Ruth's black trousers and jacket.

'Yes,' says Ruth, letting herself into her office. She has the satisfaction of thinking that she has, for once, completely silenced her head of department.

She shuts the door, hoping that everyone will assume that

she's deep in marking, and gets a rather squashed sandwich out of her bag. She hasn't had time for lunch but she needs sustenance before her three o'clock tutorial. She has just taken a mouthful of ham and cheese when there's a knock at the door. Is it Phil, come to apologise for his gaffe/find out about the funeral?

'Come in,' she says, rather indistinctly.

The door opens and a blonde woman stands framed in a sudden shaft of sunlight. For a second, Ruth thinks of Michelle, that time that she came to the cottage, to beg Ruth to see Nelson on what she thought was his deathbed. It's a memory that never ceases to fill Ruth with mingled guilt and admiration. But then she sees that this woman is much younger than Michelle and is wearing ripped jeans and a hoodie. She can't imagine Michelle in a hoodie.

'You don't know who I am, do you?' says the woman.

'Er . . .' Ruth hesitates, though she is pretty sure that she does recognise this person from some area of her life and it's not an area that makes her feel very comfortable.

'I'm Laura,' says the woman. 'Laura Nelson.'

Ah. That's it. Nelson's daughter. Kate's half-sister. Come to demand Ruth's head on a plate, by the looks of it. Salome in ripped jeans.

'Have a seat,' says Ruth, although Laura has already taken the visitor's chair.

'So,' says Laura, 'you had an affair with my dad.'

Although Ruth is, by now, expecting something of the sort, she is still thrown off guard.

'It was a long time ago,' she says at last.

'I realise that,' says Laura. 'His daughter must be about eight.'

'Eight in November,' says Ruth.

'A Scorpio like Dad. How cute.'

'I'm sorry—' Ruth begins.

'Sorry for what?' says Laura. 'For screwing my dad or getting found out?'

'Both,' says Ruth.

'He's not going to leave Mum, you know.'

'I know.'

This seems to take away some of Laura's aggression. She pushes her hair back and Ruth sees that her eyes are wet with tears. How old is Laura? In her mid-twenties, she thinks. Ruth tries to imagine how she would have reacted, at that age, if she'd found out that her father had a love child. Astounded, mainly, given that her father and late mother were ostentatiously upright Christians. But history is full of virtuous people behaving badly. She doesn't think that, whatever the circumstances, she would have confronted her father's mistress at work. Does this make her braver than Laura, or more cowardly?

'You know,' says Laura. 'I always rather admired you.'

'Really?'

'Yes. You were a professional, obviously really good at your job. Even Dad admired you. And then you were a single mother as well. Of course, I didn't realise that you weren't really single.'

'Oh I am,' says Ruth. 'Believe me.'

'Why should I believe anything you say?'

'That's up to you,' says Ruth. 'I'm sorry you're upset but there's really nothing I can do about it. I've got Kate and she deserves to see her father sometimes. Your dad's not going to leave your mum. She's been terrific about all this.'

'It's just that he lied to us,' says Laura, tears now rolling down her cheeks.

'Talk to him,' says Ruth. 'I do know one thing – he loves you very much.'

'I don't want to see him,' says Laura. 'I would like to see Katie again though. Can I come over one day?'

'Of course,' says Ruth. 'Bring Rebecca too. I'd love her to get to know you both. She'll adore you.'

She doesn't think it's worth reminding Laura that her half-sister's name is Kate.

Nelson stays late at work for a variety of reasons, some only half-acknowledged. There's a lot of work to be done on both murder cases. Michelle's mother is staying so he's not needed for moral support. And he has a superstitious feeling that the longer he stays away, the more likely it will be that Laura will be there when he gets home. She's not answering her phone and, though he's left a stream of texts saying he's sorry and that he loves her, there's been no reply, not even a sad face. Rebecca is back in Brighton and she's not answering his calls either.

Now it's nine o'clock and even Nelson can't see any reason for staying at his desk. He has organised the strategy for tomorrow: more door-to-door near Allenby Avenue, more forensic analysis, more research on the Scarning Fell area, interviews with anyone who saw John Mostyn on the day that he died. He really should be getting home, Michelle will be worrying about him. When his phone rings, he's not surprised to see his wife's name flashing up on screen.

'Hallo, love. I'm just leaving.'

'Harry!' says Michelle. 'The baby's gone!'

CHAPTER 25

'What do you mean?' he says, the room growing cold around him. 'George?'

'No.' Michelle's voice is stifled with sobs. 'Ava. Star's baby.'

Relief makes Nelson feel temporarily light-headed. He sits down at his desk.

'What do you mean, gone?'

'Star's just called me. She put Ava down in her cot and now she's vanished. She's called the police but I thought you should know as soon as possible. I told her you'd help.'

Nelson thinks fast. Control will have put the call through to the duty sergeant. Missing Persons, or Mispers, are assessed according to risk and a missing child is the highest priority of all. Uniform will probably be on the scene already. Sooner or later, Nelson and the Serious Crimes Unit will be involved. It might as well be sooner. Nelson gets the address from Michelle and promises to call round. He's about to ring Judy and ask her to meet him there when he remembers Michael. A missing child case might still be too traumatic for Judy. So he rings Tanya, who is only too pleased to leave whatever she is doing on a Monday night and join him at Star's house on Ferry Road.

Tanya is there when he arrives.

'A missing baby,' she says cheerily. 'Just like old times.'

Nelson does not dignify this with an answer.

The door is opened by Annie, last seen at the funeral. She's still in her smart black dress but her hair is loose and there's a wild look in her eyes.

'The police?' she says. 'The police are already here.'

'We're from the Serious Crimes Unit.' Nelson shows his warrant card.

Annie looks at him properly for the first time. 'So you're DCI Nelson.'

'Yes, and this is DS Tanya Fuller.'

'We're here to help,' says Tanya. 'I'm sure we'll find your baby soon.'

'It's my daughter's baby,' says Annie, but she stands aside to let them in.

The sitting room is large but it still seems very crowded. The blonde-haired girl sits sobbing on a sofa comforted by an older man. There are also two uniformed PCs, looking awkward, and another older man in a black suit.

If Judy were with him Nelson would let her take the lead, comforting Star whilst, at the same time, trying to get all the facts straight in those vital first hours. But he doesn't altogether trust Tanya so he crouches down next to Star and says, trying for his gentlest voice, 'Star. I'm DCI Nelson.

Harry Nelson. Michelle's husband. Do you think you could tell me what happened?'

Star looks at him, her face swollen with tears. 'Is Michelle here?'

'No. But she sent me. I can help you. Can you tell me what happened? Take a deep breath.' He says this because Star looks on the verge of hyperventilating. The man (her father?) pats her back and offers a glass of water. It strikes Nelson as slightly odd that it's not the mother, Annie, who's doing the comforting.

'I came back early from the wake,' says Star, 'because Ava needed a feed. Usually I don't mind breastfeeding in public but I thought it might scandalise Uncle Luke.'

The man in the dark suit, whom Nelson takes to be Uncle Luke, makes a noise of protest but Star carries on. 'I fed her and put her down in her car seat.' Her voice starts to tremble.

'In her car seat?' says Nelson.

'Yes, it doubles as a carry cot.'

'Has that gone too?'

'Yes,' says Star. She looks at Nelson, eyes wide with horror. 'Oh God. Do you think that means someone's taken her somewhere in the car? Somewhere miles away?'

'Easy, love,' says Nelson. 'Let's take things slowly. Make sure we've got all the information. So you put Ava to sleep in her car seat. Where was that? In here?'

'Yes,' says Star. 'I put her down over there, by the French windows.' As if impelled, they all look to the spot where the swagged velvet curtains cover the window. Star continues, 'Then I lay down on the sofa and I went to sleep.' She sobs, doubling up as if in pain. 'I shouldn't have gone to sleep but I was tired. I'd got up three times last night. And the funeral ... it was so sad ... I just closed my eyes.' She is sobbing uncontrollably now.

'You're doing well, love,' says Nelson. 'When was this? And was there anyone else in the house?'

His voice seems to calm Star a little. She looks up, wiping her eyes on her sleeve, which is black and slightly see-through, presumably worn for the funeral. 'No. I was on my own. Uncle Luke dropped me off but he went back to Grandma's house.'

Presumably to avoid witnessing any breastfeeding. 'What time was this?' says Nelson again.

'About seven. I fed Ava and put her down. Then, like I said, I went to sleep. When I woke up it was eight. I thought at first that Mum had come back and taken Ava upstairs but she wasn't back and nor was Dad. I rang her and texted her. I was running round the house in hysterics.'

'We came straight back,' says the father. 'And I rang the police.'

'I called Michelle,' says Star, 'because I know you're in charge of the police.'

Nelson half wishes Jo were here to hear this. 'Not quite,' he says. 'But you did well to let me know. We'll find Ava, I promise you. Have you done a proper search of the house? You'd be surprised how many times missing children turn out to be in the house all along.'

'We've searched the house thoroughly, sir,' says one of the PCs, sounding both awed and slightly resentful.

'I looked too,' says Luke. 'I came back with Annie and Dave.'

Why? Nelson wonders. He doesn't seem to be adding much in terms of help or moral support.

'And there's no other member of the family that could have popped in and taken Ava somewhere? For a walk or something like that?'

He looks back towards the window. It's pitch black outside and the wind is getting up but stranger things have happened. He remembers driving Laura round and round the block when she wouldn't sleep. Please God, make her come home tonight.

'We've asked everyone,' says Annie. 'Matt and Sienna have gone home. There's only Mum and Pete and the boys.'

'The boys' must be Karen's children with her second husband. By Nelson's reckoning they must be in their late twenties or early thirties.

'We need to do a fingertip search of the area,' says Nelson. 'Tanya, phone through to control and say that we're treating this as HR and need reinforcements here as soon as possible.' He doesn't want to say the words High Risk aloud, though, with a newborn baby and a cold March night, it's pretty obvious.

He asks the constables if they've spoken to the neighbours and they haven't. 'We'd only just got here when you arrived and we searched the house first.'

'Well, do it now,' says Nelson. 'I want a list of everyone who has been in and out since seven p.m.' He looks back at Star, sobbing on the sofa, now with a parent at either side.

He turns back to Luke. 'Could you show me the layout of the house?' he says.

They search all night. The house and garden on Ferry Street are taken apart and put together again. Police in protective clothing trawl through the nearby gardens, torches illuminating lawns and shrubbery, watched from above by curious and resentful householders. Nelson's friend Jan Adams, the famous police dog handler, arrives with Barney, a distant relative of Bruno. Barney sets off efficiently, nose down, tail waving. Jan is uncharacteristically subdued, calling her dog with strange staccato commands. They all know that a search for a missing baby rarely ends well.

From the start Nelson was worried about the proximity of the river. Is it possible that someone has taken Ava and put her in the dark water, like a horrible version of the Moses story, without the kindly princess pulling the wicker basket to shore? At midnight he calls for the frogmen and they add to the strange procession through the Lynn streets, amphibious creatures who disappear into the depths with barely a sound. But the frogmen find nothing.

At three Nelson goes home for a few hours' sleep. Michelle is up, feeding George, and they confer in whispers because of Louise sleeping next door. Michelle hasn't heard from Laura but she thinks she has been home to collect some of her belongings. Laura is in touch with Rebecca but Rebecca won't say where she is. For her part, Rebecca is angry with her father but this is almost trumped by her curiosity about Katie. Rebecca will come round. Neither of them are sure about Laura who, although generally sweet-tempered, possesses a strength of will that her parents often call stubbornness. Michelle weeps about Ava and holds George so tightly that he squeaks. 'What do you know about the family?' asks Nelson, getting into bed.

Michelle looks at him. 'You can't suspect . . .'

'The family are always the first suspects,' says Nelson, 'you know that.'

'I'm sure there's nothing like that with Star's family,' says Michelle, switching George to her other breast. 'I mean, she's living with her parents. They seem to get on well.' Nelson tries to frame another question, something about Uncle Luke and Star's obvious preference for her father over her mother, but he's asleep before he finds the right words.

The briefing is at seven. The team are all there: Tanya full of satisfaction at being the first DS on the scene, Clough chewing thoughtfully, Judy . . . Nelson finds it hard to read Judy's face. She looks pale but composed enough, making notes in her leather-bound book as she always does. Is she thinking about Michael? Is she resentful that Nelson took Tanya with him last night? Judy gives little away, a quality Nelson admires in principle but, at the moment, he feels that he's had enough of enigmatic women.

'The timeline is quite tight,' says Nelson. 'Star left the wake at six thirty and was driven back to her house by Luke Lacey. He left her at about six forty-five and drove to Karen's house, where the remaining family members were gathering. Star says she fed Ava at seven, then woke at eight to find that the baby had disappeared. She called her parents at once and they contacted the police. First responders were there at eight thirty. Fuller and I got to the house at nine eighteen.'

'What time did Luke get back to Karen's house?' asks Clough.

'That's something we've got to ascertain today,' says Nelson. 'We've got to interview all the family members. We need a clear strategy for this.'

'Luke's the one with the opportunity,' says Clough. 'What's he like?'

'Serious, smartly dressed, possibly a bit strait-laced,' says Nelson. 'Star said that she didn't want to breastfeed in front of him. Fuller, you interviewed him. What did you think?'

'He still seemed very cut up about Margaret,' says Tanya. 'As if nothing was ever the same again after she disappeared. Luke went out searching for Margaret that night. He was with his dad and it sounds as if the dad completely went to pieces. That must have had an effect on Luke. And he seemed a bit negative about Annie, Star's mother. He said she had anger management problems.'

'Were those his exact words?' says Judy.

'No,' says Tanya, with dignity, 'but he said that she had a temper when she was a child. They were close then but I got the impression that they aren't now. I mean, he didn't come rushing down as soon as the bones were found, did he? He did mention Star's baby to me, said that Annie had recently become a grandmother. He said that Star's name was really Stella.'

'Carol Dunne, the headteacher, told me that too,' says Judy. 'She taught Annie and Luke. Might be worth talking to her again.'

'Do we think this is linked to Margaret in some way?' asks Clough. 'I mean, it's the same family, the day of Margaret's funeral. Seems too much of a coincidence to me.'

Nelson is glad to see that the team have absorbed his suspicion of coincidence.

'Do you mean that the person who killed Margaret also abducted Ava?' says Tanya, ever literal.

'Not necessarily,' says Clough. 'For one thing, they would be getting on a bit now. But maybe this is an attack on Star. When I saw her I did think that she looked a bit like pictures of Margaret.'

Once again, Nelson is impressed. And, now that Clough mentions it, he can see the resemblance. Could there be a link between the two cases?

'We won't rule anything out,' he says, turning to the whiteboard. 'We need to talk to Karen and Pete and to their grown-up sons Bradley and Richard. We need to interview Star's parents, Annie and David, and Uncle Luke. We also need to talk to Star again. Johnson, are you up to doing that?'

'Of course,' says Judy.

'Fuller, you take Luke and his wife. Clough, you talk to Karen's family as you have the rapport there. It goes without saying that time is of the essence. Ava has been missing for twelve hours and she's only twenty-three days old.'

He has no trouble calculating Ava's age because she's only a day older than George.

'The best we can hope is that someone has taken her, for whatever reason, and is keeping her safe,' he says. 'But we need to move fast. I'll brief Superintendent Archer when she comes in and I expect she'll want to talk to the press. Until then, no comment.'

'There are already reporters outside,' says Clough. 'No sign of Maddie yet.'

'She'll turn up,' says Judy.

'No word from Cathbad?' says Nelson. 'No psychic insights for us?' He's only half-joking.

'He was asleep when I left,' says Judy.

Nelson always finds it hard to imagine Cathbad sleeping. Somehow he pictures him hanging from the ceiling like a bat.

CHAPTER 26

Ruth doesn't hear the news until midway through the morning. And her informant is Cathbad himself. She comes back from a lecture to find him waiting outside her office, in everyday clothing of jeans and a heavy jacket. It reminds her of the time – more than eight years ago now – that she arrived one morning to find Nelson waiting there for her with Phil. 'This is Detective Chief Inspector Harry Nelson. He wants to talk to you about a murder.'

'Hi, Cathbad,' she said, unlocking the door with her card. 'What brings you here?'

'Have you heard?' he says. 'A child has gone missing.'

'A child?' For a moment, Ruth thinks of George, that swaddled baby in Kate's arms, her half-brother.

'A relation of Margaret's, the girl whose remains were found in the stone circle. Judy's involved in the search. The child, just a baby, a few weeks old, went missing last night. They're searching the river. Everything.'

'My God,' says Ruth. 'How awful. Can it be related to Margaret in any way?'

'I don't know,' says Cathbad, sitting in her visitor's chair. 'I only had a quick call from Judy. She's interviewing the baby's mother now. Poor thing. She's only twenty-one. Almost a child herself. I know her quite well. She goes to my meditation class.'

Somehow, thinks Ruth, Cathbad manages to know everyone. But then she thinks of the mother, that primal cord that ties you to your baby, long after the physical umbilicus is cut. What must it be like to have your child wrenched from your arms?

'They'll find her,' she says. 'Nelson will find her.' She remembers how her thoughts first went to George and, even now, she can't help feeling that he's in danger in some way. She is surprised how protective she feels towards Nelson's baby, the child who, however innocently, came in the way of their happiness. She wonders what Nelson is feeling as he leads the search for this unnamed infant. Then she sees Cathbad's face and she remembers Michael.

'I'm sorry,' she says. 'This must bring it all back. How's Judy coping?'

'She'll have her professional face on,' says Cathbad. 'She won't show what she's feeling. But yes, the searching, the waiting, it brings it all back.'

'But Michael was found safe and well,' says Ruth. 'Let's hope this baby is too.'

'I pray to the goddess that she is,' says Cathbad. 'But that's not what I came for. I've had a message from Leif. A message from beyond the grave, in a way.'

'You too?' says Ruth, before she can stop herself.

Cathbad looks quite put out. 'What do you mean?'

'Leif met me here the other day. He read me part of a letter that Erik had left for him. It mentioned me and something about dancing with the stone wedding guests.'

'The letter mentioned me too,' says Cathbad. 'Erik said that he was sorry for involving me in his affairs. He wished me well and told me to dance in the stone circle.'

'I think it means Stanton Drew in Somerset,' says Ruth. 'It's a Neolithic stone circle and there's a local legend that the stones represent a wedding party who danced on the Sabbath. I rang you up to tell you about it but you were out. Teaching your meditation class, actually.'

'I know,' says Cathbad. 'Leif's been researching it too. And he wants you and me to go to Stanton Drew with him tomorrow.'

'Tomorrow?' says Ruth. 'Why?'

'I said that it might be difficult for you,' says Cathbad. 'For me too, come to that. Judy will probably be working late. I might have to take Miranda with me.'

'It's a four-hour drive,' says Ruth. 'Why can't we leave it until the weekend?'

'He was very insistent that it has to be tomorrow,' says Cathbad.

Ruth thinks. She has no lectures on a Wednesday and, as a matter of fact, Kate has been invited to a sleepover with her best friend Tasha, a midweek treat for Tasha's birthday. But Leif can't have known this and she resents the high-handed way that he's dictating the terms.

'What's so special about tomorrow?' she says.

'I don't know,' says Cathbad. 'I just have this feeling ...
I know it's stupid but I feel that Erik wants us to go. I feel
like I've been getting messages from him all day. A black cat
walking across my path, three magpies in the apple tree, a
white feather that just fell into my hand as I walked across
the campus just now.' He opens his palm to show the tiny
feather, downy and pale.

'The baby birds are starting to be born,' says Ruth, 'that's
all.'

'I know what it *is*,' says Cathbad patiently, 'just not what
it *means*.'

'I'll think about it,' says Ruth.

'You do that, Ruthie,' says Cathbad. 'Let me know. I'd
better be going back now. I'm helping in the school library
this afternoon.'

Ruth feels guilty. She never helps in the school, never
goes to PTA meetings, only attends the Christmas fair for
long enough to buy a raffle ticket and to let Kate meet
Father Christmas (Mr Evans, the Year 6 teacher, in a fat suit).
Cathbad, despite his eccentricities, is a valued member of
the school community. She really must try harder.

It's only when Cathbad has gone that she thinks of the
three magpies. Three for a girl.

Judy sees immediately that Star is still in shock. The girl
– she still seems like a girl to Judy – is sitting on the sofa
hugging her knees to her body. She is shaking and her eyes
have a glazed, unfocused look. Her parents hover around
her, clearly not sure what to do.

Judy sits next to Star. She has already worked out what she will say. It is stepping over the line to offer personal information but, in this case, she thinks it is justified.

'Star,' she says. 'I'm Judy. I'm a police officer. We met the other day when I came to talk to your mum.'

Star looks at her. She has large blue eyes that remind Judy, rather disconcertingly, of Maddie. 'Ava's gone,' she says. 'My baby's gone.'

'Star,' says Judy. 'Listen to me. I know what you're going through. My little boy was taken five years ago. It was terrible. I wanted to die. But the police found him. He was fine. He's seven now.'

Star says nothing, picking at a thread on her loose trousers – or are they pyjamas? Judy thinks she hasn't taken her words in but then she says, 'Who took him? Your little boy?'

Judy hesitates, not wanting to give a name, although the case was in the papers at the time. 'Someone who didn't mean him any harm,' she says. 'Someone . . . not quite in their right mind.'

'How did the police find him?'

'By following the clues,' says Judy. Plus guesswork and a handy medium, she adds silently. 'That's why it's important that you tell me everything that you remember about yesterday. Can you do that?'

'Yes,' says Star. Judy can hear Star's parents exhaling with relief behind her. To get them out of the room, she asks for some tea.

'I drink blessed thistle,' says Star. 'It's very good when you're breastfeeding.' Her eyes well up again.

'My partner gave me all sorts of herbal infusions when I was breastfeeding,' says Judy. 'Most of them were disgusting.'

Star manages a watery smile.

'So, can you tell me what happened yesterday, from the time you left the wake?'

'I wanted to come back to feed Ava,' says Star. 'Normally I just feed her where I am but ... I don't know ... I felt tired and sad after the funeral. I just wanted to be at home with my feet up. Also stuffy Uncle Luke was there and I'm sure he wouldn't approve of me breastfeeding in public. So I said I wanted to go home and Uncle Luke offered me a lift. He dropped me at the door, wouldn't even come in, so I just came into the sitting room and fed Ava and left her in her car seat, there by the window. Then ... Oh God ... I fell asleep.'

She starts to rock back and forth. 'I shouldn't have gone to sleep. It's all my fault.'

'It's not your fault,' says Judy, 'but you've got to hold it together, OK? For Ava's sake. Now, who knew you were at home yesterday evening?'

'Mum and Dad, of course. And the rest of the family. Granny and Granddad, Bradley and Richard.'

'Did you text any of your friends? Send a snapchat?'

'No,' says Star. 'I don't even have a smartphone. I don't approve of them really.'

Once again, Judy is reminded of Maddie, that high-minded earnestness, charming in the young, less charming when it crystallises into prejudice later.

'Do you have a boyfriend?' she asks. 'What about Ava's dad?'

'Ryan? We're not together any more.'

'Does he know about Ava going missing?' Judy thinks of the time when Michael was abducted, the added strain of having his two fathers at her side, all of them suffering in their different ways.

'I think he's abroad,' says Star vaguely. 'He hasn't even seen Ava yet.'

'What about a boyfriend?'

For the first time, some colour seeps into Ava's cheeks. 'There is someone. I met him at my meditation class.'

'You go to meditation classes?'

'Yes, at the community centre. I met Leif there.'

'Leif?' Judy's knows that her tone is too sharp.

'Yes, Leif Anderssen. He's an archaeologist. Do you know him?'

'Slightly. How long have you been going out with him?'

'Oh, we're not going out,' says Star and Judy remembers that this means something different to the new generation. She's vague about the stages: hooking up, hanging out, being exclusive. Judy's thirty-six and she's only had two serious relationships in her life.

'When did you last see Leif?'

'Last week. He met me after my class. We went for a drink but I had to come back because of Ava.'

'We'll need to speak to Leif and any other close friends,' says Judy. 'Can you make me a list?'

'OK,' says Star. She is sitting up and the shivering has stopped. Annie, coming into the room with the tea, says, 'Oh you do look better, sweetheart.' Judy thinks that Annie looks almost as harrowed as her daughter; there are dark circles under her eyes and the tray is jangling in her hands.

Star sips her blessed thistle tea. 'My boobs are agony,' she says. 'I'll have to express.'

'Do you often express?' says Judy. 'Where do you keep it?'

'In the fridge,' says Star. 'Why?'

'Can I see?'

Star's father, Dave, is in the kitchen. When he hears Judy's request he goes to look in the 'small fridge', which is hidden behind one of the shiny units. The other fridge is a massive chrome American affair with a mechanism for making ice. A two-fridge family, thinks Judy.

Dave opens the door and gives an exclamation.

'What's wrong?' says Annie.

'Star's expressed milk. It's gone.'

CHAPTER 27

'So whoever took Ava took the milk too,' says Nelson. 'That means they knew where to look. In this second fridge.'

'It also means they want to keep Ava alive,' says Judy. She's in her car, a few streets away from Star's house. It's a grim, grey day and starting to rain.

'True,' says Nelson and Judy can almost hear him pacing. 'It may be someone who thinks they have a claim on Ava. What about her father?'

'Star says he's abroad. I don't think they're in touch.'

'All the same, check him out. And his family. They might resent the fact that they're not involved in Ava's life.'

'There's another thing, boss.'

'What?'

'Star's been seeing Leif Anderssen.'

'Bloody hell. Seeing as in having a relationship?'

'I don't think it's that serious. But they've been out a few times.' Judy guesses that Nelson will be even less au fait with dating terminology than she is.

'Where did she meet him?'

'At Cathbad's meditation class.'

'Jesus. I don't like this. Leif's a coincidence too far. He was the one who discovered Margaret's body, for God's sake. One of his team, anyway.'

'I know.'

Nelson is silent for a few minutes, then he says, 'Leave Leif to me. You check out Ava's father and his family. Briefing at five.'

'OK, boss.'

He rings off, leaving Judy sitting in her car staring at the rain.

Clough doesn't like to admit it but he misses having Judy alongside him. Karen and Pete seem utterly shell-shocked by Ava's disappearance and he needs Judy's calm empathy to get the interview back on course.

'Who would take a baby?' Karen keeps asking, as if he could possibly know the answer.

'She's only tiny,' adds Pete, unhelpfully. 'A newborn.'

'We'll find her,' says Clough. 'We've got officers from four forces searching. We'll find her. But it would help if you could tell me what happened yesterday. After the . . . after Margaret's funeral.'

'The burial was terrible,' says Karen, 'seeing her coffin go into the ground. It was as if I'd lost her all over again. But, when we got back to the wake, I don't know . . . it seemed almost joyful. All the family together. It's a long time since I've had Annie and Luke in the same room.'

'Why?' asks Clough. 'Don't they get on?'

'They've always rubbed each other up the wrong way,' says Karen. 'Annie's always been a bit prickly and, after Margaret went, it got worse. She's always been a bit . . . well, forceful, and she used to niggle away at Luke all the time, saying that he was lazy, didn't pull his weight at home, that sort of thing. Luke went away to university, got a job in London and hardly ever came home. But, this weekend, they seemed really close, talking together for ages. Don't you think, Pete? You went to the allotment with them on Saturday, didn't you?'

'Yes, they seemed to be like a proper brother and sister for a change,' says Pete. His own sons, Bradley and Richard, quiet men with tattoos and closely shaven heads, sit silently in the background.

'Can you remember what time Star left the wake?' asks Clough.

'I think it was after six,' says Karen, 'because it was getting dark outside. She came to say goodbye. She wanted to get home to feed Ava. She's such a lovely mum.' She dabs at her eyes, Pete pats her on the back, ever the comforter.

'Luke drove Star and Ava home, didn't he?'

'Yes,' says Karen. 'He's got a company car. It's very comfortable.'

'Did you notice what time Luke got back?'

'After Star left, we all decided to go home,' says Karen. 'Annie stayed behind to help clear up. She's good like that. But the rest of us – me, Pete and the boys – came back here.'

'And did Luke join you here? What time was that?'

'I couldn't say,' says Karen. 'We were all sitting in here, looking at photos of Margaret.'

'Had you been home for some time?' Clough knows that he has to persist on this. It's vital to know whether Luke had time to abduct his great-niece before returning to the family party.

'I don't think so,' says Pete. 'I remember Bradley asking Luke if he'd go out and get some more beer. He wasn't drinking, you see.'

'So Luke went out again?'

'No,' Bradley cuts in. 'He was just about to but then Dave got the call from Star.'

'Dave's Star's dad?'

'Yes,' says Karen. 'They've always been close. Dave got the call and he and Annie left immediately. Luke went too, to see if he could help.'

Why? wonders Clough. Why was Luke, the man who hadn't bothered with his family for years, being so helpful all of a sudden? He hopes that Tanya is making some progress with Luke and his wife. They're staying at a smart hotel near the quay. None of this mucking-in sleeping-on-sofas stuff for them.

'Do you have any idea who could have taken Ava?' he asks. 'Any idea at all?'

'I thought Star was making it up at first,' says Bradley. 'She always used to make things up when she was little.'

'How can you say that?' says Karen. 'Annie says that she's devastated.'

'She's a good actress,' says Bradley.

'No one's that good an actress, son,' says Pete.

But Clough is married to an actress and he knows that the audience believe what they want to believe.

Nelson knows that he should stay at headquarters, masterminding the search for Ava. It's not the role of a DCI to go out interviewing suspects. And Leif's not a suspect or even a person of interest. But by early afternoon he's going stir-crazy. The rain has set in and he's pretty sure that Leif won't be doing any digging today. He tells Leah that he's popping out and takes the back stairs to avoid bumping into Super Jo.

Leif is staying in a flat overlooking the river. In fact it's very near the place where Margaret was last seen by Kim Jennings, crossing the narrow bridge in front of the Custom House. There's an entry phone but someone is coming out of the double doors so Nelson just pushes past and barges up the stairs. He always likes to take people by surprise if he can. He hammers on Leif's door, one of four identical doors on the second-floor landing. He has to restrain himself from shouting 'Police!' After a few minutes the door is opened but Nelson does not shoulder his way into the apartment. Instead he stands there, mouth slightly open.

'Dad!' says Laura. 'What are you doing here?'

CHAPTER 28

'Laura,' says Nelson. 'I was looking for Leif Anderssen.' For a moment he really believes that he's come to the wrong address.

'Leif's out,' says Laura. 'He went to the university.'

Nelson stands there staring at his daughter. He tries to frame a question but the words won't come.

'Well, if that's all . . .' Laura goes to shut the door.

'No!' With instinct born of years of policing Nelson gets his foot in the gap. 'We need to talk.'

Laura looks as if she wants to refuse but then shrugs and stands aside to let him in.

The small flat shows signs of dual occupancy. Laura's laptop on the coffee table, her trainers on the carpet. She's wearing leggings and a T-shirt as if she's just been to the gym.

'No uni today?'

'No,' says Laura. 'I start my first placement in a school next week.'

His daughter is nearly a teacher, a role Nelson regards

with utmost respect. He feels the familiar surge of pride in his first-born followed immediately by an equally familiar urge to protect her.

'Why are you living with Leif?'

'Don't tell me you're going to give me a moral lecture,' says Laura. 'You of all people.'

'Laura . . .' He takes a step towards her.

'Don't,' says Laura, backing away. 'I don't want to talk to you.'

'I'm sorry, love. Please come home.'

'No,' says Laura. 'I'm happy with Leif.'

'You don't know anything about him,' says Nelson. 'Do you know why I'm here? Because a baby has been abducted and we've been told that the baby's mother is Leif's girl-friend.' He wants to shock Laura and he succeeds. She stares at him, eyes wide. 'What?'

'She's called Star. Apparently she met Leif at Cathbad's meditation class.'

'Star?' Laura sits on the sofa. 'Oh my God.'

'Do you know her?' Nelson sits next to his daughter.

'Of course I do. I go to the same class, remember?'

But Nelson has never sorted out all of Laura's extra-curricular activities: gym, spinning, weight-training, hot yoga. She always seems to be dashing off somewhere with a mat under her arm. And it turns out that she was dashing off to one of Cathbad's lunatic fringe activities. Now he dimly remembers Laura saying that Cathbad was kind to her after the shooting last year, that he had listened and understood, something to do with them both being scientists. Nelson has never thought of Cathbad as a scientist although, when they first met, he was working at the university as a lab technician.

'Leif's not going out with Star.' Laura sounds quite contemptuous. 'They're just friends.'

'He's got a friend at UNN too,' says Nelson. 'She's called Chloe Jackson and she teaches history.' He thinks that this is news to Laura. Her eyes narrow but she says nothing.

'How do you know Leif anyway?' he asks.

'I met him outside the class one evening,' says Laura. 'Then, that day . . . when you told us . . . I went to talk to Cathbad but he was out. Leif was there, he was calling on Cathbad too. We went for a walk and we talked. He was kind, he listened.'

Then he lured Laura back to his flat, thinks Nelson. That good listener act is the oldest trick in the book.

'I need to interview Leif,' says Nelson. 'When's he back?'

'In an hour or so,' says Laura. 'He's organising some sort of trip for tomorrow.'

'Tell him to call in at the station later today,' says Nelson. 'It's important.'

'OK.' Laura isn't looking at him.

'Look, love,' says Nelson, trying for the tone that often works with Laura, though rarely with Rebecca. 'I'm just thinking about you. I'm worried about you. Mum is too.'

Laura turns towards him, her eyes full of tears. 'How is Mum?'

'She's OK. But she misses you. George does too.'

'Rubbish.' But this draws an unwilling smile. 'He only worries about his next feed.'

Nelson thinks about Ava. Is she missing her mother? Is she thinking about her next feed, delivered by the person who stole expressed milk for her?

'Bruno really misses you,' he says. 'He's pining.'

'Stop trying to stop me being cross with you.'

Nelson reaches for Laura's hand. 'I'm sorry. I really am. If I could change the past, I would.' But, even as he says this, he wonders if it's really true.

Laura pulls her hand away. 'I went to see Ruth yesterday,' she says, in a tight, hard voice that he hasn't heard before. 'At the university.'

'You did?'

'Yes. I was angry with her. I wanted to tell her that she'd broken up our family. But, when it came to it, I couldn't. She's just an ordinary woman. She said that she always knew that you weren't going to leave Mum. I actually felt a bit sorry for her.'

Nelson says nothing. Laura is having spiritual guidance from Cathbad, she's visiting Ruth at the university. It's as if all the separate areas of his life are suddenly colliding, making him feel jolted and uneasy.

'I'd like to see Katie again,' says Laura. 'I remember the time you brought her to the house. I didn't realise why you were babysitting Ruth's child. I must be so stupid.'

'Of course you're not stupid. You're a hundred times cleverer than me.'

'That's not difficult,' says Laura. Then, softening slightly, 'Katie was sweet though.'

'I think you'd like her,' says Nelson carefully.

'Ruth told me to talk to you,' says Laura. 'She was quite nice really.'

'Come home, love,' says Nelson. 'Then we can talk. All three of us. You can't stay here. I don't trust this Leif. I knew his father and he was a very strange character.'

This is a mistake. Laura stands up. 'You don't know anything about Leif.'

'He's too old for you.' He falls back on an old favourite.

'He's only thirty-five. Anyway, age is just a number.'

'Is that one of Cathbad's pearls of wisdom?'

'Get out,' says Laura, flaring up. 'Go away and leave me alone.'

'Please, love—'

'Just go,' says Laura. 'I never want to see you again.'

Tanya is finding Luke and his wife, Rina, rather hard going. She interviews them in their room at the charming Bank House Hotel which makes the occasion seem oddly intimate. Tanya sits in a chintzy armchair while the Laceys perch on the bed. She is distracted by an open suitcase on the floor. Why can't they hang their clothes up like civilised people? She and Petra have a wardrobe each.

Luke seems very nervous and keeps getting up to pace the room, once knocking his head quite hard on the sloping ceiling. Rina seems calm, almost too calm. She's a poised, elegant woman who, in Tanya's estimate, is about five kilos underweight.

'Can you tell me what happened after you left Star at her parents' house last night?' Tanya asks Luke. 'Any detail, however seemingly insignificant, might be important.'

'I saw her inside the house,' says Luke, fiddling with the tassels on one of the numerous cushions on the bed. 'Then I went back to Mum's house. I knew everyone was meeting up there.'

'Why didn't you go in with Star?' asks Tanya.

'I got the impression she wanted to be alone,' says Luke. 'She's very self-contained although she's so young.'

'Did you see anything unusual near the house? Any cars parked outside it?'

'No.' Fiddle, fiddle, fiddle. 'I don't think so.'

'What did you do next?'

'Drove straight to my mum's house.'

'What time did you get there?'

'About seven, I think.'

'Who was there?'

'Mum, Pete, Bradley and Richard. Annie and Dave arrived at about the same time as me. They'd been clearing up in the church hall.'

'What happened next?'

'Bradley wanted me to go out for some beer. I thought he'd had enough but I said I would.'

'Nothing's ever enough for Bradley,' says Rina. 'He's a borderline alcoholic.' Tanya thinks this is interesting. She gets the impression that Rina is not close to her in-laws.

'But, then, just as I was leaving, Dave said he'd had a call from Star saying Ava was missing. He and Annie left immediately. I followed them in my car.'

'Why?' says Tanya.

'Why?' Luke looks bemused.

'Yes, why? What could you do?' Tanya realises that sounds rather rude and amends it to, 'Weren't her mum and dad enough?'

'I thought they might need to someone to drive somewhere,' says Luke. 'Talk to the police, that sort of thing.'

'Luke's a professional, you see,' says Rina. 'He's used to talking to people in authority.'

But Dave is a teacher and Annie is a nurse, thinks Tanya. Both highly responsible, professional jobs. Why would they need Luke to liaise with the authorities?

'At what point did you call the police?' Tanya asks.

'Almost immediately,' says Luke. 'Star was hysterical. Annie and I had a quick search of the house. It was obvious the baby wasn't there. Dave called the police. They came very quickly,' he adds, in a conciliatory tone.

'Do you have any idea who could have taken Ava?' Tanya addresses both of them.

'No,' says Luke. 'Who would do a thing like that?'

'That's what we're trying to find out,' says Tanya, hoping that she doesn't sound too pompous. It's hard work, being nice to irritating people.

Ruth, popping into the cafeteria at lunchtime, is surprised to see a long blond ponytail in the queue in front of her.

'Leif! What are you doing here?'

'Ruth!' Leif turns in apparent delight. 'How are you?'

'Fine,' says Ruth, conscious of looking sweaty and untidy in her crumpled shirt and dark trousers. It's cold and rainy outside but, for some reason, the temperature in the Natural Sciences block is tropical.

'Did Cathbad mention tomorrow to you?' says Leif. 'Visiting Stanton Drew.'

'Yes,' says Ruth. 'It seems a long way to go.'

There's a hiatus while Leif pays for his lentil salad and carrot juice and Ruth tries to hide the fact that she's having a ham and cheese toastie. While Ruth's waiting for her food Leif turns to her with the full force of his blue-eyed charm; so like Erik, so horridly, wonderfully like Erik. 'Please, Ruth. I can't explain but I really think it's important that we do this tomorrow. Bring your daughter if you like. Surely the school will understand if it's educational?'

Shows how much you know about the British education system, thinks Ruth, collecting her toastie, steaming gently in its greaseproof paper. 'Kate's been invited on a sleepover,' she says.

'Well, then,' says Leif, spreading his arms wide. 'What's stopping you?'

And Ruth finds herself agreeing to go to the stone circle.

The briefing is a rather tense affair. They all know that time is running out. The search parties have found nothing and the press are camping outside the police station. Jo Archer keeps reminding Nelson that the eyes of the world are on them which, even if not strictly true, doesn't help with the stress levels.

'It's such a narrow window of opportunity,' says Nelson. 'Star went into the house at six forty-five, Ava was gone by eight. Someone entered the house, probably with a key – there's no sign of forced entry – took Ava and the milk and left. It must have been someone who knew the place well. Is there anything from the neighbours? Any CCTV?'

'No.' Judy is flipping through the reports. 'Nobody saw anything unusual and none of the houses have CCTV. It was a dark evening. Probably everyone was inside watching TV.'

'What about Luke?' says Nelson. 'He's still our best bet. He could have waited in the car and come back when Star was asleep.'

'But where would he put her?' says Tanya, managing to make it sound as if Ava were an inconveniently shaped parcel. 'He's staying in a hotel.'

'Bradley – Karen and Pete's son – thought that Star might be making it up,' says Clough. 'Is it worth following up that line of enquiry? Could Star just want to be the centre of attention? A bit like what's-it-called . . . Munchausen's.'

Nelson is impressed that Clough has remembered the name of the syndrome where a person invents medical symptoms in order to gain sympathy and attention. He turns to Judy. 'What did you think of Star? Is this possible?'

'It's called Facititious Disorder now,' says Judy. 'I suppose it's possible. After all, yesterday was all about Margaret, not Star. She might want to be back in the limelight. But I could swear that she's genuine. And Star's been a devoted mother up until now. I spoke to her health visitor.'

'Michelle said the same,' says Nelson. 'She said that Star seemed to really enjoy being a mum. What about the dad? Ryan? Any luck there?'

'He's in the States,' says Judy, 'working at Camp America. I saw his parents. They seemed very shocked. They knew about Ava but I don't think they've seen her yet. I got the impression that they don't want to be involved. What about possible boyfriends? Did you contact Leif Anderssen?'

'I called round but he wasn't in,' says Nelson. 'I left a message for him to come into the station later.'

'The archaeologist bloke?' says Clough. 'Could there be a link there?'

'It's a coincidence,' says Nelson, 'and I don't like coincidences. But it's hard to see why Leif would snatch Ava. And, like Fuller said earlier, where would he be keeping her?'

'What about Star's mother, Annie?' says Judy. 'She seemed really distressed today. Could she know something?'

'Karen said that Annie was a difficult character,' says Clough. 'And Pete, her stepfather, said the same. He spent a lot of time with Annie and Luke at the weekend apparently. On his allotment.'

'Pete has an allotment?' says Judy.

'Yes,' says Clough. 'Why? Lots of people do.'

Judy is flipping through her notebook. 'When we went to see Karen and Pete to ask about Scarning Fen, did either of them say that they had links to the area?'

'No,' says Clough. 'What are you getting at?'

'When I interviewed Steve and Alison Jennings, Kim's parents, they said that Pete used to live "out Swaffham way". I made a note. Look.' She pushes the page, filled with her small, neat handwriting, towards Clough. 'Swaffham's near Scarning Fen. Why didn't Pete say that when we asked him? And he's got an allotment. What if he had an allotment when he lived in Swaffham?'

'And you think he killed Margaret and buried her in his allotment?' Clough's voice is rising.

'Well, it's possible,' says Judy, rather defensively. 'Pete knew Karen when Margaret went missing, the two families were friends.'

'He killed her daughter and then married the mother?'

'It is possible,' Nelson cuts in. 'And the Swaffham link is interesting, especially the fact that Pete Benson didn't mention it when interviewed. But now our focus has to be on Ava. She's been missing for almost twenty-four hours now.'

He doesn't turn to look at the clock but everyone is conscious of the second hand moving towards six.

CHAPTER 29

Nelson almost doesn't expect Leif to obey his summons but, when he comes out of the briefing, he is told that he has a visitor in the interview suite. He's grateful to Tom Henty for putting Leif into this room because it has a two-way mirror. He spends a few minutes observing Leif who is sitting, seemingly completely at ease, in one of the armchairs (this is a so-called 'soft interviewing space' which means that it has IKEA furniture and a plastic fern). Leif is leaning back, legs crossed at the ankle, staring at the ceiling. He isn't checking his phone, as most people do now whenever they have an off-duty moment. He doesn't look nervous or ill-at-ease even though he's in a police station. He is smiling gently, hands relaxed on the chair's chintz arms. Leif is taller than his father and more heavily built. Nelson supposes that he's good-looking, although that long hair is ridiculous and his eyes are too pale and he doesn't blink enough. Still, he is pretty sure that his daughters would say that Leif is 'fit'. Well, one of his daughters clearly does think so. He pushes open the door.

'DCI Nelson.' Leif smiles in apparent delight but doesn't get up.

'Good of you to come in,' says Nelson, not smiling back.

'Laura passed on your message,' says Leif. 'It sounded urgent.'

Nelson grinds his teeth at the mention of his daughter.

'It is urgent,' he says, taking the armchair beside Leif's and moving it back slightly. 'We're conducting an inquiry into a missing child. I'm sure you've seen it on the news.'

'I don't follow the news,' says Leif. 'I try to keep myself free from negative influences.'

'Bully for you,' says Nelson. 'I'm a policeman and negative stuff is my job. I believe that Star Simmonds is a friend of yours.'

'I know her a little,' says Leif. Is it Nelson's imagination or does the Vedic calm seem to falter slightly?

'Well, it's her child that has gone missing. Ava was snatched from Star's parents' house yesterday evening.'

'Laura told me,' says Leif. 'Poor Star. How terrible. Do you have any idea who could have done it?'

Nelson ignores this. 'Your name has come up as a possible boyfriend of Star's,' he says. 'And we need to check out all her close associates. Can you tell me how you met her?'

'I went to see Cathbad after his meditation class,' says Leif. 'I wanted to talk to him about my dad. I'm working through my relationship with Erik and I knew that he and Cathbad were close. Star was there, asking Cathbad some questions about meditation. I was impressed with her open mind.'

I bet you were, thinks Nelson. 'This must have been just

after Ava was born,' he says. 'After all, she's only twenty-three days old.' Once again, the number comes automatically.

'Yes, I was impressed with that too. The fact that she was going to classes so soon after having a child.'

'So you found Star impressive,' says Nelson. 'Did you go out with her?'

'Once or twice. Just for coffee and a chat.'

'Did you ever meet Ava?'

'She had the baby with her, of course. She had her in one of those . . . what's the word? . . . baby slings.'

'Did Star ever say that she was worried about anything? Anyone threatening Ava?'

'No. She seemed delighted with the whole experience of motherhood.' This is pretty much what Michelle said, but without Leif's smug expression. Nelson wonders whether Leif's amorous intentions were thwarted by the presence of the baby in the sling. Maybe that's why Leif moved on to Laura. Be careful, he tells himself. Hitting a member of the public is never a good idea.

'When are you going back to Norway?' he asks.

'At the end of the month,' says Leif. 'The dig should be finished by then. We've had some very interesting results from the bones in the cist. They're the remains of a young girl. I'm hoping to commission a facial reconstruction.'

Nelson is rather shaken by the fact that another young girl was buried in the circle on the beach. But Leif just looks, if anything, even more pleased with himself.

'Don't leave the country without letting me know,' says Nelson, standing up to show that the interview is over.

'I won't,' says Leif. 'Good luck with the search. I will pray to the goddess for Ava.'

'Very kind of you,' says Nelson. Then he leans in. 'If you hurt my daughter,' he says, 'I'll kill you. Understand?'

Nelson tells the team to get a good night's sleep. 'There's nothing more we can do today. The search teams will keep going all night. I need you all back here tomorrow in top form.' Judy considers staying at work until the kids are in bed. All that bath, story, bedtime romping is so exhausting. But she also longs to see her children, to hold them tight and feel their solid little bodies against hers. The memories, the ones that have been hovering ever since she heard that Ava was missing, are threatening to engulf her. That terrible moment when her childminder turned to her and said, 'He's gone . . . Your friend came to pick him up . . .' The dark days afterwards, the waiting, the dreadful draining away of hope. Cathbad had saved her then. The least she can do is be at home for bath time.

She gets back to find a cosy domestic scene. Cathbad cooking vegetarian spaghetti carbonara and three of his children sitting at the kitchen table: Michael, Miranda and Maddie. Thing is watching hungrily from under the table.

'Hi, Judy,' says Maddie. 'Just in time. Dad's such a good cook.'

'Maddie's here,' says Miranda, gazing adoringly at her half-sister.

'So I see,' says Judy, searching in the fridge for wine. She suspects Maddie's motives for this visit and doesn't want to spend the entire evening avoiding the subjects of Ava or Margaret. Also, it's very rare for Maddie to call Cathbad 'Dad'.

Judy splashes wine in two glasses and passes one to Cathbad.

'Tough day?' he says, beating eggs.

'Yes,' says Judy. 'I'll tell you about it later.'

'We're going to Granny and Granddad's tomorrow,' says Michael who, as ever, is watching Judy intently.

'Are you?' says Judy, taking a gulp of native Norfolk Winbirri white. 'Why?'

'I'm going to Somerset with Ruth and Leif Anderssen,' says Cathbad. 'Apparently Erik wrote a letter to Leif before he died. In it he said that he wanted us all to meet at a stone circle called Stanton Drew. Leif wants us to go tomorrow. I asked your mum and dad if they would pick up the kids. They were delighted. They'll take Thing too.'

Judy bets they were thrilled to be asked. Her parents live locally and are devoted grandparents. Even so, she feels slightly aggrieved that Cathbad hadn't mentioned his plans to her.

'I only decided today,' says Cathbad, reading her mind. 'I thought you'd be busy at work.'

'It's pretty frantic,' says Judy. 'Ava's still missing.'

'Have you got any leads?' asks Maddie, turning in her chair. 'Can I have some wine?'

'Sorry,' says Judy. 'I forgot you were grown-up.'

Miranda laughs delightedly.

Cathbad serves the pasta, getting all that last-minute egg

and cheese stuff just right. There's an appreciative silence at the table as people eat, some more successfully than others. Cathbad, who has lived in Italy, twirls like a native, Michael cuts his up and Miranda makes slurping sounds that are only just permissible in one under five. Thing takes up his position beside Miranda, licking his lips.

'How are you getting on with the Margaret Lacey case?' asks Maddie, putting a tiny piece of pasta into her mouth. Judy never thinks that she eats enough.

'The missing child is taking precedence,' says Judy.

'Aren't they linked?' says Maddie, eyes wide. 'After all, Ava is Margaret's great-niece.'

Judy has never thought about the relationship in this way before.

CHAPTER 30

It's only when Ruth sees the jeep-like Honda that she realises that Cathbad is driving. She had assumed somehow that
Leif would be at the wheel but, come to think of it, she has
only ever seen him on a bike. She always feels that Cathbad,
too, is more comfortable on two wheels, better still on two
feet. He's a dreamy and erratic driver. Judy, on the other
hand, loves cars and always drives when the family are
together. The Honda is the family car. Judy must have taken
the sportier Fiat to work.

Ruth has already dropped Kate at her childminder's
house. Sandra will take her to school. Cathbad must have
picked up Leif on his way home from the school run. Ruth
is waiting for them and comes straight out of the house. Leif
gets out of the car, all the same.

'So this is the famous cottage,' he says. 'What a stunning
situation.'

Actually, it's a grey and misty day, the marshes and the
sea lost in a hazy, mutable light. There's something about
Leif's tone that Ruth doesn't quite like. Why is her home

'famous' to him? She remembers the last time that Erik visited her, the mad chase across the dangerous no-man's-land, a chase that ended in death.

'It's better when you can see the view,' she says, opening the back door.

'Would you prefer to sit in the front?' asks Leif.

'No, this is fine.'

At least, in the back, she won't have her foot clamped on a phantom brake.

There's actually something quite pleasant about sitting in the back. It's like being a child again, the fields and houses sliding past, the sense of being taken rather than being in charge of the journey. She has to resist the temptation to ask if they are there yet. Cathbad and Leif are talking about stone circles, ritual and sacrifice, the cycle of the seasons, the need for state funding of archaeological digs. Ruth closes her eyes.

It's a long journey though. Right across England, from coast to coast. 'Just think of the journey from Wales to Stonehenge,' says Cathbad helpfully, 'and we're not dragging massive megaliths behind us.' Ruth knows that the so-called Stonehenge bluestones were transported from Wales to Wiltshire and, whilst this was undoubtedly an impressive and mysterious achievement, she doesn't feel like discussing Neolithic building methods now. She feels tired and slightly sick, possibly the effects of Cathbad's motorway driving.

They stop for coffee and sandwiches on the M42 near Birmingham. Ruth feels slightly revived and texts Shona:

'On an adventure with Cathbad. Scary!' Leif, unable to find food pure enough for him in a motorway service station, is drinking what he says is pea protein from a flask. Cathbad eats an M&S sandwich with apparent relish. Ruth remembers a trip to Blackpool with Cathbad and Kate, six years ago. They stopped at Preston Services and Kate had wanted to ride on the Thomas the Tank Engine machine over and over again. The maddening theme tune comes back to her now and the memory makes her smile even though the holiday itself had been at best stressful and, at worst, terrifying.

Cathbad is telling Ruth an alternative Stanton Drew story. 'It's said to be impossible to count the stones,' he says, 'because they're of the devil's number. Or else no number at all. If you succeed, you drop down dead. Stone dead.' He grins and takes a swig of mineral water.

'Well it is a big site,' says Ruth. 'Bigger than Stonehenge and only slightly smaller than Avebury. Between twenty-five and thirty stones, I read.'

'You see,' says Cathbad. 'No one knows the exact number.'

It is quite exciting as they get nearer the site, the first glimpse of the sea, the picture-perfect villages, the sudden sighting of a lichened stone looming over a thatched roof. They park by the church and follow the signs 'to the stones'.

The day is still grey and overcast. The stones, when they appear, seem sullen and menacing. They are oddly shaped, bulging as if with some secret stone pregnancy, some upright, some recumbent. It's hard to get a sense of a circle, or even of a pattern. 'It used to be thought that the number and positioning of the stones corresponded to the

Pythagorean planetary system,' says Cathbad. 'The three circles correspond to the solar, lunar and earth cycles.'

'I thought you said it was impossible to count them,' says Ruth. 'And there's no sun today.' She is finding Cathbad rather irritating; he has donned his purple cloak and frequently pauses – head up, eyes closed – to 'absorb the energy of the place'. Leif is walking on ahead. He seems preoccupied, constantly checking his phone, more like a bored teenager than a spiritual seeker after truth.

The English Heritage site described the largest collection of stones as The Great Circle but, even when you are standing in the centre, it's still hard to see the shape. You probably need to see it from above, thinks Ruth, which gives rise to one of the many unanswered questions about stone circles: how did prehistoric builders manage to create a design that was best appreciated from the air? If you discount the alien theory – which Ruth does – then you are left with Cathbad's planetary system, which is unsatisfactory in its own way. Henges are also sometimes called stone gallows. The theory is that the stones form some sort of portal, either for use in some ancient ritual or, for the more fancifully inclined, a gateway between life and death. It's said that if you pass through the gateway, on the right hour of the right day, then you will see death itself.

Cathbad now has his hand on one of the stones and his face to the sky. Ruth reaches out to touch one of the megaliths. It's scratchy with lichen but oddly warm, a disconcerting sensation given the coldness of the day. Ruth snatches her hand away and, when she turns around, she has the oddest feeling that the stones have moved closer. A mist has blown in from the sea and she can't see Cathbad or Leif. For a moment it feels as if she's completely alone, at the centre of the circle, watched by its silent guardians.

'Cathbad?' she says, hearing her voice sounding high and rather panicky.

'I'm here.' He is much closer than she had thought, materialising between two boulders, his cloak bright against the grey. Irritation forgotten, she has to resist an urge to grasp hold of Cathbad's arm.

'Where's Leif?' she says.

'Probably gone to look at the other circle,' says Cathbad. 'There's a kind of avenue to the left.' He raises his voice. 'Leif!' His voice echoes against the silent stones.

'Where is he?' Even Cathbad sounds quite rattled. He calls again. 'Leif!'

'I'm over here.' Ruth can't tell where the voice is coming from. She squints at the stones forming the Great Circle. Have they moved again? Will they be trapped, unable to escape until the devil plays his wild tarantella? She can hear seagulls calling, high above the clouds, but otherwise everything is silent. Beside her Cathbad says, 'Leif! Where are you?' Then, suddenly, the mist clears and a figure is walking towards them. No, two figures. Three. Leif is in front, followed by a woman with long hair that flows back behind her.

The woman is carrying a baby.

Carol Dunne is teaching but the receptionist says that she will fetch her. Judy waits in the area with the coloured mural which, on closer inspection, depicts St Paul's and the surrounding countryside, the school a blob of red against yellow houses and green fields, the sea – or the sky – a line of blue on the horizon. On the opposite wall there's a display of photographs of 'our school family'. The road-crossing attendant with her lollipop is at the centre. There are also certificates declaring that the school is green, accessible and anti-bullying. The list of safeguarding officers adds a more sober note but Judy is pleased to see that it's up to date.

Carol arrives, as sunny and youthful as ever in a green dress and flat brown boots.

'Sorry,' she says. 'The Year 4 teacher is off sick and I'm taking her class today. I can only spare you five minutes, I'm afraid. The teaching assistant's in there but they're quite challenging today. It's the rain. Wet play and all that.' It has been drizzling all morning but now the rain is hammering against the skylight above their heads. As Judy follows Carol to her office, she sees several buckets placed at strategic intervals.

'Maintenance never ends,' says Carol. 'Sometimes I feel more like an odd-job man than a teacher. It's not what I came into the profession for.'

'I just wanted a quick word,' says Judy, taking the visitors' chair opposite Carol. The office has a view over the wet playground. A soggy banner exhorts pupils to 'Learn Well and Play Well'.

'You've heard about Ava Simmonds going missing?' says Judy.

'Yes,' says Carol. 'I heard it on the news this morning.

What a terrible thing. As if that family hasn't suffered enough.'

'I know you used to teach Star,' says Judy. 'Or Stella as she was then. We're following up every avenue in the search for Ava and one of the family made a remark about Star which I'd like to follow up.'

Carol says nothing but she is looking at Judy intently.

'One of Star's uncles suggested that she might have made the whole thing up,' says Judy. 'To gain attention, perhaps because the previous day – the funeral – had been all about Margaret. I just wanted your opinion on this theory.'

Carol holds up her hand, like the road-crossing attendant in the photograph.

'Absolutely not,' she says. 'Stella, Star, wasn't like that at all. She wasn't the most conventional child but she was actually very firmly rooted in the real world. You often do get children who lie, who embellish the truth, who crave attention, but Star wasn't one of them. She was confident, happy in herself.'

Judy has only known Star in time of crisis, but, even so, she recognises this image. Star has obviously embraced being a single parent with clear-sightedness and practicality. She attended mother and baby groups, she expressed her milk, she drank blessed thistle tea. She is living at home with both her parents in attendance. It seems very unlikely that she would harm her precious baby just to gain attention.

'In cases where children do make up stories,' says Carol, 'it's often to make themselves feel safe. If you are telling a story then you're in control of the narrative, you're empowered.'

'My son likes making up stories,' says Judy. 'Not about himself but about made-up characters. My partner says that storytelling is an essential human activity.'

Carol smiles. 'Your partner is right. Perhaps they . . .' Judy can see Carol hesitating over the pronoun, 'could come in to one of our storytelling sessions in Book Week.'

'I'm sure he'd love to,' says Judy.

'Funnily enough,' says Carol, 'I was thinking of Margaret just then. Margaret sometimes used to tell stories, part truth, part embellishment. When she went missing some of her friends said that Margaret had told them that she had a boyfriend in London. The police investigated and there was no truth behind it at all. But the fact that she told that story made me wonder . . .'

She is silent so long that Judy prompts, 'Made you wonder what?'

'As I said, telling stories makes us feel safe. Usually, as your partner says, it's a benign activity that helps us make sense of the world but sometimes . . . sometimes you have to wonder why a child feels unsafe. Inventing a boyfriend, for example, could be a way of saying that "I'm OK, someone loves me, someone will protect me."'

'You said that everyone loved Margaret.'

'Yes, she was very popular. But, after she disappeared, I did wonder if she was completely happy at home.'

'You never met her father, Bob, did you?'

'No,' says Carol, 'and I'd be very wary about throwing out

allegations of abuse, especially as the poor man is dead. But there's no doubt that shame is often at the bottom of persistent lies.'

'Shame?'

'Victims often feel shame,' says Carol. 'Shame, guilt, anger and fear. You asked me if Star fitted the profile of a compulsive liar. I would say absolutely not. But I can't say the same about Margaret. Or even Annie. I taught her too, remember? Just briefly, before I left the school.'

'Annie? Star's mother?'

'Annie was a bright girl,' says Carol, 'and, of course, she suffered a lot. Her sister disappearing, her parents breaking up. She reacted by being permanently angry. It sometimes takes children like that but I've often wondered if there could have been more going on beneath the surface. Annie and Luke both did well at school and I've heard they're happily married now but maybe there was damage that we didn't see, or weren't trained to see.'

Judy thinks about the conversation as she drives to Star's house through the rain. Is it possible that Margaret was abused and, if so, does the focus need to come back to the immediate family? She still has her suspicions about Pete. He seems nice enough, supporting Karen, always at her shoulder with a comforting pat and a kind word. But she can't forget that he denied all knowledge of Scarning Fen when he had actually lived fairly near there. And he had an allotment. Could Pete who, according to his brother-in-law, had always liked Karen, have been hanging around to abuse her children? It's a dark thought but darker things have happened.

And what about Annie? 'Damage' was the word used by Carol Dunne. If Annie too had been abused by Pete, that might account for her anger, which a few people have mentioned. Judy hasn't really seen this side of Annie. She seems a rather distant parent, hovering around Star but often appearing not to know what to do to comfort her. It's Dave who puts his arms round Star, who tells her that it's going to be all right. But, then again, in their family it's Cathbad who's the more nurturing parent. He's the one the children call if they get scared in the night. Judy provides stability and (she hopes) unconditional love. But would an outsider judge her for checking her phone messages while on the sofa watching *Peppa Pig*?

She wonders how Cathbad is getting on in Somerset. She hopes it's not raining there, Cathbad's not the best at driving in challenging conditions. She feels slightly envious of Ruth, wandering through the countryside looking at stones, while she is stuck in the grim reality of missing children. But being with Cathbad would mean spending the day with Leif, whom Judy found a rather disturbing presence. She hopes that Cathbad remembers to tell her that he's arrived safely. He has an annoying habit of leaving his phone switched off.

The house on Ferry Road already feels claustrophobic, both too big and too small. When Judy arrives, Star is huddled on the sofa, still in her pyjama-type trousers. Dave is sitting beside her and Annie is in the background, offering food, herbal tea and backrubs, all of which are rejected.

Today there is also Star's elder sister, Sienna, who has come over from Loughborough. Sienna is a tall, athletic-looking woman who seems to get on Star's nerves. 'A walk would do you good,' she keeps saying, 'get some fresh air.'

Star shivers, wrapping her arms round herself protectively. 'I'm cold,' she says, 'I never want to go outside again.'

Judy manages to get the family out of the room on various pretexts. Then she turns to Star. 'Today's the worst day,' she says. 'A whole night has gone past and you're thinking that Ava will never be found. But she will be.'

Star looks at her, eyes shadowed and huge. 'How long was your baby missing for?'

'Four days,' says Judy. 'Three nights.'

'I don't know how you survived.'

'I almost didn't,' says Judy. 'But the police found him. My colleagues found him. We're really good at this sort of stuff. We'll find Ava.'

'What's your little boy's name?'

'Michael,' says Judy, rather reluctantly. She always feels that giving away her children's names makes them vulnerable in some way.

'Does Michael remember anything about it?'

'I don't think so,' says Judy. 'Once he said the name . . . the name of the person who took him. It gave me a terrible shock but I don't think he remembers. He was only a year old.' But Michael claims to remember being born ('It was like a door being opened in space . . .') and Cathbad believes him.

'Ava's not even a month old,' says Star. 'I was looking forward to saying her age in months and not days.'

'You will,' says Judy.

'Mum and Dad are being really kind,' says Star, 'but they don't understand. Nor does Sienna. I suppose if I had a partner it might be different because he'd love Ava as much as I do. Have you got a partner?'

'Yes,' says Judy. She doesn't feel like going into the complications of Michael's paternity. 'He was really traumatised by the whole thing. But it's fine now. We've got another child. A girl.'

'That's lovely,' says Star, giving Judy a smile of such sweetness that she blinks.

'I saw Ryan's parents,' she says. 'They were very shocked. They send their . . . their best.' It's not much, coming from Ava's grandparents, but Star seems genuinely touched.

'That's nice. They're nice people. They just didn't want Ryan to be tied down with a baby. That's why they sent him away to Camp America. But I never expected anything of Ryan. I always knew that I'd be bringing Ava up on my own.'

'That's very brave.'

'I'm luckier than most single mothers,' says Star. 'I've got my parents, a nice house, lots of friends.'

Judy is working her way down the list of friends given to her by Star but it seems that most of them haven't seen Star since she gave birth. She wonders if Star is a bit lonely, despite the parents and the nice house. After all, she seemed very keen to be friends with Michelle, who is more than twenty years older than her. The boss says that Michelle is planning to visit Star this afternoon.

'Is Leif Anderssen a good friend?' she asks.

'I like Leif,' says Star. 'He's a very beautiful person. Physically, I mean. But he'll be going back to Norway soon. My next relationship has to be with someone special. Like Cathbad.'

'What?'

'Cathbad. The man who runs my meditation class. I'd like to meet someone like him. He's so spiritual and wise. He knows all the answers.'

Only if you ask the right questions, thinks Judy. She knows that she should tell Star that Cathbad is her partner but she can't find the words.

'How about some camomile tea?' she says.

The woman comes closer, wearing a homespun cloak, her hair gleaming. For a moment Ruth genuinely wonders if she has slipped through a portal and gone back in time. This could be some Neolithic woman, come to lay her baby in the centre of the stone circle and ask for blessings from the nature spirits. She could be a Bronze Age hunter-gatherer, tending the fields with her child strapped to her back.

'Ruth,' says the woman. 'Ruthie.'

It's Magda. Erik's wife. Leif's mother.

Magda passes the baby to Leif and holds out her arms. Ruth moves forward and is enfolded in a hug that smells of lavender and wood smoke. Once she had loved Magda, seen her as the mother she wanted and needed, rather than the one she had. But, since Ruth's mother has died, Ruth has started to see her in a more favourable light. She actually misses her a great deal. And Magda, like Erik, turned out to be not quite what she seemed.

'I wanted to see you.' Magda holds Ruth's face in her hands. 'I got Leif to arrange this meeting with you. With both of you.' She turns to Cathbad.

'Hallo, Magda.' Ruth can hear her own wariness in Cathbad's voice.

'The baby?' says Ruth. She turns to look at the child in Leif's arms. It is blonde and cherubic but it's not a newborn. It's not Ava.

'This is Erik's child,' says Magda, smiling at them both. 'Freya. Our miracle baby.'

Nelson is about to leave the station to visit the search teams when Leah tells him there's a call on the line.

'This is Inspector Per Amundsen from the Norwegian police. I believe you were asking about Professor Leif Anderssen.'

'Yes, I was.' Nelson always believes in double-checking. Especially when the person is question is living with his daughter.

'There are no convictions on his file. He's a well-respected academic.'

'Oh well,' says Nelson. 'Thanks for calling anyway.'

'There is just one thing,' says Inspector Amundsen, in carefully perfect English. 'There was once a complaint made against Professor Anderssen. The case was never taken any further though.'

'A complaint? What sort of complaint?'

'Assault,' says Amundsen. 'On his then girlfriend. But, as I say, she withdrew the allegations and the case never came to court. I just thought that you should know.'

'Thank you,' says Nelson. 'Thank you very much.'

CHAPTER 31

'She was a miracle,' says Magda. 'A gift from the universe.'

'Pa had his sperm frozen,' says Leif.

Ruth thinks that Leif seems different in his mother's presence. He's diminished, hard as that is to achieve when you're about six foot five and look like a Viking. He appears, in fact, to be torn between embarrassment and affection, an expression that Ruth already recognises from Kate.

They have repaired to a café because the fog is now even thicker, bringing with it a bitter cold that seems almost malevolent, cutting into their faces as they walk through the shrouded stones. Freya is cocooned in a fur-lined snow-suit but, in the café, Magda unwraps her and Ruth sees that she's an enchanting child of about eight months. She has Erik's eyes.

'We felt that Erik's DNA should be preserved,' Magda is saying, 'so he had his sperm frozen. Last year I found a wonderful host mother, a PhD student called Agnetha. I was present at the birth and Agnetha put Freya straight into my arms. It was love at first sight.'

This must mean that Freya is not genetically Magda's child, thinks Ruth. Still, genetics are not everything and Magda obviously dotes on the baby.

'I wanted us all to be together in this sacred place,' says Magda. 'So I asked Leif to arrange it.'

'That letter,' says Ruth. 'Was it really from Erik?'

'I'm sure it's what he would have wanted to write,' says Leif. 'He was so fond of you both.' He glances at Cathbad. 'But, no. It was a little tease from me. I know how much you like a puzzle, Ruth.'

A tease. Leif has dragged them all the way across the country for a tease. Rather than Erik speaking to her from beyond the grave, in fact it was just his son trying to be clever. She remembers the way she had obediently rushed home and looked up 'stone wedding guests' as if she were a student again, completing one of Erik's assignments. Will she ever stop seeking Erik's approval? She looks at Cathbad who raises his eyebrows and shrugs. She wonders if he's thinking the same thing.

'Can I hold the baby?' Cathbad asks.

'Of course.' Magda gives him a glittering smile and passes Freya across the table. The child, who was grizzling slightly, looks up at Cathbad, almost in awe, and starts to smile. Judy calls him the baby whisperer.

'It's wonderful to see you, Ruthie,' says Magda and, despite herself, Ruth feels the familiar glow that comes from basking in the all-encompassing warmth of Magda's affection.

'Great to see you,' she says.

'But I really want to see your gorgeous little girl. How old is she?'

'Seven.'

'A magical age. What is she like?'

Ruth wonders how to sum up the glory that is Kate. 'She's very bright,' she says at last. 'Interested in everything. She loves books and acting and animals. She's great.'

'She's a star,' says Cathbad.

'And you have children too, Cathbad? I know you have a daughter. She must be grown-up now.'

'Yes, Maddie – my daughter with Delilah – is twenty-four. I've got two younger children with my partner, Judy. Michael is six and Miranda is three.'

'You are blessed.'

'Yes, I am,' says Cathbad, making Freya laugh by hiding his face behind his cloak.

The waiter brings their drinks. Cathbad and Ruth have ordered sandwiches too. Leif gets out a Tupperware box of mixed seeds.

'Still eating healthily?' says Magda.

'Yes,' says Leif, sounding slightly like a sulky teenager. 'Chia seeds are high in iron and magnesium.'

Magda has asked the waiter to bring a mug of hot water. Now she puts a bottle of milk in it to warm up. Ruth thinks of the missing baby in King's Lynn, the mother longing to hold her baby and care for it, as Magda is doing now. She knows that Nelson, Judy and Clough will be working flat out but she hopes that Judy will tell Cathbad if the baby is found.

'Your baby's father,' says Magda to Ruth with a smile, taking Freya from Cathbad and settling her in the crook of her arm before giving her the bottle. 'It's the policeman, isn't it?'

Ruth is not expecting this Erik-like sixth sense. 'Yes,' she says, rather stiffly. 'His name's Harry Nelson. He's a detective chief inspector.'

'DCI Nelson?' says Leif. 'I met him yesterday.'

'Did you?' says Ruth.

'Yes,' says Leif. 'I know the girl, you see. The one whose baby went missing.'

'Her name's Star,' says Cathbad.

'I don't think Nelson cares much for me,' says Leif. 'But then, I am living with his daughter.'

'You're living with Laura?' says Ruth. She thinks of the furious girl in ripped jeans. She supposes that Laura left home after Nelson's revelation but somehow she doesn't like to think of Laura living with Leif.

Perhaps Cathbad feels the same because he says, 'I think Laura's in a vulnerable state just now.'

'Sure she is,' says Leif. 'I'm counselling her.'

He smiles at Ruth and Ruth suddenly sees the other side of the Viking; not the adventurer but the destroyer, the raider who invades Anglo-Saxon settlements and carries off their womenfolk.

She supposes that Leif himself is a message from Erik.

Michelle feels slightly nervous as Star's mother ushers her into the sitting room. She thought long and hard about bringing George. Would the sight of him cheer and distract Star? Or would he be a reminder of the missing Ava, his almost-twin? On balance she decided to leave him behind with her mum but now she feels his absence acutely. Is it possible that she's only known this baby for twenty-odd days? Now she feels lost without him. Besides, George would have given them something to talk about.

Star is on the sofa. When she sees Michelle she bursts into tears. Michelle puts her arms round her. 'There, there. It'll be all right.' This, at least, she can do. Memories of comforting the girls when they were young. Broken toys, grazed knees and – later on – arguments with friends and the unfathomable strangeness of boys. She knows what to say for all of it. Which is to say, she says nothing. 'There, there,' she says, patting Star's back. 'There, there.'

Eventually Star hiccups and pulls away, wiping her eyes on what looks like one of Ava's muslin cloths. Star's mother, Annie, offers tea which Michelle accepts because she thinks drinking something might be good for Star. She thinks that Annie looks almost as traumatised as her daughter. She can only imagine how she'd feel if this happened to one of her girls and their mythical offspring.

'I met your husband yesterday,' says Star, still hiccupping slightly. 'He's very nice.'

'Yes, he is,' says Michelle. 'And he's very good at his job. He'll find Ava. He's done it before.'

'With Judy's baby? She told me. She's nice too.'

'Yes, she is.'

'Oh, Michelle.' The tears start again, welling in Star's blue eyes and falling unchecked down her face. 'I just miss her so much. She's my baby. She needs me.'

'That's why you have to stay calm,' says Michelle. 'For Ava's sake. She'll need you when she comes home. She'll need her mum.'

Looking towards the door, Michelle sees that Annie hasn't left the room. She's standing in the doorway and she, too, has tears running down her cheeks. Go to your daughter, Michelle wants to say. Comfort her. We all need our mothers to comfort us sometimes. But they stay frozen in their positions, Star on the sofa with Michelle beside her, Annie in the doorway. They all jump when there's a knock on the door. Annie goes to answer it and comes back with Judy.

'No news,' she says immediately. 'I'm sorry.' She sits on the other side of Star.

'Hi, Michelle.'

'Hallo, Judy.'

They sit on the sofa in silence whilst, in the background, a clock chimes the hour. Three o'clock.

Nelson is feeling the frustration of being left at the station while the action goes on elsewhere. He leaves a message for Laura and asks her to ring him back but he's not really surprised when she doesn't. At half past three he gets a message from Mike Halloran, who is in charge of Forensics.

'We've got something from the search team,' he says. 'It may or may not be significant.'

This is a typical Mike phrase.

'What is it?' says Nelson.

'A piece of brown paper caught on the hedge outside the house on Ferry Road. Looks like it might be from a bag. You know, the sort you find in greengrocers sometimes.'

'A brown paper bag?'

'Yes.'

Nelson thinks of the bag containing the witch stone that was left on his doorstep. *Greetings from Jack Valentine.* But they had been sure that John Mostyn had been Nelson's mysterious Valentine. After all, he was from east Norfolk and he collected stones. The handwriting, of course, had been impossible to match. Could this possibly be linked? He can hear Tom Henty's slow voice now: *Then there's Snatch Valentine . . . Present on the doorstep with a string attached. Child goes to grab the parcel but the string moves it just out of reach. Child chases the present until it's out of sight. Child is never seen again.*

But, then again, it could just be part of a paper bag, one that had once held oranges or apples, blown by the wind onto the Simmondses' hedge.

'The hedge is quite overgrown,' Mike is saying, 'and it's the side near the road. It's possible that this bag got caught there while someone was trying to manoeuvre themselves into their car.'

'Themselves or something else. A baby in a baby seat perhaps?'

'Perhaps. We'll check it for prints, of course. Pity it's not bigger.'

It's a pity we haven't got any more evidence, thinks Nelson. It's a pity we haven't got CCTV of someone abducting Ava.

It's a pity we haven't found her. He thanks Mike and tells him to keep him informed.

Putting down the phone, Nelson paces round the office. He wants to drive to Leif's apartment and confront him but he's worried that the confrontation will end with Nelson, not Leif, being charged with assault. Better to speak to Laura first. Or should he ask Michelle to ring her? He texts Michelle but she doesn't reply. Then he remembers that Michelle is going to visit Star this afternoon. Well, he hopes that she can be some comfort to the poor girl.

Maybe he should call in on Star too? Check in with Judy, reassure the family that they're doing all they can. He picks up his jacket and phone but, as he does so, the internal line rings. 'Someone to see you, DCI Nelson. Her name's Rita Smith. She says it's about the Ava Simmonds case.'

The name means nothing to Nelson but he's willing to meet the devil himself if he'll help him find Ava. A few minutes later a middle-aged woman comes into the room, clutching a large handbag and smiling serenely.

'I'm Madame Rita,' she says. 'You consulted me when Michael Foster went missing. I spoke to a nice policeman called Clough.'

Oh Christ, it's the medium. They had only consulted her last time because Cathbad had insisted. Nelson remembers that Clough had been sure that she'd given him vital information although he remains unconvinced.

'I haven't got much time,' he says.

'No, none of us have got much time,' says Madame Rita.

'Not on this earth anyhow. But I was able to help last time so I've asked my spirit guide if he can see Ava.'

'And can he?'

'Yes. She's with lots of other motherless children.'

Despite himself, Nelson's skin prickles. 'What do you mean? Is she dead?'

'Bless you, no.' Madame Rita gives a chuckle. 'She's alive and she's not far away.'

'Any ideas as to where she might actually be?'

'As I said to Sergeant Clough five years ago, the spirits don't deal in addresses. If you can bring me something that belongs to Ava, I might be able to feel her spirit more powerfully.'

And Nelson finds himself promising to get one of Ava's possessions to give to the medium.

Outside the café it's almost dark and the fog is thicker, adding its own visual effects of smoky vapour and lowering grey cloud. Ruth and Cathbad walk ahead across the fields while Leif follows with his mother and her baby. They are looking for the Cove, the name given to the three megaliths said to depict the bride, groom and pastor. The waiter at the café told them that the stones were in the grounds of the pub, appropriately named the Druid's Arms. In fact they are lying between the church and the pub, glowing slightly in the dusk, reminding Ruth of the phosphorescence that she sometimes sees on the marshes late at night.

One of the stones looks like a petrified golf flag, a vertical post with a protrusion at the top. The other is vaguely triangular and the third is lying horizontal on the grass.

'That's the preacher,' says Cathbad.

'Why's he lying down?' says Ruth. Her breath billows around her like the fog.

'Maybe he's drunk,' says Cathbad, waving a hand towards the pub. The bench seats, complete with holes for umbrellas, are only a few metres away.

'These stones are older than the circle,' says Leif, appearing out of the gloom. 'It's thought they might have formed the portal to a tomb.'

'They found a burial chamber under here, didn't they?' says Ruth, keen to show that she too has done some research. 'There was a study in 2009.'

'And, in the seventeenth century, when some of the stones fell,' says Leif, 'human remains were found buried underneath.'

'Were there any grave goods?' asks Magda. She is clutching Freya to her chest but her tone is very much that of the archaeologist.

'A strange round object,' says Leif, 'described as being like a large horse bell.'

'Maybe it was like Victorians having bells in their coffins,' says Cathbad, 'in case they got buried alive.'

Ruth shivers. This conversation, carried out in the ghostly fog, seems unsuitable for the day's purpose. But, then again, Erik enjoyed a chat about the undead as much as the next archaeologist. She can't help thinking of the burial chamber which is, presumably, directly beneath their feet.

Magda too seems to be remembering why they're there. From her capacious nappy bag she produces a bottle of red wine. Bull's Blood.

'For the libation,' she says.

Instinctively, they all look towards Cathbad and he rises to the occasion.

'Spirits of the other world,' he says, raising his arms. 'We ask you to receive our offering. Just as water, when poured on barren earth, causes seeds to germinate and flower, may this wine restore the spirit of our dead husband, father and friend, Erik Anderssen. Though you are gone from our sight, Erik, you are never forgotten. May your ship carry you safely to Valhalla. Rest in peace and rise in glory.'

Like most of Cathbad's incantations, this is a mixture of pagan and Christian, with a bit of Norse mythology thrown in for good measure, but it's curiously effective. Cathbad takes the bottle and, from a height, pours wine onto the grass.

'Rest in peace,' echoes Leif, 'and rise in glory.'

'Farewell, dear Erik,' says Magda, holding Freya high above her head. 'May the rainbow bridge carry you to Asgard.' The baby starts to cry and Ruth doesn't blame her. They are all looking at her expectantly.

'Goodbye, Erik,' she says. It's the best she can do.

'We should all drink of the wine,' says Leif, taking an enthusiastic swig of Bull's Blood.

'I can't,' says Cathbad. 'I'm driving.'

Ruth is grateful for this piece of non-druidical common sense.

*

Nelson drives over to Star's house, knowing that he has seized on a pretext to visit the crime scene, for that is what the house in Ferry Road has become. He's clutching at straws and he knows it but there was something about Madame Rita's demeanour that means that he cannot entirely dismiss her as a crank. *She* believed what she was saying, that much was obvious, and in the face of such certainty Nelson felt his scepticism start to waver. He feels the same when he's in Cathbad's company sometimes. Doubting Thomas, he remembers, was only convinced that Jesus had come back from the dead when he put his hands into his open wounds. He is not going to wait until he sees blood. Oh ye of little faith.

It's almost dark and raining hard by the time that he gets to Ferry Road. He can just see the search team at the end of the street, their blue overalls almost invisible in the hazy light. They are concentrating on the path down to the river. Please don't let Ava be in the water. What did Madame Rita say? *She's with lots of other motherless children.* That must, at least, rule out the river.

When he approaches the house he sees Judy in the porch looking at her phone.

'Hallo, Johnson. What's the news?'

'Nothing. Star's in a pretty bad way. Michelle came round earlier. She was really good with her. Got her to eat something and have a shower. That's more than her mother or I could do.'

Michelle, Nelson thinks, was always good when the girls were upset. She usually suggested something practical: have a shower, go for a walk, drink some water. It might not have solved the problem but it gave them something to do. He must get Michelle to talk to Laura again.

'Any news from the search teams?' asks Judy.

'You heard about the brown paper bag?'

'No.'

'Halloran's team found a piece of paper on the hedge here, outside the house. They think it was from a brown paper bag.'

'Like the Jack Valentine bag?'

'That was my first thought but we mustn't jump to conclusions. Besides, we were sure that John Mostyn was Jack Valentine.'

'I know,' says Judy. 'It's just that I'm so desperate for a lead. I'm clutching at straws. Though a drinking straw would be good. It would have DNA on it.'

'I'm the same,' says Nelson. 'That medium woman came in again. Madame Rita. And I found myself agreeing to see her.'

'Really?' says Judy. 'Madame Rita gave us a clue about Michael, didn't she?'

'Cloughie always thought so but it was all so vague. It was the same this time.'

'What did she say?'

'She said that Ava was alive and that she was with other motherless children.'

'Other motherless children? Ava isn't motherless.'

'These people always talk in riddles. Madame Rita wants a possession of Ava's so that she can feel her spirit more powerfully.' He puts ironical quotation marks round these words but Judy seems to take them seriously.

'I'll pop in and get something.'

'Why are you out here anyway?' says Nelson. 'Poor signal?'

'No, I wanted to ring Cathbad. He's gone gallivanting off somewhere with Leif and Ruth and now his phone is switched off.'

'Cathbad's gone somewhere with Ruth? And Leif Anderssen?' Nelson's antenna are on full alert. 'Where have they gone?'

'To see some stone circle in Somerset.'

'Is Katie with them?'

'No, she's at school. I think she's going on a sleepover tonight. My parents are looking after Michael and Miranda.'

But Nelson has already got out his phone. 'Call me,' he texts Ruth.

It's completely dark by the time they start the drive home. The fog is thicker too. As they drive through the country roads it's as if the outside world has vanished, reminding Ruth of the road across the Saltmarsh. This time Ruth is in the front seat while Leif lounges in the back, scrolling through his phone, still slightly in his teenager persona.

Ruth is unaccountably tired (after all, she's been in the car most of the day). She closes her eyes but forces herself to reopen them. Cathbad might need a co-driver. Looking in the passenger-side mirror she sees Leif has fallen asleep, his handsome head thrown back, like a lion at rest. The motorway is a relief; lights and signposts and the reassuring presence of other cars. All of them, Ruth imagines, on their way home. Ruth and Cathbad chat about Stanton Drew and the symbolism of circles. 'A circle is totality, wholeness, perfection,' says Cathbad. 'Think of a zero. It symbolises eternity.' 'Or nothingness,' says Ruth. Kate once asked her if nought was a number. Maybe she was thinking of something altogether more profound than number bonds.

Just outside Bristol the rain starts. The windscreen wipers slick back and forth, barely coping with the torrent. Cathbad starts to hum under his breath so Ruth knows he is nervous. It's dark now but the mist is still there, billowing around them like dry ice. They join the M4, hardly able to see a few metres in front of them, lorries passing them in a sheet of spray.

'Are we there yet?' says Leif, waking up. 'Some weather, eh?'

No one answers and he goes back to sleep. Cathbad leans forward, concentrating on the road ahead. Ruth tries to keep up a flow of calming chat but, eventually, she too falls silent. Then, just before Peterborough, they see a red sign flashing in front of them. 'Road closed.'

'What shall we do?' says Ruth.

'We'll have to go across country,' says Cathbad. His knuckles are white on the wheel and he starts to hum again.

They head towards Downham Market. At first there seem to be many cars going in their direction and their presence is comforting. But, one by one, the other vehicles veer off and they are alone on the featureless road. The rain thunders against the roof and their headlights seem only to reflect the darkness back to them. It's only eight o'clock but it feels like midnight and it seems as if this road will never end. Only about an hour more, thinks Ruth. Then she'll be home, sitting on the sofa with Flint and drinking a glass of wine. She has already had a text from Tasha's mum saying the two girls are happily watching a Disney film. Before bed she'll text again just to say goodnight to Kate. Nearly home, nearly home.

Their headlights illuminate a sign for Cambridge.

'We can call in on Frank,' says Cathbad.

'I'm thinking of applying for a job there,' says Ruth.

Cathbad flicks her a quick glance. Keep your eyes on the road, thinks Ruth.

'Are you serious?'

'Well, I'm just thinking about it but I can't stay at UNN all my life. I'll never get promotion unless Phil leaves.'

'Maybe he will leave.'

'Not him. He likes being a big fish in a small pool.'

'What about you?' says Cathbad, leaning forward to see through the deluge. 'Do you want a new pool?'

'I don't know,' says Ruth, 'but recently I've been thinking that I want *something* new. I'm just not sure what it is.'

Cathbad is about to answer when, with terrifying sudden-ness, a figure rises up in front of them. A massive creature, a mythical beast crowned with horns.

She distinctly hears Leif saying 'Herne the Hunter' before the car leaves the road and crashes headlong into a ditch.

Darkness.

CHAPTER 32

By the end of the day the searchers have found nothing. Judy finds it increasingly difficult to keep Star calm. Eventually Annie calls a doctor and Star is given a sedative. She lies on the sofa, eyes open, apparently in a daze. Annie and Dave sit in the kitchen talking in hushed tones. Luke is there too and Karen, who busies herself cooking a meal which Judy is sure no one will eat. At eight o'clock Judy leaves them to go back to the station for a briefing. Outside it's pouring with rain and, although she hopes and prays that Ava is safely inside somewhere, her heart sinks. She's increasingly worried about Cathbad, who hasn't rung all day. In the car she checks her phone, hoping to hear that the travellers have safely returned. But, instead, there's a missed call from Shona Maclean.

'Shona? What's up?'

'Hi, Judy. Have you heard from Ruth?'

'No. I think she's out somewhere with Cathbad.'

'I know. She sent me a message. "On an adventure with Cathbad. Scary."'

'Scary? She must mean his driving.'

'I didn't think anything of it but I've been trying to ring her and her phone seems to be switched off.'

Judy's skin prickles. If there's one thing she knows it's that working mothers never, ever switch off their phones.

'They've gone to Stanton Drew, haven't they?' says Shona.

'Yes,' says Judy. 'How do you know?'

'Leif asked me too. He said that Erik, his father, had left a message for me, something about dancing in a stone circle. He wanted me to go to Stanton Drew today with Ruth and Cathbad but I couldn't go because I had lectures.'

'Erik seemed to leave messages for a lot of people.'

'That's what I thought. There's something fishy about it all.'

'Cathbad's phone is switched off too.'

There's a second's pause and then Shona says, 'I know it sounds silly but I looked at Ruth's Fitbit. I can see her stats because we're friends. And she's hardly done any steps today and nothing since four o'clock.'

Judy looks at the time on her dashboard. It says 20.05.

'They're probably in the car,' she says.

'I know,' says Shona. 'I was just worried. The weather's so awful too.'

Judy has never been able to shake a slight suspicion of Shona, dating back to the time when she first interviewed her about the letters, but now she feels an unprecedented rush of goodwill towards her. Whatever else she may be, Shona is clearly genuinely fond of Ruth.

'I'll let you know if I hear from them,' she says. 'I've got to get back to the station now.'

Nelson's first question is, 'Have you heard from Cathbad?'

'No. Have you heard from Ruth?'

'No. I left a message telling her to call me.' Telling not asking, notes Judy. No wonder Ruth hasn't replied.

'The A47 is closed,' says Clough, who always knows that sort of thing.

Judy relaxes slightly. Cathbad must be held up in traffic somewhere. Even so she wishes that Cathbad or Ruth would call. It's still raining heavily and Clough says that there's freezing fog on the Downham Market road.

'Let's get going,' says Nelson. They sit around the table in the briefing room. Leah has been out for sandwiches but Judy doesn't feel like eating. Clough has her share.

'Ava has been missing for forty-eight hours now,' says Nelson. 'Things are getting very serious. We think the abductor took some of Star's expressed milk but that must be running out now. Ava is only twenty-four days old. Our only real clue is a piece of brown paper caught on the hedge outside Star's parents' house. There's no CCTV in the street and none of the neighbours saw anyone entering or leaving the house on Monday evening. The family don't seem to have anything to offer although one of her uncles suggested that Star might be making it up.'

'I'm sure she isn't,' says Judy. 'And Carol Dunne, her ex-teacher, agrees. She said that Star isn't the type to make up stories. Although, interestingly, she thought that Margaret may have been the type. And Annie too. Carol taught Annie and she described her as being damaged in some way. She suggested that telling stories was a way of making children feel safe, in situations of abuse, for example.'

'Who might have been abusing Margaret?' says Clough. 'Her dad?'

'Maybe. Or her stepdad,' says Judy.

'You're not still going on about that, are you? Pete Benson wouldn't hurt a fly.'

'Appearances can be deceptive,' says Nelson. 'But it's Star and Ava we have to focus on here. Star hasn't shown any sign of compulsive lying up until now. I think we can discount that theory. How was she when you left her?'

'In a pretty bad way,' says Judy. 'The doctor had to give her a sedative.' She looks at the mobile in her lap. No messages.

'What about Uncle Luke?' says Nelson. 'He's the only one with opportunity.'

'He's with Star now,' says Judy. 'He's a bit of an oddball but seems genuinely concerned. And, even if Luke did take Ava, it comes back to the same question. Where is she now?'

'We searched the grandparents' house,' says Clough. 'They were very cooperative.'

'What about Pete's allotment?' says Judy.

'Yes,' says Clough with elaborate patience. 'The allotment has been searched as have the homes of Bradley and Richard Benson.'

'I checked all the door-to-door interviews,' says Tanya. 'Everyone says they're a lovely family, respectable jobs and all that. No scandal, except Star getting pregnant and not being married but everyone does that now. And Star was a devoted mother, by all accounts.'

'*Is* a devoted mother,' says Judy.

Nelson gives her a rather anxious look. He must be worried that she's about to crack up.

'The next thing—' he says. But they never hear what the next thing is. Judy's phone rings and she pounces on it.

'Judy,' says Cathbad. 'There's been an accident. Ruth is hurt.'

Judy insists on driving.

'You're in no fit state,' she says to Nelson. The fact that he gives way without any further argument tells her how worried he is. Cathbad and Ruth are in the King's Lynn Hospital which is only ten minutes away from the station. The roads are clear but it's still raining hard. Judy drives as fast as she dares. She's a good driver, the best on the team. This doesn't stop Nelson telling her, several times, to get a move on.

'Bloody Cathbad,' he says, pounding his knee with a fist. 'He's a danger on the roads. I'll revoke his licence.'

'It wasn't his fault,' says Judy, firing up immediately. 'He said they hit a deer.'

'What did he say about Ruth?'

Judy has told him this three times but she repeats, patiently, 'She's unconscious, he said, and the doctors are with her now. They don't know how badly hurt she is.'

'And Cathbad hasn't got a scratch on him. He's got the luck of the devil, that man.'

Both of them have completely forgotten about Leif Anderssen.

'You love Ruth, don't you?' says Judy. She would never have dared to say this normally but, just for the moment, she feels that they are equal, driving in the dark through the rain, both worried about their loved ones.

'Concentrate on the road,' growls Nelson. Then, in a different voice, 'Yes, I love her. Sometimes I think it's killing me.'

'I thought the same when I was married to Darren and in love with Cathbad,' says Judy. 'When I left Darren it was awful but the awfulness doesn't last. Sometimes you just have to be with the person you love.'

Nelson says nothing and the rain continues to fall.

CHAPTER 33

Nelson is out of the car before Judy has parked. She watches him run towards the entrance to A&E, pushing porters out of the way. Then she drives round to the car park and goes through the labyrinthine system of getting a ticket and finding a space, surely designed to give a heart attack to any worried relative. When she finally makes her way back to reception, Cathbad is there. He has a bruise on his cheek but otherwise looks exactly like his dear, infuriating self.

He comes over and wraps his arms around her. 'I'm sorry,' he says.

'At least you're safe,' says Judy, muffled in his shirt. 'Nelson says you've got the luck of the devil.'

'No, it's the angels who're on my side,' says Cathbad. 'They're looking after Ruth now.'

'Have you heard how she is?'

'No. The doctors are with her. Nelson went steaming in, of course. He said he was her next of kin.'

'Well, I think he is, in a way.'

Cathbad looks at her quizzically but obviously decides to let this go.

'They think Leif has a broken leg,' he says.

'Leif?'

'Leif Anderssen. He was in the back seat.'

'This is all his fault,' says Judy, breaking away. 'Why did he have to drag you all the way to Somerset? Shona rang up. She said he asked her too.'

'He wanted us to meet his mother and her miracle baby,' says Cathbad.

'What?'

'It's a long story. I've rung your mum and dad, by the way. They're staying the night at the house.'

'That's good,' says Judy, rather ashamed that she didn't do this herself.

'Maddie's there too,' says Cathbad, 'but I thought you'd still want your parents to stay.'

He's right but Judy doesn't quite want to articulate why she doesn't think that Maddie is an adequate babysitter.

'I feel terrible about the deer,' says Cathbad. 'Such a beautiful, noble creature. I'd like to make some reparation.'

'I'm sure there's a charity you can donate to,' says Judy.

'Do you want to go home?' Cathbad asks. 'The car's a wreck, I'm afraid. But we could go in yours.'

'I'd like to find out about Ruth first,' says Judy.

'So would I,' says Cathbad. 'I'll get us some coffee. There's a machine here somewhere.'

Judy sits on one of the nailed-down chairs in the reception area surrounded by the halt and the lame; the boy in rugby kit with his arm in a sling, the two young women chatting on their phones about a third woman who is apparently 'having her stomach pumped', the bearded man who seems to be dying of sadness, tears rolling down his cheeks. After a while Cathbad appears with two polystyrene cups. 'I put sugar in,' he says, 'for the shock.' Judy leans against Cathbad and sips the disgustingly sweet liquid. She feels ashamed of the wave of contentment that flows through her.

Ruth is floating. She's in a black sea and the devil is playing the fiddle. She's in the stone circle and the bride is dancing. She is digging through the mud and a hand is rising up to grasp hers. She sees Kate walking between two women. They seem familiar but she can't see their faces. She tries to call out but it's too difficult . . .

'Ruth.'

She sees Nelson. His face is close to hers, his brown eyes both intent and tender, an expression that she's only seen on a few, never-to-be-forgotten, occasions. She can see the small scar on his cheekbone, his dark eyelashes, the stubble on his chin.

'Ruth.'

She opens her eyes. 'Nelson. Where's Kate?'

'She's fine. She's safe. She's having a sleepover with her friend.'

'She was with two women. I didn't recognise them.'

'You were dreaming.'

Was she dreaming? But she's not asleep. She can see

Nelson but there's a blue curtain behind him and she doesn't recognise the room.

'Where am I?'

'You're in hospital. Bloody Cathbad crashed the car.'

'Herne the Hunter. We saw Herne with his antlers.'

'You hit a deer apparently. The car went off the road. It's a write-off.'

The room comes into sharper focus. It's a cubicle really and Nelson is sitting by her bed. She tries to sit up but Nelson pushes her gently back down on her pillows.

'You've got to stay quiet. That's what the doctor said. You've got concussion but they don't think there's anything else wrong with you.'

'I want to go home. I need to feed Flint.'

'That cat's as fat as a house. He won't starve because he misses a meal.'

'He's not fat. He's big-boned.'

'He'll be fine. As soon as you're discharged, I'll drive you home.'

'My head hurts,' says Ruth.

'Just lie still,' says Nelson.

Ruth closes her eyes.

For a while Nelson just watches Ruth sleep. He knows he should go and update Judy. He should go back to the station and continue the search for Ava. He should go home to his wife. But for the moment he watches Ruth. She has a bandage wound diagonally across her head which gives her an oddly rakish appearance. Her hair is in disarray and,

ELLY GRIFFITHS | 314

for the first time, he sees threads of grey in the brown. She is frowning slightly as she sleeps. Probably working out the exact date for some obscure piece of prehistorical pottery. Nelson reaches out a hand to touch her hair. It's so soft – that's something he always remembers – unlike Michelle's which is sometimes stiff with the spray she uses to keep it in perfect waves. Nelson wants to kiss Ruth but what would the nurses think? He can see a gang of them through the cubicle curtains, standing at the end of the ward, talking earnestly. As he watches, a figure passes the double doors, another nurse, large and purposeful in navy blue. Why does she look so familiar? But then it clicks. It's Annie Simmonds, Star's mother, who should be at home looking after her daughter.

Nelson gets up and goes to the ward entrance. Annie is just disappearing around a corner. Nelson follows, keeping a discreet distance between them, up two flights of stairs, along several identical corridors, characterless and institutional, punctuated by hand-washing stations and fire extinguishers. Annie is walking quickly, not looking to left or right. Finally she reaches a locked door with 'Neonatal Unit' written on it. Annie punches in a password and is admitted. The door doesn't quite shut behind her and Nelson catches it before the latch hits the lock.

Annie is moving in a kind of trance, unaware of the footsteps behind her. She is walking through a room full of Perspex cots, all of which are surrounded by monitors, wires and drips. All except one, furthest from the door. As Nelson watches, Annie approaches this cot and lifts up the baby.

'I see you've found Ava,' says Nelson.

CHAPTER 34

'This isn't Ava,' says Annie.

'Of course it is,' says Nelson. 'The perfect place to keep her, you being in charge of the neonatal unit and all. But I think her mum wants her back now, don't you?'

'This isn't Ava,' says Annie, but her face is suddenly completely blank. Nelson has seen that look many times before and it always means guilt.

'Let me see,' he says, keeping his voice quiet and reasonable. He walks between the Perspex cots. He thinks of Madame Rita. *She's with lots of other motherless children.* These babies are not so much motherless as temporarily separated from their parents but he's got to give the medium some credit all the same. Shelves at the end of the room contain baby supplies: sterilisers, blankets, changing mats. Brown paper bags full of nappies.

Annie is holding the baby tightly to her chest, wrapped in one of those blankets that seem to be mostly holes. As Nelson approaches she loosens her hold slightly and he can see a tiny face and a single curl. He has never met Ava but he's seen photographs and that silver-blonde hair is unmistakable. He feels a rush of pure relief, so strong that his head spins. He had almost given up hope of finding Ava alive.

'Annie,' he says, still trying for the calm tone, channelling Judy at her most persuasive. 'Annie. Give Ava to me. We need to get her back to Star. She's in a terrible state and this baby needs her mother.'

'I did it for Star,' says Annie. She doesn't hand over the baby but the fight seems to leave her. Her shoulders, so square and determined in their uniform, slump. 'I did it to protect Ava from him.'

'From who?'

'Pete,' says Annie, as if this is obvious. 'Pete killed Margaret and now Ava's in danger from him. Star was even talking about letting Mum and Pete look after Ava when she goes back to work. If you can call it work, pretending to cure people with massage and a bit of oil.'

'Why do you think Pete killed Margaret?' Nelson edges closer. He should have called for back-up as soon as he saw Annie. Judy is probably still in the hospital somewhere. He could arrest Annie now, seize the baby and drive off to Star with all the sirens blazing. But, right now, it seems better to stick to the softly-softly approach.

'We never liked him, me and Luke,' says Annie. 'Everyone else said that he was so nice, so dependable, such a good stepfather, nothing like our dad, the no-good alcoholic. But I loved my dad, even if he did drink and shout a bit. I thought Pete was a creep. He was always hanging round

Mum, even when Dad was still alive. I didn't see him at the street party but he must have been there, lurking somewhere. Then, that day, a week ago, DS Johnson was asking about Scarning Fen. She said that Margaret had been buried near there. Luke and I remembered that Pete was living in Swaffham when Margaret went missing. He had an allotment near Scarning Fen. We realised that he must have killed Margaret and buried her there. So I knew we had to protect Ava.'

'Why didn't you go to the police?'

'The police!' Annie snorts with contempt. 'They wouldn't believe us. I saw DS Clough with Pete. All chummy, thinking he's such a nice man, such a good husband and father. No, Luke and I knew that we were on our own.'

'Did Luke help you?'

'Yes, he took Ava when Star was asleep. I drove her straight to the hospital. I knew she'd be safe here.'

And you let your own daughter almost die from worry, thinks Nelson. It doesn't seem the moment to say this now.

'Annie,' he says, 'if Pete is guilty we'll arrest him but, right now, we need to get this baby back to her mother.'

'Mum doesn't want to see,' says Annie, sounding for all the world like an aggrieved teenager, the age she was when her sister vanished for ever. 'She thinks that Pete is such a good guy. She'll never believe the truth.'

'What about Star?' says Nelson. 'Your daughter. She wants her baby back.'

'Star never listens to me,' says Annie, as if she's talking about undone homework rather than child abduction. 'She thinks she knows it all.' But she seems to relax her hold on the bundle in the pink blanket.

Nelson seizes his moment. He texts Judy. 'Got Ava. Meet me at hospital entrance.' Then, gently, he takes the baby from her grandmother.

Judy doesn't ask any stupid questions. She is waiting by the main door and has called for back-up. When the squad cars arrive, Nelson, still holding Ava, gets in the back of one of them. Judy gets into the other car with Annie, who has been charged with child abduction. They drive fast through the empty streets. The rain has stopped but there is still a lot of water on the ground. Several times they almost aquaplane, spray flying up as if they're on a theme park ride. Holding the tiny baby, who is now making little mewing sounds, Nelson is reminded of his own daughters. They both used to love theme parks and there's a big picture in the sitting room of the four of them – Nelson, Michelle, Laura and Rebecca – on something called The Deadly Rapids. The girls are about eight and ten, gap-toothed grins above their life jackets. Please God, let Laura forgive him.

Judy has radioed ahead and Tanya and Clough are both at the house. As soon as the car comes to a halt, Star comes flying out of the house. Nelson gets out and Star snatches Ava from his arms.

'Oh my baby, my baby.'

'Come on, love,' says Nelson. 'Let's get inside. It's too cold out here for Ava.'

He can see Dave, Star's father, in the doorway, Tanya at his side. Clough comes out to meet them, a thousand questions on his face.

'How did you find her, boss?'

'Let's just get inside first.'

Nelson watches as Dave hugs Star, who is still clutching Ava to her chest. Together, father and daughter move into the house. Tanya and Clough follow. Nelson waits in the porch. He wants Star to have a few minutes with Ava before he tells her that her mother was the person who abducted her baby.

When Ruth wakes up she thinks that she only dreamed that Nelson was there. Sitting beside her bed, her hair a fiery splash of colour against the blue curtains, is Shona.

'Hi,' says Shona. 'How's the head?'

Ruth touches her forehead gingerly. 'OK, I think. A bit sore.'

'Judy rang me,' says Shona. 'They say that you can be discharged if there's someone with you tonight so I'm taking you home with me.'

Shona's home is also Phil's home so Ruth says, 'I'll be all right on my own. We don't need to tell the hospital.'

'No. I'd never forgive myself if you slipped into a coma or something,' says Shona. 'I'm all set to be Florence Nightingale and you can't dissuade me. I knew something would happen if you went off with Leif. That man's trouble. Just like his father.'

'How is Leif?' asks Ruth. 'Is he OK?'

'Judy says they think he's broken his leg,' said Shona. 'He's waiting for an X-ray.'

'I met Magda,' says Ruth. 'She had a baby. It was Erik's. Artificial insemination using his frozen sperm.'

'Too much information,' says Shona lightly but, too late, Ruth remembers that Shona was once pregnant with Erik's child and, at his insistence, had an abortion. She's not thinking clearly. It must be the bang on the head.

'We're just waiting for a doctor to discharge you,' says Shona. 'Phil's making up the spare room bed.'

'It's very kind of you,' says Ruth. 'Of you both.' On reflection she thinks that it might be rather nice to spend the night in Shona's spare room, rather than on her own in her cottage. Her head feels as if it's full of cement.

'Was Nelson here?' she asks.

'Nelson?' says Shona. 'I don't know. Judy just rang and asked if I could pick you up. Apparently they've found the baby. The one that was missing.'

'Ava?' says Ruth. 'Oh, that's great news.' Perhaps she did imagine Nelson. She remembers a dream about the devil and Nelson saying that Flint was too fat. Flint!

'I've got to go back,' she says, struggling to sit up. 'No one's fed Flint.'

'Relax,' says Shona. 'I sent a message to your neighbour, Sam. She and Ed are down for a few days. She'll feed Flint.'

'How do you know Sam?'

'Turns out we're friends on Facebook. You see, Ruth, social media does have its advantages.'

Ruth doesn't answer this, her brain is still too muzzy.

Shona sits by her bed talking about Louis and Phil and a lot of people whom Ruth doesn't know. Eventually a doctor and nurse arrive to discharge her. After the doctor has looked into Ruth's eyes with her torch and pronounced herself satisfied, the nurse says, 'Has your husband left?'

'My . . . I don't have a husband.' Has she woken up in some parallel universe where she's married with two point four children?

'Oh, sorry. I should have said your partner. The tall, dark-haired man who was with you earlier. He said he was your next of kin.'

So Nelson must have been here after all. Ruth supposes he left because Ava was found. 'He's just a friend,' she says.

'Well, he looked a very close friend,' says the nurse. 'Sitting beside you and stroking your hair.'

'Stroking my . . .'

'And he yelled at the A&E consultant earlier. Demanding to know if you were all right.'

That sounds more like Nelson.

'He can be rather domineering.'

'Tell me about it,' says the nurse. Though he doesn't say whether he's speaking from the position of a yeller or a yellee.

'Come on, Ruth,' says Shona. 'You're free. Time to go.'

There seem to be lots of police cars outside the hospital but Ruth assumes that this is just part of the routine emergency of hospital life. By the time they reach Shona's car, on the top floor of the multi-storey, she is feeling tired and rather sick. Shona must realise this because she doesn't try to talk. Instead she switches on Radio 4 and lets *Midnight News* accompany them home.

Nelson also arrives home at midnight. He presses the button to open the garage, so tired that he's almost in a dream, a weightless feeling that's not unpleasant. He feels as if he has run through a lifetime's emotions in a day but the predominant feeling now is one of satisfaction. Ava has been found, alive and well. The complications around her abduction will have to wait until another day. Tonight Star can sleep with her baby beside her.

The house is quiet when he lets himself in. No sound from George upstairs and, more worryingly, no sound from Bruno downstairs. When he doesn't hear Bruno running to meet him, nails clattering on the wooden floor, tail hitting the wall, Nelson feels a sudden lurch of fear. What has happened to his guard dog? Has he been lured away by a piece of poisoned meat? Such things have happened before. But when Nelson lets himself into the sitting room, Bruno is lying on the sofa next to Laura, both of them fast asleep.

Bruno sees him first. He opens his eyes and wags his tail but doesn't move. After a few seconds Laura sits up, rubbing her eyes.

'You're back,' says Nelson. He knows that he's grinning like a goon.

'Just for a bit,' says Laura. 'I'm going to look for my own place soon. I can't keep looking after you two for ever.'

'No, you can't,' says Nelson. 'But this is always your home. I'm so pleased to see you, love.'

He pushes Bruno aside to sit on the sofa and Laura puts her head on his shoulder. She doesn't say so but he knows that he's forgiven.

It's so much more than he deserves.

CHAPTER 35

'The trouble is,' says Nelson, 'we've got no evidence.'

The team are back in the briefing room and, despite each of them only having had a few hours' sleep, the atmosphere has changed completely. When Nelson got into the office at nine, all the admin staff stood up and applauded him. It's rare, in policing, to have so complete a success. One baby lost, one baby found. Super Jo herself even received a tepid ovation when she wafted in to congratulate Nelson. 'It's a complete good news story,' she said.

'Well, hardly,' said Nelson. 'The baby's grandmother's been charged with abduction.' Annie Simmonds has been released on bail. Nelson doesn't know whether she has gone back to the house that she shares with her daughter. Luke Lacey has also been charged with abduction though his solicitor is fighting hard for the lesser charge of wasting police time.

'The child is safe,' said Jo. 'That's all that matters for now. Do you want to do the press conference or shall I?'

'Be my guest,' said Nelson.

And now, they are tackling the next big question. Was Annie right and did Pete Benson kill Margaret, all those years ago?

'We've got a team at his old allotment near Scarning Fen,' says Nelson. 'It's owned by someone else now. SOC think there's evidence of recent digging but, then again, it *is* an allotment. We really need Ruth there to do her stuff.'

'How is Ruth?' asks Judy. She feels a bit guilty about leaving Ruth at the hospital last night. She hopes that Shona is looking after her.

'I rang her earlier,' says Nelson, not meeting Judy's eyes. 'She's OK. Just got a bit of a sore head. She wanted to go to Scarning Fen today but I told her to wait until she was feeling stronger.'

Would Ruth listen? Judy wonders.

'So, if John Mostyn's DNA was on the bones,' says Clough, who is meditatively eating a breakfast Mars bar, 'does that mean that he knew Margaret was there and that he dug up her remains and buried them on the Saltmarsh? Why?'

Unconsciously they all look towards the cage where Sonny and Fredo are curled up in the straw. As if he recognises his former owner's name, Fredo stirs and chirrups in his sleep.

'He wanted us to find them, I suppose,' says Nelson. 'That's why Mostyn wrote those letters, basing them on the ones I received about Scarlet. He must have known about the originals because he worked for the *Chronicle*. Mostyn wanted us to find Margaret. Maybe he waited all these years until the archaeological dig gave him the opportunity.'

'And then someone killed Mostyn,' says Clough. 'Was that Pete Benson too?'

'He has an alibi.' Judy is leafing through her notebook. 'Pete and Karen were both in all evening when John Mostyn was killed, watching television.'

'Married alibis don't stand up in court,' says Nelson. 'But the way that murder was committed, so cold and clinical, I can't quite see Pete Benson pulling off a crime like that.'

Clough is frowning at the hamsters. 'Why would Karen cover up for Pete if she thought that he'd murdered Margaret? Come to that, why would she stay married to him all these years? They've got grown-up children, for God's sake.'

'Annie said that Karen didn't know,' says Nelson. 'That's what she said to me. "Mum refused to see." She said that she and Luke had never liked Pete. Maybe they had their suspicions for years. It was us asking about Scarning Fen that finally decided them.'

'It's a bit extreme though, isn't it?' says Tanya. 'I mean, I always thought Luke Lacey was a bit odd but to kidnap your own niece – great-niece – like that just because of something you suspected.'

'I think it must have festered for years,' says Nelson. 'Annie and Luke might both have felt guilty about Margaret and neither of them liked their stepfather. Last weekend, seeing each other again, Margaret's funeral, it must have brought it all back. They probably worked each other up so that kidnapping Ava seemed the only thing to do.'

'*Folie à deux*,' says Judy. 'Alone, they might never have

acted, but together they convinced themselves that they were doing the right thing.'

'"It was just Annie and me again",' says Tanya. 'That's what Luke said to me when he was talking about Margaret going missing. And he said that Annie used to "make him do things". I think she was always the dominant one.'

'Annie had a serious breakdown in her late teens,' says Nelson. 'Michelle says that Star hinted as much to her, and Dave confirmed it last night. Finding Margaret, the birth of Ava, her suspicions about Pete, it must all have pushed her over the edge.'

'And Annie knew that she could keep Ava safely in the neonatal unit,' says Judy. 'She even took Star's expressed milk for her. Although I still can't believe that Annie managed to smuggle a baby into the hospital without any of the medical team knowing about it.'

'There's a safeguarding inquiry going on as we speak,' says Nelson. 'But Annie was in charge of the neonatal unit. I don't think anyone else would have challenged her. When I saw Annie last night, it was obvious that she wasn't in her right mind. The thought of putting her own daughter through something like that.'

'I never thought that Star seemed close to her mother,' says Judy. 'She obviously had a better relationship with her father.'

'Even so,' says Nelson. 'Annie put Star through hell. "Star never listens to me," she said, "she thinks she knows it all." As if it was Star's fault.'

'Star seemed remarkably calm when I saw her this

morning,' said Judy. 'She's so pleased to have Ava back that I don't think the rest has sunk in.'

Nelson is looking at the incident board. The word 'Found' is scrawled across Ava's picture but Margaret is still there, golden-haired and innocent in her bridesmaid's dress.

'We haven't got enough to arrest Pete Benson,' he says. 'But we should interview him under caution. Scare him a bit. Can you bring him in, Cloughie?'

'Sure thing,' says Clough, standing up. 'Coming, Judy?'

'I want to call in on Star again,' says Judy. 'Tanya will go with you.'

Tanya already has her coat on.

Judy finds Star sitting on the sofa with Ava in her arms.

'I can't seem to let her out of my sight,' she says. 'I think that's quite normal, considering.'

'I think so too,' says Judy. Dave, who had met her at the door, told her that Annie was staying with Sienna in Loughborough. 'I can't see how Star can ever forgive her mum,' he said, his ruddy face pale with distress, 'but Star says she can. Of course, she knows what her mum went through as a girl but, even so, she's a wonder, my daughter.'

And Star does look rather wonderful this morning, sitting in the sunlight with the glass constellation glittering above her. Ava sleeps peacefully on her lap. 'Star's a strong spirit,' Cathbad had said that morning. 'She's got a powerful sense of self-preservation. I think she'll be just fine.' As usual, it seems that Cathbad is right. Judy asks after the baby.

'The doctor checked her over last night,' says Star. 'She

said she was fine. And she'll take a bottle now, which I suppose is a good thing.'

'And how are you?' asks Judy.

'I'm just so happy to have Ava back,' says Star. 'I can't really think of anything else. But when I do think about it . . . Dad says that Mum took Ava because she thought that Granddad had killed Margaret. That's horrible. I love Granddad. He'd never do anything like that. You don't think it's true, do you? It was just Mum . . . Mum getting ill again, wasn't it?'

'We have to investigate,' says Judy. 'But the best thing you can do is put it out of your mind for now. I know it's difficult.'

'I've been meditating,' says Star. 'That helps.' She looks rather coyly up at Judy. 'The other policewoman, Tanya, she told me that Cathbad's your partner. Why didn't you tell me?'

'I don't like to talk about my private life,' says Judy. 'I'm not the important one here.'

'But you told me about your baby being abducted.'

'Because I thought it might help.'

'It did,' says Star. 'It was the only thing I clung on to during that first awful night. I'll always feel a special kinship with Michael.'

Judy wishes that she hadn't remembered the name. 'Concentrate on Ava,' she says. 'Babies are good at making you live in the present.'

'The secret of health is not to mourn for the past or worry about the future but to live in the present wisely,' says Star. 'That's what Cathbad says.'

'I think Buddha or someone said it first,' says Judy. 'But it sounds like a good idea.'

When Judy leaves the house she is irritated, if not entirely surprised, to see Maddie sitting on the low wall of the front garden. She is scrolling through her phone but looks up when Judy emerges. 'Hi.'

'Are you following me again?' says Judy.

'Is it true that Star's mum abducted Ava?'

'There's a press conference on now,' says Judy, looking at her watch. 'Why aren't you there?'

'I thought this was where the story was.' Maddie gives her a wide smile, eyes big and innocent. Even though she knows it's an act, Judy can't help smiling back.

'Let's leave the family in peace,' she says. 'Ava's back with her mother. That's all you need to know. Can I give you a lift somewhere?'

She expects Maddie to refuse – like her father, she's an indefatigable walker – but she says, 'Could you drop me in Wells? I'm meeting someone for lunch.'

'OK,' says Judy. It's not far and she enjoys the drive along the coast. After last night's rain, it's suddenly a beautiful day with the promise of spring in the air. Maddie doesn't ask any more about the case but chatters on about her flatmates and the prospect of a trip to Greece in the summer. When they get to Wells, the sea sparkling like a Sunday night TV show, boats clinking in the harbour, Maddie says, 'You can drop me here.'

Judy stops the car. They are outside a small shop, trays of

jewels catching the light, red, green and gold. Little Rocks, reads the sign.

'Who are you meeting for lunch?'

'Roxy. She's an old schoolfriend. She works here.'

Judy looks at her almost stepdaughter. Does she know about the link between this shop, and its owner Kim Jennings, and the death of Margaret Lacey? It's possible that she doesn't. Maddie was, after all, brought up in the area. She could well have a schoolfriend who works here.

Judy watches as Maddie enters the shop, the bell ringing as the door shuts behind her. She looks at the trays displayed outside, jewellery, seashells and souvenirs of sunny Norfolk. She remembers Annie's scathing description. *Full of old tat covered in glitter.* Judy gets out of the car and moves closer. There's a whole tray of seahorses: coloured stone, silver, silk and satin embroidered in bright colours.

It came to me about five years ago that Margaret had said something about a seahorse..

That's what Kim Jennings had said when Judy asked her about the day when Margaret went missing.

Seahorses.

See horses.

Pete Benson seems confused by Clough's request.

'You want to talk to me about Margaret. Why?'

'We have received some new information,' says Clough. He is finding the whole thing rather difficult. Karen and Pete have always been nice to him. They asked him to read at Margaret's funeral. Now he is having to use phrases like 'information received' and 'interview under caution'.

'Is it about Ava?' says Pete. 'Dave rang us last night and said she'd been found. He sounded odd on the phone.'

'Ava's back home with her mother,' says Clough. 'As far as I know, she's in good health.'

'But who took her?' says Karen, who also seems bemused. She is youthfully dressed in white trousers and a sparkly top but, as she hovers around her husband in the hall, she suddenly looks like an old woman. 'I keep ringing Annie,' she says, 'but she's not answering her phone.'

'Ava is safe,' says Clough. 'That's all we can tell you at present.' Keep him in the dark, Nelson had said, then we can spring the questions about Margaret. That's all very well but the boss isn't having to shepherd a confused elderly man into a police car. Karen comes out to the car with them. 'When will you be back?'

'I don't know,' says Pete. His hands are shaking.

'We'll be as quick as we can,' says Clough. He opens the back door for Pete and then gets into the passenger seat. Tanya is driving.

They drive slowly through the estate. Haig Road, Marshall Drive, Byng Place, Allenby Avenue. John Mostyn's house still has police tape outside. The windows have been boarded up, presumably to stop the locals breaking them.

'Why are you taking me to the police station?' asks Pete, querulously, from the back seat.

'There are just some questions we need to ask you,' says Clough.

'Under caution,' adds Tanya, from behind the wheel. Clough thinks that she is enjoying herself far too much.

The skewbald is still grazing in the paddock outside the house belonging to Steve and Alison Jennings. What was its name? Patch, something like that. But Steve had said that, at one time, the family had owned a few rescue horses, including Cuddles, the pony belonging to Kim Jennings.

At first Judy thinks that there's nobody in but after a few minutes the door is opened by Steve, wearing another of his woolly jumpers.

'Hallo?' He doesn't recognise her.

'Hi. I'm DS Judy Johnson. I came to talk to you the other day, about Margaret Lacey. There's something else I wanted to ask you.'

'Come in,' says Steve but Judy thinks that he looks wary. There's little trace of the cosy granddad today.

There's no trace of the grandchildren either, or of his wife. Only the elderly dog snores by the electric fire with its fake coals. Even the cockatoo's cage is covered by a cloth.

'Ali's collecting Daisy-Mae from school,' says Steve, in answer to Judy's query. He doesn't say who Daisy-Mae is.

Judy is beginning to wish she hadn't rushed over to the Jenningses' house so recklessly. She texted Clough saying where she was going but, if he's in the middle of an interview, he won't look at his phone. She should have waited for proper back-up. But she's here now, so she might as well get on with it.

'Mr Jennings,' she said. 'Did you see Margaret alone on the day that she disappeared?'

She had thought that Steve's face had changed earlier, when he saw her at the door. But she was wrong; it changes now.

'What are you talking about?' he says.

'Kim told me that Margaret said something about a sea-horse. But I think she said that she was going to see the horses, your horses.' Judy remembers Karen being quoted, in Maddie's article, as saying that Margaret had liked 'dancing and ponies and dressing up'. She thinks it was Margaret's love for ponies that had led her to accompany Steve Jennings on the sunny July day. And, after all, the man was her best friend's father; she had trusted him. What had Annie said? *There was no one strange there. It was just our friends and family.*

'What happened, Steve?' says Judy. 'Did you take Margaret back here, to your house?'

'Of course I didn't,' says Steve. 'This is slander. I'll sue.'

'You were seen,' says Judy, suddenly sure of it. 'John Mostyn saw you.'

'That nutter,' says Steve. 'You can't believe a word he says. Anyway, he's dead now. Dead men tell no tales.'

The cliché sounds very sinister in Steve's flat Norfolk accent. Suddenly, despite the fact that it is midday and she's in a sitting room filled with pictures of smiling children, with a dog snoozing on the hearthrug, Judy is afraid.

'What happened?' she says again. 'What happened to Margaret?'

Steve turns away and seems to be looking for something

in a drawer. With his back still turned, he says, 'It was an accident. I just wanted a kiss. She was a tease, that girl, prancing about in shorts and skimpy tops. "Hallo, Uncle Steve." She knew what she was doing.'

'She was twelve,' says Judy.

'Twelve going on thirty,' says Steve. He turns to face her. He's smiling now and it's a few seconds before Judy realises that he's holding a gun.

Pete still seems confused when he's ushered into Interview Room 1.

'What's going on?' he keeps saying.

'Interview with Peter Benson under caution,' says Tanya into the microphone. 'Present, DS Tanya Fuller and DS David Clough.'

'We wanted to talk to you about Margaret,' says Clough, still feeling slightly awkward. Pete fixes him with mild blue eyes, clearly thinking that Clough is his only friend in the room. 'I believe you knew the family before you married Karen. Did you know Margaret?'

Pete blinks twice. 'I did know them,' he says slowly. 'My brother-in-law Steve was a friend of Bob's, Karen's first husband. I met the family at his house a few times.'

'How well did you know Margaret?' asks Tanya.

'Not well. I mean, she was a young girl, always playing with Steve's daughters. I don't think I spoke to her more than twice. But I feel that I've come to know her since she went missing, if you know what I mean. She's a big part of our lives still.'

Clough, remembering the wall of photographs, thinks that he does know what Pete means. Marrying Karen must have meant marrying into the shared family grief.

'Were you at the King's Lynn street party on the twenty-ninth of July 1981?' asks Clough.

'No,' says Pete. 'I lived near Swaffham then. I think I watched the wedding on television at home and then went to the pub for a quick pint. I only heard about Margaret going missing when it was on the news the next day. I rang Steve. He was quite distraught.'

'You had an allotment, didn't you?' says Clough.

'Yes,' says Pete. 'I've always enjoyed gardening. I've got an allotment now too.'

'Why didn't you tell us that you used to live near Scarning Fen?' says Clough. 'We asked if you had any connection to the area.'

'I don't think I realised it was near there,' says Pete. 'I didn't recognise the name. What's all this about? Why are you asking me these questions?'

Clough glances at Tanya. They have discussed this before-hand. It's just a matter of who says the words.

'How well do you get on with your stepchildren Annie and Luke?' asks Clough.

Pete shakes his head, seeming bewildered again by the change in direction.

'Well enough, I think. They were teenagers when I married Karen. Luke was almost an adult. So things were a bit tricky sometimes. Luke had got used to being the man of the house, I think. Annie too. It was almost like she was in charge. She used to order Luke to do things and he'd do them. It was like he didn't have any free will. Both of them tried to look after Karen, they were very protective of her, but it sometimes looked like bullying to me. Things were easier when they left home to go to university. Then Karen and I had Richard and Bradley.'

'Did the siblings get on?' asks Clough.

'Yes. Annie doted on the boys when they were young. She was always good with babies. I think that's why she became a paediatric nurse. Luke was always more distant. I think I spoke to him more when he came home for Margaret's funeral than I ever have before.'

Was that because Luke already suspected him of killing his sister? thinks Clough. And was Annie, the girl who had loved babies, already planning to abduct her own daughter's child?

But Pete's mind has been moving in the same direction.

'Is this to do with Annie and Luke? Did *they* think I killed Margaret? Oh my God.'

Clough lets silence answer him.

Steve levels the gun at Judy. It looks like an old service pistol, old-fashioned but, unfortunately, still in working order. Steve's voice is now quiet and reasonable, as it was the first time Judy met him. 'I tried to kiss her,' he says. 'I took hold of her, just to steady her, but she pulled away and she fell and hit her head. There, on the fireplace.' He points at the fire surround, which is made of rough-hewn stone, a sixties attempt at antiquity. 'When I went to pick her up, there was blood coming from her head and she was an awful colour, sort of grey. I went to get something to put over her and, when I came back, she was dead. No heartbeat, nothing. I didn't know what to do. Ali and the kids were due back from the street party any minute.'

Judy remembers Kim Jennings saying that, after she had parted from Margaret, she went back to the party to sit with her 'mum and sisters'. No mention of her dad, who was presumably, at that very moment, driving Margaret away on the pretext of seeing his horses. Yet, later, Steve had been one of the men out looking for Margaret, even though he knew that she would never be found.

'Why didn't you call an ambulance when she first fell?' says Judy. 'You might have saved her.'

'I told you,' says Steve. 'I panicked. I didn't know what to do. It was a terrible shock. Imagine Kim coming back to find her friend dead on the carpet. I had to act quickly.' He actually sounds quite sorry for himself.

'What did you do?' asks Judy.

'I wrapped her in a blanket and tied her up,' says Steve, as if this is perfectly normal behaviour. 'Then I put her in the boot of my car and went to join the search party. Later that night I buried her.'

'In your brother-in-law Pete's allotment near Scarning Fen.'

'What a clever policewoman you are,' says Steve. 'Such a shame about the way you're going to die. The gun just went off accidentally, that's what I'll say. I'll probably only get a suspended sentence, what with having such a good name in the community. Devoted family man and all that.'

And that's precisely how Judy had thought of him, until about half an hour ago. She thinks of Kim Jennings and the way her face looked sad in repose. Did she somewhere, deep down, know what her father was?

'My colleagues know where I am,' says Judy. 'They'll be here any moment.'

'Rubbish,' says Steve. 'I saw your face just now. You were terrified.'

'Police!' shouts a voice behind them. 'Drop that gun!'

Steve doesn't drop it but he half turns and that's enough for Judy. She swings her arm upwards and knocks the gun from Steve's hand. Then she punches him in the stomach. He groans and doubles up, his head near the spot where Margaret breathed her last. Somehow the dog sleeps on.

Judy is bending over Steve's hunched body and putting on handcuffs.

'Call the police,' she says to Maddie.

'I have.' Maddie's voice has gone back to normal now. Where did she find that commanding tone earlier? The shout of 'Police' had almost convinced Judy herself.

Judy kneels on the carpet beside Steve, who is still breathing heavily.

'Are you OK?' says Maddie.

'I'm fine. How did you find me?'

'I followed you.' Maddie gives her a sudden grin. 'Like you're always telling me not to do. Roxy gave me a lift up here. I knew you were on to something.'

'Well, I'm very grateful,' says Judy. 'That shout was amazing. I thought you were the real thing for a moment.'

'I tried to sound like that superintendent. The one who's always doing the press conferences.'

'Jo Archer. Yeah, that's who you reminded me of.'

'Did he confess?' Maddie nods towards the crumpled figure on the hearthrug.

'Yes. This is the man who killed Margaret Lacey.' Steve mutters something indistinct. 'He'll be confessing it again later in a taped interview.'

'Can I have an exclusive afterwards?'

'You certainly can,' says Judy, as the sirens sound in the distance.

CHAPTER 36

Despite her words to Maddie, Judy half expects Steve to deny everything when he is questioned at the police station. But, in a recorded interview with Judy and Clough, live-streamed to Nelson in the viewing room, Steve Jennings describes how Margaret Lacey died. It's murder, in Judy's book, but she knows that a lawyer might try for a plea of manslaughter. Luckily Steve has waived his right to a solicitor and Judy makes sure that she gets on tape the fact that Steve didn't call for an ambulance when Margaret first fell and hit her head. He says he went for something to put over her but did he really just wait for her to die? Maybe he even hastened her death by smothering her? Traces of material were found around Margaret's jaw bone and Judy is willing to bet that Steve's DNA is on them and on the rope that bound her body. Steve is helpfully quite expansive about his feelings for Margaret, which should damn him in the eyes of any decent-minded jury. 'She knew what she was doing, that girl. She was the type who could wind men around her little finger.'

Clough, who is less good at hiding his feelings than Judy, clenches his fists under the table.

'I only wanted a kiss,' says Steve. 'Was that so bad?'

'She was twelve years old,' says Judy. She wants this clearly on the tape.

Steve laughs. 'She was no innocent, believe me. She was just like her mother. A right little prick tease. I could see it when Margaret used to come to the house. She was always looking at me under her eyelashes. Flaunting herself. Tempting me.'

'You're talking about the times when Margaret came to play with your daughter, Kim?'

'Margaret never had much time for Kim, to be honest. I think she came to see me.'

Can he really have believed this? thinks Judy, looking at the grey-haired man across the desk, even now smiling complacently, hands folded across his paunch. And what about Kim, the little girl who was always in Margaret's shadow? Did she know that her father was lusting after her schoolfriend? Judy hopes not.

'I went to kiss her,' says Steve. 'And she pulled away. I grabbed her. I knew she wanted it really. And she fell. She hit her head on the fireplace. It was an accident.'

Judy asks again about the ambulance. 'Why didn't you call for help? It's possible that you could have saved her. Didn't you want to save her?'

'I didn't know what to do,' says Steve. 'I didn't want her lying there dead on my carpet.' Judy gets Steve to recount, in painstaking detail, how he hid Margaret's body in the boot of his car, went to join the search party and later buried Margaret in his brother-in-law's allotment. She hopes that this will sound particularly cold and calculating in court.

'Did Pete know that you had killed Margaret?' asks Clough.

'No,' says Steve. 'He's a wimp, Pete. Always has been. He would have gone to pieces.'

'Didn't he notice that the ground had been disturbed?'

'No. It was a new allotment then. Pete had just dug it over and put the compost down. I gave him the horse manure. It was easy to bury her. Pete planted his vegetables on top and never knew a thing. The plants always grew well there and I always wondered whether that was due to Margaret. And my manure, of course.'

Did he really say that? Judy glances towards the camera and wonders what the boss is making of all this.

'What did you think when Pete married Margaret's mother?' she asks, really wanting to know.

'I was pleased for Pete. I never thought he'd have the guts to ask her. And she was a good-looking woman. Though she'd gone off a bit by then.'

Karen would have been in her thirties when she married Pete but Steve's tastes obviously lay in other directions. Judy wonders again about his own daughters, not to mention Steve's grandchildren and great-grandchildren.

'Are we nearly finished?' says Steve. 'I need to get home. I'm taking Daisy-Mae to her ballet class.'

'We're nearly there,' says Judy.

She can only hope that Steve's babysitting days are over.

While Steve is being charged with murder and possession of a firearm with intent to endanger life, Judy and Clough retreat to Nelson's office.

'Good work,' says Nelson. 'We've got a full confession. We'll try hard to make the murder charge stick. After all, he assaulted an under-age girl and didn't call for help when she was hurt. Bastard. What made you realise it was him?'

Judy explains about the seahorses. Nelson makes a noise that seems halfway between admiration and exasperation.

'What were you thinking of, going there without back-up?'

'I texted Clough.'

'I was in the interview room,' says Clough. 'By the time I saw your text you were back here handcuffed to Steve Jennings.'

'I know,' says Judy. 'It's not your fault. I should have waited for back-up.'

'Instead you had Maddie storming in pretending to be Jo Archer,' says Nelson. 'That I would have liked to see.'

'Is Maddie OK?'

'Seems so. She's given a statement and she's waiting for you downstairs.'

'I've promised her an exclusive.'

'She can have one as soon we've done the paperwork. She deserves it. Seems she's like her father, always turning up at the right moment.'

'She is like him,' says Judy. 'She's been driving me mad following me around but she probably saved my life today.'

'You should never have put yourself in that position,' says Nelson, glowering again.

'I know. I'm sorry.'

'So,' says Nelson, sitting down at his desk. 'We've got Margaret's killer. And we've found Ava. Not bad going.'

'We just need to solve John Mostyn's murder and we're done,' says Clough. 'Any chance that Jennings could have done it?'

'He's got an alibi,' says Judy. 'He was at home with Alison. They had the great-grandchildren staying.'

'It's another married alibi,' says Clough. 'Could be broken. Especially when the wife finds out about this.'

'I think Mostyn suspected Steve all along,' says Judy. 'Maybe he even saw him with Margaret on the day of the street party. Somehow, he must have realised that Steve had buried Margaret in Pete's allotment. Remember when we spoke to Pete? He said that he'd talked to John Mostyn about gardening. Maybe that gave him the idea.'

'Why did he dig her up and bury her at the Saltmarsh though?' says Clough.

'So we would find her,' says Judy. 'He must have read about the dig and seen his chance. There may have been some other significance too. Remember the witch stones that were found at the site? John Mostyn loved stones and the beach. Maybe that's why he buried Margaret there.' Judy still has the witch stone that John Mostyn gave her. It's in her bag and several times a day she feels for it, the smooth surface, the satisfying void at the centre.

'I still think Jennings could have killed Mostyn,' says Clough. 'Who else could benefit?'

'Dead men tell no tales,' says Judy. 'That's what Steve said to me.'

'Steve Jennings didn't kill John Mostyn,' says Nelson.

Judy finds Maddie in reception, scrolling down her phone as usual.

'Want a lift?' she says.

'Hi, Judy,' says Maddie, for all the world as if this is a casual meeting. 'That would be great. Actually, I was wondering if I could stay at your place tonight.'

'Of course,' says Judy.

'In fact, my flatmates are getting on my nerves a bit so I was wondering . . .'

'You can move in with us,' says Judy. 'Cathbad would be delighted.'

'It's only temporary,' says Maddie, putting on her backpack. 'I think I'm destined to be a nomad.'

'Maybe for a while,' says Judy. 'But I think you'll settle down one day.'

'Like Dad?'

'Just like him.'

They go towards the exit but, at the swing doors, Judy asks Maddie to wait for her and sprints back upstairs. She comes back down carrying the hamster cage.

'What's that?' says Maddie.

'Two new pets.'

The more the merrier, she thinks. And she actually means it.

By the end of the day, Ruth is feeling exhausted. Last night hadn't been too bad. Shona had been really kind, offering hot drinks and popping in several times during the night to check that Ruth was all right. And even Phil hadn't asked too many questions. After Nelson's phone call Ruth had driven today to Scarning Fen and, ignoring his advice, had examined Pete Benson's old allotment for signs of disturbance. It was difficult because the soil had been turned over fairly recently – the current allotment owners seem keen on crop rotation – but she thought that, in one place, the earth appeared darker and richer, which could point to something organic having been buried there. She took samples and filled in a report and then she drove to the hospital to see Leif. She had been feeling rather guilty about him. After all, Cathbad had Judy and she had Shona. Who was looking after Leif?

The answer is, half the hospital. Leif, his leg in plaster up to his thigh, is in a small room off the main ward but nurse after nurse comes in to enquire after his progress and to offer fruit drinks and vitamin supplements.

'I know you're fussy about your food,' says one pretty redhead, as if she has known Leif since childhood.

'You're really kind, Kerry,' says Leif. He is on first-name terms with all of them and many have signed his plaster with accompanying hearts and kisses.

'How are you feeling?' asks Ruth during a brief lull.

'OK,' says Leif, although, close up, his eyes are rather shadowed. 'We were lucky, I guess.'

'You came off worst,' says Ruth, although her head is splitting and she still feels rather sick.

'The deer came off worst.'

'Yes. Poor thing. Cathbad feels terrible about that. And about you,' she adds hastily.

'I know. He was in earlier. But it wasn't his fault. Driving conditions were terrible and the stag just appeared in front of us out of nowhere. I still think it might have been Herne the Hunter. I'm just annoyed about this,' he gestures at his leg, 'just when I need to tie up the loose ends at the dig.'

'If there's anything I can do to help,' says Ruth, although she knows she sounds unconvincing.

'Don't worry,' says Leif. 'It's really just waiting for the lab results now. And for the facial reconstruction. When I'm discharged I'm going to stay with my mother for a few days.'

So Leif does have someone to look after him, thinks Ruth, feeling slightly envious as she often does now when people mention mothers. She wonders what has happened with Laura. If she was living with Leif, she obviously isn't now.

'I'm sorry,' says Leif suddenly. 'If I hadn't dragged you all the way to Stanton Drew, this would never have happened.'

'It's OK,' says Ruth. 'It's all part of the great web. That's what Cathbad would say.'

'He did say it earlier,' says Leif. 'But I'm sorry all the same. We're still friends, aren't we?'

Were they ever friends? thinks Ruth. Erik had been her friend. Perhaps he still is. She's not sure what she thinks about the handsome wounded lion in front of her. She still doesn't quite trust him but she takes the outstretched hand and squeezes it.

'Of course we're friends,' she says. 'I have to go and collect Kate now.'

Kate is fascinated by the plaster on Ruth's forehead, which is now looking a bit grubby at the edges. She wants to hear the story of the crash again and again: the stone circle, the rain, the deer in the road.

'Remember our crash?' she says. 'With the rabbit?'

It takes Ruth a few minutes to realise that Kate is talking about the first time that she met Frank. He had literally crashed into them, driving his hired car on the wrong side of the road. There had been a dead rabbit on the verge, completely unrelated to the accident. Ruth hadn't known that Kate had noticed it.

'Are we going to see Frank today?' asks Kate after they have reminisced about the time a man with a 'funny accent like a cowboy' drove his car into them.

'Not today,' says Ruth. 'I'm too tired today.'

'I'm tired too,' boasts Kate. 'Tasha and I didn't sleep all night. We played games on her tablet and we ate Haribos at midnight.'

Kate seems lively enough when they get back, rushing to tell Flint all about her sleepover. Flint is slightly offish with Ruth for abandoning him last night but he consents to eat a special tuna supper and to sit with them while they watch some teenage TV show that Ruth is too lethargic to turn off.

Kate must be a bit tired though because, when Ruth tells

her that it's time for bed, she only puts up a token resistance. Ruth heaves herself off the sofa, ready to run the bath, when there's a fusillade of knocks on the front door. Only one person knocks like that.

'Nelson. What are you doing here?'

'Came to see how you were,' says Nelson, thrusting a rather battered bunch of carnations at her. Ruth recognises the wrapping from her nearest petrol station but she appreciates the gesture. She remembers Valentine's Day and her vision of Nelson presenting Michelle with beautifully wrapped red roses.

'Dad!' Kate comes downstairs and barrels into Nelson's chest. 'I had a sleepover last night. I ate sweets at midnight.'

'That's nice, love.' Nelson sits on the sofa and, despite often declaring herself nearly grown-up, Kate climbs onto his lap. Flint, on the other hand, walks off in disgust.

'I had a sleepover too,' says Ruth.

'Did you?' Nelson gives her a sharp look. 'Who with?'

Ruth feels like telling him to mind his own business but it seems too much hassle so she says, 'With Shona and Phil. The hospital said that I shouldn't go home on my own.'

Nelson's face seems to relax. 'But you're OK now?'

'I'm fine,' says Ruth. 'I went to Scarning Fen today.'

'I told you not to.'

'It's lucky that I don't have to do what you tell me,' says Ruth sweetly. 'I examined the soil at the allotment and I think it's possible that a body was buried there until fairly recently.'

'Oh, we've found Margaret's killer,' says Nelson.

'You have?' says Ruth. 'Who is it?'

'A family friend called Steve Jennings. It'll be in the press tomorrow, probably in an exclusive written by Maddie Henderson.'

'Maddie? How come she's involved?'

'It's a long story. Johnson made the breakthrough but nearly got killed for her efforts. Maddie saved her.'

'Wow,' says Ruth. 'That *is* a good story.'

'Will you read me a bedtime story?' Kate asks Nelson. 'I still have stories sometimes.'

So Nelson stays to read Kate a bedtime story and, afterwards, he and Ruth drink wine in front of the fire. It's almost like the first time, when Nelson turned up at Ruth's door after Scarlet's body had been found. Except, this time, they're not going to sleep together. Ruth is quite certain about that.

But it turns out that she's wrong about this too.

CHAPTER 37

Nelson and Freddie Burnett are sitting on Cromer pier. The tide is out and the sand stretches in bands of blue and gold. They have brought coffee from the café and sit companionably in deckchairs watching the cockle-pickers pulling their nets along the beach.

'It's a beautiful spot, isn't it?' says Freddie. 'I always thought that I'd end my days here.'

'It's a nice beach,' says Nelson. Though, in his opinion, it could be improved by a roller-coaster and a few donkeys.

'How are they doing?' says Freddie. 'Margaret's family?'

'Not bad,' says Nelson. 'I think it was a relief to learn the identity of Margaret's murderer, although it was a shock too, especially for Pete, the stepfather.'

'Killer was his brother-in-law, wasn't he? Are you telling me this Pete had no idea?'

'He says not and I believe him. Pete's a gentle soul. I don't think he ever realised what his brother-in-law was.'

'Scum, that's what he is,' says Freddie. 'They should throw away the key. What about the other business, with the baby?'

They have, so far, managed to keep Annie's name out of the press. It was helpful that Steve Jennings' arrest, and Maddie's exclusive on it, led the news for many days. Annie is out on bail and receiving psychiatric treatment. Her psychiatrist says that Annie abducted Ava while suffering from delusions brought on by the stress of Margaret's body being discovered. Her family seem to have accepted this and, according to Judy, Star has seen her mother and apparently forgives her. Ava is still doing well. She's currently at Nelson's house for a 'playdate' with George.

'The baby's fine,' says Nelson. 'The family are coping well. Considering.'

'What about Mostyn?' says Freddie. 'You pinning that on Jennings too?'

'Freddie,' says Nelson, 'Steve Jennings didn't kill John Mostyn. You did.'

Freddie turns to look at him, his still-bulky frame blotting out the sun.

'What are you talking about?'

'I suspected from the beginning,' says Nelson. 'It was such a professional killing. I knew it either had to be a criminal or a copper. The way he was killed, just one shot and the bullet taken away. No prints on anything. The body moved just for a bit of misdirection. Even the CCTV at the Canada Estate. The killer knew where the cameras were, they'd even covered up the logo on their coat. I did see some dark skin though. You got very tanned in Tenerife, Freddie.'

Freddie stares at him, his eyes bright in a face which is still the colour and texture of shoe leather.

'You've got no evidence.'

'Then I remembered the phone call,' says Nelson. 'You phoned me when we had Mostyn in for a DNA test.'

'I asked you if he was going to get away with it again. And you gave me some crap about doing things by the book.'

'The thing is,' says Nelson, 'you were meant to be in Tenerife but, when I checked the call location, you were ringing from Norfolk.'

'Bloody mobile phones,' says Freddie. 'There's no privacy these days.'

In Nelson's opinion, being watched is no problem if you don't break the law. But he doesn't say anything. He wishes, more than anything, that he could leave Freddie sitting on the pier enjoying his retirement. No one's going to worry too much if John Mostyn's murder goes unsolved. They've caught Margaret's killer and they've restored Ava to her mother. The golden-haired girl and the innocent baby, those are the victims that the public cares about. Not a seventy-year-old man who collected stones and lived alone with his hamsters. Funnily enough, it's the thought of Sonny and Fredo, now happily residing with Cathbad and Judy, that strengthens Nelson's resolve. John Mostyn deserves justice and Nelson, like Agatha Christie's Poirot, does not approve of murder.

'You'll have trouble making it stand up in court,' says Freddie.

'I'm confident we'll get your DNA from the scene,' says Nelson. 'It's a different world now, Freddie. It's almost impossible to get away with these things. DNA has changed everything.'

'Changed it for the worse,' says Freddie. 'There's no real policing any more.'

That depends on your definition of policing, thinks Nelson.

In a different voice, Freddie says, 'I thought you'd let him off. You're getting soft in your old age. All that "innocent until proved guilty" crap.'

'He was innocent,' says Nelson.

Freddie gives a mirthless laugh. 'Well, I know that now, don't I?'

They are both silent, looking out towards the sea, now only a line of darker blue against the sky.

'What'll I get, do you think?' says Freddie. 'Ten years with good behaviour?'

'Maybe less,' says Nelson, 'and you could serve most of it in an open prison.'

'I'm sixty-eight,' says Freddie, 'and I've got prostate cancer. I'm not going to see the outside world again.'

It's the first time that Nelson has heard about the cancer. He watches Freddie as the older man sips his coffee, eyes narrowed against the spring sunshine.

'Give me a day to get my things in order,' says Freddie. 'I'll turn myself in tomorrow. You have my word on that.'

'All right,' says Nelson. And they sit in silence, watching the tiny figures walking across the bay.

CHAPTER 38

'When are they coming?' asks Kate, for the tenth time.

'Soon,' says Ruth. 'They said eleven o'clock.'

But Kate has been watching at the window since ten. She has changed her outfit three times. She's now wearing jeans and a black top with a sparkly Hello Kitty on it. She's even tried to persuade Flint to wear a bow tie. He is currently sitting on top of Ruth's wardrobe, tail fluffed out in outrage.

Ruth, on the other hand, is feeling extremely nervous. When Laura rang her she had been expecting more abuse, not the suggestion that Laura and Rebecca should pay a visit 'to get to know Katie'. But she had known that Kate would love a visit from her half-sisters so they have fixed on this Saturday morning, a week after Steve Jennings was charged with the murder of Margaret Lacey and a retired copper called Freddie Burnett was found dead at his bungalow in Cromer, a gun at his side.

'Is this them?' squeaks Kate as a car pulls up outside.

'I think so,' says Ruth.

The two young women, one dark and one fair, look very

similar as they walk down the garden path. But, when she meets them properly, Ruth realises how different the sisters are. Rebecca immediately bonds with Kate and, within minutes, is upstairs playing Sylvanians with her. Laura, though she gives Kate a lovely hug, holds back a little. She and Ruth are left downstairs listening to sounds of riotous play from above.

'Rebecca always gets on with children,' says Laura. 'She's the one who should have been a teacher.'

Ruth is making coffee. She thinks that Laura sounds a little wistful.

'I'm sure you'll make a great teacher,' she says.

'Cathbad says that it's my calling,' says Laura. 'And I must say I did enjoy my placement.'

'I was terrified when I taught my first undergraduates,' says Ruth. 'But I love it now.'

'It must be wonderful being a university lecturer,' says Laura. 'You can really impart knowledge.'

'The longer I do it the more I wonder if I ever teach my students anything,' says Ruth. 'But, if I can make them interested in archaeology, that's the main thing. Your job is more important. You're creating lifelong learners. God, that sounds like a government pamphlet.'

Laura laughs then looks rather constrained. Perhaps she realises that she is talking and laughing with her enemy, the scarlet woman who is threatening her parents' marriage. And, remembering the night when Nelson called round with his bunch of carnations, Ruth feels guilty all over again.

'I'm back living with my parents,' says Laura. 'But I'm

looking for a flat. I want to live on my own for a bit. I've never done that before.'

'Living on your own is great,' says Ruth. 'And, if you want company, get a cat.'

Laura brightens. 'I do like cats. And we could never have one at home because of Bruno.'

Ruth wonders again what happened with Leif. Perhaps he and Laura were never really seriously involved. She hasn't seen Leif since she visited him in hospital. She assumes that he's in the West Country with Magda and her miracle baby.

They drink their coffee and Rebecca and Kate come clattering downstairs. Rebecca is wearing Kate's pirate hat and Kate has drawn a curly line on her upper lip.

'I'm a lady pirate,' she says, grabbing biscuits with both hands, 'but I've got a moustache.'

'I've got one too,' says Rebecca, 'if I don't wax it off.'

Looking at her smooth, glowing face, Ruth doubts this. All three of Nelson's daughters are beautiful, she realises. Laura in particular takes after Michelle but she, Ruth, must surely take some credit for Kate.

It's a beautiful early spring day and Ruth suggests a walk over the marshes. Anything to work off Kate's excess energy. She has no particular route in mind but she is not surprised when they find themselves following the ancient path towards the place where the wooden henge once stood. As Cathbad would say, the Saltmarsh has its own ideas about destiny. It's a long walk though and Ruth finds herself looking at her Fitbit before remembering that it got broken in the crash. She's not going to replace it. Shona is a good friend but Ruth doesn't want her knowing all about her cardiovascular fitness, such as it is.

'It's so beautiful here,' says Laura. 'You can see for miles.'

'Not what Dad says,' says Rebecca. She adopts a comedy Northern voice. 'Ee bah gum, it's full of ghosts and ghoulies.'

'Not like Blackpool,' says Laura, in the same voice. 'Now that's a proper beach.'

Kate laughs delightedly but Ruth hears the affection in the teasing and feels rather sad. This is the family life that she can never share. She and Nelson haven't spoken since the night with the carnations. Is this what her future is going to be, hanging round on the outskirts of Nelson's life with her only reward being the occasional night of (admittedly fantastic) sex? She shouldn't settle for it. She mustn't settle for it. She thinks of the still unsent job application on her computer. Can she really do it, move from UNN to Cambridge? It would be great for her career, there's no doubt about that, but what about the rest of her life? And, when it comes down to it, could she bear to leave this place, the shifting marsh, the ever-changing sky, the sand dunes suddenly giving way to sea, wide and clear under a bright blue sky?

The dig is now over so she expects the site to be deserted but, when they get nearer, they see a man standing by the trenches. At first it looks as if he has four legs but, getting closer still, Ruth sees that he is on crutches.

'Oh no,' says Laura. 'It's Leif.'

'Laura split up with Leif,' says Rebecca, 'because Dad told her that he beat up his old girlfriend.'

'That wasn't why,' says Laura. 'And Leif was never charged. He says it didn't happen.'

'They all say that,' says Rebecca.

It doesn't surprise Ruth that Nelson has been checking up on Leif. He is insanely protective where his daughters are concerned. And nor does it totally surprise her to hear about the domestic abuse. She has always suspected that there was a darkness in Leif, something ugly beneath the handsome exterior. She felt the same about Erik, she realises now.

Laura greets Leif with some embarrassment and they speak in private for a few moments. Then Leif swings himself over to talk to Ruth. Apart from the leg, he seems fit and well, his face tanned and his hair, loose today, a burnished mane.

'I'm going home tomorrow,' he says, in answer to Ruth's question. 'I just wanted a last look at this place. The stone circle.'

Ruth remembers Stanton Drew and the stones looming up out of the mist. This is an altogether friendlier place, a hymn to the sea and the sky. But it is also a place where a young girl was buried, with a witch stone at her side. And the place where John Mostyn, the Stone Man, laid Margaret to rest. The landscape itself is important, as Erik so often used to say.

'I heard that they were able to get some DNA from the bones in the cist,' says Ruth.

'Yes,' says Leif. 'Look at this fantastic reconstruction that Oscar did.'

He produces a phone and, with some difficulty because of

the crutches, scrolls down until he finds a photograph. Ruth looks at a young girl, aged about sixteen, gazing out at the world with a mixture of curiosity and defiance.

Ruth thinks of the Bronze Age girl and of Margaret Lacey, neither of whom ever lived to see adulthood. They left their mark all the same, she thinks. Kate, Laura and Rebecca have gone down to the beach and, watching them, Ruth remembers her dream, Kate walking between two unknown women. Well, they are unknown no longer. Has she any right to take Kate away from this place, away from her family? As she watches, the three sisters start to run, their footsteps dark on the white sand, soon to be washed away by the tide.

ACKNOWLEDGEMENTS

The Stone Circle mainly features real places, although characters and events are all fictional. A second circle was found near the famous Seahenge in Norfolk although the stone cist and its contents are imaginary, as is the entire story of Margaret Lacey. King's Lynn is obviously real, with its quay, Custom House and Tuesday Marketplace, but the events described in this book are all invented by me. The stone circle at Stanton Drew, too, is real and well worth a visit. Incidentally the sculptor Oscar Nilsson is also an actual person and his work can be seen at the new archaeology gallery at Brighton Museum.

Lots of people have helped with this book but I must stress that I have followed their advice only as far as it suits the plot and any subsequent mistakes are mine alone. Thanks to Linzi Harvey for being brilliant on bones as usual and to Graham Bartlett, police consultant extraordinaire, for trying to keep the procedural side of the book within the bounds of reality. Special thanks to Matt Pope and Letty Ingrey from the UCL Institute of Archaeology for coming up with Scarning Fen, which is a real place and does contain some unique flora and fauna. Thanks also to Lee Mason at Beccles Books in Suffolk for telling me about Jack Valentine. I don't think I have nearly exhausted all the myths and legends of East Anglia, let alone its archaeological wonders.

Thanks to Carol Dunne for taking part in a charity auction to become a character in this book. All proceeds go to CLIC Sargent, the charity supporting teenage cancer sufferers, so a huge thank you to Carol and everyone else who took part. Although Carol is a headteacher, she bears no resemblance to her fictional counterpart in these pages. St Paul's School is also imaginary. Thanks to Jan Adams and Marj Maccallum, previous auction winners whose namesakes are now regular returning characters.

Heartfelt thanks to my publishers Quercus and the amazing Team Elly: Therese Keating, Hannah Robinson, Olivia Mead, Laura McKerrell, Katie Sadler, David Murphy and so many others. I'm so grateful for everything you have done for me and Ruth. Special thanks, though, must go to my editor, Jane Wood. Jane has edited all my 'Elly Griffiths' books and has, in the process, become a mentor and friend. We always agreed that there would be ten Ruth books so it's only right that this eleventh should be dedicated to her, with love and thanks.

Thanks, as always, to my wonderful agent, Rebecca Carter, and all at Janklow and Nesbit. Thanks to Kirby Kim in New York and to Naomi Gibbs and all at HMH. Thanks to all the publishers around the world who publish these books with such dedication and care. Thanks to my crime writer friends for their support and to anyone who has bought my books or borrowed them from a library. I appreciate you more than I can say.

Finally, love and thanks always to my husband, Andrew, and to our children, Alex and Juliet.

EG 2019

WHO'S WHO
IN THE DR RUTH GALLOWAY
MYSTERIES

Dr Ruth Galloway

Profession: forensic archaeologist

Likes: cats, Bruce Springsteen, bones, books

Dislikes: gyms, organized religion, shopping

Ruth Galloway was born in south London and educated at University College London and Southampton University, where she met her mentor Professor Erik Anderssen. In 1997, she participated in Professor Anderssen's dig on the north Norfolk coast which resulted in the excavation of a Bronze Age henge. Ruth subsequently moved to the area and became Head of Forensic Archaeology at the University of North Norfolk. She lives in an isolated cottage on the edge of the Saltmarsh. In 2007, she was approached by DCI Harry Nelson who wanted her help in identifying bones found buried on the marshes, and her life suddenly got a whole lot more complicated.

Surprising fact about Ruth: she is fascinated by the London Underground and once attended a fancy dress party as The Angel Islington.

Harry Nelson

Profession: Detective Chief Inspector

Likes: driving fast, solving crimes, his family

Dislikes: Norfolk, the countryside, management speak, his boss

Harry Nelson was born in Blackpool. He came to Norfolk in his thirties to lead the Serious Crimes Unit, bringing with him his wife, Michelle, and their daughters, Laura and Rebecca. Nelson has a loyal team and enjoys his work. He still hankers after the North, though, and has not come to love his adopted county. Nelson thinks of himself as an old-fashioned policeman and so often clashes with Super-intendent Archer, who is trying to drag the force into the twenty-first century. Nelson is impatient and quick-tempered but he is capable of being both imaginative and sensitive. He's also cleverer than he lets on.

Surprising fact about Nelson: he's a huge Frank Sinatra fan.

Michelle Nelson

Profession: hairdresser

Likes: her family, exercising, socializing with friends

Dislikes: dowdiness, confrontation, talking about murder

Michelle married Nelson when she was twenty-four and he was twenty-six. She was happy with her life in Blackpool – two children, part-time work, her mother nearby – but encouraged Nelson to move to Norfolk for the sake of promotion. Now that her daughters are older she works as a manager for a hair salon. Michelle is beautiful, stylish, hard-working and a dedicated wife and mother. When people see her and Nelson together, their first reaction is usually, 'What *does* she see in him?'

Surprising fact about Michelle: she once played hockey for Blackpool Girls.

Michael Malone (aka Cathbad)

Profession: laboratory assistant and druid

Likes: nature, mythology, walking, following his instincts

Dislikes: rules, injustice, conventions

Cathbad was born in Ireland and came to England to study first chemistry then archaeology. He also came under the influence of Erik Anderssen though they found themselves on opposite sides during the henge dig. Cathbad was brought up as a Catholic but he now thinks of himself as a druid and shaman.

Surprising fact about Cathbad: he can play the accordion.

Shona Maclean

Profession: lecturer in English Literature

Likes: books, wine, parties

Dislikes: being ignored

Shona is a lecturer at the University of North Norfolk and one of Ruth's closest friends. They met when they both participated in the henge dig in 1997. On the face of it, Shona seems an unlikely friend for Ruth – she's outgoing and stunningly beautiful for a start – but the two women share a sense of humour and an interest in books, films and travel. They also have a lot of history together.

Surprising fact about Shona: as a child she won several Irish dancing competitions.

David Clough

Profession: Detective Sergeant

Likes: food, football, beer, his job

Dislikes: political correctness, graduate police officers

David Clough ('Cloughie' to Nelson) was born in Norfolk and joined the force at eighteen. As a youngster he almost followed his elder brother into petty crime, but a chance meeting with a sympathetic policeman led him into a surprisingly successful police career. Clough is a tough, dedicated officer but not without imagination. He admires Nelson, his boss, but has a rather competitive relationship with Sergeant Judy Johnson.

Surprising fact about Clough: He can quote the 'you come to me on my daughter's wedding day' scene from *The Godfather* off by heart.

Judy Johnson

Profession: Detective Sergeant

Likes: horses, driving, her job

Dislikes: girls' nights out, sexism, being patronised

Judy Johnson was born in Norfolk to Irish Catholic parents. She was academic at school but opted to join the police force at eighteen rather than go to university. Judy can seem cautious and steady – she married her boyfriend from school, for example – but she is actually fiercely ambitious. She resents any hint of condescension or sexism which can lead to some fiery exchanges with Clough.

Surprising fact about Judy: she's a keen card player and once won an inter-force poker competition.

Phil Trent

Profession: professor of Archaeology

Likes: money, being on television, technology

Dislikes: new age archaeologists, anonymity, being out of the loop

Phil is Ruth's head of department at the University of North Norfolk. He's ambitious and outwardly charming, determined to put the university (and himself) on the map. He thinks of Ruth as plodding and old-fashioned so is slightly put out when she begins to make a name for herself as an advisor to the police. On one hand, it's good for the image of UNN; on the other, it should have been him.

Surprising fact about Phil: at his all boys school, he once played Juliet in *Romeo and Juliet*.